Everyman, I will go with thee, and be thy guide,
In thy most need to go by thy side.

This is No. 790 of Everyman's Library

EVERYMAN'S LIBRARY

Founded 1906 by J. M. Dent (d. 1926)
Edited by Ernest Rhys (d. 1946)

FICTION

RODERICK RANDOM
BY TOBIAS SMOLLETT · INTRO-
DUCTION BY H. W. HODGES

TOBIAS GEORGE SMOLLETT, born in 1721 in Dumbartonshire and educated at Glasgow. Went to London in 1739 and in 1741 sailed as surgeon's mate on one of the vessels of the Carthagena expedition. On his return he settled in London and devoted himself to literature. Died in 1771.

RODERICK RANDOM

TOBIAS SMOLLETT

LONDON: J. M. DENT & SONS LTD.
NEW YORK: E. P. DUTTON & CO. INC.

INTRODUCTION

THE origin of the English Novel, in its modern significance and form, is to be found in the eighteenth century. Between 1740, the year in which Richardson's *Pamela* appeared, and 1771, when Smollett produced his last novel, *Humphrey Clinker*, English prose fiction was fairly established. A great quartette [1] of writers was at work to whom succeeding novelists owe a deep debt.

Revival of interest in the inventors of the eighteenth-century Novel should not derive merely from a pious and perfunctory sense of obligation. The modern writer has much to learn or re-learn by careful study in the school of Fielding and Smollett, the masters who number Thackeray and Dickens among their many illustrious disciples. It is by virtue of their intrinsic qualities, and not merely as originators of a new form of art, that Richardson, Fielding, Smollett and Sterne—each for his own essential quality—are worthy to be read to-day. More than that, they are invaluable as vivid painters of the adventurous travel, the wayside scenes, the familiar types, the social and domestic life of the eighteenth century, those scenes and sides of life which are ignored or only indirectly glanced at by the historian, the essayist, the philosopher and the writer of memoirs.

Out of the huge bulk of literary achievement in that century the work of the great novelists can least easily be spared. [2]

Tobias George Smollett, the author of *Roderick Random*, was born in 1721. Though much younger than Richardson (born 1689) and Fielding (born 1707), he was their contemporary in the field of literature. It is worth while to consider the story of his life in some detail, since the material for all his most important works is drawn from his own experience of events and places. To call *Roderick Random* an autobiography would be exaggeration, and yet the adventurous career

---

[1] Richardson, Fielding, Smollett and Sterne.
[2] The Romantic Revival, coinciding with the outbreak and course of the French Revolution, is of the nineteenth century in spirit.

of the "hero"—above all, the scenes from naval life—could have been set down by no other pen than that of Smollett.

Smollett was a Scotsman and came of a family of considerable local distinction in Dumbartonshire. His grandfather, Sir James Smollett, had been active in helping to secure the union of England and Scotland in 1707. His youngest son, Archibald, the father of the novelist, had no profession, and was dependent on Sir James, who bestowed upon him a farm near his own seat of Bonhill. There Archibald Smollett died two years after the birth of his son Tobias. Sir James saw to it that his grandchild's education was not neglected. After a good grounding at Dumbarton Grammar School the boy was sent in 1736 to attend a short course at Glasgow University as a preliminary to qualifying for the medical profession. In that same year he was apprenticed to a Dr. John Gordon. Here in Glasgow at this early age his taste for writing first appeared in the form of a tragedy called *The Regicide*. In 1739, fired by literary ambition, he resolved to seek his fortune in London with little else but his play and some letters of introduction in his pocket. In like manner, two years previously, had Samuel Johnson, with his pupil Garrick, his play *Irene* and twopence-halfpenny in his pocket, set out for London.

Like Johnson, Smollett found no help in patrons. Neither George Lyttelton nor David Garrick was willing to promote his play, which was sorry stuff and quite unactable. This lack of appreciation provoked the author to savage attacks on his so-called patrons, which afford the first of many examples shown throughout his life of his aptness in the gentle art of making enemies.

Impatient at this first failure, he next sought for employment as a medical man. Through the kindness of a fellow Scot, Sir Andrew Mitchell, he obtained a post as surgeon's mate on board a battleship in the squadron of Sir Chaloner Ogle, then about to sail as a reinforcement to Vernon's fleet in the West Indies. The War of Jenkyns's Ear—the outcome of long-standing trade jealousies with Spain—had broken out in 1739, and Ogle sailed in 1740, arriving in time to take part in the ill-fated and mismanaged expedition against Cartagena in 1741. In this wise Smollett found the opportunity to create the most original of his characters, and to paint for the benefit of posterity a series of pictures of contemporary naval life which in vigour and sharpness of drawing have never been

excelled. He was breaking new ground and he gained immediate and lasting success. When, smarting under failure and
sorely stricken with fever, Vernon's fleet returned to Jamaica,
Smollett soon retired from the Service. In the island he met
Nancy Lascelles, the daughter of an English planter, whom
he appears to have married shortly after his return to England.
In 1744 we find him in residence at a house in Downing Street,
seeking practice as a surgeon. But his interest now clearly
lay in literature. In 1745 he produced a poem entitled *The
Tears of Scotland*, and in 1746–7 he published two short satires
of no great distinction. The year 1748 marks the turning-
point of his literary career, for it saw the production of his
first and best-known novel, *Roderick Random*. Its immediate
success made Smollett a man of mark in literary London.
Yet he still seemed determined to have two strings to his bow,
for in 1750 he obtained the degree of M.D. at Aberdeen. In
that same year, however, he went to Paris in search of material
for his new novel, *Peregrine Pickle*, which appeared in 1751.
True to his resentful nature, he took occasion in both his first
novels to vent his spite upon Lyttelton, Garrick, Rich and
Cibber—upon all, in fact, whom he considered to have been
neglectful of his early merits. It was not for nothing that the
thistle was his national emblem.

He next repaired to Bath, where he not unnaturally failed
to win practice or popularity as a doctor, since he was at pains
to prove in a published pamphlet the inefficacy of the Bath
waters.

From this time onward he may be considered as a professional man of letters. He settled in Chelsea, where he was
visited by Doctor Samuel Johnson, whom he calls "the
great Cham of literature," and by Goldsmith, Garrick and
Sterne. That he never came within the charmed circle of the
great Doctor's coterie is not surprising, for he had no disposition to bow down and worship at any man's shrine but
his own. An argument between Johnson and Smollett might
well have produced a piquant situation; it would doubtless
have been sharp, and probably stormy.

On Sundays he was wont to keep open house for a small
army of eccentric hack-writers, whom he employed in his
"literary factory." A third novel, *Count Fathom*, appeared
in 1753, and then for a period of ten years he laboured un-
ceasingly, to the ruin of his health, on what would now be
called journalistic and hack-writing. Besides translations of

Don Quixote and *Gil Blas*, he edited the *Critical Review*, and found time to achieve what must surely constitute a record in rapid book-making—the issue of a History of England "from the descent of Julius Cæsar to the Treaty of Aix-la-Chapelle, 1748"—within a period of some eighteen months. If without merit as a history, the work was lucid and readable.

In 1757 a farcical play called *The Reprisal, or The Tars of Old England*, was staged successfully by Garrick. It served to patch up the old quarrel, for Smollett showed that he could be grateful as well as revengeful, by eulogising the great actor in the *Critical Review*.

In 1759 a bitter attack on the conduct of Admiral Knowles during the combined assault on Rochefort in 1757 involved Smollett in a libel action which ended with his sentence to three months' confinement in the King's Bench prison. This habitation enforced must have served him as a much needed and tolerably comfortable rest-cure, where he was able to complete his plans at leisure for the publication of a sixpenny monthly magazine, and where, characteristically, he collected much material for a new novel, *Sir Launcelot Greaves*. The first instalments of this book appeared serially in the new magazine, a method of production hitherto unknown.

Till 1763 he continued to produce an astonishing amount of hack-work at high pressure. The death in that year of his only child, a daughter to whom he was devoted, combined with overwork and financial worry, brought on a complete nervous breakdown.

In hopes of recovery he went abroad, residing in France and Italy for two years. On his return to London in 1765 he produced his *Travels through France and Italy*, a work which well deserves a re-edition for its shrewd and lively descriptions, its appreciation of the Riviera, till then but little visited, and above all for its evidence of the author's tastes and character. A careful reading of the book will lead us at least to challenge the truth of Sterne's famous portrait of "Smelfungus" [1] in the *Sentimental Journey*.

The improvement in Smollett's health was only temporary, and in 1766 another visit was paid to Bath, where he gathered material for his last novel, *Humphrey Clinker*. But before this book was written he gave to the world one more example of his old unbridled and vindictive spirit in *The History and*

[1] "He set out," says Sterne, "with the spleen and jaundice, and every object he passed by was discoloured and distorted."

Adventures of an Atom. This book was a savage satire upon
public men and public affairs, in which he struck out indis-
criminately at king and ministers. It could only have been
produced by a man who—in his own phrase—was suffering
from "systema nervosum maxime irritabile."

In December 1769 he went abroad for the last time. He
settled near Leghorn in 1770, and there wrote the latest, the
pleasantest and most "humane" of all his novels, *The
Expedition of Humphrey Clinker*.

In 1771 he died at the age of fifty-one.

The most important part of Smollett's work, that which
is destined to live, consists in his three novels, *Roderick
Random, Peregrine Pickle* and *Humphrey Clinker*. Of these
Roderick Random, the first in time, is still the best known.

The preface to the book should be carefully read, for in it
the author explains in the frankest way that *Roderick Random*
is modelled on the plan of Le Sage, who, in his *Gil Blas* "has
described the knavery and foibles of life with infinite humour
and sagacity." The structure of his story, for it cannot be said
to possess a plot, is therefore derived consciously from the
Picaresque school of writers, the best exponents of which
were Cervantes, Le Sage and Defoe. Smollett intends to
provide us with a novel depicting crowded hours of adventurous life by sea and land, in the tavern or the gambling-den,
and introducing in almost bewildering succession types of
all sorts and conditions of men.

Roderick Random may be said to possess a general value
and a special value. Its general value is best understood if
we realise that Smollett is doing with his pen what Hogarth
was doing with his brush. One cannot turn over the pages of
his book without constant reminders of the works of Hogarth.
In both artists there is a wide selection of types, the same
narrow observation of low life, the study of the fop, the
impostor, the dupe and the criminal; often the same insistence
in detail upon the brutal, the ugly, and the obscene. Only in
Smollett the tendency to caricature his subjects is far more
pronounced. We are viewing in sharp outline those sides of
society in the eighteenth century which can nowhere else be
seen from the same angle or on the same scale, save always in
the works of Henry Fielding.

But it is the special value of the book that we propose
to emphasise at greater length. In *Roderick Random* we are

given, for the first time in "true" fiction, a new set of characters taken from the quarter-decks and forecastles of His Majesty's ships. Neither Defoe nor Swift nor Fielding had the first-hand experience of the Navy, essential for the task. Indeed, the most faithful representation of naval life in the eighteenth century had hitherto appeared, not in fiction, but in Shadwell's play, *The Fair Quaker of Deal, or Humours of the Navy*, which had been produced in 1710 at Drury Lane. Yet the characters, though full of life, are not seen on active service afloat.

Smollett, then, was the first serious novelist who thought it worth while to draw from the Navy his most notable characters and his liveliest scenes. He had, as we have seen, the rare advantage of first-hand knowledge combined with peculiar power to record it faithfully.

The Navy when Smollett saw it was suffering a period of eclipse. Between the triumphs of the Great War of the Spanish Succession, which, at its conclusion in 1713, had brought us Gibraltar, Minorca, and vast territory in North America as the fruits of sea-power, and the still greater triumphs of the Seven Years' War, which by 1763 established our Canadian and Indian Empires, there lay the peace period of Walpole. This was for the Navy a period of dry-rot. The sword, being sheathed for lack of argument, was allowed to become very rusty, and the fault lay at the door of the Government. The political and financial corruption rife in the age of Walpole, rendered the honest and efficient administration of the Navy impossible. It was not that the robust fighting spirit of the seamen had declined nor the quality of the officers as a whole deteriorated, although the system which permitted commanding officers to be on active service in Parliament sometimes led to such political animosities between admirals afloat as prevented them from combining whole-heartedly even in presence of the national foe.

The lower ratings were largely recruited (as was Roderick) by way of the Press-gang, and there is abundant evidence available to support Smollett's description of impressment and of the depraved and brutal shipmates whose company he was at first forced to share. He is detailing the crude facts as he met them, and his truth is stranger than fiction. Nor can it be doubted that the living picture of his messmates in the cockpit, the loathsome nature of the food, the nauseating conditions under which it was consumed, and the callous neglect to provide reasonable quarters and comforts for the sick and wounded, was a composite presentment of what could and did happen in an "unhappy" ship, commanded by a brutal captain.

While it is not necessary to believe that there were many Captain Oakums in the Service, the early entry (often as a child), the rigour of the life, the long periods of isolation afloat and the constant exercise of tyrannical power, all tended to produce uncultured, harsh, eccentric officers. Captains of the "fine gentleman" type caricatured in the person of Captain Whiffle, were less frequently found in Smollett's day than in the Restoration times, when, as Macaulay said, there were gentlemen and seamen in the Navy, but the gentlemen were not seamen and the seamen were not gentlemen.

Professional inefficiency was certainly exceptional. Smollett's evidence has been challenged on the ground that, as a lowly surgeon's mate, he could have had but slight opportunities for close observation of his commanding officers. Yet it must be always remembered that here was a man of unusual intelligence, whose "journalistic" faculty was keenly sharpened to use the mass of new material lying at his disposal. "Every intelligent reader," he tells us in his Preface, "will at first sight perceive I have not deviated from nature in the facts, which are all true in the main, although the circumstances are altered and disguised to avoid personal satire."

It is not the Oakums, the Mackshanes and the Crampleys on whom our gaze will linger in Smollett's gallery of naval portraits. The unforgettable characters are the irascible, yet kindly, little Welsh doctor, Morgan, and the simple, downright sea-dog, Lieutenant Tom Bowling. For them, as for the honest sailor, Jack Rattlin, the author intends—as he so seldom does—that our entire sympathy should be enlisted. They have but one rival in his works, the immortal figure of Hawser Trunnion (*Peregrine Pickle*). Smollett is doing for the first time with entire success what few, excepting Marryat, have since achieved: he shows us, in his image as he was, the naval worthy of the period. He who runs may read and never doubt the truth of the descriptions.

When Roderick Random turns from the senior officers and lower ratings to criticise the conduct of the campaign by the commander-in-chief, his trenchant commentary has far less value. It is true that he is an eyewitness of the failure before Cartagena in 1741. He wrote, indeed, two further accounts of the operations, one in his *History of England*, and another in his *Compendium of Voyages*, published in 1757. His view of Admiral Vernon could hardly be dispassionate. What he had seen and suffered made it impossible for a man of his temperament, even had he possessed more knowledge, to mete out even justice to those in high command. Admiral Vernon and General Wentworth are, to him, equally deserving of blame. That is not the verdict of competent historians. Undeniably, there were faults of temper on both sides, but to Wentworth's account must be added convictions of incompetence and lethargy amounting almost to imbecility. It is strange that the fiasco at Cartagena should still be regarded primarily as a *naval* failure, since to impose on Vernon the lion's share of responsibility is wilfully to ignore the facts. Granted that his fleet was ill-equipped for its work and its standard of efficiency low, Vernon conducted the naval operations with briskness and effect. Unfortunately he was quite unable to communicate his zeal to his military colleague, who in choice and method of attack showed woeful lack of judgment.

In the dark period [1] before the sun of Anson and Hawke arose, Vernon deserved well of his country. One order of his in particular deserves to be remembered, although we have no mention of it by Smollett. In August 1740, the customary issue of half a pint of raw rum to the seamen was forbidden, and in its stead a mixture was served liberally diluted with water. The wisdom of this reform was soon apparent in a marked increase of health, discipline and general efficiency, and a corresponding decrease of sickness throughout the fleet. The issue of this order by Vernon explains the introduction of the word "grog" as applied to the watered rum, the admiral himself being familiarly known as "Old Grog," on account of his fondness for a cloak which was made of grogram.

Vernon continued to show the keenest interest in the welfare of the common seaman, until his own career on the active list came to an abrupt close in 1745. Students of naval tactics have further reason to remember him as the first to issue additional fighting instructions whereby admirals hitherto tied and bound by the strict limits of an old and stereotyped system, might find some measure of freedom in manœuvre.

[1] At this very time Anson was embarked on the famous voyage round the world (1740–4) which brought so poignantly to his notice many grievous defects of naval administration.

Sir Chaloner Ogle, who commanded the squadron in which Smollett (and Roderick) served, was a flag-officer of respectable though not of outstanding quality. Sir Charles Knowles, of whom Smollett fell foul in later years, was a zealous and studious officer, whom we know to have been keenly alive to the defects of the Service from lengthy and thoughtful memoranda submitted by him to the Admiralty.

It is just, then, to conclude that Smollett's criticisms of these senior officers are the least trustworthy part of his testimony: they are certainly the least important, for he is never at his best unless in close personal contact with his characters. After the creation of Hawser Trunnion in *Peregrine Pickle* he makes no full-dress addition to his naval portraits. The Navy as transformed by Anson was not the Navy that Smollett knew, and he had the wisdom to refrain from second-hand and "literary" presentment.

He had done enough to whet the public taste for sea fiction. A host of imitators followed in his wake, but he had no serious rival until Captain Marryat produced the wonderful series of novels depicting the Navy in which he had served for upwards of ten years during the Napoleonic Wars. Marryat owed much to Smollett, both in his method of description and in his tendency to dwell upon the unhappy sides of naval life. The midshipman's berth in *Frank Mildmay* reminds us of the cockpit in Smollett's *Thunder*, and in *Peter Simple* much of his material is autobiographical. The characters of the boatswain "Gentleman" Chucks and Midshipman Easy, like Bowling and Morgan, must have been drawn from life and will always be alive. In this mode nothing comparable has been achieved for the modern Navy by modern novelists. The material is still there, because the Navy is careful of its types and traditions, but neither "forrard" nor on the quarter-deck has the writer of genius as yet appeared to use it.

Appreciation of Smollett's work as a whole, apart from his contribution to our knowledge of the Navy in the eighteenth century, is a difficult task. This is due to a certain "method-lessness" in his writing and an almost entire absence of form or plot. This, if a defect, does not make him the less readable: he is seldom or never dull, and the varied and lively episodes in the many changes and chances of his hero's fortunes make it possible to read his *Roderick* literally at random. If one is seldom edified, one can hardly be bored in his company.

The most serious charge to be made against him is his deliberate indecency. His books are not for family use, nor for the class-room, since much of his work is tainted by the nastiness of his times. Sometimes he seems at pains to detail the coarsest incidents in the coarsest language. His insistence on the indelicate, the brutal and the bestial is a serious blot on his writing.

That he has held his own among the many giants of eighteenth-century literature is itself a proof of the enduring quality of his best books. Facts, as he himself says, are stubborn things, and it is a fact that Charles Dickens owed as deep a debt to Smollett as Thackeray did to Fielding. The reader who knows his *Pickwick* must recognise the emphasis on external eccentricities of character, the loose stringing of the episodes, the rapid changes of scene, the absence of definite plot as features common to the method of both Dickens and Smollett. The autobiography in *Copperfield*, too, is introduced in a manner that recalls *Roderick*. In both there is a similarity of humour in the sense that Ben Jonson understood that word.

On his merits as a keen observer of his age, as a humorist, as the great originator of naval types in fiction, and as the writer of vivacious and lucid prose, Smollett is entitled to a high, if not the highest, place in the illustrious ranks of British novelists. Hazlitt has summarised his merits justly when he says that his novels "always enliven, and never tire us: we take them up with pleasure, and lay them down without any strong feeling of regret."

For further detailed information on the condition of the Navy in the eighteenth century see the admirable introduction, by Mr. John Masefield, to *A Voyage Round the World* by Lord Anson (Everyman's Library, No. 510).

H. W. H.

BIBLIOGRAPHICAL LIST

COLLECTED WORKS: *Miscellaneous Works of Tobias Smollett* (novels, poems, plays, and travels), frontispieces by T. Rowlandson, 6 vols., 1790; with memoir of life and writings by R. Anderson, 6 vols., 1796; with memoir of life by J. Moore, 8 vols., 1797; with life of author, 12 vols., 1824; with memoir by T. Roscoe, 1841. *Works of Tobias Smollett*, selected and edited, with historical notes and life of author, by D. Herbert, 1870. *Works*, edited by J. P. Browne, 8 vols., 1872; edited by

Professor George Saintsbury in 12 vols., 1895, 1925. *Works of Tobias Smollett*, with introduction by W. E. Henley, in 12 vols., 1899–1901.

Novels, with memoir by Sir Walter Scott, 2 vols., 1821. Shakespeare Head Edition of *Novels*, 11 vols., 1925.

Poetical Works, with life of author, 1794; with life by Alexander Chalmers, in *The Works of the English Poets*, vol. xv, 1810; with life by S. W. Singer, 1822.

NOVELS: *The Adventures of Roderick Random*, 1748; 3rd ed., 1750; 8th ed., 1770; with six plates, 1780; with life (Cooke's ed.), 1793; illustrated by George Cruikshank, 1831; with memoir by G. H. Townsend, 1857; many other eds. until present day. Abridged by R. Lewis (Dublin), 1791. Translated into French as *Histoire et aventures de Roderik Random*, 1782; other eds., 1784 and 1804.

The Adventures of Peregrine Pickle, in which are included Memoirs of a Lady of Quality, 1751; 3rd ed., 1765; 7th ed., 1784; Cooke's ed., 1794, with plates by T. Rowlandson, 1805; illustrated by Phiz, 1857; illustrated by George Cruikshank, 1904; translated into French by the author of *Les Mœurs* as *Histoire et aventures de Sir Williams Pickle*, 1753. (For special reference to this novel see Howard S. Buck's *Study in Smollett*, 1925.)

The Adventures of Ferdinand, Count Fathom, 1753; 2nd ed., 1771, other eds., 1780, 1782; illustrated by T. Stothard, in *Novelist's Magazine*, vii, 1782; Cooke's ed., 1795; translated into French by T. P. Bertin as *Fathom et Melvil*, 1798 (?).

The Adventures of Sir Launcelot Greaves, 1762; Cooke's ed., 1793; with engravings, 1839; many other eds., until present day. Translated into French by M. de F— as *Les Aventures de Sir Launcelot Greaves*, 1824.

The Expedition of Humphry Clinker, 1771; 2nd ed., 1771, 1772; Cooke's ed., 1794; with memoir by T. Roscoe and illustrated by George Cruikshank, 1831; illustrated by Phiz, 1857; illustrated by Cruikshank and bibliography by J. H. Isaacs, 1895; with portrait and illustrated by Cruikshank, 1904; with introduction and notes by L. Rice-Oxley, 1925. Adapted as a farce by J. Cumberland, 1828.

PLAYS, POEMS, AND SATIRES: *The Regicide: or James the First of Scotland*, a tragedy, 1749; *The Reprisal, or the Tars of Old England*, a comedy, 1757; and other eds. *The Tears of Scotland*, 1746; *Advice, a Satire* (in verse), 1746; *Reproof, a Satire* (in verse), 1747; reprinted as *Advice and Reproof*, 1748, 1826. Burlesque *Ode on the Loss of a Grandmother*, 1747; *Ode to Independence*, published posthumously, 1773. *The History and Adventures of an Atom* (prose, a satire), 1769; 10th ed. 1778; other eds., 1784, 1786, 1795.

MISCELLANEOUS WORKS: Medical treatise, entitled *An Essay on the External Use of Water*, 1752. *A Complete History of England from the Descent of Julius Caesar to the Treaty of Aix-la-Chapelle*, 1748; 1st ed., 4 vols., 1757–8, 2nd ed., 11 vols. 1758–60; *Continuation of the History of England*, 5 vols. 1763–5; *The History of England from the Revolution to the Death of George the Second*, 5 vols., 1789, continued in two supplementary volumes, 1791, 'to the end of the American War and Peace of Versailles in 1783.' *Travels through France and Italy* appeared in 1766; 2nd ed., 1772; with introduction by Thomas Seccombe, 1907; translated by C. Albini Petrucci, with Lady Mary Wortley Montagu's *Letters* as *Impressioni italiane di viaggiatori inglesi del sec. xviii*, 1916.

Smollett also translated *Gil Blas*, 1749, and numerous later eds.; *Don Quixote*, 1755, and numerous later eds., several works of Voltaire, 1761; Fénelon's *Adventures of Telemachus*, 1776.

In 1756 Smollett edited the *Critical Review*; the *British Magazine* in 1760; the *Briton* from 1762 to 1763; *A Compendium of Authentic and Entertaining Voyages*, 1766.

A work attributed to Smollett is *A Faithful Narrative of the base and inhuman arts that were lately practised upon the brain of Habbakkuk Hilding*, by Drawcansir Alexander, Fencing-Master and Philomath, 1752.

BIOGRAPHIES AND STUDIES OF SMOLLETT: *Life of Tobias Smollett*, with critical observations on his works, by Robert Anderson, 1796; later eds., 1800, 1803, and 1806. *Smollett: his Life and a Selection from his Writings*, by Robert Chambers, 1867; *Life of Tobias George Smollett*, by David Hannay, with a bibliography by J. P. Anderson, 1887; *Tobias Smollett*, by W. H. Oliphant Smeaton, in Famous Scots Series, 1897; 'Fielding and Smollett,' by Harold H. Child, in *The Cambridge History of English Literature*, 1913; *A Study in Smollett, chiefly 'Peregrine Pickle,'* 1925, and *Smollett as Poet*, 1927, by Howard S. Buck; *The Life and Letters of Tobias Smollett*, by Lewis Melville, 1926; *The Letters of Tobias Smollett, M.D.*, edited by Edward J. Noyes, 1926; *Smollett et la France*, by E. Joliat, with a bibliography of translations, 1935. *A Second Letter to Dr. Samuel Johnson . . . with an impartial character of Dr. Smollett* was written by Andrew Henderson and published in 1775; *Some Account of the Family of Smollett of Bonhill*, by Joseph Irving, 1859.

CONTENTS

CONTENTS

THE ADVENTURES OF
RODERICK RANDOM

THE PREFACE

OF all kinds of satire, there is none so entertaining and universally improving, as that which is introduced, as it were, occasionally, in the course of an interesting story, which brings every incident home to life; and, by representing familiar scenes in an uncommon and amusing point of view, invests them with all the graces of novelty, while nature is appealed to in every particular.

The reader gratifies his curiosity in pursuing the adventures of a person in whose favour he is prepossessed; he espouses his cause, he sympathises with him in distress; his indignation is heated against the authors of his calamity; the humane passions are inflamed; the contrast between dejected virtue and insulting vice appears with greater aggravation; and every impression having a double force on the imagination, the memory retains the circumstance, and the heart improves by the example. The attention is not tired with a bare catalogue of characters, but agreeably diverted with all the variety of invention; and the vicissitudes of life appear in their peculiar circumstances, opening an ample field for wit and humour.

Romance, no doubt, owes its origin to ignorance, vanity, and superstition. In the dark ages of the world, when a man had rendered himself famous for wisdom or valour, his family and adherents availed themselves of his superior qualities, magnified his virtues, and represented his character and person as sacred and supernatural. The vulgar easily swallowed the bait, implored his protection, and yielded the tribute of homage and praise even to adoration; his exploits were handed down to posterity with a thousand exaggerations; they were repeated as incitements to virtue; divine honours were paid, and altars erected to his memory, for the encouragement of those who attempted to imitate his example; and hence arose the heathen mythology, which is no other than a collection of extravagant romances. As learning advanced, and genius received cultivation, these stories were embellished with the graces of poetry; that they might the better recommend themselves to the attention, they were sung in public, at festivals, for the instruction and delight of the audience; and rehearsed before battle, as incentives to deeds of glory. Thus tragedy and the epic muse were born and, in the progress of taste, arrived at perfection. It is no wonder that the ancients could not relish a fable in prose, after they had seen so many remarkable events celebrated in verse by their best poets; we, therefore, find no romance among them, during the era of their excellence, unless the Cyropædia of Xenophon may be so called; and it was not till arts and sciences began to revive, after the irruption of the Barbarians into Europe, that anything of this kind appeared. But when the minds of men were debauched, by the imposition of priest-craft, to the most absurd pitch of credulity, the authors of romance arose, and, losing sight of probability, filled their performances with the most monstrous hyperboles. If they could not equal the ancient poets in point of genius, they were resolved to excel them in fiction, and apply to the wonder rather than the judgment of their readers. Accordingly they brought necromancy to their aid, and instead of supporting the character of their heroes by dignity of sentiment and practice, distinguished them by their bodily strength, activity, and extravagance of behaviour. Although nothing could be more ludicrous and unnatural than the figures they drew, they did not want patrons and admirers, and the world actually began to be infected with the spirit of knight-errantry, when Cervantes, by an inimitable piece of ridicule, reformed the taste of mankind, representing chivalry in the right point of view, and converting romance to purposes far more useful and enter-taining, by making it assume the sock, and point out the follies of ordinary life.

The same method has been practised by other Spanish and French authors, and by none more successfully than by Monsieur Le Sage, who, in his *Adventures of Gil Blas*, has described the knavery and foibles of life, with infinite humour and sagacity. The following sheets I have modelled on his plan, taking the liberty, however, to differ from him in the execution, where I thought his particular situations were uncommon, extravagant, or peculiar to the country in which the scene is laid. The disgraces of Gil Blas are, for the most part, such as rather excite mirth than compassion: he himself laughs at them; and his transitions from distress to happiness, or at least ease, are so sudden, that neither the reader has time to pity him, nor himself to be acquainted with affliction. This conduct, in my opinion, not only deviates from probability, but prevents that generous indignation which ought to animate the reader against the sordid and vicious disposition of the world.

I have attempted to represent modest merit struggling with every difficulty to which a friendless orphan is exposed, from his own want of experience, as well as from the selfishness, envy, malice, and base indifference of mankind. To secure a favourable prepossession, I have allowed him the advantages of birth and education, which, in the series of his misfortunes, will, I hope, engage the ingenuous more warmly in his behalf; and though I foresee that some people will be offended at the mean scenes in which he is involved, I persuade myself the judicious will not only perceive the necessity of describing those situations, to which he must of course be confined, in his low state, but also find entertainment in viewing those parts of life, where the humours and passions are undisguised by affectation, ceremony, or education; and the whimsical peculiarities of disposition appear as nature has implanted them. But I believe I need not trouble myself in vindicating a practice authorised by the best writers in this way, some of whom I have already named.

Every intelligent reader will, at first sight, perceive I have not deviated from nature in the facts, which are all true in the main, although the circumstances are altered and disguised, to avoid personal satire.

It now remains to give my reasons for making the chief personage of this work a North Briton; which are chiefly these: I could at a small expense bestow on him such education as I thought the dignity of his birth and character required, which could not possibly be obtained in England, by such slender means as the nature of my plan would afford. In the next place, I could represent simplicity of manners in a remote part of the kingdom, with more propriety than in any other place near the capital; and, lastly, the disposition of the Scots, addicted to travelling, justifies my conduct in deriving an adventurer from that country.

That the delicate reader may not be offended at the unmeaning oaths which proceed from the mouths of some persons in these memoirs, I beg leave to premise, that I imagined nothing could more effectually expose the absurdity of such miserable expletives, than a natural and verbal representation of the discourse in which they occur.

APOLOGUE

A YOUNG painter, indulging a vein of pleasantry, sketched a kind of conversation-piece, representing a bear, an owl, a monkey, and an ass; and to render it more striking, humorous, and moral, distinguished every figure by some emblem of human life.

Bruin was exhibited in the garb and attitude of an old, tooth-less, drunken soldier; the owl, perched upon the handle of a coffee pot, with spectacles on his nose, seemed to contemplate a newspaper; and the ass, ornamented with a huge tie-wig (which, however, could not conceal his long ears), sat for his picture to the monkey, who appeared with the implements of painting. This whimsical group afforded some mirth, and met with general approbation, until some mischievous wag hinted that the whole was a lampoon upon the friends of the performer; an insinuation which was no sooner circulated, than those very people who applauded it before began to be alarmed, and even to fancy themselves signified by the several figures of the piece.

Among others, a worthy personage in years, who had served in the army with reputation, being incensed at the supposed outrage, repaired to the lodgings of the painter, and, finding him at home, "Hark ye, Mr. Monkey," said he, "I have a good mind to convince you, that though the bear has lost his teeth, he retains his paws, and that he is not so drunk but he can perceive your impertinence—'Sblood! sir, that toothless jaw is a d—ned scandalous libel—but don't you imagine me so chop-fallen as not to be able to chew the cud of resentment." Here he was interrupted by the arrival of a learned physician, who, advancing to the culprit with fury in his aspect, exclaimed, "Suppose the augmentation of the ass's ears should prove the diminution of the baboon's—nay, seek not to prevaricate, for by the beard of Esculapius! there is not one hair in this periwig that will not stand up in judgment to convict thee of personal abuse.—Do but observe, Captain, how this pitiful little fellow has copied the very curls—the colour, indeed, is different, but then the form and foretop are quite similar." While he thus

7

remonstrated in a strain of vociferation, a venerable senator entered, and waddling up to the delinquent, "Jackanapes!" cried he, "I will now let thee see I can read something else than a newspaper, and that, without the help of spectacles— here is your own note of hand, sirrah, for money which, if I had not advanced, you yourself would have resembled an owl, in not daring to show your face by day, you ungrateful slanderous knave!"

In vain the astonished painter declared that he had no intention to give offence, or to characterise particular persons: they affirmed the resemblance was too palpable to be over-looked; they taxed him with insolence, malice, and ingratitude; and their clamours being overheard by the public, the captain was a bear, the doctor an ass, and the senator an owl, to his dying day.

Christian reader, I beseech thee, in the bowels of the Lord, remember this example while thou art employed in the perusal of the following sheets; and seek not to appropriate to thyself that which equally belongs to five hundred different people. If thou shouldst meet with a character that reflects thee in some ungracious particular, keep thy own counsel; consider that one feature makes not a face, and that, though thou art, perhaps, distinguished by a bottle nose, twenty of thy neighbours may be in the same predicament.

THE ADVENTURES OF
RODERICK RANDOM

CHAPTER I

Of my Birth and Parentage.

I WAS born in the northern part of this united kingdom, in the house of my grandfather; a gentleman of considerable fortune and influence, who had, on many occasions, signalised himself in behalf of his country; and was remarkable for his abilities in the law, which he exercised with great success, in the station of a judge, particularly against beggars, for whom he had a singular aversion.

My father, his youngest son, falling in love with a poor relation, who lived with the old gentleman in quality of house-keeper, espoused her privately; and I was the first fruit of that marriage. During her pregnancy, a dream discomposed my mother so much, that her husband, tired with her importunity, at last consulted a Highland seer, whose favourable interpretation he would have secured beforehand by a bribe, but found him incorruptible. She dreamed she was delivered of a tennis-ball, which the devil (who, to her great surprise, acted the part of midwife) struck so forcibly with a racket, that it disappeared in an instant; and she was for some time inconsolable for the loss of her offspring; when all of a sudden, she beheld it return with equal violence, and enter the earth beneath her feet, whence immediately sprung up a goodly tree covered with blossoms, the scent of which operated so strongly on her nerves, that she awoke. The attentive sage, after some deliberation, assured my parents, that their first-born would be a great traveller; that he would undergo many dangers and difficulties, and at last return to his native land, where he would flourish in happiness and reputation. How truly this was foretold, will appear in the sequel. It was not long before some officious person informed my grandfather of certain familiarities that passed between his son and housekeeper, which alarmed him so much, that a few days after, he told my father it was high time for him to think of settling; and that he had provided a match for him, to which he could in justice have no objections. My father, finding it would be impossible to conceal his situation much longer, frankly owned what he had done, and excused himself for not having asked the consent of his father, by saying, he knew it would have been to no purpose; and that, had his inclination been known, my grandfather might have taken such measures as would have effectually put the gratification of it out of his power. He added, that no exceptions could be taken of his wife's virtue, birth, beauty, and good sense; and as for fortune, it was beneath his care. The old gentleman, who kept all his passions, except one, in excellent order, heard him to an end with great temper; and then calmly asked, how he proposed to maintain himself and spouse? He replied, he could be in no danger of wanting, while his father's tenderness remained, which he and his wife should always cultivate with the utmost veneration; that he was persuaded his allowance would be suitable to the dignity and circumstances of his family, and to the provision already made for his brothers and sisters, who were happily settled under his protection. "Your brothers and sisters," said my grandfather, "did not think it beneath them to consult me in an affair of such importance as matrimony; neither, I suppose, would you have omitted that piece of duty, had not you some secret fund in reserve, to the comforts of which I leave you, with a desire that you will this night seek out another habitation for yourself and wife, whither, in a short time, I will send you an account of the expense I have been at in your education, with a view of being reimbursed. Sir, you have made the grand tour;—you are a polite gentleman,—a very pretty gentleman;—I wish you a great deal of joy, and am your very humble servant." So saying, he left my father in a situation easily imagined. However, he did not long hesitate; for, being perfectly well acquainted with his father's disposition, he did not doubt that he was glad of this pretence to get rid of him; and his resolves being invariable as the laws of the Medes and Persians, he knew it would be to no purpose to attempt him by prayers and entreaties; so, without any further application, he betook himself with his disconsolate bed-fellow, to a farm-house, where an old servant of his mother dwelt. There they remained for some time in a situation but ill adapted to the elegance of their desires, and tenderness of their love; which, nevertheless, my father chose to endure, rather than supplicate an unnatural and inflexible parent. But my mother, foreseeing the inconvenience to which she must have been exposed, had she been delivered in this place (and her pregnancy was very far advanced), without communicating her design to her husband, went in disguise to the house of my grandfather, hoping that her tears and condition would move him to compassion, and reconcile him to an event which was now irrevocably past. She found means to deceive the servants, and was introduced as an unfortunate lady, who wanted to complain of some matrimonial grievances; it being my grandfather's particular province to decide in all cases of scandal. She was accordingly admitted into his presence; where discovering herself, she fell at his feet, and in the most affecting manner implored his forgiveness; at the same time representing the danger that threatened not only her life, but that of his own grandchild, which was about to see the light. He told her, he was sorry that the indiscretion of her and his son had compelled him to make a vow, which put it out of his power to give them any assistance; that he had already imparted his thoughts on that subject to her husband, and was surprised that they should disturb his peace with any further importunity. This said, he retired. The violence of my mother's affliction had such an effect on her constitution, that she was immediately seized with the pains of childbed; and had not an old maid-servant, to whom she was very dear, afforded her pity and assistance, at the hazard of incurring my grandfather's displeasure, she and the innocent fruit of her womb must have fallen miserable victims to his rigour and inhumanity. By the friendship of this poor woman, she was carried up to a garret, and immediately delivered of a man-child, the story of whose unfortunate birth he himself now relates. My father being informed of what had happened, flew to the embraces of his darling spouse, and, while he loaded his offspring with paternal caresses, could not forbear shedding a flow of tears, on beholding the dear partner of his heart, for whose ease he would have sacrificed the treasures of the East, stretched upon a flock bed in a miserable apartment, unable to protect her from the inclemencies of the weather. It is not to be supposed, that the old gentleman was ignorant of what passed, though he affected to know nothing of the matter, and pretended to be very much surprised, when one of his grandchildren, by his eldest son deceased, who lived with him as his heir apparent, acquainted him with the affair. He determined, therefore, to observe no medium, but immediately on the third day of her delivery, sent her a peremptory order to be gone, and turned off the servant who had preserved her life. This behaviour so exasperated my father, that he had recourse to the most dreadful imprecations; and, on his bare knees, implored that Heaven would renounce him, if ever he should forget or forgive the barbarity of his sire. The injuries which this unhappy mother received from her removal in such circumstances, and the want of necessaries where she lodged, together with her grief and anxiety of mind, soon threw her into a languishing disorder, which put an end to her life. My father, who loved her tenderly, was so affected with her death, that he remained six weeks deprived of his senses; during which time, the people where he lodged carried the infant to the old man, who relented so far, on hearing the melancholy story of his daughter-in-law's death, and the deplorable condition of his son, as to send the child to nurse; and he ordered my father to be carried home to his house, where he soon recovered the use of his reason. Whether this hardhearted judge felt any remorse for his cruel treatment of his son and daughter, or (which is more probable) was afraid his character would suffer in the neighbourhood, he professed great sorrow for his conduct to my father, whose delirium was succeeded by a profound melancholy and reserve. At length he disappeared, and notwithstanding all imaginable inquiry, could not be heard of; a circumstance which confirmed most people in the opinion of his having made away with himself in a fit of despair. How I understood the particulars of my birth, will appear in the course of these memoirs.

CHAPTER II

I grow up—Am hated by my Relations—Sent to School—Neglected by my Grandfather—Maltreated by my Master—Seasoned to Adversity —I form Cabals against the Pedant—Am debarred access to my Grandfather—Hunted by his Heir—I demolish the Teeth of his Tutor.

THERE were not wanting some who suspected my uncles of being concerned in my father's fate, on the supposition that they would all share in the patrimony destined for him; and this conjecture was strengthened by reflecting, that, in all his calamities, they never discovered the least inclination to serve him; but, on the contrary, by all the artifices in their power, fed his father's resentment, and supported his resolution of leaving him to misery and want. But people of judgment treated this situation as an idle chimera; because, had my relations been so wicked as to consult their interest by committing such an atrocious crime, the fate of my father would have extended to me too, whose life was another obstacle to their expectation. Meanwhile, I grew apace; and as I strongly resembled my father, who was the darling of the tenants, I wanted nothing which their indigent circumstances could afford: but their favour was a weak resource against the jealous enmity of my cousins; who, the more my infancy promised, conceived the more implacable hatred against me; and, before I was six years of age, had so effectually blockaded my grandfather, that I never saw him but by stealth; when I sometimes made up to his chair, as he sat to view his labourers in the field: on which occasions, he would stroke my head, bid me be a good boy, and promise to take care of me. I was soon after sent to school at a village hard by, of which he had been dictator time out of mind; but as he neither paid for my board, nor supplied me with clothes, books, and other necessaries I required, my condition was very ragged and contemptible; and the schoolmaster, who, through fear of my grandfather, taught me *gratis*, gave himself no concern about the progress I made under his instruction. In spite of all these difficulties and disgraces, I became a good proficient in the Latin tongue; and as soon as I could write tolerably, pestered my grandfather with letters to such a degree, that he sent for my master, and chid him severely for bestowing such pains on my education, telling him, that if ever I should be brought to the gallows for forgery, which he had taught me to commit, my blood would lie on his head. The pedant, who dreaded nothing more than the displeasure of his patron, assured his honour, that the boy's ability was more owing to his own genius and application, than to any instruction or encouragement he received; that, although he could not divest him of the knowledge he had already imbibed unless he would empower him to disable his fingers, he should endeavour, with God's help, to prevent his future improvement. And, indeed, he punctually performed what he had undertaken; for, on pretence that I had writ impertinent letters to my grandfather, he caused a board to be made with five holes in it, through which he thrust the fingers and thumb of my right hand, and fastened it with a whip-cord to my wrist, in such a manner as effectually debarred

me the use of my pen. But this restraint I was freed from in a
few days, by an accident which happened in a quarrel between
me and another boy, who, taking upon him to insult my poverty,
I was so incensed at his ungenerous reproach, that, with one
stroke of my machine, I cut him to the skull, to the great terror
of myself and school-fellows, who left him bleeding on the
ground, and ran to inform the master of what had happened.
I was so severely punished for this trespass, that, were I to live
to the age of Methusalem, the impression it made on me would
not be effaced; no more than the antipathy and horror I conceived for the merciless tyrant who inflicted it. The contempt
which my appearance naturally produced in all who saw me,
the continual wants to which I was exposed, and my own
haughty disposition, impatient of affronts, involved me in a
thousand troublesome adventures, by which I was at length
inured to adversity, and emboldened to undertakings far above
my years. I was often inhumanly scourged for crimes I did not
commit; because, having the character of a vagabond in the
village, every piece of mischief, whose author lay unknown, was
charged upon me. I have been found guilty of robbing orchards
I never entered, of killing cats I never hurted, of stealing gingerbread I never touched, and of abusing old women I never saw.
Nay, a stammering carpenter had eloquence enough to persuade
my master that I fired a pistol, loaded with small shot, into his
window; though my landlady and the whole family bore witness,
that I was abed fast asleep at the time when this outrage was
committed. I was once flogged for having narrowly escaped
drowning, by the sinking of a ferry boat in which I was passenger;
another time for having recovered of a bruise occasioned by a
horse and cart running over me; a third time for being bit by a
baker's dog. In short, whether I was guilty or unfortunate, the
correction and sympathy of this arbitrary pedagogue were the
same. Far from being subdued by this infernal usage, my indignation triumphed over that slavish awe which had hitherto
enforced my obedience; and the more my years and knowledge
increased, the more I perceived the injustice and barbarity of
his behaviour. By the help of an uncommon genius, and the
advice and direction of our usher, who had served my father
in his travels, I made a surprising progress in the classics,
writings, and arithmetic; so that, before I was twelve years
old, I was allowed by everybody to be the best scholar in the
school. This qualification, together with a boldness of temper,
and strength of make, which had subjected almost all my

contemporaries, gave me such influence over them, that I began to form cabals against my persecutor, and was in hopes of being able to bid him defiance in a very short time. Being at the head of a faction consisting of thirty boys, most of them of my own age, I was determined to put their metal to trial, that I might know how far they were to be depended upon, before I put my grand scheme in execution: with this view, we attacked a body of stout apprentices, who had taken possession of a part of the ground allotted to us for the scene of our diversions, and who were then playing at nine-pins on the spot: but I had the mortification to see my adherents routed in an instant, and a leg of one of them broke in his flight by the bowl, which one of our adversaries had detached in pursuit of us. This discomfiture did not hinder us from engaging them afterwards in frequent skirmishes, which we maintained by throwing stones at a distance, wherein I received many wounds, the scars of which still remain. Our enemies were so harassed and interrupted by these alarms, that they at last abandoned their conquest, and left us to the peaceable enjoyment of our own territories. It would be endless to enumerate the exploits we performed in the course of this confederacy, which became the terror of the whole village; insomuch, that when different interests divided it, one of the parties commonly courted the assistance of Roderick Random (by which name I was known), to cast the balance, and keep the opposite faction in awe. Meanwhile, I took the advantage of every play-day to present myself before my grandfather, to whom I seldom found access, by reason of his being closely besieged by a numerous family of his female grandchildren, who, though they perpetually quarrelled among themselves, never failed to join against me, as the common enemy of all. His heir, who was about the age of eighteen, minded nothing but fox-hunting, and indeed, was qualified for nothing else, notwithstanding his grandfather's indulgence, in entertaining a tutor for him at home, who at the same time performed the office of parish-clerk. This young Actæon, who inherited his grandfather's antipathy to everything in distress, never set eyes on me, without uncoupling his beagles, and hunting me into some cottage or other, whither I generally fled for shelter. In this christian amusement, he was encouraged by his preceptor, who, no doubt, took such opportunities to ingratiate himself with the rising sun, observing that the old gentleman, according to the course of nature, had not long to live, for he was already on the verge of fourscore. The behaviour of this rascally sycophant

incensed me so much, that one day, when I was beleaguered by
him and his hounds in a farmer's house, where I found protection,
I took aim at him (being an excellent marksman) with a large
pebble, which struck out four of his fore-teeth, and effectually
incapacitated him for doing the office of a clerk.

CHAPTER III

My Mother's Brother arrives—Relieves me—A Description of him—He
goes along with me to the House of my Grandfather—Is encountered by
his Dogs—Defeats them, after a bloody Engagement—Is admitted to the
old Gentleman—A Dialogue between them.

ABOUT this time, my mother's only brother, who had been long
abroad, lieutenant of a man of war, arrived in his own country;
where, being informed of my condition, he came to see me, and,
out of his slender finances, not only supplied me with what
necessaries I wanted for the present, but resolved not to leave
the country until he had prevailed on my grandfather to settle
something handsome on me for the future. This was a task to
which he was by no means equal, being entirely ignorant, not
only of the judge's disposition, but also unacquainted with
the ways of men in general, to which his education on board
had kept him an utter stranger. He was a strong-built man,
somewhat bandy-legged, with a neck like that of a bull, and a
face which (you might easily perceive) had withstood the most
obstinate assaults of the weather. His dress consisted of a
soldier's coat, altered for him by the ship's tailor, a striped
flannel jacket, a pair of red breeches, japanned with pitch, clean
grey worsted stockings, large silver buckles that covered three-
fourths of his shoes, a silver-laced hat, whose crown overlooked
the brims about an inch and a half, a black bob wig in buckle,
a check shirt, a silk handkerchief, an hanger with a brass
handle, girded to his thigh by a tarnished laced belt, and a good
oak plant under his arm. Thus equipped, he set out with me
(who, by his bounty, made a very decent appearance) for my
grandfather's house, where we were saluted by Jowler and
Cæsar, whom my cousin, young master, had let loose at our
approach. Being well acquainted with the inveteracy of these
curs, I was about to betake myself to my heels, when my uncle
seized me with one hand, brandished his cudgel with the other,
and at one blow laid Cæsar sprawling on the ground; but finding

himself attacked at the same time in the rea...
fearing Cæsar might recover, he drew his hange...
and, by a lucky stroke, severed Jowler's head...
By this time, the young fox-hunter and three ...
with pitch-forks and flails, were come to the as...
dogs, whom they found breathless on the field; ...
was so provoked at the death of his favourites, th... ...e ordered
his attendants to advance and take vengeance on their executioner, whom he loaded with all the curses and reproaches
his anger could suggest. Upon which my uncle stepped forward
with an undaunted air, at the sight of whose bloody weapon his
antagonists fell back with precipitation, when he accosted their
leader thus: "Lookee, brother, your dogs have boarded me
without provocation—what I did was in my own defence. So
you had best be civil, and let us shoot ahead clear of you."
Whether the young squire misinterpreted my uncle's desire of
peace, or was enraged at the fate of his hounds beyond his
usual pitch of resolution, I know not; but he snatched a flail
from one of his followers, and came up with a show of assaulting
the lieutenant, who, putting himself in a posture of defence,
proceeded thus: "Lookee, you lubberly son of a w——e, if you
come athwart me, 'ware your gingerbread work, I'll be foul of
your quarter, damn me." This declaration, followed by a
flourish of his hanger, seemed to check the progress of the young
gentleman's choler, who, looking behind him, perceived his
attendants had slunk into the house, shut the gate, and left
him to decide the contention by himself. Here a parley ensued,
which was introduced by my cousin's asking, "Who the devil
are you? What do you want?—Some scoundrel of a seaman,
I suppose, who has deserted, and turned thief. But don't think
you shall escape, sirrah; I'll have you hanged, you dog, I will;
your blood shall pay for that of my two hounds, you ragamuffin.
I would not have parted with them to save your whole generation
from the gallows, you ruffian, you." "None of your jaw, you
swab—none of your jaw," replied my uncle—"else I shall trim
your laced jacket for you—I shall rub you down with an oaken
towel, my boy—I shall." So saying, he sheathed his hanger
and grasped his cudgel. Meanwhile, the people of the house
being alarmed, one of my female cousins opened a window,
and asked what was the matter? "The matter!" answered the
lieutenant, "no great matter, young woman. I have business
with the old gentleman, and this spark, belike, won't allow me
to come alongside of him, that's all." After a few minutes'

.e were admitted, and conducted to my grandfather's
..er, through a lane of my relations, who honoured me with
.ry significant looks, as I passed along. When we came into
the judge's presence, my uncle, after two or three sea-bows,
expressed himself in this manner: "Your servant—your servant.
What cheer, father?—what cheer?—I suppose you don't know
me—mayhap you don't. My name is Tom Bowling; and this
here boy—you look as if you did not know him neither; 'tis
like you mayn't. He's new rigg'd, i'faith; his cloth don't shake
in the wind so much as it wont to do. 'Tis my nephew, d'ye
see, Roderick Random—your own flesh and blood, old gentleman. Don't lag astern, you dog," pulling me forward. My
grandfather (who was laid up with the gout) received this
relation, after his long absence, with that coldness of civility
which was peculiar to him; told him he was glad to see him, and
desired him to sit down. "Thank ye, thank ye, Sir, I had as lief
stand," said my uncle. "For my own part, I desire nothing of
you; but if you have any conscience at all, do something for
this poor boy, who has been used at a very unchristian rate.
Unchristian, do I call it? I am sure the Moors in Barbary have
more humanity than to leave their little ones to want. I would
fain know why my sister's son is more neglected than that there
fair-weather Jack" (pointing to the young squire, who, with
the rest of my cousins, had followed us into the room). "Is not
he as near akin to you as the other? Is not he much handsomer
and better built than that great chucklehead? Come, come—
consider, old gentleman, you are going in a short time to give
an account of your evil actions. Remember the wrongs you did
his father; and make all the satisfaction in your power, before
it be too late. The least thing you can do is to settle his father's
portion on him." The young ladies, who thought themselves
too much concerned to contain themselves any longer, set up
their throats all together against my protector, "Scurvy companion—saucy tarpaulin—rude, impertinent fellow—did he
think to prescribe to grandpapa? His sister's brat had been too
well taken care of; grandpapa was too just not to make a difference between an unnatural rebellious son, and his dutiful
loving children, who took his advice in all things"—and such
expressions, were vented against him with great violence, until
the judge at length commanded silence. He calmly rebuked my
uncle for his unmannerly behaviour, which he said he would
excuse, on account of his education. He told him he had been
very kind to the boy, whom he had kept to school seven or eight

years, although he was informed he made no progress in his learning, but was addicted to all manner of vice; which he rather believed, because he himself was witness to a barbarous piece of mischief he had committed on the jaws of his chaplain. But, however, he would see what the lad was fit for, and bind him apprentice to some honest tradesman or other, provided he would mend his manners, and behave for the future as became him. The honest tar, whose pride and indignation boiled within him, answered my grandfather, that it was true he had sent him to school, but it had cost him nothing; for he had never been at one shilling expense to furnish him with food, raiment, books, or other necessaries; so that it was not to be much wondered at, if the boy made small progress; and yet, whoever told him so, was a lying lubberly rascal, and deserved to be keel-hauled. For though he (the lieutenant) did not understand those matters himself, he was well informed as how Rory was the best scholar of his age in all the country; the truth of which he would maintain, by laying a wager of his whole half-year's pay on the boy's head (with these words, he pulled out his purse, and challenged the company). "Neither is he predicted to vice, as you affirm, but rather left like a wreck, d'ye see, at the mercy of the wind and weather by your neglect, old gentleman. As for what happened to your chaplain, I am only sorry that he did not knock out the scoundrel's brains, instead of his teeth. By the Lord, if ever I come up with him, he had better be in Greenland—that's all. Thank you for your courteous offer of binding the lad apprentice to a tradesman. I suppose you would make a tailor of him—would you? I had rather see him hanged, d'ye see. Come along, Rory, I perceive how the land lies, my boy; let's tack about—i'faith, while I have a shilling, thou shan't want a tester. B'wye, old gentleman, you're bound for the other world, but I believe damnably ill provided for the voyage." Thus ended our visit, and we returned to the village, my uncle muttering curses all the way against the old shark and the young fry that surrounded him.

CHAPTER IV

My Grandfather makes his Will—Our second Visit—He dies—His
Will is read in presence of all his living Descendants—The Disappointment
of my female Cousins—My Uncle's Behaviour.

A FEW weeks after our first visit, we were informed that the old
judge, at the end of a fit of thoughtfulness which lasted three
days, had sent for a notary, and made his will; that the distemper
had mounted from his legs to his stomach, and, being conscious
of his approaching end, he had desired to see all his descendants
without exception. In obedience to this summons, my uncle
set out with me a second time, to receive the last benediction
of my grandfather: often repeating by the road, "Ey, ey, we
have brought up the old hulk at last. You shall see,—you shall
see the effect of my admonition." When we entered his chamber,
which was crowded with his relations, we advanced to the
bedside, where we found him in his last agonies, supported by
two of his granddaughters, who sat on each side of him, sobbing
most piteously, and wiping away the froth and slaver as it
gathered on his lips, which they frequently kissed with a show
of great anguish and affection. My uncle approached them with
these words: "What! he's not aweigh? How fare ye, old gentleman?—Lord have mercy upon your sinful soul." Upon which
the dying man turned his languid eyes towards us, and Mr.
Bowling went on, "Here's poor Rory come to see you before
you die, and receive your blessing. What, man! don't despair,
—you have been a great sinner, 'tis true, what then? There's a
righteous judge above,—an't there?—He minds me no more
than a porpoise. Yes, yes, he's agoing,—the land crabs will
have him, I see that,—his anchor's apeak, i'faith." This homely
consolation scandalised the company so much, and especially
the parson, who probably thought his province invaded, that
we were obliged to retire into the other room, where, in a few
minutes, we were convinced of my grandfather's decease, by a
dismal yell uttered by the young ladies in his apartment; whither
we immediately hastened, and found his heir, who had retired
a little before into a closet, under pretence of giving vent to
his sorrow, asking, with a countenance beslubbered with tears,
if his grandpapa was certainly dead?—"Dead!" says my uncle,
looking at the body, "ay, ay, I'll warrant him as dead as a
herring. Odds fish! now my dream is out for all the world. I
thought I stood upon the forecastle, and saw a parcel of carrion

crows foul of a dead shark that floated alongside, and the devil perching on our sprit-sail yard, in the likeness of a blue bear,— who, d'ye see, jumped overboard upon the carcass, and carried it to the bottom in its claws." "Out upon thee, reprobate," cries the parson, "out upon thee, blasphemous wretch!—Dost thou think his honour's soul is in the possession of Satan?" The clamour immediately arose, and my poor uncle, being shouldered from one corner of the room to the other, was obliged to lug out in his own defence, and swear he would turn out for no man, till such time as he knew who had a title to send him adrift. "None of your tricks upon travellers," said he; "mayhap old buff has left my kinsman here his heir: if he has, it will be the better for his miserable soul. Odds bob! I'd desire no better news. I'd soon make him a clear ship, I warrant you." To avoid any further disturbance, one of my grandfather's executors, who was present, assured Mr. Bowling that his nephew should have all manner of justice; that a day should be appointed, after the funeral, for examining the papers of the deceased, in presence of all his relations; till which time every desk and cabinet in the house should remain close sealed; and that he was very welcome to be witness to this ceremony, which was immediately performed to his satisfaction. In the meantime, orders were given to provide mourning for all the relations, in which number I was included: but my uncle would not suffer me to accept of it, until I should be assured whether or not I had reason to honour his memory so far. During this interval, the conjectures of people, with regard to the old gentleman's will, were various. As it was well known he had, besides his landed estate, which was worth £700 per annum, six or seven thousand pounds at interest, some imagined, that the whole real estate (which he had greatly improved) would go to the young man whom he always entertained as his heir; and that the money would be equally divided between my female cousins (five in number) and me. Others were of opinion, that as the rest of his children had been already provided for, he would only bequeath two or three hundred pounds to each of his granddaughters, and leave the bulk of the sum to me, to atone for his unnatural usage of my father. At length the important hour arrived, and the will was produced in the midst of the expectants, whose looks and gestures formed a group that would have been very entertaining to an unconcerned spectator. But the reader can scarce conceive the astonishment and mortification that appeared, when the attorney pronounced aloud, the young squire sole heir of all his grandfather's estate, personal and real. My uncle, who had listened with great attention, sucking the head of his cudgel all the while, accompanied these words of the attorney with a stare, and *whew*, that alarmed the whole assembly. The eldest and pertest of my female competitors, who had been always very officious about my grandfather's person, inquired with a faltering accent, and visage as yellow as an orange, "If there were no legacies?" and was answered, "None at all." Upon which she fainted away. The rest, whose expectations, perhaps, were not so sanguine, supported their disappointment with more resolution; though not without giving evident marks of indignation, and grief at least as genuine as that which appeared in them at the old gentleman's death. My conductor, having kicked with his heel for some time against the wainscot, began: "So there's no legacy, friend, ha!—here's an old succubus;—but somebody's soul howls for it, damn me!" The parson of the parish, who was one of the executors, and had acted as ghostly director to the old man, no sooner heard this exclamation than he cried out, "Avaunt, unchristian reviler! avaunt!—wilt thou not allow the soul of his honour to rest in peace?" But this zealous pastor did not find himself so warmly seconded, as formerly, by the young ladies, who now joined my uncle against him, and accused him of having acted the part of a busybody with their grandpapa, whose ears he had certainly abused by false stories to their prejudice, or else he would not have neglected them in such an unnatural manner. The young squire was much diverted with this scene, and whispered to my uncle, that, if he had not murdered his dogs, he would have shown him glorious fun, by hunting a black badger (so he termed the clergyman). The surly lieutenant, who was not in an humour to relish this amusement, replied, "You and your dogs may be damned; I suppose you'll find them with your old dad, in the latitude of hell. Come, Rory—about ship, my lad,—we must steer another course, I think."—And away we went.

CHAPTER V

The Schoolmaster uses me barbarously—I form a Project of Revenge, in which I am assisted by my Uncle—I leave the Village—Am settled at an University by his generosity.

ON our way back to the village, my uncle spoke not a word during the space of a whole hour, but whistled, with great vehemence, the tune of "Why should we quarrel for riches," etc., his visage being contracted all the while into a most formidable frown. At length his pace increased to such a degree, that I was left behind a considerable way. Then he waited for me; and, when I was almost up with him, called out in a surly tone, "Bear a hand, damme! must I bring-to every minute for you, you lazy dog?" Then, laying hold of me by the arm, hauled me along, until his good nature (of which he had a great share) and reflection getting the better of his passion, he said, "Come, my boy, don't be cast down,—the old rascal is in hell,—that's some satisfaction; you shall go to sea with me, my lad.—'A light heart and a thin pair of breeches goes through the world, brave boys,' as the song goes, eh!" Though this proposal did not at all suit my inclination, I was afraid of discovering any aversion to it, lest I should disoblige the only friend I had in the world; and he was so much a seaman, that he never dreamt I could have any objection to his design, consequently gave himself no trouble in consulting my approbation. But this resolution was soon dropt, by the advice of our usher, who assured Mr. Bowling, it would be a thousand pities to baulk my genius, which would certainly, one day, make my fortune on shore, provided it received due cultivation. Upon which this generous tar determined (though he could ill afford it) to give me university education; and accordingly settled my board and other expenses, at a town not many miles distant, famous for its colleges, whither we repaired in a short time. But, before the day of our departure, the schoolmaster, who no longer had the fear of my grandfather before his eyes, laid aside all decency and restraint, and not only abused me in the grossest language his rancour could suggest, as a wicked, profligate, dull, beggarly miscreant, whom he had taught out of charity; but also inveighed in the most bitter manner against the memory of the judge (who, by the bye, had procured that settlement for him), hinting in pretty plain terms, that the old gentleman's soul was damn'd to all eternity, for his injustice in neglecting to pay for my learning. This brutal behaviour, added to the sufferings I had formerly undergone, made me think it high time to be revenged of this insolent pedagogue. Having consulted my adherents, I found them all staunch in their promises to stand by me; and our scheme was this: in the afternoon preceding the day of my departure for the university, I resolved to take the advantage of the usher's going out to make water, which he regularly did at four o'clock, and shut the great door, that he might not come in to the assistance of his superior. This being done, the assault was to be begun, by my advancing to my master, and spitting in his face. I was to be seconded by two of the strongest boys in the school, who were devoted to me; their business was to join me in dragging the tyrant to a bench, over which he was to be laid, and his bare posteriors heartily flogged with his own birch, which we proposed to wrest from him in the struggle; but if we should find him too many for us all three, we were to demand the assistance of our competitors, who should be ready to reinforce us, or oppose anything that might be undertaken for the master's relief. One of my principal assistants was called Jeremy Gawky, son and heir of a wealthy gentleman in the neighbourhood; and the name of the other, Hugh Strap, the cadet of a family which had given shoemakers to the village time out of mind. I had once saved Gawky's life, by plunging into a river, and dragging him on shore, when he was on the point of being drowned. I had often rescued him from the clutches of those whom his insufferable arrogance had provoked to a resentment he was not able to sustain; and many times saved his reputation and posteriors, by performing his exercises at school; so that it is not to be wondered at if he had a particular regard for me and my interests. The attachment of Strap flowed from a voluntary disinterested inclination, which had manifested itself on many occasions on my behalf, he having once rendered me the same service that I had done Gawky, by saving my life at the risk of his own; and often fathered offences that I had committed, for which he suffered severely, rather than I should feel the weight of the punishment I deserved. These two champions were the more willing to engage in this enterprise, because they intended to leave the school the next day as well as I, the first being ordered by his father to return into the country, and the other being bound apprentice to a barber, at a market town not far off.

In the meantime, my uncle being informed of my master's behaviour to me, was enraged at his insolence, and vowed revenge so heartily, that I could not refrain from telling him the scheme I had concerted, which he heard with great satisfaction, at every sentence squirting out a mouthful of spittle, tinctured with tobacco, of which he constantly chewed a large quid. At last, pulling up his breeches, he cried, "No, no, zounds! that won't do, neither. Howsomever, 'tis a bold undertaking, my lad, that I must say, i'faith! But lookee, lookee, how dost propose to get clear off? won't the enemy give chase, my boy? ay, ay, that he will, I warrant, and alarm the whole coast. Ah! God help thee, more slip than ballast, Rory. Let me alone for that—leave the whole to me—I'll show him the fore-topsail, I will. If so be your shipmates are jolly boys, and won't flinch, you shall see, you shall see; egad, I'll play him a salt-water trick; I'll bring him to the gangway, and anoint him with a cat-o'-nine-tails; he shall have a round dozen doubled, my lad, he shall, and be left lashed to his meditations."

We were very proud of our associate, who immediately went to work, and prepared the instrument of his revenge with great skill and expedition; after which, he ordered our baggage to be packed up, and sent off a day before our attempt, and got horses ready to be mounted, as soon as the affair should be over. At length the hour arrived, when our auxiliary, seizing the opportunity of the usher's absence, bolted in, secured the door, and immediately laid hold of the pedant by his collar, who bawled out, "Murder! thieves!" with the voice of a Stentor. Though I trembled all over like an aspen-leaf, I knew there was no time to be lost, and accordingly got up, and summoned our associates to my assistance. Strap, without any hesitation, obeyed the signal; and seeing me leap upon the master's back, ran immediately to one of his legs, which, pulling with all his force, his dreadful adversary was humbled to the ground; upon which Gawky, who had hitherto remained in his place, under the influence of an universal trepidation, hastened to the scene of action, and insulted the fallen tyrant with a loud huzza, in which the whole school joined. This noise alarmed the usher, who, finding himself shut out, endeavoured, partly by threats, and partly by entreaties, to procure admission. My uncle bade him have a little patience, and he would let him in presently; but, if he pretended to move from that place, it should fare worse with the son of a bitch, his superior, on whom he intended only to bestow a little wholesome chastisement, for his barbarous usage of Rory; "to which," said he, "you are no stranger." By this time we had dragged the criminal to a post, to which

Bowling tied him with a rope he had provided on purpose, after having secured his hands, and stript his back. In this ludicrous posture he stood (to the no small entertainment of the boys, who crowded about him, and shouted with great exultation at the novelty of the sight), venting bitter imprecations against the lieutenant, and reproaching his scholars with treachery and rebellion, when the usher was admitted, whom my uncle accosted in this manner: "Harkee, Mr. Syntax, I believe you are an honest man, d'ye see, and I have a respect for you; but, for all that, we must, for our own security, d'ye see, belay you for a short time." With these words, he pulled out some fathoms of cord, which the honest man no sooner saw, than he protested with great earnestness he would allow no violence to be offered to him; at the same time accusing me of perfidy and ingratitude. But Bowling representing that it was in vain to resist, and that he did not mean to use him with violence and indecency, but only to hinder him from raising the hue and cry against us before we should be out of their power, he allowed himself to be bound to his own desk, where he sat a spectator of the punishment inflicted on his principal. My uncle having upbraided this arbitrary wretch with his inhumanity to me, told him that he proposed to give him a little discipline for the good of his soul, which he immediately put in practice with great vigour and dexterity. This smart application to the pedant's withered posteriors, gave him such exquisite pain, that he roared like a mad bull, danced, cursed, and blasphemed, like a frantic bedlamite. When the lieutenant thought himself sufficiently revenged, he took his leave of him in these words: "Now, friend, you'll remember me the longest day you have to live; I have given you a lesson that will let you know what flogging is, and teach you to have more sympathy for the future—shout, boys, shout." This ceremony was no sooner over, than my uncle proposed they should quit the school, and convoy their old comrade Rory to a public-house, about a mile from the village, where he would treat them all. His offer being joyfully embraced, he addressed himself to Mr. Syntax, and begged him to accompany us; but this invitation he refused with great disdain, telling my benefactor he was not the man he took him to be. "Well, well, old surly," replied my uncle, shaking his hand, "thou art an honest fellow notwithstanding; and if ever I have the command of a ship, thou shalt be our schoolmaster, i'faith." So saying, he dismissed the boys, and, locking the door, left the two preceptors to console one another, while we moved forwards on our journey, attended by a numerous retinue, whom he treated according to his promise. We parted with many tears, and lay that night at an inn on the road, about ten miles short of the town where I was to remain, at which we arrived next day; and I found I had no cause to complain of the accommodations provided for me, in being boarded at the house of an apothecary, who had married a distant relation of my mother. In a few days after, my uncle set out for his ship, having settled the necessary funds for my maintenance and education.

CHAPTER VI

I make great progress in my Studies—Am caressed by everybody—My female Cousins take notice of me—I reject their Invitation—They are incensed, and conspire against me—I am left destitute by a Misfortune that befalls my Uncle—Gawky's Treachery—My Revenge.

As I was now capable of reflection, I began to consider my precarious situation; that I was utterly abandoned by those whose duty it was to protect me; and that my sole dependence was on the generosity of one man, who was not only exposed by his profession to continual dangers, which might one day deprive me of him for ever; but also, no doubt, subject to those vicissitudes of disposition which a change of fortune usually creates, or which a better acquaintance with the world might produce; for I always ascribed his benevolence to the dictates of a heart as yet undebauched by a commerce with mankind. Alarmed at these considerations, I resolved to apply myself with great care to my studies, and enjoy the opportunity in my power; this I did with such success, that, in the space of three years, I understood Greek very well, was pretty far advanced in the mathematics, and no stranger to moral and natural philosophy; logic I made no account of; but, above all things, I valued myself on my taste in the *Belles Lettres*, and a talent for poetry, which had already produced some pieces that met with a very favourable reception. These qualifications, added to a good face and shape, acquired the esteem and acquaintance of the most considerable people in town; and I had the satisfaction to find myself in some degree of favour with the ladies —an intoxicating piece of good fortune to one of my amorous complexion!—which I obtained, or, at least, preserved, by gratifying their propensity to scandal in lampooning their rivals. Two of my female cousins lived in this place with their mother, since the death of their father, who left his whole fortune equally divided between them; so that, if they were not the most beautiful, they were at least the richest toasts in town, and received daily the addresses of all the beaux and cavaliers of the country. Although I had hitherto been looked upon by them with the most supercilious contempt, my character now attracted their notice so much, that I was given to understand I might be honoured with their acquaintance, if I pleased. The reader will easily perceive that this condescension either flowed from the hope of making my poetical capacity subservient to their malice, or, at least, of screening themselves from the lash of my resentment, which they had effectually provoked. I enjoyed this triumph with great satisfaction; and not only rejected their offer with disdain, but, in all my performances, whether satire or panegyric, industriously avoided mentioning their names, even while I celebrated those of their intimates. This neglect mortified their pride exceedingly, and incensed them to such a degree, that they were resolved to make me repent of my indifference. The first stroke of their revenge consisted in their hiring a poor collegian to write verses against me, the subject of which was my own poverty, and the catastrophe of my unhappy parents. But, besides the badness of the composition (of which they themselves were ashamed), they did not find their account in endeavouring to reproach me with those misfortunes which they and their relations had brought upon me, and which, consequently, reflected much more dishonour on themselves than on me, who was the innocent victim of their barbarity and avarice. Finding this plan miscarry, they found means to irritate a young gentleman against me, by telling him I had lampooned his mistress, and so effectually succeeded in the quality of incendiaries, that this enraged lover determined to seize me next night, as I returned to my lodgings from a friend's house that I frequented. With this view, he waited in the street, attended by two of his companions, to whom he had imparted his design of carrying me down to the river, in which he proposed to have me heartily ducked, notwithstanding the severity of the weather, it being then about the middle of December. But this stratagem did not succeed; for, being apprised of their ambush, I got home another way, and, by the help of my landlord's apprentice, discharged a volley from the garret window, which did great execution upon them; and next day, occasioned so much mirth at their expense, that they found themselves under a necessity of leaving the town, until the adventure should be entirely forgotten. My cousins (though twice baffled in their expectation) did not, however, desist from persecuting me, who had now enraged them beyond a possibility of forgiveness, by detecting their malice, and preventing its effects. Neither should I have found them more humane, had I patiently submitted to their rancour, and bore, without murmuring, the rigour of their unreasonable hate; for I have found, by experience, that, though small favours may be acknowledged, and slight injuries atoned, there is no wretch so ungrateful as he whom you have most generously obliged; and no enemy so implacable as those who have done you the greatest wrong. These good-natured creatures, therefore, had recourse to a scheme which conspired, with a piece of bad news I soon after received, to give them all the satisfaction they desired. This plan was to debauch the faith of my companion and confidant, who betrayed the trust I reposed in him, by imparting to them the particulars of my small amours, which they published with such exaggerations, that I suffered very much in the opinion of everybody, and was utterly discarded by the dear creatures whose names had been called in question. While I was busy in tracing out the author of this treachery, that I might not only be revenged on him, but also vindicate my character to my friends, I one day perceived the looks of my landlady much altered when I went home to dinner, and inquiring into the cause, she screwed up her mouth, and fixing her eyes on the ground, told me her husband had received a letter from Mr. Bowling, with one enclosed for me—she was very sorry for what had happened, both for my sake and his own—people should be more cautious of their conduct. She was always afraid his brutal behaviour would bring him into some misfortune or other. As for her part, she would be very ready to befriend me, but she had a small family of her own to maintain. The world would do nothing for her if she should come to want—charity begins at home. She wished I had been bound to some substantial handicraft, such as a weaver, or a shoemaker, rather than loiter away my time in learning foolish nonsense that would never bring me in a penny—but some folks are wise and some are otherwise. I was listening to this mysterious discourse with great amazement, when her husband entered, and, without speaking a syllable, put both the letters into my hand. I received them trembling, and read what follows:

"To Mr. Roger Potion

"Sir,—This is to let you know that I have quitted the Thunder man of war, being obliged to sheer off, for killing my captain, which I did fairly on the beach at Cape Tiberoon, in the island of Hispaniola; having received his fire, and returned it, which went through his body. And I would serve the best man so that ever stept between stem and stern, if so be that he struck me, as Captain Oakum did. I am (thank God) safe among the French, who are very civil, tho' I don't understand their lingo; and I hope to be restored in a little time, for all the great friends and parliamentary interest of the captain, for I have sent over to my landlord in Deal an account of the whole affair, with our bearings and distances while we were engaged, whereby I have desired him to lay it before his Majesty, who (God bless him) will not suffer an honest tar to be wronged. My love to your spouse, and am

"Your loving friend and servant to command, while

"THOMAS BOWLING."

————

"To Roderick Random

"Dear Rory,—Don't be grieved at my misfortune; but mind your book, my lad. I have got no money to send you; but what of that?—Mr. Potion will take care of you, for the love he bears me, and let you want for nothing, and it shall go hard but I will see him one day repaid. No more at present, but rests

"Your dutiful uncle and servant till death,

"THOMAS BOWLING."

This letter (which with the other was dated from Port Louis in Hispaniola) I no sooner read, than the apothecary, shaking his head, began: "I have a very great regard for Mr. Bowling, that's certain,—and could be well content—but times are very hard. There's no such thing as money to be got—I believe 'tis all vanished under ground, for my part. Besides, I have been out of pocket already, having entertained you since the beginning of this month without receiving a sixpence,—and God knows if ever I shall;—for I believe it will go hard with your uncle. And more than that, I was thinking of giving you warning, for I want your apartment for a new 'prentice, whom I expect from the country every hour. So I desire you will this week provide yourself with another lodging." The indignation which this harangue inspired, gave me spirits to support my reverse of fortune, and to tell him, I despised his mean, selfish disposition so much, that I would starve rather than be beholden to him for one single meal. Upon which, out of my pocket-money, I paid him to the last farthing of what I owed, and assured him I would not sleep another night under his roof. This said, I sallied out in a transport of rage and sorrow, without knowing whither to fly for shelter, having not one friend in the world capable of relieving me, and only three shillings in my purse. After giving way for a few minutes to the dictates of my rage, I went and hired a small bedroom, at the rate of one shilling and sixpence per week, which I was obliged to pay per advance, before the landlord would receive me. Thither I removed my luggage; and next morning got up, with a view of craving the advice and assistance of a person who had on all occasions loaded me with caresses, and made frequent offers of friendship, while I was under no necessity of accepting them. He received me with his wonted affability, and insisted on my breakfasting with him—a favour which I did not think fit to refuse. But, when I communicated the occasion of my visit, he appeared so disconcerted, that I concluded him wonderfully affected with the misery of my condition, and looked upon him as a man of the most extensive sympathy and benevolence. He did not leave me long under this mistake; for, recovering himself from his confusion, he told me, he was grieved at my misfortune, and desired to know what had passed between my landlord Mr. Potion and me. Whereupon I recounted the conversation; and when I repeated the answer I made to his ungenerous remonstrance with regard to my leaving his house, this pretended friend affected a stare, and exclaimed, "Is it possible you could behave so ill to the man who had treated you so kindly all along!" My surprise at hearing this was not at all affected, whatever his might be; and I gave him to understand, with some warmth, that I did not imagine he would so unreasonably espouse the cause of a scoundrel, who ought to be expelled from every social community. This heat of mine gave him all the advantage he desired over me, and our discourse (after much altercation) concluded in his desiring never to see me again in that place; to which desire I yielded my consent, assuring him, that had I been as well acquainted with his principles formerly as I was now, he should never have had an opportunity of making that request;—and thus we parted.

On my return I met my comrade, Squire Gawky, whom his

father had sent, some time ago, to town, for his improvement in writing, dancing, fencing and other modish qualifications. As I had lived with him, since his arrival, on the footing of our old intimacy, I made no scruple of informing him of the lowness of my circumstances, and asking a small supply of money, to answer my present expense; upon which he pulled out a handful of halfpence, with a shilling or two among them, and swore that was all he had to keep his pocket till next quarter-day, he having lost the greatest part of his allowance the night before at billiards. Though this assertion might very well be true, I was extremely mortified at his indifference; for he neither expressed any sympathy for my mishap, nor desire of alleviating my distress; and accordingly I left him without uttering one word. But when I afterwards understood that he was the person who had formerly betrayed me to the malice of my cousins, to whom likewise he had carried the tidings of my forlorn situation, which afforded them great matter of triumph and exultation, I determined with myself to call him to a severe account; for which purpose I borrowed a sword, and wrote a challenge, desiring him to meet me at a certain time and place, that I might have an opportunity of punishing his perfidy, at the expense of his blood. He accepted the invitation: and I betook myself to the field, though not without feeling considerable repugnance to the combat, which frequently attacked me in cold sweats by the way: but the desire for revenge, the shame of retracting, and hope of conquest, conspired to repel these unmanly symptoms of fear; and I appeared on the plain with a good grace. There I waited an hour beyond the time appointed, and was not ill pleased to find he had no mind to meet me; because I should have an opportunity of exposing his cowardice, displaying my own courage, and of beating him soundly wheresoever I should find him, without any dread of the consequence. Elevated with these suggestions, which entirely banished all thoughts of my deplorable condition, I went directly to Gawky's lodgings, where I was informed of his precipitate retreat, he having set out for the country in less than an hour after he had received my billet: and I was vain enough to have the whole story inserted in the news, although I was fain to sell a gold-laced hat to my landlord, for less than half price, to defray the expense, and contribute to my subsistence.

CHAPTER VII

I am entertained by Mr. Crab—A Description of him—I acquire the Art of Surgery—Consult Crab's Disposition—Become necessary to him—An Accident happens—He advises me to launch out into the World—Assists me with money—I set out for London.

THE fumes of my resentment being dissipated, as well as the vanity of my success, I found myself deserted to all the horrors of extreme want, and avoided by mankind as a creature of a different species, or rather as a solitary being, nowise comprehended within the scheme or protection of Providence. My despair had rendered me almost quite stupefied, when I was one day told that a gentleman desired to see me at a certain public-house, whither immediately I repaired, and was introduced to one Mr. Launcelot Crab, a surgeon in town, who was engaged with two more in drinking a liquor called *popin*, composed by mixing a quartern of brandy with a quart of small beer. Before I relate the occasion of this message, I believe it will not be disagreeable to the reader if I describe the gentleman who sent for me, and mention some circumstances of his character and conduct, which may illustrate what follows, and account for his behaviour to me.

This member of the faculty was aged fifty, about five feet high, and ten round the belly; his face was capacious as a full moon, and much the complexion of a mulberry; his nose, resembling a powder-horn, was swelled to an enormous size, and studded all over with carbuncles; and his little grey eyes reflected the rays in such an oblique manner, that, while he looked a person full in the face, one would have imagined he was admiring the buckle of his shoe. He had long entertained an implacable resentment against Potion, who, though a young practitioner, was better employed than he, and once had the assurance to perform a cure whereby he disappointed and disgraced the prognostic of the said Crab. This quarrel, which was at one time upon the point of being made up by the interposition and mediation of friends, had been lately inflamed beyond a possibility of reconciliation by the respective wives of the opponents, who, chancing to meet at a christening, disagreed about precedence, proceeded from invectives to blows, and were, with great difficulty, by the gossips, prevented from converting the occasion of joy into a scene of lamentation.

The difference between these rivals was in the height of

rancour, when I received the message of Crab, who received me as civilly as I could have expected from one of his disposition; and, after desiring me to sit, inquired into the particulars of my leaving the house of Potion; which, when I had related, he said with a malicious grin, "There's a sneaking dog!—I always thought him a fellow without a soul, damn me!—a canting scoundrel, who has crept into business by his hypocrisy, and kissing the a—se of everybody." "Ay, ay," says another, "one might see with half an eye that the rascal has no honesty in him, by his going so regularly to church." This sentence was confirmed by a third, who assured his companions, that Potion was never known to be disguised in liquor but once, at a meeting of the godly, where he distinguished himself by an extempore prayer an hour long. After this preamble, Crab addressed himself to me in these words: "Well, my lad, I have heard a good character of you, and I'll do for you. You may send your things to my house when you please. I have given orders for your reception. Zounds! what does the booby stare at?—If you have no mind to embrace my courteous offer, you may let it alone, and be damned." I answered, with a submissive bow, that I was far from rejecting his friendly offer, which I would immediately accept, as soon as he should inform me on what footing I was to be entertained. "What footing! damn my blood," cried he; "d'ye expect to have a footman and a couple of horses kept for you?" "No, sir," I replied, "my expectations are not quite so sanguine. That I may be as little burdensome as possible, I would willingly serve in your shop, by which means I may save you the expense of a journeyman, or porter at least, for I understand a little pharmacy, having employed some of my leisure hours in the practice of that art while I lived with Mr. Potion: neither am I altogether ignorant of surgery, which I have studied with great pleasure and application." "Oho! you did?" says Crab. "Gentlemen, here is a complete artist!—Studied surgery! what? in books, I suppose. I shall have you disputing with me one of these days on points of my profession. You can already account for muscular motion (I warrant) and explain the mystery of the brain and nerves—ha? You are too learned for me, damn me. But let's hear no more of this stuff. Can you bleed and give a clyster, spread a plaster, and prepare a potion?" Upon my answering in the affirmative he shook his head, telling me he believed he should have little good of me, for all my promises; but, however, he would take me in for the sake of charity. I was accordingly that very night admitted to his house, and had an apartment assigned to me in the garret, which I was fain to put up with, notwithstanding the mortification my pride suffered in this change of circumstances. I was soon convinced of the real motives which induced Crab to receive me in this manner: for, besides the gratification of his revenge, by exposing the selfishness of his antagonist in opposition to his own generosity, which was all affectation, he had occasion of a young man who understood something of the profession, to fill up the place of his eldest apprentice, lately dead, not without violent suspicion of foul play from his master's brutality. The knowledge of this circumstance, together with his daily behaviour to his wife and the young apprentice, did not at all contribute to my enjoying my new situation with ease; however, as I did not perceive how I could bestow myself to better advantage, I resolved to study Crab's temper with all the application, and manage it with all the address, in my power. And it was not long before I found out a strange peculiarity of humour, which governed his behaviour towards all his dependents. I observed, when he was pleased, he was such a niggard of his satisfaction, that, if his wife or servants betrayed the least symptom of participation, he was offended to an insupportable degree of choler and fury, the effects of which they seldom failed to feel. And, when his indignation was roused, submission and soothing always exasperated it beyond the bounds of reason and humanity. I therefore pursued a contrary plan; and one day, when he honoured me with the names of ignorant whelp, and lazy ragamuffin, I boldly replied, "I was neither ignorant nor lazy, since I both understood and performed my business as well as he could do for his soul; neither was it just to call me ragamuffin, for I had a whole coat on my back, and was descended from a better family than any he could boast an alliance with." He gave tokens of great amazement at this assurance of mine, and shook his cane over my head, regarding me all the time with a countenance truly diabolical. Although I was terribly startled at his menacing looks and posture, I yet had reflection enough left to convince me I had gone too far to retract, and that this was the critical minute which must decide my future lot in his service; I therefore snatched up the pestle of a mortar, and swore, if he offered to strike me without a cause, I should see whether his skull or my weapon was hardest. He continued silent for some time, and at last broke forth into these ejaculations: "This is fine usage from a servant to a master,—very fine!—damnation!—but no matter,

you shall pay for this, you dog, you shall. I'll do your business
—yes, yes, I'll teach you to lift your hand against me." So
saying, he retired, and left me under dreadful apprehensions,
which vanished entirely at our next meeting, when he behaved
with unusual complacency, and treated me with a glass of
punch after dinner. By this conduct I got the ascendancy over
him in a short time, and became so necessary to him, in managing
his business while he was engaged at the bottle, that fortune
began to wear a kinder aspect; and I consoled myself for the
disregard of my former acquaintance with the knowledge I
daily imbibed, by a close application to the duties of my employment, in which I succeeded beyond my own expectation. I was
on very good terms with my master's wife, whose esteem I
acquired and cultivated, by representing Mrs. Potion in the
most ridiculous lights my satirical talents could invent, as well
as by rendering her some christian offices when she had been
too familiar with the dram bottle, to which she had oftentimes
recourse for consolation under the affliction she suffered from
her barbarous husband. In this manner I lived, without hearing
the least tidings of my uncle, for the space of two years, during
which time I kept little or no company, being neither in a
humour to relish, nor in a capacity to maintain much acquaintance: for the Nabal, my master, allowed me no wages; and the
small perquisites of my station scarce supplied me with the
common necessaries of life. I was no longer a pert unthinking
coxcomb, giddy with popular applause, and elevated with the
extravagance of hope: my misfortunes had taught me how little
the caresses of the world, during a man's prosperity, are to be
valued by him; and how seriously and expeditiously he ought
to set about making himself independent of them. My present
appearance, therefore, was the least of my care, which was
wholly engrossed in laying up a stock of instruction that might
secure me against the caprice of fortune for the future. I became
such a sloven, and contracted such an air of austerity, that
everybody pronounced me crestfallen; and Gawky returned
to town, without running any risk from my resentment, which
was by this time pretty much cooled, and restrained by prudential reasons so effectually, that I never so much as thought
of obtaining satisfaction for the injuries he had done me. When
I deemed myself sufficiently master of my business, I began to
cast about for an opportunity of launching into the world, in
hope of finding some provision that might make amends for the
difficulties I had undergone; but, as this could not be effected

without a small sum of money to equip me for the field, I was in the utmost perplexity how to raise it, well knowing that Crab, for his own sake, would never put me in a condition to leave him, when his interest was so much concerned in my stay. But a small accident which happened about this time determined him in my favour. This was no other than the pregnancy of his maid-servant, who declared her situation to me, assuring me, at the same time, that I was the occasion of it. Although I had no reason to question the truth of this imputation, I was not ignorant of the familiarities which had passed between her master and her; taking the advantage of which I represented to her the folly of laying the burden at my door, when she might dispose of it to much better purpose with Mr. Crab. She listened to my advice, and next day acquainted him with the pretended success of their mutual endeavours. He was far from being over-joyed at this proof of his vigour, which he foresaw might have very troublesome consequences; not that he dreaded any domestic grumblings and reproaches from his wife, whom he kept in perfect subjection; but because he knew it would furnish his rival Potion with a handle for insulting and undermining his reputation; there being no scandal equal to that of unclean-ness in the opinion of those who inhabit the part of the island where he lived. He, therefore, took a resolution worthy of himself; which was, to persuade the girl that she was not with child, but only afflicted with a disorder incident to young women, which he would easily remove. With this view (as he pretended) he prescribed for her such medicines as he thought would infallibly procure abortion; but in this scheme he was disappointed; for the maid, being advertised by me of his design, and at the same time well acquainted with her own condition, absolutely refused to follow his directions; and threatened to publish her situation to the world, if he would not immediately take some method of providing for the important occasion, which she expected in a few months. It was not long before I guessed the result of his deliberation, by his addressing himself to me, one day, in this manner: "I am surprised that a young fellow like you discovers no inclination to push his fortune in the world. Before I was of your age I was broiling on the coast of Guinea.—Damme! what's to hinder you from profiting by the war which will certainly be declared in a short time against Spain? You may easily get on board a king's ship in quality of a surgeon's mate; where you will certainly see a great deal of practice, and stand a good chance of getting prize-money."

I laid hold of this declaration, which I had long wished for, and assured him I would follow his advice with pleasure, if it was in my power; but that it was impossible for me to embrace an opportunity of that kind, as I had no friend to advance a little money to supply me with what necessaries I should want, and defray the expenses of my journey to London. He told me that few necessaries were required; and as for the expense of my journey, he would lend me money sufficient not only for that purpose, but also to maintain me comfortably in London until I should procure a warrant for my provision on board of some ship. I gave him a thousand thanks for his obliging offer (although I was very well apprised of his motive, which was no other than a design to lay the bastard to my charge after my departure), and accordingly set out in a few weeks for London, my whole fortune consisting of one suit of clothes, half a dozen of ruffled shirts, as many plain, two pair of worsted, and a like number of thread stockings, a case of pocket instruments, a small edition of Horace Wiseman's *Surgery*, and ten guineas in cash, for which Crab took my bond, bearing five per cent. interest; at the same time gave me a letter to the member of parliament for our town, which, he said, would do my business effectually.

CHAPTER VIII

I arrive at Newcastle—Meet with my old Schoolfellow Strap—We determine to walk together to London—Set out on our Journey—Put up at a solitary Ale-house—Are disturbed by a strange Adventure in the Night.

THERE is no such convenience as a waggon in this country, and my finances were too weak to support the expense of hiring a horse; I determined therefore to set out with the carriers, who transport goods from one place to another on horseback; and this scheme I accordingly put in execution on the first day of November 1739, sitting upon a pack-saddle between two baskets, one of which contained my goods in a knapsack. But, by the time we arrived at Newcastle-upon-Tyne, I was so fatigued with the tediousness of the carriage, and benumbed with the coldness of the weather, that I resolved to travel the rest of my journey on foot, rather than proceed in such a disagreeable manner.

The hostler of the inn at which we put up, understanding I

was bound for London, advised me to take my passage in a collier, which would be both cheap and expeditious, and withal much easier than to walk upwards of three hundred miles through deep roads in the winter time; a journey which, he believed, I had not the strength enough to perform. I was almost persuaded to take his advice, when, one day, stepping into a barber's shop to be shaved, the young man, while he lathered my face, accosted me thus: "Sir, I presume you are a Scotchman." I answered in the affirmative. "Pray," continued he, "from what part of Scotland?"—I no sooner told him, than he discovered great emotion, and not confining his operation to my chin and upper lip, besmeared my whole face with great agitation. I was so offended at this profusion, that, starting up, I asked him what the devil he meant by using me so? He begged pardon, telling me his joy at meeting with a countryman had occasioned some confusion in him; and craved my name. But when I declared my name was Random, he exclaimed in a rapture, "How! Rory Random?" The same, I replied, looking at him with astonishment. "What," cried he, "don't you know your old school-fellow, Hugh Strap?" At that instant, recollecting his face, I flew into his arms, and in the transport of my joy, gave him back one half of the suds he had so lavishly bestowed on my countenance; so that we made a very ludicrous appearance, and furnished a great deal of mirth for his master and shop-mates, who were witnesses of this scene. When our mutual caresses were over, I sat down again to be shaved; but the poor fellow's nerves were so discomposed by this unexpected meeting, that his hand could scarcely hold the razor, with which, never-theless, he found means to cut me in three places, in as many strokes. His master, perceiving his disorder, bade another supply his place, and after the operation was performed, gave Strap leave to pass the rest of the day with me. We retired imme-diately to my lodgings, where, calling for some beer, I desired to be informed of his adventures, which contained nothing more, than that his master dying before his time was out, he had come to Newcastle about a year ago, in expectation of journey-work, along with three young fellows of his acquaintance, who worked in the keels; that he had the good fortune of being employed by a very civil master, with whom he intended to stay till the spring, at which time he proposed to go to London, where he did not doubt of finding encouragement. When I communicated to him my situation and design, he did not approve of my taking a passage by sea, by reason of the danger of a winter voyage,

which is very hazardous along that coast, as well as the pre-
cariousness of the wind, which might possibly detain me a great
while, to the no small detriment of my fortune. Whereas, if I
would venture by land, he would bear me company, carry my
baggage all the way, and if we should be fatigued before we could
perform all the journey, it would be no hard matter for us to
find on the road either returning horses or waggons, of which
we might take the advantage for a very trifling expense. I was
so ravished at this proposal, that I embraced him affectionately,
and assured him he might command my purse to the last farthing: but he gave me to understand, he had saved money
sufficient to answer his own occasions; and that he had a friend
in London, who would soon introduce him into business in that
capital, and might possibly have it in his power to serve me also.

Having concerted the plan and settled our affairs that night,
we departed next morning by daybreak, armed with a good
cudgel each (my companion being charged with the furniture
of us both, crammed into one knapsack), and our money sewed
between the lining and waistband of our breeches, except some
loose silver for our immediate expense on the road. We travelled
all day at a round pace, but being ignorant of the proper stages,
were benighted at a good distance from any inn, so that we were
compelled to take up our lodging at a small hedge ale-house,
that stood on a by-road, about half a mile from the highway.
There we found a pedlar of our own country, in whose company
we regaled ourselves with bacon and eggs, and a glass of good
ale, before a comfortable fire, conversing all the while very
sociably with the landlord and his daughter, an hale buxom
lass, who entertained us with great good humour, and in whose
affection I was vain enough to believe I had made some progress.
About eight o'clock, we were all three, at our own desire, shown
into an apartment, furnished with two beds, in one of which
Strap and I betook ourselves to rest, and the pedlar occupied
the other, though not before he had prayed a considerable time
extempore, searched into every corner of the room, and fastened
the door on the inside with a strong iron screw, which he carried
about with him for that use. I slept very sound till midnight,
when I was disturbed by a violent motion of the bed, which
shook under me with a continual tremor. Alarmed at this
phenomenon, I jogged my companion, whom, to my no small
amazement, I found drenched in sweat, and quaking through
every limb; he told me, with a low faltering voice, that we were
undone; for there was a bloody highwayman loaded with pistols

in the next room; then bidding me make as little noise as possible, he directed me to a small chink in the board partition, through which I could see a thick-set brawny fellow, with a fierce countenance, sitting at a table with our young landlady, having a bottle of ale and a brace of pistols before him. I listened with great attention, and heard him say in a terrible tone: "Damn that son of a bitch, Smack, the coachman;—he has served me a fine trick, indeed!—but damnation seize me, if I don't make him repent it! I'll teach the scoundrel to give intelligence to others, while he is under articles with me." Our landlady endeavoured to appease this exasperated robber, by saying he might be mistaken in Smack, who perhaps kept no correspondence with the other gentleman that robbed his coach; and that, if an accident had disappointed him to-day, he might soon find opportunity enough to atone for his lost trouble. "I'll tell thee what, my dear Bett," replied he, "I never had, nor ever will, while my name is Rifle, have such a glorious booty as I missed to-day.—Zounds! there was four hundred pounds in cash to recruit men for the king's service, besides the jewels, watches, swords, and money belonging to the passengers;—had it been my fortune to have got clear off with so much treasure, I would have purchased a commission in the army, and made you an officer's lady, you jade, I would." "Well, well," cries Betty, "we must trust to Providence for that;—but did you find nothing worth taking, which escaped the other gentlemen of the road?" "Not much, faith," said the lover; "I gleaned a few things, such as a pair of pops, silver mounted (here they are); I took them loaded from the captain who had the charge of the money, together with a gold watch, which he had concealed in his breeches. I likewise found ten Portugal pieces in the shoes of a Quaker, whom the spirit moved to revile me with great bitterness and devotion. But what I value myself mostly for, is this here purchase, a gold snuff-box, my girl, with a picture on the inside of the lid; which I untied out of the tail of a pretty lady's smock." Here, as the devil would have it, the pedlar snored so loud, that the highwayman, snatching his pistols, started up, crying: "Hell and damnation! I am betrayed; who's that in the next room?" Mrs. Betty told him, he need not be uneasy; there were only three poor wearied travellers, who, missing the road, had taken up their lodging in the house, and were asleep long ago. "Travellers," says he, "spies, you b—ch! but no matter—I'll send them all to hell in an instant." He accordingly ran towards our door: when his

sweetheart interposing, assured him, there was only a couple
of poor young Scotchmen, who were too raw and ignorant to
give him the least cause of suspicion; and the third was a
Presbyterian pedlar of the same nation, who had often lodged
in the house before. This declaration satisfied the thief, who
swore he was glad there was a pedlar, for he wanted some linen.
Then, in a jovial manner, he put about the glass, mingling his
discourse to Betty with caresses and familiarities that spoke
him very happy in his amours. During that part of the conversation which regarded us, Strap had crept under the bed, where
he lay in the agonies of fear; so that it was with great difficulty
I persuaded him our danger was over, and prevailed on him to
wake the pedlar, and inform him of what he had seen and heard.
This itinerant merchant no sooner felt somebody shaking him
by the shoulder, than he started up, calling as loud as he could,
"Thieves, thieves! Lord have mercy on us!" And Rifle, alarmed
at this exclamation, jumped up, cocked one of his pistols, and
turned towards the door, to kill the first man who should enter;
for he verily believed himself beset; when his dulcinea, after
an immoderate fit of laughter, persuaded him, that the poor
pedlar, dreaming of thieves, had only cried out in his sleep.
Meanwhile my comrade had undeceived our fellow-lodger, and
informed him of his reason for disturbing him; upon which,
getting up softly, he peeped through the hole, and was so terrified
with what he saw, that, falling down on his bare knees, he put
up a long petition to Heaven, to deliver him from the hands of
that ruffian, and promised never to defraud a customer for the
future of the value of a pin's point, provided he might be rescued
from the present danger. Whether or not his disburdening his
conscience afforded him any ease, I know not; but he slipped
into bed again, and lay very quiet until the robber and his
mistress were asleep, and snored in concert; then, rising softly,
he untied a rope that was round his pack, which making fast
to one end of it, he opened the window with as little noise as
possible, and lowered his goods into the yard with great dexterity; then he moved gently to our bedside, and bade us farewell, telling us, that, as we ran no risk, we might take our rest
with great confidence, and in the morning assure the landlord
that we knew nothing of his escape; and lastly, shaking us by
the hands, and wishing us all manner of success, he let himself
drop from the window without any danger, for the ground was
not above a yard from his feet as he hung on the outside. Although
I did not think proper to accompany him in his flight, I was not

at all free from apprehension, when I reflected on what might be the effect of the highwayman's disappointment, as he certainly intended to make free with the pedlar's ware. Neither was my companion at more ease in his mind; but, on the contrary, so possessed with the dreadful idea of Rifle, that he solicited me strongly to follow our countryman's example, and so elude the fatal resentment of that terrible adventurer, who would certainly wreak his vengeance on us, as accomplices of the pedlar's elopement. But I represented to him the danger of giving Rifle cause to think we knew his profession, and suggested, that, if ever he should meet us again on the road, he would look upon us as dangerous acquaintance, and find it his interest to put us out of the way. I told him withal my confidence in Betty's good nature, in which he acquiesced; and, during the remaining part of the night, we concerted a proper method of behaviour, to render us unsuspected in the morning.

It was no sooner day, than Betty, entering our chamber, and perceiving our window open, cried out: "Ods bobs! sure you Scotchmen must have hot constitutions to lie all night with the window open, in such cold weather." I feigned to start out of sleep, and withdrawing the curtain, called, "What's the matter?" When she showed me, I affected surprise, and said, "Bless me! the window was shut when we went to bed." "I'll be hanged," said she, "if Sawney Waddle the pedlar has not got up in a dream and done it, for I heard him very obstropulous in his sleep. Sure I put a chamber-pot under his bed." With these words she advanced to the bed in which he lay, and finding the sheets cold, exclaimed, "Good lack-a-daisy! the rogue is fled!" "Fled!" cried I, with feigned amazement, "God forbid!—Sure he has not robbed us." Then springing up, I laid hold of my breeches, and emptied all my loose money into my hand; which having reckoned, I said, "Heaven be praised, our money is all safe:—Strap, look to the knapsack." He did so, and found all was right. Upon which we asked, with seeming concern, if he had stole nothing belonging to the house? "No, no," replied she, "he has stole nothing but his reckoning"; which, it seems, this pious pedlar had forgot to discharge, in the midst of his devotion. Betty, after a moment's pause, withdrew; and immediately we could hear her waken Rifle, who no sooner heard of Waddle's flight, than he jumped out of bed, and dressed, venting a thousand execrations, and vowing to murder the pedlar, if ever he should set eyes on him again: "For," said he, "the scoundrel has by this time raised the hue and cry against me." Having dressed himself in a hurry, he mounted his horse, and for that time rid us of his company, and a thousand fears that were the consequence of it. While we were at breakfast, Betty endeavoured, by all the cunning she was mistress of, to learn whether or no we suspected our fellow-lodger, whom we saw take horse; but as we were on our guard, we answered her sly questions with a simplicity she could not distrust; when, all of a sudden, we heard the trampling of a horse's feet at the door. This noise alarmed Strap so much, whose imagination was wholly engrossed by the image of Rifle, that, with a countenance as pale as milk, he cried, "O Lord! there's the highwayman returned!" Our landlady, staring, at these words, said, "What highwayman, young man?—Do you think any highwaymen harbour here?" Though I was very much disconcerted at this piece of indiscretion in Strap, I had presence of mind enough to tell her, we had met a horseman the day before, whom Strap had foolishly supposed to be a highwayman, because he rode with pistols; and that he had been terrified at the sound of a horse's feet ever since. She forced a smile at the ignorance and timidity of my comrade; but I could perceive (not without great concern) that this account was not at all satisfactory to her.

CHAPTER IX

We proceed on our Journey—Are overtaken by an Highwayman, who fires at Strap—Is prevented from shooting me by a company of Horsemen, who ride in pursuit of him—Strap is put to bed at an Inn—Adventures at that Inn.

AFTER having paid our score, and taken leave of our hostess, who embraced me tenderly at parting, we proceeded on our journey, blessing ourselves that we had come off so well. We had not walked above five miles, when we observed a man on horseback galloping after us, whom we in a short time recognised to be no other than this formidable hero who had already given us so much vexation. He stopped hard by me, and asked if I knew who he was? My astonishment had disconcerted me so much, that I did not hear his question, which he repeated with a volley of oaths and threats; but I remained as mute as before. Strap seeing my discomposure, fell upon his knees in the mud, uttering with a lamentable voice these words: "For Christ's sake, have mercy upon us, Mr. Rifle,—we know you very well."

"Oho!" cried the thief, "you do!—but you never shall be evidence against me in this world, you dog!" So saying, he drew a pistol, and fired it at the unfortunate shaver, who fell flat upon the ground, without speaking one word. My comrade's fate, and my own situation, riveted me to the place where I stood, deprived of all sense and reflection; so that I did not make the least attempt either to run away, or deprecate the wrath of this barbarian, who snapped a second pistol at me; but before he had time to prime again, perceiving a company of horsemen coming up, he rode on, and left me standing motionless as a statue, in which posture I was found by those whose appearance had saved my life. This company consisted of three men in livery, well armed, with an officer, who, as I afterwards learned, was the person from whom Rifle had taken the pocket pistols the day before; and who, making known his misfortune to a nobleman he met on the road, and assuring him his non-resistance was altogether owing to his consideration for the ladies in the coach, procured the assistance of his lordship's servants to go in quest of the plunderer. This holiday captain scampered up to me with great address, and asked who fired the pistol which he had heard. As I had not yet recovered my reason, he, before I could answer, observed a body lying on the ground: at which sight his colour changed, and he pronounced with a faltering tongue, "Gentlemen, here's murder committed! Let us alight." "No, no," said one of his followers, "let us rather pursue the murderer. Which way went he, young man?" By this time I had recollected myself so far as to tell them, that he could not be a quarter of a mile before; and to beg of one of them to assist me in conveying the corpse of my friend to the next house, in order to its being interred. The captain, foreseeing that, in case he should pursue, he must soon come to action, began to curb his horse, and give him the spur at the same time, which treatment making the creature rear up and snort, he called out, his horse was frightened, and would not proceed; at the same time wheeling him round and round, stroking his neck, whistling and wheedling him with "Sirrah, sirrah, gently, gently," etc.—"Zounds!" cried one of the servants, "sure my lord's Sorrel is not resty!"—With these words, he bestowed a lash on his buttocks, and Sorrel, disdaining the rein, sprung forward with the captain at a pace that would have soon brought him up with the robber, had not the girth, happily for him, given way, by which means he landed in the dirt, and two of his attendants continued their pursuit, without minding

his situation. Meanwhile, one of the three who remained at my
desire, turning the body of Strap, in order to see the wound
which had killed him, found him still warm, and breathing
upon which I immediately let him blood, and saw him, with
inexpressible joy, recover; he having received no other wound
than what his fear had inflicted. Having raised him upon his
legs, we walked together to an inn, about half a mile from the
place, where Strap, who was not quite recovered, went to bed
and in a little time, the third servant returned with the captain's
horse and furniture, leaving him to crawl after as well as he
could. This gentleman of the sword, upon his arrival, complained grievously of the bruise occasioned by his fall; and, on
the recommendation of the servant, who warranted my ability,
I was employed to bleed him, for which service he rewarded me
with half a crown.

The time between this event and dinner, I passed in observing
a game at cards between two farmers, an exciseman, and a
young fellow in a rusty gown and cassock, who, as I afterward
understood, was curate of a neighbouring parish. It was easy
to perceive that the match was not equal; and that the two
farmers, who were partners, had to do with a couple of sharpers
who stript them of all their cash in a very short time. But what
surprised me very much was, to hear this clergyman reply to
one of the countrymen who seemed to suspect foul play, in these
words: "Damn me, friend, d'ye question my honour?"—I did
not at all wonder to find a cheat in canonicals, this being a
character frequent in my own country; but I was scandalised
at the indecency of his behaviour, which appeared in the oath
he swore, and the bawdy songs which he sung. At last, to make
amends, in some sort, for the damage he had done to the unwary
boors, he pulled out a fiddle from the lining of his gown, and
promising to treat them at dinner, began to play most melodi-
ously, singing in concert all the while. This good humour of
the parson inspired the company with so much glee, that the
farmers soon forgot their losses, and all present went to dancing
in the yard. While we were agreeably amused in this manner,
our musician spying a horseman riding towards the inn, stopt
all of a sudden, crying out, "Gad so! gentlemen, I beg your
pardon; there's our dog of a doctor coming into the inn." He
immediately concealed his instrument, and ran towards the
gate, where he took hold of the vicar's bridle, and helped him
off, inquiring very cordially into the state of his health. This
rosy son of the Church, who might be about the age of fifty

having alighted, and entrusted the curate with his horse, stalked with great solemnity into the kitchen, where, sitting down by the fire, he called for a bottle of ale and a pipe; scarce deigning an answer to the submissive questions of those who inquired about the welfare of his family. While he indulged himself in this state, amidst a profound silence, the curate approaching him with great reverence asked if he would not be pleased to honour us with his company at dinner? To which interrogation he answered in the negative, saying, he had been to visit Squire Bumpkin, who had drank himself into a high fever at the last assizes; and that he had, on leaving his own house, told Betty he should dine at home. Accordingly, when he had made an end of his bottle and pipe, he rose and moved, with prelatical dignity, to the door, where his journeyman stood ready with his nag. He had no sooner mounted, than the facetious curate, coming into the kitchen, held forth in this manner: "There the old rascal goes, and the devil go with him.—You see how the world wags, gentlemen.—By gad, this rogue of a vicar does not deserve to live; and yet he has two livings worth £400 per annum, while poor I am fain to do all his drudgery, and ride twenty miles every Sunday to preach, for what? why, truly, for £20 a year. I scorn to boast of my own qualifications; but —comparisons are odious. I should be glad to know how this swag-bellied doctor deserves to be more at ease than me. He can loll in his elbow chair at home, indulge himself in the best of victuals and wine, and enjoy the conversation of Betty, his housekeeper. You understand me, gentlemen. Betty is the doctor's poor kinswoman, and a pretty girl she is; but no matter for that:—ay, and a dutiful girl to her parents, whom she visits regularly every year, though I must own, I could never learn in what county they live.—My service t'ye, gentlemen."—By this time dinner being ready, I waked my companion, and we ate all together with great cheerfulness. When our meal was ended, and every man's share of the reckoning adjusted, the curate went out on pretence of some necessary occasion, and mounting his horse, left the two farmers to satisfy the host in the best manner they could. We were no sooner informed of this piece of finesse, than the exciseman, who had been silent hitherto, began to open with a malicious grin: "Ay, ay, this is an old trick of Shuffle: I could not help smiling when he talked of treating. You must know this is a very curious fellow. He picked up some scraps of learning while he served young Lord Trifle at the university. But what he most excels in is pimping

No man knows his talents better than I; for I was valet de chambre to Squire Tattle, an intimate companion of Shuffle's lord. He got himself into a scrape, by pawning some of his lordship's clothes, on which account he was turned away; but, as he was acquainted with some particular circumstances of my lord's conduct, he did not care to exasperate him too much, and so made interest for his receiving orders, and afterwards recommended him to the curacy which he now enjoys. However, the fellow cannot be too much admired for his dexterity in making a comfortable livelihood, in spite of such a small allowance. You hear he plays a good stick, and is really diverting in company. These qualifications make him agreeable wherever he goes; and, as for playing at cards, there is not a man within three counties a match for him: the truth is, he is a damnable cheat; and can shift a card with such address, that it is impossible to discover him." Here he was interrupted by one of the farmers, who asked why he had not justice enough to acquaint them with these particulars before they engaged in play? The exciseman replied, without any hesitation, that it was none of his business to intermeddle between man and man; besides, he did not know they were ignorant of Shuffle's character, which was notorious to the whole country. This did not satisfy the other, who taxed him with abetting and assisting the curate's knavery, and insisted on having his share of the winnings returned; this demand the exciseman as positively refused, affirming, that whatsoever sleights Shuffle might practise on other occasions, he was very certain that he had played on the square with them, and would answer it before any bench in Christendom; so saying, he got up, and having paid his reckoning, sneaked off. The landlord thrusting his neck into the passage, to see if he was gone, shook his head, saying, "Ah! Lord help us, if every sinner was to have his deserts.—Well, we victuallers must not disoblige the exciseman.—But I know what:—if parson Shuffle and he were weighed together, a straw thrown into either scale would make the balance kick the beam.—But, masters, this is under the rose," continued Boniface, with a whisper.

CHAPTER X

The Highwayman is taken—We are detained as Evidence against him
—Proceed to the next Village—He escapes—We arrive at another Inn,
where we go to bed—In the night we are awaked by a dreadful Adventure
—Next night we lodge at the house of a Schoolmaster—OurTreatment there.

STRAP and I were about to depart on our journey, when we
perceived a crowd on the road coming towards us, shouting and
hallooing all the way. As it approached, we could discern a man
on horseback in the middle, with his hands tied behind him,
whom we soon knew to be Rifle. This highwayman, not being
so well mounted as the two servants who went in pursuit of
him, was soon overtaken, and, after having discharged his pistols,
made prisoner without any further opposition. They were carrying him in triumph, amidst the acclamations of the country
people, to a justice of peace in a neighbouring village, but stopt
at our inn to join their companion, and take refreshment. When
Rifle was dismounted, and placed in the yard, within a circle of
peasants armed with pitchforks, I was amazed to see what a
pitiful dejected fellow he now appeared, who had but a few hours
before filled me with such terror and confusion. My companion
was so much encouraged by this alteration in his appearance,
that, going up to the thief, he presented his clenched fists to
his nose, and declared he would either cudgel or box with the
prisoner for a guinea, which he immediately produced, and began
to strip, but was dissuaded from this adventure by me, who
represented to him the folly of the undertaking, as Rifle was now
in the hands of justice, which would, no doubt, give us all satisfaction enough. But what made me repent of our impertinent
curiosity, was our being detained by the captors as evidence
against him, when we were just going to set forward. However,
there was no remedy; we were obliged to comply; and accordingly joined in the cavalcade, which luckily took the same road
that we had proposed to follow. About the twilight we arrived
at the place of our destination; but, as the justice was gone to
visit a gentleman in the country, with whom (we understood)
he would probably stay all night, the robber was confined in an
empty garret three stories high, from which it seemed impossible
for him to escape. This, nevertheless, was the case; for next
morning, when they went upstairs to bring him before the
justice, the bird was flown, having got out at the window upon
the roof, from whence he continued his route along the tops of

the adjoining houses, and entered another garret window, where he skulked until the family were asleep, at which time he ventured downstairs, and let himself out by the street door, which was found open. This event was a great disappointment to those that apprehended him, who were flushed with hopes of the reward; but gave me great joy, as I was permitted now to continue my journey without any further molestation. Resolving to make up for the small progress we had hitherto made, we this day travelled with great vigour, and before night reached a market-town, twenty miles from the place from whence we set out in the morning, without meeting any adventure worth notice. Here having taken up our lodging at an inn, I found myself so fatigued, that I began to despair of performing our journey on foot, and desired Strap to inquire if there were any waggon, return-horses, or other cheap carriage in this place, to depart for London next day. He was informed, that the waggon from Newcastle to London had halted there two nights ago; and that it would be an easy matter to overtake it, if not the next day, at farthest the day after the next. This piece of news gave us some satisfaction; and, after having made a hearty supper on hashed mutton, we were shown to our room, which contained two beds, the one allotted for us, and the other for a very honest gentleman, who, we were told, was then drinking below. Though we could have very well dispensed with his company, we were glad to submit to this disposition, as there was not another bed empty in the house; and accordingly went to rest, after having secured our baggage under the bolster. About two or three o'clock in the morning, I was waked out of a very profound sleep, by a dreadful noise in the chamber, which did not fail to throw me into an agony of consternation, when I heard these words pronounced with a terrible voice: "Blood and wounds! run the halbert into the guts of him that's next you, and I'll blow the other's brains out presently." This dreadful salutation had no sooner reached the ears of Strap, than, starting out of bed, he ran against somebody in the dark, and overturned him in an instant; at the same time bawling out, "Fire! murder! fire!" a cry which in a moment alarmed the whole house, and filled our chamber with a crowd of naked people. When lights were brought, the occasion of all this disturbance soon appeared; which was no other than our fellow-lodger, whom we found lying on the floor scratching his head, with a look testifying the utmost astonishment at the concourse of apparitions that surrounded him.—This honest gentleman was, it seems, a recruiting serjeant, who, having listed two country fellows overnight, dreamed they had mutinied, and threatened to murder him and the drummer who was along with him. This made such an impression on his imagination, that he got up in his sleep, and expressed himself as above. When our apprehension of danger vanished, the company beheld one another with great surprise and mirth; but what attracted the notice of everyone, was our landlady, with nothing on but her shift, and a large pair of buckskin breeches, with the backside before, which she had slipped on in the hurry, and her husband, with her petticoat about his shoulders. One had wrapt himself in a blanket, another was covered with a sheet, and the drummer, who had given his only shirt to be washed, appeared *in cuerpo*, with the bolster rolled about his middle. When this affair was discussed, everybody retired to his own apartment, the serjeant slipped into bed, and my companion and I slept without any further disturbance till morning, when we got up, went to breakfast, paid our reckoning, and set forward, in expectation of overtaking the waggon; in which hope, however, we were disappointed for that day. As we exerted ourselves more than usual, I found myself quite spent with fatigue, when we entered a small village in the twilight. We inquired for a public-house, and were directed to one of a very sorry appearance. At our entrance, the landlord, who seemed to be a venerable old man, with long grey hair, rose from a table placed by a large fire in a very neat paved kitchen, and, with a cheerful countenance, accosted us in these words: *"Salvete, pueri, ingredimini."* I was not a little pleased to hear our host speak Latin, because I was in hope of recommending myself to him by my knowledge in that language; I therefore answered, without hesitation— *"Dissolve frigus, ligna super foco—large reponens."* I had no sooner pronounced these words, than the old gentleman, running toward me, shook me by the hand, crying, *"Fili mi dilectissime ! unde venis ? a superis, ni fallor !"* In short, finding we were both read in the classics, he did not know how to testify his regard enough; but ordered his daughter, a jolly rosy-cheeked damsel, who was his sole domestic, to bring us a bottle of his *quadrimum*, repeating from Horace at the same time, *"Deprome quadrimum Sabina, O Thaliarche, merum diota."* This *quadrimum* was excellent ale of his own brewing, of which he told us he had always an amphora four years old for the use of himself and friends. In the course of our conversation, which was interlarded with scraps of Latin, we understood that this facetious person was a schoolmaster, whose income being small, he was fain to keep a glass of good liquor for the entertainment of passengers, by which he made shift to make the two ends of the year meet. "I am this day," said he, "the happiest old fellow in his Majesty's dominions. My wife, rest her soul, is in heaven. My daughter is to be married next week; but the two chief pleasures of my life are these" (pointing to the bottle and a large edition of Horace that lay on the table). "I am old, 'tis true,—what then? the more reason I should enjoy the small share of life that remains, as my friend Flaccus advises: *Tu ne quæsieris (scire nefas) quem mihi, quem tibi finem dii dederint. Carpe diem, quam minimum credula postero.*" As he was very inquisitive about our affairs, we made no scruple of acquainting him with our situation, which, when he had learned, he enriched us with advices how to behave in the world, telling us, that he was no stranger to the deceits of mankind. In the meantime, he ordered his daughter to lay a fowl to the fire for supper, for he was resolved this night to regale his friends—*permittens divis cætera.* While our entertainment was preparing, our host recounted the adventures of his own life, which, as they contain nothing remarkable, I forbear to rehearse. When we had fared sumptuously, and drank several bottles of his *quadrimum*, I expressed a desire of going to rest, which was with some difficulty complied with, after he had informed us, that we should overtake the waggon by noon next day; and that there was room enough in it for half a dozen, for there were only four passengers as yet in that convenience. Before my comrade and I fell asleep, we had some conversation about the good humour of our landlord, which gave Strap such an idea of his benevolence, that he positively believed we should pay nothing for our lodging and entertainment. "Don't you observe," said he, "that he has conceived a particular affection for us; nay, even treated us at supper with extraordinary fare, which to be sure, we should not of ourselves have called for?" I was partly of Strap's opinion; but the experience I had of the world made me suspend my belief till the morning, when, getting up betimes, we breakfasted with our host and his daughter on hasty-pudding and ale, and desired to know what we had to pay. "Biddy will let you know, gentlemen," said he, "for I never mind these matters. Money matters are beneath the concern of one who lives upon the Horatian plan. *Crescentem sequitur cura pecuniam.*" Meanwhile, Biddy having consulted a slate that hung in the corner, told us, our reckoning came to 8s. 7d. "Eight shillings and sevenpence!"

cried Strap; "'tis impossible—you must be mistaken, young woman." "Reckon again, child," says her father, very deliberately; "perhaps you have miscounted." "No, indeed, father," she replied, "I know my business better." I could contain my indignation no longer, but said, it was an unconscionable bill, and demanded to know the particulars; upon which the old man got up, muttering, "Ay, ay, let us see the particulars—that's but reasonable." And, taking pen, ink, and paper, wrote the following items:

	s.	d.
To bread and beer	0	6
To a fowl and sausages	2	6
To four bottles *quadrim*.	2	0
To fire and tobacco	0	7
To lodging	2	0
To breakfast	1	0
	8	7

As he had not the appearance of a common publican, and had raised a sort of veneration in me by his demeanour the preceding night, it was not in my power to upbraid him as he deserved; therefore I contented myself with saying, I was sure he did not learn to be an extortioner from Horace. He answered, I was but a young man, and did not know the world, or I would not tax him with extortion, whose only aim was to live "*contentus parvo,* and keep off *importuna pauperies.*" My fellow-traveller could not so easily put up with this imposition; but swore he should either take one-third of the money, or go without. While we were engaged in this dispute, I perceived the daughter go out, and conjecturing the occasion, immediately paid the exorbitant demand, which was no sooner done, than Biddy returned with two stout fellows, who came in on pretence of taking their morning draught; but in reality to frighten us into compliance. Just as we departed, Strap, who was half distracted on account of this piece of expense, went up to the schoolmaster, and grinning in his face, pronounced with great emphasis, "*Semper avarus eget.*" To which the pedant replied, with a malicious smile, "*Animum rege, qui, nisi paret, imperat.*"

CHAPTER XI

We descry the Waggon—Get into it—Arrive at an Inn—Our Fellow-travellers described—A Mistake is committed by Strap, which produces strange things.

WE travelled half a mile without exchanging one word; my thoughts being engrossed by the knavery of the world, to which I must be daily exposed; and the contemplation of my finances, which began sensibly to diminish. At length Strap, who could hold no longer, addressed me thus: "Well, fools and their money are soon parted. If my advice had been taken, that old skinflint should have been damn'd before he had got more than the third of his demand.—'Tis a sure sign you came easily by your money, when you squander it away in this manner. Ah, God help you, how many bristly beards must have I mowed before I earned four shillings and threepence halfpenny, which is all thrown to the dogs? How many days have I sat weaving hair, till my toes were numbed by the cold, my fingers cramp'd, and my nose as blue as the sign of the periwig that hung over the door? What the devil was you afraid of? I would have engaged to box with any one of those fellows that came in, for a guinea. I'm sure I have beat stouter men than either of them." And indeed my companion would have fought anybody, when his life was in no danger; but he had a mortal aversion to firearms, and all instruments of death. In order to appease him, I assured him, no part of this extraordinary expense should fall upon his shoulders; at which declaration he was affronted, and told me, he would have me to know, that, although he was a poor barber's boy, he had a soul to spend his money with the best squire of the land. Having walked all day at a great pace, without halting for a refreshment, we descried, towards the evening, to our inexpressible joy, the waggon about a quarter of a mile before us; and by the time we reached it, were both of us so weary, that I verily believe it would have been impracticable for us to have walked one mile farther. We therefore bargained with the driver, whose name was Joey, to give us a cast to the next stage for a shilling; at which place we should meet the master of the waggon, with whom we might agree for the rest of the journey.

Accordingly, the convenience stopped, and Joey having placed the ladder, Strap (being loaded with our baggage) mounted first; but, just as he was getting in, a tremendous voice assailed his ears in these words: "God's fury! there shall no passengers come here." The poor shaver was so disconcerted at this exclamation, which both he and I imagined proceeded from the mouth of a giant, that he descended with great velocity, and a countenance as white as paper. Joey perceiving our astonishment, called with an arch sneer, "Waunds, coptain, whay woan't you sooffer the poor waggoneer to meake a penny? Coom, coom, young man, get oop, get oop, never moind the coptain—I'se not afear'd of the coptain." This was not encouragement sufficient to Strap, who could not be prevailed upon to venture up again; upon which I attempted, though not without a quaking heart, when I heard the same voice muttering like distant thunder, "Hell and the devil confound me, if I don't make you smart for this!" However, I crept in, and by accident, got an empty place in the straw, which I immediately took possession of, without being able to discern the faces of my fellow-travellers in the dark. Strap following with the knapsack on his back, chanced to take the other side, and, by a jolt of the carriage, pitched directly upon the stomach of the captain, who bellowed out in a most dreadful manner, "Blood and thunder, where's my sword?" At these words, my frighted comrade started up, and at one spring bounced against me with such force, that I thought he was the supposed son of Anak, who intended to press me to death. In the meantime, a female voice cried, "Bless me! what is the matter, my dear?" "The matter?" replied the captain, "damn my blood! my guts are squeezed into a pancake, by that Scotchman's hump." Strap, trembling all the while at my back, asked him pardon, and laid the blame of what had happened upon the jolting of the waggon; and the woman who spoke before, went on: "Ay, ay, my dear, it is our own fault; we may thank ourselves for all the inconveniences we meet with. I thank God I never travelled so before. I'm sure, if my lady or Sir John was to know where we are, they would not sleep this night for vexation. I wish to God we had writ for the chariot: I know we shall never be forgiven."—"Come, come, my dear," replied the captain, "it don't signify fretting now—we shall laugh it over as a frolic—I hope you will not suffer in your health. I shall make my lord very merry with our adventures in the diligence." This discourse gave me such a high notion of the captain and his lady, that I durst not venture to join in the conversation. But immediately after, another female voice began: "Some people give themselves a great many needless airs—better folks than any here have travelled in waggons before now. Some of us have rode in coaches and chariots, with three footmen behind them, without making so much fuss about it. What then? we are now all upon a footing therefore let's be sociable and merry. What do you say, Isaac? Is not this a good motion, you doting rogue? Speak, you old cent. per cent. fornicator. What desperate debts are you thinking of? What mortgage are you planning? Well, Isaac, positively you shall never gain my favour till you turn over a new leaf, grow honest, and live like a gentleman. In the meantime, give me a kiss, you old fumbler." These words, accompanied with a hearty smack, enlivened the person to whom they were addressed to such a degree, that he cried in a transport, though with a faltering voice, "Ah! you wanton baggage—upon my credit, you are a waggish girl, he, he, he." This laugh introduced a fit of coughing, which almost suffocated the poor usurer (such, we afterwards found, was the profession of this our fellow-traveller). About this time I fell asleep, and enjoyed a comfortable nap, till such time as we arrived at the inn where we put up. Here, having alighted from the waggon, I had an opportunity of viewing the passengers in order as they entered. The first who appeared was a brisk airy girl, about twenty years old, with a silver-laced hat on her head, instead of a cap, a blue stuff riding-suit trimmed with silver, very much tarnished, and a whip in her hand. After her came limping an old man, with a worsted night-cap, buttoned under his chin, and a broad-brimmed hat slouched over it, an old rusty blue cloak tied about his neck, under which appeared a brown surtout, that covered a threadbare coat and waistcoat and, as we afterwards discerned, a dirty flannel jacket. His eyes were hollow, bleared, and gummy; his face was shrivelled into a thousand wrinkles, his gums were destitute of teeth, his nose sharp and drooping, his chin peaked and prominent, so that, when he mumped or spoke, they approached one another like a pair of nut-crackers; he supported himself on an ivory-headed cane; and his whole figure was a just emblem of winter, famine, and avarice. But how was I surprised, when I beheld the formidable captain in the shape of a little thin creature, about the age of forty, with a long withered visage, very much resembling that of a baboon, through the upper part of which two little grey eyes peeped: he wore his own hair in a queue that reached to his rump, which immoderate length, I suppose, was the occasion of a baldness that appeared on the crown of his head, when he deigned to take off his hat, which was very much of the size and cock of

Pistol's. Having laid aside his greatcoat, I could not help admiring the extraordinary make of this man of war: he was about five feet and three inches high, sixteen inches of which went to his face and long scraggy neck; his thighs were about six inches in length, his legs resembling spindles or drum-sticks, two feet and a half, and his body, which put me in mind of extension without substance, engrossed the remainder; so that, on the whole, he appeared like a spider or grasshopper erect, and was almost a *vox et præterea nihil*. His dress consisted of a frock of what is called bearskin, the skirts of which were about half a foot long, an hussar waistcoat, scarlet breeches, reaching half-way down his thigh, worsted stockings, rolled up almost to his groin, and shoes with wooden heels at least two inches high: he carried a sword very near as long as himself in one hand, and with the other conducted his lady, who seemed to be a woman of his own age, and still retained some remains of an agreeable person; but so ridiculously affected, that, had I not been a novice in the world, I might have easily perceived in her the deplorable vanity and second-hand airs of a lady's woman. We were all assembled in the kitchen, when Captain Weazel (for that was his name) desired a room with a fire for himself and spouse, and told the landlord they would sup by themselves. The innkeeper replied, that he could not afford them a room by themselves; and as for supping, he had prepared victuals for the passengers in the waggon, without respect of persons; but if he could prevail on the rest to let him have his choice in a separate manner, he should be very well pleased. This was no sooner said, than all of us declared against the proposal; and Miss Jenny, our other female passenger, observed, that, if Captain Weazel and his lady had a mind to sup by themselves, they might wait until we should have done. At this hint, the captain put on a martial frown, and looked very big, without speaking; while his yoke-fellow, with a disdainful toss of her nose, muttered something about "Creature!" which Miss Jenny overhearing, stept up to her, saying, "None of your names, good Mrs. Abigail. Creature, quotha—I'll assure you, no such creature as you, neither—no ten pound sneaker—no quality coupler."—Here the captain interposed, with a "Damme, madam, what do you mean by that?"—"Damn you, sir, who are you?" replied Miss Jenny; "who made you a captain, you pitiful, trencher-scraping, pimping curler?—'Sdeath! the army is come to a fine pass, when such fellows as you get commissions —what, I suppose you think I don't know you?—Egad, you

and your helpmate are well met—a cast-off mistress and a
bald valet de chambre are well yoked together." "Blood and
wounds!" cried Weazel, "d'ye question the honour of my wife
madam!—Hell and damnation! No man in England durst say
so much. I would flea him—carbonado him! Fury and destruction! I would have his liver for my supper." So saying, he drew
his sword and flourished with it, to the great terror of Strap
while Miss Jenny, snapping her fingers, told him, she did not
value his resentment a louse. In the midst of this quarrel the
master of the waggon alighted, who understanding the cause
of the disturbance, and fearing the captain and his lady would
take umbrage, and leave his carriage, was at great pains to have
everything made up, which he at last accomplished, and we
sat down to supper all together. At bedtime we were shown to
our apartments: the old usurer, Strap, and I, to one room;
the captain, his wife, and Miss Jenny, to another. About midnight, my companion's bowels being disordered, he got up, in
order to go backward; but, in his return, mistaking one door
for another, entered Weazel's chamber, and without any
hesitation, went to bed to his wife, who was fast asleep; the
captain being at another end of the room, groping for some
empty vessel, in lieu of his own chamber-pot, which was leaky;
as he did not perceive Strap coming in, he went towards his own
bed, after having found a convenience; but no sooner did he
feel a rough head, covered with a cotton night-cap, than it
came into his mind, that he had mistaken Miss Jenny's bed
instead of his own, and that the head he felt was that of some
gallant, with whom she had made an assignation. Full of this
conjecture, and scandalised at the prostitution of his apartment, he snatched up the vessel he had just before filled, and
emptied it at once on the astonished barber and his own wife,
who waking at that instant, broke forth into lamentable cries,
which not only alarmed the husband beyond measure, but
frightened poor Strap almost out of his senses; for he verily
believed himself bewitched; especially when the incensed captain
seized him by the throat, with a volley of oaths, asking him
how he durst have the presumption to attempt the chastity of
his wife. Poor Strap was so amazed and confounded, that he
could say nothing, but, "I take God to witness, she's a virgin
for me." Mrs. Weazel, enraged to find herself in such a pickle,
through the precipitation of her husband, arose in her shift,
and with the heel of her shoe, which she found by the bedside,
belaboured the captain's bald pate, till he roared, "Murder."

"I'll teach you to empty your stink-pots on me," cried she, "you pitiful hop-o'-my-thumb coxcomb. What! I warrant you're jealous, you man of lath. Was it for this I condescended to take you to my bed, you poor withered sapless twig." The noise occasioned by this adventure had brought the master of the waggon and me to the door, where we overheard all that passed with great satisfaction. In the meantime, we were alarmed with the cry of "Rape! murder! rape!" which Miss Jenny pronounced with great vociferation.—"O! you vile abominable old villain," said she, "would you rob me of my virtue? But I'll be revenged of you, you old goat! I will—Help! for heaven's sake! help!—I shall be ravished—ruined! help!" Some servants of the inn, hearing this cry, came running upstairs with lights, and such weapons as chance afforded, when we beheld a very diverting scene. In one corner stood the poor captain, shivering in his shirt, which was all torn to rags, with a woeful visage, scratched all over by his wife, who had by this time wrapped the counterpane about her, and sat sobbing on the side of her bed. In the other end lay the old usurer, sprawling on Miss Jenny's bed, with his flannel jacket over his shirt, and his tawny meagre limbs exposed to the air; while she held him fast by the two ears, and loaded him with execrations. When we asked what was the matter, she affected to weep; told us, she was afraid that wicked rogue had ruined her in her sleep; and bade us take notice of what we saw, for she intended to make use of our evidence against him. The poor wretch looked like one more dead than alive, and begged to be released; a favour which he had no sooner obtained, than he protested she was no woman, but a devil incarnate; that she had first seduced his flesh to rebel, and then betrayed him. "Yes, cockatrice," continued he, "you know you laid this snare for me, but you shan't succeed, for I will hang myself before you shall get a farthing off me." So saying, he crawled to his own bed, groaning all the way. We then advanced to the captain, who told us, "Gentlemen, here has been a damned mistake; but I'll be reveng'd on him who was the occasion of it. That Scotchman who carries the knapsack shall not breathe this vital air another day, if my name be Weazel. My dear, I ask you ten thousand pardons; you are sensible I could mean no harm to you."—"I know not what you meant," replied she, sighing, "but I know I have got enough to send me to my grave." At length they were reconciled. The wife was complimented with a share of Miss Jenny's bed (her own being overflowed), and the master of the waggon invited

Weazel to sleep the remaining part of the night with him. I retired to mine, where I found Strap mortally afraid, he having stole away in the dark, while the captain and his lady were at loggerheads.

CHAPTER XII

Captain Weazel challenges Strap, who declines the Combat—An Affair between the Captain and me—The Usurer is fain to give Miss Jenny five Guineas for a Release—We are in danger of losing a Meal—The Behaviour of Weazel, Jenny, and Joey, on that occasion—An Account of Captain Weazel and his Lady—The Captain's Courage tried—Isaac's Mirth at the Captain's expense.

NEXT morning I agreed to give the master of the waggon ten shillings for my passage to London, provided Strap should be allowed to take my place when I should be disposed to walk— at the same time I desired him to appease the incensed captain, who had entered the kitchen with a drawn sword in his hand, and threatened, with many oaths, to sacrifice the villain who attempted to violate his bed: but it was to no purpose for the master to explain the mistake, and assure him of the poor lad's innocence, who stood trembling behind me all the while. The more submission that appeared in Strap, the more implacable seemed the resentment of Weazel, who swore he must either fight him, or he would instantly put him to death. I was extremely provoked at this insolence, and told him, it could not be supposed that a poor barber lad would engage a man of the sword at his own weapon; but I was persuaded he would wrestle or box with him. To which proposal Strap immediately gave assent, by saying, he would box with him for a guinea. Weazel replied, with a look of disdain, that it was beneath any gentleman of his character to fight like a porter, or even to put himself on a footing, in any respect, with such a fellow as Strap. "Odds bodikins!" cries Joey, "sure, coptain, yaw would not commit moorder! Here's a poor lad that is willing to make atoonement for his offence; and an that woan't satisfie yaw, offers to fight yaw fairly. An' yaw woan't box, I dare say, he will coodgel with yaw,—woan't yaw, my lad?"—Strap, after some hesitation, answered, "Yes, yes, I'll cudgel with him." But this expedient being also rejected by the captain, I began to smell his character, and, tipping Strap the wink, told the company that I had always heard it said, the person who receives a challenge should have the choice of the weapons; this therefore being the rule in point of honour, I would venture to promise, on the head of my companion, that he would even fight Captain Weazel at sharps, but it should be with such sharps as Strap was best acquainted with, namely, razors. At my mentioning razors, I could perceive the captain's colour change, while Strap, pulling me by the sleeve, whispered with great eagerness, "No, no, no; for the love of God, don't make any such bargain." At length Weazel recovering himself, returned towards me, and, with a ferocious countenance, asked, "Who the devil are you? will you fight me?" With these words, putting himself in a posture, I was grievously alarmed at seeing the point of a sword within half a foot of my breast; and, springing to one side, snatched up a spit that stood in the chimney-corner, with which I kept my formidable adversary at bay, who made a great many half-longes, skipping backward at every push, till at last I pinned him up in a corner, to the no small diversion of the company. While he was in this situation, his wife entered, and, seeing her husband in these dangerous circumstances, uttered a dreadful scream: in this emergency, Weazel demanded a cessation, which was immediately granted; and at last was contented with the submission of Strap, who, falling upon his knees before him, protested the innocence of his intention, and asked pardon for the mistake he had committed. This affair being ended without bloodshed, we went to breakfast, but missed two of our company, namely, Miss Jenny and the usurer. As for the first, Mrs. Weazel informed us, that she had kept her awake all night with her groans; and that, when she rose in the morning, Miss Jenny was so much indisposed, that she could not proceed on her journey. At that instant, a message came from her to the master of the waggon, who immediately went to her chamber, followed by us all. She told him in a lamentable tone, that she was afraid of a miscarriage, owing to the fright she received last night from the brutality of Isaac; and, as the event was uncertain, desired the usurer might be detained to answer for the consequence. Accordingly, this ancient Tarquin was found in the waggon, whither he had retired to avoid the shame of last night's disgrace, and brought by force to her presence. He no sooner appeared, than she began to weep and sigh most piteously, and told us, if she died, she would leave her blood upon the head of that ravisher. Poor Isaac turned up his eyes and hands to heaven, prayed that God would deliver him from the machinations of that Jezebel; and assured us, with tears in his eyes, that his being found in bed with her was the result of her own invitation. The waggoner understanding the case, advised Isaac to make it up, by giving her a sum of money; to which advice he replied, with great vehemence, "A sum of money!—a halter for the cockatrice!"—"Oh! 'tis very well," said Miss Jenny: "I see it is in vain to attempt that flinty heart of his by fair means. Joey, be so good as to go to the justice, and tell him there is a sick person here, who wants to see him on an affair of consequence." At the name of justice, Isaac trembled, and, bidding Joey stay, asked with a quivering voice, what she would have? She told him, that as he had not perpetrated his wicked purpose, she would be satisfied with a small matter. And though the damage she might sustain in her health might be irreparable, she would give him a release for an hundred guineas. "An hundred guineas!" cried he, in an ecstasy, "an hundred furies! Where should a poor wretch like me have an hundred guineas? If I had so much money, d'ye think I should be found travelling in a waggon at this season of the year?" "Come, come," replied Jenny, "none of your miserly artifice here. You think I don't know Isaac Rapine, the money-broker, in the Minories. Ah! you old rogue! many a pawn have you had of me and my acquaintance, which was never redeemed." Isaac finding it was in vain to disguise himself, offered twenty shillings for a discharge, which she absolutely refused under fifty pounds. At last, however, she was brought down to five, which he paid, with great reluctancy, rather than be prosecuted for a rape. After which accommodation the sick person made shift to get into the waggon, and we set forwards in great tranquillity, Strap being accommodated with Joey's horse, the driver himself choosing to walk. This morning and forenoon we were entertained with an account of the valour of Captain Weazel, who told us he had once knocked down a soldier that made game of him; tweaked a drawer by the nose, who found fault with his picking his teeth with a fork, at another time; and that he had moreover challenged a cheesemonger, who had the presumption to be his rival:—for the truth of which exploits he appealed to his wife. She confirmed whatever he said, and observed, "The last affair happened that very day on which I received a love-letter from Squire Gobble; and don't you remember, my dear, I was prodigiously sick that very night with eating ortolans, when my Lord Diddle took notice of my complexion's being altered, and my lady was so alarmed that she had wellnigh fainted." "Yes, my dear," replied the captain, "you know,

my lord said to me, with a sneer, 'Billy, Mrs. Weazel is certainly
breeding.' And I answered cavalierly, 'My lord, I wish I could
return the compliment.' Upon which the whole company broke
out into an immoderate fit of laughter; and my lord, who loves
a repartee dearly, came round and bussed me."

We travelled in this manner five days, without interruption,
or meeting anything worth notice; Miss Jenny, who soon
recovered her spirits, entertaining us every day with diverting
songs, of which she could sing a great number; and rallying her
old gallant, who, notwithstanding, would never be reconciled
to her. On the sixth day, while we were about to sit down to
dinner, the innkeeper came and told us, that three gentlemen,
just arrived, had ordered the victuals to be carried to their
apartment, although he had informed them that they were
bespoke by the passengers in the waggon. To which information
they had replied, "The passengers in the waggon might be
damned,—their betters must be served before them—they
supposed it would be no hardship on such travellers to dine upon
bread and cheese for one day." This was a terrible disappointment to us all; and we laid our heads together how to remedy
it; when Miss Jenny observed, that Captain Weazel, being by
profession a soldier, ought in this case to protect and prevent
us from being insulted. But the captain excused himself, saying,
he would not for all the world be known to have travelled in a
waggon; swearing at the same time, that, could he appear with
honour, they should eat his sword sooner than his provision.
Upon this declaration, Miss Jenny, snatching his weapon, drew
it, and ran immediately into the kitchen, where she threatened
to put the cook to death if he did not send the victuals into our
chamber immediately. The noise she made brought the three
strangers down, one of whom no sooner perceived her, than he
cried, "Ha! Jenny Ramper! what the devil brought thee
hither?" "My dear Jack Rattle!" replied she, running into his
arms, "is it you? Then Weazel may go to hell for a dinner—
I shall dine with you." They consented to this proposal with a
great deal of joy; and we were on the point of being reduced
to a very uncomfortable meal, when Joey, understanding the
whole affair, entered the kitchen with a pitchfork in his hand, and
swore he would be the death of any man who should pretend
to seize the victuals prepared for the waggon. This menace had
like to have produced fatal consequences; the three strangers
drawing their swords, and being joined by their servants, and
we ranging ourselves on the side of Joey; when the landlord

interposing, offered to part with his own dinner to keep the peace, which was accepted by the strangers; and we sat down at table without any further molestation. In the afternoon, I chose to walk along with Joey, and Strap took my place. Having entered into a conversation with this driver, I soon found him to be a merry, facetious, good-natured fellow, and withal very arch. He informed me, that Miss Jenny was a common girl upon the town; who falling into company with a recruiting officer, he carried her down in the stage-coach from London to New-castle, where he had been arrested for debt, and was now in prison; upon which she was fain to return to her former way of life, by this conveyance. He told me likewise, that one of the gentleman's servants whom we left at the inn, having accident-ally seen Weazel, immediately knew him, and acquainted Joey with some particulars of his character. That he had served my Lord Frizzle in quality of valet de chambre many years, while he lived separate from his lady. But, upon their reconciliation, she expressly insisted upon Weazel's being turned off, as well as the woman he kept; when his lordship, to get rid of them both with a good grace, proposed that he should marry his mistress, and he would procure a commission for him in the army. This expedient was agreed to; and Weazel is now, by his lordship's interest, ensign in ——'s regiment. I found he and I had the same sentiments with regard to Weazel's courage, which we resolved to put to the trial, by alarming the passengers with the cry of "A highwayman!" as soon as an horseman should appear. This scheme we put in practice towards the dusk, when we descried a man on horseback approaching us. Joey had no sooner intimated to the people in the waggon, that he was afraid we should be all robbed, than a general consternation arose. Strap jumped out of the waggon, and hid himself behind a hedge. The usurer put forth ejaculations, and made a rustling among the straw, which made us conjecture he had hid some-thing under it. Mrs. Weazel, wringing her hands, uttered lament-able cries; and the captain, to our great amazement, began to snore; but this artifice did not succeed; for Miss Jenny, shaking him by the shoulder, bawled out, " 'Sdeath! captain, is this time to snore, when we are going to be robbed? Get up, for shame, and behave like a soldier and a man of honour." Weazel pre-tended to be in a great passion for being disturbed, and swore he would have his nap out if all the highwaymen in England surrounded him. "Damn my blood! what are you afraid of?" continued he, at the same time trembling with such agitation, that the whole carriage shook. This singular piece of behaviour incensed Miss Ramper so much that she cried, "Damn your pitiful soul, you are as arrant a poltroon as ever was drummed out of a regiment.—Stop the waggon, Joey—let me get out, and by God, if I have rhetoric enough, the thief shall not only take your purse, but your skin also." So saying, she leapt out with great agility. By this time the horseman came up with us, and happened to be a gentleman's servant well known to Joey, who communicated the scheme, and desired him to carry it on a little further, by going up to the waggon, and questioning those within. The stranger consenting for the sake of diversion, approached it, and in a terrible tone, demanded, "Who have we got here?" Isaac replied, with a lamentable voice, "Here's a poor miserable sinner, who has got a small family to maintain, and nothing in the world wherewithal, but these fifteen shillings, which if you rob me of, we must all starve together." "Who's that sobbing in the other corner?" said the supposed highwayman. "A poor unfortunate woman," answered Mrs. Weazel, "upon whom I beg you for Christ's sake to have compassion." "Are you maid or wife?" said he. "Wife, to my sorrow," cried she. "Who or where is your husband?" continued he. "My husband," replied Mrs. Weazel, "is an officer in the army, and was left sick at the last inn where we dined." "You must be mistaken, madam," said he, "for I myself saw him get into the waggon this afternoon.—But pray what smell is that? Sure your lap-dog has befouled himself; let me catch hold of the nasty cur, I'll teach him better manners." Here he laid hold of one of Weazel's legs, and pulled him out from under his wife's petticoats, where he had concealed himself. The poor trembling captain, being detected in this inglorious situation, rubbed his eyes, and affecting to wake out of sleep, cried, "What's the matter?—what's the matter?" "The matter is not much," answered the horseman, "I only called in to inquire after your health, and so adieu, most noble captain." So saying, he clapt spurs to his horse, and was out of sight in a moment. It was some time before Weazel could recollect himself, but at length re-assuming the big look, he said, "Damn the fellow! why did he ride away, before I had time to ask him how his lord and lady do?—Don't you remember Tom, my dear?" addressing himself to his wife. "Yes," replied she, "I think I do remember something of the fellow—but you know I seldom converse with people of his station." "Hey-day," cried Joey, "do yaw knaw the young mon, coptain?" "Know him," said Weazel, "many a time has he filled a glass of Burgundy for me at my Lord Trippet's table." "And what may his neame be, coptain?" said Joey. "His name!—his name," replied Weazel, "is Tom Rinser." "Waunds!" cried Joey, "a has changed his own neame then! for I'se lay a wager he was christened John Trotter." This observation raised a laugh against the captain, who seemed very much disconcerted; when Isaac broke silence, and said, "It was no matter who or what he was, since he has not proved the robber we suspected. And we ought to bless God for our narrow escape." "Bless God," said Weazel, "bless the devil! for what? had he been a highwayman, I should have eat his blood, body, and guts, before he had robbed me, or anyone in this diligence." "Ha, ha, ha!" cried Miss Jenny, "I believe you will eat all you kill indeed, captain." The usurer was so well pleased at the event of this adventure, that he could not refrain from being severe, and took notice, that Captain Weazel seemed to be a good Christian, for he had armed himself with patience and resignation, instead of carnal weapons, and worked out his salvation with fear and trembling. This piece of satire occasioned a great deal of mirth at Weazel's expense, who muttered a great many oaths, and threatened to cut Isaac's throat. The usurer taking hold of this menace, said, "Gentlemen and ladies, I take you all to witness, that my life is in danger from this bloody-minded officer. I'll have him bound over to the peace." This second sneer procured another laugh against him, and he remained crestfallen during the remaining part of our journey.

CHAPTER XIII

Strap and I are terrified by an Apparition—Strap's Conjecture—The Mystery explained by Joey—We arrive at London—Our Dress and Appearance described—We are insulted in the Street—An Adventure in an Ale-house—We are imposed upon by a waggish Footman—Set to rights by a Tobacconist—Take Lodgings—Dive for a Dinner—An Accident at our Ordinary.

WE arrived at our inn, supped, and went to bed; but Strap's distemper continuing, he was obliged to rise in the middle of the night, and taking the candle in his hand, which he had left burning for the purpose, he went down to the house of office, whence, in a short time, he returned in a great hurry, with his hair standing on end, and a look betokening horror and astonishment. Without speaking a word, he set down the light, and jumped into bed behind me, where he lay and trembled with great violence. When I asked him what was the matter? he replied, with a broken accent, "God have mercy on us!—I have seen the devil!" Though my prejudice was not quite so strong as his, I was not a little alarmed at this exclamation: and much more so, when I heard the sound of bells approaching our chamber, and felt my bed-fellow cling close to me, uttering these words, "Christ have mercy upon us!—there he comes!" At that instant a monstrous overgrown raven entered our chamber, with bells at his feet, and made directly towards our bed. As this creature is reckoned in our country a common vehicle for the devil and witches to play their pranks in, I verily believed we were haunted, and, in a violent fright, shrunk under the bed-clothes. This terrible apparition leapt upon the bed, and, after giving us several severe dabs with its beak through the blankets, hopped away and vanished. Strap and I recommended ourselves to the protection of Heaven with great devotion; and, when we no longer heard the noise, ventured to peep up and take breath. But we had not been long freed from this phantom, when another appeared, that had well-nigh deprived us both of our senses. We perceived an old man enter the room, with a long white beard that reached to his middle; there was a certain wild peculiarity in his eyes and countenance that did not savour of this world; and his dress consisted of a brown stuff coat, buttoned behind and at the wrists, with an odd-fashioned cap of the same stuff upon his head. I was so amazed, that I had not power to move my eyes from such a ghastly object, but lay motionless, and saw him come straight up to me. When he reached the bed, he wrung his hands, and cried, with a voice that did not seem to belong to a human creature, "Where is Ralph?" I made no reply; upon which he repeated, in an accent still more preternatural, "Where is Ralpho?" He had no sooner pronounced these words, than I heard the sound of the bells at a distance; which the apparition having listened to, tripped away, and left me almost petrified with fear. It was a good while before I could recover myself so far as to speak; and when at length I turned to Strap, I found him in a fit, which, however, did not last long. When he came to himself, I asked his opinion of what had happened; and he assured me, that the first must certainly be the soul of some person damned, which appeared by the chains about his legs (for his fears had magnified the creature to the bigness of a horse, and the sound of small morrice-bells to the clanking of massy chains). As for the old man, he took it to be the spirit of somebody murdered long ago in this place, which had power granted to it to torment the assassin in the shape of a raven, and that Ralpho was the name of the said murderer. Although I had not much faith in this interpretation, I was too much troubled to enjoy any sleep, and in all my future adventures never passed a night so ill. In the morning, Strap imparted the whole affair to Joey, who, after an immoderate fit of laughter, explained the matter, by telling him the old man was the landlord's father, who had been an idiot some years, and diverted himself with a tame raven, which, it seems, had hopped away from his apartment in the night, and induced him to follow it to our chamber, where he had inquired after it, under the name of Ralpho.

Nothing remarkable happened during the remaining part of our journey, which continued six or seven days longer. At length we entered the great city, and lodged all night at the inn where the waggon put up. Next morning, all the passengers parted different ways: while my companion and I sallied out to inquire for the member of parliament, to whom I had a letter of recommendation from Mr. Crab. As we had discharged our lodging at the inn, Strap took up our baggage and marched behind me in the street, with the knapsack on his back, as usual, so that we made a very whimsical appearance. I had dressed myself to the greatest advantage—that is, put on a clean ruffled shirt, and my best thread stockings. My hair, which was of the deepest red, hung down upon my shoulders, as lank and straight as a pound of candles; and the skirts of my coat reached to the middle of my leg; my waistcoat and breeches were of the same piece, and cut in the same taste; and my hat very much resembled a barber's bason, in the shallowness of the crown, and narrowness of the brim. Strap was habited in a much less awkward manner; but a short crop-eared wig that very much resembled Scrub's in the play, and the knapsack on his back, added to what is called a queer phiz, occasioned by a long chin, hook nose, and high cheek-bones, rendered him on the whole a very fit subject of mirth and pleasantry. As we walked along, Strap, at my desire, inquired of a carman, whom we met, whereabouts Mr. Cringer lived; and was answered by a stare, accompanied with the word, "Anan!" Upon which I came up in order to explain the question, but had the misfortune to be unintelligible likewise, the carman damning us for a lousy Scotch guard, and whipping his horses, with a "Gee ho!" which nettled me to the quick, and roused the indignation of Strap so far, that, after the fellow was gone a good way, he told me he would fight him for a farthing. While we were deliberating upon what was to be done, an hackney coachman driving softly along, and perceiving us standing by the kennel, came up close to us, and calling, "A coach, master!" by a dexterous management of the reins, made his horses stumble in the wet, and bedaub us all over with mud. After which exploit, he drove on, applauding himself with a hearty laugh, in which several people joined, to my great mortification; but one, more compassionate than the rest, seeing us strangers, advised me to go into an ale-house and dry myself. I thanked him for his advice, which I immediately complied with; and going into the house he pointed out, called for a pot of beer, and sat down by a fire in the public room, where we cleaned ourselves as well as we could. In the meantime, a wag, who sat in a box, smoking his pipe, understanding by our dialect that we were from Scotland, came up to me, and, with a grave countenance, asked how long I had been caught? As I did not know the meaning of this question, I made no answer; and he went on, saying, it could not be a great while, for my tail was not yet cut; at the same time, taking hold of my hair, and tipping the wink to the rest of the company, who seemed highly entertained with his wit. I was incensed at this usage, but afraid of resenting it, because I happened to be in a strange place, and perceived the person who spoke to me was a brawny fellow, for whom I thought myself by no means a match. However, Strap having either more courage, or less caution, could not put up with the insults that I suffered; but told him, in a peremptory tone, "He was an uncivil fellow for making so free with his betters." Then the wit, going towards him, asked what he had got in his knapsack? "Is it oatmeal, or brimstone, Sawney?" said he, seizing him by the chin, which he shook, to the inexpressible diversion of all present. My companion, feeling himself assaulted in such an opprobrious manner, disengaged himself in a trice, and lent his antagonist such a box on the ear, as made him stagger to the other side of the room; and in a moment, a ring was formed for the combatants. Seeing Strap beginning to strip, and my blood being heated with indignation, which banished all other thoughts, I undressed myself to the skin in an instant, and declared, that as the affront that occasioned the quarrel was offered to me, I would fight it out myself; upon which one or two cried out, "That's a brave Scotch boy; you shall have fair play, by God." This assurance gave me fresh spirits, and going up to my adversary, who, by his pale countenance, did not seem much inclined to the battle, I struck him so hard on the stomach, that he reeled over the bench, and fell to the ground. Then I attempted to keep him down, in order to improve my success, according to the manner of my own country, but was restrained by the spectators, one of whom endeavoured to raise up my opponent, but in vain; for he protested he would not fight, for he was not quite recovered of a late illness. I was very well pleased with this excuse, and immediately dressed myself, having acquired the good opinion of the company for my bravery, as well as of my comrade Strap, who shook me by the hand, and wished me joy of the victory. After having drank our pot, and dried our clothes, we inquired of the landlord if he knew Mr. Cringer, the member of parliament, and were amazed at his replying in the negative; for we imagined, he must be altogether as conspicuous here as in the borough he represented; but he told us we might possibly hear of him as we passed along. We betook ourselves, therefore, to the street, where, seeing a footman standing at a door, we made up to him, and asked if he knew where our patron lived? This member of the party-coloured fraternity, surveying us both very minutely, said he knew Mr. Cringer very well, and bade us turn down the first street on our left, then turn to the right, and then to the left again, after which perambulation we would observe a lane, through which we must pass, and at the other end we should find an alley that led to another street, where we should see the sign of the Thistle and Three Pedlars, and there he lodged. We thanked him for his information, and went forwards, Strap telling me, that he knew this person to be an honest friendly man, by his countenance, before he opened his mouth; in which opinion I acquiesced, ascribing his good manners to the company he daily saw in the house where he served. We followed his directions punctually, in turning to the left and to the right, and to the left again; but, instead of seeing a lane before us, found ourselves at the side of the river, a circumstance that perplexed us not a little; and my fellow-traveller ventured to pronounce, that we had certainly missed our way. By this time we were pretty much fatigued with our walk, and not knowing how to proceed, I went into a small snuff shop hard by, encouraged by the sign of the Highlander, where I found, to my inexpressible satisfaction, the shop-keeper was my countryman. He was no sooner informed of our peregrination, and the directions we had received from the footman, than he informed us, we had been imposed upon, telling us, Mr. Cringer lived in the other end of the town; and that it would be to no purpose for us to go thither to-day, for by that time he was gone to the House. I then asked if he could recommend us to a lodging. He readily gave us a line to one of his acquaintance, who kept a chandler's shop not far from St. Martin's Lane; there we hired a bedroom, up two pair of stairs, at the rate of two shillings per week, so very small, that, when the bed was let down, we were obliged to carry out every other piece of furniture that belonged to the apartment, and use the bedstead by way of chairs. About dinner-time our landlord asked us how we proposed to live? to which interrogation we answered, that we would be directed by him. "Well, then," says he, "there are two ways of eating in this town, for people of your condition—the one more creditable and expensive than the other; the first is, to dine at an eating-house, frequented by well-dressed people only; and the other is called diving, practised by those who are either obliged or inclined to live frugally." I gave him to understand, that, provided the last was not infamous, it would suit much better with our circumstances than the other. "Infamous," cried he, "God forbid! there are many creditable people, rich people, ay, and fine people, that dive every day. I have seen many a pretty gentleman, with a laced waistcoat, dine in that manner very comfortably for threepence halfpenny, and go afterwards to the coffee-house, where he made a figure with the best lord in the land; but your own eyes shall bear witness —I will go along with you to-day, and introduce you." He accordingly conducted us to a certain lane, where stopping, he bade us observe him, and do as he did; and, walking a few paces, dived into a cellar, and disappeared in an instant. I followed his example, and descending very successfully, found myself in the middle of a cook's shop, almost suffocated with the steams of boiled beef, and surrounded by a company of hackney coachmen, chairmen, draymen, and a few footmen out of place, or on board wages, who sat eating shin of beef, tripe, cowheel, or sausages, at separate boards, covered with cloths which turned my stomach. While I stood in amaze, undetermined whether to sit down or walk upwards again, Strap, in his descent missing one of the steps, tumbled headlong into this infernal ordinary, and overturned the cook, as she carried a porringer of soup to one of the guests. In her fall, she dashed the whole mess against the legs of a drummer, belonging to the foot-guards, who happened to be in her way, and scalded him so miserably, that he started up, and danced up and down, uttering a volley of execrations, that made my hair stand on end. While he entertained the company in this manner, with an eloquence peculiar to himself, the cook got up, and, after a hearty curse on the poor author of this mischance, who lay under the table, scratching his rump with a woeful countenance, emptied a salt-cellar in her hand, and stripping down the patient's stocking, which brought the skin along with it, applied the contents to the sore. This poultice was scarce laid on, when the drummer, who had begun to abate of his exclamation, broke forth into such a hideous yell, as made the whole company tremble; then, seizing a pewter pint pot that stood by him, squeezed the sides of it together, as if it had been made of pliant leather, grinding his teeth at the same time with a most horrible grin. Guessing the cause of this violent transport, I bade the woman wash off the salt, and then bathe the part with oil, which she did, and procured him immediate ease. But here another difficulty occurred, which was no other than the land-lady's insisting on his paying for the pot he had rendered useless. He swore he would pay for nothing but what he had eaten, and bade her be thankful for his moderation, or else he would prosecute her for damages. Strap, foreseeing the whole affair would lie at his door, promised to satisfy the cook, and called for a dram of gin to treat the drummer, which entirely appeased him, and composed all animosities. After this accommodation, our landlord and we sat down at a board, and dined upon shin of beef most deliciously; our reckoning amounting to twopence halfpenny each, bread and small beer included.

CHAPTER XIV

We visit Strap's Friend—A Description of him—His Advice—We go to Mr. Cringer's House—Are denied Admittance—An Accident befalls Strap—His Behaviour thereupon—An extraordinary Adventure occurs, in the course of which I lose all my Money.

IN the afternoon my companion proposed to call at his friend's house, which, we were informed, was in the neighbourhood; whither we accordingly went, and were so lucky as to find him at home. This gentleman, who had come from Scotland three or four years before, kept a school in town, where he taught the Latin, French, and Italian languages; but what he chiefly

professed was the pronunciation of the English tongue, after a
method more speedy and uncommon than any practised here-
tofore; and, indeed, if his scholars spoke like their master, the
latter part of his undertaking was certainly performed to a tittle;
for, although I could easily understand every word of what I
had heard hitherto since I entered England, three parts in four
of his dialect were as unintelligible to me as if he had spoke in
Arabic or Irish. He was a middle-sized man, and stooped very
much, though not above the age of forty; his face frightfully
pitted with the small-pox, and his mouth extended from ear
to ear. He was dressed in a nightgown of plaid, fastened about
his middle with a serjeant's old sash, and a tie-periwig, with a
fore-top three inches high, in the fashion of King Charles the
Second's reign. After he had received Strap (who was related to
him) very courteously, he inquired of him who I was, and, being
informed, took me by the hand, telling me he was at school
with my father. When he understood my situation, he assured
me that he would do me all the service in his power, both by
his advice and otherwise; and, while he spoke these words, eyed
me with great attention, walking round me several times, and
muttering, "O Christ! O Christ! fat a saight is here?" I soon
guessed the reason of his ejaculation, and said, "I suppose, sir,
you are not pleased with my dress?" "Dress!" answered he,
"you may caal it fat you please in your country, but I vaw to
Gad, 'tis a masquerade here. No Christian will admit such a
figure into his hawse. Upon my conscience! I wonder the dogs
did not hunt you. Did you pass through St. James's Market?
God bless my eye-saight! you look like a cousin-german of
Ouran Outang."—I began to be a little serious at this discourse,
and asked him if he thought I should obtain entrance to-morrow
at the house of Mr. Cringer, on whom I chiefly depended for an
introduction into business. "Mr. Cringer, Mr. Cringer," replied
he, scratching his cheek, "may be a very honest gentleman—
I know nothing to the contrary; but is your sole dependence
upon him? Who recommended you to him?" I pulled out
Mr. Crab's letter, and told him the foundation of my hopes;
at which he stared at me, and repeated, "Christ!" I began to
conceive bad omens from this behaviour of his, and begged he
would assist me with his advice, which he promised to give me
frankly; and, as a specimen, directed us to a periwig warehouse
in the neighbourhood, in order to be accommodated; laying
strong injunctions on me not to appear before Mr. Cringer till
I had parted with these carroty locks, which he said were

sufficient to beget an antipathy against me in all mankind. And, as we were going to pursue this advice, he called me back, and bade me be sure to deliver my letter into Mr. Cringer's own hand. As we walked along, Strap triumphed greatly in our reception with his friend, who, it seems, had assured him he would, in a day or two, provide for him with some good master; and "Now," says he, "you shall see how I shall fit you with a wig. There's ne'er a barber in London, and that's a bold word, can palm a rotten caul or a pennyweight of dead hair upon me." And, indeed, this zealous adherent did wrangle so long with the merchant that he was desired twenty times to leave the shop, and see if he could get one cheaper elsewhere. At length I made choice of a good handsome bob, for which I paid ten shillings, and returned to our lodging, where Strap in a moment rid me of that hair which had given the schoolmaster so much offence.

We got up next day betimes, having been informed that Mr. Cringer gave audience by candlelight to all his dependants, he himself being obliged to attend the levee of my Lord Terrier at break of day; because his lordship made one at the minister's between eight and nine o'clock. When we came to Mr. Cringer's door, Strap, to give me an instance of his politeness, ran to the knocker, which he employed so loud and so long that he alarmed the whole street; and a window opening in the second story of the next house, a chamber-pot was discharged upon him so successfully that the poor barber was wet to the skin, while I, being luckily at some distance, escaped the unsavoury deluge. In the meantime a footman opening the door, and seeing nobody in the street but us, asked with a stern countenance if it was I who made such a damned noise, and what I wanted? I told him I had business with his master, whom I desired to see. Upon which he clapped the door in my face, telling me I must learn better manners before I could have access to his master. Vexed at this disappointment, I turned my resentment against Strap, whom I sharply reprimanded for his presumption; but he, not in the least regarding what I said, wrung the urine out of his periwig, and, lifting up a large stone, flung it with such force against the street door of that house from whence he had been bedewed, that the lock giving way, it flew wide open, and he took to his heels, leaving me to follow him as I could. Indeed there was no time for deliberation; I therefore pursued him with all the speed I could exert, until we found ourselves about the dawn in a street we did not know. Here, as we wandered along

gaping about, a very decent sort of a man passing by me, stopped
of a sudden, and took up something, which having examined,
he turned and presented it to me with these words: "Sir, you
have dropped half a crown." I was not a little surprised at this
instance of honesty, and told him it did not belong to me; but
he bade me recollect, and see if all my money was safe: upon
which I pulled out my purse (for I had bought one since I came
to town), and reckoning my money in my hand, which was now
reduced to five guineas seven shillings and twopence, assured
him I had lost nothing. "Well, then," says he, "so much the
better—this is a godsend; and, as you two were present when I
picked it up, you are entitled to equal shares with me." I was
astonished at these words, and looked upon this person to be a
prodigy of integrity, but absolutely refused to take any part of
the sum. "Come, gentlemen," said he, "you are too modest—
I see you are strangers; but you shall give me leave to treat
you with a whet this cold, raw morning." I would have declined
this invitation, but Strap whispered to me that the gentleman
would be affronted, and I complied. "Where shall we go?"
said the stranger; "I am quite ignorant of this part of the town."
I informed him that we were in the same situation: upon which
he proposed to go into the first public-house we should find open;
and, as we walked together, he began in this manner. "I find
by your tongues you are from Scotland, gentlemen. My grandmother by the father's side was of your country; and I am so
prepossessed in its favour that I never meet a Scotchman but
my heart warms. The Scots are a very brave people. There is
scarce a great family in the kingdom that cannot boast of some
exploits performed by its ancestors many hundred years ago.
There's your Douglases, Gordons, Campbells, Hamiltons. We
have no such ancient families here in England. Then you are all
very well educated. I have known a pedlar talk in Greek and
Hebrew, as well as if they had been his mother tongue. And,
for honesty, I once had a servant, his name was Gregory Mac-
gregor: I would have trusted him with untold gold."—This
eulogium on my native country gained my affection so strongly
that I believe I could have gone to death to serve the author;
and Strap's eyes swam in tears. At length, as we passed through
a dark narrow lane, we perceived a public-house, which we
entered, and found a man sitting by the fire smoking a pipe,
with a pint of purl before him. Our new acquaintance asked us
if ever we had drank egg-flip? To which question we answering
in the negative, he assured us of a regale, and ordered a quart

to be prepared, calling for pipes and tobacco at the same time. We found this composition very palatable, and drank heartily; the conversation (which was introduced by the gentleman) turning upon the snares that young inexperienced people are exposed to in this metropolis. He described a thousand cheats that are daily practised upon the ignorant and unwary; and warned us of them with so much good nature and concern, that we blessed the opportunity which threw us in his way. After we had put the can about for some time, our new friend began to yawn, telling us he had been up all night with a sick person; and proposed we should have recourse to some diversion to keep him awake. "Suppose," said he, "we should take a hand at whist for pastime. But let me see, that won't do, there's only three of us; and I cannot play at any other game. The truth is, I seldom or never play, but out of complaisance, or at such a time as this, when I am in danger of falling asleep." Although I was not much inclined to gaming, I felt no aversion to pass an hour or two at cards with a friend; and knowing that Strap understood as much of the matter as I, made no scruple of saying, "I wish we could find a fourth hand." While we were in this perplexity, the person whom we found in the house at our entrance overhearing our discourse, took the pipe from his mouth very gravely, and accosted us thus: "Gentlemen, my pipe is out, you see" (shaking the ashes into the fire), "and rather than you should be baulked, I don't care if I take a hand with you for a trifle; but remember I won't play for anything of consequence." We accepted this proffer with pleasure. Having cut for partners, it fell to my lot to play with him against our friend and Strap, for threepence a game. We were so successful, that, in a short time, I was half a crown gainer; when the gentleman whom we had met in the street observing he had no luck to-day, proposed to leave off, or change partners. By this time I was inflamed with my good fortune and the expectation of improving it, as I perceived the two strangers played but indifferently. Therefore, I voted for giving him his revenge; and, cutting again, Strap and I, to our mutual satisfaction, happened to be partners. My good fortune attended me still; and in less than an hour we had got thirty shillings of their money; for, as they lost, they grew the keener, and doubled stakes every time. At last the inconstant goddess began to veer about; and we were very soon stripped of all our gains, and about forty shillings of our own money. This loss mortified me extremely, and had a visible effect on the muscles of Strap's face, which lengthened apace; but our antagonists perceiving our condition, kindly permitted us to retrieve our loss, and console ourselves with a new acquisition. Then my companion wisely suggested it was time to be gone; upon which the person who had joined us in the house began to curse the cards, and muttered that we were indebted to fortune only for what we had got, no part of our success being owing to our good play. This insinuation nettled me so much, that I challenged him to a game of piquet for a crown; and he was with difficulty persuaded to accept the invitation. This contest ended in less than an hour, to my inexpressible affliction, who lost every shilling of my own money, Strap absolutely refusing to supply me with a sixpence. The gentleman at whose request we had come in, perceiving, by my disconsolate looks, the situation of my heart, which well nigh bursted with grief and resentment, when the other stranger got up and went away with my money, began in this manner: "I am truly afflicted at your bad luck, and would willingly repair it, was it in my power. But what in the name of goodness could provoke you to tempt your fate so long? It is always a maxim with gamesters to pursue success as far as it will go, and to stop whenever fortune shifts about. You are a young man, and your passions too impetuous; you must learn to govern them better. However, there is no experience like that which is bought; you will be the better for this the longest day you have to live. As for the fellow who has got your money, I don't half like him. Did not you observe me tip you the wink to leave off in time?" I answered, "No." "No," continued he, "you was too eager to mind anything but the game. But harkee," said he, in a whisper, "are you satisfied of that young man's honesty? his looks are a little suspicious; but I may be mistaken; he made a great many grimaces while he stood behind you; this is a very wicked town." I told him I was very well convinced of my comrade's integrity, and that the grimaces he mentioned were doubtless owing to his anxiety at my loss "Oho! if that be the case, I ask his pardon. Landlord, see what's to pay."—The reckoning amounted to eighteenpence, which having discharged, the gentleman shook us both by the hand, and, saying he should be glad to see us again, departed.

CHAPTER XV

Strap moralises—Presents his Purse to me—We inform our Landlord of my Misfortune—He unravels the Mystery—I present myself to Cringer—He recommends and turns me over to Mr. Staytape—I become acquainted with a Fellow-dependant, who explains the Characters of Cringer and Staytape—And informs me of the Method to be pursued at the Navy Office and Surgeons' Hall—Strap is employed.

IN our way to our lodging, after a profound silence on both sides, Strap, with a hideous groan, observed, that we had brought our pigs to a fine market. To this observation I made no reply; and he went on, "God send us well out of this place; we have not been in London eight and forty hours, and I believe we have met with eight and forty thousand misfortunes.—We have been jeered, reproached, buffeted, pissed upon, and at last stripped of our money; and I suppose by and by we shall be stripped of our skins.—Indeed, as to the money part of it, that was owing to our own folly; Solomon says, *Bray a fool in a mortar, and he will never be wise.* Ah! God help us, an ounce of prudence is worth a pound of gold." This was no time for him to tamper with my disposition, already mad with my loss, and inflamed with resentment against him for having refused me a little money to attempt to retrieve it. I therefore turned towards him with a stern countenance, and asked, who he called fool? Being altogether unaccustomed to such looks from me, he stood still, and stared in my face for some time; then, with some confusion, uttered, "Fool! I called nobody fool but myself; I am sure I am the greatest fool of the two, for being so much concerned at other people's misfortunes: but *nemo omnibus horis sapit*—that's all, that's all." Upon which a silence ensued, that brought us to our lodging, where I threw myself upon the bed in an agony of despair, resolved to perish rather than apply to my companion, or any other body, for relief; but Strap, who knew my temper, and whose heart bled within him at my distress, after some pause came to the bedside, and, putting a leathern purse into my hand, burst into tears, crying, "I know what you think; but I scorn your thoughts. There's all I have in the world; take it, and I'll perhaps get more for you before that be done. If not, I'll beg for you, steal for you, go through the wide world with you, and starve with you; for though I be a poor cobbler's son, I am no scout." I was so touched with the generous passion of this poor creature, that I could not refrain from weeping also; and we mingled our tears together for some time. Upon examining the purse, I found in it two half-guineas and half a crown, which I would have returned to him, saying, he knew better than I how to manage it; but he absolutely refused my proposal, and told me, it was more reasonable and decent that he should depend upon me who was a gentleman, than that I should be controlled by him.

After this friendly contest was over, and our minds more at ease, we informed our landlord of what had happened to us, taking care to conceal the extremity to which we were reduced. He no sooner heard the story, than he assured us we had been grievously imposed upon by a couple of sharpers, who were associates; and that this polite, honest, friendly, humane person, who had treated us so civilly, was no other than a rascally money-dropper, who made it his business to decoy strangers in that manner to one of his own haunts, where an accomplice or two were always waiting to assist in pillaging the prey he had run down. Here the good man recounted a great many stories of people who had been seduced, cheated, pilfered, beat, nay even murdered by such villains. I was confounded at the artifice and wickedness of mankind; and Strap, lifting up his eyes and hands to heaven, prayed that God would deliver him from such scenes of iniquity; for surely the devil had set up his throne in London. Our landlord being curious to know what reception we had met with at Mr. Cringer's, we acquainted him with the particulars; at which he shook his head, and told us, we had not gone the right way to work; that there was nothing to be done with a member of parliament without a bribe; that the servant was commonly infected with the master's disease, and expected to be paid for his work, as well as his betters. He therefore advised me to give the footman a shilling the next time I should desire admittance to my patron, or else I should scarce find an opportunity to deliver my letter. Accordingly, next morning, when the door was opened, I slipped a shilling into his hand, and told him I had a letter for his master. I found the good effects of my liberality; for the fellow let me in immediately, and taking the letter out of my hand, desired me to wait in a kind of passage for an answer. In this place I continued standing for three-quarters of an hour, during which time I saw a great many young fellows, whom I formerly knew in Scotland, pass and repass, with an air of familiarity, in their way to and from the audience chamber; while I was fain to stand shivering in the cold, and turn my back to them, that they might not perceive the lowness of my condition. At length Mr. Cringer came

out to see a young gentleman to the door, who was no other than
Squire Gawky, dressed in a very gay suit of clothes. At parting,
Mr. Cringer shook him by the hand, and told him he hoped to
have the pleasure of his company at dinner; then turning about
towards me, asked what were my commands? When he understood I was the person who had brought the letter from Mr.
Crab, he affected to recollect my name, which, however, he
pretended he could not do, till he had consulted the letter again;
to save him that trouble, I told him my name was Random.
Upon which he went on, "Ay, ay, Random, Random, Random
—I think I remember the name"; and very well he might, for
this very individual, Mr. Cringe, had many a time rode before
my grandfather's cloak-bag in quality of a footman. "Well,"
says he, "you propose to go on board a man of war, as surgeon's
mate." I replied by a low bow. "I believe it will be a difficult
matter," continued he, "to procure a warrant, there being
already such a swarm of Scotch surgeons at the Navy Office, in
expectation of the next vacancy, that the commissioners are
afraid of being torn to pieces, and have actually applied for a
guard to protect them. However, some ships will soon be put
in commission, and then we shall see what's to be done." So
saying, he left me exceedingly mortified at the different reception
Mr. Gawky and I had met with from this upstart, proud, mean
member, who, I imagined, would have been glad of an opportunity to be grateful for the obligations he owed to my family.

At my return, I was surprised with the agreeable news of
Strap's being employed, on the recommendation of his friend
the schoolmaster, by a periwig maker in the neighbourhood,
who allowed him five shillings per week, besides bed and board.
I continued to dance attendance every other morning at the
levee of Mr. Cringer, during a fortnight, in which time I became
acquainted with a young fellow of my own country and profession, who also depended on the member's interest; but was
treated with much more respect than I, both by the servants
and master, and often admitted into a parlour, where there
was a fire, for the convenience of the better sort of those who
waited for him. Thither I was never permitted to penetrate,
on account of my appearance, which was not at all fashionable:
but was obliged to stand blowing my fingers in a cold lobby,
and take the first opportunity of Mr. Cringer's going to the door
to speak with him. One day, while I enjoyed this occasion, a
person was introduced, whom Mr. Cringer no sooner saw, than,
running towards him, he saluted him with a bow to the very

ground, and afterwards shaking him by the hand with great heartiness and familiarity, called him his good friend, and asked very kindly after Mrs. Staytape and the young ladies; then, after a whisper which continued some minutes, wherein I overheard the word *honour* repeated several times with great emphasis, Mr. Cringer introduced me to this gentleman, as to a person whose advice and assistance I might depend upon, and having given me his direction, followed me to the door, where he told me, I need not give myself the trouble to call at his house any more, for Mr. Staytape would do my business. At that instant my fellow-dependant coming out after me, overheard the discourse of Mr. Cringer, and making up to me in the street, accosted me very civilly. This address I looked upon as no small honour, considering the figure he made; for he was dressed in a blue frock with a gold button, a green silk waistcoat trimmed with gold, black velvet breeches, white silk stockings, silver buckles, a gold-laced hat, a Spencer wig, and a silver-hilted hanger, with a fine clouded cane in his hand. "I perceive," says he, "you are but lately come from Scotland; pray what may your business with Mr. Cringer be? I suppose it is no secret—and I may possibly give you some advice that may be serviceable; for I have been surgeon's second mate on board of a seventy-gun ship, and consequently know a good deal of the world." I made no scruple to disclose my situation, which when he had learned, he shook his head, and told me he had been pretty much in the same circumstances about a year ago; that he had relied on Cringer's promises, until his money (which was considerable), as well as his credit, was quite exhausted; and when he wrote to his relations for a fresh supply, instead of money, he received nothing but reproaches, and the epithets of "idle," "debauched fellow": that, after he had waited at the Navy Office many months for a warrant, to no purpose, he was fain to pawn some of his clothes, which raised a small sum, wherewith he bribed the secretary, who soon procured a warrant for him, notwithstanding he had affirmed the same day, that there was not one vacancy: that he had gone on board, where he remained nine months; at the end of which the ship was put out of commission; and he said the company were to be paid off in Broad Street the very next day: that his relations, being reconciled to him, had charged him to pay his devoirs regularly to Mr. Cringer, who had informed them by letter that his interest alone had procured the warrant; in obedience to which command, he came to his levee every morning as I saw, though he looked upon him to be a very pitiful scoundrel. In conclusion, he asked me if I had yet passed at Surgeons' Hall? To which question I answered, I did not so much as know it was necessary. "Necessary!" cried he. "O Lord, O Lord! I find I must instruct you—come along with me, and I'll give you some information about that matter." So saying, he carried me into an ale-house, where he called for some beer, and bread and cheese, on which we breakfasted. While we sat in this place, he told me I must first go to the Navy Office, and write to the board, desiring them to order a letter for me to the Surgeons' Hall, that I might be examined touching my skill in surgery: that the surgeons, after having examined me, would give me my qualification sealed up in form of a letter directed to the commissioners, which qualification I must deliver to the secretary of the board, who would open it in my presence, and read the contents. After which I must employ my interest to be provided for as soon as possible. That the expense of this qualification, for second mate of a third rate, amounted to thirteen shillings, exclusive of the warrant, which cost him half a guinea and half a crown, besides the present to the secretary, which consisted of a three-pound-twelve piece. This calculation was like a thunderbolt to me, whose whole fortune did not amount to twelve shillings. I accordingly made him acquainted with this part of my distress, after having thanked him for his information and advice. He condoled me on this occasion; but bade me be of good cheer, for he had conceived a friendship for me, and would make all things easy. He was run out at present, but to-morrow or next day he was certain of receiving a considerable sum, of which he would lend me what would be sufficient to answer my exigencies. This frank declaration pleased me so much, that I pulled out my purse, and emptied it before him, begging him to take what he pleased for pocket expenses, until he should receive his own money. With a good deal of pressing he was prevailed upon to take five shillings, telling me that he might have what money he wanted at any time for the trouble of going into the city; but as he had met with me, he would defer his going thither till to-morrow, when I should go along with him, and he would put me in a way of acting for myself, without any servile dependence on that rascal Cringer, much less on the lousy tailor to whom he heard him turn me over. "How," cried I; "is Mr. Staytape a tailor?" "No less, I'll assure you," answered he; "and I confess, more likely to serve you than the member; for, provided you can entertain him with politics and conundrums, you may have credit with him for as many and as rich clothes as you please." I told him, I was utterly ignorant of both, and so incensed at Cringer's usage, that I would never set foot within his door again. After a good deal more conversation, my new acquaintance and I parted, having made an appointment to meet the next day at the same place, in order to set out for the city. I went immediately to Strap, and related everything which had happened; but he did not at all approve of my being so forward to lend money to a stranger, especially as we had already been so much imposed upon by appearances. "However," said he, "if you are sure he is a Scotchman, I believe you are safe."

CHAPTER XVI

My new Acquaintance breaks an Appointment—I proceed by myself to the Navy Office—Address myself to a Person there, who assists me with his Advice—Write to the Board—They grant me a Letter to the Surgeons at the Hall—Am informed of the Beau's Name and Character—Find him—He makes me his Confidant in an Amour—Desires me to pawn my Linen, for his Occasions—I recover what I lent him—Some curious Observations of Strap on that Occasion—His Vanity.

IN the morning I rose and went to the place of rendezvous, where I waited two hours in vain; and was so exasperated against him for breaking his appointment, that I set out for the city by myself, in hopes of finding the villain, and being revenged on him for his breach of promise. At length I found myself at the Navy Office, which I entered, and saw crowds of young fellows walking below, many of whom made no better appearance than myself. I consulted the physiognomy of each, and at last made up to one whose countenance I liked; and asked if he could instruct me in the form of the letter which was to be sent to the board, to obtain an order for examination. He answered me in broad Scotch, that he would show me the copy of what he had writ for himself, by the direction of another who knew the form; and accordingly pulled it out of his pocket for my perusal; and told me that, if I was expeditious, I might send it in to the board before dinner, for they did no business in the afternoon. He then went with me to a coffee-house hard by, where I wrote the letter, which was immediately delivered to the messenger; who told me I might expect an order to-morrow about the same time. Having transacted this piece of business, my mind was a good deal composed; and as I met with so much civility from this stranger, I desired further acquaintance with him, fully resolved, however, not to be deceived by him so much to my prejudice as I had been by the beau. He agreed to dine with me at the cook's shop which I frequented; and on our way thither, carried me to Change, where I was in some hopes of finding Mr. Jackson (for that was the name of the person who had broke his appointment). I sought him there to no purpose, and on our way towards the other end of the town, imparted to my companion his behaviour towards me. Upon which, he gave me to understand, that he was no stranger to the name of Beau Jackson (so he was called at the Navy Office), although he did not know him personally; that he had the character of a good-natured careless fellow, who made no scruple of borrowing from anybody that would lend; that most people who knew him believed he had a good principle at bottom; but his extravagance was such, he would probably never have it in his power to manifest the honesty of his intention. This account made me sweat for my five shillings, which I nevertheless did not altogether despair of recovering, provided I could find out the debtor. This young man likewise added another circumstance of Squire Jackson's history, which was, that being destitute of all means to equip himself for sea, when he received his last warrant, he had been recommended to a person who lent him a little money, after he had signed a will and power, entitling that person to lift his wages when they should become due, as also to inherit his effects in case of his death. That he was still under the tutorage and direction of that gentleman, who advanced him small sums from time to time upon his security at the rate of fifty per cent. But at present his credit was very low, because his funds would do little more than pay what he had already received, this moderate interest included. After the stranger (whose name was Thomson) had entertained me with this account of Jackson, he informed me that he himself had passed for third mate of a third rate, about four months ago; since which time, he had constantly attended at the Navy Office in hope of a warrant, having been assured from the beginning, both by a Scotch member and one of the commissioners to whom the member recommended him, that he should be put into the first vacancy; notwithstanding which promise, he had the mortification to see six or seven appointed to the same station almost every week: that now, being utterly impoverished, his sole hope consisted in the promise of a friend lately come to town, to lend him a small matter, for a present to the secretary, without which he was persuaded he might wait a thousand years to no purpose. I conceived a mighty liking for this young fellow, which (I believe) proceeded from the similitude of our fortunes. We spent the whole day together; and, as he lived at Wapping, I desired him to take a share of my bed. Next day we returned to the Navy Office, where, after being called before the board, and questioned about the place of my nativity and education, they ordered a letter to be made out for me, which, upon paying half a crown to the clerk, I received, and delivered into the hands of the clerk at Surgeons' Hall, together with a shilling for his trouble in registering my name. By this time my whole stock was diminished to two shillings, and I saw not the least prospect of relief, even for present subsistence, much less to enable me to pay the fees at Surgeons' Hall for my examination, which would come on in a fortnight. In this state of perplexity, I consulted Strap, who assured me, he would pawn everything he had in the world, even to his razors, before I should want. But this expedient I absolutely rejected, telling him, I would a thousand times rather list for a soldier, of which I had some thoughts, than be any longer a burden to him. At the word soldier, he grew pale as death, and begged, on his knees, I would think no more of that scheme. "God preserve us all in our right wits!" cried he; "would you turn soldier, and perhaps be sent abroad against the Spaniards, where you must stand and be shot at like a woodcock?—Heaven keep cold lead out of my carcass! and let me die in a bed like a Christian, as all my fore-fathers have done. What signifies all the riches and honours of this life, if one enjoys not content? And, in the next, there is no respect of persons. Better be a poor honest barber with a good conscience, and time to repent of my sins upon my death-bed, than be cut off (God bless us) by a musket-shot, as it were in the very flower of one's age, in the pursuit of riches and fame. What signify riches, my dear friend? do not they make unto themselves wings? as the wise man saith; and does not Horace observe, *Non domus et fundus, non æris acervus et auri Ægroto domini deduxit corpore febres, Non animo curas*? I could more-over mention many other sayings in contempt of riches, both from the Bible and other good books; but, as I know you are not very fond of those things, I shall only assure you that, if you take on to be a soldier, I will do the same; and then if we should both be slain, you will not only have your own blood to answer for, but mine also; and peradventure the lives of all those whom we shall kill in battle. Therefore, I pray you, consider whether you will sit down contented with small things, and share the fruits of my industry in peace, till Providence shall send better tidings; or, by your despair, plunge both our souls and bodies into everlasting perdition, which God of his infinite mercy forbid." I could not help smiling at this harangue, which was delivered with great earnestness, the tears standing in his eyes all the time; and promised to do nothing of that sort without his consent and concurrence. He was much comforted with this declaration; and told me in a few days he should receive a week's wages, which should be at my service; but advised me, in the meantime, to go in quest of Jackson, and recover, if possible, what he had borrowed of me. I accordingly trudged about from one end of the town to the other for several days, without being able to learn anything certain concerning him: and, one day, being extremely hungry, and allured by the steams that regaled my nostrils from a boiling cellar, I went down with an intention to gratify my appetite with two-pennyworth of beef; when, to my no small surprise, I found Mr. Jackson sitting at dinner with a footman. He no sooner perceived me than he got up and shook me by the hand, saying, he was glad to see me, for he intended to have called at my lodgings in the afternoon. I was so well pleased with this rencontre, and the apologies he made for not keeping his appointment, that I forgot my resentment, and sat down to dinner, with the happy expectation of not only recovering my own money before we should part, but also of reaping the benefit of his promise to lend me wherewithal to pass examination; and this hope my sanguine complexion suggested, though the account Thomson gave me of him ought to have moderated my expectation. When we had feasted sumptuously, he took his leave of the footman, and adjourned with me to an ale-house hard by, where, after shaking me by the hand again, he began thus: "I suppose you think me a sad dog, Mr. Random, and I do confess that appearances are against me. But I dare say you will forgive me, when I tell you, my not coming at the time appointed was owing to a peremptory message I received from a certain lady, whom, harkee (but this is a great secret), I am to marry very soon. You think this strange, perhaps, but it is not less true for all that—a five thousand pounder, I'll assure you, besides expectations. For my own part, devil take me if I know what any woman can see engaging about me—but a whim, you know; and then one would not baulk one's good fortune. You saw that footman who dined with us—he's one of the honestest fellows that ever wore a livery. You must know, it was by his means I was introduced to her, for he made me first acquainted with her woman, who is his mistress; ay, many a crown has he and his sweetheart had of my money; but what of that? things are now brought to a bearing. I have—come a little this way—I have proposed marriage, and the day is fixed; she's a charming creature; writes like an angel. O Lord! she can repeat all the English tragedies as well as e'er a player in Drury Lane! and indeed is so fond of plays, that, to be near the stage, she has taken lodgings in a court hard by the theatre. But you shall see—you shall see—here's the last letter she sent me."—With these words, he put it into my hand, and I read, to the best of my remembrance, as follows:

"DEER KREETER,—As you are the animable hopjack of my contemplayshins, your aydear is infernally skimming before my keymerycal fansee, when Murfy sends his puppies to the heys of slipping mortals; and when Febus shines from his merrydying throne. Whereupon, I shall canseeif old whorie time has lost his pinners, as also Cupid his harrows, until thou enjoy sweet propose in the loafseek harms of thy faithfool to commend.
"CLAYRENDER.

"Wingar Yeard, Doory Lane,
    January 12*th*."

While I was reading, he seemed to be in an ecstasy, rubbing his hands, and bursting out into fits of laughter; at last he caught hold of my hand, and, squeezing it, cried, "There is style for you! what do you think of this billet-doux?" I answered, "It might be sublime for aught I knew, for it was altogether above my comprehension."—"Oho!" said he, "I believe it is both tender and sublime—she's a divine creature! and so doats upon me! Let me see, what shall I do with this money, when I have once got it into my hands? In the first place, I shall do for you—I'm a man of few words; but, say no more, that's determined—whether would you advise me to purchase some post, by which I may rise in the state; or lay out my wife's fortune in land, and retire to the country at once?" —I gave my opinion without hesitation, that he could not do better than buy an estate and improve; especially since he had already seen so much of the world. Then I launched out into the praises of a country life, as described by the poets whose works I had read. He seemed to relish my advice, but withal told me, that, although he had seen a great deal of the world both by land and sea, having cruised three whole months in the Channel, yet he should not be satisfied until he had visited France, which he proposed to do before he should settle; and to carry his wife along with him. I had nothing to object to his proposal; and asked how soon he hoped to be happy? "As to that," he replied, "nothing obstructs my happiness, but the want of a little ready cash; for you must know, my friend in the city has gone out of town for a week or two; and I unfortunately missed my pay at Broad Street, by being detained too long by the dear charmer; but, there will be a recall at Chatham next week, whither the ship's books are sent, and I have commissioned a friend in that place to receive the money." "If that be all," said I, "there's no great harm in deferring your marriage a few days."—"Yes, faith! but there is," said he, "you don't know how many rivals I have, who would take all advantages against me. I would not baulk the impatience of her passion for the world; the least appearance of coldness and indifference would ruin all: and such offers don't occur every day." I acquiesced in this observation, and inquired how he intended to proceed: at this question, he rubbed his chin, and said, "Why, truly, I must be obliged to some friend or other—do you know of nobody that would lend me a small sum for a day or two?"—I assured him, I was such an utter stranger in London, that I did not believe I could borrow a guinea if my life depended upon it. "No!" said he, "that's hard—that's hard. I wish I had anything to pawn; upon my soul you have got excellent linen" (feeling the sleeve of my shirt); "how many shirts of that kind have you got?"—I answered, "Six ruffled and six plain";—at which he testified great surprise, and swore that no gentleman ought to have more than four. "How many d'ye think I have got?" continued he. "But this and another, as I hope to be saved! I dare say we shall be able to raise a good sum out of your superfluity—let me see—let me see—each of these shirts is worth sixteen shillings at a moderate computation; now suppose we pawn them for half-price, eight times eight is sixty-four, that's three pounds four; zounds! that will do; give me your hand."—"Softly, softly, Mr. Jackson," said I, "don't dispose of my linen without my consent; first pay me the crown you owe me, and then we shall talk of other matters." He protested he had not above one shilling in his pocket, but that he would pay me out of the first of my money raised from the shirts. This piece of assurance incensed me so much, that I swore that I would not part with him until I had received satisfaction for what I had lent him; and, as for the shirts, I would not pawn one of them to save him from the gallows. At his expression he laughed aloud, and then complained that it was damn'd hard, that I should refuse him a trifle that would infallibly enable him not only to make his own fortune, but mine also. "You talk of pawning my shirts," said I, "suppose you should sell this hanger, Mr. Jackson? I believe it would fetch a good round sum."—"No, hang it," said he, "I can't appear decently without my hanger, or egad it should go." However, seeing me inflexible with regard to my linen, he at length unbuckled his hanger, and, showing me the sign of the three blue balls, desired me to carry it thither and pawn it for two guineas. This office I would by no means have performed, had I seen any likelihood of having my money otherwise; but not willing, out of a piece of false delicacy, to neglect the only opportunity I should perhaps ever have, I ventured into a pawn-broker's shop, where I demanded two guineas on the pledge, in the name of Thomas Williams. "Two guineas!" said the pawn-broker, looking at the hanger; "this piece of goods has been here several times before for thirty shillings; however, since I believe the gentleman to whom it belongs will redeem it, he shall have what he wants", and accordingly, he paid me the money, which I carried to the house where I had left Jackson, and, calling for change, counted out to him seven and thirty shillings, reserving the other five for myself. After looking at the money some time, he said, "Damn it! it don't signify—this won't do my business; so you may as well take half a guinea, or a whole one, as the five shillings you have kept." I thanked him kindly; but I refused to accept of any more than was my due, because I had no prospect of repaying it. Upon which declaration he stared in my face, and told me I was excessively raw, or I would not talk in that manner. "Blood!" cried he, "I have a very bad opinion of a young fellow who won't borrow of his friend when he is in want; 'tis the sign of a sneaking spirit. Come, come, Random, give me back the five shillings, and take this half-guinea, and if ever you are able to pay me, I believe you will; if not, damn me if ever I ask it." When I reflected on my present necessity, I suffered myself to be persuaded; and, after making my acknow-ledgments to Mr. Jackson, who offered to treat me with a play, I returned to my lodgings with a much better opinion of this gentleman than I had in the morning; and at night imparted my day's adventures to Strap, who rejoiced at the good luck,

saying, "I told you, if he was a Scotchman, you was safe enough
and who knows but this marriage may make us all? You have
heard, I suppose, as how a countryman of ours, a journeyman
baker, ran away with a great lady of this town, and now keeps
his coach. Ecod! I say nothing; but yesterday morning, as I
was a-shaving a gentleman at his own house, there was a young
lady in the room—a fine buxom wench, i'faith! and she threw
so many sheep's eyes at a certain person whom I shall not name,
that my heart went knock, knock, knock, like a fulling mill,
and my hand sh—sh—shook so much that I sliced a piece of
skin off the gentleman's nose. Whereby he swore a deadly oath,
and was going to horsewhip me, when she prevented him, and
made my peace. *Omen haud malum !* Is not a journeyman barber
as good as a journeyman baker? The only difference is, the baker
uses flour for the belly, and the barber uses it for the head.
And as the head is a more noble member than the belly, so is a
barber more noble than a baker; for what's the belly without
the head? Besides, I am told he could neither read nor write;
now you know I can do both, and, moreover, speak Latin. But
I will say no more, for I despise vanity; nothing is more vain
than vanity." With these words he pulled out of his pocket a
wax candle's end, which he applied to his forehead; and, upon
examination, I found he had combed his own hair over the
toupee of his wig, and was indeed in his whole dress become a
very smart shaver. I congratulated him on his prospect with a
satirical smile, which he understood very well; and, shaking
his head, observed I had very little faith, but the truth would
come to light in spite of my incredulity.

CHAPTER XVII

I go to Surgeons' Hall, where I meet with Mr. Jackson—Am examined—
A fierce Dispute arises between two of the Examiners—Jackson disguises
himself to attract Respect—Is detected—In hazard of being sent to
Bridewell—He treats us at a Tavern—Carries us to a Night House—
A troublesome Adventure there—We are committed to the Round-house
—Carried before a Justice—His Behaviour.

WITH the assistance of this faithful adherent, who gave me
almost all the money he earned, I preserved my half-guinea
entire till the day of examination, when I went with a quaking
heart to Surgeons' Hall, in order to undergo that ceremony.
Among a crowd of young fellows who walked in the outward

hall, I perceived Mr. Jackson, to whom I immediately went up, and inquiring into the state of his amour, understood it was still undetermined by reason of his friend's absence, and the delay of the recall at Chatham, which put it out of his power to bring it to a conclusion. I then asked what his business was in this place? He replied, he was resolved to have two strings to his bow, that in case the one failed he might use the other; and, with this view, he was to pass that night for a higher qualification. At that instant a young fellow came out from the place of examination with a pale countenance, his lip quivering, and his looks as wild as if he had seen a ghost. He no sooner appeared, than we all flocked about him with the utmost eagerness to know what reception he had met with; which, after some pause, he described, recounting all the questions they had asked, with the answers he made. In this manner we obliged no less than twelve to recapitulate, which, now the danger was past, they did with pleasure, before it fell to my lot: at length the beadle called my name, with a voice that made me tremble as much as if it had been the sound of the last trumpet: however, there was no remedy: I was conducted into a large hall, where I saw about a dozen of grim faces sitting at a long table; one of whom bade me come forward, in such an imperious tone that I was actually for a minute or two bereft of my senses. The first question he put to me was, "Where was you born?" To which I answered, "In Scotland."—"In Scotland," said he; "I know that very well; we have scarce any other countrymen to examine here; you Scotchmen have overspread us of late as the locusts did Egypt: I ask you in what part of Scotland was you born?" I named the place of my nativity, which he had never before heard of: he then proceeded to interrogate me about my age, the town where I served my time, with the term of my apprenticeship; and when I informed him that I served three years only, he fell into a violent passion; swore it was a shame and a scandal to send such raw boys into the world as surgeons; that it was a great presumption in me, and an affront upon the English, to pretend to sufficient skill in my business, having served so short a time, when every apprentice in England was bound seven years at least; that my friends would have done better if they had made me a weaver or shoemaker, but their pride would have me a gentleman, he supposed, at any rate, and their poverty could not afford the necessary education. This exordium did not at all contribute to the recovery of my spirits, but, on the contrary, reduced me to such a situation that

I was scarce able to stand; which being perceived by a plump gentleman who sat opposite to me, with a skull before him, he said, Mr. Snarler was too severe upon the young man; and turning towards me, told me, I need not be afraid, for nobody would do me any harm; then bidding me take time to recollect myself, he examined me touching the operation of the trepan, and was very well satisfied with my answers. The next person who questioned me was a wag, who began by asking if I had ever seen amputation performed; and I replying in the affirmative, he shook his head, and said, "What! upon a dead subject, I suppose?" "If," continued he, "during an engagement at sea, a man should be brought to you with his head shot off, how would you behave?" After some hesitation, I owned such a case had never come under my observation, neither did I remember to have seen any method of cure proposed for such an accident, in any of the systems of surgery I had perused. Whether it was owing to the simplicity of my answer, or the archness of the question, I know not, but every member at the board deigned to smile, except Mr. Snarler, who seemed to have very little of the *animal risibile* in his constitution. The facetious member, encouraged by the success of his last joke, went on thus: "Suppose you was called to a patient of a plethoric habit, who had been bruised by a fall, what would you do?" I answered, I would bleed him immediately. "What," said he, "before you had tied up his arm?" But this stroke of wit not answering his expectation, he desired me to advance to the gentleman who sat next to him; and who, with a pert air, asked what method of cure I would follow in wounds of the intestines. I repeated the method of cure as it is prescribed by the best chirurgical writers; which he heard to an end, and then said, with a supercilious smile, "So you think by such treatment the patient might recover?"—I told him I saw nothing to make me think otherwise. "That may be," resumed he, "I won't answer for your foresight; but did you ever know of a case of this kind succeed?" I answered I did not; and was about to tell him I had never seen a wounded intestine; but he stopped me, by saying, with some precipitation, "Nor never will. I affirm, that all wounds of the intestines, whether great or small, are mortal."—"Pardon me, brother," says the fat gentleman, "there is very good authority——"—Here he was interrupted by the other, with "Sir, excuse me, I despise all authority. *Nullius in verba.* I stand upon my own bottom."—"But, sir, sir," replied his antagonist, "the reason of the thing shows——"—"A fig for reason," cried this sufficient member, "I laugh at reason, give me ocular demonstration." The corpulent gentleman began to wax warm, and observed that no man acquainted with the anatomy of the parts would advance such an extravagant assertion. This innuendo enraged the other so much that he started up, and in a furious tone exclaimed, "What, sir! do you question my knowledge in anatomy?" By this time, all the examiners had espoused the opinion of one or other of the disputants, and raised their voices all together, when the chairman commanded silence, and ordered me to withdraw. In less than a quarter of an hour I was called in again, received my qualification sealed up, and was ordered to pay five shillings. I laid down my half-guinea upon the table, and stood some time, until one of them bade me begone; to this I replied, I will, when I have got my change; upon which another threw me five shillings and sixpence, saying, I should not be a true Scotchman if I went away without my change. I was afterwards obliged to give three shillings and sixpence to the beadles, and a shilling to an old woman who swept the hall. This disbursement sunk my finances to thirteen-pence halfpenny, with which I was sneaking off, when Jackson perceiving it came up to me and begged I would tarry for him, and he would accompany me to the other end of the town, as soon as his examination should be over. I could not refuse this to a person that was so much my friend; but I was astonished at the change of his dress, which was varied in half an hour from what I have already described, to a very grotesque fashion. His head was covered with an old smoked tie-wig that did not boast one crooked hair, and a slouched hat over it, which would have very well have become a chimney-sweeper or a dustman; his neck was adorned with a black crape, the ends of which he had twisted, and fixed in the buttonhole of a shabby great-coat that wrapped up his whole body; his white silk stockings were converted into black worsted hose; and his countenance was rendered venerable by wrinkles, and a beard of his own painting. When I expressed my surprise at this metamorphosis, he laughed, and told me, it was done by the advice and assistance of a friend who lived over the way, and would certainly produce something very much to his advantage; for it gave him the appearance of age, which never fails of attracting respect. I applauded his sagacity, and waited with impatience for the effects of it. At length he was called in, but whether the oddness of his appearance excited a curiosity more than usual in the board, or his behaviour was not suitable to his figure, I know not; he was

discovered to be an impostor, and put into the hands of the
beadle, in order to be sent to Bridewell. So that instead of seeing
him come out with a cheerful countenance and a surgeon's
qualification in his hand, I perceived him led through the outward hall as a prisoner, and was very much alarmed and anxious
to know the occasion; when he called with a lamentable voice
and piteous aspect to me, and some others who knew him,
"For God's sake, gentlemen, bear witness that I am the same
individual John Jackson, who served as surgeon's second mate
on board the *Elizabeth*, or else I shall go to Bridewell." It
would have been impossible for the most austere hermit that
ever lived to have refrained from laughing at his appearance
and address; we therefore indulged ourselves a good while at
his expense, and afterwards pleaded his cause so effectually
with the beadle, who was gratified with half a crown, that the
prisoner was dismissed, and, in a few moments, resumed his
former gaiety; swearing, since the board had refused his money,
he would spend it every shilling before he went to bed in treating
his friends; at the same time inviting us all to favour him with
our company. It was now ten o'clock at night, and as I had a
great way to walk, through streets that were utterly unknown
to me, I was prevailed upon to be of their party, in hopes he
would afterwards accompany me to my lodgings, according to
his promise. He conducted us to his friend's house, who kept
a tavern over the way, where we continued drinking punch,
until the liquor mounted up to our heads, and made us all
extremely frolicsome: I in particular was so much elevated,
that nothing would serve me but a wench, at which demand
Jackson expressed much joy, and assured me I should have my
desire before we parted. Accordingly, when we had paid the
reckoning, we sallied out, roaring and singing; and were conducted by our leader to a place of nocturnal entertainment,
where I immediately attached myself to a fair one, with whom
I proposed to spend the remaining part of the night; but she
not relishing my appearance, refused to grant my request before
I should have made her an acknowledgment; which not suiting
with my circumstances, we broke off our correspondence, to
my no small mortification and resentment, because I thought
the mercenary creature had not done justice to my merit. In
the meantime, Mr. Jackson's dress had attracted the inclinations
and assiduities of two or three nymphs, who loaded him with
caresses, in return for the arrack punch with which he treated
them; till at length, notwithstanding the sprightly sallies of

those charmers, sleep began to exert his power over us all; and
our conductor called, "To pay." When the bill was brought,
which amounted to twelve shillings, he put his hand in his
pocket, but might have saved himself the trouble, for his purse
was gone. This accident disconcerted him a great deal at first;
but, after some recollection, he seized the two dulcineas who
sat by him, one in each hand, and swore, if they did not immediately restore his money, he would charge a constable with
them. The good lady at the bar, seeing what passed, whispered
something to the drawer, who went out; and then, with great
composure, asked what was the matter. Jackson told her he
was robbed, and swore, if she refused him satisfaction, he would
have her and her whores committed to Bridewell. "Robbed,"
cried she, "robbed in my house! Gentlemen and ladies, I take
you all to witness, this person has scandalised my reputation."
At that instant seeing the constable and watch enter, she proceeded, "What! you must not only endeavour by your false
aspersions to ruin my character, but even commit an assault
upon my family! Mr. Constable, I charge you with this uncivil
person, who has been guilty of a riot here; I shall take care
and bring an action against him for defamation." While I was
reflecting on this melancholy event, which had made me quite
sober, the lady whose favours I had solicited, being piqued at
some repartee that passed between us, cried, "They are all
concerned"; and desired the constable to take us all into custody; an arrest which was performed instantly, to the utter
astonishment and despair of us all, except Jackson, who having
been often in such scrapes, was very little concerned, and charged
the constable in his turn with the landlady and her whole bevy:
upon which we were carried all together prisoners to the Round-
house; where Jackson, after a word of comfort to us, informed
the constable of his being robbed, to which he said he would
swear next morning before the justice. "Ay, ay," says the bawd,
"we shall see whose oath will most signify." In a little time the
constable calling Jackson into another room, spoke to him thus:
"I perceive that you and your company are strangers, and am
very sorry for your being involved in such an ugly business.
I have known this woman a great while; she has kept a notorious
house in the neighbourhood this many years, and, although
often complained of as a nuisance, still escapes, through her
interest with the justices, to whom she, and all of her employment, pay contribution quarterly for protection. As she charged
me with you first, her complaint will have the preference;

and she can procure evidence to swear whatever she shall please to desire of them. So that unless you can make it up before morning, you and your companions may think yourselves happily quit for a month's hard labour in Bridewell. Nay, if she should swear a robbery or assault against you, you will be committed to Newgate, and tried next sessions at the Old Bailey for your life." This last piece of information had such an effect upon Jackson, that he agreed to make it up, provided his money might be restored. The constable told him, that, instead of retrieving what he had lost, he was pretty certain it would cost him some more before they would come to any composition. But, however, he had compassion on him, and would, if he pleased, sound them about a mutual release. The unfortunate beau thanked him for his friendship, and returning to us, acquainted us with the substance of this dialogue; while the constable, desiring to speak in private with our adversary, carried her into the next room, and pleaded our cause so effectually, that she condescended to make him umpire; he accordingly proposed an arbitration, to which we gave our assent; and he fined each party in three shillings, to be laid out in a bowl of punch, wherein we drowned all animosities, to the inexpressible joy of my two late acquaintances and me, who had been in the state of the damned ever since Jackson mentioned Bridewell and Newgate. By the time we had finished our bowl, to which, by the by, I had contributed my last shilling, it was morning; and I proposed to move homeward, when the constable gave me to understand he could discharge no prisoners, but by order of the justice, before whom we must appear. This renewed my chagrin; and I cursed the hour in which I had yielded to Jackson's invitation. About nine o'clock we were escorted to the house of a certain justice, not many miles distant from Covent Garden; who no sooner saw the constable enter with a train of prisoners at his heels, than he saluted him as follows: "So, Mr. Constable, you are a diligent man—What den of rogues have you been scouring?" Then looking at us, who appeared very much dejected, he continued, "Ay, ay, thieves, I see—old offenders —Oh, your humble servant, Mrs. Harridan! I suppose these fellows have been taken robbing your house—yes, yes, here's an old acquaintance of mine—you have used expedition," said he to me, "in returning from transportation; but we shall save you the trouble for the future—the surgeons will fetch you from your next transportation at their expense." I assured his worship he was mistaken in me, for he had never seen me in his life before. To this declaration he replied, "How! you impudent rascal, dare you say so to my face? Do you think I am to be imposed upon by that northern accent which you have assumed? but it shan't avail you—you shall find me too far north for you. Here, clerk, write this fellow's *mittimus*. His name is Patrick Gahagan." Here Mr. Jackson interposed, and told him I was a Scotchman lately come to town, descended of a good family, and that my name was Random. The justice looked upon this assertion as an outrage upon his memory, on which he valued himself much; and strutting up to Jackson, with a fierce countenance, put his hands in his sides, and said, "Who are you, sir? Do you give me the lie? Take notice, gentlemen, here's a fellow who affronts me upon the bench; but I'll lay you fast, sirrah, I will; for notwithstanding your laced jacket, I believe you are a notorious felon." My friend was so much abashed at this menace, which was thundered out with great vociferation, that he changed colour, and remained speechless. This confusion his worship took for a symptom of guilt, and to complete his discovery, continued his threats: "Now, I am convinced you are a thief—your face discovers it—you tremble all over—your conscience won't lie still—you'll be hanged, sirrah," raising his voice, "you'll be hanged; and happy had it been for the world, as well as your own miserable soul, if you had been detected and cut off in the beginning of your career. Come hither, clerk, and take this man's confession." I was in an agony of consternation, when the constable, going into another room with his worship, acquainted him with the truth of the story; which having learned, he returned with a smiling countenance, and addressing himself to us all, said it was always his way to terrify young people, when they came before him, that his threats might make a strong impression on their minds, and deter them from engaging in scenes of riot and debauchery, which commonly ended before the judge. Thus having cloaked his own want of discernment under the disguise of paternal care, we were dismissed, and I found myself as much lightened as if a mountain had been lifted off my breast.

CHAPTER XVIII

I carry my Qualification to the Navy Office—The Nature of it—The Behaviour of the Secretary—Strap's Concern for my Absence—A Battle between him and a Blacksmith—The troublesome Consequences of it—His Harangue to me—His Friend the Schoolmaster recommends me to a French Apothecary, who entertains me as a Journeyman.

I WOULD willingly have gone home to sleep, but was told by my companions, that we must deliver our letters of qualification at the Navy Office before one o'clock; accordingly we went thither, and gave them to the secretary, who opened and read them; and I was mightily pleased to find myself qualified for second mate of a third rate. When he had stuck them altogether on a file, one of our company asked if there were any vacancies? to which interrogation he answered, No. Then I ventured to inquire if any ships were to be put in commission soon? At which question he surveyed me with a look of ineffable contempt, and, pushing us out of his office, locked the door, without deigning us another word. We went downstairs, and conferred together on our expectations, when I understood that each of them had been recommended to one or other of the commissioners, and each of them promised the first vacancy that should fall; but that none of them relied solely upon that interest, without a present to the secretary, with whom some of the commissioners went snacks. For which reason each of them had provided a small purse; and I was asked what I proposed to give? This was a vexatious question to me, who, far from being in a capacity to gratify a ravenous secretary, had not wherewithal to purchase a dinner. I therefore answered, I had not yet determined what to give; and sneaked off towards my own lodgings, cursing my fate all the way, and inveighing with much bitterness against the barbarity of my grandfather, and the sordid avarice of my relations, who left me a prey to contempt and indigence. Full of these disagreeable reflections, I arrived at the house where I lodged, and relieved my landlord from great anxiety on my account; for this honest man believed I had met with some dismal accident, and that he should never see me again. Strap, who had come to visit me in the morning, understanding I had been abroad all night, was almost distracted, and, after having obtained leave of his master, had gone in quest of me, though he was even more ignorant of the town than I. Not being willing to inform my landlord of my adventure,

I told him I had met with an acquaintance at Surgeons' Hall, with whom I spent the evening and night, but being very much infested by bugs, I had not slept much, and therefore intended to take a little repose; so saying, I went to bed, and desired to be awakened, if Strap should happen to come while I should be asleep. I was accordingly roused by my friend himself, who entered my chamber about three o'clock in the afternoon; and presented a figure to my eyes that I could scarce believe real. In short, this affectionate shaver, setting out towards Surgeons' Hall, had inquired for me there to no purpose; from thence he found his way to the Navy Office, where he could hear no tidings of me, because I was unknown to everybody then present; he afterwards went upon Change, in hopes of seeing me upon the Scotch walk, but without success. At last, being almost in despair of finding me, he resolved to ask everybody he met in the street, if perchance anyone could give him information about me; and actually put his resolution in practice, in spite of the scoffs, curses, and reproaches with which he was answered; until a blacksmith's 'prentice, seeing him stop a porter with a burden on his back, and hearing his question, for which he received a hearty curse, called to him, and asked if the person he inquired after was not a Scotchman? Strap replied with great eagerness, "Yes, and had on a brown coat with long skirts." "The same," said the blacksmith, "I saw him pass by an hour ago." "Did you so?" cried Strap, rubbing his hands. "Odd! I am very glad of that—which way went he?" "Towards Tyburn in a cart," said he, "if you make good speed, you may get thither time enough to see him hanged." This piece of wit incensed my friend to such a degree, that he called the blacksmith scoundrel, and protested he would fight him for half a farthing. "No, no," said the other, stripping, "I'll have none of your money—you Scotchmen seldom carry any about with you—but I'll fight you for love." There was a ring immediately formed by the mob; and Strap, finding he could not get off honourably without fighting, at the same time burning with resentment against his adversary, quitted his clothes to the care of the multitude, and the battle began with great violence on the side of Strap, who in a few minutes exhausted his breath and spirits on his patient antagonist, who sustained the assault with great coolness, till, finding the barber quite spent, he returned the blows he had lent him with such interest, that Strap, after having received three falls on the hard stones, gave out, and allowed the blacksmith to be the better man. The

victory being thus decided, it was proposed to adjourn to a
cellar hard by, and drink friends. But when my friend began to
gather up his clothes, he perceived that some honest person or
other had made free with his shirt, neckcloth, hat, and wig,
which were carried off; and probably his coat and waistcoat
would have met with the same fate, had they been worth stealing.
It was in vain for him to make a noise, which only yielded mirth
to the spectators; he was fain to get off in this manner, which
he accomplished with much difficulty, and appeared before me
all besmeared with blood and dirt. Notwithstanding this misfortune, such was his transport at finding me safe and sound,
that he had almost stifled and stunk me to death with his
embraces. After he had cleaned himself, and put on one of my
shirts, and a woollen nightcap, I recounted to him the particulars
of my night's campaign, which filled him with admiration, and
made him repeat with great energy an observation which was
often in his mouth, namely, "that surely London is the devil's
drawing-room." As neither of us had dined, he desired me to
get up; and the milkwoman coming round at that instant, he
went downstairs, and brought up a quart, with a penny brick,
on which we made a comfortable meal. He then shared his money
with me, which amounted to eighteenpence, and left me, with
an intention to borrow an old wig and hat of his friend the
schoolmaster.

He was no sooner gone than I began to consider my situation
with great uneasiness, and revolved all the schemes my imagination could suggest, in order to choose and pursue someone that
might procure me bread; for it is impossible to express the pangs
I felt, when I reflected on the miserable dependence in which I
lived at the expense of a poor barber's boy. My pride took the
alarm, and having no hopes of succeeding at the Navy Office,
I came to a resolution of enlisting in the foot-guards next day,
be the event what it would. This extravagant design, by flattering my disposition, gave great satisfaction; and I was charging
the enemy at the head of my own regiment, when Strap's
return interrupted my reverie. The schoolmaster had made
him a present of the tie-wig which he wore when I was introduced
to him, together with an old hat, whose brims would have overshadowed a Colossus. Though Strap had ventured to wear them
in the dusk, he did not choose to entertain the mob by day;
therefore went to work immediately, and reduced them both
to a moderate size. While he was employed in this office, he
addressed me thus: "To be sure, Mr. Random, you are born a

gentleman, and have a great deal of learning—and indeed look like a gentleman; for, as to person, you may hold up your head with the best of them. On the other hand, I am a poor but honest cobbler's son—my mother was as industrious a woman as ever broke bread, till such time as she took to drinking, which you very well know—but everybody has failings—*humanum est errare*. Now, for myself, I am a poor journeyman barber, tolerably well made, and understand some Latin, and have a smattering of Greek—but what of that? perhaps I might also say that I know a little of the world—but that is to no purpose —though you be gentle and I simple, it does not follow but that I who am simple may do a good office to you who are gentle. Now this is the case—my kinsman the schoolmaster—perhaps you did not know how nearly he is related to me—I'll satisfy you in that presently—his mother and my grandmother's sister's nephew—no, that's not it—my grandfather's brother's daughter —rabbit it! I have forgot the degree, but this I know, he and I are cousins seven times removed." My impatience to know the good office he had done me got the better of my temper, and interrupted him at this place, with "Damn your relation and pedigree! if the schoolmaster or you can be of any advantage to me, why don't you tell me without all this preamble?" When I pronounced these words with some vehemence, Strap looked at me for some time with a grave countenance, and then went on: "Surely my pedigree is not to be damn'd, because it is not so noble as yours. I am very sorry to see such an alteration in your temper of late—you was always fiery, but now you are grown as crabbed as old Periwinkle the drunken tinker, on whom you and I, God forgive us, played so many unlucky tricks, while we were at school. But I will no longer detain you in suspense, because, doubtless, nothing is more uneasy than doubt —*dubio, procul dubio, nil dubius*. My friend, or relation, or which you will, or both, the schoolmaster, being informed of the regard I have for you—for, you may be sure, I did not fail to let him know your good qualities—by the bye, he has undertaken to teach you the pronunciation of the English tongue, without which, he says, you will be unfit for business in this country. I say my relation has spoke in your behalf to a French apothecary who wants a journeyman; and, on his recommendation, you may have fifteen pounds per year, bed and board, whenever you please." I was too much interested in this piece of news to entertain it with indifference; but, jumping up, insisted on Strap's immediately accompanying me to the house of his

friend, that I might not lose this opportunity through the least
delay or neglect on my part. We were informed that the schoolmaster was in company at a public-house in the neighbourhood,
whither we repaired, and found him drinking with the very
individual apothecary in question. When he was called to the
door at our desire, and observed my impatience, he broke out
into his usual term of admiration: "O Christ! I suppose, when
you heard of this offer, you did not take leisure enough to come
downstairs, but leapt out of the window; did you overturn no
porter nor oyster-woman in your way! It is a mercy of God you
did not knock your brains out against some post in your career.
O' my conscience! I believe, had I been in the inmost recesses
of my habitation,—the very *penetralia*,—even in bed with my
wife, your eagerness would have surmounted bolts, bars, decency,
and everything. The den of Cacus or *Sanctum Sanctorum* could
not have hid me from you. But come along, the gentleman of
whom I spoke is in the house, I will present you to him forthwith." When I entered the room, I perceived four or five people
smoking, one of whom the schoolmaster accosted thus: "Mr.
Lavement, here's the young man of whom I spoke to you." The
apothecary, who was a little old withered man, with a forehead
about an inch high, a nose turned up at the end, large cheek-
bones that helped to form a pit for his little grey eyes, a great
bag of loose skin hanging down on each side in wrinkles like the
alforjas of a baboon; and a mouth so accustomed to that contraction which produces grinning, that he could not pronounce
a syllable without discovering the remains of his teeth, which
consisted of four yellow fangs, not improperly, by anatomists,
called *canine*. This person, I say, after having eyed me some time,
said, "Oho, 'tis very well, Mons. Concordance;—young man,
you are ver welcome, take one coup of bierre—and come to
mine house to-morrow morning: Mons. Concordance vil show
you de way." Upon this I made my bow, and as I went out of
the room, could hear him say, *"Ma foi! c'est un beau garçon,
c'est un gaillard."* As I had, by my own application, while I
served Crab, acquired the French tongue well enough to read
authors written in that language, and understand anything
that occurred in conversation, I determined to pretend ignorance
to my new master, that he and his family, whom I supposed
to be of the same country, not being on the reserve before me,
might possibly discover something in discourse which would
either yield me amusement or advantage. Next morning Mr.
Concordance carried me to the apothecary's house, where the

bargain was made, and orders given to provide an apartment for me immediately. But, before I entered upon business, the schoolmaster recommended me to his tailor, who gave me credit for a suit of clothes to be paid out of the first moiety of my wages, and they were begun upon that very day; he afterwards accommodated me with a new hat, on the same terms, so that, in a few days, I hoped to make a very fashionable appearance. In the meantime, Strap conveyed my baggage to the place allotted for me, which was a back room up two pair of stairs, furnished with a pallet for me to lie upon, a chair without a back, an earthen chamber-pot without a handle, a bottle by way of candlestick, and a triangular piece of glass instead of a mirror, the rest of its ornaments having been lately removed to one of the garrets, for the convenience of the servant of an Irish captain, who lodged in the first floor.

CHAPTER XIX

The Characters of Mr. Lavement, his Wife, and Daughter—Some Anecdotes of the Family—The Mother and Daughter rivals—I am guilty of a Mistake that gives me present Satisfaction, but is attended with troublesome Consequences.

NEXT day, while I was at work in the shop, a bouncing damsel, well dressed, came in, on pretence of finding a phial for some use or other; and taking an opportunity when she thought I did not mind her, of observing me narrowly, went away with a silent look of disdain. I easily guessed her sentiments, and my pride took the resolution of entertaining the same indifference and neglect towards her. At dinner, the maids, with whom I dined in the kitchen, gave me to understand that this was my master's only daughter, who would have a very handsome fortune, on account of which, and her beauty, a great many young gentlemen made their addresses to her; that she had been twice on the brink of marriage, but disappointed by the stinginess of her father, who refused to part with a shilling to promote the match; for which reason the young lady did not behave to her father with all the filial veneration that might be expected. In particular, she harboured the most perfect hatred for his countrymen, in which disposition she resembled her mother, who was an English woman; and by the hints they dropped, I learned the grey mare was the better horse; that she was a matron of a high spirit, which was often manifested at the expense of her dependants; that she loved diversions, and looked upon Miss as her rival in all parties; which, indeed, was the true cause of all her disappointments, for, had the mother been hearty in her interest, the father would not have ventured to refuse her demands. Over and above this intelligence, I, of myself, soon made more discoveries. Mr. Lavement's significant grins at his wife, while she looked another way, convinced me that he was not at all content with his lot; and his behaviour in presence of the captain made me believe his chief torment was jealousy. As for my own part, I was considered in no other light than that of a menial servant, and had been already six days in the house without being honoured with one word from either mother or daughter, the latter (as I understood from the maids) having, at table, one day expressed some surprise that her papa should entertain such an awkward mean-looking journeyman. I was nettled at this piece of information, and next Sunday (it being my turn to take my diversion) dressed myself in my new clothes, to the greatest advantage, and, vanity apart, made no contemptible figure. After having spent most of the day in company with Strap and some of his acquaintance, I came home in the afternoon, and was let in by Miss, who, not knowing me, dropped a low curtsey as I advanced, which I returned with a profound bow, and shut the door. By the time I had turned about, she had perceived her mistake, and changed colour, but did not withdraw. The passage being narrow, I could not get away without jostling her; so I was forced to remain where I was, with my eyes fixed on the ground, and my face glowing with blushes. At length her vanity coming to her assistance, she went away tittering, and I could hear her pronounce the word "Creature." From this day forward, she came into the shop fifty times every day, upon various pretences, and put in practice so many ridiculous airs, that I could easily perceive her opinion of me was changed, and that she did not think me altogether an unworthy conquest. But my heart was so steeled against her charms by pride and resentment, which were two chief ingredients in my disposition, that I remained insensible to all her arts; and, notwithstanding some advances she made, could not be prevailed upon to yield her the least attention. This neglect soon banished all the favourable impressions she felt for me, and the rage of a slighted woman took place in her heart; this she manifested not only in all the suggestions her malice could invent to my prejudice with her father, but also in procuring for me such servile employments as she hoped would

ufficiently humble my spirit. One day, in particular, she ordered
me to brush my master's coat, but I refusing, a smart dialogue
ensued, which ended in her bursting into tears of rage; when her
mother interposing, and examining into the merits of the cause,
determined it in my favour; and this good office I owed not to
any esteem or consideration she had for me, but solely to the
desire of mortifying her daughter, who on this occasion observed,
that let people be never so much in the right, there were some
folks who would never do them justice; but, to be sure, they had
their reasons for it, which some people were not ignorant of,
although they despised their little arts. This insinuation of
some people and *some folks*, put me upon observing the behaviour
of my mistress more narrowly for the future; and it was not long
before I had reason to believe that she looked upon her daughter
as a rival in the affections of Captain O'Donnell, who lodged
in the house. In the meantime, my industry and knowledge gained
me the good will of my master, who would often say in French,
"*Mardie ! c'est un bon garçon.*" He had a great deal of business;
but as he was mostly employed among his fellow-refugees, his
profits were small. However, his expense for medicines was not
great, for he was the most expert man at a succedaneum of any
apothecary in London; so that I have been sometimes amazed
to see him, without the least hesitation, make up a physician's
prescription, though he had not in his shop one medicine
mentioned in it. Oyster shells he could invent into crab's eyes;
common oil into oil of sweet almonds; syrup of sugar, into
balsamic syrup; Thames water, into aqua cinnamoni; turpentine,
into capivi; and a hundred more costly preparations were
produced in an instant, from the cheapest and coarsest drugs of
the *materia medica*: and when any common thing was ordered
for a patient, he always took care to disguise it in colour or
taste, or both, in such a manner as that it could not possibly
be known. For which purpose cochineal and oil of cloves were of
great service. Among many nostrums which he possessed, there
was one for the venereal disease, that brought him a good deal
of money; and this he concealed so artfully from me, that I
could never learn its composition. But during the eight months
I staid in his service, he was so unfortunate in the use of it, that
three parts in four of those who took it were fain to confirm
the cure by a salivation under the direction of another doctor.
This bad success, in all appearance, attached him the more to
his specific; and before I left him, I may venture to say, he
would have sooner renounced the Trinity, notwithstanding

his being a good Huguenot, than his confidence in the never-failing power of this remedy. Mr. Lavement had attempted more than once to introduce a vegetable diet into his family, by launching out into the praise of roots and greens, and decrying the use of flesh, both as a physician and philosopher; but all his rhetoric could not make one proselyte to his opinion; and even the wife of his bosom declared against the proposal. Whether it was owing to the little regard she paid to her husband's admonition in this particular, or to the natural warmth of her constitution, I know not; but this lady's passions became every day more and more violent, till at last she looked upon decency as an unnecessary restraint; and one afternoon, when her husband was abroad, and her daughter gone to visit, ordered me to call a hackney coach, in which she and the captain drove towards Covent Garden. Miss came home in the evening, and, supping at her usual hour, went to bed. About eleven o'clock my master entered, and asked if his wife was gone to sleep; upon which I told him my mistress went out in the afternoon, and was not yet returned. This was like a clap of thunder to the poor apothecary, who, starting back, cried, "*Mort de ma vie!* vat you tell a me? My wife not at home!" At that instant a patient's servant arrived with a prescription for a draught, which my master taking, went into the shop to make it up with his own hand. While he rubbed the ingredients in a glass mortar, he inquired of me whether or not his wife went out alone; and no sooner heard that she was in company with the captain than, with one blow, he split the mortar into a thousand pieces, and grinning like the head of a bass viol, exclaimed, "*Ah, traitresse!*" It would have been impossible for me to have preserved my gravity a minute longer, when I was happily relieved by a rap at the door, which I opened, and perceived my mistress coming out of the coach; she flounced immediately into the shop, and addressed her husband thus: "I suppose you thought I was lost, my dear—Captain O'Donnell has been so good as to treat me with a play." "Play, play," replied he, "oho! yes, by gar, I believe ver prettie play." "Bless me!" said she, "what's the matter?" "Vat de matter?" cried he, forgetting all his former complaisance, "by gar, you be one damn dog's wife—*ventre bleu!* me vill show you vat it is to put one horn upon mine head. *Pardieu!* le Capitaine O'Donnell be one——" Here the captain, who had been all the while at the door discharging the coach, entered, and said, with a terrible voice, "Damme! what am I?" Mr. Lavement, changing his tone, immediately saluted him with, *"Oh, serviteur, Monsieur le Capitaine, vous êtes un gallant homme—ma femme est fort obligée."* Then, turning about towards me, pronounced with a low voice, *"Et diablement obligeante, sans doute."*—"Harkee, Mr. Lavement," said the captain, "I am a man of honour, and I believe you are too much of a gentleman to be offended at the civility I show your wife." This declaration had such an effect on the apothecary, that he resumed all the *politesse* of a Frenchman, and with the utmost prostration of compliment, assured the captain that he was perfectly well satisfied with the honour he had done his wife. Matters being thus composed, everybody went to rest. Next day I perceived, through a glass door that opened from the shop into the parlour, the captain talking earnestly to Miss, who heard him with a look that expressed anger mingled with scorn; which, however, he at last found means to mollify, and sealed his reconciliation with a kiss. This circumstance soon convinced me of the occasion of the quarrel; but notwithstanding all my vigilance, I could never discover any other commerce between them. In the meanwhile, I had reason to believe I had inspired one of the maids with tender sentiments for me; and one night, when I thought every other person in the house asleep, I took the opportunity of going to reap the fruits of my conquest, her bedfellow having the day before gone to Richmond to visit her parents. Accordingly, I got up, and, naked as I was, explored my way in the dark to the garret where she lay. I was ravished to find the door open, and moved softly to her bedside, transported with the hope of completing my wishes. But what horrors of jealousy and disappointment did I feel, when I found her asleep, fast locked in the arms of a man, whom I easily guessed to be no other than the captain's servant! I was upon the point of doing some rash thing, when the noise of a rat scratching behind the wainscot put me to flight, and I was fain to get back to my own bed in safety. Whether this alarm had disordered my mind, or that I was led astray by the power of destiny, I know not; but, instead of turning to the left hand when I descended to the second story, I pursued the contrary course, and mistook the young lady's bedchamber for my own. I did not perceive my mistake before I had run against the bedposts, and then it was not in my power to retreat undiscovered; for the nymph being awake, felt my approach, and, with a soft voice, bade me make less noise, lest the Scotch booby in the next room should overhear us. This hint was sufficient to inform me of the nature of the assignation; and

as my passions, at any time high, were then in a state of exalt-
ation, I resolved to profit by my good fortune. Without any
more ceremony, therefore, I made bold to slip into bed to this
charmer, who gave me as favourable a reception as I could
desire. Our conversation was very sparing on my part; but she
upbraided the person whom I represented with his jealousy of
me, whom she handled so roughly, that my resentment had well-
nigh occasioned a discovery more than once; but I was consoled
for her hatred of me by the revenge I enjoyed in understanding
from her own mouth that it was now high time to salve her
reputation by matrimony; for she had reason to fear she could
not much longer conceal the effects of their mutual intercourse.
While I was meditating an answer to this proposal, I heard a
noise in my room, like something heavy falling down upon the
floor; upon which I started up, and, creeping to the door of my
chamber, observed by moonlight the shadow of a man groping
his way out; so I retired to one side to let him pass, and saw him
go downstairs as expeditiously as he could. It was an easy
matter to divine that this was the captain, who, having over-
slept himself, had got up at last to keep his assignation; and
finding my door open, had entered my apartment instead of
that of his mistress, where I supplied his place; but finding his
mistake, by falling over my chair, he was afraid the noise might
alarm the family, and, for that reason, made off, delaying the
gratification of his desires till another opportunity. By this time
I was satisfied; and, instead of returning to the place from
whence I came, retreated to my own castle, which I fortified
by bolting the door, and, in the congratulation of my own
happiness, fell asleep. But the truth of this adventure could
not be long concealed from my young mistress, who next day
came to an explanation with the captain, upon his lamenting
his last night's disappointment, and begging pardon for the
noise he had made. Their mutual chagrin, when they came to
the knowledge of what had happened, may be easily con-
jectured, though each had a peculiar grief unfelt by the other;
for she was conscious of not only having betrayed to me the
secrets of her commerce with him, but also of having incensed
me by the freedoms she had taken with my name, beyond a
hope of reconciliation. On the other hand, his jealousy suggested
that her sorrow was all artifice, and that I had supplied his place
with her own privity and consent. That such was the situation
of their thoughts, will appear in the sequel; for that very day
she came into the shop where I was alone, and fixing her eyes,

swimming in tears, upon me, sighed most piteously. But I was proof against her distress, by recollecting the epithets with which she had honoured me the night before; and believing that the good reception I enjoyed was destined for another, therefore I took no notice of her affliction; and she had the mortification to find her disdain returned fourfold. However, from thenceforward she thought proper to use me with more complaisance than usual, knowing that it was in my power at any time to publish her shame. By these means my life became much more agreeable, though I never could prevail upon myself to repeat my nocturnal visit; and, as I every day improved in my knowledge of the town, I shook off my awkward air by degrees, and acquired the character of a polite journeyman apothecary.

CHAPTER XX

I am assaulted and dangerously wounded—Suspect O'Donnell, and am confirmed in my Opinion—Concert a Scheme of Revenge, and put it in execution—O'Donnell robs his own Servant, and disappears—I make my Addresses to a Lady, and am miraculously delivered from her Snare.

ONE night, about twelve o'clock, as I returned from visiting a patient at Chelsea, I received a blow on my head from an unseen hand that stretched me senseless on the ground; and was left for dead, with three stabs of a sword in my body. The groans I uttered, when I recovered the use of my reason, alarmed the people of a solitary alehouse that stood near the spot where I lay, and they were humane enough to take me in and send for a surgeon, who dressed my wounds, and assured me they were not mortal. One of them penetrated through the skin and muscles of one side of my belly in such a manner, that doubtless the assassin imagined he had run me through the entrails. The second slanted along one of my ribs; and the last, which was intended for the finishing stroke, having been directed to my heart, the sword snapped upon my breastbone, and the point remained sticking in the skin. When I reflected upon this event, I could not persuade myself that I had been assaulted by a common footpad; because it is not usual for such people to murder those they rob, especially when they meet with no resistance; and I found my money and everything else about me (but my carcass) safe. I concluded, therefore, that I must either have been mistaken for another, or obliged to the private

E 79°

resentment of some secret enemy for what had happened; and as I could remember nobody who had the least cause of complaint against me, except Captain O'Donnell and my master's daughter, my suspicion settled upon them, though I took care to conceal it, that I might the sooner arrive at confirmation. With this view I went home in a chair about ten o'clock in the morning; and as the chairman supported me into the house, met the captain in the passage, who no sooner saw me than he started back, and gave evident signs of guilty confusion, which he would have accounted for from the surprise occasioned by seeing me in such a condition. My master having heard my story, condoled me with a good deal of sympathy, and when he understood my wounds were not dangerous, ordered me to be carried upstairs to bed; though not without some opposition from his wife, who was of opinion it would be better for me to go to an hospital, where I should be more carefully attended. My meditation was employed in concerting with myself some method of revenge against Squire O'Donnell and his inamorata, whom I looked upon as the authors of my misfortune; when Miss (who was not at home at my arrival) entered my chamber, and, saying she was sorry for the accident that had befallen me, asked me if I suspected anybody to be the assassin: upon which I fixed my eyes stedfastly upon her, and answered, "Yes." She discovered no symptom of confusion; but replied hastily, "If that be the case, why don't you take out a warrant to have him apprehended? It will cost but a trifle; if you have no money, I'll lend you." This frankness not only cured me of my suspicion with respect to her, but even staggered my belief with regard to the captain, of whose guilt I resolved to have further proof before I should enterprise anything in the way of revenge. I thanked her kindly for her generous offer; which, however, I had no occasion to accept, being determined to do nothing rashly: for though I could plainly perceive the person who attacked me to be a soldier, whose face I thought was familiar to me, I could not swear with a safe conscience to any particular man; and, granting I could, my prosecution of him would not much avail. This uncertainty I pretended, lest the captain, hearing from her that I knew the person who wounded me, might think proper to withdraw before I could be in a condition to requite him. In two days I was up, and able to do a little business, so that Mr. Lavement made shift to carry on his practice without hiring another journeyman in my room. The first thing I attempted towards a certain discovery of my secret enemy, was to get into O'Donnell's apartment while he was abroad in an undress, and examine his sword, the point of which being broke off, I applied the fragment that was found sticking in my body, and found it answered the fractured part exactly. There was no room left for doubt; and all that remained was to fix upon a scheme of revenge, which almost solely engrossed my thoughts during the space of eight nights and days. Sometimes I was tempted to fall upon him in the same manner as he had practised upon me, and kill him outright. But this assault my honour opposed as a piece of barbarous cowardice, in which he was not to be imitated. At other times I entertained thoughts of demanding satisfaction in an honourable way; but was diverted from this undertaking by considering the uncertainty of the event, and the nature of the injury he had done me, which did not entitle him to such easy terms. At last I determined to pursue a middle course; and actually put my design in execution after this manner. Having secured the assistance of Strap and two of his acquaintance whom he could depend upon, we provided ourselves with disguises, and I caused the following letter to be delivered to him by one of our associates in livery one Sunday evening:

"SIR,—If I may be allowed to judge from appearance, it will not be disagreeable to you to hear that my husband is gone to Bagshot to visit a patient, and will not return till to-morrow night; so that if you have anything to propose to me (as your behaviour on many occasions has seemed to insinuate), you will do well to embrace the present opportunity of seeing

"Yours, etc."

This letter was signed with the name of an apothecar wife who lived in Chelsea, of whom I had heard O'Donnell an admirer. Everything succeeded to our wish. The am hero hastened towards the place of assignation; and countered by us in the very place where he had assa We rushed upon him all at once, secured his sword, his clothes even to the skin, which we scourged till he was blistered from head to foot, notwiths eloquence of his tears and supplications. Whe with the stripes I had bestowed, we carried of we hid in a hedge near the place, and left find his way home in the best manner he to be there before him. I afterwards way to the lodgings of a friend who town, he was picked up by the watch, who carried him to the Round-house, from whence he sent for clothes to his lodgings; and next morning arrived at the door in a chair, wrapped up in a blanket he had borrowed; for his body was so sore and swelled, that he could not bear to be confined in his wearing apparel. He was treated with the utmost tenderness by my mistress and her daughter, who vied with each other in their care and attendance of him; but Lavement himself could not forbear expressing his joy, by several malicious grins, while he ordered me to prepare an unguent for his sores. As to myself, nobody can doubt my gratification when I had every day an opportunity of seeing my revenge protracted on the body of my adversary, by the ulcers of which I had been the cause; and indeed I not only enjoyed the satisfaction of having flayed him alive, but another also which I had not foreseen. The story of his being attacked and stripped in such a place having been inserted in the news, gave information to those who found his clothes next day whither to bring them; and accordingly he retrieved everything he had lost, except a few letters, among which was that which I had writ to him in the name of the apothecary's wife. This and the others, which, it seems, were all on the subject of love (for this Hibernian hero was one of those people who are called fortune-hunters), fell into the hands of a certain female author, famous for the scandal she published, who, after having embellished them with some ~~nts~~ of her own invention, gave them to the town in ~~was~~ very much shocked on reflecting, that I might ~~the~~ occasion of a whole family's unhappiness, on ~~letter~~ I had written; but was eased of that ~~when~~ I understood that the Chelsea apothecary ~~law~~-suit against the printer for defamation; ~~whole~~ as a piece of forgery committed by ~~appeared~~. But whatever might be his ~~two~~ ladies seemed to entertain a ~~as~~ the pamphlet appeared, I ~~patient~~ considerably diminish, ~~It~~ was impossible for him ~~more~~ than of the occasion ~~himself~~ of having deserved ~~he~~ was glad to come off so ~~muttering~~ curses and threats ~~imagined~~, having got an ~~wife~~, had taken revenge of

him in the manner described. By the time he got a new scarf
skin, his character was become so notorious, that he thought
it high time for him to decamp; and his retreat he performed
in one night without beat of drum, after having robbed his
own servant of everything that belonged to him, except the
clothes he had on his back. A few days after he disappeared,
Mr. Lavement, for his own security, took into custody a large
old trunk which he had left; and, as it was very heavy, made no
question that the contents were sufficient to indemnify him for
what O'Donnell owed in lodging. But a month being elapsed
without hearing any tidings of this adventurer, and my master
being impatient to know what the trunk contained, he ordered
me to break it open in his presence, which task I performed
with the pestle of our great mortar, and discovered, to his
inexpressible astonishment and mortification, a heap of stones.

About this time my friend Strap informed me of an offer he
had to go abroad with a gentleman, in quality of valet de
chambre, and at the same time assured me, that whatever
advantage he might propose to himself from this prospect, he
could not bear the thoughts of parting from me; so much was
he attached to my fortune. In spite of all the obligations I owed
to this poor honest fellow, ingratitude is so natural to the heart
of man, that I began to be tired of his acquaintance; and now
that I had contracted other friendships which appeared more
creditable, was even ashamed to see a journeyman barber inquiring after me with the familiarity of a companion. I therefore, on pretence of consulting his welfare, insisted upon his
accepting the proposal, which he at last determined to embrace
with great reluctance; and in a few days took his leave of me,
shedding a flood of tears, which I could not behold without
emotion. I now began to look upon myself as a gentleman in
reality—learned to dance of a Frenchman whom I had cured of a
fashionable distemper—frequented plays during the holidays
—became the oracle of an alehouse, where every dispute was
referred to my decision—and at length contracted an acquaintance with a young lady, who found means to make a conquest
of my heart, and upon whom I prevailed, after much attendance
and solicitation, to give me a promise of marriage. As this
beautiful creature passed for a rich heiress, I blessed my good
fortune, and was actually on the point of crowning all my wishes
by matrimony, when one morning I went to her lodgings, and
her maid being abroad, took the privilege of a bridegroom to
enter her chamber, where, to my utter confusion, I found her

in bed with a man. Heaven gave me patience and presence of
mind enough to withdraw immediately; and I thanked my
stars a thousand times for the happy discovery, by which I
resolved to profit so much as to abandon all thoughts of marriage
for the future.

CHAPTER XXI

Squire Gawky comes to lodge with my Master—Is involved in a trouble-
some Affair, out of which he is extricated by me—He marries my Master's
Daughter—They conspire against me, and I am found guilty of Theft—
Discharged—Deserted by my Friends—I hire a Room in St. Giles's—
Where, by accident, I find the Lady to whom I made my Addresses in a
miserable condition—I relieve her.

WHILE I enjoyed myself at large in this temper of mind, Mr.
Lavement let his first floor to my countryman and acquaintance,
Squire Gawky, who, by this time, had got a lieutenancy in the
army, and such a martial ferocity in his appearance, that I was
afraid he would remember what had happened between us in
Scotland, and atone for his breach of appointment then, by his
punctuality now; but, whether he had actually forgot me, or
was willing to make me believe so, he betrayed not the least
symptom of recognition at sight of me, and I remained quite
cured of my apprehension; though I had occasion, not long
after, to be convinced that, howsoever his externals might be
altered, he was at bottom the same individual Gawky whom I
have already described. For, coming home late one night from
the house of a patient, I heard a noise in the street, and, as I
approached, perceived two gentlemen in custody of three watch-
men. The prisoners, who were miserably disfigured with dirt,
complained bitterly of the loss of their hats and wigs; and one
of them, whom, by his tongue, I knew to be a Scotchman,
lamented most piteously, offering a guinea for his liberty, which
the watchman refused, alleging that one of his companions
was wounded grievously, and that he must stand to the consequence. My prejudice in favour of my country was so strong,
that I could not bear to see anybody belonging to it in distress,
and therefore, with one blow of my faithful cudgel, knocked
down the watchman who had hold of the person for whom I was
chiefly concerned. He was no sooner disengaged, than he betook
himself to his heels, and left me to maintain the dispute as I
should think proper; and, indeed, I came off but scurvily;
for, before I could avail myself of my speed, I received a blow

on the eye from one of the other two that had well-nigh deprived me of the use of that organ. However, I made shift to get home, where I was informed of Captain Gawky's being robbed and abused by a company of footpads, and was ordered by my master to prepare an emollient glyster and paregoric draught, in order to allay and compose the ferment of his spirits, occasioned by the barbarous treatment he had undergone, while he took twelve ounces of blood from him immediately. When I had inquired into the particulars of this adventure, and understood, by the servant, that he came in just before me, without hat and wig, I made no scruple of believing him to be the person I had released, and was confirmed in my belief upon hearing his voice, to which, before that event, I had been so long a stranger. My eye being considerably swelled and inflamed, I could not reflect upon my enterprise without cursing my own folly, and even resolving to declare the truth of the whole story, in order to be revenged on the cowardly wretch for whom I had suffered. Accordingly, next day, after he had told, in the presence of my master, his wife, and daughter, who came to visit him, a thousand lies concerning the prowess he had shown in making his escape, I ventured to explain the mystery, and, calling in the evidence of my contused eye, upbraided him with cowardice and ingratitude. Gawky was so astonished at this discourse, that he could not answer one word; and the rest of the company stared at one another; till, at length, my mistress reprimanded me for my insolent behaviour, and threatened to turn me away for my presumption. Upon which Gawky, having recollected himself, observed, as the young man might have mistaken another person for him, he could forgive his insinuations, more especially as he seemed to have suffered for his civility; but advised me to be more certain in my conjectures for the future, before I ventured to publish them to the prejudice of any man. Miss applauded the captain's generosity in pardoning one who had so villainously aspersed him, and I began to imagine her praise was not at all disinterested. But the apothecary, who, perhaps, had more penetration, or less partiality, than his wife and daughter, differed from them in his sentiments of the matter, and expressed himself to me in the shop in this manner: "Ah! mon pauvre Roderique! you ave more of de veracité dan of de prudence—bot mine vife and dater be diablement sage, and Mons. le Capitaine un fanfaron, pardieu!" This eulogium on his wife and daughter, though spoken ironically by him, was nevertheless literally just; by espousing the cause of Gawky,

the one obliged a valuable lodger, and the other acquired a
husband at a juncture when one was absolutely necessary; for
the young lady, finding the effects of her correspondence with
O'Donnell becoming plainer and plainer every day, insinuated
herself so artfully into the affection of this new lodger, that in
less than a fortnight, on pretence of going to a play, they drove
away together to the Fleet, where they were coupled; from
thence removed to a bagnio, where the marriage was consum-
mated; and in the morning came home, where they asked her
father's and mother's blessing. The prudent parents, notwithstanding the precipitation with which the match was carried
on, did not think fit to refuse their approbation; for the apothecary was not ill pleased to find his daughter married to a young
man of good prospect, who had not mentioned to him one
syllable on the article of her dowry; and his wife was rejoiced
at being rid of a rival in her gallants, and a spy upon her
pleasures. Nor was I without self-enjoyment at this event,
when I reflected upon the revenge I had unwittingly taken
upon my enemy, in making him a cuckold by anticipation. But
I little dreamed what a storm of mischief was brewing against
me, whilst I thus indulged myself. Whatever face Gawky put
on the matter, my discovery of the adventure before related,
and the reproaches I vented against him, had stung him to the
soul, and cherished the seeds of enmity so strongly in his breast,
that he, it seems, imparted his indignation to his wife, who being
as desirous as himself to compass the ruin of one that not only
slighted her caresses, but was able on any occasion to discover
particulars not at all advantageous to her character, readily
joined in a conspiracy against me, which, had it taken effect
as they expected, would infallibly have brought me to an
ignominious death.

My master having several times missed large quantities of
medicines, of which I could give no account, at last lost all
patience, and, in plain terms, taxed me with having embezzled
them for my own use. As I could only oppose my single asever-
ation to his suspicion, he told me one day, "By gar, your vord
not be give me de satisfaction—me find necessaire to chercher
for my medicine, pardonnez-moi—il faut chercher—me demand
le clef of your coffre à cette heure." Then raising his voice to
conceal the fright he was in, lest I should make any opposition,
he went on, "Oui, foutre, I charge you rendez le clef of your
coffre—moi—si, moi qui vous parle." I was fired with so much
resentment and disdain at this accusation, that I burst into

ears, which he took for a sign of my guilt: and pulling out my
key, told him he might satisfy himself immediately, though he
would not find it so easy to satisfy me for the injury my repu-
ation had suffered from his unjust suspicion. He took the key,
and mounted up to my chamber, attended by the whole family;
saying, "Hé bien, nous verrons—nous verrons." But what was
my horror and amazement, when, on opening my chest, he
pulled out a handful of the very things that were missing, and
pronounced, "Ah ha! vous êtes bien venus—mardie, Mons.
Roderique, you be fort innocent." I had not power to utter one
word in my own vindication, but stood motionless and silent,
while everybody present made their respective remarks on what
appeared against me. The servants said they were sorry for my
misfortune, and went away repeating, "Who would have
thought it?" My mistress took occasion, from this detection,
to rail against the practice of employing strangers in general;
and Mrs. Gawky, after having observed that she never had a
good opinion of my fidelity, proposed to have me carried before
a justice, and committed to Newgate immediately. Her husband
was actually upon the stairs in his way for a constable, when
Mr. Lavement, knowing the cost and trouble of a prosecution
to which he must bind himself, and at the same time dreading
lest some particulars of my confession might affect his practice,
called out, "Restez, mon fils! restez, it be véritablement one
grand crime which dis pauvre diable have committed—bot
peut-être de good God give him de penitence, and me vill not
have upon mine head de blood of one sinner." The captain and
his lady used all the christian arguments their zeal could suggest,
to prevail on the apothecary to pursue me to destruction, and
represented the injustice he did to the community of which he
was a member, in letting a villain escape, who would not fail
of doing more mischief in the world, when he should reflect on
his coming off so easily now. But their eloquence made no
impression on my master, who, turning to me, said, "Go,
miserable, go from mine house, quick, quick—and make reparation for your mauvaise actions." By this time my indignation
had roused me from the stupefaction in which I had hitherto
remained, and I began in this manner: "Sir, appearances, I
own, condemn me; but you are imposed upon as much as I am
abused. I have fallen a sacrifice to the rancour of that scoundrel,"
pointing to Gawky, "who has found means to convey your goods
hither, that the detection of them might blast my reputation,
and accomplish my destruction. His hatred of me is owing to a
* E 790

consciousness of his having wronged me in my own country for which injury he, in a cowardly manner, refused me the satisfaction of a gentleman. He knows, moreover, that I am no stranger to his dastardly behaviour in this town, which I have recounted before; and he is unwilling that such a testimony of his ingratitude and pusillanimity should live upon the earth. For this reason he is guilty of the most infernal malice to bring about my ruin. And I am afraid, madam," turning to Mrs Gawky, "you have too easily entered into the sentiments of your husband. I have often found you my enemy, and am well acquainted with the occasion of your being so, which I don't at present think proper to declare; but I would not advise you, for your own sake, to drive me to extremity." This address enraged her so much, that, with a face as red as scarlet, and the eyes of a fury, she strutted up to me, and, putting her hands on her sides, spit in my face, saying I was a scandalous villain, but she defied my malice; and that, unless her papa would prosecute me like a thief as I was, she would not stay another night under his roof. At the same time Gawky, assuming a big look, told me he scorned what lies I could invent against him: but that, if I pretended to asperse his wife, he would put me to death, by God. To this threat I answered, "I wish to God I could meet with thee in a desert, that I might have an opportunity of punishing thee for thy perfidy towards me, and rid the world of such a rascal. What hinders me this moment," said I, seizing an old bottle that stood by, "from doing myself that justice?" I had no sooner armed myself in this manner, than Gawky and his father-in-law retired in such a hurry, that the one overturned the other, and they rolled together downstairs; while my mistress swooned away with fear; and her daughter asked if I intended to murder her? I gave her to understand, that nothing was farther from my intention: that I would leave her to the stings of her own conscience, but was firmly resolved to slit her husband's nose, whenever fortune should offer a convenient opportunity. Then going downstairs, I met Lavement coming up trembling with the pestle in his hand, and Gawky behind, armed with his sword, pushing him forward. I demanded a parley, and having assured them of my pacific disposition, Gawky exclaimed, "Ah! villain! you have killed my dear wife." And the apothecary cried, "Ah! coquin! vere is my shild?" "The lady," said I, "is above stairs, unhurt by me, and will a few months hence, I believe, reward your concern." Here she called to them, and desired they would let he wretch go, and trouble themselves no further about him. To which request her father consented, observing, nevertheless, hat my conversation was fort mysterieuse. Finding it impossible o vindicate my innocence, I left the house immediately, and vent to the schoolmaster, with an intention of clearing myself o him, and asking his advice with regard to my future conduct; but, to my inexpressible vexation, was told he was gone to the country, where he would stay two or three days. I returned with a design of consulting some acquaintances I had acquired in my master's neighbourhood; but my story had taken air, hrough the officiousness of the servants, and not one of my friends would vouchsafe me a hearing. Thus I found myself, by the iniquity of mankind, in a much more deplorable condition than ever: for though I had been formerly as poor, my reputation was without blemish, and my health unimpaired till now; but at present my good name was lost, my money gone, my friends were alienated, my body was infected by a distemper contracted in the course of an amour, and my faithful Strap, who alone could yield me pity and assistance, absent I knew not where.

The first resolution I could take in this melancholy conjuncture, was to remove my clothes to the house of the person with whom I had formerly lodged, where I remained two days, in hopes of getting another place, by the interest of Mr. Concordance, to whom I made no doubt of being able to vindicate my character; but in this supposition I reckoned without my host, for Lavement took care to be beforehand with me, and when I attempted to explain the whole affair to the schoolmaster, I found him so prepossessed against me, that he would scarce hear me to an end; but when I had finished my justification, shook his head, and beginning with his usual exclamation, "O Christ!" said, "That won't go down with me. I am very sorry I should have the misfortune of being concerned in the affair, but, however, shall be more cautious for the future. I will trust no man from henceforward—no, not my father who begat me—nor the brother who lay with me in my mother's womb. Should Daniel rise from the dead, I would think him an impostor, and were the genius of Truth to appear, would question its veracity." I told him, that one day it was possible he might be convinced of the injury I had suffered, and repent of his premature determination. To which remark he answered, the proof of my innocence would make his bowels to vibrate with joy; "but till that shall happen," continued he, "I must beg to have no manner of connection with you—my reputation

is at stake—O my good God! I shall be looked upon as your
accomplice and abettor—people will say Jonathan Wild was
but a type of me—boys will hoot at me as I pass along, and the
cinder-wenches belch forth reproaches wafted in a gale impregnated with gin—I shall be notorious—the very butt of slander
and cloak of infamy." I was not in a humour to relish the climax
of expressions upon which this gentleman valued himself in all
his discourses; but, without any ceremony, took my leave
cursed with every sentiment of horror which my situation could
suggest. I considered, however, in the intervals of my despondence, that I must in some shape suit my expense to my calamitous circumstances; and with that view hired an apartment
in a garret near St. Giles's, at the rate of ninepence per week.
In this place I resolved to perform my own cure, having first
pawned three shirts to purchase medicines and support for
the occasion.

One day when I sat in this solitary retreat, musing upon the
unhappiness of my fate, I was alarmed by a groan that issued
from a chamber contiguous to mine, into which I immediately
ran, and found a woman stretched on a miserable truckle bed,
without any visible signs of life. Having applied a smelling-bottle to her nose, the blood began to revisit her cheeks, and
she opened her eyes; but, good heavens! what were the emotions
of my soul, when I discovered her to be the same individual lady
who had triumphed over my heart, and to whose fate I had
almost been inseparably joined! Her deplorable situation filled
my breast with compassion, and every tender idea reviving
in my imagination, I flew into her embrace. She knew me
immediately; and, straining me gently in her arms, shed a
torrent of tears, which I could not help increasing. At length,
casting a languishing look at me, she pronounced, with a feeble
voice, "Dear Mr. Random, I do not deserve this concern at
your hands. I am a vile creature who had a base design upon
your person; suffer me to expiate that and all my other crimes
by a miserable death, which will not fail to overtake me in a
few hours." I encouraged her as much as I could; told her I
forgave all her intentions with regard to me; and that, although
my circumstances were extremely low, I would share my last
farthing with her. In the meantime, I begged to know the immediate cause of that fit from which she had just recovered, and
said I would endeavour by my skill to prevent any more such
attacks. She seemed very much affected with this expression,
took my hand and pressed it to her lips, saying, "You are too

enerous!—I wish I could live to express my gratitude; but
las! I perish for want." Then, shutting her eyes, she relapsed
nto another swoon. Such extremity of distress must have
waked the most obdurate heart to sympathy and compassion.
What effect, then, must it have had on mine, that was naturally
prone to every tender passion? I ran downstairs, and sent my
andlady to a chemist's shop for some cinnamon water; while I,
eturning to this unfortunate creature's chamber, used all the
means in my power to bring her to herself. This aim, with much
lifficulty, I accomplished, and made her drink a glass of the
cordial to recruit her spirits; then I prepared a little mulled
ed wine and a toast, which having taken, she found herself
thoroughly revived, and informed me that she had not tasted
food for eight and forty hours before. As I was impatient to
know the occasion and nature of her calamity, she gave me to
understand, that she was a woman of the town by profession:
that, in the course of her adventures, she found herself dangerously infected with a distemper to which all of her class are
particularly subject; that her malady gaining ground every
day, she became loathsome to herself and offensive to others;
when she resolved to retire to some obscure corner, where she
might be cured with as little noise and expense as possible;
that she had accordingly chosen this place of retreat, and put
herself into the hands of an advertising doctor, who having
fleeced her of all the money she had, or could procure, left her
three days ago in a worse condition than that in which he found
her: that, except the clothes on her back, she had pawned or
sold everything that belonged to her, to satisfy that rapacious
quack, and quiet the clamour of her landlady, who still persisted in her threats to turn her out into the street. After having
moralised upon these particulars, I proposed that she should
lodge in the same room with me, an expedient that would save
some money; and assured her I would undertake her cure as
well as my own, during which she should partake of all the
conveniences that I could afford to myself. She embraced my
offer with unfeigned acknowledgment; and I began to put it in
practice immediately. I found in her not only an agreeable
companion, whose conversation greatly alleviated my chagrin,
but also a careful nurse, who served me with the utmost fidelity
and affection. One day, while I testified my surprise that a
woman of her beauty, good sense, and education (for she had
a large portion of each) could be reduced to such an infamous
and miserable way of life as that of a prostitute,—she answered,

with a sigh, "These very advantages were the cause of my undoing." This remarkable reply inflamed my curiosity to such a degree, that I begged she would favour me with the particulars of her story, and she complied in these words:

CHAPTER XXII

The History of Miss Williams.

My father was an eminent merchant in the city, who, having in the course of trade suffered very considerable losses, retired in his old age, with his wife, to a small estate in the country, which he had purchased with the remains of his fortune. At the time I, being but eight years of age, was left in town for the convenience of education, boarded with an aunt, who was a rigid Presbyterian, and who confined me so closely to what she called the duties of religion, that, in time, I grew weary of her doctrines, and by degrees conceived an aversion for the good books she daily recommended to my perusal. As I increased in age, and appeared with a person not disagreeable, I contracted a good deal of acquaintance among my own sex, one of whom, after having lamented the restraint I was under from the narrowness of my aunt's sentiments, told me I must now throw off the prejudices of opinion imbibed under her influence and example, and learn to think for myself; to which purpose she advised me to read Shaftesbury, Tindal, Hobbes, and all the books that are remarkable for their deviation from the old way of thinking, and, by comparing one with another, I should soon be able to form a system of my own. I followed her advice; and, whether it was owing to my prepossession against what I had formerly read, or the clearness of argument in these my new instructors, I know not, but I studied them with pleasure, and in a short time became a professed Freethinker. Proud of my new improvement, I argued in all companies, and that with such success, that I soon acquired the reputation of a philosopher, and few people durst undertake me in a dispute. I grew vain upon my good fortune, and at length pretended to make my aunt a proselyte to my opinion; but she no sooner perceived my drift, than, taking the alarm, she wrote to my father an account of my heresy, and conjured him, as he tendered the good of my soul, to remove me immediately from the dangerous place where I had contracted such sinful principles. Accordingly my father ordered me into the country, where I arrived in the fifteenth year of my age; and, by his command, gave him a detail of all the articles of my faith, which he did not find so unreasonable as they had been represented. Finding myself suddenly deprived of the company and pleasures of the town, I grew melancholy, and it was some time before I could relish my situation. But solitude became every day more and more familiar to me; and I consoled myself in my retreat with the enjoyment of a good library, at such times as I was not employed in the management of the family (for my mother had been dead three years), in visiting, or some other party of rural diversion. Having more imagination than judgment, I addicted myself too much to poetry and romance; and, in short, was looked upon as a very extraordinary person by everybody in the country where I resided. I had one evening strayed, with a book in my hand, into a wood that bordered on the high road, at a little distance from my father's house, when a certain drunken squire riding by perceived me, and crying, "Zounds! there's a charming creature!" alighted in a moment, caught me in his arms, and treated me so rudely, that I shrieked as loud as I could; and, in the meantime, opposed his violence with all the strength that rage and resentment could inspire. During this struggle, another horseman came up, who, seeing a lady so unworthily used, dismounted, and flew to my assistance. My ravisher, mad with disappointment, or provoked with the reproaches of the other gentleman, quitted me, and running to his horse, drew a pistol from the saddle, and fired at my protector, who happily receiving no damage, went up, and, with the butt-end of his whip, laid him prostrate on the ground, before he could use the other, which his antagonist immediately seized, and clapping to the squire's breast, threatened to put him to death for his cowardice and treachery. In this dilemma I interposed and begged his life, which was granted to my request, after he had asked pardon, and swore his intention was only to obtain a kiss. However, my defender thought proper to unload the other pistol, and throw away the flints, before he gave him his liberty. This courteous stranger conducted me home, where my father, having learned the signal service he had done me, loaded him with caresses, and insisted on his lodging that night at our house. If the obligation he had conferred upon me justly inspired me with sentiments of gratitude, his appearance and conversation seemed to entitle him to somewhat more. He was about the age of two and twenty, among the tallest of the middle size; had chestnut-coloured hair, which he wore tied up in a ribbon; a high polished forehead, a nose inclining to the aquiline, lively blue eyes, red pouting lips, teeth as white as snow, and a certain openness of countenance—but what need I describe any more particulars of his person? I hope you will do me the justice to believe I do not flatter, when I say he was the exact resemblance of you; and, if I had not been well acquainted with his family and pedigree, I should have made no scruple of concluding that you was his brother. He spoke little, and seemed to have no reserve; for what he said was ingenuous, sensible, and uncommon. In short, said she, bursting into tears, he was formed for the ruin of our sex. His behaviour was modest and respectable; but his looks were so significant, that I could easily observe he secretly blessed the occasion that introduced him to my acquaintance. We learned from his discourse that he was the eldest son of a wealthy gentleman in the neighbourhood, to whose name we were no strangers; that he had been to visit an acquaintance in the country, from whose house he was returning home when my shrieks brought him to my rescue. All night long my imagination formed a thousand ridiculous expectations. There was so much of knight-errantry in this gentleman's coming to the relief of a damsel in distress, with whom he immediately became enamoured, that all I had read of love and chivalry recurred to my fancy, and I looked upon myself as a princess in some region of romance, who, being delivered from the power of a brutal giant or satyr by a generous Oroondates, was bound in gratitude, as well as led by inclination, to yield my affections to him without reserve. In vain did I endeavour to chastise these foolish conceits, by reflections more reasonable and severe. The amusing images took full possession of my mind, and my dreams represented my hero sighing at my feet in the language of a despairing lover. Next morning after breakfast he took his leave, when my father begged the favour of further acquaintance with him; to which request he replied by a compliment to him, and a look to me so full of eloquence and tenderness, that my whole soul received the soft impression. In a short time he repeated his visit; and, as a recital of the particular steps he pursued to ruin me would be too tedious and impertinent, let it suffice to say, he made it his business to insinuate himself into my esteem, by convincing me of his good sense, and at the same time flattering my understanding. This task he performed in the most artful manner, by seeming to contradict me often through misapprehension, that I might have an opportunity of clearing myself the more to my own honour. Having thus secured my good opinion, he began to give me some tokens of a particular passion, founded on a veneration for the qualities of my mind, and, as an accidental ornament, admired the beauties of my person; till at length, being fully persuaded of his conquest, he chose a proper season for the theme, and disclosed his love in terms so ardent and sincere, that it was impossible for me to disguise the sentiments of my heart, and he received my approbation with the most lively transport. After this mutual declaration, we contrived to meet more frequently in private interviews, where we enjoyed the conversation of one another, in all the elevation of fancy and impatience of hope that reciprocal adoration can inspire. He professed his honourable intentions, of which I made no question, lamented the avaricious disposition of his father, who had destined him for the arms of another, and vowed eternal fidelity with such an appearance of candour and devotion, that I became a dupe to his deceit, and, in an evil hour, crowned his eager desire with full possession.—Cursed be the day on which I gave away my innocence and peace for a momentary gratification, which has entailed upon me such misery and horror! cursed be my beauty, that first attracted the attention of my seducer! cursed be my education, that, by refining my sentiments, made my heart the more susceptible! cursed be my good sense, that fixed me to one object, and taught me the preference I enjoyed was but my due! Had I been ugly, nobody would have tempted me; had I been ignorant, the charms of my person would not have atoned for the coarseness of my conversation; had I been giddy, my vanity would have divided my inclinations, and my ideas would have been so diffused, that I should never have listened to the enchantments of one alone.

But, to return to my unfortunate story; we gave a loose to guilty pleasure, which, for some months, banished every other concern. At last, by degrees, his visits became less frequent, and his behaviour less warm. I perceived his coldness—my heart took the alarm—my tears reproached him—and I insisted upon the performance of his promise to espouse me, that, whatever should happen, my reputation might be safe. He seemed to acquiesce in my proposal, and left me on pretence of finding a proper clergyman to unite us in the bands of wedlock. But, alas! the inconstant had no intention to return. I waited a whole week with the utmost impatience; sometimes doubting his honour, at other times inventing excuses for him, and

condemning myself for harbouring the least suspicion of his faith.
At length I understood from a gentleman who dined at our
house that this perfidious wretch was on the point of setting
out for London with his bride, to buy clothes for their approaching nuptials. This information distracted me! the more so, as
I found myself some months gone with child, and reflected that
it would be impossible to conceal my disgrace, which would not
only ruin the character I had acquired in the country, but also
bring the grey hairs of an indulgent parent with sorrow to the
grave. Rage took possession of my soul; I denounced a thousand
imprecations and formed as many schemes of revenge against
the traitor who had undone me! Then my resentment would
subside into silent sorrow. I recalled the tranquillity I had lost,
I wept over my infatuation, and sometimes a ray of hope would
intervene, and for a moment cheer my drooping heart; I would
revolve all the favourable circumstances of his character, repeat
the vows he made, ascribe his absence to the vigilance of a
suspicious father, who compelled him to a match his soul
abhorred, and comfort myself with the expectation of seeing
him before the thing should be brought to any terms of agreement. But how vain was my imagination! The villain left me
without remorse; and in a few days the news of his marriage
was spread all over the country. My horror was then incon-
ceivable! and had not the desire of revenge diverted the resolution, I should infallibly have put an end to my miserable life.
My father observed the symptoms of my despair; and, though
I have good reason to believe he guessed the cause, was at a
great deal of pains to seem ignorant of my affliction, while he
endeavoured, with paternal fondness, to alleviate my distress.
I saw his concern, which increased my anguish, and raised my
fury against the author of my calamity to an implacable degree.
Having furnished myself with a little money, I made an elopement from this unhappy parent in the night-time, and about
break of day arrived at a small town, from whence a stage coach
set out for London, in which I embarked, and next day alighted
in town; the spirit of revenge having supported me all the way
against every other reflection. My first care was to hire a lodging,
in which I kept myself very retired, having assumed a feigned
name, that my character and situation might be the better
concealed. It was not long before I found out the house of my
ravisher, whither I immediately repaired in a transport of rage,
determined to act some desperate deed for the satisfaction of
my despair, though the hurry of my spirits would not permit

me to concert or resolve upon a particular plan. When I demanded admission to Lothario (so let me call him), I was desired to send up my name and business; but this I refused, telling the porter I had business for his master's private ear. Upon which I was conducted into a parlour until he should be informed of my request. There I remained about a quarter of an hour, when a servant entered, and told me his master was engaged with company, and begged to be excused at that time. My temper could hold out no longer; I pulled a poignard from my bosom where I had concealed it, and, rushing out, flew upstairs like a fury, exclaiming, "Where is this perfidious villain! could I once plunge this dagger into his false heart, I should then die satisfied." The noise I made alarmed not only the servants, but the company also, who, hearing my threats, came forwards to the staircase to see what was the matter. I was seized, disarmed, and withheld by two footmen; and, in this situation, felt the most exquisite torture in beholding my undoer approach with his young wife. I could not endure the sight, was deprived of my senses, and fell into a severe fit, during which I know not how I was treated; but when I recovered the use of reflection, found myself on a bed in a paltry apartment, where I was attended by an old woman, who asked a thousand impertinent questions relating to my condition; and informed me that my behaviour had thrown the whole family into confusion; that Lothario affirmed I was mad, and proposed to have me sent to Bedlam; but my lady persuaded herself there was more in my conduct than he cared should be known, and had taken to her bed on bare suspicion, having first ordered that I should be narrowly looked to. I heard all she said without making any other reply than desiring she would do me the favour to call a chair; but this, she told me, could not be done without her master's consent, which, however, was easily procured, and I was conveyed to my own lodgings in a state of mind that baffles all description. The agitation of my thoughts produced a fever, which brought on a miscarriage; and I believe it is well for my conscience that Heaven thus disposed of my burden; for, let me own to you with penitence and horror, if I had brought a living child into the world, my frenzy would have prompted me to sacrifice the little innocent to my resentment of the father's infidelity.

After this event my rage abated, and my hate became more deliberate and calm; when, one day, my landlady informed me that there was a gentleman below who desired to see me, he having something of consequence to impart, which he was sure would contribute to my peace of mind. I was exceedingly alarmed at this declaration, which I attempted to interpret a thousand ways; and before I came to any determination he entered my room, with an apology for intruding upon me against my knowledge or consent. I surveyed him some time, and not being able to recollect his face, demanded, with a faltering accent, what his business was with me? Upon which he desired I would give him a particular audience, and he did not doubt of communicating something that would conduce to my satisfaction and repose. As I thought myself sufficiently guarded against any violence, I granted his request, and bid the woman withdraw. The stranger, then advancing, gave me to understand that he was well acquainted with the particulars of my story, having been informed of them from Lothario's own mouth; that, from the time he knew my misfortunes, he had entertained a detestation for the author of them; which had of late been increased and inflamed to a desire of revenge, by a piece of dishonourable conduct towards him; that, hearing of my melancholy situation, he had come with an intention of offering his assistance and comfort, and was ready to espouse my quarrel, and forthwith take vengeance on my seducer, provided I would grant him one consideration, which, he hoped, I should see no reason to refuse. Had all the artifice of hell been employed in composing a persuasive, it could not have had a more instantaneous or favourable effect than this discourse had upon me. I was transported with a delirium of gloomy joy; I hugged my companion in my arms, and vowed, that if he would make good his promise, my soul and body should be at his disposal. The contract was made; he devoted himself to my revenge, undertook to murder Lothario that very night, and to bring me an account of his death before morning. Accordingly, about two of the clock, he was introduced into my chamber, and assured me my perfidious lover was no more; that, although he was not entitled to such an honourable proceeding, he had fairly challenged him to the field, where he upbraided him with his treachery towards me, for whom, he told me, his sword was drawn, and after a few passes left him weltering in his blood. I was so savaged by my wrongs that I delighted in the recital of this adventure, made him repeat the particulars, feasted my eyes with the blood that remained on his clothes and sword, and yielded up my body as a recompense for the service he had done me. My imagination was so engrossed with these ideas, that in my sleep I dreamed Lothario appeared before me, pale, mangled, and bloody, blamed my rashness, protested his innocence, and pleaded his own cause so pathetically, that I was convinced of his fidelity, and waked in a horror of remorse. My bedfellow endeavoured to soothe, console, and persuade me that I had but barely done justice to myself. I dropped asleep again, and the same apparition returned to my fancy. In short, I passed the night in great misery, and looked upon my avenger with such abhorrence, that in the morning, perceiving my aversion, he insinuated there was still a possibility of Lothario's recovery; it was true he left him wounded on the ground, but not quite dead; and perhaps his hurts might not be mortal. At these words I started up, bade him fly for intelligence, and, if he could not bring me tidings of Lothario's safety, at least consult his own, and never return, for I was resolved to surrender myself to justice, and declare all that I knew of the affair, that, if possible, I might expiate my own guilt, by incurring the rigours of a sincere repentance and ignominious death. He very coolly represented the unreasonableness of my prejudice against him, who had done nothing but what his love of me inspired, and honour justified; that now he had, at the risk of his life, been subservient to my revenge, I was about to discard him as an infamous agent occasionally necessary; and that, even if he should be so lucky as to bring news of Lothario's safety, it was probable my former resentment might revive, and I would upbraid him of having failed in his undertaking. I assured him that, on the contrary, he should be dearer to me than ever, as I then should be convinced he acted more on the principles of a man of honour than on those of a mercenary assassin, and scorned to take away the life of an adversary, how inveterate soever, which fortune had put in his power. "Well, then, madam," said he, "whatever may have happened, I shall find it no difficult matter to acquit myself in point of honour." And took his leave, in order to inquire into the consequences of his duel. I was now more sensible than ever of the degrees of guilt and misery; all the affliction I had suffered hitherto was owing to my own credulity and weakness, and my conscience could not accuse me of venial crimes; but now that I looked upon myself as a murderer, it is impossible to express the terrors of my imagination, which was incessantly haunted by the image of the deceased, and my bosom stung with the most exquisite agonies, of which I saw no end. At length Horatio (for so I shall call my keeper) returned, and, telling me I had nothing to fear, delivered into my hands a billet containing these words:

"MADAM,—As I understand it is of consequence to your peace, I take this liberty to inform you, that the wounds received from Horatio are not mortal. This satisfaction my humanity could not deny, even to a person who has endeavoured to disturb the repose, as well as destroy the life of

"LOTHARIO."

Being well acquainted with this hand, I had no reason to suspect an imposition in this letter, which I read over in a transport of joy, and caressed Horatio so much that he appeared the happiest man alive. Thus was I won from despair by the menaces of a greater misfortune than that which depressed me. Griefs are like usurpers, the most powerful deposes all the rest. But my raptures were not lasting; that very letter, which, in a manner, re-established my tranquillity, in a little time banished my peace. His unjust reproaches, while they waked my resentment, recalled my former happiness, and filled my soul with rage and sorrow. Horatio, perceiving the situation of my mind, endeavoured to divert my chagrin, by treating me with all the amusements and entertainments of the town. I was gratified with every indulgence I could desire, introduced into the company of other kept mistresses, by whom uncommon deference was paid to me; and I began to lose all remembrance of my former condition, when an accident brought it back to view, with all its interesting circumstances. Diverting myself one day with some newspapers which I had not before perused, the following advertisement attracted my attention:

"Whereas, a young gentlewoman disappeared from her father's house, in the county of ——, about the end of September, on account, as is supposed, of some uneasiness of mind, and has not been as yet heard of. Whoever will give any information about her to Mr. ——, of Gray's Inn, shall be handsomely rewarded; or if she will return to the arms of her disconsolate parent, she will be received with the utmost tenderness, whatever reason she may have to think otherwise, and may be the means of prolonging the life of a father, already weighed down almost to the grave with age and sorrow."

This pathetic remonstrance had such an effect on me, that I was fully resolved to return, like the prodigal son, and implore forgiveness of him who gave me life; but, alas! upon inquiry, I found he had paid his debt to nature a month before, lamenting my absence to his last hour, having left his fortune to a stranger, as a mark of his resentment of my unkind and undutiful behaviour. Penetrated with remorse on this occasion, I sank into the most profound melancholy, and considered myself as the immediate cause of his death. I lost all relish for company, and indeed most of my acquaintance no sooner perceived my change of temper than they abandoned me. Horatio, disgusted at my insensibility, or, which is more probable, cloyed with possession, became colder and colder every day, till at last he left me altogether, without making any apology for his conduct, or securing me against the miseries of want, as a man of honour ought to have done, considering the share he had in my ruin; for I afterwards learned that the quarrel between Lothario and him was a story trumped up to rid the one of my importunities, and give the other the enjoyment of my person, which, it seems, he lusted after, upon seeing me at the house of my seducer. Reduced to this extremity, I cursed my simplicity, uttered horrid imprecations against the treachery of Horatio, and, as I became every day more familiarised to the loss of innocence, resolved to be revenged on the sex in general, by practising their own arts upon themselves. Nor was an opportunity long wanting; an old gentlewoman, under pretence of sympathising, visited me, and, after having condoled me on my misfortunes, and professed a disinterested friendship, began to display the art of her occupation in encomiums on my beauty, and invectives against the wretch who had forsaken me; insinuating withal, that it would be my own fault if I did not still make my fortune by the extraordinary qualifications with which nature had endowed me. I soon understood her drift, and gave her such encouragement to explain herself, that we came to an agreement immediately to divide the profits of my prostitution accruing from such gallants as she should introduce to my acquaintance. The first stroke of my dissimulation was practised upon a certain judge, to whom I was recommended by this matron as an innocent creature just arrived from the country. He was so transported with my appearance and feigned simplicity, that he paid a hundred guineas for the possession of me for one night only, during which I behaved in such a manner as to make him perfectly well pleased with his purchase.

CHAPTER XXIII

HER story was here interrupted by a rap at the door, which I no sooner opened, than three or four terrible fellows rushed in, one of whom accosted my fellow-lodger thus: "Madam, your servant, you must do me the favour to come along with me—I have got a writ against you." While the bailiff, for so he was, spoke thus, his followers surrounded the prisoner, and began to handle her very roughly. This treatment incensed me so much, that I snatched up the poker, and would certainly have used it in defence of the lady, without any regard to the strength and number of her adversaries, had she not begged me, with a composure of countenance for which I could not account, to use no violence in her behalf, which could be of no service to her, but might be very detrimental to myself. Then, turning to the leader of this formidable troop, she desired to see the writ, and having perused it, said, with a faltering voice, "I am not the person whose name is here mentioned; arrest me at your peril." "Ay, ay, madam," replied the catchpole, "we shall prove your identity. In the meantime, whether will you be pleased to be carried to my house, or to jail?" "If I must be confined," said she, "I would rather be in your house than in a common jail." "Well, well," answered he, "if you have money enough in your pocket, you shall be entertained like a princess." But when she acquainted him with her poverty, he swore he never gave credit, and ordered one of his myrmidons to call a coach to carry her to the Marshalsea at once. While they waited for the convenience, she took me aside, and bade me be under no concern on her account, for she knew how to extricate herself from this difficulty very soon, and, perhaps, gain something by the occasion. Although her discourse was a mystery to me, I was very well pleased with her assurance, and when the coach came to the door, offered to accompany her to prison; to which proposal, after much entreaty, she consented. When we arrived at the gate of the Marshalsea, our conductor alighted, and having demanded entrance, presented the writ to the turnkey, who no sooner perceived the name of Elizabeth Cary, than he cried,

"Ah, hah! my old acquaintance, Bett!—I am glad to see thee with all my heart." So saying, he opened the coach door, and helped her to dismount; but when he observed her face, he started back, saying, "Zounds! who have we got here?" The bailiff, alarmed at this interrogation, cried, with some emotion, "Who the devil should it be, but the prisoner, Elizabeth Cary?" The turnkey replied, "That Elizabeth Cary!—I'll be damned if that's Elizabeth Cary, more than my grandmother. Damn my blood, I know Bett Cary as well as if I had made her." Here the lady thought fit to interpose and tell the catchpole, if he had taken her word for it at first, he might have saved himself and her a great deal of trouble. "It may be so," answered he, "but, by God, I'll have further evidence that you are not the person before you and I part." "Yes, yes," said she, "you shall have further evidence to your cost." Then we adjourned into the lodge, and called for a bottle of wine, where my companion wrote a direction to two of her acquaintance, and begged the favour of me to go to their lodgings, and request them to come to her immediately. I found them together in a house in Bridges Street, Drury Lane; and as they were luckily unengaged, they set out with me in a hackney-coach, without hesitation, after I had related the circumstances of the affair, which flattered them with the hopes of seeing a bailiff trounced; for there is an antipathy as natural between the whores and bailiffs, as that subsisting between mice and cats. Accordingly, when they entered the lodge, they embraced the prisoner very affectionately by the name of Nancy Williams, and asked how long she had been nabbed, and for what? On hearing the particulars of her adventure repeated, they offered to swear before a justice of peace that she was not the person mentioned in the writ, whom, it seems, they all knew; but the bailiff, who was by this time convinced of his mistake, told them that he would not put them to that trouble. "Ladies," said he, "there's no harm done; you shall give me leave to treat you with another bottle, and then we'll part friends." This proposal was not at all relished by the sisterhood; and Miss Williams told him, sure he did not imagine her such a fool as to be satisfied with a paltry glass of sour wine. Here the turnkey interrupted her, by affirming with an oath, that the wine was as good as ever was tipped over tongue. "Well," continued she, "that may be, but was it the best of champagne, it is no recompense for the damage I have suffered, both in character and health, by being wrongfully dragged to jail. At this rate, no innocent person is safe, since an officer of justice, out of malice, private pique, or mistake, may injure and oppress the subject with impunity. But, thank heaven, I live under the protection of laws that will not suffer such insults to pass unpunished, and I know very well how to procure redress." Mr. Vulture (for that was the bailiff's name), finding he had to deal with one who would not be imposed upon, began to look very sullen and perplexed, and leaning his forehead on his hand, entered into a deliberation with himself, which lasted a few minutes, and then broke out in a volley of dreadful curses against the old b——ch, our landlady, as he called her, for having misinformed him. After much wrangling and swearing, the matter was referred to the decision of the turnkey, who, calling for the other bottle, mulcted the bailiff in all the liquor that had been drank, coach-hire, and a couple of guineas, for the use of the plaintiff. The money was immediately deposited, Miss Williams gratified the two evidences with one half, and, putting the other in her pocket, drove home with me, leaving the catchpole grumbling over his loss, yet pleased in the main, for having so cheaply got clear of a business that might have cost him ten times the sum, and his place to boot. This guinea was a very seasonable relief to us, who were reduced to great necessity, six of my shirts, and almost all my clothes, except those on my back, having been either pawned or sold for our maintenance, before this happened. As we resented the behaviour of our landlady, our first care was to provide ourselves with another lodging, whither we removed the next day, with an intention to keep ourselves as retired as possible, until our cure should be completed. When we were fixed in our new habitation, I entreated her to finish the story of her life, which she pursued in this manner:

The success of our experiment on the judge encouraged us to practise the same deceit on others, and my virginity was five times sold to good purpose. But this harvest lasted not long, my character taking air, and my directress deserting me for some new game. Then I took lodgings near Charing Cross, at two guineas per week, and began to entertain company in a public manner; but my income being too small to defray my expense, I was obliged to retrench, and enter into articles with the porters of certain taverns, who undertook to find employment enough for me, provided I would share my profits with them. Accordingly, I was almost every night engaged with company, among whom I was exposed to every mortification, danger, and abuse, that flows from drunkenness, brutality, and disease. How miserable is the condition of a courtesan, whose business it is to soothe, suffer, and obey the dictates of rage, insolence, and lust! As my spirit was not sufficiently humbled to the will, nor my temper calculated for the conversation of my gallants, it was impossible for me to overcome an aversion I felt for my profession, which manifested itself in a settled gloom on my countenance, and disgusted those sons of mirth and riot so much, that I was frequently used in a shocking manner, and kicked downstairs with disgrace. The messengers seeing me disagreeable to their benefactors and employers, seldom troubled me with a call, and I began to find myself almost totally neglected. To contribute towards my support, I was fain to sell my watch, rings, trinkets, with the best part of my clothes; and I was one evening musing by myself on the misery before me, when I received a message from a bagnio, whither I repaired in a chair, and was introduced to a gentleman dressed like an officer, with whom I supped in a sumptuous manner, and, after drinking a hearty glass of champagne, went to bed. In the morning, when I awoke, I found my gallant had got up, and, drawing aside the curtain, could not perceive him in the room. This circumstance gave me some uneasiness; but as he might have retired on some necessary occasion, I waited a full hour for his return, and then in the greatest perplexity rose up and rang the bell. When the waiter came to the door he found it locked, and desired admittance, which I granted, after observing, with great surprise, that the key remained on the inside, as when we went to bed. I no sooner inquired for the captain, than the fellow, staring with a distracted look, cried, "How, madam! is not he a-bed?" And when he was satisfied as to that particular, ran into a closet adjoining to the chamber, the window of which he found open. Through this the adventurer had got upon a wall, from whence he dropped down into a court and escaped, leaving me to be answerable, not only for the reckoning, but also for a large silver tankard and posset bowl, which he had carried off with him. It is impossible to describe the consternation I was under, when I saw myself detained as a thief's accomplice; for I was looked upon in that light, and carried before a justice, who, mistaking my confusion for a sign of guilt, committed me, after a short examination, to Bridewell, having advised me, as the only means to save my life, to turn evidence and impeach my confederate. I now concluded the vengeance of Heaven had overtaken me, and that I must soon finish my career by an ignominious death. This reflection sunk so deep into my soul, that I was for some days deprived of my reason, and actually believed myself in hell, tormented by fiends: indeed, there needs not a very extravagant imagination to form that idea; for, of all the scenes on earth, that of Bridewell approaches nearest the notion I had always entertained of the infernal regions. Here I saw nothing but rage, anguish, and impiety; and heard nothing but groans, curses, and blasphemy. In the midst of this hellish crew, I was subjected to the tyranny of a barbarian, who imposed upon me tasks that I could not possibly perform, and then punished my incapacity with the utmost rigour and inhumanity. I was often whipped into a swoon, and lashed out of it, during which miserable intervals I was robbed by my fellow-prisoners of everything about me, even to my cap, shoes, and stockings: I was not only destitute of necessaries, but even of food; so that my wretchedness was extreme. Not one of my acquaintance, to whom I imparted my situation, would grant me the least succour or regard, on pretence of my being committed for theft; and my landlord refused to part with some of my own clothes, which I sent for, because I was indebted to him for a week's lodging. Overwhelmed with calamity, I grew desperate, and resolved to put an end to my grievances and life together: for this purpose I got up in the middle of the night, when I thought everybody around me asleep, and fixing one end of my handkerchief to a large hook in the ceiling, that supported the scales on which the hemp is weighed, I stood upon a chair, and making a noose on the other end, put my neck into it, with an intention to hang myself; but before I could adjust the knot, I was surprised and prevented by two women who had been awake all the while, and suspected my design. In the morning my attempt was published among the prisoners and punished with thirty stripes; the pain of which co-operating with my disappointment and disgrace, bereft me of my senses, and threw me into an ecstasy of madness, during which I tore the flesh from my bones with my teeth, and dashed my head against the pavement; so that they were obliged to set a watch over me, to restrain me from doing further mischief to myself and others. This fit of frenzy continued three days, at the end of which I grew calm and sullen; but, as the desire of making away with myself still remained, I came to a determination of starving myself to death, and with that view refused all sustenance. Whether it was owing to the want of opposition, or to the weakness of nature, I know not, but on the second day of

ny fast I found my resolution considerably impaired, and the
calls of hunger almost insupportable. At this critical conjuncture,
a lady was brought into the prison with whom I had contracted
an acquaintance while I lived with Horatio: she was then on
the same footing as I was, but afterwards quarrelling with her
gallant, and not finding another to her mind, altered her scheme
of life, and set up her coffee-house among the hundreds of Drury,
where she entertained gentlemen with claret, arrack, and the
choice of half a dozen of damsels, who lived in her house. This
serviceable matron having neglected to gratify a certain justice
for the connivance she enjoyed, was indicted at the quarter
sessions, in consequence of which her bevy was dispersed, and
herself committed to Bridewell. She had not been long there,
before she learned my disaster, and coming up to me, after a
compliment of condolence, inquired into the particulars of my
fate. While we were engaged in discourse together, the master
came and told me that the fellow on whose account I had suffered
was taken; that he had confessed the theft, and cleared me of
any concern in the affair; for which reason, he, the master, had
orders to discharge me; and that I was from that moment free.
This piece of news soon banished all thoughts of death, and
had such an instantaneous effect on my countenance, that Mrs.
Coupler (the lady then present), hoping to find her account in
me, very generously offered to furnish me with what necessaries
I wanted, and take me into her own house, as soon as she should
compromise matters with the justices. The conditions of her
offer were, that I should pay three guineas weekly for my
board, and a reasonable consideration besides for the use of
such clothes and ornaments as she should supply me with, to be
deducted from the first profits of my embraces. These were
hard terms; but not to be rejected by one who was turned out
helpless and naked into the wide world, without a friend to pity
or assist her. I therefore embraced her proposal; and she being
bailed in a few hours, took me home with her in a coach. As I
was by this time conscious of having formerly disgusted my
admirers by my reserved and haughty behaviour, I now endeavoured to conquer that disposition; and the sudden change of
my fortune giving me a flow of spirits, I appeared in the most
winning and gay manner I could assume. Having the advantage
of a good voice and education, I exerted my talents to the
uttermost, and soon became the favourite with all company.
This success alarmed the pride and jealousy of Mrs. Coupler,
who could not bear the thoughts of being eclipsed; she therefore

made a merit of her envy, and whispered among the customer that I was unsound. There needed no more to ruin my reputatio and blast my prosperity; everybody shunned me with marks of aversion and disdain; and, in a very short time, I was as solitar as ever. Want of gallants was attended with want of money t satisfy my malicious landlady, who, having purposely give me credit to the amount of eleven pounds, took out a wri against me, and I was arrested in her own house. Though th room was crowded with people when the bailiff entered, no one of them had compassion enough to mollify my prosecutrix far less to pay the debt. They even laughed at my tears; and one of them bade me be of good cheer, for I should not want admirer in Newgate. At that instant, a sea lieutenant came in, and seeing my plight, began to inquire into the circumstances of my mis fortune; when this wit advised him to keep clear of me, for I was a fire-ship. "A fire-ship!" replied the sailor; "more like a poor galley in distress, that has been boarded by such a fire ship as you; if so be as that is the case, she stands in more need of assistance. Hark'ee, my girl, how far have you over-run the constable?" I told him that the debt amounted to eleven pounds, besides the expense of the writ—"An' that be all," said he, "you shan't go to the bilboes this bout." And taking out his purse, paid the money, discharged the bailiff, and telling me I had got into the wrong port, advised me to seek out a more convenient harbour, where I could be safely hove down, for which purpose he made me a present of five guineas more. I was so touched with this singular piece of generosity, that, for some time, I had not power to thank him. However, as soon as I had recollected myself, I begged the favour of him to go with me to the next tavern, where I explained the nature of my disaster, and convinced him of the falsehood of what was reported to my prejudice so effectually, that he from that moment attached himself to me; and we lived in great harmony together, until he was obliged to go to sea, where he perished in a storm.

Having lost my benefactor, and almost consumed the remains of his bounty, I saw myself in danger of relapsing into my former necessity, and began to be very uneasy at the prospect of bailiffs and jails; when one of the sisterhood, a little stale, advised me to take lodgings in a part of the town where I was unknown, and pass for an heiress, by which artifice I might entrap some-body to be my husband, who would possibly be able to allow me a handsome maintenance, or at worst screen me from the dread and danger of a prison, by becoming liable for whatever debts I should contract. I approved of this scheme, towards the execution of which my companion clubbed her wardrobe, and undertook to live with me in quality of my maid; with the proviso that she should be reimbursed, and handsomely considered out of the profits of my success. She was immediately detached to look out for a convenient place, and that very day hired a genteel apartment in Park Street, where I moved in a coach loaded with her baggage and my own. I made my first appearance in a blue riding-habit trimmed with silver; and my maid acted her part so artfully, that, in a day or two, my fame was spread all over the neighbourhood, and I was said to be a rich heiress just arrived from the country. This report brought a swarm of gay young fellows about me; but I soon found them out to be all indigent adventurers like myself, who crowded to me like crows to a carrion, with a view of preying upon my fortune. I maintained, however, the appearance of wealth as long as possible, in hopes of gaining some admirer more for my purpose; and at length attracted the regard of one who would have satisfied my wishes; and managed matters so well, that a day was actually fixed for our nuptials. In the interim, he begged leave to introduce an intimate friend to me; which request I could not refuse. I had the extreme mortification and surprise to see next night, in that friend, my old keeper, Horatio; who no sooner beheld me, than he changed colour; but had presence of mind to advance and salute me, bidding me, with a low voice, be under no apprehension, for he would not expose me. In spite of this assurance, I could not recover myself so far as to entertain them, but withdrew to my chamber, on pretence of a severe headache, to the no small concern of my adorer, who took his leave in the tenderest manner, and went off with his friend.

Having imparted my situation to my companion, she found it high time for us to decamp, and that without any noise, because we were not only indebted to our landlady, but also to several tradesmen in the neighbourhood. Our retreat, therefore, was concerted and executed in this manner:—having packed up all our clothes and movables in small parcels, she, on pretence of fetching cordials for me, carried them, at several times, to the house of an acquaintance, where she likewise procured a lodging, to which we retired in the middle of the night, when every other body in the house was asleep. I was now obliged to aim at lower game, and accordingly spread my nets among tradespeople; but found them all too phlegmatic or cautious for my art and attractions; till at last I became acquainted with you, on whom I practised all my dexterity; not that I believed you had any fortune, or expectation of one, but that I might transfer the burden of such debts as I had incurred, or should contract, from myself to another; and at the same time avenge myself of your sex, by rendering miserable one who bore such a resemblance to the wretch who ruined me; but Heaven preserved you from my snares, by the discovery you made, which was owing to the negligence of my maid in leaving the chamber door unlocked, when she went to buy sugar for breakfast. The person in bed with me was a gentleman whom I had allured the night before, as he walked homeward, pretty much elevated with liquor; for by this time my condition was so low, that I was forced to turn out in the twilight in the streets, in hopes of prey. When I found myself detected and forsaken by you, I was fain to move my lodging, and dwell two pair of steps higher than before. My companion, being disappointed in her expectations, left me, to trade upon her own bottom, and I had no other resource than to venture forth like the owls in the dark, to pick up a precarious and uncomfortable subsistence. I have often sauntered between Ludgate Hill and Charing Cross a whole winter night, exposed not only to the inclemency of the weather, but likewise to the rage of hunger and thirst, without being so happy as to meet with one cully; then creep up to my garret in a deplorable draggled condition, sneak to bed, and try to bury my appetite and sorrows in sleep. When I lighted on some rake or tradesman reeling home drunk, I frequently suffered the most brutal treatment, in spite of which I was obliged to affect gaiety and good humour, though my soul was stung with resentment and disdain, and my heart loaded with grief and affliction. In the course of these nocturnal adventures, I was infected with the disease that, in a short time, rendered me the object of my own abhorrence, and drove me to the retreat where your benevolence rescued me from the jaws of death.

So much candour and good sense appeared in this lady's narration, that I made no scruple of believing every syllable of what she said; and expressed my astonishment at the variety of miseries she had undergone in so little time; for all her misfortunes had happened within the compass of two years. I compared her situation with my own, and found it a thousand times more wretched. I had endured hardships, 'tis true; my whole life had been a series of such; and when I looked forward, the prospect was not much bettered; but then they were become habitual to me, and consequently I could bear them with less difficulty. If one scheme of life should not succeed, I could have recourse to another, and so to a third, veering about to a thousand different shifts, according to the emergencies of my fate, without forfeiting the dignity of my character beyond a power of retrieving it, or subjecting myself wholly to the caprice and barbarity of the world. On the other hand, she had known and relished the sweets of prosperity; she had been brought up under the wings of an indulgent parent, in all the delicacies to which her sex and rank entitled her; and, without any extravagance of hope, entertained herself with the view of uninterrupted happiness through the whole scene of life. How fatal then, how tormenting, how intolerable must her reverse of fortune be!—a reverse that not only robs her of these external comforts, and plunges her into all the miseries of want, but also murders her peace of mind, and entails upon her the curse of eternal infamy! Of all professions, I pronounce that of a courtesan the most deplorable, and her of all courtesans the most unhappy. She allowed my observation to be just in the main, but at the same time affirmed, that, notwithstanding the disgraces which had fallen to her share, she had not been so unlucky in the condition of a prostitute, as many others of the same community. "I have often seen," said she, "while I strolled about the streets at midnight, a number of naked wretches reduced to rags and filth, huddled together like swine in a corner of a dark alley; some of whom, but eighteen months before, I had known the favourites of the town, rolling in affluence, and glittering in all the pomp of equipage and dress. And indeed the gradation is easily conceived. The most fashionable woman of the town is as liable to contagion as one in a much humbler sphere; she infects her admirers, her situation is public; she is avoided, neglected, unable to support her usual appearance, which, however, she strives to maintain as long as possible; her credit fails; she is obliged to retrench, and become a night-walker; her malady gains ground; she tampers with her constitution and ruins it; her complexion fades; she grows nauseous to everybody; finds herself reduced to a starving condition; is tempted to pick pockets; is detected; committed to Newgate, where she remains in a miserable condition till she is discharged, because the plaintiff will not appear to prosecute her. Nobody will afford her lodgings; the symptoms of her distemper are grown outrageous; she sues to be admitted into an hospital where she is cured at the expense of her nose; she is turned out naked into the streets, depends upon the addresses of the lowest class, is fain to allay the rage of hunger and cold with gin, degenerates into a brutal insensibility, rots and dies upon a dunghill. Miserable wretch that I am! perhaps the same horrors are decreed for me! No," cried she, after some pause, "I shall never live to such extremity of distress! my own hand shall open a way for my deliverance, before I arrive at that forlorn period!" Her condition filled me with sympathy and compassion; I revered her qualifications, looked upon her as unfortunate, not criminal, and attended her with such care and success, that, in less than two months, her health, as well as my own, was perfectly re-established. As we often conferred upon our mutual affairs, and interchanged advice, a thousand different projects were formed, which, upon further canvassing, appeared impracticable. We would have gladly gone to service, but who would take us in without recommendation? At length an expedient occurred to her, of which she intended to lay hold, and this was to procure, with the first money she should earn, the homely garb of a country wench, go to some village at a good distance from town, and come up in a waggon, as a fresh girl for service; by which means she might be provided for in a manner much more suitable to her inclination than her present way of life.

CHAPTER XXIV

I am reduced to great Misery—Assaulted on Tower Hill by a Press-gang, who put me on board a Tender—My Usage there—My arrival on board of the *Thunder* Man of War, where I am put in Irons, and afterwards released by the good offices of Mr. Thomson, who recommends me as Assistant to the Surgeon—He relates his own Story, and makes me acquainted with the Characters of the Captain, Surgeon and First Mate.

I APPLAUDED the resolution of Miss Williams, who, a few days after, was hired in quality of bar-keeper by one of the ladies who had witnessed in her behalf at the Marshalsea, and who since that time had got credit with a wine merchant, whose favourite she was, to set up a convenient house of her own. Thither my fellow-lodger repaired, after having taken leave of me with a torrent of tears, and a thousand protestations of eternal gratitude; assuring me she would remain in this situation

no longer than she should pick up money sufficient to put her
other design in execution.

As for my own part, I saw no resource but the army or navy,
between which I hesitated so long, that I found myself reduced
to a starving condition. My spirit began to accommodate itself
to my beggarly fate, and I became so mean as to go down towards
Wapping, with an intention to inquire for an old schoolfellow,
who, I understood, had got the command of a small coasting
vessel, then in the river, and implore his assistance. But my
destiny prevented this abject piece of behaviour; for, as I
crossed Tower Wharf, a squat tawny fellow, with a hanger by
his side, and a cudgel in his hand, came up to me, calling, "Yo,
ho! brother, you must come along with me." As I did not like
his appearance, instead of answering his salutation, I quickened
my pace, in hope of ridding myself of his company; upon
which he whistled aloud, and immediately another sailor
appeared before me, who laid hold of me by the collar and began
to drag me along. Not being of a humour to relish such treatment, I disengaged myself of the assailant, and with one blow
of my cudgel, laid him motionless on the ground; and perceiving
myself surrounded in a trice by ten or a dozen more, exerted
myself with such dexterity and success, that some of my opponents were fain to attack me with drawn cutlasses; and, after
an obstinate engagement, in which I received a large wound on
my head, and another on my left cheek, I was disarmed, taken
prisoner, and carried on board a pressing tender, where, after
being pinioned like a malefactor, I was thrust down into the
hold among a parcel of miserable wretches, the sight of whom
well-nigh distracted me. As the commanding officer had not
humanity enough to order my wounds to be dressed, and I
could not use my own hands, I desired one of my fellow-captives,
who was unfettered, to take a handkerchief out of my pocket
and tie it round my head to stop the bleeding. He pulled out
my handkerchief, 'tis true; but, instead of applying it to the
use for which I designed it, went to the grating of the hatchway,
and with astonishing composure, sold it before my face to a
bum-boat woman [1] then on board, for a quart of gin, with which
he treated my companions, regardless of my circumstances
and entreaties.

I complained bitterly of this robbery to the midshipman on

[1] A bum-boat woman is one who sells bread, cheese, greens, liquor,
and fresh provisions to the sailors, in a small boat that lies alongside
the ship.

deck, telling him at the same time, that unless my hurts were dressed I should bleed to death. But compassion was a weakness of which no man could justly accuse this person, who, squirting a mouthful of dissolved tobacco upon me through the gratings told me, "I was a mutinous dog, and that I might die and be damned." Finding there was no other remedy, I appealed to patience, and laid up this usage in my memory, to be recalled at a fitter season. In the meantime, loss of blood, vexation, and want of food contributed, with the noisome stench of the place, to throw me into a swoon; out of which I was recovered by a tweak of the nose, administered by the tar who stood sentinel over us, who at the same time regaled me with a draught of flip, and comforted me with the hopes of being put on board the *Thunder* next day, where I should be freed of my handcuffs, and cured of my wounds by the doctor. I no sooner heard him name the *Thunder*, than I asked if he had belonged to that ship long? and he giving me to understand he had belonged to her five years, I inquired if he knew Lieutenant Bowling? "Know Lieutenant Bowling," said he,—"odds my life! and that I do! and a good seaman he is, as ever stepp'd upon forecastle,—and a brave fellow as ever crack'd bisket; none of your Guinea pigs, —nor your fresh-water, wishy-washy, fair-weather fowls. Many a taut gale of wind has honest Tom Bowling and I weathered together. Here's his health with all my heart, wherever he is, aloft or alow—in heaven or in hell—all's one for that—he needs not be ashamed to show himself." I was so much affected with this eulogium, that I could not refrain from telling him that I was Lieutenant Bowling's kinsman; in consequence of which connection he expressed an inclination to serve me, and, when he was relieved, brought some cold boiled beef in a platter, and biscuit, on which we supped plentifully, and afterwards drank another can of flip together. While we were thus engaged, he recounted a great many exploits of my uncle, who, I found, was very much beloved by the ship's company, and pitied for the misfortune that had happened to him in Hispaniola, which I was very glad to be informed was not so great as I imagined; for Captain Oakum had recovered of his wounds, and actually at that time commanded the ship. Having, by accident, in my pocket, my uncle's letter, written from Port Louis, I gave it to my benefactor, whose name was Jack Rattlin, for his perusal; but honest Jack told me frankly he could not read, and desired to know the contents; which I immediately communicated. When he heard that part of it in which he says he had writ to his landlord in Deal, he cried, "Body o' me!—that was old Ben Block—he was dead before the letter came to hand. Ey, ey, had Ben been alive, Lieutenant Bowling would have had no occasion to skulk so long. Honest Ben was the first man that taught him to hand, reef, and steer.—Well, well, we must all die, that's certain,—we must all come to port sooner or later—at sea, or on shore; we must be fast moored one day; death's like the best bower anchor, as the saying is, it will bring us all up." I could not but signify my approbation of the justness of Jack's reflections; and inquired into the occasion of the quarrel between Captain Oakum and my uncle; which he explained in this manner: "Captain Oakum, to be sure, is a good man enough,—besides he's my commander;—but what's that to me?—I do my duty, and value no man's anger of a rope's end. —Now the report goes, as how he's a lord, or baron knight's brother, whereby, d'ye see me, he carries a strait arm, and keeps aloof from his officers, thô'f, mayhap, they may be as good men in the main as he. Now we lying at anchor in Tuberoon Bay, Lieutenant Bowling had the middle watch, and as he always kept a good look-out, he made, d'ye see, three lights in the offing, whereby he ran down to the great cabin for orders, and found the captain asleep; whereupon he waked him, which put him in a main high passion, and he swore woundily at the lieutenant, and called him lousy Scotch son of a whore (for I being then sentinel in the steerage, heard all), and swab, and lubber, whereby the lieutenant returned the salute, and they jawed together, fore and aft, a good spell, till at last the captain turned out, and laying hold of a rattan, came athwart Mr. Bowling's quarter; whereby he told the captain, that, if he was not his commander, he would heave him overboard, and demanded satisfaction ashore; whereby, in the morning watch, the captain went ashore in the pinnace, and afterwards the lieutenant carried the cutter ashore; and so they, leaving their boats' crews on their oars, went away together; and so, d'ye see, in less than a quarter of an hour we heard firing, whereby we made for the place, and found the captain lying wounded on the beach, and so brought him on board to the doctor, who cured him in less than six weeks. But the lieutenant clapp'd on all the sail he could bear, and had got far enow ahead before we knew anything of the matter; so that we could never after get sight of him, for which we were not sorry, because the captain was mainly wroth, and would certainly have done him a mischief;—for he afterwards caused him to be run on the

ship's books, whereby he lost all his pay, and if he should b
taken, would be tried as a deserter."

This account of the captain's behaviour gave me no advan
tageous idea of his character; and I could not help lamentin
my own fate, that had subjected me to such a commande
However, making a virtue of necessity, I put a good face on th
matter, and next day was, with the other pressed men, put o
board of the *Thunder*, lying at the Nore. When we came along
side, the mate who guarded us thither ordered my handcuf
to be taken off, that I might get on board the easier. This circum
stance being perceived by some of the company, who stoo
upon the gang-boards to see us enter, one of them called to Jac
Rattlin, who was busied in doing this friendly office for me
"Hey, Jack, what Newgate galley have you boarded in th
river as you came along? Have we not thieves enow among u
already?" Another, observing my wounds, which remaine
exposed to the air, told me that my seams were uncaulked, an
that I must be new payed. A third, seeing my hair clotte
together with blood, as it were, into distinct cords, took notic
that my bows were manned with the red ropes, instead of m
side. A fourth asked me if I could not keep my yards squar
without iron braces? And, in short, a thousand witticisms o
the same nature were passed upon me before I could get up th
ship's side. After we had been all entered upon the ship's book
I inquired of one of my shipmates where the surgeon was, tha
I might have my wounds dressed, and had actually got as fa
as the middle deck (for our ship carried eighty guns), in my wa
to the cockpit, when I was met by the same midshipman wh
had used me so barbarously in the tender. He, seeing me free
from my chains, asked, with an insolent air, who had released
me? To this question I foolishly answered, with a countenance
that too plainly declared the state of my thoughts, "Whoever
did it, I am persuaded did not consult you in the affair." I had
no sooner uttered these words, than he cried, "Damn you, you
saucy son of a bitch, I'll teach you to talk so to your officer."
So saying, he bestowed on me several severe stripes with a
supple-jack he had in his hand; and, going to the commanding
officer, made such a report of me, that I was immediately put
in irons by the master-at-arms, and a sentinel placed over me.
Honest Rattlin, as soon as he heard of my condition, came to
me, and administered all the consolation he could, and then
went to the surgeon in my behalf, who sent one of his mates
to dress my wounds. This mate was no other than my old friend

Thomson, with whom I became acquainted at the Navy Office, as before mentioned. If I knew him at first sight, it was not easy for him to recognise me, disfigured with blood and dirt, and altered by the misery I had undergone. Unknown as I was to him, he surveyed me with looks of compassion, and handled my sores with great tenderness. When he had applied what he thought proper, and was about to leave me, I asked him if my misfortunes had disguised me so much that he could not recollect my face? Upon this address, he observed me with great earnestness for some time, and at length protested he could not recollect one feature of my countenance. To keep him no longer in suspense, I told him my name; which, when he heard, he embraced me with affection, and professed his sorrow in seeing me in such a disagreeable situation. I made him acquainted with my story; and when he heard how inhumanly I had been used in the tender, he left me abruptly, assuring me I should see him again soon. I had scarce time to wonder at his sudden departure, when the master-at-arms came to the place of my confinement, and bade me follow him to the quarter-deck, where I was examined by the first lieutenant, who commanded the ship in the absence of the captain, touching the treatment I had received in the tender from my friend the midshipman, who was present to confront me. I recounted the particulars of his behaviour to me, not only in the tender, but since my being on board the ship, part of which being proved by the evidence of Jack Rattlin, and others who had no great devotion for my oppressor, I was discharged from confinement, to make way for him, who was delivered to the master-at-arms to take his turn in the bilboes. And this was not the only satisfaction I enjoyed; for I was, at the request of the surgeon, exempted from all other duty than that of assisting his mates in making and administering medicines to the sick. This good office I owed to the friendship of Mr. Thomson, who had represented me in such a favourable light to the surgeon, that he demanded me of the lieutenant to supply the place of his third mate, who was lately dead. When I had obtained this favour, my friend Thomson carried me down to the cockpit, which is the place allotted for the habitation of the surgeon's mates; and when he had shown me their berth, as he called it, I was filled with astonishment and horror. We descended by divers ladders to a space as dark as a dungeon, which I understood was immersed several feet under water, being immediately above the hold. I had no sooner approached this dismal gulf, than my nose was saluted with an intolerable stench of putrefied cheese and rancid butter, that issued from an apartment at the foot of the ladder, resembling a chandler's shop, where, by the faint glimmering of a candle, I could perceive a man with a pale meagre countenance, sitting behind a kind of desk, having spectacles on his nose, and a pen in his hand. This, I learned of Mr. Thomson, was the ship's steward, who sat there to distribute provision to the several messes, and to mark what each received. He therefore presented my name to him, and desired I might be entered in his mess; then, taking a light in his hand, conducted me to the place of his residence, which was a square of about six feet, surrounded with the medicine chest, that of the first mate, his own, and a board, by way of table, fastened to the after powder-room; it was also enclosed with canvas, nailed round to the beams of the ship, to screen us from the cold, as well as from the view of the midshipmen and quarter-masters, who lodged within the cable-tiers on each side of us. In this gloomy mansion, he entertained me with some cold salt pork, which he brought from a sort of locker fixed above the table; and, calling for the boy of the mess, sent for a can of beer, of which he made excellent flip to crown the banquet. By this time I began to recover my spirits, which had been exceedingly depressed by the appearance of everything about me, and could no longer refrain from asking the particulars of Mr. Thomson's fortune since I had seen him in London. He told me that, being disappointed in his expectations of borrowing money to gratify the rapacious secretary at the Navy Office, he found himself utterly unable to subsist any longer in town, and had actually offered his service in quality of mate to the surgeon of a merchant's ship bound to Guinea, on the slaving trade; when, one morning, a young fellow, of whom he had some acquaintance, came to his lodgings, and informed him that he had seen a warrant made out in his name at the Navy Office for surgeon's second mate of a third rate. This unexpected piece of good news he could scarcely believe to be true, more especially as he had been found qualified at Surgeons' Hall for third mate only; but, that he might not be wanting to himself, he went thither to be assured, and actually found it so. Whereupon, demanding his warrant, it was delivered to him, and the oaths administered immediately. That very afternoon he went to Gravesend in the tilt-boat, from whence he took a place in the tide-coach for Rochester; next morning, got on board the *Thunder*, for which he was appointed, then lying in the harbour at Chatham; and the same day was mustered by the clerk of the cheque. And well it was for him that such expedition was used; for, in less than twelve hours after his arrival, another William Thomson came on board, affirming that he was the person for whom the warrant was expedited, and that the other was an impostor. My friend was grievously alarmed at this accident—the more so, as his name-sake had very much the advantage over him both in assurance and dress. However, to acquit himself of the suspicion of imposture, he produced several letters, written from Scotland to him in that name, and recollecting that his indentures were in a box on board, he brought them up, and convinced all present that he had not assumed a name which did not belong to him. His competitor, enraged that they should hesitate in doing him justice (for, to be sure, the warrant had been designed for him), behaved with so much indecent heat, that the commanding officer, who was the same gentleman I had seen, and the surgeon, were offended at his presumption, and making a point of it with their friends in town, in less than a week got the first confirmed in his station. "I have been on board," said he, "ever since, and, as this way of life is become familiar to me, have no cause to complain of my situation. The surgeon is a good-natured indolent man; the first mate, who is now on shore on duty, is, indeed, a little proud and choleric, as all Welshmen are, but, in the main, a friendly honest fellow. The lieutenants I have no concern with; and as for the captain, he is too much of a gentleman to know a surgeon's mate, even by sight."

CHAPTER XXV

The Behaviour of Mr. Morgan—His Pride, Displeasure, and Generosity—The Economy of our Mess described—Thomson's further Friendship—The Nature of my Duty explained—The Situation of the Sick.

WHILE he was thus discoursing to me, we heard a voice on the cockpit ladder pronounce with great vehemence, in a strange dialect, "The devil and his dam blow me from the top of Mounch-denny, if I go to him before there is something in my pelly; let his nose be as yellow as saffron, or as plue as a pell, look you, or green as a leek, 'tis all one." To this declaration somebody answered, "So it seems my poor messmate must part his cable for want of a little assistance. His fore-top-sail is loose already; and, besides, the doctor ordered you to overhaul him; but I

* F 790

see you don't mind what your master says." Here he was interrupted with, "Splunter and oons! you lousy tog, who do you call my master? Get you gone to the doctor, and tell him my birth, and education, and my abilities, and moreover my behaviour is as good as his, or any shentleman's (no disparagement to him) in the whole world. Got pless my soul! does he think, or conceive, or imagine, that I am a horse, or an ass, or a goat, to trudge backwards and forwards, and upwards and downwards, and by sea and by land, at his will and pleasures? Go your ways, you rapscallion, and tell Dr. Atkins, that I desire and request that he will give a look to the tying man, and order something for him if he be dead or alive, and I will see him take it by and by, when my craving stomach is satisfied, look you." At this the other went away, saying that if they should serve him so when he was dying, by God, he would be foul of them in the other world. Here Mr. Thomson let me know that the person we heard was Mr. Morgan, the first mate, who was just come on board from the hospital, whither he had attended some of the sick in the morning. At the same time I saw him come into the berth. He was a short thick man, with a face garnished with pimples, a snub nose turned up at the end, an excessive wide mouth, and little fiery eyes, surrounded with skin puckered up in innumerable wrinkles. My friend immediately made him acquainted with my case; when he regarded me with a very lofty look, but without speaking, set down a bundle he had in his hand, and approached the cupboard, which, when he had opened, he exclaimed in a great passion, "Got is my life! all the pork is gone, as I am a Christian!" Thomson then gave him to understand, that as I had been brought on board half famished, he could do no less than entertain me with what was in the locker; and the rather as he had bid the steward enter me in the mess. Whether this disappointment made Mr. Morgan more peevish than usual, or he rather thought himself too little regarded by his fellow-mate, I know not, but, after some pause, he went on in this manner, "Mr. Thomson, perhaps you do not use me with all the good manners, and complaisance, and respect, look you, that becomes you, because you have not vouchsafed to advise with me in this affair. I have, in my time, look you, been a man of some weight and substance, and consideration, and have kept house and home, and paid scot and lot, and the king's taxes; ay, and maintained a family to boot. And moreover, also, I am your senior, and your elder, and your petter, Mr. Thomson." "My elder I'll allow you to be, but not my better," cried Thomson with some heat. "Got is my Saviour, and witness too," said Morgan, with great vehemence, "that I am more elder, and therefore more petter, by many years, than you." Fearing this dispute might be attended with some bad consequence, I interposed, and told Mr. Morgan I was very sorry for having been the occasion of any difference between him and the second mate; and that rather than cause the least breach in their good understanding, I would eat my allowance by myself, or seek admission into some other company. But Thomson, with more spirit than discretion, as I thought, insisted upon my remaining where he had appointed me; and observed, that no man possessed of generosity and compassion would have any objection to it, considering my birth and talents, and the misfortunes I had of late so unjustly undergone. This was touching Mr. Morgan on the right key, who protested with great earnestness that he had no objection to my being received in the mess; but only complained that the ceremony of asking his consent was not observed. "As for a shentleman in distress," said he, shaking me by the hand, "I lofe him as I lofe my own powels; for, Got help me! I have had vexations enough upon my own pack." And, as I afterwards learned, in so saying, he spoke no more than what was true; for he had been once settled in a very good situation in Glamorganshire, and was ruined by being security for an acquaintance. All differences being composed, he untied his bundle, which consisted of three bunches of onions, and a great lump of Cheshire cheese, wrapped up in a handkerchief; and, taking some biscuit from the cupboard, fell to with a keen appetite, inviting us to a share of the repast. When he had fed heartily on his homely fare, he filled a large cup, made of a cocoa-nut shell, with brandy, and drinking it off, told us, "Prandy was the pest menstruum for onion and sheese." His hunger being appeased, he began to be in better humour; and being inquisitive about my birth, no sooner understood that I was descended of a good family, than he discovered a particular good will to me on that account, deducing his own pedigree in a direct line from the famous Caractacus, king of the Britons, who was first the prisoner and afterwards the friend of Claudius Cæsar. Perceiving how much I was reduced in point of linen, he made me a present of two good ruffled shirts, which, with two more of check which I received from Mr. Thomson, enabled me to appear with decency. Meanwhile the sailor whom Mr. Morgan had sent to the doctor, brought a prescription for his messmate, which, when the Welshman had read, he got up to prepare it, and asked if the man was "Tead or alive." "Dead!" replied Jack, "if he was dead he would have no occasion for doctor's stuff. No, thank God, death han't as yet boarded him, but they have been yard-arm and yard-arm these three glasses." "Are his eyes open?" continued the mate. "His starboard eye," said the sailor, "is open, but fast jammed in his head; and the haulyards of his under jaw have given way.". "Passion of my heart!" cried Morgan, "the man is as pad as one would desire to be! Did you feel his pulses?" To this the other replied with, "Anan?" Upon which this Cambro-Briton, with great earnestness and humanity, ordered the tar to run to his messmate, and keep him alive till he should come with the medicine, "And then," said he, "you shall, perad-venture, pehold what you shall see." The poor fellow, with great simplicity, ran to the place where the sick man lay, but, in less than a minute, returned with a woeful countenance, and told us his comrade had struck. Morgan, hearing this, exclaimed, "Mercy upon my salvation! why did you not stop him till I came?" "Stop him," said the other, "I hailed him several times, but he was too far on his way, and the enemy had got possession of his close quarters; so that he did not mind me." "Well, well," said he, "we all owe Heaven a teath. Go your ways, you ragamuffin, and take an example, and a warning, look you, and repent of your misteets." So saying, he pushed the seaman out of the berth.

While he entertained us with reflections suitable to this event, we heard the boatswain pipe to dinner, and immediately the boy belonging to our mess ran to the locker, from whence he carried off a large wooden platter, and in a few minutes returned with it full of boiled peas, crying, "Scaldings," all the way as he came. The cloth, consisting of a piece of an old sail, was instantly laid, covered with three plates, which, by the colour, I could with difficulty discern to be metal, and as many spoons of the same composition, two of which were curtailed in the handles, and the other abridged in the lip. Mr. Morgan himself enriched this mess with a lump of salt butter, scooped from an old gallipot, and a handful of onions shorn, with some pounded pepper. J was not very much tempted with the appearance of this dish, of which, nevertheless, my messmates ate heartily, advising me to follow their example, as it was banyan-day, and we could have no meat till next noon. But I had already laid in sufficient for the occasion; and therefore desired to be excused, expressing a curiosity to know the meaning of banyan-day.

They told me that on Mondays, Wednesdays, and Fridays, the ship's company had no allowance of meat, and that these meagre days were called banyan-days, the reason of which they did not know; but I have since learned they take their denomination from a sect of devotees in some parts of the East Indies who never taste flesh.

After dinner, Thomson led me round the ship, showed me the different parts, described their uses, and, as far as he could, made me acquainted with the particulars of the discipline and economy practised on board. He then demanded of the boatswain an hammock for me, which was slung in a very neat manner by my friend, Jack Rattlin; and as I had no bed-clothes, procured credit for me with the purser for a mattress and two blankets. At seven o'clock in the evening, Morgan visited the sick, and having ordered what was proper for each, I assisted Thomson in making up his prescriptions: but when I followed him with the medicines into the sick-berth or hospital, and observed the situations of the patients, I was much less surprised that people should die on board, than that any sick person should recover. Here I saw about fifty miserable distempered wretches, suspended in rows, so huddled one upon another, that not more than fourteen inches space was allotted for each with his bed and bedding; and deprived of the light of day, as well as of fresh air; breathing nothing but a noisome atmosphere of the morbid steams exhaling from their own excrements and diseased bodies, devoured with vermin hatched in the filth that surrounded them, and destitute of every convenience necessary for people in that helpless condition.

CHAPTER XXVI

A disagreeable Accident happens to me in the discharge of my Office —Morgan's Nose is offended—A Dialogue between him and the Ship's Steward—Upon examination, I find more causes of Complaint than one —My Hair is cut off—Morgan's Cookery—The Manner of Sleeping on Board —I am waked in the Night by a dreadful Noise.

I COULD not comprehend how it was possible for the attendants to come near those who hung on the inside towards the sides of the ship, in order to assist them, as they seemed barricadoed by those who lay on the outside, and entirely out of the reach of all visitation. Much less could I conceive how my friend Thomson would be able to administer clysters, that were ordered for some in that situation; when I saw him thrust his wig in his pocket, and strip himself to his waistcoat in a moment, then creep on all-fours under the hammocks of the sick, and, forcing up his bare pate between two, keep them asunder with one shoulder, until he had done his duty. Eager to learn the service, I desired he would give me leave to perform the next operation of that kind; and he consenting, I undressed myself after his example, and crawling along, the ship happened to roll; this motion alarming me, I laid hold of the first thing that came within my grasp with such violence, that I overturned it, and soon found by the smell that issued upon me, I had not unlocked a box of the most delicious perfume: it was well for me that my nose was none of the most delicate, else I know not how I might have been affected by this vapour, which diffused itself all over the ship, to the utter discomposure of everybody who tarried on the same deck: neither was the consequence of this disgrace confined to my sense of smelling only; for I felt my misfortunes more ways than one. That I might not, however, appear altogether disconcerted in this my first essay, I got up, and pushing my head with great force between two hammocks, towards the middle, where the greatest resistance was, I made an opening indeed, but, not understanding the knack of dexterously turning my shoulder to maintain my advantage, had the mortification to find myself stuck up as it were in a pillory, and the weight of three or four people bearing on each side of my neck, so that I was in danger of strangulation. While I remained in this defenceless posture, one of the sick men, rendered peevish by his distemper, was so enraged at the smell I had occasioned, and the rude shock he had received from me in my elevation, that, with many bitter reproaches, he seized me by the nose, which he tweaked so unmercifully, that I roared with anguish. Thomson, perceiving my condition, ordered one of the waiters to my assistance, who with much difficulty disengaged me from this situation, and hindered me from taking vengeance of the sick man, whose indisposition would not have screened him from the effects of my indignation.

After having made an end of our ministry for that time, we descended to the cockpit, my friend comforting me for what had happened with a homely proverb, which I do not choose to repeat. When we had descended half-way down the ladder, Mr. Morgan, before he saw us, having intelligence by his nose of the approach of something extraordinary, cried, "Got have mercy upon my senses! I believe the enemy has poarded us in a stink-pot!" Then directing his discourse to the steward, from whom he imagined the odour proceeded, he reprimanded him severely for the freedoms he took among gentlemen of birth, and threat-ened to smoke him like a padger with sulphur, if he ever should presume to offend his neighbours with such smells for the future. The steward, conscious of his own innocence, replied, with some warmth, "I know of no smells but those of your own making." This repartee introduced a smart dialogue, in which the Welsh-man undertook to prove, that though the stench he complained of did not flow from the steward's own body, he was, never-theless, the author of it, by serving out damaged provisions to the ship's company; and in particular, putrefied cheese, from the use of which only, he affirmed, such unsavoury steams could arise. Then he launched out into the praise of good cheese, of which he gave the analysis; he explained the different kinds of that commodity, with the methods practised to make and preserve it; and concluded with observing, that, in yielding good cheese, the county of Glamorgan might vie with Cheshire itself, and was much superior to it in the produce of goats and putter. I gathered from this conversation, that, if I entered in my present pickle, I should be no welcome guest; and therefore desired Mr. Thomson to go before and represent my calamity; at which the first mate expressing some concern, went upon deck immediately, taking his way through the cable-tier, and by the main hatchway, to avoid encountering me, desiring me to clean myself as soon as possible, for he intended to regale himself with a dish of salmagundy and a pipe. Accordingly I set about this disagreeable business, and soon found that I had more causes of complaint than I at first imagined; for I per-ceived some guests had honoured me with their company, whose visit I did not at all think seasonable; neither did they seem inclined to leave me in a hurry, for they were in possession of my chief quarters, where they fed without reserve at the expense of my blood. But considering it would be much easier to extir-pate this ferocious colony in the infancy of their settlement, than after they should be multiplied and naturalised to the soil, I took the advice of my friend, who, to prevent such misfortunes, went always close shaved, and made the boy of our mess cut off my hair, which had been growing since I left the service of Lavement; and the second mate lent me an old bob-wig, to supply the loss of that covering. This affair being ended, and everything adjusted in the best manner my circumstances would permit, the descendant of Caractacus returned, and ordering the boy to bring a piece of salt beef from the brine, cut off a slice and mixed it with an equal quantity of onions, which seasoning with a moderate proportion of pepper and salt, he brought it into a consistence of oil and vinegar. Then tasting the dish, assured us it was the best salmagundy that he had ever made, and recommended it to our palate with such heartiness, that I could not help doing honour to his preparation. But I had no sooner swallowed a mouthful than I thought my entrails were scorched, and endeavoured, with a deluge of small beer, to allay the heat it occasioned. Supper being over, Mr. Morgan having smoked a couple of pipes, and supplied the moisture he had expended with as many cans of flip, of which we all partook, a certain yawning began to admonish me that it was high time to repair by sleep the injury I had suffered from want of rest the preceding night; which being perceived by my companions, whose time of repose was now arrived, they proposed we should turn in, or, in other words, go to bed. Our hammocks, which hung parallel to one another on the outside of the berth, were immediately unlashed, and I beheld my messmates spring with great agility into their respective nests, where they seemed to lie concealed, very much at their ease. But it was some time before I could prevail upon myself to trust my carcass at such a distance from the ground, in a narrow bag, out of which I imagined I should be apt, on the least motion in my sleep, to tumble down at the hazard of breaking my bones. I suffered myself, however, to be persuaded, and, taking a leap to get in, threw myself quite over with such violence that, had I not luckily got hold of Thomson's hammock, I should have pitched upon my head on the other side, and in all likelihood fractured my skull. After some fruitless efforts, I succeeded at last; but the apprehension of the jeopardy in which I believed myself withstood all the attacks of sleep, till towards the morning watch, when, in spite of my fears, I was overpowered with slumber, though I did not long enjoy this comfortable situation; being aroused with a noise so loud and shrill, that I thought the drums of my ears were burst by it; this was followed by a dreadful summons pronounced by a hoarse voice, which I could not understand. While I was debating with myself whether or not I should wake my companion, and inquire into the occasion of this disturbance, I was informed by one of the quarter-masters, who passed by me with a lantern in his hand, that the noise that alarmed me was occasioned by the boatswain's mates, who called up the larboard watch, and that I must lay my account with such interruption every morning at the same hour. Being now more assured of my safety, I addressed myself again to rest, and slept till eight o'clock, when rising, and breakfasting with my comrades on biscuit and brandy, the sick were visited and assisted as before; after which visitation my good friend Thomson explained and performed another piece of duty, to which I was a stranger. At a certain hour in the morning, the boy of the mess went round all the decks, ringing a small hand-bell, and, in rhymes composed for the occasion, invited all those who had sores to repair before the mast, where one of the doctor's mates attended, with applications to dress them.

CHAPTER XXVII

I acquire the friendship of the Surgeon, who procures a Warrant for me, and makes me a present of Clothes—A Battle between a Midshipman and me—The Surgeon leaves the Ship—The Captain comes on board with another Surgeon—A Dialogue between the Captain and Morgan—The Sick are ordered to be brought upon the Quarter-deck and examined—The Consequences of that Order—A Madman accuses Morgan, and is set at Liberty by command of the Captain, whom he instantly attacks and pommels without mercy.

WHILE I was busied with my friend in this practice, the doctor chanced to pass by the place where we were, and, stopping to observe me, appeared very well satisfied with my method of application; and afterwards sent for me to his cabin, where, having examined me touching my skill in surgery, and the particulars of my fortune, he interested himself so far in my behalf as to promise his assistance in procuring a warrant for me, seeing I had been already found qualified at Surgeons' Hall for the station I filled on board; and in this good office he the more cordially engaged, when he understood I was nephew to Lieutenant Bowling, for whom he expressed a particular regard. In the meantime, I could learn from his discourse that he did not intend to go to sea again with Captain Oakum, having, as he thought, been indifferently used by him during the last voyage.

While I lived tolerably easy, in expectation of preferment, I was not altogether without mortifications, which I not only suffered from the rude insults of the sailors and petty officers, among whom I was known by the name of *Loblolly Boy*, but also from the disposition of Morgan, who, though friendly in the main, was often very troublesome with his pride, which expected a good deal of submission from me, and delighted in recapitulating the favours which I had received at his hands.

About six weeks after my arrival on board, the surgeon bidding me follow him into his cabin, presented a warrant to me, by which I was appointed surgeon's third mate on board the *Thunder*. This he had procured by his interest at the Navy Office; as also another for himself, by virtue of which he was removed into a second rate. I acknowledged his kindness in the strongest terms my gratitude could suggest, and professed my sorrow at the prospect of losing so valuable a friend, to whom I hoped to have recommended myself still further by my respectful and diligent behaviour. But his generosity did not stop here; for, before he left the ship, he made me a present of a chest and some clothes, that enabled me to support the rank to which he had raised me. I found my spirit revive with my good fortune; and, now I was an officer, resolved to maintain the dignity of my station against all opposition or affronts. Nor was it long before I had occasion to exert my resolution. My old enemy, the midshipman, whose name was Crampley, entertaining an implacable animosity against me for the disgrace he had suffered on my account, had since that time taken all opportunities of reviling and ridiculing me, when I was not entitled to retort this bad usage. And even after I had been rated on the books and mustered as surgeon's mate, he did not think fit to restrain his insolence. In particular, being one day present while I dressed a wound in a sailor's leg, he began to sing a song which I thought highly injurious to the honour of my country, and therefore signified my resentment by observing, that the Scots always laid their account with finding enemies among the ignorant, insignificant, and malicious. This unexpected piece of assurance enraged him to such a degree, that he lent me a blow on the face, which I verily thought had demolished my cheekbone; I was not slow in returning the obligation, and the affair began to be very serious, when by accident Mr. Morgan and one of the master's mates, coming that way, interposed, and inquiring into the cause, endeavoured to promote a reconciliation; but finding us both exasperated to the uttermost, and bent against accommodation, they advised us either to leave our difference undecided till we should have an opportunity of terminating it on shore, like gentlemen, or else choose a proper place on board, and bring it to an issue by boxing. This last expedient was greedily embraced by us both; and being forthwith conducted to the ground proposed, we stripped in a moment, and began a very furious contest, in which I soon found myself inferior to my antagonist, not so much in strength and agility, as in skill, which he had acquired in the school of Hockley-in-the-Hole and Tottenham Court. Many cross-buttocks did I sustain, and pegs on the stomach without number, till at last my breath being quite gone, as well as my vigour wasted, I grew desperate, and collecting all my strength in one effort, threw in at once, head, hands, and feet, with such violence, that I drove my antagonist three paces backward into the main hatchway, down which he fell, and pitching upon his head and right shoulder, remained without sense and motion. Morgan, looking down and seeing him lie in that condition, cried, "Upon my conscience, as I am a Christian sinner, look you, I believe his pattles are all ofer; but I take you all to witness that there was no treachery in the case, and that he has suffered by the chance of war." So saying, he descended to the deck below, to examine into the situation of my adversary; and left me very little pleased with my victory, as I found myself not only terribly bruised, but likewise in danger of being called to account for the death of Crampley. But this fear vanished when my fellow-mate, having by bleeding him in the jugular brought him to himself, and inquired into the state of his body, called up to me to be under no concern, for the midshipman had received no other damage than as pretty a luxation of the *os humeri* as one would desire to see on a summer's day. Upon this information, I crawled down to the cockpit, and acquainted Thomson with the affair, who, providing himself with bandages, etc., necessary for the occasion, went up to assist Mr. Morgan in the reduction of the dislocation. When this was successfully performed, they wished me joy of the event of the combat; and the Welshman, after observing, that, in all likelihood, the ancient Scots and Britons were the same people, bade me "praise Got for putting mettlo in my pelly, and strength in my limbs to support it." I acquired such reputation by this ren-contre (which lasted twenty minutes), that everybody became more cautious in behaviour towards me; though Crampley, with his arm in a sling, talked very high, and threatened to seize the first opportunity of retrieving on shore the honour he had lost by an accident, from which I could justly claim no merit.

About this time, Captain Oakum, having received sailing

orders, came on board, and brought along with him a surgeon of his own country, who soon made us sensible of the loss we suffered in the departure of Doctor Atkins; for he was grossly ignorant, and intolerably assuming, false, vindictive, and unforgiving; a merciless tyrant to his inferiors, an abject sycophant to those above him. In the morning after the captain came on board, our first mate, according to custom, went to wait on him with a sick-list, which when this grim commander had perused, he cried, with a stern countenance, "Blood and oons! sixty-one sick people on board of my ship! Harkee, you sir, I'll have no sick in my ship, by God." The Welshman replied, he should be very glad to find no sick people on board; but while it was otherwise, he did no more than his duty in presenting him with a list. "You and your list may be damned," said the captain, throwing it at him, "I say, there shall be no sick in this ship while I have the command of her." Mr. Morgan being nettled at this treatment, told him, his indignation ought to be directed to Got Almighty, who visited his people with distempers, and not to him, who contributed all in his power towards their cure. The bashaw not being used to such behaviour in any of his officers, was enraged to fury at this satirical insinuation; and stamping with his foot, called him insolent scoundrel, threatening to have him pinioned to the deck, if he should presume to utter another syllable. But the blood of Caractacus being thoroughly heated, disdained to be restricted by such a command, and began to manifest itself in, "Captain Oagum, I am a shentleman of birth and parentage, look you, and peradventure I am moreover——" Here his harangue was broke off by the captain's steward, who, being Morgan's countryman, hurried him out of the cabin before he had time to exasperate his master to a greater degree: and this would certainly have been the case; for the indignant Welshman could hardly be hindered, by his friend's arguments and entreaties, from re-entering the presence-chamber and defying Captain Oakum to his teeth. He was, however, appeased at length, and came down to the berth, where, finding Thomson and me at work preparing medicines, he bade us leave off our labour and go to play, for the captain, by his sole word and power, and command, had driven sickness a-pegging to the tevil, and there was no more malady on board. So saying, he drank off a gill of brandy, sighed grievously three times, poured forth an ejaculation of "Got pless my heart, liver, and lungs!" and then began to sing a Welsh song with great earnestness of visage, voice and gesture,

I could not conceive the meaning of this singular phenomenon, and saw by the looks of Thomson, who at the same time shook his head, that he suspected poor Cadwallader's brains were unsettled. He perceiving our amazement, told us he would explain the mystery; but at the same time bade us take notice, that he had lived poy, patchelor, married man, and widower almost forty years, and, in all that time, there was no man nor mother's son in the whole world who durst use him so ill as Captain Oagum had done. Then he acquainted us with the dialogue that passed between them, as I have already related it; and had no sooner finished this narration, than he received a message from the surgeon to bring the sick-list to the quarter-deck, for the captain had ordered all the patients thither to be reviewed. This inhuman order shocked us extremely, as we knew it would be impossible to carry some of them on the deck without imminent danger of their lives; but, as we likewise knew it would be to no purpose for us to remonstrate against it, we repaired to the quarter-deck in a body, to see this extraordinary muster; Morgan observing by the way, that the captain was going to send to the other world a great many evidences to testify against himself. When we appeared upon deck, the captain bade the doctor, who stood bowing at his right hand, look at these lazy lubberly sons of bitches, who were good for nothing on board but to eat the king's provision, and encourage idleness in the skulkers. The surgeon grinned approbation, and taking the list, began to examine the complaints of each, as they could crawl to the place appointed. The first who came under his cognisance was a poor fellow just freed of a fever, which had weakened him so much that he could hardly stand. Mr. Mackshane (for that was the doctor's name) having felt his pulse, protested he was as well as any man in the world; and the captain delivered him over to the boatswain's mate, with orders that he should receive a round dozen at the gang-way immediately, for counterfeiting himself sick; but before the discipline could be executed, the man dropped down on the deck, and had well-nigh perished under the hands of the executioner. The next patient to be considered, laboured under a quartan ague, and being then in his interval of health, discovered no other symptoms of distemper than a pale meagre countenance and emaciated body; upon which, he was declared fit for duty, and turned over to the boatswain: but being resolved to disgrace the doctor, died upon the forecastle next day during his cold fit. The third complained of a pleuritic stitch and spitting of blood; for which Doctor Mackshane prescribed exercise at the pump, to promote expectoration: but whether this was improper for one in his situation, or that it was used to excess, I know not; for in less than half an hour he was suffocated with a deluge of blood that issued from his lungs. A fourth, with much difficulty, climbed to the quarter-deck, being loaded with a monstrous ascites or dropsy, that invaded his chest so much, he could scarce fetch his breath; but his disease being interpreted into fat, occasioned by idleness and excess of eating, he was ordered, with a view to promote perspiration, and enlarge his chest, to go aloft immediately: it was in vain for this unwieldy wretch to allege his utter incapacity; the boatswain's driver was commanded to whip him up with a cat-o'-nine-tails: the smart of this application made him exert himself so much, that he actually arrived at the puttock shrouds; but when the enormous weight of his body had nothing else to support it than his weakened arms, either out of spite or necessity, he quitted his hold and plumped into the sea, where he must have been drowned, had not a sailor, who was in a boat alongside, saved his life, by keeping him afloat till he was hoisted on board by a tackle. It would be tedious and disagreeable to describe the fate of every miserable object that suffered by the inhumanity and ignorance of the captain and surgeon, who so wantonly sacrificed the lives of their fellow-creatures. Many were brought up in the height of fevers, and rendered delirious by the injuries they received in the way. Some gave up the ghost in the presence of their inspectors; and others, who were ordered to their duty, languished a few days at work among their fellows, and then departed without any ceremony. On the whole, the number of the sick was reduced to less than a dozen; and the authors of this reduction were applauding themselves for the services they had done to their king and country, when the boatswain's mate informed his honour that there was a man below lashed to his hammock by the direction of the doctor's mate, and that he begged hard to be released; affirming he had been so maltreated only for a grudge Mr. Morgan bore him, and that he was as much in his senses as any man aboard. The captain hearing this, darted a severe look at the Welshman, and ordered the man to be brought up immediately: upon which Morgan protested with great fervency, that the person in question was as mad as a March hare; and begged, for the love of Got, they would at least keep his arms pinioned during his examination, to prevent him from doing mischief. This request the commander granted for his own sake, and the patient was produced, who insisted upon his being in his right wits with such calmness and strength of argument, that everybody present was inclined to believe him, except Morgan, who affirmed there was no trusting to appearances; for he himself had been so much imposed upon by his behaviour two days before, that he had actually unbound him with his own hands, and had well-nigh been murdered for his pains. This was confirmed by the evidence of one of the waiters, who declared he had pulled this patient from the doctor's mate, whom he had gotten down and almost strangled. To this the man answered, that the witness was a creature of Morgan's, and was suborned to give his testimony against him by the malice of the mate, whom the defendant had affronted, by discovering to the people on board that Mr. Morgan's wife kept a gin-shop in Rag Fair. This anecdote produced a laugh at the expense of the Welshman, who, shaking his head with some emotion, said, "Ay, ay, 'tis no matter. Got knows, it is an arrant falsehood." Captain Oakum, without any further hesitation, ordered the fellow to be unfettered; at the same time threatening to make Morgan exchange situations with him for his spite. But the Briton no sooner heard the decision in favour of the madman, than he got up the mizen shrouds, crying to Thomson and me to get out of his reach, for we would see him play the devil with a vengeance. We did not think fit to disregard his caution, and accordingly got up on the poop, whence we beheld the maniac, as soon as he was released, fly at the captain like a fury, crying, "I'll let you know, you scoundrel, that I am commander of this vessel," and pommel him without mercy. The surgeon, who went to the assistance of his patron, shared the same fate; and it was with the utmost difficulty that he was mastered at last, after having done great execution among those who opposed him.

CHAPTER XXVIII

The Captain, enraged, threatens to put the Madman to death with his own Hand—Is diverted from that Resolution by the Arguments and Persuasions of the First Lieutenant and Surgeon—We set sail for St. Helen's, join the Fleet under the command of Sir C——n——r O——le, and proceed for the West Indies—Are overtaken by a terrible Tempest—My friend Jack Rattlin has his Leg broke by a Fall from the Main-yard —The Behaviour of Dr. Mackshane—Jack opposes the Amputation of his Limb, in which he is seconded by Morgan and me, who undertake the Cure, and perform it successfully.

THE captain was carried into his cabin, so enraged with the treatment he had received, that he ordered the fellow to be brought before him, that he might have the pleasure of pistolling him with his own hand; and would certainly have satisfied his revenge in this manner, had not the first lieutenant remonstrated against it, by observing, that, in all appearance, the fellow was not mad but desperate; that he had been hired by some enemy of the captain to assassinate him, and therefore ought to be kept in irons till he could be brought to a courtmartial, which, no doubt, would sift the affair to the bottom, by which means important discoveries might be made, and then sentence the criminal to a death adequate to his demerits. This suggestion, improbable as it was, had the desired effect upon the captain, being exactly calculated for the meridian of his intellects; more especially as Dr. Mackshane espoused this opinion, in consequence of his previous declaration that the man was not mad. Morgan finding there was no more damage done, could not help discovering, by his countenance, the pleasure he enjoyed on this occasion; and while he bathed the doctor's face with an embrocation, ventured to ask him whether he thought there were more fools or madmen on board? But he would have been wiser in containing this sally, which his patient carefully laid up in his memory, to be taken notice of at a more fit season. Meanwhile, we weighed anchor, and on our way to the Downs, the madman, who was treated as a prisoner, took an opportunity while the sentinel attended him at the head, to leap overboard, and frustrate the revenge of the captain. We staid not long at the Downs, but took the benefit of the first easterly wind to go round to Spithead; where having received on board provisions for six months, we sailed from St. Helen's in the grand fleet bound for the West Indies, on the ever-memorable expedition of Carthagena.

It was not without great mortification I saw myself on the

point of being transported to such a distant and unhealthy climate, destitute of every convenience that could render such a voyage supportable; and under the dominion of an arbitrary tyrant, whose command was almost intolerable. However, as these complaints were common to a great many on board, I resolved to submit patiently to my fate, and contrive to make myself as easy as the nature of the case would allow. We got out of the Channel with a prosperous breeze, which died away, leaving us becalmed about fifty leagues to the westward of the Lizard. But this state of inaction did not last long; for next night our maintop sail was split by the wind, which in the morning increased to a hurricane. I was wakened by a most horrible din, occasioned by the play of the gun carriages upon the deck above, the cracking of cabins, the howling of the wind through the shrouds, the confused noise of the ship's crew, the pipes of the boatswain and his mates, the trumpets of the lieutenants, and the clanking of the chain pumps. Morgan, who had never been at sea before, turned out in a great hurry, crying, "Got have mercy and compassion upon us! I believe we have got upon the confines of Lucifer and the damned!" while poor Thomson lay quaking in his hammock, putting up petitions to Heaven for our safety. I rose and joined the Welshman, with whom (after having fortified ourselves with brandy) I went above; but, if my sense of hearing was startled before, how must my sight have been appalled in beholding the effects of the storm! The sea was swelled into billows mountain high, on the top of which our ship sometimes hung as if it was about to be precipitated to the abyss below! Sometimes we sunk between two waves that rose on each side higher than our topmast head, and threatened, by dashing together, to overwhelm us in a moment! Of all our fleet, consisting of a hundred and fifty sail, scarce twelve appeared, and these driving under their bare poles, at the mercy of the tempest. At length the mast of one of them gave way, and tumbled overboard with a hideous crash! Nor was the prospect in our own ship much more agreeable; a number of officers and sailors ran backward and forward with distraction in their looks, hallooing to one another, and undetermined what they should attend to first. Some clung to the yards, endeavouring to unbend the sails that were split into a thousand pieces flapping in the wind; others tried to furl those which were yet whole, while the masts, at every pitch, bent and quivered like twigs, as if they would have shivered into innumerable splinters! While I considered this scene with equal terror and astonishment, one of the main braces broke, by the shock whereof two sailors were flung from the yard's arm into the sea, where they perished, and poor Jack Rattlin was thrown down upon the deck at the expense of a broken leg. Morgan and I ran immediately to his assistance, and found a splinter of the shinbone thrust by the violence of the fall through the skin. As this was a case of too great consequence to be treated without the authority of the doctor, I went down to his cabin to inform him of the accident, as well as to bring up dressings, which we always kept ready prepared. I entered his apartment without any ceremony, and by the glimmering of a lamp, perceived him on his knees, before something that very much resembled a crucifix; but this I will not insist upon, that I may not seem too much a slave to common report, which indeed assisted my conjecture on this occasion, by representing Dr. Mackshane as a member of the Church of Rome. Be this as it will, he got up in a sort of confusion, occasioned, I suppose, by his being disturbed in his devotion, and, in a trice, snatched the subject of my suspicion from my sight.

After making an apology for my intrusion, I acquainted him with the situation of Rattlin, but could by no means prevail upon him to visit him on deck, where he lay. He bade me desire the boatswain to order some of the men to carry him down to the cockpit, and in the meantime, said he, I will direct Thomson to get ready the dressings. When I signified to the boatswain the doctor's desire, he swore a terrible oath, that he could not spare one man from the deck, because he expected the mast would go by the board every minute. This piece of information did not at all contribute to my peace of mind; however, as my friend Rattlin complained very much, with the assistance of Morgan, I supported him to the lower deck, whither Mr. Mackshane, after much entreaty, ventured to come, attended by Thomson, with a box full of dressings, and his own servant, who carried a whole set of capital instruments. He examined the fracture and the wound, and concluding, from a livid colour extending itself upon the limb, that a mortification would ensue, resolved to amputate the leg immediately. This was a dreadful sentence to the patient, who, recruiting himself with a quid of tobacco, pronounced, with a woeful countenance, "What! is there no remedy, doctor?—must I be dock'd?—can't you splice it?" "Assuredly, Doctor Mackshane," said the first mate, "with submission, and deference, and veneration to your superior abilities, and opportunities, and stations, look you, I do appre-

hend, and conjecture, and aver, that there is no occasion nor
necessity to smite off this poor man's leg." "God Almighty
bless you, dear Welshman!" cried Rattlin, "may you have fair
wind and weather wheresoever you're bound, and come to an
anchor in the Road of Heaven at last." Mackshane, very much
incensed at his mate's differing in opinion from him so openly,
answered, that he was not bound to give an account of his
practice to him; and, in a peremptory tone, ordered him to
apply the tourniquet; at the sight of which, Jack, starting up,
cried, "Avast, avast! damn my heart, if you clap your nippers
on me, till I know wherefore! Mr. Random, won't you lend a
hand towards saving my precious limb? Odds heart, if Lieutenant Bowling was here, he would not suffer Jack Rattlin's
leg to be chopped off like a piece of old junk." This pathetic
address to me, joined to my inclination to serve my honest
friend, and the reasons I had to believe there was no danger in
delaying the amputation, induced me to declare myself of the
first mate's opinion, and affirm that the preternatural colour
of the skin was owing to an inflammation occasioned by a
contusion, and common in all such cases, without any indication
of an approaching gangrene. Morgan, who had a great opinion
of my skill, manifestly exulted in my fellowship, and asked
Thomson's sentiments of the matter, in hopes of strengthening
our association with him too; but he, being of a meek disposition,
and either dreading the enmity of the surgeon, or speaking the
dictates of his own judgment, in a modest manner, espoused
the opinion of Mackshane, who, by this time, having consulted
with himself, determined to act in such a manner as to screen
himself from censure, and at the same time revenge himself
on us for our arrogance in contradicting him. With this view
he asked if we would undertake to cure the leg at our peril—
that is, be answerable for the consequence. To this question
Morgan replied, that the lives of his creatures are in the hands
of Got alone; and it would be great presumption in him to
undertake for an event that was in the power of his Maker, no
more than the doctor could promise to cure all the sick to whom
he administered his assistance; but if the patient would put
himself under our direction, we would do our endeavour to bring
his distemper to a favourable issue, to which, at present, we
saw no obstruction. I signified my concurrence; and Rattlin
was so overjoyed, that, shaking us both by the hands, he swore
nobody else should touch him, and if he died, his blood should
be upon his own head. Mr. Mackshane, flattering himself with

the prospect of our miscarriage, went away, and left us to manage it as we should think proper. Accordingly, having sawed off part of the splinter that stuck through the skin, we reduced the fracture, dressed the wound, applied the eighteen-tailed bandage, and put the leg in a box, *secundum artem*. Everything succeeded according to our wish, and we had the satisfaction of not only preserving the poor fellow's leg, but likewise of rendering the doctor contemptible among the ship's company, who had all their eyes on us during the course of this cure, which was completed in six weeks.

CHAPTER XXIX

Mackshane's Malice—I am taken up and imprisoned for a Spy—Morgan meets with the same Fate—Thomson is tampered with to turn Evidence against us—Disdains the Proposal, and is maltreated for his Integrity—Morgan is released to assist the Surgeon during an Engagement with some French Ships of War—I remain fettered on the Poop, exposed to the Enemy's Shot, and grow delirious with Fear—Am comforted after the Battle by Morgan, who speaks freely of the Captain—Is overheard by the Sentinel, who informs against him, and again imprisoned—Thomson grows desperate, and, notwithstanding the Remonstrances of Morgan and me, goes overboard in the Night.

IN the meantime, the storm subsided into a brisk gale, that carried us into the warm latitudes, where the weather became intolerable, and the crew very sickly. The doctor left nothing unattempted towards the completion of his vengeance against the Welshman and me. He went among the sick, under pretence of inquiring into their grievances, with a view of picking up complaints to our prejudice; but finding himself frustrated in that expectation, by the good will we had procured from the patients by our diligence and humanity, he took the resolution of listening to our conversation, by hiding himself behind the canvas that surrounded our berth. Here, too, he was detected by the boy of our mess, who acquainted us with this piece of behaviour; and one night, while we were picking a large bone of salt beef, Morgan discerned something stir on the outside of our hangings, which immediately interpreting to be the doctor, he tipt me the wink, and pointed to the place, where I could perceive somebody standing; upon which I snatched up the bone, and levelled it with all my force at him, saying, "Whoever you are, take that for your curiosity." It had the desired effect, for we heard the listener tumble down, and afterwards crawl to his own cabin. I applauded myself much for this feat, which turned out one of the most unlucky exploits of my life, Mack-shane from that time marking me out for destruction. About a week after this exploit, as I was going my rounds among the sick, I was taken prisoner, and carried to the poop by the master-at-arms, where I was loaded with irons and stapled to the deck, on pretence that I was a spy on board, and had con-spired against the captain's life. How ridiculous soever this imputation was, I did not fail to suffer by it all the rigour that could be shown to the worst of criminals, being exposed in this miserable condition to the scorching heat of the sun by day, and the unwholesome damps by night, during the space of twelve days, in which I was neither brought to trial, nor examined touching the probability of the charge. I had no sooner recovered the use of my reflection, which had been quite overthrown by this accident, than I sent for Thomson, who, after condoling me on the occasion, hinted that I owed this misfortune to the hatred of the doctor, who had given an information against me to the captain, in consequence of which I was arrested, and all my papers seized. While I was cursing my capricious fate, I saw Morgan ascend the poop, guarded by two corporals, who made him sit down by me, that he might be pinioned in the same machine. Notwithstanding my situation, I could scarce refrain from laughing at the countenance of my fellow-prisoner, who, without speaking one word, allowed his feet to be enclosed in the rings provided for that purpose; but when they pretended to fasten him on his back, he grew outrageous, and drawing a large couteau from his side-pocket, threatened to rip up the belly of the first man that should approach him, in order to treat him in such an unworthy manner. They were preparing to use him very roughly, when the lieutenant on the quarter-deck called up to them to let him remain as he was. He then crept towards me, and taking me by the hand, bade me "put my trust in Got"; and looking at Thomson, who sat by us trembling, with a pale visage, told him there were two more rings for his feet, and he should be glad to find him in such good company. But it was not the intention of our adversary to include the second mate in our fate; him he excepted, to be his drudge in attending the sick, and, if possible, his evidence against us. With this view, he sounded him afar off, but finding his integrity incorruptible, harassed him so much out of spite, that, in a short time, this mild creature grew weary of his life. While I and my fellow-prisoner comforted each other in our tribulation, the admiral discovered four sail to leeward, and made signal for our ship and four more to chase: hereupon everything was cleared for an engagement; and Mackshane, foreseeing he should have occasion for more assistants than one, obtained Morgan's liberty; while I was left in this deplorable posture to the chance of battle. It was almost dark when we came up with the sternmost chase, which we hailed, and inquired who they were: they gave us to understand they were Frenchmen of war; upon which Captain Oakum commanded them to send their boat on board of him; but they refused, telling him, if he had any business with them, to come on board of their ship: he then threatened to pour in a broadside upon them, which they promised to return. Both sides were as good as their word; and the engagement began with great fury. The reader may guess how I passed my time, lying in this helpless situation, amidst the terrors of a sea-fight; expecting every moment to be cut asunder, or dashed in pieces by the enemy's shot! I endeavoured to compose myself as much as possible, by reflecting that I was not a whit more exposed than those who were stationed about me; but when I beheld them employed without intermission in annoying the foe, and encouraged by the society and behaviour of one another, I could easily perceive a wide difference between their condition and mine: however, I concealed my agitation as well as I could, till the head of the officer of the marines, who stood near me, being shot off, bounced from the deck athwart my face, leaving me well-nigh blinded with brains. I could contain myself no longer, but began to bellow with all the strength of my lungs: when a drummer coming towards me, asked if I was wounded? and before I could answer, received a great shot in his belly, which tore out his entrails, and he fell flat on my breast. This accident entirely bereft me of all discretion: I redoubled my cries, which were drowned in the noise of the battle; and finding myself disregarded, lost all patience and became frantic: I vented my rage in oaths and execrations, till my spirits being quite exhausted, I remained quiet and insensible of the load that oppressed me. The engagement lasted till broad day, when Captain Oakum, finding that he was like to gain neither honour nor advantage by the affair, pretended to be undeceived by seeing their colours; and hailing the ship with whom he had fought all night, protested he believed them Spaniards, and the guns being silenced on each side, ordered the barge to be hoisted out, and went on board the French commodore. Our loss amounted to ten killed and eighteen wounded, most part of whom afterwards died. My fellow-mates had no sooner despatched their business in the cockpit, than, full of friendly concern, they came to visit me. Morgan ascending first, and seeing my face almost covered with brains and blood, concluded I was no longer a man for this world; and calling to Thomson with great emotion, bade him come up and take his last farewell of his comrade and countryman, who was posting to a better place, where there were no Mackshanes nor Oakums to asperse and torment him. "No," said he, taking me by the hand, "you are going to a country where there is more respect shown to unfortunate shentlemen, and where you will have the satisfaction of peholding your adversaries tossing upon pillows of purning primstone." Thomson, alarmed at this apostrophe, made haste to the place where I lay, and sitting down by me, with tears in his eyes, inquired into the nature of my calamity. By this time I had recollected myself so far as to be able to converse rationally with my friends, whom, to their great satisfaction, I immediately undeceived with regard to their apprehension of my being mortally wounded. After I had got myself disengaged from the carnage in which I wallowed, and partaken of a refreshment which my friends brought along with them, we entered into discourse upon the hardships we sustained, and spoke very freely of the authors of our misery: but our discourse being overheard by the sentinel who guarded me, he was no sooner relieved, than he reported to the captain every syllable of our conversation, according to the orders he received. The effect of this information soon appeared in the arrival of the master-at-arms, who replaced Morgan in his former station; and gave the second mate a caution to keep a strict guard over his tongue, if he did not choose to accompany us in our confinement. Thomson, foreseeing that the whole slavery of attending the sick and wounded, as well as the cruelty of Mackshane, must now fall upon his shoulders, grew desperate at the prospect, and, though I never heard him swear before, imprecated dreadful curses on the heads of his oppressors, declaring that he would rather quit life altogether, than be much longer under the power of such barbarians. I was not a little startled at his vivacity, and endeavoured to alleviate his complaints, by representing the subject of my own, with as much aggravation as it would bear, by which comparison he might see the balance of misfortune lay on my side, and take an example from me of fortitude and submission, till such time as we could procure redress, which, I hoped, was not far off, considering that we should probably be in a harbour in less than three days, where we should have an opportunity of preferring our complaints to the admiral. The Welshman joined in my remonstrance, and was at great pains to demonstrate that it was every man's duty, as well as interest, to resign himself to the divine will, and look upon himself as a sentinel upon duty, who is by no means at liberty to leave his post before he is relieved. Thomson listened attentively to what we said, and at last, shedding a flood of tears, shook his head, and left us without making any reply. About eleven at night he came to see us again, with a settled gloom on his countenance, and gave us to understand that he had undergone excessive toil since he saw us, and in recompense had been grossly abused by the doctor, who taxed him with being confederate with us, in a design of taking away his life, and that of the captain. After some time spent in mutual exhortation, he got up, and squeezing me by the hand, with an uncommon fervour, cried, "God bless you both"; and left us to wonder at his singular manner of parting with us, which did not fail to make a deep impression on us.

Next morning when the hour of visitation came round, this unhappy young man was missing, and, after strict search, supposed to have gone overboard in the night; and this was certainly the case.

CHAPTER XXX

We lament the Fate of our Companion—The Captain offers Morgan his Liberty, which he refuses to accept—We are brought before him and examined—Morgan is sent back into Custody, whither also I am remanded, after a curious Trial.

THE news of this event affected my fellow-prisoner and me extremely, as our unfortunate companion had justly acquired, by his amiable disposition, the love and esteem of us both; and the more we regretted his untimely fate, the greater horror we conceived for the villain who was undoubtedly the occasion of it. This abandoned miscreant did not discover the least symptom of concern for Thomson's death, although he must have been conscious to himself of having driven him by ill-usage to that fatal resolution; but desired the captain to set Morgan at liberty again, to look after the patients. Accordingly, one of the corporals was sent up to unfetter him; but he protested he would not be

eleased until he should know for what he was confined; nor
would he be a tennis-ball, nor a shuttlecock, nor a drudge, nor
scullion, to any captain under the sun. Oakum, finding him
obstinate, and fearing it would not be in his power to exercise
his tyranny much longer with impunity, was willing to show
some appearance of justice, and therefore ordered us both to be
brought before him on the quarter-deck, where he sat in state,
with his clerk on one side, and his counsellor Mackshane on the
other. When we approached, he honoured us with this salutation:
"So, gentlemen, damn my blood! many a captain in the navy
would have ordered you both to be tucked up to the yard's
arm, without either judge or jury, for the crimes you have been
guilty of; but, damn my blood! I have too much good nature,
in allowing such dogs as you to make your defence." "Captain
Oakum," said my fellow-sufferer, "certainly it is in your power
(Got help the while) to tuck us all up at your will, and desire,
and pleasures. And perhaps it would be petter for some of us
to be tucked up, than undergo the miseries to which we have
been exposed. So may the farmer hang his kids for his diversion,
and amusement, and mirth; but there is such a thing as justice,
if not upon earth, surely in heaven, that will punish with fire
and primstone all those who take away the lives of innocent
people out of wantonness and parparity, look you. In the meantime, I shall be glad to know the crimes laid to my charge, and
see the person who accuses me." "That you shall," said the
captain; "here, doctor, what have you to say?" Mackshane
stepping forward, hemmed a good while, in order to clear his
throat, and, before he began, Morgan accosted him thus:
"Doctor Mackshane, look in my face—look in the face of an
honest man, who abhors a false witness as he abhors the tevil,
and Got be judge between you and me." The doctor, not minding
his conjuration, made the following speech, as near as I can
remember: "I'll tell you what, Mr. Morgan, to be sure what
you say is just, in regard to an honest man, and if so be it
appears as how you are an honest man, then it is my opinion
that you deserve to be acquitted, in relation to that there affair;
or I tell you what, Captain Oakum is resolved for to do everybody justice. As for my own part, all that I have to allege is,
that I have been informed you have spoken disrespectful words
against your captain, who, to be sure, is the most honourable
and generous commander in the king's service, without disparagement or exception of man, woman, or child." Having
uttered this elegant harangue, on which he seemed to plume

himself, Morgan replied, "I do partly guess, and conceive, ar
understand your meaning, which I wish could be more explici
but, however, I do suppose I am not to be condemned upo
bare hearsay; or if I am convicted of speaking disrespectful
of Captain Oakum, I hope there is no treason in my words
"But there's mutiny, by God, and that's death by the articl
of war," cried Oakum. "In the meantime let the witnesses I
called." Hereupon Mackshane's servant appeared, and the bo
of our mess, whom they had seduced and tutored for the purpos
The first declared that Morgan, as he descended the cockp
ladder one day, cursed the captain, and called him a sava,
beast, saying he ought to be hunted down as an enemy
mankind. "This," said the clerk, "is a strong presumption of
design formed against the captain's life. For why? It presuppos
malice aforethought, and a criminal intention *a priori*." "Right
said the captain to this miserable grub, who had been a
attorney's boy, "you shall have law enough; here's Cook ar
Littlejohn for it." This evidence was confirmed by the bo
who affirmed he heard the first mate say that the captain ha
no more bowels than a bear, and the surgeon had no more brai
than an ass. Then the sentinel, who heard our discourse on th
poop, was examined, and informed the court that the Welshma
assured me, Captain Oakum and Doctor Mackshane would to
upon billows of burning brimstone in hell for their barbarit
The clerk observed that there was an evident prejudicatic
which confirmed the former suspicion of a conspiracy again
the life of Captain Oakum; for, because, how would Morgan s
positively pronounce that the captain and surgeon would I
damned, unless he had an intention to make away with the:
before they could have time to repent? This sage explanatic
had great weight with our noble commander, who exclaime
"What have you to say to this, Taffy? you seem to be taken a
aback, brother, ha!" Morgan was too much of a gentleman t
disown the text, although he absolutely denied the truth
the comment. Upon which the captain, strutting up to hir
with a ferocious countenance, said, "So, Mr. Son of a b—l
you confess you honoured me with the names of bear and beas
and pronounced my damnation? Damn my heart! I have a goo
mind to have you brought to a court-martial, and hanged, yo
dog." Here Mackshane, having occasion for an assistant, inte
posed, and begged the captain to pardon Mr. Morgan, with h
wonted goodness, upon condition that he, the delinquent, shou
make such submission as the nature of the misdemeanou

emanded. Upon which the Cambro-Briton, who on this occasion would have made no submission to the Great Mogul, surrounded with his guards, thanked the doctor for his mediation, and acknowledged himself in the wrong for calling the image of God a peast. "But," said he, "I spoke by metaphor, and parable, and comparison, and types; as we signify meekness by a lamb, lechery by a goat, and craftiness by a fox, so we liken ignorance to an ass, and brutality to a bear, and fury to a tiger; therefore I made use of these similes to express my sentiments, look you, and what I said before Got, I will not unsay before man or peast neither." Oakum was so provoked at this insolence, as he termed it, that he ordered him forthwith to be carried to the place of his confinement, and his clerk to proceed on the examination of me. The first question put to me was touching the place of my nativity, which I declared to be the north of Scotland. The north of Ireland, more like," cried the captain; "but we shall bring you up presently." He then asked what religion I professed; and when I answered, "The Protestant," swore I was as arrant a Roman as ever went to mass. "Come, come, clerk," continued he, "catechise him a little on this subject." But before I relate the particulars of the clerk's inquiries, it will not be amiss to inform the reader that our commander himself was an Hibernian, and, if not shrewdly belied, a Roman Catholic to boot. "You say you are a Protestant," said the clerk; "make the sign of the cross with your fingers—so; and swear upon it to that affirmation." When I was about to perform this ceremony, the captain cried, with some emotion, "No, no, damme! I'll have no profanation, neither. But go on with your interrogations." "Well, then," proceeded my examiner, "how many sacraments are there?" To which I replied, "Two." "What are they?" said he. I answered, "Baptism and the Lord's Supper." "And so you would explode confirmation and marriage altogether?" said Oakum; "I thought this fellow was a rank Roman." The clerk, though he was bred under an attorney, could not refrain from blushing at this blunder, which he endeavoured to conceal by observing, that these decoys would not do with me, who seemed to be an old offender. He went on with asking if I believed in transubstantiation; but I treated the notion of a real presence with such disrespect, that his patron was scandalised at my impiety, and commanded him to proceed to the plot. Whereupon this miserable pettifogger told me, there was great reason to suspect me of being a spy on board; and that I had entered into a conspiracy with Thomson,

and others not yet detected, against the life of Captain Oakum,
which accusation they pretended to support by the evidence of
our boy, who declared he had often heard the deceased Thomson
and me whispering together, and could distinguish the words
"Oakum, rascal, poison, pistol." By which expressions it
appeared we did intend to use sinister means to accomplish his
destruction; that the death of Thomson seemed to confirm this
conjecture; who, either feeling the stings of remorse, for being
engaged in such a horrid confederacy or fearing a discovery, by
which he must have infallibly suffered an ignominious death,
had put a fatal period to his own existence. But what established
the truth of the whole was a book in ciphers, found among my
papers, which exactly tallied with one found in his chest, after
his disappearance. This, he observed, was a presumption very
near proof positive, and would determine any jury in Christendom to find me guilty. In my own defence, I alleged that I had
been dragged on board at first very much against my inclination,
as I could prove by the evidence of some people now in the ship;
consequently could have no design of becoming spy at the time,
and ever since had been entirely out of the reach of any correspondence that could justly entail that suspicion upon me. As
for conspiring against my captain's life, it could not be supposed
that any man in his right wits would harbour the least thought
of such an undertaking, which he could not possibly perform
without certain infamy and ruin to himself, even if he had
all the inclination in the world. That, allowing the boy's evidence
to be true (which I affirmed was false and malicious), nothing
conclusive could be gathered from a few incoherent words.
Neither was the fate of Mr. Thomson a circumstance more
favourable for the charge; for I had in my pocket a letter which
too well explained that mystery, in a very different manner from
that which was supposed. With these words I produced the
following letter, which Jack Rattlin brought to me the very day
after Thomson disappeared; and told me it was committed to
his care by the deceased, who made him promise not to deliver
it sooner. The clerk, taking it out of my hand, read aloud the
contents, which were these:

"DEAR FRIEND,—I am so much oppressed with the fatigue
I daily and nightly undergo, and the barbarous usage of Doctor
Mackshane, who is bent on your destruction, as well as mine,
that I am resolved to free myself from this miserable life, and
before you receive this, shall be no more. I could have wished

to die in your good opinion, which I am afraid I shall forfeit
by the last act of my life; but if you cannot acquit me, I know
you will at least preserve some regard for the memory of an
unfortunate young man who loved you. I recommend it to you
to beware of Mackshane, whose revenge is implacable. I wish
all prosperity to you and Mr. Morgan, to whom pray offer
my last respects, and beg to be remembered as your unhappy
friend and countryman,

"WILLIAM THOMSON."

This letter was no sooner read, than Mackshane, in a transport
of rage, snatched it out of the clerk's hands and tore it into a
thousand pieces, saying it was a villainous forgery, contrived
and executed by myself. The captain and clerk declared themselves of the same opinion, although I insisted on having the
remains of it compared with other writings of Thomson, which
they had in their possession; and I was ordered to answer the
last article of my accusation, namely, the book of ciphers found
among my papers. "That is easily done," said I; "what you are
pleased to call ciphers, are no other than the Greek characters,
in which, for my amusement, I kept a diary of everything
remarkable that has occurred to my observation, since the
beginning of the voyage till the day on which I was put in irons;
and the same method was practised by Mr. Thomson, who
copied mine." "A very likely story!" cried Mackshane; "what
occasion was there for using Greek characters, if you were not
afraid of discovering what you had wrote? But what d'ye talk
of Greek characters? D'ye think I am so ignorant of the Greek
language, as not to distinguish its letters from these, which are
no more Greek than Chinese? No, no, I will not give up my
knowledge of the Greek for you, nor none that ever came from
your country." So saying, with an unparalleled effrontery, he
repeated some gibberish, which by the sound seemed to be
Irish, and made it pass for Greek with the captain, who, looking
at me with a contemptuous sneer, exclaimed, "Ah! ah! have you
caught a tartar?" I could not help smiling at the consummate
assurance of this Hibernian, and offered to refer the dispute to
anybody on board who understood the Greek alphabet. Upon
which Morgan was brought back, and being made acquainted
with the affair, took the book and read a whole page in English
without hesitation, deciding the controversy in my favour. The
doctor was so far from being out of countenance at this detection,
that he affirmed Morgan was in the secret, and repeated from

his own invention. Oakum said, "Ay, ay, I see they are both in a story"; and dismissed my fellow-mate to his cock-loft, although I proposed that he and I should read and translate separately any chapter or verse in the Greek Testament in his possession by which it would appear whether we or the surgeon spoke truth. Not being endued with eloquence enough to convince the captain that there could be no juggle nor confederacy in this expedient, I begged to be examined by some unconcerned person on board who understood Greek. Accordingly the whole ship's company, officers, and all, were called upon deck, among whom it was proclaimed, that if any of them could speak Greek, he or they so qualified should ascend the quarter-deck immediately. After some pause, two foremast men came up and professed their skill in that language, which, they said, they acquired during several voyages to the Levant, among the Greeks of the Morea. The captain exulted much in this declaration, and put my journal-book into the hands of one of them, who candidly owned he could neither read nor write: the other acknowledged the same degree of ignorance, but pretended to speak the Greek lingo with any man on board; and addressing himself to me pronounced some sentences of a barbarous corrupted language which I did not understand. I asserted that the modern Greek was as different from that spoken and written by the ancients as the English used now from the old Saxon spoke in the time of Hengist; and as I had only learned the true original tongue in which Homer, Pindar, the Evangelists, and other great men of antiquity wrote, it could not be supposed that I should know anything of an imperfect Gothic dialect that rose on the ruin of the former, and scarce retained any traces of the old expression. But if Doctor Mackshane, who pretended to be master of the Greek language, could maintain a conversation with these seamen, I would retract what I had said, and be content to suffer any punishment he should think proper to inflict. I had no sooner uttered these words, than the surgeon, knowing one of these fellows to be his countryman, accosted him in Irish, and was answered in the same brogue; then a dialogue ensued between them, which they affirmed to be in Greek, after having secured the secrecy of the other tar, who had his cue in the language of the Morea from his companion, before they could venture to assert such an intrepid falsehood. "I thought," said Oakum, "we should discover the imposture at last. Let the rascal be carried back to his confinement. I find he must dangle." Having nothing further to urge in my own behalf, before a

ourt so prejudiced with spite, and fortified with ignorance
against truth, I suffered myself to be re-conducted peaceably
to my fellow-prisoner, who hearing the particulars of my trial,
lifted up his hands and eyes to heaven, and uttered a dreadful
groan; and not daring to disburden his thoughts to me by
speech, lest he might be overheard by the sentinel, burst forth
into a Welsh song, which he accompanied with a thousand
contortions of face, and violent gestures of body.

CHAPTER XXXI

I discover a Subornation against me, by means of a Quarrel between
two of the Evidences; in consequence of which I am set at Liberty, and
prevail upon Morgan to accept of his Freedom on the same Terms—
Mackshane's Malice—We arrive at Jamaica, from whence, in a short
time, we beat up to Hispaniola, in conjunction with the West India
Squadron—We take in Water, sail again, and arrive at Carthagena—
Reflections on our Conduct there.

MEANWHILE, a quarrel happened between the two modern
Greeks; the one, to be revenged of the other, came and discovered
to us the mystery of Mackshane's dialogue, as I have explained
it above. This detection coming to the ears of the doctor, who
was sensible that, now we were in sight of Jamaica, we should
have an opportunity of clearing ourselves before a court-martial,
and, at the same time, of making his malice and ignorance
conspicuous, he interceded for us with the captain so effectually,
that, in a few hours, we were set at liberty, and ordered to
return to our duty. This was a happy event for me, my whole
body being blistered by the sun, and my limbs benumbed by
want of motion. But I could scarce persuade the Welshman to
accept of this indulgence, he persisting in his obstinacy to
remain in irons until he should be discharged by a court-martial,
which he believed would also do him justice on his enemies.
At length I represented to him the precarious issue of a trial,
the power and interest of his adversaries, and flattered his
revenge with the hope of wreaking his resentment with his own
hands upon Mackshane after our return to England. This last
argument had more weight with him than all the rest, and
prevailed upon him to repair with me to the cockpit, which I
no sooner entered than the idea of my departed friend presented
itself to my remembrance, and filled my eyes with tears. We
discharged from our mess the boy who acted so perfidiously,
notwithstanding his tears, entreaties, and professions of

penitence for what he had done; but not before he had confessed that the surgeon had bribed him to give evidence against us with a pair of stockings and a couple of old check shirts, of which his servant had since plundered him.

The keys of our chests and lockers being sent to us by the doctor, we detained the messenger until we had examined the contents; and my fellow-mate finding all his Cheshire cheese consumed to a crust, his brandy exhausted, and his onions gone, was seized with a fit of choler, which he discharged on Mackshane's man in oaths and execrations, threatening to prosecute him as a thief. The fellow swore in his turn that he never had the keys in his possession till that time, when he received them from his master, with orders to deliver them to us. "As Got is my judge," cried Morgan, "and my salfation, and my witness, whosoever has pilfered my provisions, is a lousy, peggarly, rascally knave! and by the soul of my grandsire! I will impeach, and accuse, and indict him of a roppery, if I did but know who he is."—Had this misfortune happened at sea, where we could not repair the loss, in all probability this descendant of Caractacus would have lost his wits entirely; but, when I observed how easy it would be to remedy this paltry mischance, he became more calm, and reconciled himself to the occasion. A little while after this transport, the surgeon came into the berth, under pretence of taking something out of the medicine chest, and with a smiling aspect, wished us joy of our deliverance, which, he said, he had been at great pains to obtain of the captain, who was very justly incensed at our behaviour; but he (the doctor) had passed his word for our future conduct, and he hoped we should give him no cause to repent of his kindness. He expected, no doubt, an acknowledgment from us for this pretended piece of service, as well as a general amnesty of what was past; but he had to do with people who were not quite so apt to forgive injuries as he imagined, or to forget that, if our deliverance was owing to his mediation, our calamity was occasioned by his malice. I therefore sat silent, while my companion answered, "Ay, ay, 'tis no matter. Got knows the heart —there is a time for all things, as the wise man saith, there is a time for throwing away stones, and a time to gather them up again." He seemed to be disconcerted at this reply, and went away in a pet, muttering something about "ingratitude" and "fellows," of which we did not think fit to take any notice.

Our fleet having joined another that waited for us, lay at anchor about a month in the harbour at Port Royal in Jamaica, during which time something of consequence was certainly transacted; notwithstanding the insinuations of some who affirmed we had no business at all in that place; that, in order to take the advantage of the season proper for our enterprise, the West India squadron, which had previous notice of our coming, ought to have joined us at the west end of Hispaniola, with necessary stores and refreshments, from whence we could have sailed directly for Carthagena, before the enemy could put themselves in a good posture of defence, or, indeed, have an inkling of our design. Be this as it will, we sailed from Jamaica, and, in ten days or a fortnight, beat up against the wind as far as the Isle of Vache, with an intention, as was said, to attack the French fleet, then supposed to be lying near that place; but, before we arrived, they had sailed for Europe, having first despatched an advice-boat to Carthagena, with an account of our being in those seas, as also of our strength and destination. We loitered here some days longer, taking in wood and brackish water, in the use whereof, however, our admiral seemed to consult the health of the men, by restricting each to a quart a day. At length we set sail, and arrived in a bay to the windward of Carthagena, where we came to an anchor, and lay at our ease ten days longer. Here again certain malicious people took occasion to blame the conduct of their superiors, by saying that, in so doing, they not only unprofitably wasted time, which was very precious, considering the approach of the rainy season, but also allowed the Spaniards to recollect themselves from the terror occasioned by the approach of an English fleet, at least three times as numerous as ever appeared in that part of the world before. But, if I might be allowed to give my opinion of the matter, I would ascribe this delay to the generosity of our chiefs, who scorned to take any advantage that fortune might give them, even over an enemy. At last, however, we weighed, and anchored again somewhat nearer the harbour's mouth, where we made shift to land our marines, who encamped on the beach in despite of the enemy's shot, which knocked a good many of them on the head. This piece of conduct, in choosing a camp under the walls of an enemy's fortification, which, I believe, never happened before, was practised, I presume, with a view to accustoming the soldiers to stand fire, who were not as yet much used to discipline, most of them having been taken from the plough-tail a few months before. This expedient again has furnished matters for censure against the ministry, for sending a few raw recruits on such an important enterprise, while so many veteran regiments lay inactive at home. But surely our governors had their reasons for so doing, which possibly may be disclosed with other secrets of the deep. Perhaps they were loth to risk their best troops on such desperate service; or the colonel and field officers of the old corps, who, generally speaking, enjoyed their commissions as sinecures or pensions, for some domestic services tendered to the court, refused to embark in such a dangerous and precarious undertaking; for which refusal, no doubt, they are much to be commended.

CHAPTER XXXII

Our Land Forces being disembarked, erect a Fascine Battery—Our Ship is ordered, with four more, to batter the Fort of Boca Chica—Mackshane's Cowardice—The Chaplain's frenzy—Honest Rattlin loses one Hand—His Heroism, and Reflections on the Battle—Crampley's Behaviour to me during the heat of the Fight.

OUR forces, being landed and stationed as I have already mentioned, set about erecting a fascine battery to cannonade the principal fort of the enemy, and in something more than three weeks it was ready to open. That we might do the Spaniards as much honour as possible, it was determined, in a council of war, that five of our largest ships should attack the fort on one side, while the battery, strengthened by two mortars and twenty-four cohorns, should ply it on the other.

Accordingly the signal for our ship to engage, among others, was hoisted, we being advertised the night before to make everything clear for that purpose; and in so doing, a difference happened between Captain Oakum and his well-beloved cousin and counsellor Mackshane, which had well-nigh terminated in an open rupture. The doctor, who had imagined there was no more danger of being hurt by the enemy's shot in the cockpit than in the centre of the earth, was lately informed that a surgeon's mate had been killed in that part of the ship, by a cannon-ball from two small redoubts that were destroyed before the disembarkation of our soldiers; and therefore insisted upon having a platform raised for the convenience of the sick and wounded in the after-hold, where he deemed himself more secure than on the deck above. The captain, offended at this extraordinary proposal, accused him of pusillanimity, and told him there was no room in the hold for such an occasion; or if there was, he could not expect to be indulged more than the rest of the surgeons of the navy, who used the cockpit for that purpose. Fear rendering Mackshane obstinate, he persisted in his demand, and showed his instructions by which it was authorised. The captain swore these instructions were dictated by a parcel of lazy poltroons who were never at sea; nevertheless, he was obliged to comply and sent for the carpenter to give him orders about it: but, before any such measure could be taken, our signal was thrown out, and the doctor compelled to trust his carcass in the cockpit, where Morgan and I were busy in putting our instruments and dressings in order.

Our ship, with others destined for this service, immediately weighed, and, in less than half an hour, came to an anchor before the castle of Boca Chica, with a spring upon our cable; and the cannonading (which, indeed, was terrible!) began. The surgeon, after having crossed himself, fell flat on the deck; and the chaplain and purser, who were stationed with us in quality of assistants, followed his example, while the Welshman and I sat upon a chest looking at one another with great discomposure, scarce able to refrain from the like prostration. And, that the reader may know it was not a common occasion that alarmed us thus, I must inform him of the particulars of this dreadful din that astounded us. The fire of the Spaniards proceeded from eighty-four great guns, beside a mortar and small arms, in Boca Chica, thirty-six in Fort St. Joseph, twenty in two fascine batteries, and four men-of-war, mounting sixty-four guns each. This was answered by our land battery, mounted with twenty-one cannon, two mortars, and twenty-four cohorns, and five great ships of eighty or seventy guns, that fired without intermission. We had not been many minutes engaged, when one of the sailors brought another on his back to the cockpit, where he tossed him down like a bag of oats, and pulling out his pouch, put a large chew of tobacco in his mouth, without speaking a word. Morgan immediately examined the condition of the wounded man, and cried out, "As I shall answer now, the man is as tead as my great-grandfather." —"Dead," said his comrade, "he may be dead now, for aught I know, but I'll be damned if he was not alive when I took him up."—So saying, he was about to return to his quarters, when I bade him carry the body along with him and throw it overboard.—"Damn the body!" said he, "I think 'tis fair enough if I take care of my own." My fellow-mate, snatching up the amputation knife, pursued him half-way up the cockpit ladder, crying, "You lousy rascal, is this the churchyard, or the charnel-house, or the sepulchre, or the Golgotha of the ship?" but was stopped in his career by one calling, "Yo ho, avast there—scaldings." "Scaldings!" answered Morgan, "Got knows, 'tis hot enough, indeed: who are you?" "Here's one," replied the voice. And I immediately knew it to be that of my honest friend, Jack Rattlin, who, coming towards me, told me, with great deliberation, he was come to be docked at last, and discovered the remains of one hand which had been shattered to pieces with a grape-shot. I lamented with unfeigned sorrow his misfortune, which he bore with heroic courage, observing that every shot had its commission. It was well it did not take him in the head; or, if it had, what then? he should have died bravely fighting for his king and country: death was a debt which every man owed, and must pay; and that now was as well as another time. I was much pleased and edified with the maxims of this sea philosopher, who endured the amputation of his left hand without shrinking; the operation being performed, at his request, by me, after Mackshane, who was with difficulty prevailed to lift his head from the deck, had declared there was a necessity for his losing the limb. While I was employed in dressing the stump, I asked Jack's opinion of the battle, who, shaking his head, frankly told me, he believed we should do no good; "For why? because instead of dropping anchor close under shore, where we should have had to deal with one corner of Boca Chica only, we had opened the harbour, and exposed ourselves to the whole fire of the enemy from their shipping and Fort St. Joseph, as well as from the castle we intended to cannonade; that, besides, we lay at too great a distance to damage the walls, and three parts in four of our shot did not take place; for there was scarce anybody on board who understood the pointing of a gun. Ah! God help us!" continued he, "if your kinsman Lieutenant Bowling had been here, we should have had other guesswork."

By this time our patients had increased to such a number, that we did not know which to begin with; and the first mate plainly told the surgeon that, if he did not get up immediately and perform his duty, he would complain of his behaviour to the admiral, and make application for his warrant. This remonstrance effectually roused Mackshane, who was never deaf to an argument in which he thought his interest was concerned; he therefore rose up, and in order to strengthen his resolution, had recourse more than once to a case-bottle of rum, which he freely communicated to the chaplain and purser, who had as much need of such extraordinary inspiration as himself: being thus supported, he went to work, and arms and legs were hewed down without mercy. The fumes of the liquor mounting into the parson's brain, conspired, with his former agitation of spirits, to make him quite delirious; he stripped himself to the skin, and besmearing his body with blood, could scarce be withheld from running upon deck in that condition. Jack Rattlin, scandalised at this deportment, endeavoured to allay his transports with reason; but, finding all he said ineffectual, and great confusion occasioned by his frolics, he knocked him down with his right hand, and by threats kept him quiet in that state of humiliation. But it was not in the power of rum to elevate the purser, who sat on the floor, wringing his hands, and cursing the hour in which he left his peaceable profession of a brewer in Rochester, to engage in such a life of terror and disquiet. While we diverted ourselves at the expense of this poor devil, a shot happened to take us between wind and water, and, its course being through the purser's store-room, made a terrible havoc and noise among the jars and bottles in its way, and disconcerted Mackshane so much, that he dropped his scalpel, and, falling down on his knees, pronounced his *paternoster* aloud; the purser fell backward, and lay without sense or motion; and the chaplain grew so outrageous, that Rattlin with one hand could not keep him under; so that we were obliged to confine him in the surgeon's cabin, where he was no doubt guilty of a thousand extravagances. Much about this time, my old antagonist Crampley came down, with express orders, as he said, to bring me up to the quarter-deck, to dress a slight wound the captain had received by a splinter; his reason for honouring me in particular with this piece of service being, that, in case I should be killed or disabled by the way, my death or mutilation would be of less consequence to the ship's company than that of the doctor or his first mate. At another time, perhaps, I might have disputed this order, to which I was not bound to pay the least regard; but as I thought my reputation depended upon my compliance, I was resolved to convince my rival that I was no more afraid than he of exposing myself to danger. With this view I provided myself with dressings, and followed him immediately to the quarter-deck, through a most infernal scene of slaughter, fire, smoke, and uproar! Captain Oakum, who leaned against the mizenmast, no sooner saw me approach in my shirt, with the sleeves tucked up to my armpits, and my hands dyed with blood, than he signified his displeasure by a frown, and asked why the doctor himself did not come? I told him Crampley had singled me out, as if by express command; at which reply he seemed surprised, and threatened to punish the midshipman for his presumption after the engagement: in the meantime I was sent back to my station, and ordered to tell Mackshane that the captain expected him immediately. I got safe back, and delivered my commission to the doctor, who flatly refused to quit the post assigned to him by his instructions; whereupon Morgan, who, I believe, was jealous of my reputation for courage, undertook the affair, and ascended with great intrepidity. The captain, finding the surgeon obstinate, suffered himself to be dressed, and swore he would confine Mackshane as soon as the service should be over.

CHAPTER XXXIII

A Breach being made in the Walls, our Soldiers give the Assault, and take the Place without Opposition—Our Sailors at the same time become Masters of all the other Strengths near Boca Chica, and take possession of the Harbour—The good Consequence of the Success—We move nearer the Town—Find two Forts deserted, and the Channel blocked up with sunk Vessels; which, however, we find means to clear—Land our Soldiers at La Quinta—Repulse a body of Militia—Attack the Castle of St. Lazar, and are forced to retreat with great Loss—The remains of our Army are re-embarked—An Effort of the Admiral to take the Town—The Economy of our Expedition described.

HAVING cannonaded the fort during the space of four hours, we were all ordered to slip our cables and sheer off; but next day the engagement was renewed, and continued from the morning till the afternoon, when the enemy's fire from Boca Chica slackened, and towards evening was quite silenced. A breach being made on the other side by our land battery, large enough to admit a middle-sized baboon, provided he could find means to climb up to it,—our general proposed to give the assault that very night, and actually ordered a detachment on that duty. Providence stood our friend upon this occasion, and put it into the hearts of the Spaniards to abandon the fort, which might have been maintained by resolute men till the day of judgment, against all the force we could exert in the attack; and while our soldiers took possession of the enemy's ramparts without resistance, the same good luck attended a body of sailors, who made themselves masters of Fort St. Joseph, the fascine batteries, and one Spanish man-of-war; the other three being burnt or sunk by the foe, that they might not fall into our hands. The taking of these forts, in the strength of which the Spaniards chiefly confided, made us masters of the outward harbour, and occasioned great joy among us; as we laid our accounts with finding little or no opposition from the town; and, indeed, if a few great ships had sailed up immediately, before they had recovered from the confusion and despair that our unexpected success had produced among them, it is not impossible that we might have finished the affair to our satisfaction, without any more bloodshed; but this step our heroes disdained, as a barbarous insult over the enemy's distress, and gave them all the respite they could desire, in order to recollect themselves. In the meantime, Mackshane, taking the advantage of this general exultation, waited on our captain, and pleaded his cause so effectually, that he was re-established in his good graces; and as for Crampley, there was no more notice taken of his behaviour towards me during the action. But of all the consequences of the victory, none was more grateful than plenty of fresh water, after we had languished five weeks on the allowance of a purser's quart *per diem* for each man, in the torrid zone, where the sun was vertical, and the expense of bodily fluid so great, that a gallon of liquor could scarce supply the waste of twenty-four hours; especially as our provision consisted of putrid salt beef, to which the sailors gave the name of Irish horse; salt pork of New England, which, though neither fish nor flesh, savoured of both; bread from the same country, every biscuit whereof, like a piece of clock-work, moved by its own internal impulse, occasioned by the myriads of insects that dwelt within it; and butter served out by the gill, that tasted like train-oil thickened with salt. Instead of small beer, each man was allowed three half-quarterns of brandy or rum, which were distributed every morning, diluted with a certain quantity of his water, without either sugar or fruit to render it palatable; for which reason, this composition was, by the sailors, not unaptly styled *Necessity*. Nor was this limitation of simple element owing to a scarcity of it on board, for there was at this time water enough in the ship for a voyage of six months, at the rate of half a gallon per day to each man: but this fast must, I suppose, have been enjoined by way of penance on the ship's company for their sins; or rather with a view to mortify them into a contempt of life, that they might thereby become more resolute and regardless of danger. How simply, then, do those people argue, who ascribe the mortality among us to our bad provision and want of water; and affirm that a great many

valuable lives might have been saved, if the useless transports
had been employed in fetching fresh stock, turtle, fruit, and
other refreshments from Jamaica, and other adjacent islands,
for the use of the army and fleet! seeing, it is to be hoped, that
those who died went to a better place, and those who survived
were the more easily maintained. After all, a sufficient number
remained to fall before the walls of St. Lazar, where they
behaved like their own country mastiffs, which shut their
eyes, run into the jaws of a bear, and have their heads crushed
for their valour.

But to return to my narration. After having put garrisons
into the forts we had taken, and re-embarked our soldiers and
artillery, a piece of service that detained us more than a week,
we ventured up to the mouth of the inner harbour, guarded by
a large fortification on one side, and a small redoubt on the other,
both of which were deserted before our approach, and the entrance of the harbour blocked up by several old galleons, and
two men-of-war that the enemy had sunk in the channel. We
made shift, however, to open a passage for some ships, that
favoured a second landing of our troops, at a place called La
Quinta, not far from the town, where, after a faint resistance
from a body of Spaniards who opposed their disembarkation,
they encamped with a design of besieging the castle of St.
Lazar, which overlooked and commanded the city. Whether
our renowned general had nobody in his army who knew how
to approach it in form, or that he trusted entirely to the fame
of his arms, I shall not determine; but, certain it is, a resolution
was taken in a council of war to attack the place with musketry
only. This was put in execution, and succeeded accordingly;
the enemy giving them such a hearty reception, that the greatest
part of the detachment took up their everlasting residence on
the spot. Our chief, not relishing this kind of complaisance in
the Spaniards, was wise enough to retreat on board with the
remains of his army, which, from eight thousand able men
landed on the beach near Boca Chica, was now reduced to
fifteen hundred fit for service. The sick and wounded were
squeezed into certain vessels, which thence obtained the name
of hospital-ships, though methinks they scarce deserved such
a creditable title, seeing few of them could boast of their surgeon,
nurse, or cook; and the space between decks was so confined,
that the miserable patients had not room to sit upright in their
beds. Their wounds and stumps being neglected, contracted
filth and putrefaction, and millions of maggots were hatched

amidst the corruption of their sores. This inhuman disregard was imputed to the scarcity of surgeons; though it is well known that every great ship in the fleet could have spared one at least for this duty; an expedient which would have been more than sufficient to remove this shocking inconvenience. But, perhaps, the general was too much of a gentleman to ask a favour of this kind from his fellow-chief, who, on the other hand, would not derogate so much from his own dignity, as to offer such assistance unasked; for I may venture to affirm that, by this time, the demon of Discord, with her sooty wings, had breathed her influence upon our counsels; and it might be said of these great men (I hope they will pardon the comparison) as of Cæsar and Pompey, the one could not brook a superior, and the other was impatient of an equal; so that, between the pride of one, and insolence of another, the enterprise miscarried, according to the proverb, "Between two stools, the backside falls to the ground." Not that I would be thought to liken any public concern to that opprobrious part of the human body, though I might with truth assert, if I durst use such a vulgar idiom, that the nation did hang an a—se at its disappointment on this occasion; neither would I presume to compare the capacity of our heroic leaders to any such wooden convenience as a joint-stool, or a close-stool, but only to signify by this simile the mistake the people committed in trusting to the union of two instruments that were never joined.

A day or two after the attempt on St. Lazar, the admiral ordered one of the Spanish men-of-war we had taken to be mounted with sixteen guns, and manned with detachments from our great ships, in order to batter the town. Accordingly she was towed into the inner harbour in the night, and moored within half a mile of the walls, against which she began to fire at daybreak; and continued about six hours exposed to the opposition of at least thirty pieces of cannon, which at length obliged our men to set her on fire, and get off as well as they could in their boats. This piece of conduct afforded matter of speculation to all the wits either in the army or navy, who were at last fain to acknowledge it was a stroke of policy above their comprehension. Some entertained such an irreverent opinion of the admiral's understanding, as to think he expected the town would surrender to his floating battery of sixteen guns. Others imagined his sole intention was to try the enemy's strength, by which he should be able to compute the number of great ships that would be necessary to force the town to a

capitulation. But this last conjecture soon appeared groundless
inasmuch as no ships of any kind whatever were afterward
employed on that service. A third sort swore that no othe
cause could be assigned for this undertaking, than that whic
induced Don Quixote to attack the windmill. A fourth class
and that the most numerous, though, without doubt, compose
of the sanguine and malicious, plainly taxed this commande
for want of honesty, as well as sense; and alleged that he ough
to have sacrificed private pique to the interest of his country
that, where the lives of so many brave fellow-citizens wer
concerned, he ought to have concurred with the general, withou
being solicited, or even desired, towards their preservation an
advantage; that, if his arguments could not dissuade him from
a desperate enterprise, it was his duty to have rendered it a
practicable as possible, without running extreme hazard; tha
this could have been done, with a good prospect of success, by
ordering five or six large ships to batter the town, while th
land forces stormed the castle; by these means a considerabl
diversion would have been made in favour of those troops, who
in their march to the assault, and in their retreat, suffered much
more from the town than from the castle; that the inhabitants
seeing themselves vigorously attacked on all hands, would hav
been divided, distracted, and confused, and, in all probability
unable to resist the assailants. But all these suggestions surely
proceeded from ignorance and malevolence, or else the admira
would not have found it such an easy matter, at his return to
England, to justify his conduct to a ministry at once so upright
and discerning. True it is, that those who undertook to vindicate
him on the spot, asserted that there was not water enough for
our great ships near the town; though this was a little unfortunately urged, because there happened to be pilots in the fleet
perfectly well acquainted with the soundings of the harbour,
who affirmed there was water enough for five eighty-gun ships
to lie abreast, almost up at the very walls. The disappointments
we suffered occasioned a universal dejection, which was not at
all alleviated by the objects that daily and hourly entertained
our eyes, nor by the prospect of what must have inevitably
happened, had we remained much longer in this place. Such was
the economy in some ships, that, rather than be at the trouble
of interring the dead, the commanders ordered their men to
throw their bodies overboard, many without either ballast or
winding-sheet; so that numbers of human carcasses floated in
the harbour, until they were devoured by sharks and carrion

rows, which afforded no agreeable spectacle to those who
survived. At the same time the wet season began, during which
, deluge of rain falls from the rising to the setting of the sun,
without intermission; and that no sooner ceases, than it begins
to thunder and lighten with such continual flashing, that one
can see to read a very small print by the illumination.

CHAPTER XXXIV

An Epidemic Fever rages among us—We abandon our Conquests—I
am seized with the Distemper—Write a Petition to the Captain, which is
rejected—I am in danger of Suffocation through the Malice of Crampley;
and relieved by a Serjeant—My Fever increases—The Chaplain wants
to confess me—I obtain a favourable Crisis—Morgan's Affection for me
proved—The Behaviour of Mackshane and Crampley towards me—
Captain Oakum is removed into another Ship, with his beloved Doctor—
Our new Captain described—An Adventure of Morgan.

THE change of the atmosphere, occasioned by this phenomenon,
conspired, with the stench that surrounded us, the heat of the
climate, our own constitutions impoverished by bad provisions,
and our despair, to introduce the bilious fever among us, which
raged with such violence, that three-fourths of those whom it
invaded died in a deplorable manner; the colour of their skin
being, by the extreme putrefaction of the juices, changed into
that of soot.

Our conductors, finding things in this situation, perceived it
was high time to relinquish our conquests; and this we did, after
having rendered their artillery useless, and blown up their walls
with gunpowder. Just as we sailed from Boca Chica on our
return to Jamaica, I found myself threatened with the symptoms
of this terrible distemper; and knowing very well that I stood
no chance for my life if I should be obliged to lie in the cockpit,
which by this time was grown intolerable, even to people in
health, by reason of the heat and unwholesome smell of decayed
provision, I wrote a petition to the captain, representing my
case, and humbly imploring his permission to lie among the
soldiers in the middle deck, for the benefit of the air: but I
might have spared myself the trouble; for this humane commander refused my request, and ordered me to continue in the
place allotted for the surgeon's mates, or else to be contented
to lie in the hospital, which, by the bye, was three degrees more
offensive and more suffocating than our own berth below.

Another in my condition, perhaps, would have submitted to his fate, and died in a pet; but I could not brook the thoughts of perishing so pitifully, after I had weathered so many gales of hard fortune. I therefore, without minding Oakum's injunction, prevailed upon the soldiers, whose good will I had acquired, to admit my hammock among them, and actually congratulated myself upon my comfortable situation; which Crampley no sooner understood, than he signified to the captain my contempt of his orders, and was invested with the power to turn me down again into my proper habitation. This barbarous piece of revenge incensed me so much against the author, that I vowed, with bitter imprecations, to call him to a severe account, if ever it should be in my power; and the agitation of my spirits increased my fever to a violent degree. While I lay gasping for breath in this infernal abode, I was visited by a serjeant, the bones of whose nose I had reduced and set to rights, after they had been demolished by a splinter during our last engagement. He being informed of my condition, offered me the use of his berth in the middle deck, which was enclosed with canvas, and well aired by a porthole that remained open within it. I embraced this proposal with joy, and was immediately conducted to the place, where I was treated, while my illness lasted, with the utmost tenderness and care by this grateful halberdier, who had no other bed for himself than a hen-coop, during the whole passage. Here I lay, and enjoyed the breeze; notwithstanding which, my malady gained ground, and at length my life was despaired of, though I never lost hopes of recovery, even when I had the mortification to see, from my cabin window, six or seven thrown overboard every day, who died of the same distemper. This confidence, I am persuaded, conduced a great deal to the preservation of my life, especially when joined to another resolution I took at the beginning, namely, to refuse all medicine, which I could not help thinking co-operated with the disease, and, instead of resisting putrefaction, promoted a total degeneracy of the vital fluid. When my friend Morgan, therefore, brought his diaphoretic boluses, I put them in my mouth, 'tis true, but without any intention of swallowing them; and, when he went away, spit them out, and washed my mouth with water-gruel: I seemingly complied in this manner, that I might not affront the blood of Caractacus, by a refusal which might have intimated a diffidence of his physical capacity; for he acted as my physician, Doctor Mackshane never once inquiring about me, or even knowing where I was. When my distemper was at the height, Morgan thought my case desperate; and, after having applied a blister to the nape of my neck, squeezed my hand, bidding me, with a woeful countenance, recommend myself to Got and my Reteemer; then taking his leave, desired the chaplain to come and administer some spiritual consolation to me; but before he arrived, I made shift to rid myself of the troublesome application the Welshman had bestowed on my back. The parson having felt my pulse, inquired into the nature of my complaints, hemmed a little, and began thus: "Mr. Random, God out of his infinite mercy hath been pleased to visit you with a dreadful distemper, the issue of which no man knows. You may be permitted to recover, and live many days on the face of the earth; and, which is more probable, you may be taken away and cut off in the flower of your youth. It is incumbent on you, therefore, to prepare for the great change, by repenting sincerely of your sins; of this there cannot be a greater sign, than an ingenuous confession, which I conjure you to make, without hesitation or mental reservation; and when I am convinced of your sincerity, I will then give you such comfort as the situation of your soul will admit of. Without doubt, you have been guilty of numberless transgressions to which youth is subject, as swearing, drunkenness, whoredom, and adultery; tell me, therefore, without reserve, the particulars of each, especially the last, that I may be acquainted with the true state of your conscience: for no physician will prescribe for his patient until he knows the circumstances of his disease." As I was not under any apprehensions of death, I could not help smiling at the chaplain's inquisitive remonstrance, which I told him savoured more of the Roman than of the Protestant Church, in recommending auricular confession; a thing, in my opinion, not at all necessary to salvation, and which, for that reason, I declined. This reply disconcerted him a little; however, he explained away his meaning, in making learned distinctions between what was absolutely necessary and what was only convenient; then proceeded to ask what religion I professed. I answered, that I had not as yet considered the difference of religions, consequently had not fixed on any one in particular, but that I was bred a presbyterian. At this word the chaplain expressed great astonishment, and said he could not apprehend how a presbyterian was entitled to any post under the English Government. Then he asked if I had ever received the sacrament, or taken the oaths; to which questions I replying in the negative, he held up his hands, assured me he could do me no service, wished I might not be in a state of reprobation, and returned to his messmates, who were making merry in the ward-room round a table well stored with bumbo [1] and wine. This insinuation, terrible as it was, had not such an effect upon me as the fever, which, soon after he had left me, grew outrageous; I began to see strange chimeras, and concluded myself on the point of becoming delirious: in the meantime, being in great danger of suffocation, I started up in a kind of frantic fit, with an intention to plunge myself into the sea; and as my friend the serjeant was not present, would certainly have cooled myself to some purpose, had I not perceived a moisture upon my thigh, as I endeavoured to get out of my hammock. The appearance of this revived my hopes, and I had reflection and resolution enough to take advantage of this favourable symptom, by tearing the shirt from my body, and sheets from my bed, and wrapping myself in a thick blanket, in which enclosure, for about a quarter of an hour, I felt the pains of hell; but it was not long before I was recompensed for my suffering, by a profuse sweat that, bursting from the whole surface of my skin, in less than two hours relieved me from all my complaints, except that of weakness; and left me as hungry as a kite.

I enjoyed a very comfortable nap, after which I was regaling myself with the agreeable reverie of my future happiness, when I heard Morgan, on the outside of the curtain, ask the serjeant if I was alive still? "Alive!" cried the other, "God forbid he should be otherwise! he has lain quiet these five hours, and I do not choose to disturb him, for sleep will do him great service." "Ay," said my fellow-mate, "he sleeps so sound, look you, that he will never waken till the great trump blows. Got be merciful to his soul! He has paid his debt like an honest man. Ay, and moreover he is at rest from all persecutions, and troubles, and afflictions, of which, Got knows, and I know, he had his own share. Ochree! Ochree! he was a promising youth, indeed." So saying, he groaned grievously, and began to whine in such a manner, as persuaded me he had a real friendship for me. The serjeant, alarmed at his words, came into the berth, and while he looked upon me, I smiled, and tipped him the wink: he immediately guessed my meaning, and, remaining silent, Morgan was confirmed in his opinion of my being dead: whereupon he approached with tears in his eyes, in order to indulge his grief with the sight of the object. And I counterfeited death so well, by fixing my eyes, and dropping my under-jaw,

[1] Bumbo is a liquor composed of rum, sugar, water, and nutmeg.

hat he said, "There he lies, no petter than a lump of clay, Got elp me"; and observed, by the distortion of my face, that I ust have had a strong struggle. I should not have been able o contain myself much longer, when he began to perform the ust duty of a friend, in closing my eyes and my mouth; upon hich I suddenly snapped at his fingers, and discomposed him o much, that he started back, turned pale as ashes, and stared ke the picture of Horror. Although I could not help laughng at his appearance, I was concerned for his situation, and tretched out my hand, telling him I hoped to live and eat some almagundy of his making in England. It was some time before e could recollect himself so far as to feel my pulse, and inquire nto the particulars of my disease. But when he found I had njoyed a favourable crisis, he congratulated me upon my good ortune, not failing to ascribe it, under Got, to the blister he had pplied to my back at his last visit. "Which, by the bye," said te, "must now be removed and dressed." He was actually going o fetch dressings, when I, feigning astonishment, said, "Bless ne! sure you never applied a blister to me; there is nothing on ay back, I assure you." But he could not be convinced till he ad examined it, and then endeavoured to conceal his confusion, by expressing his surprise in finding the skin untouched, and the plaster missing. In order to excuse myself for paying so little egard to his prescription, I pretended to have been insensible vhen it was put on, and to have pulled it off afterwards in a fit of delirium. This apology satisfied my friend, who on this occasion abated a good deal of his stiffness in regard to punctilio; and as we were now safely arrived at Jamaica, where I had the benefit of fresh provisions and other refreshments, I recovered trength every day, and, in a short time, my health and vigour were perfectly re-established. When I got up at first, and was ust able to crawl about the deck with a staff in my hand, I met Doctor Mackshane, who passed by me with a disdainful look, and did not vouchsafe to honour me with one word. After him came Crampley, who, strutting up to me, with a fierce countenance, pronounced, "Here's fine discipline on board, when such lazy skulking sons of bitches as you are allowed, on pretence of sickness, to lollop at your ease, while your betters are kept to hard duty!" The sight and behaviour of this malicious scoundrel enraged me so much, that I could scarce refrain from laying my cudgel across his pate; but when I considered my present feebleness, and the enemies I had in the ship, who wanted only a pretence to ruin me, I restrained my passion, and contented

myself with telling him, I had not forgot his insolence an
malice, and that I hoped we should meet one day on shore. A
this declaration he grinned, shook his fist, and swore he longe
for nothing more than such an opportunity.

Meanwhile our ship was ordered to be heaved down, victualle
and watered, for her return to England; and our captain, fo
some reason or other, not thinking it convenient for him t
revisit his native country at this time, exchanged with a gentle
man who, on the other hand, wished for nothing so much as t
be safe without the tropic; all his care and tenderness of himsel
being insufficient to preserve his complexion from the injurie
of the sun and weather.

Our tyrant having left the ship, and carried his favourit
Mackshane along with him, to my inexpressible satisfaction
our new commander came on board in a ten-oared barge, over
shadowed with a vast umbrella, and appeared in everything
the reverse of Oakum, being a tall, thin, young man, dresse
in this manner: a white hat, garnished with a red feather
adorned his head, from whence his hair flowed upon his shoulder
in ringlets, tied behind with a ribbon. His coat, consisting o
pink-coloured silk lined with white, by the elegance of the cur
retired backward, as it were to discover a white satin waistcoa
embroidered with gold, unbuttoned at the upper part to display
a brooch set with garnets, that glittered in the breast of his
shirt, which was of the finest cambric, edged with right Mechlin
The knees of his crimson velvet breeches scarcely descended
so low as to meet his silk stockings, which rose without spot or
wrinkle on his meagre legs, from shoes of blue Meroquin, studded
with diamond buckles, that flamed forth rivals to the sun.
A steel-hilted sword, inlaid with gold, and decked with a knot
of ribbon which fell down in a rich tassel, equipped his side;
and an amber-headed cane hung dangling from his wrist. But
the most remarkable parts of his furniture were, a mask on his
face, and white gloves on his hands, which did not seem to be
put on with an intention to be pulled off occasionally, but
were fixed with a curious ring on the little finger of each hand.
In this garb Captain Whiffle, for that was his name, took
possession of the ship, surrounded with a crowd of attendants,
all of whom, in their different degrees, seemed to be of their
patron's disposition; and the air was so impregnated with
perfumes, that one may venture to affirm the clime of Arabia
Felix was not half so sweet-scented. My fellow-mate, observing
no surgeon among his train, thought he had found an occasion

too favourable for himself to be neglected; and remembering the old proverb, "Spare to speak, and spare to speed," resolved to solicit the new captain's interest immediately, before any other surgeon could be appointed for the ship. With this view he repaired to the cabin in his ordinary dress, consisting of a check shirt and trousers, a brown linen waistcoat, and a nightcap of the same (neither of them very clean), which, for his future misfortune, happened to smell strong of tobacco. Entering without any ceremony into this sacred place, he found Captain Whiffle reposing on a couch, with a wrapper of fine chintz about his body, and a muslin cap bordered with lace about his head; and, after several low congees, began in this manner: "Sir, I hope you will forgive, and excuse, and pardon the presumption of one who has not the honour of being known unto you, but who is, nevertheless, a shentleman porn and pred, and moreover has had misfortunes, Got help me, in the world." Here he was interrupted by the captain, who, on seeing him, had started up with great amazement at the novelty of the apparition; and having recollected himself, pronounced, with a look and tone signifying disdain, curiosity, and surprise, "Zauns! who art thou?" "I am surgeon's first mate on board of this ship," replied Morgan, "and I most vehemently desire and beseech you, with all submission, to be pleased to condescend, and vouchsafe to inquire into my character, and my pehaviour, and my deserts, which, under Got, I hope will entitle me to the vacancy of surgeon." As he proceeded in his speech, he continued advancing towards the captain, whose nostrils were no sooner saluted with the aromatic flavour that exhaled from him, than he cried, with great emotion, "Heaven preserve me! I am suffocated! Fellow, fellow, away with thee. Curse thee, fellow! get thee gone. I shall be stunk to death!" At the noise of his outcries, his servants ran into his apartment, and he accosted them thus: "Villains! cut-throats! traitors! I am betrayed! I am sacrificed!—Will you not carry that monster away? or must I be stifled with the stench of him! oh! oh!" With these interjections he sunk down upon his settee in a fit; his valet de chambre plied him with a smelling-bottle, one footman chafed his temples with Hungary water, another sprinkled the floor with spirits of lavender, a third pushed Morgan out of the cabin; who, coming to the place where I was, sat down with a demure countenance, and, according to his custom, when he received an indignity which he durst not revenge, began to sing a Welsh ditty. I guessed he was under some agitation of spirits, and desired to know the cause; but, instead of answering me directly, he asked, with great emotion, if I thought him a monster and a stinkard? "A monster and a stinkard!" said I, with some surprise; "did anybody call you so?" "Got is my judge," replied he, "Captain Fifle did call me both; ay, and all the water in the Tawy will not wash it out of my remembrance. I do affirm, and vouch, and maintain, with my soul, and my pody, and my plood, look you, that I have no smells about me, but such as a Christian ought to have, except the effluvia of tobacco, which is a cephalic, odoriferous, aromatic herb, and he is a son of a mountain goat who says otherwise. As for my being a monster, let that be as it is: I am as Got was pleased to create me, which, peradventure, is more than I shall aver of him who gave me that title; for I will proclaim it before the world, that he is disguised, and transfigured, and transmogrified with affectation and whimsies, and that he is more like a papoon than one of the human race."

CHAPTER XXXV

Captain Whiffle sends for me—His Situation described—His Surgeon arrives, prescribes for him, and puts him to Bed—A Bed is put up for Mr. Simper contiguous to the State-room, which, with other parts of the Captain's behaviour, gives the Ship's Company a very unfavourable idea of their Commander—I am detained in the West Indies by the Admiral, and go on board of the *Lizard* Sloop of War in quality of Surgeon's Mate, where I make myself known to the Surgeon, who treats me very kindly —I go on Shore, sell my Ticket, purchase Necessaries, and, at my return on Board, am surprised at the sight of Crampley, who is appointed Lieutenant of the Sloop—We sail on a Cruise—Take a Prize, in which I arrive at Port Morant, under the Command of my Messmate, with whom I live in great Harmony.

HE was going on with an eulogium upon the captain, when I received a message to clean myself, and go up to the great cabin; and with this command I instantly complied, sweetening myself with rose water from the medicine chest. When I entered the room, I was ordered to stand by the door, until Captain Whiffle had reconnoitred me at a distance with a spy-glass. He having consulted one sense in this manner, bade me advance gradually, that his nose might have intelligence before it could be much offended. I therefore approached with great caution and success, and he was pleased to say, "Ay, this creature is tolerable." I found him lolling on his couch with a languishing air, his head

supported by his valet de chambre, who, from time to time,
applied a smelling-bottle to his nose. "Vergette," said he, in a
squeaking tone, "dost thou think this wretch (meaning me)
will do me no injury? may I venture to submit my arm to him?"
"Pon my vord," replied the valet, "I do tink dat dere be great
occasion for your honour losing one small quantity of blodt;
and the young man ave quelque chose of de bonne mien."
"Well, then," said his master, "I think I must venture." Then,
addressing himself to me, "Hast thou ever blooded anybody
but brutes? But I need not ask thee, for thou wilt tell me a
most damnable lie." "Brutes, Sir," answered I, pulling down
his glove, in order to feel his pulse, "I never meddle with
brutes." "What the devil art thou about?" cried he; "dost
thou intend to twist off my hand? God's curse! my arm is
benumbed up to the very shoulder! Heaven have mercy upon
me! must I perish under the hands of savages? What an unfortunate dog was I, to come on board without my own surgeon,
Mr. Simper!" I craved pardon for having handled him so roughly,
and, with the utmost care and tenderness, tied up his arm with
a fillet of silk. While I was feeling for the vein, he desired to
know how much blood I intended to take from him, and when
I answered, "Not above twelve ounces," started up with a look
full of horror, and bade me be gone, swearing I had a design
upon his life. Vergette appeased him with difficulty, and opening
a bureau, took out a pair of scales, in one of which was placed
a small cup; and putting them into my hands, told me the
captain never lost above an ounce and three drachms at one
time. While I prepared for this important evacuation, there
came into the cabin a young man gaily dressed, of a very delicate
complexion, with a kind of languid smile on his face, which
seemed to have been rendered habitual by a long course of
affectation. The captain no sooner perceived him, than, rising
hastily, he flew into his arms, crying, "O! my dear Simper!
I am excessively disordered! I have been betrayed, frighted,
murdered by the negligence of my servants, who suffered a
beast, a mule, a bear, to surprise me, and stink me into convulsions with the fumes of tobacco." Simper, who by this time
I found was obliged to art for the clearness of his complexion,
assumed an air of softness and sympathy, and lamented, with
many tender expressions of sorrow, the sad accident that had
thrown him into that condition; then feeling his patient's pulse
on the outside of his glove, gave it as his opinion that his disorder was entirely nervous, and that some drops of tincture of

castor, and liquid laudanum would be of more service to him than bleeding, by bridling the inordinate sallies of his spirits, and composing the fermentation of his bile. I was therefore sent to prepare this prescription, which was administered in a glass of sack posset; after the captain had been put to bed, and orders sent to the officers on the quarter-deck, to let nobody walk on that side under which he lay.

While the captain enjoyed his repose, the doctor watched over him, and indeed became so necessary, that a cabin was made for him contiguous to the state-room, where Whiffle slept, that he might be at hand in case of accidents in the night. Next day, our commander being happily recovered, gave orders, that none of the lieutenants should appear upon deck without a wig, sword, and ruffles; nor any midshipman, or other petty officer, be seen with a check shirt, or dirty linen. He also prohibited any person whatever, except Simper and his own servants, from coming into the great cabin, without first sending in to obtain leave. These singular regulations did not prepossess the ship's company in his favour; but on the contrary, gave scandal an opportunity to be very busy with his character, and accusing him of maintaining a correspondence with the surgeon not fit to be named.

In a few weeks, our ship being under sailing orders, I was in hopes of revisiting my native country in a very short time, when the admiral's surgeon came on board, and sending for Morgan and me to the quarter-deck, gave us to understand there was a great scarcity of surgeons in the West Indies; that he was commanded to detain one mate out of every great ship that was bound for England; and desired us to agree between ourselves, before the next day at that hour, which of us should stay behind. We were thunderstruck at this proposal, and stared at one another some time without speaking; at length the Welshman broke silence, and offered to remain in the West Indies, provided the admiral would give him a surgeon's warrant immediately: but he was told there was no want of chief surgeons, and that he must be contented with the station of mate, till he should be further provided for in due course. Whereupon Morgan flatly refused to quit the ship for which the Commissioners of the Navy had appointed him; and the other told him as plainly, that if we could not determine the affair by ourselves before to-morrow morning, he must cast lots and abide by his chance. When I recalled to my remembrance the miseries I had undergone in England, where I had not one friend to promote my interest, or favour my advancement in the navy, and, at the same time, reflected on the present dearth of surgeons in the West Indies, and the unhealthiness of the climate, which every day almost reduced the number, I could not help thinking my success would be much more certain and expeditious, by my staying where I was, than by returning to Europe. I therefore resolved to comply with a good grace, and next day, when we were ordered to throw dice, told Morgan he need not trouble himself, for I would voluntarily submit to the admiral's pleasure. This frank declaration was commended by the gentleman, who assured me it should not fare the worse with me for my resignation. Indeed, he was as good as his word, and that very afternoon procured a warrant, appointing me surgeon's mate of the *Lizard* sloop of war, which put me on a footing with every first mate in the service.

My ticket being made out, I put my chest and bedding on board a canoe that lay alongside, and having shook hands with my trusty friend the serjeant, and honest Jack Rattlin, who was bound for Greenwich Hospital, I took my leave of Morgan with many tears, after we had exchanged our sleeve-buttons as remembrances of each other. Having presented my new warrant to the captain of the *Lizard*, I inquired for the doctor, whom I no sooner saw, than I recollected him to be one of those young fellows with whom I had been committed to the roundhouse during our frolic with Jackson, as I have related before. He received me with a good deal of courtesy, and when I put him in mind of our former acquaintance, expressed great joy at seeing me again, and recommended me to an exceeding good mess, composed of the gunner and master's mate. As there was not one sick person in the ship, I got leave to go ashore next day with the gunner, who recommended me to a Jew that bought my ticket at the rate of forty per cent. discount; and having furnished myself with what necessaries I wanted, returned on board in the evening, and, to my surprise, found my old antagonist Crampley walking upon deck. Though I did not fear his enmity, I was shocked at his appearance, and communicated my sentiments on that subject to Mr. Tomlins the surgeon, who told me that Crampley, by dint of some friends about the admiral, had procured a commission, constituting him lieutenant on board the *Lizard*; and advised me, now he was my superior officer, to behave with some respect towards him, or else he would find a thousand opportunities of using me ill. This advice was a bitter potion to me, whom pride and resentment had rendered utterly incapable of the least submission to, or even of a reconciliation with, the wretch who had on many occasions treated me so inhumanly. However, I resolved to have as little connection as possible with him, and to ingratiate myself as much as I could with the rest of the officers, whose friendship might be a bulwark to defend me from the attempts of his malice.

In less than a week we sailed on a cruise, and, having weathered the east end of the island, had the good fortune to take a Spanish barcolongo, with her prize, which was an English ship bound for Bristol, that sailed from Jamaica a fortnight before without convoy. All the prisoners who were well we put on shore on the north side of the island; the prizes were manned with Englishmen, and the command of the barcolongo given to my friend the master's mate, with orders to carry them into Port Morant, and there to remain until the *Lizard's* cruise should be ended, at which time she would touch at the same place in her way to Port Royal. With him I was sent to attend the wounded Spaniards as well as Englishmen, who amounted to sixteen, and to take care of them on shore, in a house that was to be hired as an hospital. This destination gave me a great deal of pleasure, as I should for some time be freed from the arrogance of Crampley, whose inveteracy against me had already broke out on two or three occasions since he was become a lieutenant. My messmate, who very much resembled my uncle, both in figure and disposition, treated me on board of the prize with the utmost civility and confidence; and, among other favours, made me a present of a silver-hilted hanger, and a pair of pistols mounted with the same metal, which fell to his share in plundering the enemy. We arrived safely at Morant, and going on shore, pitched upon an empty storehouse, which we hired for the reception of the wounded, who were brought to it next day, with beds and other necessaries; and four of the ship's company appointed to attend them and obey me.

CHAPTER XXXVI

A strange Adventure—In consequence of which I am extremely happy —Crampley does me ill offices with the Captain: but his Malice is defeated by the Good Nature and Friendship of the Surgeon—We return to Port Royal—Our Captain gets the Command of a larger Ship, and is succeeded by an old Man—Brayl is provided for—We receive Orders to sail for England.

WHEN my patients were all in a fair way, my companion and commander, whose name was Brayl, carried me up the country to the house of a rich planter, with whom he was acquainted; where we were sumptuously entertained, and, in the evening, set out on our return to the ship. When we had walked about a mile by moonlight, we perceived a horseman behind us, who, coming up, wished us *good even*, and asked which way we went? His voice, which was quite familiar to me, no sooner struck my ear than, in spite of all my resolution and reflection, my hair bristled up, and I was seized with a violent fit of trembling, which Brayl misinterpreting, bade me be under no concern. I told him he was mistaken in the cause of my disorder; and, addressing myself to the person on horseback, said, "I could have sworn by your voice that you were a dear friend of mine, if I had not been certain of his death." To this address, after some pause, he replied, "There are many voices as well as faces that resemble one another; but pray, what was your friend's name?" I satisfied him in that particular, and gave a short detail of the melancholy fate of Thomson, not without many sighs and some tears. A silence ensued, which lasted some minutes, and then the conversation turned on different subjects, till we arrived at a house on the road, where the horseman alighted, and begged with so much earnestness that we would go in and drink a bowl of punch with him, that we could not resist. But if I was alarmed at his voice, what must my amazement be when I discovered by the light the very person of my lamented friend! Perceiving my confusion, which was extreme, he clasped me in his arms, and bedewed my face with tears. It was some time ere I recovered the use of my reason, overpowered with this event, and longer still before I could speak; so that all I was capable of was to return his embraces, and to mingle the overflowings of my joy with his; whilst honest Brayl, affected with the scene, wept as fast as either of us, and signified his participation of our happiness by hugging us both, and capering about the room like a madman. At length I retrieved the use of my tongue, and cried, "Is it possible, can you be my friend Thomson? No certainly, alas! he was drowned! and I am now under the deception of a dream!" He was at great pains to convince me of his being the individual person whom I regretted, and, bidding me sit down and compose myself, promised to explain his sudden disappearance from the *Thunder*, and to account for his being at present in the land of the living. This task he acquitted himself of, after I had drank a glass of punch, and recollected my spirits, by informing us that, with a determination to rid himself of a miserable existence he had gone in the night-time to the head, while the ship was on her way, from whence he slipped down as softly as he could by the bows into the sea, where, after he was heartily ducked, he began to repent of his precipitation, and, as he could swim very well, kept himself above water, in hopes of being taken up by some of the ships astern; that, in this situation, he hailed a large vessel, and begged to be taken in, but was answered that she was a heavy sailer, and therefore they did not choose to lose time by bringing to; however, they threw an old chest overboard for his convenience, and told him that some of the ships astern would certainly save him; that no other vessel came within sight or cry of him for the space of three hours, during which time he had the mortification to find himself in the middle of the ocean alone, without other support or resting-place but what a few crazy boards afforded; till at last he discerned a small sloop steering towards him, upon which he set up his throat, and had the good fortune to be heard and rescued from the dreary waste by their boat, which was hoisted out on purpose. "I was no sooner brought on board," continued he, "than I fainted, and when I recovered my senses, found myself in bed regaled with a most noisome smell of onions and cheese, which made me think, at first, that I was in my own hammock, alongside of honest Morgan, and that all which had passed was no more than a dream. Upon inquiry I understood that I was on board of a schooner belonging to Rhode Island, bound for Jamaica, with a cargo of geese, pigs, onions, and cheese; and that the master's name was Robertson, by birth a North Briton, whom I knew at first sight to be an old school-fellow of mine. When I discovered myself to him he was transported with surprise and joy, and begged to know the occasion of my misfortune, which I did not think fit to disclose, because I knew his notions with regard to religion were very severe and confined; therefore contented myself with telling him, I fell overboard by accident; but made no scruple of explaining the nature of my disagreeable station, and of acquainting him with my determined purpose never to return to the *Thunder* man-of-war. Although he was not of my opinion in that particular, knowing that I must lose my clothes, and what pay was due to me, unless I went back to my duty; yet, when I described the circumstances of the hellish life I led, under the tyrannic sway of Oakum and Mackshane; and, among other grievances, hinted a dissatisfaction at the irreligious deportment of my shipmates, and the want of the true Presbyterian gospel doctrine; he changed his sentiments, and conjured me with great vehemence and zeal to lay aside all thought of rising in the navy; and, that he might show how much he had my interest at heart, undertook to provide for me in some shape or other, before he should leave Jamaica. This promise he performed to my heart's desire, by recommending me to a gentleman of fortune, with whom I have lived ever since, in quality of surgeon and overseer to his plantations. He and his lady are now at Kingston, so that I am, for the present, master of this house, to which, from my soul, I bid you welcome, and hope you will favour me with your company during the remaining part of the night."—I needed not a second invitation; but Mr. Brayl, who was a diligent and excellent officer, could not be persuaded to sleep out of the ship: however, he supped with us, and, after having drank a cheerful glass, set out for the vessel, which was not above three miles from the place, escorted by a couple of stout negroes, whom Mr. Thomson ordered to conduct him. Never were two friends more happy in the conversation of each other than we, for the time it lasted. I related to him the particulars of our attempt upon Carthagena, of which he had heard but an imperfect account; and he gratified me with a narration of every little incident of his life since we parted. He assured me it was with the utmost difficulty he could resist his inclination of coming down to Port Royal to see Morgan and me, of whom he had heard no tidings since the day of our separation; but that he was restrained by the fear of being detained as a deserter. He told me that, when he heard my voice in the dark, he was almost as much surprised as I was at seeing him afterwards; and, in the confidence of friendship, disclosed a passion he entertained for the only daughter of the gentleman with whom he lived, who, by his description, was a very amiable young lady, and did not disdain his addresses; that he was very much favoured by her parents, and did not despair obtaining their consent to the match; which would at once render him independent of the world. I congratulated him on his good fortune, which he protested should never make him forget his friends; and towards morning we betook ourselves to rest.

Next day he accompanied me to the ship, where Mr. Brayl entertained him at dinner, and we having spent the afternoon together, he took his leave of us in the evening, after he had forced upon me ten pistoles, as a small token of his affection. In short, while we staid here, we saw one another every day, and generally ate at the same table, which was plentifully supplied by him with all kinds of poultry, butchers' meat, oranges, limes, lemons, pineapples, Madeira wine, and excellent rum; so that this small interval of ten days was by far the most agreeable period of my life.

At length the *Lizard* arrived; and my patients being all fit for duty, they and I were ordered on board of her, where I understood from Mr. Tomlins that there was a dryness between the lieutenant and him on my account; that rancorous villain having taken the opportunity of my absence to fill the captain's ears with a thousand scandalous stories to my prejudice; among other things, affirming that I had once been transported for theft, and that, when I was in the *Thunder* man-of-war, I had been whipped for the same crime. The surgeon, on the other hand, having heard my whole story from my own mouth, defended me strenuously, and, in the course of that good-natured office, recounted all the instances of Crampley's malice against me while I remained on board of that ship; which declaration, while it satisfied the captain of my innocence, made the lieutenant as much my defender's enemy as mine. This infernal behaviour of Crampley, with regard to me, added such fuel to my former resentment, that, at certain times, I was quite beside myself with the desire of revenge, and was even tempted to pistol him on the quarter-deck, though an infamous death must inevitably have been my reward. But the surgeon, who was my confidant, argued against such a desperate action so effectually, that I stifled the flame which consumed me for the present, and resolved to wait for a more convenient opportunity. In the meantime, that Mr. Tomlins might be the more convinced of the wrongs I suffered by this fellow's slander, I begged he would go and visit Mr. Thomson, whose wonderful escape I had made him acquainted with, and inquire of him into the particulars of my conduct while he was my fellow-mate. This request the surgeon complied with, more through curiosity to see a person whose fate had been so extraordinary, than to confirm his good opinion of me, which, he assured me, was already firmly established. He therefore set out for the dwelling-place of my friend, with a letter of introduction from me; and, being received with all the civility and kindness I expected, returned to the ship, not only satisfied with my character beyond the power of doubt or insinuation, but also charmed with the affability and conversation of Thomson, who loaded him and me with presents of fresh stocks, liquors, and fruit. As he would not venture to come and see us on board, lest Crampley should know and detain him, when the time of our departure approached, I obtained leave to go and bid him farewell. After we had vowed an everlasting friendship, he pressed upon me a purse with four doubloons, which I refused as long as I could, without giving umbrage; and, having cordially embraced each other, I returned on board, where I found a small box, with a letter directed for me, to the care of Mr. Tomlins. Knowing the superscription to be of Thomson's handwriting, I opened it with some surprise, and learned that this generous friend, not contented with loading me with the presents already mentioned, had sent, for my use and acceptance, half a dozen fine shirts, and as many linen waistcoats and caps, with twelve pair of new thread stockings.—Being thus provided with money, and all necessaries for the comfort of life, I began to look upon myself as a gentleman of some consequence, and felt my pride dilate apace.

Next day we sailed for Port Royal, where we arrived safely with our prizes; and, as there was nothing to do on board, I went ashore, and, having purchased a laced waistcoat, with some other clothes, at a sale, made a swaggering figure for some days among the taverns, where I ventured to play a little at hazard, and came off with fifty pistoles in my pocket. Meanwhile, our captain was promoted to a ship of twenty guns, and the command of the *Lizard* given to a man turned of fourscore, who had been lieutenant since the reign of King William, and, notwithstanding his long service, would have probably died in that station, had he not applied some prize money he had lately received, to make interest with his superiors. My friend Brayl was also made an officer about the same time, after he had served in quality of a midshipman and mate five and twenty years. Soon after these alterations the admiral pitched upon our ship to carry home despatches for the ministry; and we set sail for England, having first scrubbed her bottom, and taken in provision and water for the occasion.

CHAPTER XXXVII

We depart for Europe—A Misunderstanding arises between the Captain and Surgeon, through the scandalous Aspersions of Crampley—The Captain dies—Crampley tyrannises over the Surgeon, who falls a Victim to his Cruelty—I am also ill-used—The Ship strikes—The Behaviour of Crampley and the Seamen on that Occasion—I get on Shore, challenge the Captain to single Combat—Am treacherously knocked down, wounded and robbed.

Now that I could return to my native country in a creditable way, I felt excessive pleasure in finding myself out of sight of that fatal island, which has been the grave of so many Europeans and as I was accommodated with everything to render the passage agreeable, I resolved to enjoy myself as much as the insolence of Crampley would permit. This insidious slanderer had found means already to cause a misunderstanding between the surgeon and captain, who, by his age and infirmities, was rendered intolerably peevish, his disposition having also been soured by a long course of disappointments. He had a particular aversion to all young men, especially to surgeons, whom he considered as unnecessary animals on board of a ship; and, in consequence of these sentiments, never consulted the doctor notwithstanding his being seized with a violent fit of the gout and gravel; but applied to a cask of Holland gin, which was his sovereign prescription against all distempers. Whether he was at this time too sparing, or took an overdose of his cordial, certain it is, he departed in the night without any ceremony, which indeed was a thing he always despised, and was found stiff next morning, to the no small satisfaction of Crampley, who succeeded to the command of the vessel. For that very reason, Mr. Tomlins and I had no cause to rejoice at this event, fearing that the tyranny of our new commander would now be as unlimited as his power. The first day of his command justified our apprehension. For, on pretence that the decks were too much crowded, he ordered the surgeon's hen-coops, with all his fowls, to be thrown overboard, and at the same time prohibited him and me from appearing on the quarter-deck. Mr. Tomlins could not help complaining of these injuries, and, in the course of his expostulation, dropped some hasty words, of which Crampley taking hold, confined him to his cabin, where, in a few days, for want of air, he was attacked by a fever, which soon put an end to his life, after he had made his will, by which he bequeathed all his estate, personal and real, to his sister, and left to me his watch and instruments, as memorials of his friendship. I was penetrated with grief on this melancholy occasion; the more because there was nobody on board to whom I could communicate my sorrows, or of whom I could receive the least consolation or advice. Crampley was so far from discovering the least remorse for his barbarity at the news of the surgeon's death, that he insulted his memory in the most abusive manner, and affirmed he had poisoned himself out of pure fear, dreading to be brought to a court-martial for mutiny; for which reason he would not suffer the service of the dead to be read over his body before it was thrown overboard.

Nothing but a speedy deliverance could have supported me under the brutal sway of this bashaw, who, to render my life the more irksome, signified to my messmates a desire that I should be expelled from their society. This was no sooner hinted, than they granted his request; and I was fain to eat in a solitary manner by myself during the rest of the passage, which however soon drew to a period.

We had been seven weeks at sea, when the gunner told the captain that, by his reckoning, we must be in soundings, and desired he would order the lead to be heaved. Crampley swore he did not know how to keep the ship's way, for we were not within a hundred leagues of soundings, and therefore he would not give himself the trouble to cast the lead. Accordingly we continued our course all that afternoon and night, without shortening sail, although the gunner pretended to discover Scilly light, and next morning protested in form against the captain's conduct, for which he was put in confinement. We discovered no land all that day, and Crampley was still so infatuated as to neglect sounding; but at three o'clock in the morning the ship struck, and remained fast on a sandbank. This accident alarmed the whole crew; the boat was immediately hoisted out; but, as we could not discern which way the shore lay, we were obliged to wait for daylight. In the meantime the wind increased, and the waves beat against the sloop with such violence, that we expected she would have gone to pieces. The gunner was released and consulted. He advised the captain to cut away the mast, in order to lighten her; this expedient was performed without success. The sailors, seeing things in a desperate situation, according to custom, broke up the chests belonging to the officers, dressed themselves in their clothes, drank their liquors without ceremony; and drunkenness, tumult, and confusion ensued. In the midst of this uproar I went below, to secure my own effects; and found the carpenter's mate hewing down the purser's cabin with his hatchet, whistling all the while with great composure. When I asked his intention in so doing, he replied very calmly, "I only want to taste the purser's rum, that's all, master." At that instant the purser coming down, and seeing his effects going to wreck, complained bitterly of the injustice done to him, and asked the fellow what occasion he had for liquor, when, in all likelihood, he should be in eternity in a few minutes. "All's one for that," said the plunderer, "let us live while we can." "Miserable wretch that thou art," cried the purser, "what must be thy lot in the other world, if thou diest in the commission of robbery?" "Why, hell, I suppose," replied the other, with great deliberation, while the purser fell upon his knees, and begged of Heaven that we might not all perish for the sake of one Jonas. During this dialogue, I clothed myself in my best apparel, girded on my hanger, stuck my pistols loaded in my belt, disposed of all my valuable movables about my person, and came upon deck with a resolution of taking the first opportunity to get on shore, which, when the day broke, appeared at the distance of three miles ahead. Crampley, finding his efforts to get the ship off ineffectual, determined to consult his own safety, by going into the boat, which he had no sooner done, than the ship's company followed so fast, that she would have sunk alongside, had not someone wiser than the rest cut the rope and put off. But before this happened, I had made several attempts to get in, and was always balked by the captain, who was so eager in excluding me, that he did not mind the endeavours of any other body. Enraged at this inhuman partiality, and seeing the rope cut, I pulled one of my pistols from my belt, and cocking it, swore I would shoot any man who would presume to obstruct my entrance. So saying, I leaped with my full exertion, and got on board of the boat with the loss of the skin of my shins. I chanced in my descent to overturn Crampley, who no sooner got up than he struck at me several times with a cutlass, and ordered the men to throw me overboard; but they were too anxious about their own safety to mind what he said. Though the boat was very deeply loaded, and the sea terribly high, we made shift to get upon dry land in less than an hour after we parted from the sloop. As soon as I set foot on terra firma, my indignation, which had boiled so long within me, broke out against Crampley, whom I immediately challenged to single combat, presenting my pistols, that he might take his choice: he took one without hesitation, and before I could cock the other, fired in my face, throwing the pistol after the shot. I felt myself stunned, and imagining the bullet had entered my brain, discharged mine as quick as possible, that I might not die unrevenged; then flying upon my antagonist, knocked out several of his fore teeth with the butt-end of the piece, and would certainly have made an end of him with that instrument, had he not disengaged himself, and seized his cutlass, which he had given to his servant when he received the pistol. Seeing him armed in this manner, I drew my hanger, and having flung my pistol at his head, closed with him in a transport of fury, and thrust my weapon into his mouth, which it enlarged on one side to his ear. Whether the smart of this wound disconcerted him, or the unevenness of the ground made him reel, I know not, but he staggered some paces back: I followed close, and with one stroke cut the tendons of the back of his hand, upon which his cutlass dropped and he remained defenceless. I know not with what cruelty my rage might have inspired me, if I had not at that instant been felled to the ground by a blow on the back part of my head, which deprived me of all sensation. In this deplorable situation, exposed to the rage of an incensed barbarian, and the rapine of an inhuman crew, I remained for some time; and whether any disputes arose among them during the state of my annihilation, I cannot pretend to determine; but in one particular they seem to have been unanimous, and acted with equal dexterity and despatch; for, when I recovered the use of understanding, I found myself alone in a desolate place, stripped of my clothes, money, watch, buckles, and everything but my shoes, stockings, breeches, and shirt. What a discovery must this have been to me, who but an hour before was worth sixty guineas in cash! I cursed the hour of my birth, the parents that gave me being, the sea that did not swallow me up, the poignard of the enemy, which could not find the way to my heart, the villainy of those who had left me in that miserable condition; and, in the ecstasy of despair, resolved to lie still where I was, and perish.

CHAPTER XXXVIII

I get up and crawl into a Barn, where I am in danger of perishing through the fear of the Country People—Their Inhumanity—I am succoured by a reputed Witch—Her Story—Her Advice—She recommends me as a Valet to a single Lady, whose character she explains.

BUT, as I lay ruminating, my passion insensibly abated; I considered my situation in quite another light from that in which it appeared to me at first, and the result of my deliberation was to rise, if I could, and crawl to the next inhabited place for assistance. With some difficulty I got upon my legs, and having examined my body, found I had received no other injury than two large contused wounds, one on the fore, and another on the hinder part of my head, which seemed to be occasioned by the same weapon, namely, the butt-end of a pistol. I looked towards the sea, but could discern no remains of the ship, so that I concluded she was gone to pieces, and that those who remained in her had perished. But, as I afterwards learned, the gunner, who had more sagacity than Crampley, observing that it was flood when he left her, and that she would probably float at high water, made no noise about getting on shore, but continued on deck, in hopes of bringing her safe into some harbour, after the commander should have deserted her; for which piece of service he expected, no doubt, to be handsomely rewarded. This scheme he accordingly executed, and was promised great things by the Admiralty for saving his majesty's ship; but I never heard he reaped the fruits of his expectation. As for my own part, I directed my course towards a small cottage I perceived, and, in the road, picked up a seaman's old jacket, which I suppose the thief who dressed himself in my clothes had thrown away; this was a very comfortable acquisition to me, who was almost stiff with cold. I therefore put it on, and as my natural heat revived, my wounds, which had left off bleeding, burst out afresh; so that, finding myself excessively exhausted, I was about to lie down in the fields, when I discovered a barn on my left hand, within a few yards of me. Thither I made shift to stagger, and finding the door open, went in, but saw nobody; however, I threw myself upon a truss of straw, hoping to be soon relieved by some person or other. I had not lain here many minutes, when I saw a countryman come in with a pitchfork in his hand, which he was upon the point of thrusting into the straw that concealed me, and, in all probability, would have done my business, had I not uttered a dreadful groan, after having essayed in vain to speak. This melancholy note alarmed the clown, who started back, and discovering a body all besmeared with blood, stood trembling, with the pitchfork extended before him, his hair bristling up, his eyes staring, his nostrils dilated, and his mouth wide open. At another time I should have been much diverted by this figure, which preserved the same attitude very near ten minutes; during which time I made many unsuccessful efforts to implore his compassion and assistance, but my tongue failed me, and my language was only a repetition of groans. At length an old man arrived, who, seeing the other in such a posture, cried, "Mercy upon en! the leaad's bewitched;—why, Dick, beest thou besayd thyself?" Dick, without moving his eyes from the object that terrified him, replied, "O vather! vather! here be either the devil or a dead mon! I doan't know which o' en, but a groans woundily." The father, whose eyesight was none of the best, pulled out his spectacles, and having applied them to his nose, reconnoitred me over his son's shoulder; but no sooner did he behold me, than he was seized with a fit of shaking even more violent than Dick's, and, with a broken accent, addressed me thus: "In the name of the Vather, Zun, and Holy Ghost, I charge you, an you been Satan, to be gone to the Red Zea; but an you be a murdered man, speak, that you may have a christom burial." As I was not in a condition to satisfy him in this particular, he repeated his conjuration to no purpose; and they continued a good while in the agonies of fear. At length the father proposed that the son should draw nearer, and take a more distinct view of the apparition; but Dick was of opinion that his father should advance first, as being an old man past his labour, and if he received any mischief, the loss would be the smaller; whereas he himself might escape, and be useful in his generation. This prudential reason had no effect upon the senior, who still kept Dick between me and him. In the meantime, I endeavoured to raise one hand as a signal of distress, but had only strength sufficient to produce a rustling among the straw, which discomposed the young peasant so much, that he sprung out at the door, and overthrew his father in his flight. The old gentleman would not spend time in getting up, but crawled backwards like a crab, with great speed, till he had got over the threshold, mumbling exorcisms all the way. I was excceedingly mortified to find myself in danger of perishing through the ignorance and cowardice of these clowns, and felt my spirits decay apace, when an old woman entered the barn, followed by the two fugitives, and with great intrepidity advanced to the place where I lay, saying, "If it be the devil I fear en not, and for a dead mon, a can do us no harm." When she saw my condition, she cried, "Here be no devil, but in youren fool's head. Here be a poor miserable wretch, bleeding to death, and if a dies, we must be at the charge of burying him; therefore, Dick, go vetch the old wheel-barrow, and put en in, and carry en to goodman Hodge's back door; he is more able than we to lay out money upon poor vagrants." Her advice was taken, and immediately put in execution. I was rolled to the other farmer's door, where I was tumbled out like a heap of dung, and would certainly have fallen a prey to the hogs, if my groans had not disturbed the family, and brought some of them out to view my situation. But Hodge resembled the Jew more than the good Samaritan, and ordered me to be carried to the house of the parson, whose business it was to practise as well as to preach charity; observing that it was sufficient for him to pay his quota towards the maintenance of the poor belonging to his own parish. When I was set down at the vicar's gate, he fell into a mighty passion, and threatened to excommunicate him who sent, as well as those who brought me, unless they would move me immediately to another place. About this time, I fainted with the fatigue I had undergone, and, afterwards, understood that I was bandied from door to door through a whole village, nobody having humanity enough to administer the least relief to me, until an old woman, who was suspected of witchcraft by the neighbourhood, hearing of my distress, received me into her house, and having dressed my wounds, brought me to myself with cordials of her own preparing. I was treated with great care and tenderness by this grave matron, who, after I had recovered some strength, desired to know the particulars of my last disaster. This piece of satisfaction I could not refuse to one who had saved my life; therefore related all my adventures, without exaggeration or reserve. She seemed surprised at the vicissitudes I had undergone, and drew a happy presage of my future life from my past sufferings; then launched out into the praise of adversity with so much ardour and good sense, that I concluded she was a person who had seen better days, and conceived a longing desire to hear her story. She perceived my drift by some words I dropped, and smiling, told me, there was nothing either entertaining or extraordinary in the course of her fortune; but, however, she would communicate it to me in consideration of the confidence I had reposed in her. "It is of little consequence," said she, "to tell the names of my parents, who are dead many years ago; let it suffice to assure you, they were wealthy, and had no other child than me; so that I was looked upon as heiress to a considerable estate, and teased with addresses on that account. Among the number of my admirers, there was a young gentleman of no fortune, whose sole dependence was on his promotion in the army, in which at that time he bore a lieutenant's commission. I conceived an affection for this amiable officer, which, in a short time, increased to a violent passion, and, without entering into minute circumstances, married him privately. We had not enjoyed one another long, in stolen interviews, when he was ordered with his regiment to Flanders; but, before he set out, it was agreed between us that he should declare our marriage to my father by letter, and implore his pardon for the step we had taken without his approbation. This discovery was made while I was abroad visiting; and just as I was about to return home, I received a letter from my father, importing, that since I had acted so undutifully and meanly as to marry a beggar, without his privity or consent, to the disgrace of his family, as well as the disappointment of his hopes, he renounced me to the miserable fate I had entailed on myself, and charged me never to set foot within his doors again. This rigid sentence was confirmed by my mother, who, in a postscript, gave me to understand that her sentiments were exactly conformable to those of my father, and that I might save myself the trouble of making any applications, for her resolutions were unalterable. Thunderstruck with my evil fortune, I called a coach and drove to my husband's lodgings, where I found him waiting the event of his letter. Though he could easily divine, by my looks, the issue of his declaration, he read with great steadiness the epistle I had received; and, with a smile full of tenderness, which I shall never forget, embraced me, saying, '*I believe the good lady, your mother, might have spared herself the trouble of the last part of her postscript. Well, my dear Betty, you must lay aside all thoughts of a coach, till I can procure the command of a regiment.*' This unconcerned behaviour, while it enabled me to support my reverse of fortune, at the same time endeared him to me the more, by convincing me of his disinterested views in espousing me. I was next day boarded in company with the wife of another officer, who had long been the friend and confidant of my husband, at a village not far from London, where they parted with us in the most melting manner, went to Flanders, and were killed in sight of one another, at the Battle of the Wood. Why should I tire you with a description of our unutterable sorrow at the fatal news of this event, the remembrance of which now fills my aged eyes with tears! When our grief subsided a little, and reflection came to our aid, we found ourselves deserted by the whole world, and in danger of perishing by want; whereupon, we made application for the pension, and were put upon the list. Then, vowing eternal friendship, sold our jewels and superfluous clothes, retired to this place, which is in the county of Sussex, bought this little house, where we lived many years in a solitary manner, indulging our mutual sorrow, till it pleased Heaven to call away my companion two years ago; since which time I have lingered out an unhappy being, in hopes of a speedy dissolution, when I promise myself the eternal reward of all my cares. In the meantime," continued she, "I must inform you of the character I bear among the neighbours:—My conversation being different from that of the inhabitants of the village, my recluse way of life, my skill in curing distempers, which I acquired from books since I settled here—and lastly, my age, have made the common people look upon me as something preternatural, and I am actually at this hour believed to be a witch. The parson of the parish, whose acquaintance I have not been at much pains to cultivate, taking umbrage at my supposed disrespect, has contributed not a little towards the confirmation of this opinion, by dropping certain hints to my prejudice among the vulgar, who are also very much scandalised at my entertaining this poor tabby cat, with the collar about her neck, which was a favourite of my deceased companion."

The whole behaviour of this venerable person was so primitive, innocent, sensible, and humane, that I contracted a filial respect for her, and begged her advice with regard to my future conduct, as soon as I was in a condition to act for myself. She dissuaded me from a design I had formed of travelling to London, in hopes of retrieving my clothes and pay, by returning to my ship, which by this time, I read in the newspaper, was safely arrived in the river Thames: "Because," said she, "you run the hazard of being treated not only as a deserter in quitting the sloop, but also as a mutineer in assaulting your commanding officer, to the malice of whose revenge you will moreover be exposed." She then promised to recommend me as a servant to a single lady of her acquaintance, who lived in the neighbourhood with her nephew, who was a young fox-hunter of great fortune, where

I might be very happy, provided I could bear the disposition and manners of my mistress, which were somewhat whimsical and particular. But, above all things, she counselled me to conceal my story, the knowledge of which would effectually poison my entertainment; for it was a maxim among most people of condition, that no gentleman in distress ought to be admitted into a family as a domestic, lest he become proud, lazy, and insolent. I was fain to embrace this humble proposal, because my affairs were desperate; and in a few days was hired by this lady to serve in quality of her footman; having been represented by my hostess as a young man who was bred up to the sea by his relations against his will, and had suffered shipwreck, which had increased his disgust to that way of life so much, that he rather chose to go into service on shore, than enter himself on board of any other ship. Before I took possession of my new place, she gave me a sketch of my mistress's character, that I might know better how to regulate my conduct. "Your lady," said she, "is a maiden of forty years, not so remarkable for her beauty, as her learning and taste, which is famous all over the country. Indeed, she is a perfect female virtuoso; and so eager after the pursuit of knowledge, that she neglects her person even to a degree of sluttishness; this negligence, together with her contempt of the male part of the creation, gives her nephew no great concern, as by these means he will probably keep her fortune, which is considerable, in the family. He therefore permits her to live in her own way, which is something extraordinary, and gratifies her in all her whimsical desires. Her apartment is at some distance from the other inhabited parts of the house, and consists of a dining-room, bed-chamber, and study. She keeps a cook-maid, waiting-woman, and footman of her own; and seldom eats or converses with any of the family but her niece, who is a very lovely creature, and humours her aunt often to the prejudice of her own health, by sitting up with her whole nights together; for your mistress is too much of a philosopher to be swayed by the customs of the world, and never sleeps or eats like other people. Among other odd notions, she professes the principles of Rosicrutius; and believes the earth, air, and sea are inhabited by invisible beings, with whom it is possible for the human species to entertain correspondence and intimacy, on the easy condition of living chaste. As she hopes one day to be admitted into an acquaintance of this kind, she no sooner heard of me and my cat, than she paid me a visit, with a view, as she has since owned, to be introduced to my familiar, and was greatly mortified to find herself disappointed in her expectation. Being, by this visionary turn of mind, abstracted as it were from the world, she cannot advert to the common occurrences of life; and therefore is frequently so absent, as to commit very strange mistakes and extravagances, which you will do well to rectify and repair as your prudence shall suggest."

CHAPTER XXXIX

My Reception by that Lady—I become enamoured of Narcissa—Recount the Particulars of my last Misfortune—Acquire the good Opinion of my Mistress—An Account of the young Squire—I am made acquainted with more Particulars of Narcissa's Situation—Conceive a mortal Hatred against Sir Timothy—Examine my Lady's Library and Performances—Her extravagant Behaviour.

FRAUGHT with these useful instructions, I repaired to the place of her habitation, and was introduced by the waiting-woman to the presence of my lady, who had not before seen me. She sat in her study, with one foot on the ground, and the other upon a high stool at some distance from her seat; her sandy locks hung down in a disorder I cannot call beautiful, from her head, which was deprived of its coif, for the benefit of scratching with one hand, while she held a stump of a pen in the other. Her forehead was high and wrinkled; her eyes were large, grey, and prominent; her nose was long, sharp, and aquiline; her mouth of vast capacity; her visage meagre and freckled, and her chin peaked like a shoemaker's paring-knife; her upper lip contained a large quantity of plain Spanish, which, by continual falling, had embroidered her neck, that was not naturally very white; and the breast of her gown, that flowed loose about her with a negligence truly poetic, discovering linen that was very fine, and to all appearance never *washed but in Castalian streams.* Around her lay heaps of books, globes, quadrants, telescopes, and other learned apparatus. Her snuff-box stood at her right hand; at her left hand lay her handkerchief, sufficiently used; and a convenience to spit in appeared on one side of her chair. She being in a reverie when we entered, the maid did not think proper to disturb her; so that we waited some minutes unobserved, during which time she bit the quill several times, altered her position, made many wry faces, and at length, with an air of triumph, repeated aloud:

Nor dare th' immortal gods my rage oppose.

Having committed her success to paper, she turned towards the door, and perceiving us, cried, "What's the matter?"—"Here's the young man," replied my conductress, "whom Mrs. Sagely recommended as a footman to your ladyship." On this information she stared in my face a considerable time, and then asked my name, which I thought proper to conceal under that of John Brown. After having surveyed me with a curious eye, she broke out into, "O! ay, thou wast shipwrecked, I remember. Whether didst thou come on shore on the back of a whale or a dolphin?" To this I answered I had swam ashore without any assistance.—Then she demanded to know if I had ever been at the Hellespont, and swam from Sestos to Abydos. I replied in the negative. Upon which she bade the maid order a suit of new livery for me, and instruct me in the articles of my duty. So saying, she spit in her snuff-box, and wiped her nose with her cap, which lay on the table instead of a handkerchief. We returned to the kitchen, where I was regaled by the maids, who seemed to vie with each other in expressing their regard for me; and from them I understood that my business consisted in cleaning knives and forks, laying the cloth, waiting at table, carrying messages, and attending my lady when she went abroad. There was a very good suit of livery in the house, which had belonged to my predecessor, deceased, and it fitted me exactly; so that there was no occasion for employing a tailor on my account. I had not long been equipped in this manner, when my lady's bell rung; upon which I ran upstairs, and found her stalking about the room in her shift and under-petticoat only: I would have immediately retired as became me, but she bade me come in, and air a clean shift for her; which operation I having performed with some backwardness, she put it on before me without any ceremony, and I verily believe was ignorant of my sex all that time, as being quite absorbed in contemplation. About four o'clock in the afternoon, I was ordered to lay the cloth, and place two covers, which I understood were for my mistress and her niece, whom I had not as yet seen. Though I was not very dexterous at this work, I performed it pretty well for a beginner; and, when dinner was upon the table, saw my mistress approach, accompanied by the young lady, whose name, for the present, shall be Narcissa. So much sweetness appeared in the countenance and carriage of this amiable apparition, that my heart was captivated at first sight, and, while dinner lasted, I gazed upon her without intermission. Her age seemed to be seventeen, her stature tall, her shape unexceptionable; her hair, that fell down upon her ivory neck in ringlets, black as jet; her arched eyebrows of the same colour; her eyes piercing, yet tender; her lips of the consistence and hue of cherries; her complexion clear, delicate, and healthy; her aspect noble, ingenuous, and humane; and the whole person so ravishingly delightful, that it was impossible for any creature endued with sensibility, to see without admiring, and admire without loving her to excess! I began to curse the servile station that placed me so far beneath the regard of this idol of my adoration! and yet I blessed my fate, that enabled me to enjoy daily the sight of so much perfection! When she spoke, I listened with pleasure; but when she spoke to me, my soul was thrilled with an ecstasy of tumultuous joy! I was even so happy as to be the subject of their conversation. For Narcissa having observed me, said to her aunt, "I see your new footman is come." Then addressing herself to me, asked with ineffable complacency if I was the person who had been so cruelly used by robbers? When I satisfied her in this, she expressed a desire of knowing the other particulars of my fortune, both before and since my being shipwrecked. Hereupon (as Mrs. Sagely had counselled me) I told her that I had been bound apprentice to the master of a ship, contrary to my inclination, which ship had foundered at sea; that I and four more, who chanced to be on deck when she went down, made shift to swim to the shore, when my companions, after having overpowered me, stripped me to the shirt, and left me, as they imagined, dead of the wounds I received in my own defence. Then I related the circumstances of my being found in a barn, with the inhuman treatment I met with from the country people and parson; the description of which, I perceived, drew tears from the charming creature's eyes! When I had finished my recital, my mistress said, "*Ma foil le garçon est bien fait!*" To which opinion Narcissa assented, with a compliment to my understanding in the same language, that flattered my vanity extremely.

The conversation, among other subjects, turned upon the young squire, whom my lady inquired after under the title of the Savage; and was informed by her niece that he was still in bed, repairing the fatigue of last night's debauch, and recruiting strength and spirits to undergo a fox-chase to-morrow morning, in company with Sir Timothy Thicket, Squire Bumper, and a great many other gentlemen of the same stamp, whom he had invited on that occasion; so that, by daybreak, the whole house would be in an uproar. This was a very disagreeable piece of news to the virtuoso, who protested she would stuff her ears with cotton when she went to bed, and take a dose of opium to make her sleep the more sound, that she might not be disturbed and distracted by the clamour of the brutes.

When their dinner was over, I and my fellow-servants sat down to ours in the kitchen, where I understood that Sir Timothy Thicket was a wealthy knight in the neighbourhood, between whom and Narcissa a match had been projected by her brother, who promised at the same time to espouse Sir Timothy's sister; by which means, as their fortunes were pretty equal, the young ladies would be provided for, and their brothers be never the poorer; but that the ladies did not concur in the scheme, each of them entertaining a hearty contempt for the person allotted to her for a husband by this agreement. This information begat in me a mortal aversion to Sir Timothy, whom I looked upon as my rival, and cursed in my heart for his presumption. Next morning, by daybreak, being awakened by the noise of the hunters and hounds, I arose to view the cavalcade, and had a sight of my competitor, whose accomplishments, the estate excluded, did not seem brilliant enough to give me much uneasiness with respect to Narcissa, who, I flattered myself, was not to be won by such qualifications as he was master of, either as to person or mind. My mistress, notwithstanding her precaution, was so much disturbed by her nephew's company, that she did not rise till five o'clock in the afternoon; so that I had an opportunity of examining her study at leisure, to which examination I was strongly prompted by my curiosity. Here I found a thousand scraps of her own poetry, consisting of three, four, ten, twelve, and twenty lines, on an infinity of subjects, which, as whim inspired, she had begun, without constancy or capacity to bring to any degree of composition. But, what was very extraordinary in a female poet, there was not the least mention made of love in any of her performances. I counted fragments of five tragedies, the titles of which were, "The Stern Philosopher—The Double Murder—The Sacrilegious Traitor—The Fall of Lucifer—and The Last Day." From whence I gathered, that her disposition was gloomy, and her imagination delighted with objects of horror. Her library was composed of the best English historians, poets, and philosophers; of all the French critics and poets, and of a few books in Italian, chiefly poetry, at the head of which were Tasso and Ariosto, pretty much used. Besides these, translations of the classics into French, but not one book in Greek or Latin; a circumstance that discovered her ignorance in these languages. After having taken a full view of this collection, I retired, and, at the usual time, was preparing to lay the cloth, when I was told by the maid that her mistress was still in bed, and had been so affected with the notes of the hounds in the morning, that she actually believed herself a hare beset by the hunters; and begged a few greens to munch for breakfast. When I expressed my surprise at this unaccountable imagination, she gave me to understand that her lady was very much subject to whims of this nature; sometimes fancying herself an animal, sometimes a piece of furniture, during which conceited transformations it was very dangerous to come near her, especially when she represented a beast; for that, lately, in the character of a cat, she had flown at her, and scratched her face in a terrible manner; that, some months ago, she prophesied the general conflagration was at hand, and nothing would be able to quench it but her water, which, therefore, she kept so long that her life was in danger; and she must needs have died of the retention, had they not found an expedient to make her evacuate, by kindling a bonfire under her chamber window, and persuading her that the house was in flames; upon which, with great deliberation, she bade them bring all the tubs and vessels they could find, to be filled, for the preservation of the house, into one of which she immediately discharged the cause of her distemper. I was also informed that nothing contributed so much to the recovery of her reason as music, which was always administered on those occasions by Narcissa, who played perfectly well on the harpsichord, and to whom she, the maid, was just then going to intimate her aunt's disorder. She was no sooner gone than I was summoned by the bell to my lady's chamber, where I found her sitting squat on her hams on the floor, in the manner of puss when she listens to the outcries of her pursuers. When I appeared, she started up with an alarmed look, and sprung to the other side of the room to avoid me, whom, without doubt, she mistook for a beagle thirsting after her life. Perceiving her extreme confusion, I retired, and, on the staircase, met the adorable Narcissa coming up, to whom I imparted the situation of my mistress. She said not a word, but, smiling with unspeakable grace, went into her aunt's apartment, and in a little time my ears were ravished with the effects of her skill. She accompanied the instrument with a voice so sweet and melodious, that I did not wonder at the surprising change it produced on the spirits of my mistress, which were soon composed to peace and sober reflection.

About seven o'clock the hunters arrived, with the skins of two foxes and one badger, carried before them as trophies of their success. And, when they were about to sit down to dinner, or supper, Sir Timothy Thicket desired that Narcissa would honour the table with her presence. But this request, notwithstanding her brother's threats and entreaties, she refused, on pretence of attending her aunt, who was indisposed; so I enjoyed the satisfaction of seeing my rival mortified. But this disappointment made no great impression on him, who consoled himself with the bottle, of which the whole company became so enamoured, that, after a most horrid uproar of laughing, singing, swearing, dancing, and fighting, they were all carried to bed in a state of utter oblivion. My duty being altogether detached from the squire and his family, I led a pretty easy and comfortable life, drinking daily intoxicating draughts of love from the charms of Narcissa, which brightened on my contemplation every day more and more. Inglorious as my station was, I became blind to my own unworthiness, and even conceived hopes of one day enjoying this amiable creature, whose affability greatly encouraged these presumptuous thoughts.

CHAPTER XL

My Mistress is surprised at my Learning—Communicates her Performance to me—I impart some of mine to her—Am mortified at her faint Praise—Narcissa approves of my Conduct—I gain an involuntary Conquest over the Cook maid and Dairy-maid—Their mutual Resentment and Insinuations—The Jealousy of their Lovers.

DURING this season of love and tranquillity, my muse, which had lain dormant so long, awoke, and produced several small performances on the subject of my flame; but, as it concerned me nearly to remain undiscovered in my real character and sentiments, I was under a necessity of mortifying my desire of praise, by confining my works to my own perusal and applause. In the meantime I strove to insinuate myself into the good opinion of both ladies; and succeeded so well, by my diligence and dutiful behaviour, that, in a little time, I was at least a favourite servant; and frequently enjoyed the pleasure of hearing myself mentioned in French and Italian, with some degree of warmth and surprise, by the dear object of all my wishes, as a person who had so much of the gentleman in my appearance and discourse, that she could not for her soul treat me like a common lacquey. My prudence and modesty were not long proof against these bewitching compliments. One day, while I waited at dinner, the conversation turned upon a knotty passage of Tasso's *Jerusalem*, which, it seems, had puzzled them both. After a great many unsatisfactory conjectures, my mistress, taking the book out of her pocket, turned up the place in question, and read the sentence over and over without success; at length, despairing of finding the author's meaning, she turned to me, saying, "Come hither, Bruno, let us see what fortune will do for us; I will interpret to thee what goes before and what follows this obscure paragraph, the particular words of which I will also explain, that thou mayest, by comparing one with another, guess the sense of that which perplexes us." I was too vain to let slip this opportunity of displaying my talents, therefore, without hesitation, read and explained the whole of that which had disconcerted them, to the utter astonishment of both. Narcissa's face and lovely neck were overspread with blushes, from which I drew a favourable omen, while her aunt, after having stared at me a good while with a look of amazement, exclaimed, "In the name of heaven! Who art thou?" I told her I had picked up a smattering of Italian during a voyage up the Straits. At this explanation she shook her head, and observed that no smatterer could read as I had done. She then desired to know if I understood French? To which question I answered in the affirmative. She asked if I was acquainted with Latin and Greek? I replied, "A little."—"Oho!" continued she, "and with philosophy and mathematics I suppose?" I owned I knew something of each. Then she repeated her stare and interrogation. I began to repent my vanity, and, in order to repair the fault I had committed, said it was not to be wondered at if I had a tolerable education, for learning was so cheap in my country, that every peasant was a scholar; but I hoped her ladyship would think my understanding no exception to my character. She was pleased to answer, "No, no, God forbid." But during the rest of the time they sat at table, they behaved with remarkable reserve.

This alteration gave me great uneasiness; and I passed the night without sleep, in melancholy reflections on the vanity of young men, which prompts them to commit so many foolish actions, contrary to their own sober judgment. Next day, however, instead of profiting by this self-condemnation, I yielded still more to the dictates of the principle I had endeavoured to chastise, and, if fortune had not befriended me more than prudence could expect, I should have been treated with the contempt it deserved. After breakfast, my lady, who was a true author, bade me follow her into the study, where she expressed herself thus: "Since you are so learned, you cannot be void of taste; therefore I am to desire your opinion of a small perform-ance in poetry which I lately composed. You must know I have planned a tragedy, the subject of which shall be the murder of a prince before the altar, where he is busy at his devotions. After the deed is perpetrated, the regicide will harangue the people with the bloody dagger in his hand; and I have already composed a speech, which I think will suit the character extremely; here it is." Then taking up a scrap of paper, she read, with violent emphasis and gesture, as follows:

> Thus have I sent the simple king to hell,
> Without or coffin, shroud, or passing bell;
> To me what are divine and human laws?
> I court no sanction but my own applause!
> Rapes, robb'ries, treasons, yield my soul delight;
> And human carnage gratifies my sight:
> I drag the parent by the hoary hair,
> And toss the sprawling infant on my spear, ⎫
> While the fond mother's cries regale mine ear, ⎭
> I fight, I vanquish, murder friends and foes:
> Nor dare th' immortal gods my rage oppose.

Though I did great violence to my understanding in praising this unnatural rhapsody, I nevertheless extolled it as a produc-tion that of itself deserved immortal fame; and besought her ladyship to bless the world with the fruits of those uncommon talents Heaven had bestowed upon her. She smiled with a look of self-complacency, and, encouraged by the incense I had offered, communicated all her poetical works, which I applauded one by one, with as little candour as I had shown at first. Satiated with my flattery, which, I hope, my situation justified, she could not in conscience refuse me an opportunity of shining in my turn; and, therefore, after a compliment to my nice discernment and taste, observed that, doubtless, I must have produced something in that way myself, which she desired to see. This was a temptation I could by no means resist. I owned that, while I was at college, I wrote some small de-tached pieces, at the desire of a friend who was in love, and at her request repeated the following verses, which indeed my love for Narcissa had inspired.

ON CELIA,

PLAYING ON THE HARPSICHORD AND SINGING

When Sappho struck the quiv'ring wire,
The throbbing breast was all on fire:
And, when she rais'd the vocal lay,
The captive soul was charm'd away.

But had the nymph possess'd with these,
Thy softer, chaster power to please:
Thy beauteous air of sprightly youth,
Thy native smiles of artless truth;

The worm of grief had never prey'd
On the forsaken love-sick maid:
Nor had she mourn'd an hapless flame,
Nor dash'd on rocks her tender frame.

My mistress paid me a cold compliment on my versification, which, she said, was elegant enough, but the subject beneath the pen of a true poet. I was extremely nettled at her indifference, and looked at Narcissa, who by this time had joined us, for her approbation; but she declined giving her opinion, protesting she was no judge of these matters; so that I was forced to retire, very much balked in my expectation, which was generally a little too sanguine. In the afternoon, however, the waiting-maid assured me that Narcissa had expressed her approbation of my performance with great warmth, and desired her to procure a copy of it, as for herself, that she (Narcissa) might have an opportunity to peruse it at pleasure. I was elated to an extravagant pitch at this intelligence, and immediately transcribed a fair copy of my ode, which was carried to the dear charmer, together with another on the same subject, as follows:

Thy fatal shafts unerring move,
I bow before thine altar, Love!
I feel thy soft resistless flame
Glide swift through all my vital frame!

For while I gaze, my bosom glows,
My blood in tides impetuous flows;
Hope, fear, and joy alternate roll,
And floods of transport whelm my soul!

My falt'ring tongue attempts in vain,
In soothing murmurs to complain;
My tongue some secret magic ties,
My murmurs sink in broken sighs!

Condemn'd to nurse eternal care,
And ever drop the silent tear,
Unheard, I mourn, unknown I sigh,
Unfriended live, unpity'd die!

Whether or not Narcissa discovered my passion, I could not learn from her behaviour, which, though always benevolent to me, was henceforth more reserved and less cheerful. While my thoughts aspired to a sphere so far above me, I had unwittingly made a conquest of the cook-wench and dairy-maid, who became so jealous of each other, that, if their sentiments had been refined by education, it is probable one or other of them would have had recourse to poison or steel to be avenged of her rival; but, as their minds were happily adapted to their humble station, their mutual enmity was confined to scolding and fisticuffs, in which exercises they were both well skilled. My good fortune did not long remain a secret; for it was disclosed by the frequent broils of these heroines, who kept no decorum in their encounters. The coachman and gardener, who paid their devoirs to my admirers, each to his respective choice, alarmed at my success, laid their heads together, in order to concert a plan of revenge; and the former having been educated at the academy at Tottenham Court, undertook to challenge me to single combat. He accordingly, with many opprobrious invectives, bade me defiance, and offered to box me for twenty guineas. I told him that, although I believed myself a match for him, even at that work, I would not descend so far below the dignity of a gentleman as to fight like a porter; but if he had anything to say to me, I was his man at blunderbuss, musket, pistol, sword, hatchet, spit, cleaver, fork, or needle; nay, I swore that, should he give his tongue any more saucy liberties at my expense, I would crop his ears without any ceremony. This rhodomontade, delivered with a stern countenance and resolute tone, had the desired effect upon my antagonist, who, with some confusion, sneaked off, and gave his friend an account of his reception. The story taking air among the servants, procured for me the title of Gentleman John, with which I was sometimes honoured, even by my mistress and Narcissa, who had been informed of the whole affair by the chambermaid. In the meantime, the rival queans expressed their passion by all the ways in their power; the cook entertained me with choice bits, the dairy-maid with stroakings; the first would often encourage me to discover myself by complimenting me upon my courage and learning, and observing, that if she had a husband like me, to maintain order, and keep accounts, she could make a great deal of money by setting up an eating-house at London, for gentlemen's servants on board wages. The other courted my affection by showing her own importance, and telling me that many a substantial farmer in the neighbourhood would be glad to marry her; but she was resolved to please her eye, if she should plague her heart. Then she would launch out into the praise of my proper person, and say she was sure I would make a good husband, for I was very good-natured. I began to be uneasy at the importunities of these inamoratas, whom, at another time, perhaps, I might have pleased without the disagreeable sauce of matrimony; but at present my whole soul was engrossed by Narcissa, and I could not bear the thoughts of doing anything derogatory of the passion I entertained for her.

CHAPTER XLI

Narcissa being in Danger from the Brutality of Sir Timothy is rescued by me, who revenge myself on my Rival—I declare my Passion, and retreat to the Seaside—Am surrounded by Smugglers and carried to Boulogne—Find my Uncle, Lieutenant Bowling, in great Distress, and relieve him—Our Conversation.

AT certain intervals, my ambition would revive; I would despise myself for my tame resignation to my sordid fate, and revolve an hundred schemes for assuming the character of a gentleman, to which I thought myself entitled by birth and education. In these fruitless suggestions time stole away unperceived, and I had already remained eight months in the station of a footman, when an accident happened that put an end to my servitude, and for the present banished all hopes of succeeding in my love.

Narcissa went one day to visit Miss Thicket, who lived with her brother, within less than a mile of our house, and was persuaded to walk home in the cool of the evening, accompanied by Sir Timothy, who having a good deal of the brute in him, was instigated to use some unbecoming familiarities with her, encouraged by the solitariness of a field through which they passed. The lovely creature was incensed at his rude behaviour, for which she reproached him in such a manner, that he lost all regard to decency, and actually offered violence to this pattern of innocence and beauty. But Heaven would not suffer so much goodness to be violated; and sent me, who, passing by accident near the place, was alarmed with her cries, to her succour. What were the emotions of my soul when I beheld Narcissa, almost sinking beneath the brutal force of this satyr! I flew like lightning to her rescue, and he perceiving me, quitted his prey, and drew his hanger to chastise my presumption. My indignation was too high to admit one thought of fear; so that, rushing upon him, I struck his weapon out of his hand, and used my cudgel so successfully, that he fell to the ground, and lay, to all appearance, without sense. Then I turned to Narcissa, who had swooned, and sitting down by her, gently raised her head, and supported it on my bosom, while, with my hand around her waist, I kept her in that position. My soul was thrilled with tumultuous joy at feeling the object of my dearest wishes within my arms; and while she lay insensible, I could not refrain from applying my cheek to hers, and ravishing a kiss. In a little time, the blood began to revisit her face; she opened her enchanting eyes, and having recollected her late situation, said, with a look full of tender acknowledgment, "Dear John, I am eternally obliged to you!" So saying, she made an effort to rise, in which I assisted her, and she proceeded to the house, leaning upon me all the way. I was a thousand times tempted by this opportunity to declare my passion, but the dread of disobliging her restrained my tongue. We had not moved an hundred paces from the scene of her distress, when I perceived Sir Timothy rise and walk homeward; a circumstance which, though it gave me some satisfaction, inasmuch as I thereby knew I had not killed him, filled me with just apprehension of his resentment, which I found myself in no condition to withstand; especially when I considered his intimacy with our squire, to whom I knew he could justify himself for what he had done, by imputing it to his love, and desiring his brother Bruin to take the same liberty with his sister, without any fear of offence. When we arrived at the house, Narcissa assured me she would exert all her influence in protecting me from the revenge of Thicket, and likewise engage her aunt in my favour. At the same time, pulling out her purse, offered it as a small consideration for the service I had done her. But I stood too much upon the punctilios of love, to incur the least suspicion of being mercenary, and refused the present, by saying I had merited nothing by barely doing my duty. She seemed astonished at my disinterestedness, and blushed; I felt the same suffusion, and, with a downcast eye and broken accent, told her I had one request to make, which if her generosity would grant, I should think myself fully recompensed for an age of misery. She changed colour at this preamble, and, with great confusion, replied, she hoped my good sense would hinder me from asking anything she was bound in honour to refuse, and therefore bade me signify my desire. Upon which I kneeled, and begged to kiss her hand. She immediately, with an averted look, stretched it out; I imprinted on it an ardent kiss, and bathing it with my tears, cried, "Dear Madam, I am an unfortunate gentleman, and love you to distraction, but would have died a thousand deaths rather than make this declaration under such a servile appearance, were I not determined to yield to the rigour of my fate, to fly from your bewitching presence, and bury my presumptuous passion in eternal silence." With these words I rose and went away, before she could recover her spirits so far as to make any reply. My first care was to go and consult Mrs. Sagely, with whom I had maintained a friendly correspondence ever since I left her house. When she understood my situation, the good woman, with real concern, condoled me on my unhappy fate, and approved of my resolution to leave the country, as being perfectly well acquainted with the barbarous disposition of my rival, "who by this time," said she, "has no doubt meditated a scheme of revenge. Indeed I cannot see how you will be able to elude his vengeance; being himself in the commission, he will immediately grant warrants for apprehending you; and as almost all the people in this country are dependent on him or his friend, it will be impossible for you to find shelter among them. If you should be apprehended, he will commit you to jail, where you may possibly languish in great misery till the next assizes, and then be transported for assaulting a magistrate." While she thus warned me of my danger, we heard a knocking at the door, which threw us both into consternation, as, in all probability, it was occasioned by my pursuers: whereupon this generous old lady, putting two guineas into my hand, with tears in her eyes, bade me for God's sake to get out at the back door, and consult my safety as Providence should direct me. There was no time for deliberation. I followed her advice, and escaped by the benefit of a dark night to the seaside, where, while I ruminated on my next excursion, I was all of a sudden surrounded by armed men, who, having bound my hands and feet, bade me make no noise, on pain of being shot, and carried me on board of a vessel, which I soon perceived to be a smuggling cutter. This discovery gave me some satisfaction at first, because I concluded myself safe from the resentment of Sir Timothy. But when I found myself in the hands of ruffians, who threatened to execute me for a spy, I would have thought myself happily quit for a year's imprisonment, or even transportation. It was in vain for me to protest my innocence. I could not persuade them that I had taken a solitary walk to their haunt, at such an hour, for merely my own amusement; and I did not think it my interest to disclose the true cause of my retreat, because I was afraid they would have made their peace with justice, by surrendering me to the penalty of the law. What confirmed their suspicion was, the appearance of a custom-house yacht, which gave them chase, and had well-nigh made a prize of the vessel; when they were delivered from their fears by a thick fog, which effectually screened them, and favoured their arrival at Boulogne. But before they got out of sight of their pursuer, they held a council of war about me; and some of the most ferocious among them would have thrown me overboard, as a traitor who had betrayed them to their enemies; but others, more considerate, alleged that, if they put me to death, and should afterwards be taken, they could expect no mercy from the legislature, which would never pardon outlawry aggravated by murder. It was therefore determined by a plurality of votes, that I should be set on shore in France, and left to find my passage back to England as I should think proper, this being punishment sufficient for the bare suspicion of a crime in itself not capital. Although this favourable determination gave me great pleasure, the apprehension of being robbed would not suffer me to be perfectly at ease. To prevent this calamity, as soon as I was untied, in consequence of the foresaid decision, I tore a small hole in one of my stockings, into which I dropped six guineas, reserving half a piece and some silver in my pocket, that finding something, they might not be tempted to make any further inquiry. This was a very necessary precaution; for when we came within sight of the French shore, one of the smugglers told me I must pay for my passage. To this declaration I replied, that my passage was none of my own seeking; therefore they could not expect a reward from me for transporting me into a strange country by force. "Damn me!" said the outlaw, "none of your palaver; but let me see what money you have got." So saying, he thrust his hand into my pocket without any ceremony, and emptied it of the contents. Then casting an eye at my hat and wig, which captivated his fancy, he took them off, and clapping his own on my head, declared that a fair exchange was no robbery. I was fain to put up with the bargain, which was by no means favourable to me; and a little while after we went all on shore together.

I resolved to take my leave of these desperadoes without much ceremony, when one of them cautioned me against appearing to their prejudice, if ever I returned to England, unless I had a mind to be murdered; for which service, he assured me, the gang never wanted agents. I promised to observe his advice, and departed for the Upper Town, where I inquired for a cabaret, or public-house, into which I went, with an intention of taking some refreshment. In the kitchen, five Dutch sailors sat at breakfast, with a large loaf, a firkin of butter, and a cag of brandy, the bung of which they often applied to their mouths with great perseverance and satisfaction. At some distance from them I perceived another person in the same garb, sitting in a pensive solitary manner, entertaining himself with a whiff of tobacco from the stump of a pipe as black as jet. The appearance of distress never failed to attract my regard and compassion. I approached this forlorn tar with a view to offer him my assistance; and, notwithstanding the alteration of dress, and disguise of a long beard, I discovered in him my long-lost and lamented uncle and benefactor, Lieutenant Bowling! Good Heaven! what were the agitations of my soul, between the joy of finding again such a valuable friend, and the sorrow of seeing him in such a low condition! The tears gushed down my cheeks: I stood motionless and silent for some time; at length, recovering the use of speech, exclaimed, "Gracious God! Mr. Bowling!" My uncle no sooner heard his name mentioned, than he started up, crying with some surprise, "Halloa!" and after having looked at me steadfastly, without being able to recollect me, said, "Did you call me, brother?" I told him I had something extraordinary to communicate, and desired him to give me the hearing for a few minutes in another room; but he would by no means consent to this proposal, saying, "Avast there, friend; none of your tricks upon travellers; if you have anything to say to me, do it above board; you need not be afraid of being overheard; here are none who understand our lingo."

Though I was loth to discover myself before company, I could no longer refrain from telling him I was his own nephew, Roderick Random. On this information, he considered me with great earnestness and astonishment, and recalling my features, which, though enlarged, were not entirely altered since he had seen me, came up, and shook me by the hand very cordially, protesting he was glad to see me well. After some pause, he went on thus: "And yet, my lad, I am sorry to see you under such colours; the more so, as it is not in my power, at present, to change them for the better, times being very hard with me." With these words, I could perceive a tear trickle down his furrowed cheeks, which affected me so much, that I wept bitterly. Imagining my sorrow was the effect of my own misfortunes, he comforted me with observing, that life was a voyage in which we must expect to meet with all weathers; sometimes it was calm, sometimes rough; that a fair gale often succeeded a storm; that the wind did not always sit one way, and that despair signified nothing; but that resolution and skill were better than a stout vessel; for why? because they require no carpenter, and grow stronger the more labour they undergo. I dried up my tears, which I assured him were not shed for my own distress, but for his, and begged leave to accompany him into another room, where we could converse more at our ease. There I recounted to him the ungenerous usage I had met with from Potion; at which relation he started up, stalked across the room three or four times in a great hurry, and, grasping his cudgel, cried, "I would I were alongside of him—that's all—I would I were alongside of him!" I then gave him a detail of all my adventures and sufferings, which affected him more than I could have imagined; and concluded with telling him that Captain Oakum was still alive, and that he might return to England when he would to solicit his affairs, without danger or molestation. He was wonderfully pleased with this piece of information, of which, however, he said he could not at present avail himself, for want of money to pay his passage to London. This objection I soon removed, by putting five guineas into his hand, and telling him I thought myself extremely happy in having an opportunity of manifesting my gratitude to him in his necessity. But it was with the utmost difficulty I could prevail upon him to accept of two, which he affirmed were more than sufficient to defray the necessary expense. After this friendly contest was over, he proposed we should have a mess of something: "For," said he, "it has been banyan-day with me a great while. You must know I was shipwrecked five days ago, near a place called Lisieux, in company with those Dutchmen who are now drinking below; and having but little money when I came ashore, it was soon spent, because I let them have share and share while it lasted. Howsomever, I should have remembered the old saying, *Every hog his own apple*: for when they found my hold unstowed, they went all hands to shooling and begging, and because I would not take a spell at the same duty, refused to give me the least assistance; so that I have not broke bread these two days." I was shocked at the extremity of his distress, and ordered some bread, cheese, and wine to be brought immediately, to allay his hunger, until a fricassee of chickens could be prepared. When he had recruited his spirits with this homely fare, I desired to know the particulars of his peregrination since the accident at Cape Tiberoon; which were briefly these: the money he had about him being all spent at Port Louis, the civility and hospitality of the French cooled to such a degree, that he was obliged to list on board of one of their king's ships as a common foremast man, to prevent himself from starving on shore. In this situation he continued two years, during which time he had acquired some knowledge of their language, and the reputation of a good seaman: the ship he belonged to was ordered home to France, where she was laid up, as unfit for service, and he was received on board of one of Monsieur D'Antin's squadron, in quality of quarter-master; which office he performed in a voyage to the West Indies, where they engaged with our ship as before related; but his conscience upbraiding him for serving the enemies of his country, he quitted the ship at the same place where he first listed, and got to Curaçoa in a Dutch vessel; there he bargained with a skipper bound to Europe, to work for his passage to Holland, from whence he was in hopes of hearing from his friends in England; but was cast away, as he mentioned before, on the French coast, and must have been reduced to the necessity of travelling on foot to Holland, and begging for his subsistence on the road, or of entering on board of another French man-of-war, at the hazard of being treated as a deserter, if Providence had not sent me to his succour. "And now, my lad," continued he, "I think I shall steer my course directly to London, where I do not doubt of being replaced, and of having the R taken off me by the Lords of the Admiralty, to whom I intend to write a petition setting forth my case. If I succeed, I shall have wherewithal to give you some assistance, because, when I left the ship, I had two years' pay due to me: therefore I desire to know whither you are bound; and besides, perhaps, I may have interest enough to procure a warrant appointing you surgeon's mate of the ship to which I shall belong. For the beadle of the Admiralty is my good friend; and he and one of the under-clerks are sworn brothers, and that under-clerk has a good deal to say with one of the upper clerks, who is very well known to the under-secretary who, upon his recommendation, I hope will recommend my affair to the first secretary; and he again will speak to one of the lords in my behalf: so that you see I do not want friends to assist me on occasion—as for the fellow Crampley, tho'f I know him not, I am sure he is neither seaman nor officer, by what you have told me, or else he could never be so much mistaken in his reckoning, as to run the ship on shore on the coast of Sussex, before he believed himself in soundings; neither, when that accident happened, would he have left the ship until she had been stove to pieces, especially when the tide was making; wherefore, by this time, I do suppose he has been tried by a court-martial, and executed for his cowardice and misconduct." I could not help smiling at the description of my uncle's ladder, by which he proposed to climb to the attention of the Board of Admiralty; and though I knew the world too well to confide in such dependence myself, I would not discourage him with doubts; but asked if he had no friend in London who would advance a small sum of money to enable him to appear as he ought, and make a small present to the under-secretary, who might possibly despatch his business the sooner on that account. He scratched his head, and, after some recollection, replied, "Why, yes, I believe Daniel Whipcord the ship-chandler in Wapping would not refuse me such a small matter. I know I can have what credit I want, for lodging, liquor, and clothes: but as to money I won't be positive: had honest Block been living, I should not have been at a loss." I was heartily sorry to find a worthy man so destitute of friends, when he had such need of them; and looked upon my own situation as less miserable than his, because I was better acquainted with the selfishness and roguery of mankind, consequently less liable to disappointment and imposition.

CHAPTER XLII

He takes his Passage in a Cutter for Deal—We are accosted by a Priest, who proves to be a Scotchman—His Profession of Friendship—He is affronted by the Lieutenant, who afterwards appeases him by Submission —My Uncle embarks—I am introduced by a Priest to a Capuchin, in whose Company I set out for Paris—The Character of my Fellow-traveller— An Adventure on the Road—I am shocked at his Behaviour.

WHEN our repast was ended, we walked down to the harbour, where we found a cutter that was to sail for Deal in the evening, and Mr. Bowling agreed for his passage. In the meantime, we sauntered about the town to satisfy our curiosity, our conversation turning on the subject of my designs, which were not as yet fixed: neither can it be supposed that my mind was at ease, when I found myself reduced almost to extreme poverty, in the midst of foreigners, among whom I had not one acquaintance to advise or befriend me. My uncle was sensible of my forlorn condition, and pressed me to accompany him to England, where he did not doubt of finding some sort of provision for me: but, besides the other reasons I had for avoiding that kingdom, I looked upon it, at this time, as the worst country in the universe for a honest man to live in; and therefore determined to remain in France, at all events. I was confirmed in this resolution by a reverend priest, who passing by at this time, and overhearing us speak English, accosted us in the same language, telling us he was our countryman, and wishing it might be in his power to do us any service. We thanked this grave person for his courteous offer, and invited him to drink a glass with us, which he did not think proper to refuse, and we went altogether into a tavern of his recommending. After having drank to our healths in a bumper of good Burgundy, he began to inquire into our situation, particularly the place of our nativity, which we no sooner named, than he started up, and wringing our hands with great fervour, shed a flood of tears, crying, "I come from the same part of the country! perhaps you are my own relations." I was on my guard against his caresses, which I suspected very much, when I remembered the adventure of the money-dropper; but, without any appearance of diffidence, observed, that as he was born in that part of the country, he must certainly know our families, which, howsoever mean our present appearance might be, were none of the most obscure or inconsiderable. Then I discovered our names, to which I found he was no stranger: he had known my grandfather personally; and, notwithstanding an absence of fifty years from Scotland, recounted so many particulars of the families in the neighbourhood, that my scruples were entirely removed, and I thought myself happy in his acquaintance. In the course of our conversation, I disclosed my condition without reserve, and displayed my talents to such advantage, that the old father looked upon me with admiration, and assured me that if I stayed in France, and listened to reason, I could not fail of making my fortune, to which he would contribute all in his power.

My uncle began to be jealous of the priest's insinuation, and very abruptly declared that, if ever I should renounce my religion, he would break off all connection and correspondence with me; for it was his opinion, that no honest man would swerve from the principles in which he was bred, whether Turkish, Protestant, or Roman. The father, affronted at this declaration, with great vehemence began a long discourse setting forth the danger of obstinacy, and shutting one's eyes against the light: he said that ignorance would be no plea towards justification, when we had opportunities of being better informed; and that, if the minds of people had not been open to conviction, the Christian religion could not have been propagated in the world; and we should now be in a state of Pagan darkness and barbarity. He endeavoured to prove, by some texts of Scripture, and many quotations from the fathers, that the Pope was the successor of St. Peter, and vicar of Jesus Christ; that the Church of Rome was the true Holy Catholic Church; and that the Protestant faith was an impious heresy and damnable schism, by which many millions of souls would suffer everlasting perdition. When he had finished this sermon, which I thought he pronounced with more zeal than discretion, he addressed himself to my uncle, and desired to know his objections to what had been said. The lieutenant, whose attention had been wholly engrossed by his own affairs, took the pipe out of his mouth, and replied, "As for me, friend, d'ye see, I have no objection to what you say; it may be either true or false for what I know; I meddle with nobody's affairs but my own; the gunner to his linstock, and the steersman to the helm, as the saying is. I trust to no creed but the compass, and do unto every man as I would be done by; so that I defy the Pope, the Devil, and the Pretender; and hope to be saved as well as another." This association of persons gave great offence to the friar, who protested in a mighty passion, that if Mr. Bowling had not been his countryman, he would have caused him to be imprisoned for his insolence. I ventured to disapprove of my uncle's rashness, and appeased the old gentleman by assuring him, there was no offence intended by my kinsman, who, by this time, sensible of his error, shook the injured party by the hand, and asked pardon for the freedom he had taken. Matters being amicably compromised, he invited us to come and see him in the afternoon at the convent to which he belonged, and took his leave for the present; when my uncle recommended it strongly to me to persevere in the religion of my forefathers, whatever advantages I might propose to myself by a change, which could not fail of disgracing myself, and dishonouring my family. I assured him, no consideration should induce me to forfeit his friendship and good opinion on that score; at which assurance he discovered great satisfaction, and put me in mind of dinner, which we immediately bespoke, and, when it was ready, ate together.

I imagined my acquaintance with the Scottish priest, if properly managed, might turn out to my advantage, and therefore resolved to cultivate it as much as I could. With this view we visited him at his convent, according to his invitation, where he treated us with wine and sweetmeats, and showed us everything that was remarkable in the monastery. Having been thus entertained, we took our leave, though not before I had promised to see him next day; and the time fixed for my uncle's embarking being come, I accompanied him to the harbour, and saw him on board. We parted not without tears, after we had embraced, and wished one another all manner of prosperity; and he entreated me to write to him often, directing to Lieutenant Bowling, at the sign of the Union Flag, near the Hermitage, London.

I returned to the house in which we had met, where I passed the night in a very solitary manner, reflecting on the severity of my fate, and endeavouring to project some likely scheme of life for the future; but my invention failed me; I saw nothing but insurmountable difficulties in my way, and was ready to despair at the miserable prospect! That I might not, however, neglect any probable means, I got up in the morning and went directly to the father, whose advice and assistance I implored. He received me very kindly, and gave me to understand that there was one way of life in which a person of my talents could not fail of making a great figure. I guessed his meaning, and told him once for all, I was fully determined against any alteration in point of religion, therefore, if his proposal regarded the Church, he might save himself the trouble of explaining it. He shook his head and sighed, saying, "Ah! son, son, what a glorious prospect is here spoiled by your stubborn prejudice! Suffer yourself to be persuaded by reason, and consult your temporal welfare, as well as the concerns of your eternal soul. I can, by my interest, procure your admission as a noviciate into this convent, where I will superintend and direct you with a truly paternal affection." Then he launched out into the praises of a monastic life, which no noise disturbs, no cares molest, and no danger invades; where the heart is weaned from carnal attachments, the grosser appetites subdued and chastised, and the soul wafted to divine regions of philosophy and truth, on the wings of studious contemplation. But his eloquence was lost upon me, whom two considerations enabled to withstand his temptations; namely, my promise to my uncle, and my aversion to an ecclesiastical life; for, as to the difference of religion, I looked upon it as a thing of too small moment to come in competition with a man's fortune. Finding me immovable on this head, he told me he was more sorry than offended at my noncompliance, and still ready to employ his good offices in my behalf. "The same erroneous maxims," said he, "that obstruct your promotion in the Church, will infallibly prevent your advancement in the army; but if you can brook the condition of a servant, I am acquainted with some people of rank at Versailles, to whom I can give you letters of recommendation, that you may be entertained by some one of them in quality of *maître d'hôtel*; and I do not doubt that your qualifications will soon entitle you to a better provision." I embraced his offer with great eagerness; and he appointed me to come back in the afternoon, when he would not only give me letters, but likewise introduce me to a Capuchin of his acquaintance, who intended to set out for Paris next morning, in whose company I might travel, without being at the expense of one livre during the whole journey. This piece of good news gave me infinite pleasure; I acknowledged my obligation to the benevolent father in the most grateful expressions; and he performed his promise to a tittle, in delivering the letters, and making me acquainted with the Capuchin, with whom I departed next morning by break of day.

It was not long before I discovered my fellow-traveller to be a merry facetious fellow, who, notwithstanding his profession and appearance of mortification, loved good eating and drinking better than his rosary, and paid more adoration to a pretty girl than to the Virgin Mary, or St. Genevieve. He was a thick brawny young man, with red eyebrows, a hook nose, a face covered with freckles; and his name was Frère Balthazar. His order did not permit him to wear linen, so that, having little occasion to undress himself, he was none of the cleanliest animals in the world; and his constitution was naturally so strongly scented, that I always thought it convenient to keep -to the windward of him in our march. As he was perfectly well known on the road, we fared sumptuously without any cost, and the fatigue of our journey was much alleviated by the good humour of my companion, who sung an infinite number of catches on the subjects of love and wine. We took up our lodging the first night at a peasant's house not far from Abbeville, where we were entertained with an excellent ragout, cooked by our landlord's daughters, one of whom was very handsome. After having eaten heartily, and drank a sufficient quantity of small wine,

we were conducted to a barn, where we found a couple of carpets
spread upon clean straw for our reception. We had not lain in
this situation above half an hour, when we heard somebody
knock softly at the door, upon which Balthazar got up, and let
in our host's two daughters, who wanted to have some private
conversation with him in the dark; when they had whispered
together for some time, the Capuchin came to me and asked if
I was insensible to love, and so hard-hearted as to refuse a share
of my bed to a pretty maid, who had a *tendre* for me? I must
own, to my shame, that I suffered myself to be overcome by
my passion, and with great eagerness seized the occasion, when
I understood the amiable Nanette was to be my bedfellow. In
vain did my reason suggest the respect that I owed to my dear
mistress Narcissa; the idea of that lovely charmer rather in
creased than allayed the ferment of my spirits; and the young
paysanne had no reason to complain of my remembrance. Early
in the morning, the kind creatures left us to our repose, which
lasted till eight o'clock, when we got up, and were treated at
breakfast with chocolate and *l'eau de vie* by our paramours,
of whom we took a tender leave, after my companion had
confessed and given them absolution. While we proceeded on
our journey, the conversation turned upon the night's adventure,
being introduced by the Capuchin, who asked me how I liked my
lodging: I declared my satisfaction, and talked in rapture of
the agreeable Nanette; at which he shook his head, and smiling
said she was a *morceau pour la bonne bouche*. "I never valued
myself," continued he, "upon anything so much as the conquest of Nanette; and, vanity apart, I have been pretty fortunate
in my amours." This information shocked me not a little, as I
was well convinced of his intimacy with her sister; and though
I did not care to tax him with downright incest, I professed my
astonishment at his last night's choice, when, I supposed, the
other was at his devotion. To this hint he answered that, besides
his natural complaisance to the sex, he had another reason to
distribute his favours equally between them, namely, to preserve
peace in the family, which could not otherwise be maintained;
that, moreover, Nanette had conceived an affection for me, and
he loved her too well to balk her inclination; more especially
when he had an opportunity of obliging his friend at the same
time. I thanked him for this instance of his friendship, though
I was extremely disgusted at his want of delicacy, and cursed
the occasion that threw me in his way. Libertine as I was, I
could not bear to see a man behave so wide of the character he

assumed; I looked upon him as a person of very little worth or honesty, and should have even kept a wary eye upon my pocket, if I had thought he could have any temptation to steal. But I could not conceive the use of money to a Capuchin, who is obliged, by the rules of his order, to appear like a beggar, and enjoys all other necessaries of life gratis; besides, my fellow-traveller seemed to be of a complexion too careless and sanguine to give me any apprehension on that score; so that I proceeded with great confidence, in expectation of being soon at my journey's end.

CHAPTER XLIII

We lodge at a House near Amiens, where I am robbed by the Capuchin, who escapes while I am asleep—I go to Noyons in search of him, but without success—Make my Condition known to several People, but find no Relief —Grow desperate—Join a Company of Soldiers—Enlist in the Regiment of Picardy—We are ordered into Germany—I find the Fatigues of the March almost intolerable—Quarrel with my Comrade in a Dispute about Politics—He challenges me to the Field, wounds and disarms me.

THE third night of our pilgrimage we passed at a house near Amiens, where Balthazar being unknown, we supped upon indifferent fare and sour wine, and were fain to lie in a garret upon an old mattress, which, I believe, had been in the possession of ten thousand myriads of fleas, time out of mind. We did not invade their territory with impunity: in less than a minute we were attacked by stings innumerable; in spite of which, however, we fell fast asleep, being excessively fatigued with our day's march, and did not wake till nine next morning, when seeing myself alone, I started up in a terrible fright, and examining my pockets, found my presaging fear too true! My companion had made free with my cash, and left me to seek my way to Paris by myself! I randown stairs immediately; and with a look full of grief and amazement, inquired for the mendicant, who, they gave me to understand, had set out four hours before, after having told them I was a little indisposed, and desired I might not be disturbed, but be informed when I should awake that he had taken the road to Noyons, where he would wait for my coming at the Coq d'Or. I spoke not a word, but with a heavy heart directed my course to that place, at which I arrived in the afternoon, fainting with weariness and hunger; but learned to my utter confusion, that no such person had been there! It was happy for me that I had a good deal of resentment in my constitution, which animated me on such occasions against the villainy of mankind, and enabled me to bear misfortunes otherwise intolerable. Boiling with indignation, I discovered to the host my deplorable condition, and inveighed with great bitterness against the treachery of Balthazar; at which he shrugged up his shoulders, and, with a peculiar grimace in his countenance, said he was sorry for my misfortune; but there was no remedy like patience. At that instant some guests arrived, to whom he hastened to offer his service, leaving me mortified at his indifference, and fully persuaded that an inn-keeper is the same sordid animal all the world over. While I stood in the porch, forlorn and undetermined, venting ejaculations of curses against the thief who robbed me, and the old priest who recommended him to my friendship, a young gentleman richly dressed, attended by a valet de chambre and two servants in livery, arrived at the inn. I thought I perceived a great deal of sweetness and good nature in his countenance; therefore he had no sooner alighted than I accosted him, and, in a few words, explained my situation: he listened with great politeness, and, when I had made an end of my story, said, "Well, Monsieur, what would you have me to do?" I was effectually abashed at this interrogation, which I believe no man of common sense or generosity could make, and made no other reply than a low bow: he returned the compliment still lower, and tript into an apartment, while the landlord let me know, that my standing there to interrupt company gave offence, and might do him infinite prejudice. He had no occasion to repeat his insinuation; I moved from the place immediately; and was so much transported with grief, anger, and disdain, that a torrent of blood gushed from my nostrils. In this ecstasy I quitted Noyons, and betook myself to the fields, where I wandered about like one distracted, till my spirits were quite exhausted, and I was obliged to throw myself down at the root of a tree, to rest my wearied limbs. Here my rage forsook me; I began to feel the importunate cravings of nature, and relapsed into silent sorrow and melancholy reflection. I revolved all the crimes I had been guilty of, and found them so few and venial, that I could not comprehend the justice of that Providence, which, after having exposed me to so much wretchedness and danger, left me a prey to famine at last in a foreign country, where I had not one friend or acquaintance to close my eyes, and do the last offices of humanity to my miserable carcass. A thousand times I wished myself a bear, that I might retreat to woods and deserts, far from the hospitable haunts of man, where I could live by my own talents, independent of treacherous friends and supercilious scorn.

As I lay in this manner groaning over my hapless fate, I heard the sound of a violin, and raising my head, perceived a company of men and women dancing on the grass at some distance from me. I looked upon this to be a favourable season for distress to attract compassion, when every selfish thought is banished, and the heart dilated with mirth and social joy; wherefore I got up and approached this happy people, whom I soon discovered to be a party of soldiers, with their wives and children, unbending and diverting themselves at this rate, after the fatigue of a march. I had never before seen such a parcel of scarecrows together, neither could I reconcile their meagre gaunt looks, their squalid and ragged attire, and every other external symptom of extreme woe, with this appearance of festivity. I saluted them, however, and was received with great politeness; after which they formed a ring and danced around me. This jollity had a wonderful effect upon my spirits! I was infected with their gaiety, and, in spite of my dismal situation, forgot my cares, and joined in their extravagance. When we had recreated ourselves a good while at this diversion, the ladies spread their manteaus on the ground, upon which they emptied their knapsacks of some onions, coarse bread, and a few flasks of poor wine. Being invited to a share of the banquet, I sat down with the rest, and in the whole course of my life never made a more comfortable meal. When our repast was ended, we got up again to dance; and now that I found myself refreshed, I behaved to the admiration of everybody. I was loaded with a thousand compliments and professions of friendship; the men commended my person and agility, and the women were loud in praise of my *bonne grace*; the sergeant in particular expressed so much regard for me, and described the pleasures of a soldier's life with so much art, that I began to listen to his proposal of enlisting me in the service; and the more I considered my own condition, the more I was convinced of the necessity I was under to come to a speedy determination. Having, therefore, maturely weighed the circumstances *pro* and *con*, I signified my consent, and was admitted into the regiment of Picardy, said to be the oldest corps in Europe. The company to which this command belonged was quartered at a village not far off, whither we marched next day, and I was presented to my captain, who seemed very well pleased with my appearance, gave me a crown to drink, and ordered me to be accommodated with clothes, arms, and accoutrements. Then I sold my livery suit, purchased linen, and, as I was at great pains to learn the exercise, in a very short time became a complete soldier.

It was not long before we received orders to join several more regiments, and march with all expedition into Germany, in order to reinforce Mareschal Duc de Noailles, who was then encamped with his army on the side of the river Mayne, to watch the motions of the English, Hanoverians, Austrians, and Hessians, under the command of the Earl of Stair. We began our march accordingly, and then I became acquainted with that part of a soldier's life to which I had been hitherto a stranger. It is impossible to describe the hunger and thirst I sustained, and the fatigue I underwent in a march of so many hundred miles; during which I was so much chafed with the heat and motion of my limbs, that in a very short time the inside of my thighs and legs was deprived of skin, and I proceeded in the utmost torture. This misfortune I owed to the plumpness of my constitution, which I cursed, and envied the withered condition of my comrades, whose bodies could not spare juice enough to supply a common issue, and were indeed proof against all manner of friction. The continual pain I felt made me fretful, and my peevishness was increased by the mortification of my pride in seeing those miserable wretches, whom a hard gale of wind would have scattered through the air like chaff, bear those toils with alacrity under which I was ready to sink.

One day, while we enjoyed a halt, and the soldiers with their wives had gone out to dance, according to custom, my comrade stayed at home with me on pretence of friendship, and insulted me with his pity and consolation! He told me, though I was young and tender at present, I would soon be seasoned to the service; and he did not doubt but I should have the honour to contribute in some measure to the glory of the king. "Have courage, therefore, my child," said he, "and pray to the good God that you may be as happy as I am, who have had the honour of serving Lewis the Great, and of receiving many wounds in helping to establish his glory." When I looked upon the contemptible object that pronounced these words, I was amazed at the infatuation that possessed him; and could not help expressing my astonishment at the absurdity of a rational being, who thinks himself highly honoured in being permitted to encounter abject poverty, oppression, famine, disease, mutilation, and evident death, merely to gratify the vicious ambition of a prince, by whom his sufferings were disregarded, and his name utterly unknown. I observed that, if his situation was the consequence of compulsion, I would praise his patience and fortitude in bearing his lot; if he had taken up arms in defence of his injured country, he was to be applauded for his patriotism; or, if he had fled to this way of life as a refuge from a greater evil, he was justifiable in his own conscience, though I could have no notion of misery more extreme than that he suffered; but to put his condition on the footing of conducing to the glory of his prince, was no more than professing himself a desperate slave, who voluntarily underwent the utmost wretchedness and peril, and committed the most flagrant crimes, to soothe the barbarous pride of a fellow-creature, his superior in nothing but the power he derived from the submission of such wretches as him. The soldier was very much affronted at the liberty I took with his king, which he said nothing but my ignorance could excuse. He affirmed that the characters of princes were sacred, and ought not to be profaned by the censure of their subjects, who were bound by their allegiance to obey their commands, of what nature soever, without scruple or repining; and advised me to correct the rebellious principles I had imbibed among the English, who, for their insolence to their kings, were notorious all over the world, even to a proverb.

In vindication of my countrymen, I repeated all the arguments commonly used to prove that every man has a natural right to liberty; that allegiance and protection are reciprocal; that, when the mutual tie is broken by the tyranny of the king, he is accountable to the people for his breach of contract, and subject to the penalty of the law; and that those insurrections of the English, which are branded with the name of rebellion by the slaves of arbitrary power, were no other than glorious efforts to rescue that independence which was their birthright, from the ravenous claws of usurping ambition. The Frenchman, provoked at the little deference I paid to the kingly name, lost all patience, and reproached me in such a manner that my temper forsook me, and I clenched my fist, with an intention to give him a hearty box on the ear. Perceiving my design, he started back, and demanded a parley; upon which I cnecked my indignation, and he gave me to understand that a Frenchman never forgave a blow; therefore, if I was not weary of my life, I would do well to spare him that mortification, and do him the honour of measuring my sword with his, like a gentleman. I took his advice, and followed him to a field hard by, where indeed I was

* I 790

ashamed at the pitiful figure of my antagonist, who was a poor little, shivering creature, decrepit with age, and blind of one eye But I soon found the folly of judging from appearances, being at the second pass wounded in the sword-hand, and immediately dis armed with such a jerk, that I thought the joint was dislocated I was no less confounded than enraged at this event, especially as my adversary did not bear his success with all the moderation that might have been expected; for he insisted upon my asking pardon for affronting his king and him. This proposal I would by no means comply with, but told him it was a mean con descension, which no gentleman in his circumstances ought to propose, nor any in my situation ought to perform; and that if he persisted in his ungenerous demand, I would in my turn claim satisfaction with my musket, when we should be more upon a par than with the sword, of which he seemed so much master.

CHAPTER XLIV

In order to be revenged, I learn the Science of Defence—We join the Mareschal Duc de Noailles—Are engaged with the Allies at Dettingen and put to Flight—The Behaviour of the French Soldiers on that Occasion —I industriously seek another Combat with the old Gascon, and vanquish him in my turn—Our Regiment is put into Winter-quarters at Rheims, where I find my friend Strap—Our Recognition—He supplies me with Money, and procures my Discharge—We take a Trip to Paris; from whence, by the way of Flanders, we set out for London, where we safely arrive.

HE was disconcerted at this declaration, to which he made no reply, but repaired to the dancers, among whom he recounted his victory, with many exaggerations and gasconades; while I, taking up my sword, went to my quarters and examined my wound, which I found was of no consequence. The same day, an Irish drummer, having heard of my misfortune, visited me, and, after having condoled me on the chance of war, gave me to understand that he was master of the sword, and would, in a very short time, instruct me so thoroughly in that noble science, that I should be able to chastise the old Gascon for his insolent boasting at my expense. This friendly office he proffered on pretence of the regard he had for his countrymen; but I after-wards learned the true motive was no other than a jealousy he entertained of a correspondence between the Frenchman and his wife, which he did not think proper to resent in person. Be this as it will, I accepted his offer, and practised his lessons with such application, that I soon believed myself a match for my conqueror. In the meantime we continued our march, and arrived at the camp of Mareschal Noailles, the night before the battle of Dettingen. Notwithstanding the fatigue we had undergone, our regiment was one of those that were ordered next day to cross the river, under the command of the Duc de Gramont, to take possession of a narrow defile, through which the Allies must of necessity have passed at a great disadvantage, or remain where they were, and perish for want of provision, if they would not condescend to surrender at discretion. How they suffered themselves to be pent up in this manner, it is not my province to relate; I shall only observe, that, when we had taken possession of our ground, I heard an old officer, in conversation with another, express a surprise at the conduct of Lord Stair, who had the reputation of a good general. But it seems, at this time, that nobleman was overruled, and only acted in an inferior character; so that no part of the blame could be imputed to him, who declared his disapprobation of the step, in consequence of which the whole army was in the utmost danger; but Providence or Destiny acted miracles in their behalf, by disposing the Duc de Gramont to quit his advantageous post, pass the defile and attack the English, who were drawn up in order of battle on the plain, and who handled us so roughly, that, after having lost a great number of our men, we turned our backs without ceremony, and fled with such precipitation, that many hundreds perished in the river, through pure fear and confusion; for the enemy was so generous, that they did not pursue us one inch of ground; and if our consternation would have permitted, we might have retreated with great order and deliberation. But, notwithstanding the royal clemency of the King of Great Britain, who headed the Allies in person, and, no doubt, put a stop to the carnage, our loss amounted to 5000 men, among whom were many officers of distinction. Our miscarriage opened a passage for the foe to Hanau, whither they immediately marched, leaving their sick and wounded in the care of the French, who next day took possession of the field of battle, buried the dead, and treated the living with humanity. This circumstance was a great consolation to us, who thence took occasion to claim the victory; and the genius of the French nation never appeared more conspicuous than now, in the rhodomontades they uttered on the subject of their generosity and courage. Every man, by his own account, performed feats that eclipsed all the heroes of antiquity. One compared himself to a lion retiring at leisure from his cowardly pursuers, who keep at a wary distance, and gall him with their darts. Another likened himself to a bear who retreats with his face to the enemy, who dare not assail him; and the third assumed the character of a desperate stag, that turns upon the hounds and keeps them at bay. There was not a private soldier engaged who had not, by the prowess of his single arm, demolished a whole platoon, or put a squadron of horse to flight; and, among others, the meagre Gascon extolled his exploits above those of Hercules or Charlemagne. As I still retained my resentment for the disgrace I suffered in my last rencontre with him, and, now that I thought myself qualified, longed for an opportunity to retrieve my honour, I magnified the valour of the English with all the hyperboles I could imagine, and decried the pusillanimity of the French in the same style, comparing them to hares flying before greyhounds, or mice pursued by cats; and passed an ironical compliment on the speed he exerted in his flight, which, considering his age and infirmities, I said was surprising. He was stung to the quick by this sarcasm, and, with an air of threatening disdain, bade me know myself better, and remember the correction I had lately received from him for my insolence; he might not always be in the humour of sparing a wretch who abused his goodness. To this innuendo I made no reply but a kick in the breech, which overturned him in an instant. He started up with wonderful agility, and, drawing his sword, attacked me with great fury. Several people interposed; but when he informed them of its being an affair of honour, they retired, and left us to decide the battle by ourselves. I sustained his onset with little damage, having only received a small scratch on my right shoulder, and seeing his breath and vigour almost exhausted, assaulted him in my turn, closed with him, and wrested his sword out of his hand in the struggle. Having thus acquired the victory, I desired him to beg his life; to which demand he made no answer, but shrugged up his shoulders to his ears, expanded his hands, elevated the skin on his forehead and eyebrows, and depressed the corners of his mouth in such a manner, that I could scarce refrain from laughing aloud at his grotesque appearance. That I might, however, mortify his vanity, which triumphed without bounds over my misfortune, I thrust his sword up to the hilt in something (it was not a tansy) that lay smoking on the plain, and joined the rest of the soldiers with an air of tranquillity and indifference.

There was nothing more of moment attempted by either of the armies during the remaining part of the campaign, which being ended, the English marched back to the Netherlands; part of our army was detached to French Flanders, and our regiment ordered into winter quarters in Champagne. It was the fate of the grenadier company, to which I now belonged, to lie at Rheims, where I found myself in the utmost want of everything; my pay, which amounted to five sols a day, far from supplying me with necessaries, being scarce sufficient to procure a wretched subsistence, to keep soul and body together; so that I was, by hunger and hard duty, brought down to the meagre condition of my fellow-soldiers, and my linen reduced from three tolerable shirts to two pair of sleeves and necks, the bodies having been long ago converted into spatterdashes; and, after all, I was better provided than any private man in the regiment. In this urgency of my affairs, I wrote to my uncle in England, though my hopes from that quarter were not at all sanguine, for the reasons I have already explained; and, in the meantime, had recourse to my old remedy, patience, consoling myself with the flattering suggestions of a lively imagination, that never abandoned me in distress.

One day, while I stood sentinel at the gate of a general officer, a certain nobleman came to the door followed by a gentleman in mourning, to whom, at parting, I heard him saying, "You may depend upon my good offices." This assurance was answered by a low bow of the person in black, who, turning to go away, discovered to me the individual countenance of my old friend and adherent Strap. I was so much astonished at the sight, that I lost the power of utterance, and before I could recollect myself, he was gone without taking any notice of me. Indeed, had he stayed, I scarcely should have ventured to accost him; because, though I was perfectly well acquainted with the features of his face, I could not be positively certain as to the rest of his person, which was very much altered for the better since he left me at London; neither could I perceive by what means he was enabled to appear in the sphere of a gentleman, to which, while I knew him, he had not even the ambition to aspire. But I was too much concerned in the affair to neglect further inform-ation, and therefore took the first opportunity of asking the porter if he knew the gentleman to whom the marquis spoke. The Swiss told me his name was Monsieur d'Estrapes; that he had been valet de chambre to an English gentleman lately deceased; and that he was very much regarded by the marquis for his fidelity to his master, between whom and that nobleman a very intimate friendship had subsisted. Nothing could be more agreeable to me than this piece of intelligence, which banished all doubt of it being my friend, who had found means to frenchify his name as well as his behaviour since we parted. As soon therefore, as I was relieved, I went to his lodging, according to a direction given me by the Swiss, and had the good fortune to find him at home. That I might surprise him the more, I concealed my name and business, and only desired the servant of the house to tell Monsieur d'Estrapes that I begged the honour of half an hour's conversation with him. He was confounded and dismayed at the message, when he understood it was sent by a soldier. Though he was conscious to himself of no ; he, all that he had heard of the Bastille appeared to his imagination with aggravated horror, and it was not before I had waited a considerable time, that he had resolution enough to let the servant show me upstairs.

When I entered his chamber, he returned my bow with great civility, and endeavoured, with forced complaisance, to disguise his fear, which appeared in the paleness of his face, the wildness of his looks, and the shaking of his limbs. I was diverted at his consternation, which redoubled when I told him in French, I had business for his private ear, and demanded a particular audience. The valet being withdrawn, I asked in the same language if his name was d'Estrapes? to which he answered, with a faltering tongue, "The same, at your service." "Are you a Frenchman?" said I. "I have not the honour of being a Frenchman born," replied he, "but I have an infinite veneration for the country." I then desired he would do me the honour to look at me; which he no sooner did, than, struck with my appearance, he started back, and cried in English, "O Jesus! sure it can't! No, 'tis impossible!" I smiled at his interjections, saying, "I suppose you are too much of a gentleman to own your friend in adversity." When he heard me pronounce these words in our own language he leaped upon me in a transport of joy, hung about my neck, kissed me from ear to ear, and blubbered like a great schoolboy who had been whipt.—Then observing my dress, he set up his throat, crying, "O Lord! O Lord! that ever I should live to see my dearest friend reduced to the condition of a foot-soldier in the French service! Why did you consent to my leaving you?—But I know the reason—you thought you had got more creditable friends, and grew ashamed of my acquaintance.—Ah! Lord help us! though I was a little hortsighted, I was not altogether blind. And though I did not complain, I was not the less sensible of your unkindness, which vas indeed the only thing that induced me to ramble abroad, he Lord knows whither; but I must own it has been a lucky amble for me, and so I forgive you, and may God forgive you; —O Lord! O Lord! is it come to this?" I was nettled at the charge, which, though just, I could not help thinking unseasonable, and told him with some tartness, that, whether his suspicions were well or ill grounded, he might have chosen a more convenient opportunity of introducing them; and that the question now was, whether or no he found himself disposed to lend me any assistance. "Disposed!" replied he with great emotion, "I thought you had known me so well, as to assure yourself, without asking, that I and all that belongs to me are at your command. In the meantime, you shall dine with me, and I will tell you something that, perhaps, will not be displeasing unto you." Then wringing my hand, he said, "It makes my heart bleed to see you in that garb!" I thanked him for his invitation, which, I observed, could not be unwelcome to a person who had not eaten a comfortable meal these seven months. But I had another request to make, which I begged he would grant before dinner, and that was the loan of a shirt; for although my back had been many weeks a stranger to any comfort of that kind, my skin was not yet familiarised to the want of it. He stared in my face, with a woeful countenance, at this declaration, which he could scarce believe, until I explained it by unbuttoning my coat and disclosing my naked body; a circumstance that shocked the tender-hearted Strap, who, with tears in his eyes, ran to a chest of drawers, and, taking out some linen, presented to me a very fine ruffled holland shirt, and cambric neckcloth, assuring me he had three dozen of the same kind at my service. I was ravished at this piece of good news, and having accommodated myself in a moment, hugged my benefactor for his generous offer, saying I was overjoyed to find him undebauched by prosperity, which seldom fails to corrupt the heart. He bespoke for dinner some soup and bouillé, a couple of pullets roasted, and a dish of asparagus, and in the interim entertained me with biscuit and Burgundy; after which repast, he entreated me to gratify his longing desire of knowing every circumstance of my fortune since his departure from London. This request I complied with, beginning at the adventure of Gawky, and relating every particular event in which I had been concerned from that day to the present hour.

During the recital, my friend was strongly affected, according to the various situations described. He started with surprise, glowed with indignation, gaped with curiosity, smiled with pleasure, trembled with fear, and wept with sorrow, as the vicissitudes of my life inspired these different passions; and when my story was ended, signified his amazement on the whole by lifting up his eyes and hands, and protesting, that though I was a young man, I had suffered more than all the blessed martyrs.

After dinner, I desired in my turn to know the particulars of his peregrination, and he satisfied me in a few words, by giving me to understand that he had lived a year at Paris with his master, who in that time having acquired the language, as well as the fashionable exercises, to perfection, made a tour of France and Holland, during which excursion he was so unfortunate to meet with three of his own countrymen on their travels, in whose company he committed such excesses, that his constitution failed, and he fell into a consumption; that, by the advice of physicians, he went to Montpellier for the benefit of good air, and recovered so well in six weeks, that he returned to Rheims, seemingly in good health, where he had not continued above a month, when he was seized with a looseness that carried him off in ten days, to the unspeakable sorrow of all who knew him, and especially of Strap, who had been very happy in his service, and given such satisfaction, that his master, on his deathbed, recommended him to several persons of distinction, for his diligence, sobriety, and affection, and left him by will his wearing apparel, gold watch, sword, rings, ready money, and all the movables he had in France, to the value of three hundred pounds, "which I now," said he, "in the sight of God and man, surrender to your absolute disposal. Here are my keys, take them, I beseech you, and God give you joy of the possession." My brain was almost turned by the sudden change of fortune, which I could scarce believe real; however, I positively refused this extravagant offer of my friend, and put him in mind of my being a soldier; at which hint he started, crying, "Odso! that's true—we must procure your discharge. I have some interest with a nobleman who is able to do me that favour." We consulted about this affair, and it was determined that Monsieur d'Estrapes should wait upon the marquis in the morning, and tell him he had by accident found his brother, whom he had not seen for many years before, a private soldier in the regiment of Picardy, and implore that nobleman's interest for his discharge. In the meantime we enjoyed ourselves over a bottle of good Burgundy, and spent the evening in concerting schemes for our future conduct, in case I should be so lucky as to get rid of the army. The business was to make ourselves easy for life by means of his legacy, a task very difficult, and, in the usual methods of laying out money, altogether impracticable; so that after much canvassing, we could come to no resolution that night, but when we parted, recommended the matter to the serious attention of each other. As for my own part, I puzzled my imagination to no purpose. When I thought of turning merchant, the smallness of our stock, and the risk of seas, enemies, and markets, deterred me from that scheme. If I should settle as a surgeon in my own country, I would find the business already overstocked; or, if I pretended to set up in England, must labour under want of friends, and powerful opposition, obstacles insurmountable by the most shining merit. Neither should I succeed in my endeavours to rise in the state, inasmuch as I could neither flatter nor pimp for courtiers, nor prostitute my pen in defence of a wicked and contemptible administration. Before I could form any feasible project, I fell asleep, and my fancy was blessed with the image of the dear Narcissa, who seemed to smile upon my passion, and offer her hand as a reward for all my toils.

Early in the morning, I went to the lodgings of my friend, whom I found exulting over his happy invention; for I no sooner entered his apartment, than he addressed himself to me in these words, with a smile of self-applause: "Well, Mr. Random, a lucky thought may come into a fool's head sometimes. I have hit it; I'll hold you a button my plan is better than yours, for all your learning. But you shall have the preference in this, as in all other things; therefore proceed, and let us know the effects of your meditation, and then I will impart my own simple excogitations." I told him that not one thought had occurred to me that deserved the least notice, and signified my impatience to be acquainted with the fruits of his reflection. "As we have not," said he, "money sufficient to maintain us during a tedious expectation, it is my opinion that a bold push must be made; and I see none so likely to succeed, as your appearing in the character of a gentleman (which is your due), and making your addresses to some lady of fortune, who can render you independent at once. Nay, don't stare; I affirm that this scheme is both prudent and honourable; for I would not have you throw yourself away upon an old, toothless, wheezing dame, whose breath would stink you into a consumption in less than three months. Neither would I advise you to assume the character of a wealthy squire, as your common fortune-hunters do, by which means many a poor lady is cheated into matrimony, and, instead of enjoying the pomp and grandeur that was promised, sees her dowry seized by her husband's rapacious creditors, and herself reduced to misery and despair. No, I know you have a soul that disdains such imposition, and are master of qualifications, both of mind and body, which alone entitle you to a match that will set you above the world. I have clothes in my possession that a duke need not be ashamed to wear. I believe they will fit you as they are; if not, there are plenty of tailors in France. Let us take a short trip to Paris, and provide ourselves with all other necessaries, then set out for England, where I intend to do myself the honour of attending you in quality of a valet. This expedient will save you the expense of a servant, shaving, and dressing; and I doubt not but, by the blessing of God, we shall bring matters to a speedy and fortunate issue." Extravagant as this proposal was, I listened to it with pleasure, because it flattered my vanity, and indulged a ridiculous hope I began to entertain of inspiring Narcissa with a mutual flame.

After breakfast, Monsieur d'Estrapes went to pay his devoirs to the marquis, and was so successful in his application, that I obtained a discharge in a few days, upon which we set out for Paris. Here I had time to reflect and congratulate myself upon this sudden transition of fate, which, to bear with moderation, required some degree of philosophy and self-denial. This truth will be more obvious, if I give a detail of the particulars, to the quiet possession of which I was raised in an instant, from the most abject misery and contempt. My wardrobe consisted of five fashionable coats, full mounted, two of which were plain, one of cut velvet, one trimmed with gold, and another with silver lace; two frocks, one of white drab with large plate buttons, the other of blue, with gold binding; one waistcoat of gold brocade; one of blue satin, embroidered with silver; one of green silk, trimmed with broad figured gold lace; one of black silk, with fringes; one of white satin, one of black cloth, and one of scarlet; six pair of cloth breeches, one pair of crimson, and another of black velvet; twelve pair of white silk stockings, as many of black silk, and the same number of fine cotton; one hat, laced with gold, *point d'Espagne*, another with silver lace scolloped, a third with gold binding, and a fourth plain; three dozen of fine ruffled shirts, as many neckcloths; one dozen of cambric handkerchiefs, and the like number of silk. The other movables which I possessed, by the generosity and friendship of Strap, were a gold watch, with a chased case; two valuable diamond rings; two mourning swords, one with a silver handle, and a fourth, cut steel, inlaid with gold; a diamond stock-buckle, and a set of stone buckles for the knees and shoes; a pair of silver-mounted pistols, with rich housings; a gold-headed cane, and a snuff-box of tortoiseshell, mounted with gold, having the picture of a lady in the top. The gentleman left many other things of value, which my friend had converted into cash before I met with him; so that, over and above these particulars, our stock in ready money amounted to something more than two hundred pounds.

Thus equipped, I put on the gentleman of figure, and, attended by my honest friend, who was contented with the station of my valet, visited the Louvre, examined the gallery of Luxembourg, and appeared at Versailles, where I had the honour of seeing his Most Christian Majesty eat a considerable quantity of olives. During the month I spent at Paris, I went several times to court, the Italian comedy, opera, and play-house, danced at a masquerade—and, in short, saw everything remarkable in and about that capital. Then we set out for England by the way of Flanders, passed through Brussels, Ghent, and Bruges, and took shipping at Ostend, from whence, in fourteen hours, we arrived at Deal, hired a post-chaise, and, in twelve hours more, got safe to London, having disposed of our heavy baggage in the waggon.

CHAPTER XLV

I inquire for my Uncle, and understand he is gone to Sea—Take Lodgings at Charing Cross—Go to the Play, where I meet with an Adventure—Dine at an Ordinary; the Guests described—Become acquainted with Medlar and Doctor Wagtail.

As soon as we alighted at the inn, I despatched Strap to inquire for my uncle at the Union Flag, in Wapping; and he returned in a little time with an account of Mr. Bowling's having gone to sea, mate of a merchant-ship, after a long and unsuccessful application and attendance at the Admiralty; where, it seems, the interest he depended upon was not sufficient to reinstate him, or recover the pay that was due to him when he quitted the *Thunder*.

Next day I hired very handsome lodgings, not far from Charing Cross, and, in the evening, dressed myself in a plain suit of true Paris cut, and appeared in a front box at the play, where I saw a good deal of company, and was vain enough to believe that I was observed with an uncommon degree of attention and applause. This silly conceit intoxicated me so much, that I was guilty of a thousand ridiculous coquetries; and I dare say, how favourable soever the thoughts of the company might be at my first appearance, they were soon changed, by my absurd behaviour, into pity or contempt. I rose and sat down, covered and uncovered my head twenty times between the acts; pulled out my watch, clapped it to my ear, wound it up, set it, gave it the hearing again; displayed my snuff-box, affected to take snuff, that I might have an opportunity of showing my brilliant, and wiped my nose with a perfumed handkerchief; then dangled my cane, and adjusted my sword-knot, and acted many more fooleries of the same kind, in hopes of obtaining the character of a pretty fellow, in the acquiring of which I found two considerable obstructions in my disposition, namely, a natural reserve, and jealous sensibility. Fain would I have entered into conversation with the people around me, but I was restrained by the fear of being censured for my assurance, as well as by reflecting that I was more entitled to a compliment of this kind from them, than they to such condescension from a stranger like me. How often did I redden at the frequent whispers and loud laughter of my fellow-beaus, which I imagined were excited by me! and how often did I envy the happy indifference of those choice spirits who beheld the distress of the scene without discovering the least symptom of approbation or concern! My attention was engaged in spite of myself, and I could not help weeping with the heroine of the stage; though I practised a great many shifts to conceal this piece of unpolite weakness. When the play was ended, I sat waiting for an opportunity of handing some lady to her coach; but every one was attended by such a number of officious gallants, that for a long time I was balked in my expectation. At length, however, I perceived a very handsome creature, genteelly dressed, sitting by herself in a box, at some distance from me; upon which I went up to her and offered my service. She seemed to be in some confusion, thanked me for my complaisance, and with a tender look declined giving me

the trouble; looking at her watch, and testifying her surprise
at the negligence of her footman, whom she had ordered to have
a chair ready for her at that hour. I repeated my entreaty with
all the eloquence and compliment I was master of; and, in the
event, she was prevailed upon to accept of a proposal I made
to send my servant for a chair or coach: accordingly, Strap was
detached for that purpose, and returned without success. By
this time the playhouse was quite empty, and we were obliged
to retire. As I led her through the passage, I observed five or
six young fellows of fashion standing in a corner, one of whom,
as I thought, tipt my charmer the wink, and when we were past,
I heard them set up a loud laugh. This note aroused my attention,
and I was resolved to be fully satisfied of this lady's character
before I should have any nearer connection with her. As no
convenience appeared, I proposed to conduct her to a tavern,
where we might stay a few minutes, till my servant could fetch
a coach from the Strand. She seemed particularly shy of trusting
herself in a tavern with a stranger; but at last yielded to my
pathetic remonstrances, rather than endanger her health by
remaining in a cold damp thoroughfare. Having thus far succeeded, I begged to know what wine she would be pleased to
drink a glass of; but she professed the greatest aversion to all
sorts of strong liquors; and it was with much difficulty that I
could persuade her to eat a jelly. In the meantime, I endeavoured
to alleviate the uneasiness she discovered, by saying all the
agreeable things I could think of; at which she would often sigh,
and regard me with a languishing look, that seemed however
too near akin to the lewd leer of a courtesan. This discovery,
added to my former suspicion, while it put me upon my guard
against her arts, divested me of reserve, and enabled me to
entertain her with gaiety and freedom. In the course of our
conversation, I pressed her to allow me the honour of waiting
upon her next day at her lodgings; a request which she, with
many apologies, refused, lest it should give umbrage to Sir
John, who was of a disposition apt to be fretted with trifles.
This information, by which I was to understand that her husband
was a knight, did not check my addresses, which became more
and more importunate, and I was even hardy enough to ravish
a kiss. But, O Heavens! instead of banqueting on the ambrosial
flavour that her delicacy of complexion promised, I was almost
suffocated with the steams of Geneva! An exhalation of this
kind, from a mouth which had just before declared an utter
abhorrence of all spirituous liquors, not only changed my

doubts into certainty, but my raptures into loathing; and it
would have been impossible for me to have preserved common
complaisance five minutes longer, when my servant returned
with the coach. I took the advantage of this occasion, and
presented my hand to the lady, who put in practice against me
the whole artillery of her charms, ogling, languishing, sighing,
and squeezing, with so little reserve, that Strap perceived her
tenderness, and rubbed his hands with joy as he followed us to
the door; but I was proof against all her endearments, and
handed her into the coach with an intention to take my leave
immediately. She guessed my design, and invited me to her
house, whispering, that now Sir John was gone to bed, she
could have the pleasure of my conversation for half an hour
without interruption. I told her there was no mortification
I would not undergo, rather than endanger the repose of her
ladyship; and bidding the coachman drive on, wished her a
good night. She lost all temper at my indifference, and stopping
the coach at the distance of about twenty yards from me,
popped out her head, and bawled with the lungs of a fish-woman,
"Damn you, you dog, won't you pay the coach-hire?" As I
made no answer, she held forth against me with an eloquence
peculiar to herself; calling me a pitiful fellow, scoundrel, and
an hundred such appellations; concluding with an oath that,
for all my appearance, she believed I had got no money in
my pocket.

Having thus vented her indignation, she ordered the coachman to proceed, and I returned to the tavern, where I bespoke
something for supper, very well pleased at the issue of this
adventure. I dispensed with the attendance of the waiter at
table, on pretence that my own servant was present, and when
we were alone, said to Strap, "Well, Monsieur d'Estrapes, what
do you think of this lady?" My friend, who had not opened
his mouth since her departure, could make no other reply than
the monosyllable, "Think!" which he pronounced with a note
of fear and astonishment. Surprised at this emphasis, I surveyed my valet, and perceiving a wildness in his looks asked
if he had seen his grandfather's ghost? "Ghost!" said he, "I am
sure I have seen a devil incarnate! Who would have thought
that so much devilish malice and Billingsgate could lurk under
such sweetness of countenance and modesty of behaviour?
Ah! God help us! *Fronti nulla fides—nimium ne crede colori—*
but we ought to down on our knees and bless God for delivering
us from the jaws of that painted sepulchre." I was pretty much

of Strap's opinion, and though I did not believe myself in any danger from the allurements of that sisterhood, I determined to act with great circumspection for the future, and shun all commerce of that kind, as equally prejudicial to my purse and constitution.

My next care was to introduce myself into a set of good acquaintance; for which purpose I frequented a certain coffee-house, noted for the resort of good company, English as well as foreigners, where my appearance produced all the civilities and advances I could desire. As there was an ordinary in the same house, I went upstairs to dinner with the other guests, and found myself at a table with thirteen people, the greatest part of whom were better dressed than myself. The conversation, which was mostly carried on in French, turned chiefly on politics; and I soon found the whole company was in the French interest, myself excepted, and a testy old gentleman, who contradicted everything that was advanced in favour of his Most Christian Majesty, with a surliness truly English. But this trusty patriot, who had never been out of his own country, and drew all his maxims and notions from prejudice and hear-say, was very unequal to his antagonists, who were superior to him in learning and experience, and often took the liberty of travellers in asserting things which were not strictly true, because they thought themselves in no danger of being detected by him. The claim of the Queen of Spain to the Austrian dominions in Italy was fully explained and vindicated by a person who sat opposite to me, and, by the solemnity of his manner, and the richness of his apparel, seemed to be a foreign ambassador. This dissertation produced another on the Pragmatic Sanction, handled with great warmth by a young gentleman at my right hand, dressed in a green frock trimmed with gold, who justified the French king for his breach of that contract, and affirmed that he could not have observed it without injuring his own glory. Although I was not at all convinced by this gentleman's arguments, I could not help admiring his vivacity, which I imagined must be the effect of his illustrious birth and noble education, and accordingly rated him in my conjecture as a young prince on his travels. The discourse was afterwards shifted by an old gentleman of a very martial appearance, to the last campaign, when the battle of Dettingen was fought over again, with so many circumstances to the honour of the French, and disadvantage of the Allies, that I began to entertain some doubts of my having been there in person, and took the liberty to mention some objections to what he advanced. This freedom introduced a dispute, which lasted a good while, to the mortification of all present; and was at last referred to the determination of a grave person, whom they styled Doctor, and who, under a show of great moderation, decided it against me, with so little regard to truth, that I taxed him with partiality in pretty severe terms, to the no small entertainment of the true English politician, who rejoiced at my defence of a cause he had so often espoused without success.

My opponent, pleased with the victory he had gained, affected a great deal of candour, and told me he should not have been so positive if he had not been at great pains to inform himself of each particular. "Indeed," said he, "I am convinced that, the previous steps considered, things could not happen otherwise; for we generals who have seen service, though we may not be on the spot ourselves, know, by the least sketch of the disposition, what must be the event." He then censured, with great freedom, every circumstance of the conduct of those who commanded the Allies; from thence made a transition to the ministry, which he honoured with many invectives for employing people who had neither experience nor capacity, to the prejudice of old officers who had been distinguished for both, dropped many hints of his own importance, and concluded with observing that the French and Spaniards knew better how to value generals of merit; the good effects of which are seen in the conquests they gain, and the admirable discipline of their troops, which are, at the same time, better clothed and paid than any soldiers in the universe. These remarks furnished the green knight with an opportunity of launching out in the praise of the French Government in general, civil as well as military; on which occasion he made many odious comparisons to the disadvantage of the English. Everybody, almost, assented to the observations he made; and the doctor gave his sanction by saying, the people in France were undoubtedly the happiest subjects in the world. I was so much astonished and confounded at their infatuation and effrontery, that I had not power to utter one word in opposition to their assertions; but my morose associate could not put up with the indignity that was offered to Old England, and therefore, with a satirical grin, addressed himself to the general in these words: "Sir, sir, I have often heard it said, 'She's a villainous bird that befouls her own nest.' As for what those people who are foreigners say, I don't mind it, they know no better; but you, who were bred and born, and have got your bread under the English Government, should have more regard to gratitude, as well as truth, in censuring your native country. If the ministry have thought fit to lay you aside, I suppose they have their own reason for so doing; and you ought to remember that you still live on the bounty of this nation. As for these gentlemen" (meaning the prince and ambassador), "who make so free with our constitution, laws, and genius of our people, I think they might show a little more respect for their benefactors, who, I must own, are to blame in harbouring, protecting, and encouraging such ungrateful vagrants as they are." At these words, the chevalier in green started up in a great passion, and, laying his hand on the hilt of his hanger, exclaimed, "Ha, *foutre!*" The Englishman, on the other hand, grasping his cane, cried, "Don't *foutre* me, sirrah, or, by God, I'll knock you down." The company interposed, the Frenchman sat down again, and his antagonist proceeded: "Lookee, Monsieur, you know very well that, had you dared to speak so freely of the administration of your own country in Paris as you have done of ours in London, you would have been sent to the Bastille without ceremony, where you might have rotted in a dungeon, and never seen the light of the sun again. Now, sir, take my word for it, although our constitution screens us from such oppression, we want not laws to chastise the authors of seditious discourse; and if I hear another syllable out of your mouth in contempt or prejudice of this kingdom, I will give you a convincing proof of what I advance, and have you laid by the heels for your presumption." This declaration had an effect on the company as sudden as surprising. The young prince became supple as a spaniel; the ambassador trembled; the general sat silent and abashed; and the doctor, who, it seems, had felt the rod of power, grew pale as death, and assured us all that he had no intention to affront any person or people. "Your principles, doctor," resumed the old gentleman, "are no secret—I have nothing to say to you upon that head; but am very much surprised that a man who despises us so much, should, notwithstanding, live among us, when he has no visible motive for so doing. Why don't you take up your habitation in your beloved France, where you may rail at England without censure?" To this remonstrance the doctor thought proper to make no reply; and an unsocial silence ensued; which I perceiving, took notice that it was pity such idle disputes, maintained very often through whim or diversion, should create any misunderstanding among gentlemen of good sense; and proposed to drink down all animosity in another bottle. This motion was applauded by the whole company; the wine was brought, and the English champion, declaring he had no spleen against any man for differing in opinion from him, any more than for difference of complexion, drank to the good health of all present; the compliment was returned, and the conversation once more became unreserved, though more general than before. Among other topics, the subject of war was introduced, on which the general declaimed with great eloquence, recounting many of his own exploits by way of illustration. In the course of his harangue, he happened to mention the word *épaulement*, upon which the testy gentleman asked the meaning of that term. "I'll tell you what an épaulement is," replied he; "I never saw an épaulement but once, and that was at the siege of Namur; in a council of war, Monsieur Cohorn, the famous engineer, affirmed that the place could not be taken. 'Yes,' said the Prince of Vaudemont, 'it may be taken by an épaulement.' This was immediately put in execution, and, in twenty-four hours, Mareschal Boufflers was fain to capitulate." Here he made a full stop; and the old gentleman repeated the question, "But pray what is an épaulement?" To this interrogation the officer made no reply, but rung the bell and called for a bill, which being brought, he threw down his proportion of the reckoning, and, telling the company he would show them an épaulement when his majesty should think fit to entrust him with the command of our army abroad, strutted away with great dignity. I could not imagine why he was so shy of explaining one of the most simple terms of fortification, which I forthwith described as a side-work, composed of earth, gabions, or fascines; but I was very much surprised when I afterwards understood that his reserve proceeded from his ignorance. Having paid our bill, we adjourned to the coffee-room, where my fellow-labourer insisted on treating me with a dish, giving me to understand at the same time, that I had acquired his good opinion, both with respect to my principles and understanding. I thanked him for his compliment, and professing myself an utter stranger in this part of the world, begged he would have the goodness to inform me of the quality and characters of the people who dined above. This request was a real favour to one of his disposition, which was no less communicative than curious; he therefore complied with great satisfaction, and told me, to my extreme astonishment, that the supposed young prince was a dancer at one of the theatres, and the ambassador no other than a fiddler belonging to the opera. "The doctor," said he, "is a Roman Catholic priest, who sometimes appears in the character of an officer, and assumes the name of Captain; but more generally takes the garb, title, and behaviour, of a physician, in which capacity he wheedles himself into the confidence of weak-minded people, and, by arguments no less specious than false, converts them from their religion and allegiance. He has been in the hands of justice more than once for such practices; but he is a sly dog, and manages matters with so much craft, that, hitherto, he has escaped for a short imprisonment. As for the general, you may see he has owed his promotion more to his interest than his capacity; and, now that the eyes of the ministry are opened, his friends dead, or become inconsiderable, he is struck off the list, and obliged to put up with a yearly pension. In consequence of this reduction, he is become malcontent, and inveighs against the government, in all companies, with so little discretion, that I am surprised at the lenity of the administration in overlooking his insolence; but the truth of the matter is, he owes his safety to his weakness and want of importance. He has seen a little, and but a little, service; and yet, if you would take his word for it, there has not been a great action performed in the field since the Revolution in which he was not principally concerned. When a story is told of any great general, he immediately matches it with one of himself, though he is often unhappy in his invention, and commits such gross blunders in the detail, that everybody is in pain for him. Cæsar, Pompey, and Alexander the Great are continually in his mouth; and as he reads a good deal without any judgment to digest it, his ideas are confused, and his harangues as unintelligible as infinite; for, once he begins, there is no chance of his leaving off speaking while one person remains to yield attention; therefore the only expedient I know for putting a stop to his loquacity, is to lay hold of some incongruity he has uttered, and demand an explanation; or ask the meaning of some difficult term that he knows by name only. This method will effectually put him to silence, if not to flight, as it happened when I inquired about an *épaulement*. Had he been acquainted with the signification of that word, his triumph would have been intolerable, and we must have quitted the field first, or been worried with impertinence." Having thus gratified my curiosity, the old gentleman began to discover his own, in questions relating to myself, to which I thought proper to return ambiguous answers. "I presume, sir," said he, "you have travelled." I answered, "Yes." "I dare say you would find it very expensive," said he. I replied, "To be sure, one cannot travel without money." "That I know by experience," said he, "for I myself take a trip to Bath or Tunbridge every season; and one must pay sauce for what he has on the road, as well in other countries as in this.—That's a very pretty stone in your ring,—give me leave, sir,—the French have attained a wonderful skill in making compositions of this kind. Why, now, this looks almost as well as a diamond." "Almost as well, sir," said I, "why not altogether? I am sure, if you understand anything of jewels, you must perceive at first sight that this stone is a real diamond, and that of a very fine water. Take it in your hand and examine it." He did so, with some confusion, and returned it, saying, "I ask your pardon, I see it is a true brilliant of immense value." I imagined his respect for me increased after this inquiry; therefore, to captivate his esteem the more, I told him I would show him a seal of composition, engraved after a very valuable antique; upon which I pulled out my watch, with a rich gold chain, adorned with three seals set in gold, and an opal ring. He viewed each of them with great eagerness, handled the chain, admired the chased case, and observed that the whole must have cost me a vast sum of money. I affected indifference, and replied in a careless manner, "Some trifle of sixty or seventy guineas." He stared in my face for some time, and then asked if I was an Englishman? I answered in the negative. "You are from Ireland then, sir, I presume," said he. I made the same reply. "O! perhaps," said he, "you was born in one of our settlements abroad." I still answered, "No." He seemed very much surprised, and said he was sure I was not a foreigner. I made no reply, but left him upon the tenterhooks of impatient uncertainty. He could not contain his anxiety, but asked pardon for the liberties he had taken, and, to encourage me the more to disclose my situation, displayed his own without reserve: "I am," said he, "a single man, have a considerable annuity, on which I live according to my own inclination, and make the ends of the year meet very comfortably. As I have no estate to leave behind me, I am not troubled with the importunate officiousness of relations or legacy hunters, and I consider the world as made for me, not me for the world: it is my maxim therefore to enjoy it while I can, and let futurity shift for itself." While he thus indulged his own talkative vein, and at the same time, no doubt, expected a retaliation from me, a young man entered dressed in black velvet, and an enormous tie-wig, with an air in which natural levity and affected solemnity were so jumbled together, that, on the whole, he appeared a burlesque on all decorum. The ridiculous oddity danced up to the table at which we sat, and, after a thousand grimaces, asked my friend, by the name of Mr. Medlar, if we were not engaged upon business. My companion put on a surly countenance, and replied, "No great business—Doctor,—but however——" "O! then," cried the physician, "I must beg your indulgence a little,—pray pardon me, gentlemen.—Sir," said he, addressing himself to me, "your most humble servant, I hope you will forgive me, sir—I must beg the favour to sit, sir—Sir, I have something of consequence to impart to my friend, Mr. Medlar—Sir, I hope you will excuse my freedom in whispering, sir." Before I had time to give this complaisant person my permission, Mr. Medlar cried, "I'll have no whispering; if you have anything to say to me, speak with an audible voice." The doctor seemed a little disconcerted at this exclamation, and, turning again to me, made a thousand apologies for pretending to make mystery of anything, a piece of caution which he said was owing to his ignorance of my connection with Mr. Medlar; but, now he understood I was a friend, he would communicate what he had to say in my hearing. He then began, after two or three hems, in this manner: "You must know, sir, I am just come from dinner at my Lady Flareit's" (then addressing himself to me), "a lady of quality, sir, at whose table I have the honour of dining sometimes. There was Lady Stately, and my Lady Larum, and Mrs. Dainty, and Miss Biddy Gigler, upon my word, a very good-natured young lady, with a very pretty fortune, sir. There were also my Lord Straddle, Sir John Shrug, and Mr. Billy Chatter, who is actually a very facetious young gentleman. So, sir, her ladyship seeing me excessively fatigued, for she was the last of fifteen patients, people of distinction, sir, whom I had visited this forenoon—insisted upon my staying to dinner, though, upon my word, I protest I had no appetite; however, in compliance with her ladyship's request, sir, I sat down, and the conversation turning upon different subjects, among other things, Mr. Chatter asked very earnestly when I saw Mr. Medlar. I told him I had not had the pleasure of seeing you these nineteen hours and a half; for you may remember, sir, it was nearly about that time; I won't be positive to a minute.— 'No!' says he, 'then I desire you will go to his lodgings immediately after dinner, and see what's the matter with him, for he must certainly be very bad from having eat last night such a vast quantity of raw oysters.'" The crusty gentleman, who, from the solemnity of his delivery, expected something extra-ordinary, no sooner heard his conclusion, than he started up in a testy humour, crying, "Pshaw! pshaw! damn your oysters"; and walked away after a short compliment of, "Your servant, sir," to me. The doctor got up also, saying, "I vow and protest, upon my word, I am actually amazed," and followed Mr. Medlar to the bar, which was hard by, where he was paying for his coffee; there he whispered so loud, that I could overhear, "Pray who is this gentleman?" His friend replied hastily, "I might have known that before now, if it had not been for your imper-tinent intrusion," and walked off very much disappointed. The ceremonious physician returned immediately, and sat down by me, asking a thousand pardons for leaving me alone; and giving me to understand, that what he had communicated to Mr. Medlar at the bar was an affair of the last importance, that would admit of no delay. He then called for some coffee, and launched out into the virtues of that berry, which, he said, in cold phlegmatic constitutions, like his, dried up the superfluous moisture, and braced the relaxed nerves. He told me it was utterly unknown to the ancients; and derived its name from an Arabian word, which I might easily perceive by the sound and termination. From this topic he transferred his disquisitions to the verb *drink*, which he affirmed was improperly applied to the taking of coffee, inasmuch as people did not drink, but sip or sipple that liquor; that the genuine meaning of drinking is to quench one's thirst, or commit a debauch by swallowing wine; that the Latin word, which conveyed the same idea, was *bibere* or *potare*, and that of the Greeks *pinein* or *poteein*, though he was apt to believe they were differently used on different oc-casions. For example: to drink a vast quantity, or, as the vulgar express it, to drink an ocean of liquor, was in Latin *potare*, and in Greek *poteein*; and, on the other hand, to use it moderately, was *bibere*, and *pinein*; that this was only a conjecture of his own, which, however, seemed to be supported by the word *bibulous*, which is particularly applied to the pores of the skin, that can only drink a very small quantity of the circumambient moisture, by reason of the smallness of their diameters; whereas, from the verb *poteein* is derived the substantive *potamos*, which signifies a river, or vast quantity of liquor. I could not help smiling at this learned and important investigation; and, to recommend myself the more to my new acquaintance, whose disposition I was by this time well informed of, I observed, that what he alleged did not, to the best of my remembrance, appear in the writings of the ancients: for Horace uses the words *poto* and *bibo* indifferently for the same purpose, as in the twentieth ode of his First Book:

> Vile potabis modicis Sabinum cantharis,——
> ——et prœlo domitam Caleno tu bibes uvam.

That I had never heard of the verb *poteein*, but that *potomos*, *potema*, and *potos* were derived from *pino*, *poso*, *pepoka*; in consequence of which the Greek poets never used any other word for festal drinking. Homer describes Nestor at his cups in these words:

> Nestora d'ouk elathen iache *pinonta* per empes.

And Anacreon mentions it on the same occasion almost in every page:

> *Pinonti* de oinon hedun.
> Otan *pino* ton oinon.
> Opliz' ego dc *pino*.

And in a thousand other places. The doctor, who, doubtless, intended by his criticism to give me a high idea of his erudition, was infinitely surprised to find himself schooled by one of my appearance; and after a considerable pause, cried, "Upon my word! you are in the right, sir—I find I have not considered this affair with my usual accuracy." Then accosting me in Latin, which he spoke very well, the conversation was maintained a full two hours, on a variety of subjects, in that language; and indeed, he spoke so judiciously, that I was convinced, notwithstanding his whimsical appearance, and attention to trifles, that he was a man of extensive knowledge, especially in books; he looked upon me, as I afterwards understood from Mr. Medlar, as a prodigy in learning, and proposed that very night, if I was not engaged, to introduce me to several young gentlemen of fortune and fashion, with whom he had an appointment at the Bedford Coffee-house.

CHAPTER XLVI

Wagtail introduces me to a set of fine Gentlemen, with whom I spend
the Evening at a Tavern—Our Conversation—The Characters of my new
Companions—The Doctor is roasted—The Issue of our Debauch.

I ACCEPTED his offer with pleasure, and we went thither in a
hackney coach, where I saw a great number of gay figures
fluttering about, most of whom spoke to the doctor with great
familiarity. Among the rest stood a group of them round the
fire, whom I immediately knew to be the very persons who had
the night before, by their laughing, alarmed my suspicion of the
lady who had put herself under my protection. They no sooner
perceived me enter with Dr. Wagtail, for that was my companion's name, than they tittered and whispered one to another;
and I was not a little surprised to find that these were the
gentlemen to whose acquaintance he designed to recommend
me; for when he observed them together, he told me who they
were, and desired to know by what name he should introduce
me. I satisfied him in that particular, and he advanced with
great gravity, saying, "Gentlemen, your most obedient—give
me leave to introduce my friend Mr. Random to your society."
Then turning to me, "Mr. Random, this is Mr. Bragwell—Mr.
Banter, sir—Mr. Chatter—my friend Mr. Slyboot, and Mr.
Ranter, sir." I saluted each of them in order, and when I came
to take Mr. Slyboot by the hand, I perceived him to thrust his
tongue in his cheek, to the no small entertainment of the company; but I did not think proper to take any notice of it on this
occasion. Mr. Ranter, too, who I afterwards learned was a
player, displayed his talents, by mimicking my air, features,
and voice, while he returned my compliment. This feat I should
not have been so sensible of, had not I seen him behave in the
same manner to my friend Wagtail, when he made up to them
at first. But for once I let him enjoy the fruits of his dexterity
without question or control, resolved, however, to chastise his
insolence at a more convenient opportunity. Mr. Slyboot,
guessing I was a stranger, asked if I had been lately in France;
and when I answered in the affirmative, inquired if I had seen
the Luxembourg Gallery. I told him I had considered it more
than once with great attention. Upon this, a conversation
ensued, in which I discovered him to be a painter. While we
were discoursing upon the particulars of this famous collection,
I overheard Banter ask Dr. Wagtail where he had picked up

this Mr. Random. To which question the physician answered, "Upon my word, a mighty pretty sort of a gentleman—a man of fortune, sir—he has made the grand tour, and seen the best company in Europe, sir." "What, he told you so, I suppose?" said the other; "I take him to be neither more nor less than a French valet de chambre." "Oh! barbarous, barbarous!" cried the doctor; "this is actually, upon my word, altogether unaccountable. I know all his family perfectly well, sir; he is of the Randoms of the north—a very ancient house, sir, and a distant relation of mine." I was extremely nettled at the conjecture of Mr. Banter, and began to entertain a very indifferent opinion of my company in general; but as I might possibly, by their means, acquire a more extensive and agreeable acquaintance, I determined to bear these little mortifications as long as I could, without injuring the dignity of my character. After having talked for some time on the weather, plays, politics, and other coffee-house subjects, it was proposed that we should spend the evening at a noted tavern in the neighbourhood, whither we repaired in a body. Having taken possession of a room, called for French wine, and bespoke supper, the glass went about pretty freely, and the characters of my associates opened upon me more and more. It soon appeared that the doctor was entertained as a butt for the painter and player to exercise their wit upon, for the diversion of the company. Mr. Ranter began the game by asking him what was good for a hoarseness, lowness of spirits, and indigestion, for he was troubled with all these complaints to a very great degree? Wagtail immediately undertook to explain the nature of his case, and in a very prolix manner harangued upon prognostics, diagnostics, symptomatics, therapeutics, inanition, and repletion; then calculated the force of the stomach and lungs in their respective operations; ascribed the player's malady to a disorder in these organs, proceeding from hard drinking and vociferation, and prescribed a course of stomachics, with abstinence from venery, wine, loud speaking, laughing, singing, coughing, sneezing, or hallooing. "Pah, pah," cried Ranter, interrupting him, "the remedy is worse than the disease. I wish I knew where to find some tinder-water." "Tinder-water!" said the doctor; "upon my word I don't apprehend you, Mr. Ranter." "Water extracted from tinder," replied the other, "an universal specific for all distempers incident to man. It was invented by a learned German monk, who, for a valuable consideration, imparted the secret to Paracelsus." "Pardon me," cried the painter, "it was first used by Solomon, as appears by a Greek manuscript in his own handwriting, lately found at the foot of Mount Lebanon, by a peasant who was digging for potatoes." "Well," said Wagtail, "in all my vast reading I never met with such a preparation! neither did I know, till this minute, that Solomon understood Greek, or that potatoes grew in Palestine." Here Banter interposed, saying he was surprised that Doctor Wagtail should make the least doubt of Solomon's understanding Greek, when he is represented to us as the wisest and best-educated prince in the world; and as for potatoes, they were transplanted thither from Ireland, in the time of the Crusades, by some knights of that country. "I profess," said the doctor, "there is nothing more likely—I would actually give a vast sum for a sight of that manuscript, which must be inestimable—and if I understood the process, would set about it immediately." The player assured him the process was very simple—that he must cram a hundredweight of dry tinder into a glass retort, and distilling it by the force of animal heat, it would yield half a scruple of insipid water, one drop of which is a full dose. "Upon my integrity!" exclaimed the credulous doctor, "this is very amazing! and extraordinary! that a *caput mortuum* shall yield any water at all—I must own I have always been an enemy to specifics, which I thought inconsistent with the nature of the animal economy; but certainly the authority of Solomon is not to be questioned. I wonder where I shall find a glass retort large enough to contain such a vast quantity of tinder, the consumption of which must undoubtedly raise the price of paper —or where I shall find animal heat sufficient to warm such a mass." Slyboot informed him that he might have a retort blown for him as big as a church; and that the easiest method of raising the vapour by animal heat, would be to place it in the middle of an infirmary for feverish patients, who might lie upon mattresses around, and in contact with it. He had no sooner pronounced these words, than Wagtail exclaimed, in a rapture, "An admirable expedient, as I hope to be saved! I will positively put it in practice." This simplicity of the physician furnished excellent diversion for the company, who, in their turns, sneered at him in ironical compliments, which his vanity swallowed as the genuine sentiments of their hearts. Mr. Chatter, impatient of so long a silence, now broke out, and entertained us with a catalogue of all the people who danced at the last Hampstead assembly, with a most circumstantial account of the dress and ornaments of each, from the lappets of the ladies to the shoe-buckles of the men; concluding with telling Bragwell that his mistress Melinda was there, and seemed to miss him; and soliciting his company at the next occasion of that kind. "No, no, damn me," said Bragwell, "I have something else to mind than dangling after a parcel of giddy-headed girls; besides, you know my temper is so unruly, that I am apt to involve myself in scrapes, when a woman is concerned. The last time I was there I had an affair with Tom Trippet." "O! I remember that," cried Banter; "you lugged out before the ladies; and I commend you for so doing, because you had an opportunity of showing your manhood without running any risk." "Risk!" said the other, with a fierce countenance; "damn my blood! I fear no risks. I ain't afraid of lugging out against any man that wears a head, damme! 'tis well known I have drawn blood more than once, and lost some too; but what does that signify?" The player begged this champion to employ him as his second the next time he intended to kill, for he wanted to see a man die of a stab, that he might know how to act such a part the more naturally on the stage. "Die!" replied the hero; "no, by God! I know better things than to incur the verdict of a Middlesex jury—I should look upon my fencing-master to be an ignorant son of a bitch, if he had not taught me to prick any part of my antagonist's body that I please to disable." "Oho!" cried Slyboot, "if that be the case, I have a favour to ask. You must know I am employed to paint a Jesus on the cross; and my purpose is to represent him at that point of time when the spear is thrust into his side. Now, I should be glad if you would, in my presence, pink some impertinent fellow into convulsions, without endangering his life, that I may have an opportunity of taking a good clever agony from nature. The doctor will direct you where to enter, and how far to go; but pray let it be as near the left side as possible." Wagtail, who took this proposal seriously, observed that it would be a very difficult matter to penetrate into the left side of the thorax without hurting the heart, and of consequence killing the patient; but he believed it was possible for a man of a very nice hand, and exact knowledge of anatomy, to wound the diaphragma somewhere about the skirts, which might induce a singultus, without being attended with death; that he was ready to demonstrate the insertion of that muscle to Mr. Bragwell; but desired to have no concern with the experiment, which might essentially prejudice his reputation, in case of miscarriage. Bragwell was as much imposed upon by the painter's waggery as the doctor, and declined engaging in the affair, saying he had a very great regard for Mr. Slyboot, but had laid it down as a maxim, never to fight except when his honour was engaged. A thousand jokes of this kind were uttered; the wine circulated; supper was served in; we ate heartily; returned to the bottle; Bragwell became noisy and troublesome; Banter grew more and more severe; Ranter rehearsed; Slyboot made faces at the whole company; I sung French catches, and Chatter kissed me with great affection; while the doctor, with a woeful countenance, sat silent, like a disciple of Pythagoras. At length it was proposed by Bragwell that we should scour the hundreds, sweat the constable, maul the watch, and then reel soberly to bed.

While we deliberated on this expedition, the waiter came into the room and asked for Doctor Wagtail; when he understood he was present, he told him there was a lady below to inquire for him; at which message the physician started from his melancholy contemplation, and, with a look of extreme confusion, assured the company he could not possibly be the person wanted, for he had no connection with any lady whatever, and bade the drawer tell her so. "For shame!" cried Banter, "would you be so impolite as to refuse a lady the hearing? perhaps she comes for a consultation. It must be some extraordinary affair that brings a lady to a tavern at this time o' night. Mr. Ranter, pray do the doctor's baisemains to the lady, and squire her hither." The player immediately staggered out, and returned, leading in, with much ceremony, a tall strapping wench, whose appearance proclaimed her occupation. We received her with the utmost solemnity, and with a good deal of entreaty she was persuaded to sit, when a profound silence ensued, during which she fixed her eyes, with a disconsolate look, on the doctor, who was utterly confounded at her behaviour, and returned her melancholy fourfold. At length, after a good many piteous sighs, she wiped her eyes, and accosted him thus: "What! not one word of comfort? Will nothing soften that stony heart of thine? Not all my tears! not all my affliction! not the inevitable ruin thou hast brought upon me! Where are thy vows, thou faithless perjured man? Hast thou no honour — no conscience — no remorse for thy perfidious conduct towards me?—Answer me, wilt thou at last do me justice, or must I have recourse to heaven or hell for my revenge?" If poor Wagtail was amazed before she spoke, what must his confusion be on hearing this address! His natural paleness changed into a ghastly clay colour, his eyes rolled, his lips trembled, and he answered, in an accent not to be described, "Upon my word, honour, and salvation! madam, you are actually mistaken in my person. I have a most particular veneration for your sex, and am actually incapable of injuring any lady in the smallest degree, madam; —besides, madam, to the best of my recollection, I never had the honour of seeing you before, as I hope to be saved, madam!" "How, traitor!" cried she, "dost thou disown me then?— Mistaken! no, too well I know that fair bewitching face; too well I know the false enchanting tongue!—Alas! gentlemen, since the villain compels me, by his unkindness, to expose myself and him, know that this betrayer, under the specious pretence of honourable addresses, won my heart, and, taking advantage of his conquest, robbed me of my virgin treasure, and afterwards abandoned me to my fate! I am now four months gone with child by him, turned out of doors by my relations, and left a prey to misery and want! Yes, thou barbarian," said she, turning to Wagtail, "thou tiger, thou succubus! too well thou knowest my situation—but I will tear out thy faithless heart, and deliver the world from such a monster." So saying, she sprung forward at the doctor, who with incredible agility jumped over the table, and ran behind Bragwell, while the rest of us endeavoured to appease the furious heroine. Although everybody in the company affected the utmost surprise, I could easily perceive it was a scheme concerted among them to produce diversion at the doctor's expense; and being under no concern about the consequence, I entered into the confederacy, and enjoyed the distress of Wagtail, who, with tears in his eyes, begged the protection of the company, declaring himself as innocent of the crime laid to his charge, as the fœtus in utero; and hinting, at the same time, that nature had not put it into his power to be guilty of such a trespass. "Nature!" cried the lady; "there was no nature in the case—he abused me by the help of charms and spells; or else how is it possible that any woman could have listened to the addresses of such a scarecrow? Were these owlish eyes made for ogling; that carrion complexion to be admired; or that mouth like a horse-shoe to be kissed? No, no, you owe your success to your philtres, to your drugs and incantations; and not to your natural talents, which are in every respect mean and contemptible." The doctor now thought he had got an opportunity of vindicating himself effectually; and desired the complainant to compose herself but for half an hour, in which he undertook to prove the absurdity of believing in the power of incantations, which were only idle dreams of ignorance and superstition. He accordingly pronounced a very learned discourse upon the nature of ideas, the power and independence of the mind, the properties of stimulating medicines, the difference between a proneness to venery, which many simples would create, and a passion limited to one object, which can only be the result of sense and reflection; and concluded with a pathetic remonstrance, setting forth his unhappiness in being persecuted with the resentment of a lady whom he had never injured, nor ever seen before that occasion, and whose faculties were, in all likelihood, so much impaired by her misfortunes, that an innocent person was in danger of being ruined by her disorder. He had no sooner finished his harangue than the forlorn princess renewed her lamentations, and cautioned the company against his eloquence, which, she said, was able to bias the most impartial bench in Christendom. Banter advised him to espouse her immediately, as the only means to salve his reputation, and offered to accompany him to the Fleet for that purpose; but Slyboot proposed that a father should be purchased for the child, and a comfortable alimony settled on the mother. Ranter promised to adopt the infant gratis. Wagtail was ready to worship him for his generosity; and, though he persisted in protesting his innocence, condescended to everything, rather than his unblemished character should be called in question. The lady rejected the proposal, and insisted on matrimony. Bragwell took up the cudgels for the doctor, and undertook to rid him of her importunity for half a guinea; upon which Wagtail, with great eagerness, pulled out his purse and put it into the hands of his friend, who, taking half a piece out of it, gave it to the plaintiff, and bade her thank God for her good fortune. When she had received this bounty, she affected to weep, and begged, since the physician had renounced her, he would at least vouchsafe her a parting kiss. This he was prevailed upon to grant, with great reluctance, and went up with his usual solemnity to salute her; when she laid hold of his cheek with her teeth and held fast, while he roared with anguish, to the unspeakable diversion of all present. When she thought proper to release him, she dropped a low curtsey to the company, and quitted the room, leaving the doctor in the utmost horror, not so much on account of the pain, as the apprehension of the consequence of the bite; for by this time he was convinced of her being mad. Banter prescribed the actual cautery, and put the poker in the fire to be heated, in order to sear the place.

The player was of opinion that Bragwell should scoop out the part affected with the point of his sword; but the painter prevented both these dreadful operations by recommending a balsam he had in his pocket, which never failed to cure the bite of a mad dog. So saying, he pulled out a small bladder of black paint; with which he instantly anointed not only the sore, but the greatest part of the patient's face, and left it in a frightful condition. In short, the poor creature was so harassed with fear and vexation, that I pitied him extremely, and sent him home in a chair, contrary to the inclination of everybody present.

This freedom of mine gave umbrage to Bragwell, who testified his displeasure by swearing a few threats, without making any application; which being perceived by Slyboot, who sat by me, he, with a view of promoting a quarrel, whispered to me that he thought Bragwell used me very ill; but every man was the best judge of his own affairs. I answered aloud, that I would neither suffer Mr. Bragwell nor him to use me ill with impunity, and that I stood in no need of his counsel in regard to the regulation of my conduct. He thought proper to ask a thousand pardons, and assured me he meant no offence; while Bragwell feigned himself asleep, that he might not be obliged to take notice of what passed. But the player, who had more animal spirits and less discretion than Slyboot, unwilling to let the affair rest where he had dropped it, jogged Mr. Bragwell, and told him softly that I called him names, and threatened to cudgel him. This particular I understood by his starting, and crying, "Blood and wounds! you lie! No man durst treat me so ignominiously—Mr. Random, did you call me names, and threaten to drub me?" I denied the imputation, and proposed to punish the scoundrel who endeavoured to foment disturbance in the company. Bragwell signified his approbation, and drew his sword; I did the same, and accosted the actor in these words: "Lookee, Mr. Ranter, I know you possess all the mimicry and mischievous qualities of an ape, because I have observed you put them all in practice more than once to-night, on me and others; now I want to see if you resemble one in nimbleness also; therefore I desire you to leap over this sword without hesitation." So saying, I held it parallel to the horizon, at the distance of about three feet from the floor, and called, "Once —twice—thrice, and away"; but, instead of complying with my command, he snatched his hat and hanger, and assuming the looks, swagger, and phrase of Pistol, burst out into the following exclamation: "Ha! must I then perform inglorious prank of sylvan ape in mountain forest caught! Death rock me asleep, abridge my doleful days, and lay my head in fury's lap. Have we not Hiren here?" This buffoonery did not answer his expectation, for by this time the company was bent on seeing him in a new character. Mr. Banter desired me to hold my sword a foot or two higher, that he might have the better opportunity of exerting himself. The painter told him, if he performed well, he would recommend him as a vaulter to the proprietors of Saddler's Wells; and Bragwell, crying "Leap for the king," applied the point of the sword to the player's posteriors with such success, that he swung over in a trice, and, finding the door unguarded, vanished in a twinkling; glad, no doubt, of having paid his share of the reckoning so easily.

It being now near two o'clock in the morning, we discharged the bill, and sallied out into the street. The painter slunk away without taking his leave. Billy Chatter, being unable to speak or stand, was sent to a bagnio; and Banter and I accompanied Bragwell to Moll King's coffee-house, where, after he had kicked half a dozen hungry whores, we left him asleep on a bench, and directed our course towards Charing Cross, near which place both he and I lodged.

The natural dryness of my companion being overcome by liquor, he honoured me by the way with many compliments and professions of friendship, for which I made suitable acknowledgments, and told him I thought myself happy in having, by my behaviour, removed the unfavourable opinion he entertained of me at first sight. He was surprised at this declaration, and begged me to explain myself: upon which I mentioned what I had overheard him say of me to Wagtail in the coffee-house. He laughed, and made an apology for his freedom, assuring me that my appearance had very much prepossessed him in my favour; and what he said was only intended as a joke on the doctor's solemnity. I was highly pleased at being undeceived in this particular, and not a little proud of the good opinion of this wit, who shook me by the hand at parting, and promised to meet me next day at the ordinary.

CHAPTER XLVII

Strap communicates to me a Conquest he had made of a Chandler's Widow—Finds himself miserably mistaken—I go to the Opera—Admire Melinda—Am cautioned by Banter—Go to the Assembly at Hampstead —Dance with that young Lady—Receive an insolent Message from Bragwell, whose Metal is soon cooled—Am in favour with my Mistress, whom I visit next day; and am bubbled out of eighteen Guineas at Cards— Strap triumphs at my Success but is astonished at my Expense—Banter comes to my Lodging, is very sarcastic at my expense, and borrows five Guineas from me, as a proof of his Friendship.

In the morning before I got up, Strap came into my chamber, and, finding me awake, hemmed several times, scratched his head, cast his eyes upon the ground, and, with a very foolish kind of simper upon his face, gave me to understand he had something to communicate. "By your countenance," said I, "I expect to hear good tidings." "Indifferent," replied he, tittering; "that is, hereafter as it shall be. You must know I have some thoughts of altering my condition." "What!" cried I, astonished, "a matrimonial scheme? O rare Strap! thou hast got the heels of me at last." "N'—no less, I assure you," said he, bursting into a laugh of self-approbation; "a tallow-chandler's widow, that lives hard by, has taken a liking to me— a fine jolly dame, as plump as a partridge. She has a well-furnished house, a brisk trade, and a good deal of the ready. I may have her for the asking. She told a friend of mine, a brother footman, that she would take me out of a stinking clout. But I refused to give my final answer till I knew your opinion of the matter." I congratulated Monsieur d'Estrapes upon his conquest, and approved of the scheme, provided he could be assured of those circumstances of her fortune; but advised him to do nothing rashly, and give me an opportunity of seeing the lady before matters should be brought to a conclusion. He assured me he would do nothing without my consent and approbation, and that very morning, while I was at breakfast, introduced his inamorata to my acquaintance. She was a short thick woman, about the age of thirty-six, and had a particular prominence of belly, which I perceived at first sight, not without some suspicion of foul play. I desired her, however, to sit, and treated her with a dish of tea; the discourse turned upon the good qualities of Strap, whom I represented as a prodigy of sobriety, industry, and virtue.—When she took her leave, he followed her to the door, and returned licking his lips, and asked if I did not think she was a luscious creature. I made no mystery of my apprehension, but declared my sentiments of her without reserve; at which he was not surprised, telling me he had observed the same symptom, but had been informed by his friend that she was only liver-grown, and would in a few months be as small in the waist as ever. "Yes," said I, "a few weeks I believe will do the business. In short, Strap, it is my opinion that you are egregiously imposed upon; and that this friend is no other than a rascal who wants to palm his trull upon you for a wife, that he may at once deliver himself from the importunities of the mother, and the expense of her bantling; for which reason I would not have you trust implicitly to the report he makes of her wealth, which is inconsistent with his behaviour; nor run your head precipitately into a noose, that you may afterwards wish exchanged for the hangman's." He seemed very much startled at my insinuation, and promised to look twice before he leaped; saying, with some heat, "Odds, if I find his intention is to betray me, we shall see which of us is the better man." My prediction was verified in less than a fortnight; her great belly producing an infant, to the unspeakable amazement of Strap, who was, before this happened, inclinable to believe I had refined a little too much in my penetration. His false friend disappeared; and in a few days after an execution was issued against her goods and household furniture, which were seized by the creditors.

Meanwhile I met my friend Banter at the ordinary, and in the evening went to the opera with him and Mr. Chatter, who pointed out Melinda in one of the boxes, and offered to introduce me to her, observing at the same time, that she was a reigning toast worth ten thousand pounds. This piece of information made my heart bound with joy, and I discovered great eagerness to accept the proposal; upon which he assured me I should dance with her at the next assembly, if he had any influence in that quarter. So saying, he went round, spoke to her some minutes, and, as I imagined, pointed at me; then returning, told me, to my inexpressible pleasure, that I might depend upon what he had promised, for she was now engaged as my partner. Banter, in a whisper, gave me to understand that she was an incorrigible coquette, who would grant the same favour to any young fellow in England of a tolerable appearance, merely to engage him among the herd of her admirers, that she might have the pleasure of seeing them daily increase; that she was of a cold insensible disposition, dead to every passion but vanity, and so blind to merit, that he would lay any wager the wealthiest fool should carry her at last. I attributed a good deal of this intelligence to the satirical turn of my friend, or resentment for having himself suffered a rebuff from the lady in question; and, at any rate, trusted so much to my own accomplishments, as to believe no woman could resist the ardour of my addresses.

Full of this confidence I repaired to Hampstead, in company with Billy Chatter, my Lord Hobble, and Doctor Wagtail. There I saw a very brilliant assembly, before whom I had the honour to walk a minuet with Melinda, who charmed me with her frank manner and easiness of behaviour. Before the country dances began, I received a message, by a person I did not know, from Bragwell, who was present, importing that nobody who knew him presumed to dance with Melinda while he was there in person; and that I would do well to relinquish her without noise, because he had a mind to lead up a country dance with her. This extraordinary intimation, which was delivered in the lady's hearing, did not at all discompose me, who by this time was pretty well acquainted with the character of my rival. I therefore, without the least symptom of concern, bade the gentleman tell Mr. Bragwell that, since I was so happy as to obtain the lady's consent, I should not be solicitous about his; and desired the bearer himself to bring me no such impertinent message for the future. Melinda affected a sort of confusion, and pretended to wonder that Mr. Bragwell should give himself such liberties with regard to her, who had no manner of connection with the fellow. I laid hold of this opportunity to display my valour, and offered to call him to account for his insolence, a proposal which she absolutely refused under pretence of consulting my safety; though I could perceive by the sparkling of her eyes, that she would not have thought herself affronted in being the subject of a duel. I was by no means pleased with this discovery of her thoughts, which not only argued the most unjustifiable vanity, but likewise the most barbarous indifference; however, I was allured by her fortune, and resolved to gratify her pride, in making her the occasion of a public quarrel between me and Bragwell, who, I was pretty certain, would never drive matters to a dangerous extremity.

While we danced together, I observed this formidable rival at one end of the room, encircled with a cluster of beaux, to whom he talked with great vehemence, casting many big looks at me from time to time: I guessed the subject of his discourse, and as soon as I had handed my partner to her seat, strutted up to the place where he stood, and cocking my hat in his face,

demanded aloud if he had anything to say to me. He answered
with a sullen tone, "Nothing at present, sir"; and turned about
upon his heel. "Well," said I, "you know where I am to be
found at any time." His companions stared at one another,
and I returned to the lady, whose features brightened at my
approach, and immediately a whisper ran through the whole
room; after which so many eyes were turned upon me, that I
was ready to sink with confusion. When the ball broke up, I led
her to her coach, and, like a true French gallant, would have
got up behind it, in order to protect her from violence on the
road; but she absolutely refused my offer, and expressed her
concern that there was not an empty seat for me within the
vehicle.

Next day in the afternoon, I waited on her at her lodgings,
by permission, in company with Chatter, and was very civilly
received by her mother, with whom she lived; there were a
good many fashionable people present, chiefly young fellows,
and immediately after tea, a couple of card tables were set, at
one of which I had the honour to play with Melinda, who, in
less than three hours, made shift to plunder me of eight guineas.
I was well enough content to lose a little money with a good
grace, that I might have an opportunity in the meantime to
say soft things, which are still most welcome when attended
with good luck; but I was by no means satisfied of her fair play,
a circumstance that shocked me not a little, and greatly impaired
my opinion of her disinterestedness and delicacy. However,
I was resolved to profit by this behaviour, and treat her in my
turn with less ceremony; accordingly, I laid close siege to her,
and finding her not at all disgusted with the gross incense I
offered, that very night made a declaration of love in plain
terms. She received my addresses with great gaiety, and pretended to laugh them off; but, at the same time, treated me with
such particular complacency, that I was persuaded I had made
a conquest of her heart, and concluded myself the happiest
man alive. Elevated with these flattering ideas, I sat down again
to cards after supper, and with great cheerfulness suffered
myself to be cheated of ten guineas more.

It was late before I took my leave, after being favoured with
a general invitation; and when I got into bed, the adventures
of the day hindered me from sleeping. Sometimes I pleased
myself with the hopes of possessing a fine woman with ten
thousand pounds; then I would ruminate on the character I
had heard of her from Banter, and compare it with the circum-

stances of her conduct towards me, which seemed to bear too
great a resemblance to the picture he had drawn. This introduced
a melancholy reflection on the expense I had undergone, and
the smallness of my funds to support it, which, by the bye, were
none of my own. In short, I found myself involved in doubts
and perplexities, that kept me awake the greatest part of the
night.

In the morning, Strap, with whom I had not conversed for
two days, presented himself with the utensils for shaving me;
upon which, I asked his opinion of the lady whom he had seen
me conduct to her coach at Hampstead. "Odd! she's a delicious
creature," cried he, "and, as I am informed, a great fortune.
I am sorry you did not insist on going home with her. I dare say
she would not have refused your company; for she seems to be
a good-humoured soul." "There's a time for all things," said I.
"You must know, Strap, I was in company with her till one
o'clock this morning." I had no sooner pronounced these words
than he began to caper about the room, and snap his fingers,
crying, in a transport, "The day's our own!—the day's our
own!" I gave him to understand that his triumph was a little
premature, and that I had more difficulties to surmount than
he was aware of. Then I recounted to him the intelligence I had
received from Banter, at which he changed colour, shook his
head, and observed there was no faith in woman. I told him I
was resolved to make a bold push notwithstanding, although I
foresaw it would lead me into a great expense; and bade him
guess the sum I had lost last night at cards. He scratched his
chin, and protested his abhorrence of cards, the very name of
which being mentioned, made him sweat with vexation, as it
recalled the money-dropper to his remembrance: "But, however," said he, "you have to do with other-guess people now.
Why, I suppose, if you had a bad run last night, you would
scarce come off for less than ten or twelve shillings." I was
mortified at this piece of simplicity, which I imagined, at that
time, as all affected, by way of reprimand for my folly; and
asked with some heat, if he thought I spent the evening in a
cellar with chairmen and bunters; giving him to know at the
same time that my expense had amounted to eighteen guineas.
It would require the pencil of Hogarth to express the astonishment and concern of Strap on hearing this piece of news. The
bason in which he was preparing the lather for my chin, dropped
out of his hands, and he remained some time immovable in that
ludicrous attitude, with his mouth open, and his eyes thrust

forward considerably beyond their station; but remembering my disposition, which was touchy and impatient of control, he smothered his chagrin, and attempted to recollect himself. With this view, he endeavoured to laugh, but, in spite of his teeth, broke into a whimper, took up his wash-ball and pewter pot, scrubbed my beard with the one, and discharged the other upon my face. I took no notice of his confusion, but after he had fully recovered himself, put him in mind of his right, and assured him of my readiness to surrender his effects whenever he should think proper to demand them. He was nettled at my insinuation, which he thought proceeded from my distrust of his friendship; and begged I would never talk to him in that strain again, unless I had a mind to break his heart.

This good creature's unalterable friendship for me, affected me with the most grateful sentiments, and acted as a spur to my resolution of acquiring a fortune, that I might have it in my power to manifest my generosity in my return. For this purpose I determined to bring matters to a speedy conclusion with Melinda; well knowing that a few such nights as the last would effectually incapacitate me from prosecuting that or any other advantageous amour.

While my meditation was busied in planning out my future conduct, Mr. Banter favoured me with a visit; and, after breakfast, asked how I had passed the preceding evening. I answered, I was very agreeably entertained at a private house. "Yes," said he, with a sarcastic smile, "you deserved something extraordinary for the price you paid." I was surprised at this remark, and pretended ignorance of his meaning. "Come, come, Random," continued he, "you need not make a mystery of it to me, the whole town has it. I wish that foolish affair between you and Bragwell at Hampstead had been less public. It has set all the busybodies at work to find out your real character and situation; and you cannot imagine what conjectures have already circulated at your expense. One suspects you to be a Jesuit in disguise; another thinks you are an agent from the Pretender; a third believes you to be an upstart gamester, because nobody knows anything of your family or fortune; a fourth is of opinion that you are an Irish fortune hunter." This last hypothesis touched me so nearly, that, to conceal my confusion, I was fain to interrupt his detail, and damn the world for an envious meddling community, that would not suffer a gentleman to live without molestation. He took no notice of this apostrophe, but went on, "For my own part, I neither know, nor desire to know,

who or what you are; this I am certain of, that few people make
a mystery of their origin or situation, who can boast of anything
advantageous in either; and my own opinion of the matter is,
that you have raised yourself by your industry from nothing to
the appearance you now maintain, and which you endeavour to
support by some matrimonial scheme." Here he fixed his eyes
stedfastly upon me, and perceiving my face covered with blushes,
told me, now he was confirmed in his opinion;—"Look ye,
Random," said he, "I have divined your plan, and am confident
it will never succeed. You are too honest, and too ignorant of the
town, to practise the necessary cheats of your profession, and
detect the conspiracies that will be formed against you. Besides,
you are downright bashful—what the devil! set up for a fortune
hunter before you have conquered the sense of shame! Perhaps
you are entitled by your merit, and I believe you are, to a richer
and better wife than Melinda; but, take my word for it, she is
not to be won at that rate; or, if you are so lucky as to carry her,
between you and me, you may say as Teague did, *By my soul,
I have gained a loss!* She would take care to spend her fortune in
a twinkling, and soon make you sick of her extravagance." I
was alarmed by his discourse, while I resented the freedom of
it, and expressed my disgust, by telling him he was mistaken
in my intentions, and desiring he would give me leave to regulate
my conduct according to the dictates of my own reason. He
made an apology for the liberty he had taken, and ascribed it to
the warmth of his friendship for me; as an uncommon instance
of which, he borrowed five guineas, assuring me there were
very few people in the world whom he would so far favour with
his confidence. I gave him the money, and professed myself so
well convinced of his sincerity, that he had no occasion to put it
to such extraordinary proofs for the future. "I thought," said
he, "to have asked five pieces more, but hearing you was bubbled
of eighteen last night, I presumed you might be out of cash, and
resolved to model my demand accordingly." I could not help
admiring the cavalier behaviour of this spark, of whom I desired
to know his reason for saying I was bubbled. He then gave me
to understand, that, before he came to my lodgings, he had beat
up Tom Tossle, who, having been present, informed him of the
particulars, rehearsed all the fine things I said to Melinda, with
which he proposes to entertain the town; and, among other
circumstances, assured him, my mistress cheated with so little
art, that nobody but a mere novice could have been imposed upon.

The thoughts of becoming a subject of raillery for coxcombs, and losing my money to boot, stung me to the quick; but I made a virtue of my indignation, and swore that no man should, with impunity, either asperse the character of Melinda, or turn my behaviour into ridicule. He replied, in a dry manner, that I would find it an Herculean task to chastise everybody who would laugh at my expense; and as for the character of Melinda, he did not see how it could suffer by what was laid to her charge; for that cheating at cards, far from being reckoned a blemish among people of fashion, was looked upon as an honourable indication of superior genius and address. "But let us waive this subject," said he, "and go to the coffee-house, in order to make a party for dinner."

CHAPTER XLVIII

We repair to the Coffee-house, where we overhear a curious Dispute between Wagtail and Medlar, which is referred to our Decision—The Doctor gives an Account of his Experiment—Medlar is roasted by Banter at the Ordinary—The old Gentleman's Advice to me.

BEING as willing to drop the theme, as he to propose it, I accompanied him thither, where we found Mr. Medlar and Dr. Wagtail disputing upon the word *Custard*, which the physician affirmed should be spelled with a *G*, because it was derived from the Latin verb *gustare*, "to taste." But Medlar pleaded custom in behalf of *C*, observing that, by the doctor's rule, we ought to change pudding into budding, because it is derived from the French word *Boudin:* and in that case why not retain the original orthography and pronunciation of all the foreign words we have adopted; by which means our language would become a dissonant jargon, without standard or propriety. The controversy was referred to us; and Banter, notwithstanding his real opinion to the contrary, decided it in favour of Wagtail: upon which the peevish annuitant arose, and uttering the monosyllable "Pish!" with great emphasis, removed to another table.

We then inquired of the doctor what progress he had made in the experiment of distilling tinder-water; and he told us he had been at all the glass-houses about town, but could find nobody who would undertake to blow a retort large enough to hold the third part of the quantity prescribed; but he intended to try the process on as much as would produce five drops, which would be sufficient to prove the specific, and then he would make it a parliamentary affair; that he had already purchased a considerable weight of rags, in reducing which to tinder he had met with a misfortune, which had obliged him to change his lodgings; for he had gathered them in a heap on the floor and set fire to them with a candle, on the supposition that the boards would sustain no damage, because it is the nature of flame to ascend; but by some very extraordinary accident, the wood was invaded, and began to blaze with great violence, which disordered him so much, that he had not presence of mind enough to call for assistance, and the whole house must have been consumed, with him in the midst of it, had not the smoke that rolled out of the windows in clouds, alarmed the neighbourhood, and brought people to his succour. That he had lost a pair of black velvet breeches and a tie-wig in the hurry, besides the expense of the rags, which were rendered useless by the water used to quench the flame, and the damage of the floor, which he was compelled to repair. That his landlord, believing him distracted, had insisted on his quitting his apartment at a minute's warning, and he was put to incredible inconvenience; but now he was settled in a very comfortable house, and had the use of a large paved yard for preparing his tinder: so that he hoped in a very short time to reap the fruits of his labour.

After having congratulated the doctor on his prospect, and read the papers, we repaired to an auction of pictures, where we entertained ourselves an hour or two. From thence we adjourned to the Mall, and after two or three turns went back to dinner, Banter assuring us that he intended to roast Medlar at the ordinary; and, indeed, we were no sooner set than this Cynic began to execute his purpose, by telling the old gentleman that he looked extremely well, considering the little sleep he had enjoyed last night. To this compliment Medlar made no reply but by a stare, accompanied with a significant grin; and Banter went on thus: "I don't know whether most to admire, the charity of your mind, or the vigour of your body. Upon my soul, Mr. Medlar, you do generous things with the best taste of any man I know: you extend your compassion to real objects, and exact only such returns as they are capable of making. You must know, gentlemen," said he, turning to the company, "I had been up most part of the night with a friend who is ill of a fever, and on my return home this morning chanced to pass by a gin shop still open, whence issued a confused sound of mirth and jollity: upon which I popped in my head, and perceived Mr. Medlar dancing bare-headed in the midst of ten or twenty ragged bunters, who rejoiced at his expense. But indeed, Mr. Medlar, you ought not to sacrifice your constitution to your benevolence. Consider you grow old apace; and therefore have a reverend care of your health, which must certainly be very much impaired by these nocturnal expeditions." The testy senior could no longer contain himself, but cried hastily, "'Tis well known that your tongue is no slander." "I think," said the other, "you might spare that observation, as you are very sensible that my tongue has done you signal service on many occasions. You may remember that when you made your addresses to the fat widow, who kept a public-house at Islington, there was a report spread very much to the prejudice of your manhood, which coming to the ears of your mistress, you was discarded immediately, and I brought matters to a reconciliation, by assuring her you had three bastards at nurse in the country: how you ruined your own affair afterwards, it is neither my business nor inclination to relate." This anecdote, which had no other foundation than in Banter's own invention, afforded a good deal of mirth to everybody present, and provoked Mr. Medlar beyond all sufferance; so that he started up in a mighty passion, and, forgetting that his mouth was full, bespattered those who sat next to him, while he discharged his indignation in a volley of oaths, and called Banter insignificant puppy, impertinent jackanapes, and an hundred such appellations; telling the company he had invented these false malicious aspersions, because he would not lend him money to squander away among rooks and whores. "A very likely story," said Banter, "that I should attempt to borrow money of a man who is obliged to practise a thousand shifts to make his weekly allowance hold out till Saturday night. Sometimes he sleeps four and twenty hours at a stretch, by which means he saves three meals, besides coffee-house expense. Sometimes he is fain to put up with bread and cheese and small beer for dinner; and sometimes he regales on two pennyworth of ox-cheek in a cellar." "You are a lying miscreant," cried Medlar, in an ecstasy of rage, "I can always command money enough to pay your tailor's bill, which I am sure is no trifle; and I have a good mind to give you a convincing proof of my circumstances, by prosecuting you for defamation, sirrah." By this time the violence of his wrath had deprived him of his appetite, and he sat silent, unable to swallow one mouthful, while his tormentor enjoyed his mortification and increased his chagrin by advising him to lay in plentifully for his next day's fast.

Dinner being ended, we came downstairs to the coffee-room, and Banter went away to keep an appointment, saying, he supposed he should see Wagtail and me in the evening at the Bedford coffee-house. He was no sooner gone, than the old gentleman took me aside and said, he was sorry to see me so intimate with that fellow, who was one of the most graceless rakes about town, and had already wasted a good estate and constitution upon harlots; that he had been the ruin of many a young man, by introducing them into debauched company, and setting a lewd example of all manner of wickedness; and that, unless I was on my guard, he would strip me in a short time both of my money and reputation. I thanked him for his information, and promised to conduct myself accordingly, wishing, however, his caution had been a few hours more early, by which means I might have saved five guineas. Notwithstanding this intelligence, I was inclinable to impute some part of the charge to Medlar's revenge for the liberties taken with him at dinner; and, therefore, as soon as I could disengage myself, applied to Wagtail for his opinion of the character in question; resolved to compare their accounts, allowing for the prejudice of each, and to form my judgment upon both, without adhering strictly to either. The doctor assured me that he was a very pretty gentleman of family and fortune; a scholar, a wit, a critic, and perfectly well acquainted with the town; that his honour and courage were unquestionable, though some extravagances he had been guilty of, and his talents for satire, had procured him enemies, and made some people shy of his acquaintance. From these different sketches, I concluded that Banter was a young fellow of some parts, who had spent his fortune, but retained his appetites, and fallen out with the world, because he could not enjoy it to his wish.

I went to the Bedford coffee-house in the evening, where I met my friends, from thence proceeded to the play, and afterwards carried them home to my lodgings, where we supped in great good humour.

CHAPTER XLIX

I receive a Challenge—The Consequences of it—The Quarrel being made up, am put in Arrest, by the Care and Affection of Strap—But immediately released upon explaining my Affair—The Behaviour of Mr. Oregan and his two Friends—I visit Melinda whom I divert with an Account of the Duel—Propose Marriage—She refers the Matter to her Mother, of whom I make a solemn Demand of her Daughter—The old Lady's Behaviour—I am discarded—Resent their Disdain.

WHEN I was ready to go abroad next day, Strap brought me a letter, *To Mr. Random, Esq. These*—Which, upon opening, I found contained a challenge, conceived in these very extraordinary terms:

"SIR,—Whereas I am informed that you make love to Miss Melinda Goosetrap—This is to let you know that she is under promise of marriage to me; and that I am at this present waiting at the back of Montague House, with a pair of good pistols in my hand; and if you will keep your appointment, I will make your tongue confess (after the breath is out of your body) that you do not deserve her so well as

"Yours, etc.

"ROURK OREGAN."

I guessed from the style and subscription of this billet that my rival was a true Milesian, and was not a little uneasy at the contents, especially that part in which he asserted his right to my mistress by promise, a circumstance I did not know how to reconcile to her good sense and penetration. However, this was no time for me to decline the defiance, because the success of my addresses might in a great measure depend upon my behaviour in that affair. I therefore immediately loaded my pistols, and betook myself in a hackney coach to the place appointed, where I found a tall, raw-boned man, with a hard-featured countenance, and black bushy beard, walking by himself, wrapped up in a shabby great-coat, over which his own hair descended in a leathern queue from his head, that was covered with a greasy hat trimmed with a tarnished *point d'Espagne*. He no sooner perceived me advancing, than he pulled a pistol from his bosom, and presenting it at me, snapped it without the least preamble. Alarmed at this rude salutation, I made a stand; and before he could adjust his other piece, fired one of mine at him, without doing any damage. By this time he was ready with his second, that flashed in the pan without

going off. Upon which he called, with a true Tipperary cadence,
"Fire away, honey,"—and began to hammer his flint with great
deliberation. But I was resolved to make use of the advantage
fortune had given me; and therefore stepped up, without
throwing away my fire, desiring him to ask his life, or prepare
for another world; but this stout Hibernian refused to condescend, and complained bitterly of my having quitted my ground
before he could return my shot; saying I ought to go back to my
station, and let him have an equal chance with me. I endeavoured to persuade him that I had given him a double chance
already; and it was my business to prevent him from enjoying
a third;—but now, since I had an opportunity, I demanded a
parley, and desired to know his condition, and reason for calling
me to the field, who, to the best of my remembrance, far from
having done him an injury, had never before seen him. He told
me that he was a gentleman of fortune, who had spent all he
had, and hearing that Melinda had got ten thousand pounds,
he intended to make himself master of that sum by espousing
her, and was determined, in an honourable way, to cut the
throats of all those who stood between him and his hopes. I
then demanded to know the foundation of his hopes; and, now
that I had seen him, being more and more astonished at the
circumstance of the promise, desired that he would explain
that mystery. He gave me to understand that he trusted entirely
to his birth and personal merit; that he had frequently written
to Melinda, setting forth his claim and pretensions, but she was
never kind enough to send an answer, or even to admit him
into her presence; and that the promise he mentioned in his
letter was made by his friend Mr. Gahagan, who assured him
that no woman could resist a man of his appearance. I could
not forbear laughing to excess at the simplicity of my rival,
who did not seem to relish my mirth, but began to be very
serious. Upon which I endeavoured to appease him by giving
him my word and honour, that, far from prejudicing his
addresses to the lady, I would represent him to her in the most
favourable light I could with any regard to truth; but he must
not be surprised if she should remain blind to his deserts, for
nothing was more capricious than a woman's mind, and the
affection of that sex was seldom purchased with virtue alone.
That my declaration might have the better effect, I took notice
of his dishabille, and professing sorrow at seeing a gentleman
reduced, slipped two guineas into his hand; at sight of which
he threw away his pistols, and, hugging me in his arms, cried,

"Arrah, by Jesus now, you are the best friend I have met with these seven long years." When I had suffered some minutes in his embrace, he quitted me, and picking up his rusty arms, wished the devil might burn him if he should give me any further trouble about womankind.

The quarrel being thus amicably composed, I begged leave to look at his pistols, which I found so crazy and so foul, that I believe it was happy for him neither of them was discharged, for one of them would certainly have split in the going off, and he would, in all probability, have lost his hand in the explosion; but what gave me a lively idea of the man's character was to find, upon examination, that one of them had been loaded without being primed, and the other primed without a charge.

While we walked home together, I expressed a desire of knowing my friend's history; and he informed me of his having served in the German army as a volunteer against the Turks; that, for his behaviour at the siege of Belgrade, he had been honoured with an ensign's commission, and afterwards promoted to the rank of lieutenant, in which station it was his misfortune to affront his captain, who challenged him to the field, and was killed in the duel, upon which he was obliged to retreat;—that he had been in England some years soliciting his friends for provision in the British army; but being hitherto unsuccessful, was desired by Mr. Gahagan to turn his thoughts to matrimony, and make his fortune by an advantageous match; in consequence of which advice, he had made up to Melinda, and having heard, by means of an Irish footman in the family, that I was her chief favourite, had called me out, in hopes of removing by my death the greatest obstruction to his desires; but now he was convinced of my honour and generosity, he swore by the Blessed Virgin, he would think of her no more, if there was not another woman in the world. As a farther proof of his veracity, which I did not at all doubt, he opened an old iron snuff-box, and pulled out his commission in the Imperial army, and his captain's challenge, which he preserved as testimonials of his character. I was so well convinced of this poor man's honesty and courage, that I determined to speak in his behalf to some of my acquaintance, who might recommend his case to the consideration of those who could provide for him; and in the meantime to accommodate him with a few clothes, by which his appearance would be much mended, and himself enabled to renew his solicitations in person.

As we walked along, conversing socially together, we were

met by a file of musketeers, and Strap at their head, who no sooner approached, than, with a frantic look, he cried, "Seize them!—in the name of God! seize them."—We were accordingly surrounded, and put in arrest by the corporal, who was commanding officer; but Captain Oregan disengaged himself and ran with such speed towards Tottenham Court Road, that he was out of sight in a moment. When my arms were delivered up, and myself secured, Strap became a little more composed, and asked pardon for the liberty he had taken, which he hoped I would excuse, as it proceeded from his affection. He then told me, that, suspecting the letter (which by the bye was brought by the author himself) contained something extraordinary, he had peeped through the keyhole, and seen me load my pistols; upon which he ran down to Whitehall, and applied to the officer on guard for a party to put me in arrest; but before he returned, I was gone in a coach; that he had inquired which way I went, and having heard that duels were commonly fought at the back of Montague House, he conducted the guard to this place, where he thanked God for having found me safe and sound. I gave him to understand that I forgave his officious concern for once, but cautioned him in pretty severe terms of making me the subject of idle conversation for the future; then, turning to the corporal, thanked him for his care, and gave him a crown to drink with his men, assuring him that the rencontre was over long before he came up, and everything compromised, as he might observe by our behaviour; as a farther proof of which he would find, upon examination, that one of my pistols had been discharged;—but this civil person, without giving himself or me any further trouble, received the bounty with a thousand bows and acknowledgments, and returning the pistols, released me immediately.

He was not gone a hundred yards, when my friend Oregan came up, in order to rescue me, with two tatterdemalions whom he had engaged for that purpose about the purlieus of St. Giles's: one of them was armed with a musket that wanted a lock, and another with a rusty broadsword; but their dress surpassed all description. When he understood I was already free, he made an apology for his abrupt departure, and introduced me to his two companions: first, to counsellor Fitzclabber, who, he told me, was then employed in compiling a history of the kings of Munster, from Irish manuscripts; and then to his friend Mr. Gahagan, who was a profound philosopher and politician, and had projected many excellent schemes for the good of his country. But it seems these literati had been very ill rewarded for their ingenious labours; for between them both there was but one shirt and a half-pair of breeches. I thanked them very kindly for their readiness to assist me, and having offered my service in my turn, bade them good morrow, desiring Oregan to accompany me to my lodgings, where he was fitted with decent clothes from my wardrobe, so much to his satisfaction, that he swore eternal gratitude and friendship for me, and, at my request, recounted all the adventures of his life.

In the afternoon I waited on Melinda, who received me with great kindness and familiarity, and laughed excessively at my adventure with the Irishman, to whose wishes she was no stranger, having more than a dozen letters in her possession, which he had wrote to her on the subject of love, and which, for my entertainment, she submitted to my perusal. Having made ourselves merry at the expense of this poor admirer, I seized the opportunity of her mother's going out of the room, and introduced my own passion, which I recommended to her with all the ardour and eloquence I was master of. I flattered, sighed, and swore, entreated, and acted a thousand extravagances, in hopes of making some impression on her heart; but she heard everything I said without discovering the least emotion; and other company came in before she would vouchsafe one serious reply. After tea, the cards were brought in, according to custom, and it was my good fortune to have Melinda for my partner; by which means, instead of losing, I came off with five guineas clear gain.

I soon became acquainted with a good many people of fashion, and spent my time in the modish diversion of the town, such as plays, operas, masquerades, drums, assemblies, and puppet-shows; chiefly in company with Melinda, whom I cultivated with all the eagerness and address that my prospect could inspire, and my education afford; I spared neither my person nor my purse to gratify her vanity and pride; my rivals were intimidated, and indeed outshone; and, after all, I began to fear that the dear creature had not a heart to lose. At last, finding myself unable to support the expense of this amour much longer, I was determined to bring the matter to a crisis; and one evening, while we were together by ourselves, complained of her indifference, described the tortures of suspense to a lovesick mind, and pressed her to disclose her sentiments of matrimony and me, with such earnestness, that she could not, with all her art, shift the subject, but was obliged to come to an éclaircissement. She told me with a careless air, that she had no objection to my person, and, if I could satisfy her mother in other particulars, I should not find her averse to the match; but she was resolved to do nothing in such a momentous concern without the advice and consent of her parent. This was no very agreeable declaration to me, whose aim had been to win her inclination first, and then secure my conquest by private marriage, to which I flattered myself she would express no reluctance. That I might not, however, desert my cause before it was desperate, I waited on her mother, and with great formality demanded the daughter in marriage. The good lady, who was a very notable woman, behaved with great state and civility; thanked me for the honour I intended her family; and said, that she did not doubt that I was in all respects qualified to make a woman happy; but it concerned her, as a parent anxious about the welfare of her child, to inquire into the particulars of my fortune, and know what settlement I proposed to make. To this intimation, which would have utterly disconcerted me if I had not expected it, I replied, without hesitation, that, though my fortune was very small, I was a gentleman by birth and education, would maintain her daughter in the sphere of a gentlewoman, and settle her own dowry on her and her heirs for ever. This careful matron did not seem to relish my proposal, but observed, with a demure countenance, that there was no necessity for settling that upon her child which was her own already: however, if I pleased, her lawyer should confer with mine upon the matter; and, in the meantime, she desired I would favour her with the perusal of my rent-roll. Notwithstanding the vexation I was under, I could scarce forbear laughing in her face, at the mention of my rent-roll, which was, indeed, a severe piece of satire on my pretensions. I frankly owned I had no landed estate; and told her that I could not exactly specify the sum I was master of, until I had regulated my affairs, which were at present in some disorder; but that I would take an opportunity of satisfying her upon that head very soon.

It was not long before I took my leave, and returned to my lodgings in a very melancholy mood, persuaded that I had nothing more to expect from that quarter. I was confirmed in this opinion next day, when I went back with a view of explaining myself more fully to the old gentlewoman; and was told by the footman that his ladies were not at home, although I had seen Melinda through the blinds at the parlour window as

I went up to the door. Incensed at this affront, I quitted the door, without saying one word, and as I repassed the parlour, bowed to Miss, who still remained in the same situation, securely screened, as she thought, from view.

This disappointment gave me more uneasiness on Strap's account than my own; for I was in no danger of dying for love of Melinda; on the contrary, the remembrance of my charming Narcissa was a continual check upon my conscience, during the whole course of my addresses; and perhaps contributed to the bad success of my scheme, by controlling my raptures, and condemning my design.

There was a necessity for informing my companion of everything that happened to me, and I performed this piece of duty in an affected passion, swearing I would be his packhorse no longer, and desiring him to take the management of his affairs into his own hands. This finesse had the desired effect; for, instead of grumbling over my miscarriage, Strap was frightened at the passion I feigned, and begged me, for the love of God, to be appeased; observing, that, although we had suffered a great loss, it was not irreparable; and if fortune frowned to-day, she might perhaps smile to-morrow. I pretended to acquiesce in his remarks, praise his equanimity, and promise to improve my misfortune. He, on the other hand, pretended to be perfectly well satisfied with my conduct, and conjured me to follow the dictates of my own reflection; but, in spite of all his affectation, I perceived his inward affliction, and his visage sensibly increased in longitude from that day.

CHAPTER L

I long to be revenged on Melinda—Apply to Banter for his Assistance —He contrives a Scheme for that Purpose, which is put in Execution with great Success—I make an Attempt on the Heart of Miss Gripewell, but am disappointed—Grow melancholy at my Disappointment, and have recourse to the Bottle—Receive a Billet-doux—Am ravished with the Contents—Find myself involved in an Intrigue, which I imagined would make my Fortune—Am confounded at my Mistake, which banishes all Thoughts of Matrimony.

IN the meantime, my attention was wholly engrossed in search of another mistress and the desire of being revenged on Melinda, in both which schemes I was very much assisted by Billy Chatter, who was such a necessary creature among the ladies, that in all private dances he engaged the men. To him therefore

I applied, desiring he would introduce me to a partner of some figure at the next private assembly, for the sake of a frolic, the intention of which I would afterwards communicate. Billy, who had heard something of the difference between Melinda and me, immediately smoked part of my design, and thinking I only wanted to alarm her jealousy a little, promised to gratify my desire, by matching me with a partner worth thirty thousand pounds, whom the ladies of this end of the town had lately taken under their management and protection. Upon further inquiry, I found this person's name was Miss Biddy Gripewell; that her father, who had been a pawnbroker, died intestate, by which means all his substance descended to his daughter, who was so little a favourite, that, could the old man have prevailed with his own rapacious disposition to part with as much money as would have paid the expense of a will, she would have inherited a sixth part of his fortune; that, during his life, far from being educated in a way suitable to such great expectations, she was obliged to live like a servant wench, and do the most menial offices in the family. But his funeral was no sooner performed, than she assumed the fine lady, and found so many people of both sexes to flatter, caress, and instruct her, that, for want of discretion and experience, she was grown insufferably vain and arrogant, and pretended to no less than a duke or earl at least for her husband. That she had the misfortune to be neglected by the English quality, but a certain poor Scottish lord was then making interest to be introduced to her acquaintance. In the meantime, she was fallen into the hands of a notable lady, who had already disposed of her to a lieutenant of foot, a distant relation of her ladyship's, though Miss, as yet, knew nothing of the affair. And, lastly, that, if I proposed to dance with her, I must give him leave to represent me as a knight or foreign count at least. I was ravished at this piece of information, and consented, for one night, to personate a French marquis, that I might the easier fulfil my revenge.

Having made the appointment with Chatter, I went to Banter's lodgings, as I had by this time conceived a great opinion of his penetration and knowledge; and, after I had enjoined secrecy, told him every circumstance of my disgrace with Melinda, and imparted the plan I had projected to mortify that proud coquette, desiring his advice in improving, and assistance in executing the scheme. Nothing could be more agreeable to his misanthropical temper, than an account of her behaviour and my resentment. He applauded my resolution, and proposed that I should not only provide myself with a proper partner, but also procure such an one for Miss Goosetrap as should infallibly entail upon her the ridicule of all her acquaintance. For this purpose he mentioned his barber, who, he said, was an exceeding coxcomb, lately come from Paris, whose absurd affectation and grimace would easily pass upon her for the sprightly politesse of a gentleman improved by travel. I hugged him for this hint; and he assured me, it would be no difficult matter to make him believe that Melinda, having seen him by accident, was captivated by his appearance, and longed for his acquaintance. He actually engaged him on this pretence, and painted his good fortune in such colours, that the poor shaver was quite beside himself with joy. He was immediately fitted with a tawdry suit of clothes belonging to Banter, and by him recommended to Chatter, as a very pretty fellow just returned from his travels. Mr. Billy, who acted as a gentleman usher to a great many of the fair sex in and about town, undertook at once to bespeak Melinda in his behalf; and everything happened according to my wish.

At the time appointed, I appeared dressed to the best advantage; and, in the character of Marquis, had the honour of opening the ball with the rich heiress, who attracted the eyes of the whole company by the prodigious number of jewels with which she was adorned. Among others, I perceived Melinda, who could no more conceal her envy than astonishment at my success. Her curiosity was still more flagrant and tormenting, for she had never seen Miss Gripewell before; and Chatter, who alone could give her any satisfaction on that head, was engaged in conversation at the other end of the room. I observed her impatience, and exulted in her chagrin; and after my partner was set, took the opportunity of passing by her to make a slight bow without stopping; which completed my triumph and her indignation. She changed colour, bridled up, assumed an air of disdain, and flirted her fan with such a fury, that it went to pieces in a moment, to the no small entertainment of those who sat near and observed her.

At length the metamorphosed barber took her out, and acted his part with such ridiculous extravagance, that the mirth of the whole company was excited at his expense, and his partner so much ashamed, that, before the country-dances began, she retired in great confusion, under pretence of being taken suddenly ill, and was followed by her gallant, who, no doubt, imagined her indisposition was nothing but love; and laid hold of the occasion of conducting her home, to comfort her with an assurance of his entertaining a reciprocal passion. They were no sooner gone, than an inquisitive whisper of "Who is he?" ran round the room; and Chatter could give no other intelligence about him, than that he was a man of fortune just returned from his travels. I, who alone was acquainted with his real quality, affected ignorance, well knowing that female curiosity would not rest satisfied with such a general account, and that the discovery would proceed with a better grace from anybody than me.

Meanwhile, I was tempted by the richness of the prize, to practise upon Miss Gripewell's heart, but soon found it too well fortified with pride and indifference to yield to any efforts in my own character, and I neither would nor could preserve the title I had borrowed longer than that night.

As I expected, everything came to light next day. The barber, in pure simplicity of heart, detected himself to Melinda, and discovered the foundation of his hopes. She sickened at the affront, and was ashamed to show her face in public for many weeks after this accident. Poor Chatter found it impossible to justify himself to her satisfaction; was in utter disgrace with Miss Gripewell, for having imposed me upon her as a nobleman; and suffered very much in his character and influence among the ladies in general.

Finding my finances diminished more than one half, and my project as little advanced as on the first day of my arrival in town, I began to despair of my success, and grew melancholy at the prospect of approaching want. To dispel the horrors of this fiend, I had recourse to the bottle and kept more company than ever. I became particularly attached to the playhouse, conversed with the actors behind the scenes, grew acquainted with a body of Templars, and in a short time commenced a professed wit and critic. Indeed I may say, without vanity, that I was much better qualified than any one of my companions, who were, generally speaking, of all the creatures I ever conversed with, the most ignorant and assuming. By means of these avocations, I got the better of care, and learned to separate my ideas in such a manner, that whenever I was attacked by a gloomy reflection, I could shove it aside, and call in some agreeable reverie to my assistance. This was not the case with Strap, who practised a thousand shifts to conceal the sorrow that preyed upon his carcass, and reduced him to the resemblance of a mere skeleton.

While I thus posted, in a thoughtless manner, towards poverty,

I one day received, by the penny-post, a letter written in a
woman's hand, containing a great many high-flown compliments,
warm protestations of love, couched in a very poetical style,
an earnest desire of knowing whether or not my heart was
engaged, by leaving an answer at a certain place, directed to
R.B. and the whole subscribed, "Your incognita." I was transported with joy on reading the contents of this billet-doux,
which I admired as a masterpiece of tenderness and elegance,
and was already up to the ears in love with the author, whom
my imagination represented as a lady of fortune, in the bloom
of youth and beauty. Elevated with this conjecture, I went to
work, and exhausted my invention in composing an answer
suitable to the sublimity of her style, and the ardour of her
sentiments. I expressed my admiration of her wit in terms the
most hyperbolical; and while I acknowledged myself unworthy
of her regard, declared myself enamoured of her understanding;
and, in the most pathetic manner, implored the honour of an
interview. Having finished this performance, and communicated
it to Strap, who skipped about for joy, I despatched him with
it to the place appointed, which was the house of a milliner not
far from Bond Street, and desired him to keep watch near the
door for some time, that he might discover the person who
should call for it. In less than an hour he returned with a joyful.
countenance, and told me that soon after he had delivered
the letter, a chairman was called, to whom it was given, with
directions to carry it to the house of a rich gentleman in the
neighbourhood, whither he (Strap) followed him, and saw it
put into the hands of a waiting-woman, who paid the messenger,
and shut the door. That, upon inquiry at an alehouse hard by,
where he called for a pint of beer, he understood the gentleman
to whom the house belonged had an only daughter, very handsome, who would inherit his whole estate, and who certainly
was the author of the billet I had received. I was of the same
opinion, and hugging myself in the happy prospect, dressed
immediately, and passed in great state by the house that contained my unknown admirer. Nor was my vanity disappointed;
for I perceived a beautiful young creature standing at one of
the windows of the dining-room, who, I imagined, observed me
with more than common curiosity. That I might indulge her
view, and at the same time feast my own, I affected to stop,
and gave orders to Strap, in the street, just opposite to her
station, by which means I had an opportunity of seeing her
more distinctly, and of congratulating myself on having made a

conquest of so much perfection. In a few minutes she retired, and I betook myself to the ordinary, in a rapture of hope, which deprived me of appetite for that meal, and sent me home in the evening to indulge my contemplation.

Early next day, I was favoured with another epistle from my unknown charmer, signifying her unutterable joy at the receipt of mine, which, while it made a tender of my heart, convinced her of the value of it. Above all things, she professed extreme pleasure in finding me so much attached to her understanding, a circumstance that not only flattered her in the most sensible part, but at the same time argued my own sagacity. As for the interview I desired, she assured me that I could not be more eager for such an occasion than she; but she must not only sacrifice a little more to decorum, but be satisfied of my honourable intentions, before she would grant that request: meanwhile, she gave me to understand, that although she might owe some deference to the opinion of certain persons, she was resolved, in an affair that so nearly concerned her happiness, to consult her own inclination, preferable to the advice of the whole world; especially as she was urged to such condescension by no consideration of fortune, what she depended upon being her own without restriction or control. Struck with admiration at the philosophy and self-denial of my mistress, who seemed insensible of the beauty she possessed, and, in particular, ravished with that piece of intelligence by which I learned her fortune was independent, I resumed the pen, launched out into encomiums on the dignity of her sentiments, affected to undervalue the charms of external beauty, pretended to ground my passion on the qualities of her mind, complained of her rigour in sacrificing my repose to an over-scrupulous regard to decorum, and declared the purity of my designs in the most solemn and pathetic vows. This performance being sealed and directed, was sent to the place appointed by Strap, who, that we might be still the more confirmed in our belief, renewed his watch, and in a little time brought back the same information as before, with this addition, that Miss Sparkle (the name of my correspondent), looking out at the window, no sooner saw the messenger arrive, than she shut the casement in a sort of beautiful confusion, and disappeared; eager, no doubt, to hear from the dear object of her love.

My doubts now vanished, the long-expected port appeared, and I looked upon myself as perfectly secure of that happiness I had been in quest of so long. After dinner, I sauntered, in company with Doctor Wagtail, to that part of the town in which my inamorata lived; and as he was a mere register, inquired of him into the name, character, and fortune of everybody who possessed a good house in the streets through which we passed; when it came to his turn to mention Sir John Sparkle, he represented him as a man of an immense estate and narrow disposition, who mewed up his only child, a fine young lady, from the conversation of mankind, under the strict watch and inspection of an old governante, who was either so honest, envious, or insatiable, that nobody had been, as yet, able to make her a friend, or get access to her charge, though numbers attempted it every day; not so much on account of her expectations from her father, who, being a widower, might marry again and have sons, as for a fortune of twelve thousand pounds left her by an uncle of which she could not be deprived. This piece of news exactly tallying with the last part of the letter I had been honoured with in the morning, had such an effect on me, that any man, except Wagtail, might have observed my emotion; but his attention was too much engrossed by the contemplation of his own importance, to suffer him to be affected with the deportment of any other body, unless it happened to be so particular that he could not help taking notice of it.

When I had disengaged myself from him, whose conversation grew insipid to me, I went home and made Strap acquainted with the fruit of my researches. This faithful squire was almost choked with transports, and even wept with joy; but whether on account of himself or me, I shall not pretend to determine. Next day a third billet-doux was brought to me, containing many expressions of tenderness, mingled with some affecting doubts, about the artifice of man, the inconsistency of youth, and the jealousy often attending the most sincere passion; withal desiring I would excuse her, if she should try me a little longer, before she declared herself beyond the power of retracting. These interesting scruples added fuel to my flame, and impatience to my hope; I redoubled my complaints of her indifference, and pressed her to an assignation with such fervid entreaties that in a few days, she consented to meet me at the house of that milliner who had forwarded all my letters. During the interval between the date of her promise and the hour of appointment my pride soared beyond all reason and description; I lost all remembrance of the gentle Narcissa, and my thoughts were wholly employed in planning triumphs over the malice and contempt of the world.

At length the happy hour arrived, I flew to the place of rendezvous, and was conducted into an apartment, where I had not waited ten minutes, when I heard the rustling of silk, and the sound of feet ascending the stairs. My heart took the alarm and beat quick; my cheeks glowed, my nerves thrilled, and my knees shook with ecstasy! I perceived the door opening, saw a gold brocade petticoat advance, and sprung forward to embrace my charmer! Heaven and earth!—how shall I paint my situation, when I found Miss Sparkle converted into a wrinkled hag, turned of seventy! I was struck dumb with amazement, and petrified with horror! This ancient Urganda perceived my disorder, and approaching with a languishing air, seized my hand, asking, in a squeaking tone, if I was indisposed. Her monstrous affectation completed the disgust I had conceived for her at first appearance; and it was a long time before I could command myself so much as to behave with common civility. At length, however, I recollected myself, and pronounced an apology for my behaviour, which, I said, proceeded from a dizziness that seized me all of a sudden. My hoary dulcinea, who, no doubt, had been alarmed at my confusion, no sooner learned the cause to which I now ascribed it, than she discovered her joy in a thousand amorous coquetries, and assumed the sprightly airs of a girl of sixteen. One while, she ogled me with her dim eyes, quenched in rheum; then, as if she was ashamed of that freedom, she affected to look down, blush, and play with her fan; then toss her head, that I might not perceive a palsy that shook it, ask some childish questions with a lisping accent, giggle and grin with her mouth shut, to conceal the ravages of time upon her teeth; leer upon me again, sigh piteously, fling herself about in her chair to show her agility, and act a great many more absurdities that youth and beauty can alone excuse. Shocked as I was at my disappointment, my disposition was incapable of affronting any person who loved me; I therefore endeavoured to put a good face on the matter for the present, resolved to drop the whole affair as soon as I should get clear of her company. With this view, I uttered some civil things, and, in particular, desired to know the name and condition of the lady who had honoured me so much. She told me her name was Withers; that she lived with Sir John Sparkle in quality of governess to his only daughter, in which situation she had picked up a comfortable sufficiency to make her easy for life; that she had the pleasure of seeing me at church, where my appearance and deportment made such an impression upon her

L 79⁰

heart, that she could enjoy no ease until she had inquired into my character, which she found so amiable in all respects, that she yielded to the violence of her inclination, and ventured to declare her passion, with too little regard, perhaps, to the decorum of her sex; but she hoped I would forgive a trespass of which I myself was, in some measure, the cause, and impute her intrusion to the irresistible dictates of love. No decayed rake ever swallowed a bolus with more reluctance than I felt in making a reply suitable to this compliment, when, instead of the jewel, I found the crazy casket only in my power; and yet my hopes began to revive a little, when I considered that, by carrying on the appearance of an intrigue with the duenna, I might possibly obtain access to her charge. Encouraged by this suggestion, my temper grew more serene, my reserve wore off, I talked *en cavalier*, and even made love to this antiquated coquette, who seemed extremely happy in her adorer, and spread all her allurements to make her imagined conquest more secure. The good woman of the house treated us with tea and sweetmeats and afterwards withdrew, like a civil experienced matron as she was. Left to our mutual endearments, Miss Withers (for she was still a maiden) began to talk of matrimony, and expressed so much impatience in all her behaviour, that had she been fifty years younger, I might possibly have gratified her longing without having recourse to the church; but this step my virtue, as well as interest, forbade. When the inclinations of an old maid settle upon a young fellow, he is persecuted with her addresses; but should he once grant her the favour, he will never be able to disentangle himself from her importunities and reproaches. It was my business to defer the ceremony as long as possible, under the most specious pretences, with a view of becoming acquainted with Miss Sparkle in the meantime; and I did not despair of success, when I considered that, in the course of our correspondence, I should, in all probability, be invited to visit my mistress in her own apartment, and by these means have an opportunity of conversing with her charming ward. Pleased with this prospect, my heart dilated with joy, I talked in raptures to the stale governante, and kissed her shrivelled hand with great devotion. She was so much transported with her good fortune, that she could not contain her ecstasy, but flew upon me like a tigress, and pressed her skinny lips to mine; when (as it was no doubt concerted by her evil genius) a dose of garlic she had swallowed that morning, to dispel wind I suppose, began to operate with such a sudden explosion, that human nature, circumstanced as I was, could not endure the shock with any degree of temper. I lost all patience and reflection, flung away from her in an instant, snatched my hat and cane, and ran downstairs as if the devil had me in pursuit, and could scarce refrain the convulsion of my bowels, which were grievously offended by the perfume that assaulted me. Strap, who waited my return with impatience, seeing me arrive in the utmost disorder, stood motionless with apprehension, and durst not inquire into the cause.

After I had washed my mouth more than once, and recruited my spirits with a glass of wine, I recounted to him every particular of what had happened; to which he made no other reply for some time, than lifting up his eyes, clasping his hands, and uttering a hollow groan. At length he observed, in a melancholy tone, that it was a thousand pities my organs were so delicate as to be offended with the smell of garlic. "Ah! God help us," said he, "'tis not the steams of garlic—no, nor of something else, that would give me the least uneasiness; see what it is to be a cobbler's son." I replied hastily, "I wish, then, you would go and retrieve my miscarriage." At this suggestion he started, forced a smile, and left the room, shaking his head. Whether the old gentlewoman resented my abrupt departure so much that her love changed into disdain, or was ashamed to see me on account of her infirmity, I know not; but I was never troubled again with her passion.

CHAPTER LI

I cultivate an Acquaintance with two Noblemen—Am introduced to Earl Strutwell—His kind Promises and Invitation—The Behaviour of his Porter and Lacquey—He receives me with an appearance of uncommon Affection—Undertakes to speak in my Behalf to the Minister—Informs me of his Success, and wishes me joy—Introduces a Conversation about Petronius Arbiter—Falls in love with my Watch, which I press upon him —I make a Present of a Diamond Ring to Lord Straddle—Impart my good Fortune to Strap and Banter, who disabuses me, to my utter Mortification.

BAFFLED hitherto in my matrimonial schemes, I began to question my talents for the science of fortune-hunting, and to bend my thoughts towards some employment under the government; with the view of procuring which, I cultivated the acquaintance of Lords Straddle and Swillpot, whose fathers were men of interest at court. I found these young noblemen as open to my advances as I could desire. I accompanied them in their midnight rambles, and often dined with them at taverns, where I had the honour of paying the reckoning.

I one day took the opportunity, while I was loaded with protestations of friendship, to disclose my desire of being settled in some sinecure, and to solicit their influence in my behalf. Swillpot, squeezing my hand, said I might depend upon his service, by God. The other swore that no man would be more proud than he to run my errands. Encouraged by these declarations, I ventured to express an inclination to be introduced to their fathers, who were able to do my business at once. Swillpot frankly owned he had not spoke to his father these three years; and Straddle assured me his father having lately disobliged the minister, by subscribing his name to a protest in the House of Peers, was thereby rendered incapable of serving his friends at present; but he undertook to make me acquainted with Earl Strutwell, who was hand and glove with a certain person who ruled the roast. This offer I embraced with many acknowledgments, and plied him so closely, in spite of a thousand evasions, that he found himself under a necessity of keeping his word, and actually carried me to the levee of this great man, where he left me in a crowd of fellow-dependants, and was ushered to a particular closet audience; from whence in a few minutes he returned with his lordship, who took me by the hand, assured me he would do me all the service he could, and desired to see me often. I was charmed with my reception, and although I had heard that a courtier's promise is not to be depended upon, I thought I discovered so much sweetness of temper and candour in this earl's countenance, that I did not doubt of finding my account in his protection. I resolved, therefore, to profit by this permission, and waited on him next audience day, when I was favoured with a particular smile, squeeze of the hand, and a whisper, signifying that he wanted half an hour's conversation with me in private, when he should be disengaged, and for that purpose desired me to come and drink a dish of chocolate with him to-morrow morning. This invitation, which did not a little flatter my vanity and expectation, I took care to observe, and went to his lordship's house at the time appointed. Having rapped at the gate, the porter unbolted and kept it half open, placing himself in the gap, like soldiers in a breach, to dispute my passage. I asked if his lord was stirring? He answered with a surly aspect, "No." "At what hour does he commonly rise?"

said I. "Sometimes sooner, sometimes later," said he, closing the door upon me by degrees. I then told him, I was come by his lordship's own appointment; to which intimation this Cerberus replied, "I have received no orders about the matter"; and was upon the point of shutting me out, when I recollected myself all of a sudden, and, slipping a crown into his hand, begged as a favour that he would inquire, and let me know whether or not the earl was up. The grim janitor relented at the touch of my money, which he took with all the indifference of a tax-gatherer, and showed me into a parlour, where, he said, I might amuse myself till such time as his lord should be awake. I had not sat ten minutes in this place, when a footman entered, and, without speaking, stared at me; I interpreted this piece of his behaviour into, "Pray, sir, what is your business?" and asked the same question I had put to the porter, when I accosted him first. The lacquey made the same reply and disappeared before I could get any further intelligence. In a little time he returned, on pretence of poking the fire, and looked at me again with great earnestness; upon which I began to perceive his meaning, and tipped him with half a crown, desired he would be so good as to fall upon some method of letting the earl know that I was in the house. He made a low bow, said "Yes, sir," and vanished. This bounty was not thrown away, for in an instant he came back, and conducted me to a chamber, where I was received with great kindness and familiarity by his lordship, whom I found just risen, in his morning gown and slippers. After breakfast, he entered into a particular conversation with me about my travels, the remarks I had made abroad, and examined me to the full extent of my understanding. My answers seemed to please him very much; he frequently squeezed my hand, and looking at me with a singular complacency in his countenance, bade me depend upon his good offices with the ministry in my behalf. "Young men of your qualifications," said he, "ought to be cherished by every administration. For my own part, I see so little merit in the world, that I have laid it down as a maxim, to encourage the least appearance of genius and virtue to the utmost of my power—you have a great deal of both; and will not fail of making a figure one day, if I am not mistaken, but you must lay your account with mounting by gradual steps to the summit of your fortune. Rome was not built in a day. As you understand the languages perfectly well, how would you like to cross the sea as secretary to an embassy?" I assured his lordship, with great eagerness, that nothing could be more agreeable to my inclination. Upon which he bade me make myself easy, my business was done, for he had a place of that kind in his view. This piece of generosity affected me so much, that I was unable for some time to express my gratitude, which at length broke out in acknowledgments of my own unworthiness, and encomiums on his benevolence. I could not even help shedding tears at the goodness of this noble lord, who no sooner perceived them, than he caught me in his arms, and hugged and kissed me with a seemingly paternal affection. Confounded at this uncommon instance of fondness for a stranger, I remained a few moments silent and ashamed, then rose and took my leave, after he had assured me that he would speak to the minister in my favour that very day; and desired that I would not for the future give myself the trouble of attending at his levee, but come at the same hour every day when he should be at leisure, that is, three times a week.

Though my hopes were now very sanguine, I determined to conceal my prospect from everybody, even from Strap, until I should be more certain of success; and, in the meantime, give my patron no respite from my solicitations. When I renewed my visit, I found the street door open to me, as if by enchantment; but, in my passage towards the presence room, I was met by the valet de chambre, who cast some furious looks at me, the meaning of which I could not comprehend. The earl saluted me at entrance with a tender embrace, and wished me joy of his success with the premier, who, he said, had preferred his recommendation to that of two other noblemen very urgent in behalf of their respective friends, and absolutely promised that I should go to a certain foreign court, in quality of secretary to an ambassador and plenipotentiary, who was to set out in a few weeks, on an affair of vast importance to the nation. I was thunderstruck with my good fortune, and could make no other reply than kneel, and attempt to kiss my benefactor's hand; which submission he would not permit, but, raising me up, pressed me to his breast with surprising emotion, and told me he had now taken upon himself the care of making my fortune. What enhanced the value of the benefit still more, was his making light of the favour, and shifting the conversation to another subject. Among other topics of discourse, that of the *Belles Lettres* was introduced, upon which his lordship held forth with great taste and erudition, and discovered an intimate knowledge of the authors of antiquity. "Here's a book," said he, taking one from his bosom, "written with great elegance and spirit, and though the subject may give offence to some narrow-minded people, the author will always be held in esteem by every person of wit and learning." So saying, he put into my hand Petronius Arbiter, and asked my opinion of his wit and manner. I told him that, in my opinion, he wrote with great ease and vivacity, but was withal so lewd and indecent, that he ought to find no quarter or protection among people of morals and taste. "I own," replied the earl, "that his taste in love is generally decried, and indeed condemned by our laws; but perhaps that may be more owing to prejudice and misapprehension, than to true reason and deliberation. The best man among the ancients is said to have entertained that passion; one of the wisest of their legislators has permitted the indulgence of it in his commonwealth; the most celebrated poets have not scrupled to avow it. At this day it prevails not only over all the East, but in most parts of Europe; in our own country it gains ground apace, and in all probability will become in a short time a more fashionable vice than simple fornication. Indeed, there is something to be said in vindication of it; for, notwithstanding the severity of the law against offenders in this way, it must be confessed that the practice of this passion is unattended with that curse and burden upon society, which proceeds from a race of miserable and deserted bastards, who are either murdered by their parents, deserted to the utmost want and wretchedness, or bred up to prey upon the commonwealth. And it likewise prevents the debauchery of many a young maiden, and the prostitution of honest men's wives; not to mention the consideration of health, which is much less liable to be impaired in the gratification of this appetite, than in the exercise of common venery, which, by ruining the constitutions of our young men, has produced a puny progeny, that degenerates from generation to generation. Nay, I have been told, that there is another motive, perhaps more powerful than all these, that induces people to cultivate this inclination, namely, the exquisite pleasure attending its success."

From this discourse, I began to be apprehensive that his lordship, finding I had travelled, was afraid I might have been infected with this spurious and sordid desire abroad, and took this method of sounding my sentiments on the subject. Fired at this supposed suspicion, I argued against it with great warmth, as an appetite unnatural, absurd, and of pernicious consequence;

and declared my utter detestation and abhorrence of it in these
lines of the satirist:

> Eternal infamy the wretch confound
> Who planted first that vice on British ground!
> A vice! that, 'spite of sense and nature, reigns
> And poisons genial love, and manhood stains.

The earl smiled at my indignation, told me he was glad to
find my opinion of the matter so conformable to his own, and
that what he had advanced was only to provoke me to an
answer, with which he professed himself perfectly well pleased.
After I had enjoyed a long audience, I happened to look at
my watch, in order to regulate my motions by it; and his lordship
observing the chased case, desired to see the device and examine
the execution, which he approved, with some expressions of
admiration. Considering the obligations I lay under to his lordship, I thought there could not be a fitter opportunity than the
present to manifest in some shape my gratitude; I therefore
begged he would do me the honour to accept of the watch as a
small testimony of the sense I had of his lordship's generosity;
but he refused it in a peremptory manner, and said he was sorry
I should entertain such a mercenary opinion of him, observing
at the same time, that it was the most beautiful piece of work-
manship he had ever seen, and desiring to know where he could
have such another. I begged a thousand pardons for the freedom
I had taken, which I hoped he would impute to nothing else but
the highest veneration for his person; told him that, as it came
to my hand by accident in France, I could give him no information about the maker, for there was no name on the inside; and
once more humbly entreated that he would indulge me so far as
to use it for my sake. He was still positive in refusing it, but was
pleased to thank me for my generous offer, saying it was a
present that no nobleman need be ashamed receiving; though
he was resolved to show his disinterestedness with regard to me,
for whom he had conceived a particular friendship; and insisted,
if I was willing to part with the watch, upon knowing what it
had cost, that he might at least indemnify me by refunding
the money. On the other hand, I assured his lordship that I
should look upon it as an uncommon mark of distinction, if
he would take it without further question; and, rather than disoblige me, he was at last persuaded to put it in his pocket, to
my no small satisfaction, who took my leave immediately,
after having received a kind squeeze, and an injunction
to depend upon his promise.

Buoyed up with this reception, my heart opened; I gave away a guinea among the lacqueys who escorted me to the door, flew to the lodgings of Lord Straddle, upon whom I forced my diamond ring as an acknowledgment for the great service he had done me, and from thence hied me home, with an intent of sharing my happiness with honest Strap. I determined, however, to heighten his pleasure by depressing his spirits at first, and then bringing in the good news with double relish. For this purpose, I affected the appearance of disappointment and chagrin, and told him in an abrupt manner that I had lost the watch and diamond. Poor Hugh, who had been already harassed into a consumption by intelligence of this sort, no sooner heard these words, than, unable to contain himself, he cried, with distraction in his looks, "God in heaven forbid!" I could carry on the farce no longer, but, laughing in his face, told him everything that had passed as above recited. His features were immediately unbended, and the transition was so affecting, that he wept with joy, called my Lord Strutwell by the appellations of Jewel, Phœnix, *Rara avis*; and praising God that there was still some virtue left among our nobility. Our mutual congratulations being over, we gave way to our imaginations, and anticipated our happiness by prosecuting our success through the different steps of promotion, till I arrived at the rank of prime minister, and he to that of my first secretary.

Intoxicated with these ideas, I went to the ordinary, where, meeting with Banter, I communicated the whole affair in confidence to him, concluding with an assurance that I would do him all the service in my power. He heard me to an end with great patience, then regarding me a good while with a look of disdain, pronounced, "So your business is done, you think?" "As good as done, I believe," said I. "I'll tell you," replied he, "what will do it still more effectually, a halter!—'Sdeath! if I had been such a gull to two such scoundrels as Strutwell and Straddle, I would, without any more ado, tuck myself up." Shocked at this exclamation, I desired him, with some confusion, to explain himself; upon which he gave me to understand, that Straddle was a poor contemptible wretch, who lived by borrowing and pimping for his fellow-peers; that, in consequence of this last capacity, he had doubtless introduced me to Strutwell, who was so notorious for a passion for his own sex, that he was amazed his character had never reached my ears; and that, far from being able to obtain for me the post he had promised, his interest at court was so low, that he could scarce provide for

a superannuated footman once a year, in the customs or excise
That it was a common thing for him to amuse strangers whom
his jackals ran down, with such assurances and caresses as he had
bestowed on me, until he had stripped them of their cash, and
everything valuable about them—very often of their chastity,
and then leave them a prey to want and infamy. That he allowed
his servants no other wages than that part of the spoil which
they could glean by their industry; and the whole of his conduct
towards me was so glaring, that nobody who knew anything of
mankind could have been imposed upon by his insinuations.

I leave the reader to judge how I relished this piece of information, which precipitated me from the most exalted pinnacle of
hope, to the lowest abyss of despondence; and well-nigh determined me to take Banter's advice, and finish my chagrin with
a halter. I had no room to suspect the veracity of my friend,
because, upon recollection, I found every circumstance of
Strutwell's behaviour exactly tallying with the character he
had described. His hugs, embraces, squeezes, and eager looks,
were now no longer a mystery, no more than his defence of
Petronius, and the jealous frown of his valet de chambre, who,
it seems, had been the favourite pathic of his lord.

CHAPTER LII

I attempt to recover my Watch and Jewel, but to no purpose—Resolve
to revenge myself on Strutwell by my Importunity—Am reduced to my
last Guinea—Obliged to inform Strap of my Necessity, who is almost
distracted with the News—But, nevertheless, obliged to pawn my best
Sword for present Subsistence—That small Supply being exhausted, I am
almost stupefied with my Misfortunes—Go to the Gaming-table, by the
Advice of Banter, and come off with unexpected Success—Strap's Ecstasy
—Mrs. Gawky waits upon me, professes Remorse for her Perfidy, and
implores my Assistance—I do myself a piece of Justice by her Means, and
afterwards reconcile her to her Father.

I WAS so confounded, that I could make no reply to Banter,
who reproached me with great indignation for having thrown
away upon rascals that which, had it been converted into ready
money, would have supported the rank of a gentleman for some
months, and enable me, at the same time, to oblige my friends.
Stupefied as I was, I could easily divine the source of his concern,
but sneaked away in a solitary manner, without yielding the
least answer to his expostulations, and began to deliberate with
myself in what manner I should attempt to retrieve the movables

I had so foolishly lost. I should have thought it no robbery to take them again by force, could I have done it without any danger of being detected; but as I could have no such opportunity, I resolved to work by finesse, and go immediately to the lodgings of Straddle, where I was so fortunate as to find him. "My lord," said I, "have just now recollected that the diamond I had the honour of presenting to you is loosened a little in the socket, and there is a young fellow just arrived from Paris who is reckoned the best jeweller in Europe; I knew him in France, and if your lordship will give me leave, will carry the ring to him to be set to rights." His lordship was not to be caught in this snare; he thanked me for my offer, and told me, that having himself observed the defect, he had already sent it to his own jeweller to be mended. And, indeed, by this time, I believe it was in the jeweller's hands, though not in order to be mended, for it stood in need of no alteration.

Balked in this piece of politics, I cursed my simplicity, but resolved to play a surer game with the earl, which I thus devised. I did not doubt of being admitted into familiar conversation with him as before, and hoped by some means to get the watch into my hand; then, on pretence of winding or playing with it, drop it on the floor, when in all probability the fall would disorder the work so as to stop its motion. This event would furnish me with an opportunity of insisting upon carrying it away, in order to be repaired; and then I should have been in no hurry to bring it back. What pity it was I could not find an occasion of putting this fine scheme in execution! When I went to renew my visit to his lordship, my access to the parlour was as free as ever; but after I had waited some time, the valet de chambre came in with his lordship's compliments, and a desire to see me to-morrow at his levee, he being at present so much indisposed that he could not see company. I interpreted this message into a bad omen, and came away muttering curses against his lordship's politeness, and ready to go to loggerheads with myself for being so egregiously duped. But that I might have some satisfaction for the loss I had sustained, I besieged him closely at his levee, and persecuted him with my solicitations; not without faint hopes, indeed, of reaping something more from my industry than the bare pleasure of making him uneasy; though I could never obtain another private hearing, during the whole course of my attendance; neither had I resolution enough to undeceive Strap, whose looks in a little time were so whetted with impatience, that, whenever I came home, his eyes devoured me, as it were, with eagerness of attention. At length, however finding myself reduced to my last guinea, I was compelled to disclose my necessity, though I endeavoured to sweeten the discovery by rehearsing to him the daily assurances I received from my patron. But these promises were not of efficacy sufficient to support the spirits of my friend, who no sooner understood the lowness of my finances, than, uttering a dreadful groan, he exclaimed, "In the name of God, what shall we do?" In order to comfort him, I said that many of my acquaintance, who were in a worse condition than we, supported, notwith-standing, the character of gentlemen; and, advising him to thank God that we had as yet incurred no debt, proposed he should pawn my sword of steel inlaid with gold, and trust to my discretion for the rest. This expedient was wormwood and gall to poor Strap, who, in spite of his invincible affection for me, still retained notions of economy and expense suitable to the narrowness of his education; nevertheless, he complied with my request, and raised seven pieces on the sword in a twinkling. This supply, inconsiderable as it was, made me as happy for the present as if I had kept five hundred pounds in bank; for by this time I was so well skilled in procrastinating every troublesome reflection, that the prospect of want seldom affected me very much, let it be ever so near. And now, indeed, it was nearer than I imagined; my landlord having occasion for money, put me in mind of my being indebted to him five guineas in lodging, and telling me he had a sum to make up, begged I would excuse his importunity, and discharge the debt. Though I could ill spare so much cash, my pride took the resolution of disbursing it. This I did in a cavalier manner, after he had written a discharge, telling him with an air of scorn and resentment, I saw he was resolved that I should not be long in his books; while Strap, who stood by, and knew my circum-stances, wrung his hands in secret, gnawed his nether lip, and turned yellow with despair. Whatever appearance of indifference my vanity enabled me to put on, I was thunderstruck with this demand, which I had no sooner satisfied, than I hastened into company, with a view of beguiling my cares with conversation, or of drowning them with wine.

After dinner, a party was accordingly made in the coffee-house, from whence we adjourned to the tavern, where, instead of sharing the mirth of the company, I was as much chagrined at their good humour as a damned soul in hell would be at a glimpse of heaven. In vain did I swallow bumper after bumper:

the wine had lost its effect upon me, and, far from raising my
dejected spirits, could not even lay me asleep. Banter, who was
the only intimate I had (Strap excepted), perceived my anxiety,
and, when we broke up, reproached me with pusillanimity, for
being cast down at any disappointment that such a rascal as
Strutwell could be the occasion of. I told him I did not at all
see how Strutwell's being a rascal alleviated my misfortune;
and gave him to understand, that my present grief did not so
much proceed from that disappointment, as from the low ebb
of my fortune, which was sunk to something less than two
guineas. At this declaration, he cried, "Psha! is that all?"
and assured me there was a thousand ways of living in town
without a fortune, he himself having subsisted many years
entirely by his wit. I expressed an eager desire of being acquainted with some of these methods; and he, without further
expostulation, bade me follow him. He conducted me to a house
under the piazzas in Covent Garden, which we entered, and
having delivered our swords to a grim fellow, who demanded
them at the foot of the staircase, ascended to the second story,
where I saw multitudes of people standing round two gaming-
tables, loaded in a manner with gold and silver. My conductor
told me this was the house of a worthy Scotch lord, who using
the privilege of his peerage, had set up public gaming-tables,
from the profits of which he drew a comfortable livelihood. He
then explained the difference between the *sitters* and the *betters*;
characterised the first as old rooks, and the last as bubbles; and
advised me to try my fortune at the silver table, by betting a
crown at a time. Before I would venture anything, I considered
the company more particularly; and there appeared such a
group of villainous faces, that I was struck with horror and
astonishment at the sight! I signified my surprise to Banter,
who whispered in my ear that the bulk of those present were
sharpers, highwaymen, and apprentices, who, having embezzled
their masters' cash, made a desperate push in this place to make
up their deficiencies. This account did not encourage me to
hazard any part of my small pittance; but at length, being
teased by the importunities of my friend, who assured me there
was no danger of being ill-used, because people were hired by
the owner to see justice done to everybody, I began by risking
one shilling, and in less than an hour my winning amounted
to thirty. Convinced by this time of the fairness of the game,
and animated with success, there was no need of further per-
suasion to continue the play. I lent Banter (who seldom had

any money in his pocket) a guinea, which he carried to the gold table, and lost in a moment. He would have borrowed another, but finding me deaf to his arguments, went away in a pet. Meanwhile, my gain advanced to six pieces, and my desire for more increased in proportion; so that I moved to the higher table, where I laid half-a-guinea on every throw; and fortune still favouring me, I became a sitter, in which capacity I remained until it was broad day; when I found myself, after many vicissitudes, one hundred and fifty guineas in pocket.

Thinking it now high time to retire with my booty, I asked if anybody would take my place, and made a motion to rise; upon which an old Gascon, who sat opposite to me, and of whom I had won a little money, started up with fury in his looks, crying, *"Restez, foutre, restez, il faut donner moi mon ravanchio!"* At the same time, a Jew who sat near the other, insinuated that I was more beholden to art than fortune for what I had got; that he had observed me wipe the table very often, and that some of the divisions seemed to be greasy. This intimation produced a great deal of clamour against me, especially among the losers, who threatened with many oaths and imprecations to take me up by a warrant as a sharper, unless I would compromise the affair by refunding the greatest part of my winning. Though I was far from being easy under this accusation, I relied upon my innocence, threatened in my turn to prosecute the Jew for defamation, and boldly offered to submit my cause to the examination of any justice in Westminster; but they knew themselves too well to put their characters on that issue, and finding I was not to be intimidated into any concession, dropped their plea, and made way for me to withdraw. I would not, however, stir from the table until the Israelite had retracted what he had said to my disadvantage, and asked pardon before the whole assembly.

As I marched out with my prize, I happened to tread upon the toes of a tall, rawboned fellow, with a hooked nose, fierce eyes, black, thick eyebrows, a pigtail wig of the same colour, and a formidable hat pulled over his forehead, who stood gnawing his fingers in the crowd, and no sooner felt the application of my shoe-heel, than he roared out in a tremendous voice, "Blood and wounds! you son of a whore, what's that for?" I asked pardon with a great deal of submission, and protested I had no intention of hurting him. But the more I humbled myself, the more he stormed, and insisted upon gentlemanly satisfaction, at the same time provoking me with scandalous names that I could not put up with; so that I gave a loose to my passion, returned his Billingsgate, and challenged him to follow me down to the piazzas. His indignation cooling as mine warmed, he refused my invitation, saying he would choose his own time, and returned towards the table, muttering threats, which I neither dreaded, nor distinctly heard; but descending with great deliberation, received my sword from the doorkeeper, whom I gratified with a guinea, according to the custom of that place, and went home in a rapture of joy.

My faithful valet, who had sat up all night in the utmost uneasiness on my account, let me in with his face beslubbered with tears, and followed me to my chamber, where he stood silent like a condemned criminal, in expectation of hearing that every shilling was spent. I guessed the situation of his thoughts, and, assuming a sullen look, bade him fetch me some water to wash. He replied, without lifting his eyes from the ground, "In my simple conjecture you have more occasion for rest, not having, I suppose, slept these four-and-twenty hours." "Bring me some water," said I in a peremptory tone; upon which he sneaked away shrugging his shoulders. Before he returned, I had spread my whole stock on the table in the most ostentatious manner; so that, when it first saluted his view, he stood like one entranced, and having rubbed his eyes more than once, to assure himself of his being awake, broke out into, "Lord have mercy upon us! what a vast treasure is here!" "'Tis all our own, Strap," said I; "take what is necessary, and redeem the sword immediately." He advanced towards the table, stopped short by the way, looked at the money and me by turns, and, with a wildness in his countenance, produced from joy checked by distrust, cried, "I dare say it is honestly come by." To remove his scruples, I made him acquainted with the whole story of my success, which when he heard, he danced about the room in an ecstasy, crying, "God be praised! a white stone! —God be praised! a white stone!" so that I was afraid the sudden change of fortune had disordered his intellects, and that he was run mad with joy. Extremely concerned at this event, I attempted to reason him out of his frenzy, but to no purpose; for, without regarding what I said, he continued to frisk up and down, and repeat his rhapsody of "God be praised! a white stone!" At last I rose in the utmost consternation, and, laying violent hands upon him, put a stop to his extravagance by fixing him down to a settee that was in the room. This constraint banished his delirium; he started as if just awoke, and, terrified at my behaviour, cried, "What is the matter?" When he learned the cause of my apprehension, he was ashamed of his transports, and told me that in mentioning the white stone, he alluded to the *dies fasti* of the Romans, *albo lapide notati*.

Having no inclination to sleep, I secured my cash, dressed, and was just going abroad, when the servant of the house told me there was a gentlewoman at the door, who wanted to speak with me. Surprised at this information, I bade Strap show her up, and in less than a minute saw a young woman of a shabby, decayed appearance, enter my room. After half-a-dozen curtseys, she began to sob, and told me her name was Gawky; upon which information I immediately recollected the features of Miss Lavement, who had been the first occasion of my misfortunes. Though I had all the reason in the world to resent her treacherous behaviour to me, I was moved at her distress, and professing my sorrow at seeing her so reduced, desired her to sit, and inquired into the particulars of her situation. She fell upon her knees, and implored my forgiveness for the injuries she had done me, protesting before God that she was forced, against her inclination, into that hellish conspiracy which had almost deprived me of my life, by the entreaties of her husband, who having been afterwards renounced by his father, on account of his marriage with her, and unable to support a family on his pay, left his wife at her father's house, and went with the regiment to Germany, where he was broke for misbehaviour at the battle of Dettingen, since which time she had heard no tidings of him. She then gave me to understand, with many symptoms of penitence, that it was her misfortune to bear a child four months after marriage, by which event her parents were so incensed, that she was turned out of doors with the infant, that died soon after; and had hitherto subsisted in a miserable, indigent manner, on the extorted charity of a few friends, who were now quite tired of giving. That not knowing where or how to support herself one day longer, she had fled for succour even to me, who, of all mankind, had the least cause to assist her, relying upon the generosity of my disposition, which, she hoped, would be pleased with this opportunity of avenging itself in the noblest manner on the wretch who had wronged me. I was very much affected with her discourse, and having no cause to suspect the sincerity of her repentance, raised her up, freely pardoned all she had done against me, and promised to befriend her as much as lay in my power.

Since my last arrival in London, I had made no advances

to the apothecary, imagining it would be impossible for me to
make my innocence appear, so unhappily was my accusation
circumstanced. Strap indeed had laboured to justify me to the
schoolmaster; but, far from succeeding in his attempt, Mr.
Concordance dropped all correspondence with him, because
he refused to quit his connection with me. Things being in this
situation, I thought a fairer opportunity of vindicating my
character could not offer than that which now presented itself.
I therefore stipulated with Mrs. Gawky, that, before I would
yield her the least assistance, she should do me the justice to
clear my reputation, by explaining upon oath, before a magistrate, the whole of the conspiracy, as it had been executed
against me. When she had given me this satisfaction, I presented
her with five guineas, a sum so much above her expectation,
that she could scarce believe the evidence of her senses, and was
ready to worship me for my benevolence. The declaration, signed
with her own hand, I sent to her father, who, upon recollecting
and comparing the circumstances of my charge, was convinced
of my integrity, and waited on me next day, in company with
his friend the schoolmaster, to whom he had communicated my
vindication. After mutual salutation, Monsieur Lavement began
a long apology for the unjust treatment I had received; but I
saved him a good deal of breath, by interrupting his harangue,
and assuring him that, far from entertaining a resentment
against him, I thought myself obliged to his lenity, which allowed
me to escape, after such strong presumptions of guilt appeared
against me. Mr. Concordance, thinking it now his turn to speak,
observed that Mr. Random had too much candour and sagacity
to be disobliged at their conduct, which, all things considered,
could not have been otherwise, with any honesty of intention.
"Indeed," said he, "if the plot had been unravelled to us by any
supernatural intelligence, if it had been whispered by a genie,
communicated by a dream, or revealed by an angel from on high,
we should have been to blame in crediting ocular demonstration:
but as we are left in the midst of mortality, it cannot be expected
we should be incapable of imposition. I do assure you, Mr.
Random, no man on earth is more pleased than I am at this
triumph of your character; and as the news of your misfortune
panged me to the very entrails, this manifestation of your
innocence makes my midriff quiver with joy." I thanked him
for his concern, desired them to undeceive those of their
acquaintance who judged harshly of me, and, having treated
them with a glass of wine, represented to Lavement the

deplorable condition of his daughter, and pleaded her cause so effectually, that he consented to settle a small annuity on her for life; but could not be persuaded to take her home, because her mother was so much incensed that she would never see her.

CHAPTER LIII

I purchase new Clothes—Reprimand Strutwell and Straddle—Banter proposes another Matrimonial Scheme—I accept of his Terms—Set out for Bath in a Stage Coach, with the young Lady and her Mother—The Behaviour of an Officer and Lawyer—Our Fellow-travellers described—A smart Dialogue between my Mistress and the Captain.

HAVING finished this affair to my satisfaction, I found myself perfectly at ease, and looking upon the gaming-table as a certain resource for a gentleman in want, became more gay than ever. Although my clothes were almost as good as new, I grew ashamed of wearing them, because I thought everybody, by this time, had got an inventory of my wardrobe. For which reason I disposed of a good part of my apparel to a salesman in Monmouth Street for half the value, and bought two new suits with the money. I likewise purchased a plain gold watch, despairing of recovering that which I had so foolishly given to Strutwell, whom, notwithstanding, I still continued to visit at his levee, until the ambassador he had mentioned set out with a secretary of his own choosing. I thought myself then at liberty to expostulate with his lordship, whom I treated with great freedom in a letter, for amusing me with vain hopes, when he neither had the power nor inclination to provide for me. Nor was I less reserved with Straddle, whom I in person reproached for misrepresenting to me the character of Strutwell, which I did not scruple to aver was infamous in every respect. He seemed very much enraged at my freedom, talked a great deal about his quality and honour, and began to make some comparisons which I thought so injurious to mine, that I demanded an explanation with great warmth; and he was mean enough to equivocate, and condescend in such a manner, that I left him with a hearty contempt of his behaviour.

About this time, Banter, who had observed a surprising and sudden alteration in my appearance and disposition, began to inquire very minutely into the cause; and as I did not think fit to let him know the true state of the affair, lest he might make free with my purse, on the strength of having proposed the scheme that filled it, I told him that I had received a small supply from a relation in the country, who at the same time had promised to use all his interest, which was not small, in soliciting some post for me that should make me easy for life. "If that be the case," said Banter, "perhaps you won't care to mortify yourself a little, in making your fortune another way. I have a relation who is to set out for Bath next week, with an only daughter, who, being sickly and decrepit, intends to drink the waters for the recovery of her health. Her father, who was a rich Turkey merchant, died about a year ago, and left her with a fortune of twenty thousand pounds, under the sole management of her mother, who is my kinswoman. I would have put in for the plate myself, but there is a breach at present between the old woman and me. You must know, that some time ago I borrowed a small sum of her, and promised, it seems, to pay it before a certain time; but being disappointed in my expectation of money from the country, the day elapsed without my being able to take up my note; upon which she wrote a peremptory letter, threatening to arrest me, if I did not pay the debt immediately. Nettled at this precise behaviour, I sent a damned severe answer, which enraged her so much that she actually took out a writ against me. Whereupon, finding the thing grow serious, I got a friend to advance the money for me, discharged the debt, went to her house, and abused her for her unfriendly dealing. She was provoked by my reproaches, and scolded in her turn. The little deformed urchin joined her mother with such virulence and volubility of tongue, that I was fain to make my retreat, after having been honoured with a great many scandalous epithets, which gave me plainly to understand that I had nothing to hope from the esteem of the one, or the affection of the other. As they are both utter strangers to life, it is a thousand to one that the girl will be picked up by some scoundrel or other at Bath, if I don't provide for her otherwise. You are a well-looking fellow, Random, and can behave as demurely as a Quaker. Now, if you will give me an obligation for five hundred pounds, to be paid six months after your marriage, I will put you in a method of carrying her in spite of all opposition."

This proposal was too advantageous for me to be refused. The writing was immediately drawn up and executed; and Banter giving me notice of the time when, and the stage coach in which they were to set out, I bespoke a place in the same convenience, and having hired a horse for Strap, who was charmed with the prospect, set forward accordingly.

As we embarked before day, I had not the pleasure for some time of seeing Miss Snapper (that was the name of my mistress), nor even of perceiving the number and sex of my fellow-travellers, although I guessed that the coach was full, by the difficulty I found in seating myself. The first five minutes passed in a general silence, when, all of a sudden, the coach heeling to one side, a boisterous voice pronounced, "To the right and left, cover your flanks, damme! whiz!" I easily discovered by the tone and matter of this exclamation, that it was uttered by a son of Mars; neither was it hard to conceive the profession of another person who sat opposite to me, and observed that we ought to have been well satisfied of the security before we entered upon the premises. These two sallies had not the desired effect. We continued a good while as mute as before, till at length the gentleman of the sword, impatient of longer silence, made a second effort, by swearing he had got into a meeting of Quakers. "I believe so, too," said a shrill voice at my left hand, "for the spirit of folly begins to move." "Out with it, then, madam," replied the soldier. "You seem to have no occasion for a midwife," cried the lady. "Damn my blood!" exclaimed the other, "a man can't talk to a woman, but she immediately thinks of a midwife." "True, sir," said she, "I long to be delivered." "What! of a mouse, madam?" said he. "No, sir," said she, "of a fool." "Are you far gone with a fool?" said he. "Little more than two miles," said she. "By Gad, you are a wit, madam!" cried the officer. "I wish I could with any justice return the compliment," said the lady. "Zounds, I have done," said he. "Your bolt is soon shot, according to the old proverb," said she. The warrior's powder was quite spent; the lawyer advised him to drop the prosecution; and a grave matron, who sat on the left hand of the victorious wit, told her she must not let her tongue run so fast among strangers. This reprimand, softened with the appellation of *child*, convinced me that the satirical lady was no other than Miss Snapper, and I resolved to regulate my conduct accordingly. The champion finding himself so smartly handled, changed his battery, and began to expatiate on his own exploits. "You talk of shot, madam," said he, "damme! I have both given and received some shot in my time. I was wounded in the shoulder by a pistol-ball at Dettingen, where—I say nothing—but by Gad! if it had not been for me—all's one for that—I despise boasting, damme! whiz!" So saying, he whistled one part and hummed another of "Black Joke"; then addressing himself to the lawyer, went on thus: "Wouldn't you think it damned hard, after having, at the risk of your life, recovered the standard of a regiment, that had been lost, to receive no preferment for your pains! I don't choose to name no names, sink me! but howsomever, this I will refer, by Gad; and that is this, a musketeer of the French guards, having taken a standard from a certain cornet of a certain regiment, damme! was retreating with his prize as fast as his horse's heels could carry him, sink me! Upon which I snatched up a firelock that belonged to a dead man, damme! whiz! and shot his horse under him, damn my blood! The fellow got upon his feet, and began to repose me; upon which I charged my bayonet breast high, and ran him through the body, by Gad! One of his comrades coming to his assistance, shot me in the shoulder, as I told you before; another gave me a confusion on the head with the butt-end of his carbine; but, damme! that did not signify. I killed one, put the other to flight, and, taking up the standard, carried it off very deliberately. But the best joke of all was, the son of a bitch of a cornet who had surrendered it in a cowardly manner, seeing it in my possession, demanded it from me, in the front of the line. 'Damn my blood,' says he, 'where did you find my standard?' says he. 'Damn my blood,' said I, 'where,' said I, 'did you lose it?' said I. 'That's nothing to you,' says he—''tis my standard,' says he, 'and by Gad I'll have it,' says he. 'Damnation seize me,' says I, 'if you shall,' says I, 'till I have first delivered it to the general,' says I; and accordingly I went to the headquarters, after the battle, and delivered it to my Lord Stair, who promised to do for me, but I am no more than a poor lieutenant still, damn my blood."

Having vented this repetition of expletives, the lawyer owned he had not been requited according to his desert; observed, that the labourer is always worthy of his hire, and asked if the promise was made before witnesses, because in that case the law would compel the general to perform it;—but understanding that the promise was made over a bottle, without being restricted to time or terms, he pronounced it not valid in law, proceeded to inquire into the particulars of the battle, and affirmed, that although the English had drawn themselves into a premunire at first, the French managed their cause so lamely in the course of the dispute, that they would have been utterly nonsuited, had they not obtained a *noli prosequi*. In spite of these enlivening touches, the conversation was likely to suffer another long interruption; when the lieutenant, unwilling to conceal any of his accomplishments that could be displayed in his present situation, offered to regale the company with a song; and interpreting our silence into a desire of hearing, began to warble a fashionable air, the first stanza of which he pronounced thus:

> "Would you task the moon-ty'd hair,
> To yon flagrant beau repair;
> Where waving with the popling vow,
> The bantling fine will shelter you, etc."

The sense of the rest he perverted as he went on, with such surprising facility, that I could not help thinking he had been at some pains to burlesque the performance. Miss Snapper ascribed it to the true cause, namely ignorance; and when he asked her how she relished his music, answered, that, in her opinion, the music and the words were much of a piece. "O damn my blood!" said he, "I take that as a high compliment; for everybody allows the words are damnable fine." "They may be so," replied the lady, "for aught I know, but they are above my comprehension." "I ain't obliged to find you comprehension, madam, curse me!" cried he. "No, nor to speak sense neither," said she. "Damn my heart," said he, "I'll speak what I please." Here the lawyer interposed by telling him there were some things he must not speak. And upon being defied to give an instance, mentioned treason and defamation. "As for the king," cried the soldier, "God bless him—I eat his bread, and have lost blood in his cause, therefore I have nothing to say to him—but, by Gad, I dare say anything to any other man." "No," said the lawyer, "you dare not call me a rogue." "Damme, for what?" said the other. "Because," replied the counsellor, "I should have a good action against you, and recover." "Well, well," cried the officer, "if I dare not call you a rogue, I dare think you one, damme." This stroke of wit he accompanied with a loud laugh of self-approbation, which unluckily did not affect the audience, but effectually silenced his antagonist, who did not open his mouth for the space of an hour, except to clear his pipe with three *hems*, which, however, produced nothing.

CHAPTER LIV

Day breaking, I have the Pleasure of viewing the Person of Miss Snapper, whom I had not seen before—The Soldier is witty upon me—Is offended—Talks much of his Valour—Is reprimanded by a grave Gentlewoman—We are alarmed with the Cry of Highwaymen—I get out of the Coach and stand in my own Defence—They ride off without having attacked us—I pursue them—One of them is thrown from his Horse and taken—I return to the Coach—Am complimented by Miss Snapper—The Captain's Behaviour on this Occasion—The Prude reproaches me in a Soliloquy—I upbraid her in the same Manner—The Behaviour of Mrs. Snapper at Breakfast disobliges me—The Lawyer is witty upon the Officer, who threatens him.

IN the meantime, day breaking in upon us, discovered to one another the faces of their fellow-travellers, and I had the good fortune to find my mistress not quite so deformed nor disagreeable as she had been represented to me. Her head, indeed, bore some resemblance to a hatchet, the edge being represented by her face; but she had a certain delicacy in her complexion, and a great deal of vivacity in her eyes, which were very large and black; and though the protuberance of her breast, when considered alone, seemed to drag her forwards, it was easy to perceive an equivalent on her back which balanced the other, and kept her body in equilibrio. On the whole, I thought I should have great reason to congratulate myself, if it should be my fate to possess twenty thousand pounds encumbered with such a wife. I began therefore to deliberate about the most probable means of acquiring the conquest, and was so much engrossed by this idea, that I scarce took any notice of the rest of the people in the coach, but revolved my project in silence; while the conversation was maintained as before, by the object of my hopes, the son of Mars, and the barrister, who by this time had recollected himself, and talked in terms as much as ever. At length a dispute happened which ended in a wager, to be determined by me, who was so much absorbed in contemplation, that I neither heard the reference nor the question, which was put to me by each in his turn; affronted at my supposed contempt, the soldier, with great vociferation, swore I was either dumb or deaf, if not both, and that I looked as if I could not say Boh to a goose. Aroused at this observation, I fixed my eyes upon him, and pronounced with emphasis the interjection *Boh!* Upon which he cocked his hat in a fierce manner, and cried, "Damme, sir, what d'ye mean by that?" Had I intended to answer him, which by the bye was not my design, I should have been anticipated by Miss, who told him, my meaning was to show that I could cry Boh to a goose; and laughed very heartily at my laconic reproof. Her explanation and mirth did not help to appease his wrath, which broke out in several martial insinuations, such as—"I do not understand such freedoms, damme! Damn my blood! I'm a gentleman, and bear the king's commission. 'Sblood! some people deserve to have their noses pulled for their impertinence." I thought to have checked these ejaculations by a frown; because he had talked so much of his valour, that I had long ago rated him as an ass in a lion's skin; but this expedient did not answer my expectation; he took umbrage at the contraction of my brows, swore he did not value my sulky looks a fig's end, and protested he feared no man breathing. Miss Snapper said she was very glad to find herself in company with a man of so much courage, who, she did not doubt, would protect us from all attempts of highwaymen during our journey. "Make yourself perfectly easy on that head, madam," replied the officer; "I have got a pair of pistols (here they are) which I took from a horse officer at the battle of Dettingen—they are double loaded, and if any highwayman in England robs you of the value of a pin while I have the honour of being in your company, damn my heart." When he had expressed himself in this manner, a prim gentlewoman, who had sat silent hitherto, opened her mouth and said, she wondered how any man could be so rude as to pull out such weapons before ladies. "Damme, madam," cried the champion, "if you are so much afraid at sight of a pistol, how d'ye propose to stand fire if there should be occasion?" She then told him, that if she thought he could be so unmannerly as to use firearms in her presence, whatever might be the occasion, she would get out of the coach immediately, and walk to the next village, where she might procure a convenience to herself. Before he could make any answer, my dulcinea interposed, and observed, that, far from being offended at a gentleman's using his arms in his own defence, she thought herself very lucky in being along with one by whose valour she stood a good chance of saving herself from being rifled. The prude cast a disdainful look at Miss, and said that people who have but little to lose are sometimes the most solicitous about preserving it. The old lady was affronted at this innuendo, and took notice that people ought to be very well informed before they spoke slightingly of other people's fortunes, lest they discover their own envy, and make themselves ridiculous. The daughter declared that she did not pretend to vie with anybody in point of riches; and if the lady who insisted upon non-resistance would promise to indemnify us for all the loss we should sustain, she would be one of the first to persuade the captain to submission, in case we should be attacked. To this proposal, reasonable as it was, the reserved lady made no other reply than a scornful glance and a toss of her head. I was very well pleased with the spirit of my mistress; and even wished for an opportunity of distinguishing my courage under her eye, which I believed could not fail of prepossessing her in my favour; when, all of a sudden, Strap rode up to the coach door, and told us in a great fright that two men on horseback were crossing the heath (for by this time we had passed Hounslow), and made directly towards us. This piece of information was no sooner delivered than Mrs. Snapper began to scream, her daughter grew pale, the other lady pulled out her purse to be in readiness, the lawyer's teeth chattered, while he pronounced, "'Tis no matter—we'll sue the county, and recover." The captain gave evident signs of confusion; and I, after having commanded the coachman to stop, opened the door, jumped out, and invited the warrior to follow me; but finding him backward and astonished, took his pistols, and giving them to Strap, who had by this time alighted, and trembled very much, I mounted on horseback, and taking my own, which I could better depend upon, from the holsters, cocked them both, and faced the robbers, who were now very near us. Seeing me ready to oppose them on horseback, and another man armed afoot, they made a halt at some distance to reconnoitre us, and, after having rode round us twice, myself still facing about as they rode, went off the same way as they came, at a hand-gallop. A gentleman's servant coming up with a horse at the same time, I offered him a crown to assist me in pursuing them: which he no sooner accepted, then I armed him with the officer's pistols, and we galloped after the thieves, who, trusting to the swiftness of their horses, stopped till we came within shot of them, and then firing at us, put their nags to the full speed. We followed them as fast as our beasts could carry us; but not being so well mounted as they, our efforts would have been to little purpose, had not the horse of one of them stumbled, and thrown his rider with such violence over his head, that he lay senseless when we came up, and was taken without the least opposition; while his comrade consulted his own safety in flight, without regarding the distress of his friend. We scarce had time to make ourselves masters of his arms, and tie his hands together, before he recovered his senses, when learning his situation, he affected surprise, demanded to know by what authority we used a gentleman in that manner, and had the impudence to threaten us with a prosecution for robbery. In the meantime we perceived Strap coming up with a crowd of people, armed with different kinds of weapons; and among the rest a farmer, who no sooner perceived the thief, whom we had secured, than he cried with great emotion, "There's the fellow who robbed me an hour ago of twenty pounds in a canvas bag." He was immediately searched, and the money found exactly as it had been described. Upon which we committed him to the charge of the countryman, who carried him to the town of Hounslow, which it seems the farmer had alarmed; and I, having satisfied the footman for his trouble, according to promise, returned with Strap to the coach, where I found the captain and lawyer busy in administering smelling-bottles and cordials to the grave lady, who had gone into a fit at the noise of the firing.

When I had taken my seat, Miss Snapper, who from the coach had seen everything that happened, made me a compliment on my behaviour, and said she was glad to see me returned, without having received any injury: her mother, too, owned herself obliged to my resolution; and the lawyer told me that I was entitled by act of parliament to a reward of forty pounds, for having apprehended a highwayman. The soldier observed, with a countenance in which impudence and shame struggling produced some disorder, that if I had not been in such a damned hurry to get out of the coach, he would have secured the rogues effectually, without all this bustle and loss of time, by a scheme which my heat and precipitation ruined. "For my own part," continued he, "I am always extremely cool on these occasions." "So it appeared, by your trembling," said the young lady. "Death and damnation," cried he, "your sex protects you, madam; if any man on earth durst tell me so much, I'd send him to hell, damn my heart! in an instant." So saying, he fixed his eyes upon me, and asked if I had seen him tremble? I answered without hesitation, "Yes." "Damme, sir," said he, "d'ye doubt my courage?" I replied, "Very much." This declaration quite disconcerted him. He looked blank, and pronounced with a faltering voice, "O! 'tis very well—damn my blood! I shall find a time." I signified my contempt of him by thrusting my tongue in my cheek, which humbled him so much, that he scarce swore another oath aloud during the whole journey.

The precise lady having recruited her spirits by the help of some strong waters, began a soliloquy, in which she wondered that any man, who pretended to maintain the character of a gentleman, could, for the sake of a little paltry coin, throw persons of honour into such quandaries as might endanger their lives; and professed her surprise that women were not ashamed to commend such brutality; at the same time vowing, that for the future she would never set foot in a stage coach, if a private convenience could be had for love or money.

Nettled at her remarks, I took the same method of conveying my sentiments, and wondered in my turn that any woman of common sense should be so unreasonable as to expect that people who had neither acquaintance or connection with her, would tamely allow themselves to be robbed and maltreated, merely to indulge her capricious humour. I likewise confessed my astonishment at her insolence and ingratitude in taxing a person with brutality, who deserved her approbation and acknowledgment; and vowed that if ever she should be assaulted again, I would leave her to the mercy of the spoiler, that she might know the value of my protection.

This person of honour did not think fit to carry on the altercation any further, but seemed to chew the cud of her resentment with the crestfallen captain, while I entered into discourse with my charmer, who was the more pleased with my conversation, as she had conceived a very indifferent opinion of my intellects from my former silence. I should have had cause to be equally satisfied with the sprightliness of her genius, could she have curbed her imagination with judgment; but she laboured under such a profusion of talk, that I dreaded her unruly tongue, and felt by anticipation the horrors of an eternal clack! However, when I considered, on the other hand, the joys attending the possession of twenty thousand pounds, I forgot her imperfections, seized occasion by the forelock, and endeavoured to insinuate myself into her affection. The careful mother kept a strict watch over her, and though she could not help behaving civilly to me, took frequent opportunities of discouraging our communication, by reprimanding her for being so free with strangers, and telling her she must learn to speak less, and think more. Abridged of the use of speech, we conversed with our eyes, and I found the young lady very eloquent in this kind of discourse. In short, I had reason to believe that she was sick of the old gentlewoman's tuition, and that I should find it no difficult matter to supersede her authority.

When we arrived at the place where we were to breakfast, I alighted, and helped my mistress out of the coach, as well as her mother, who called for a private room to which they withdrew, in order to eat by themselves. As they retired together, I perceived that Miss had got more twists from nature, than I had before observed, for she was bent sideways in the figure like an S, so that her progression very much resembled that of a crab. The prude also chose the captain for her messmate, and ordered breakfast for two only to be brought into another separate room; while the lawyer and I, deserted by the rest of the company, were fain to put up with each other. I was a good deal chagrined at the stately reserve of Mrs. Snapper, who I thought did not use me with all the complaisance I deserved; and my companion declared that he had been a traveller for twenty years, and never knew the stage-coach rules so much infringed before. As for the honourable gentlewoman, I could not conceive the meaning of her attachment to the lieutenant; and asked the lawyer if he knew for which of the soldier's virtues she admired him? The counsellor facetiously replied, "I suppose the lady knows him to be an able conveyancer, and wants him to make a settlement in tail." I could not help laughing at the archness of the barrister, who entertained me during breakfast with a great deal of wit of the same kind, at the expense of our fellow-travellers; and among other things said, he was sorry to find the young lady saddled with such encumbrances.

When we had made an end of our repast, and paid our reckoning, we went into the coach, took our places, and bribed the driver with sixpence to revenge us on the rest of his fare, by hurrying them away in the midst of their meal. This task he performed to our satisfaction, after he had disturbed their enjoyment with his importunate clamour. The mother and daughter obeyed the summons first, and coming to the coach door, were obliged to desire the coachman's assistance to get in, because the lawyer and I had agreed to show our resentment by our neglect. They were no sooner seated, than the captain appeared as much heated as if he had been pursued a dozen miles by an enemy; and immediately after him came the lady, not without some marks of disorder. Having helped her up, he entered himself, growling a few oaths against the coachman for his impertinent interruption; and the lawyer comforted him by saying, that if he had suffered a *nisi prius* through the obstinacy of the defendant, he might have an opportunity to join issue at the next stage. This last expression gave offence to the grave gentlewoman, who told him, if she was a man, she would make him repent of such obscenity, and thanked God she had never been in such company before. At this insinuation, the captain thought himself under a necessity of espousing the lady's cause; and accordingly threatened to cut off the lawyer's ears, if he should give his tongue any such liberties for the future. The poor counsellor begged pardon, and universal silence ensued.

CHAPTER LV

I resolve to ingratiate myself with the Mother, and am favoured by Accident—The precise Lady finds her Husband, and quits the Coach—The Captain is disappointed of his Dinner—We arrive at Bath—I accompany Miss Snapper to the Long Room, where she is attacked by Beau Nash, and turns the laugh against him—I make Love to her, and receive a Check—Squire her to an Assembly, where I am blessed with a sight of my dear Narcissa, which discomposes me so much, that Miss Snapper, observing my Disorder, is at pains to discover the Cause—Is piqued at the Occasion, and, in our way Home, pays me a sarcastic Compliment—I am met by Miss Williams, who is Maid and Confidante of Narcissa—She acquaints me with her Lady's regard for me while under the disguise of a Servant, and describes the transports of Narcissa on seeing me at the Assembly in the character of a Gentleman—I am surprised with an account of her Aunt's Marriage, and make an Appointment to meet Miss Williams next day.

DURING this unsocial interval, my pride and interest maintained a severe conflict on the subject of Miss Snapper, whom the one represented as unworthy of notice, and the other proposed as the object of my whole attention: the advantages and disadvantages attending such a match were opposed to one another by my imagination; and at length my judgment gave it so much in favour of the first, that I resolved to prosecute my scheme with all the address in my power. I thought I perceived some concern in her countenance, occasioned by my silence, which she, no doubt, imputed to my disgust at her mother's behaviour; and as I believe the old woman could not fail of ascribing my muteness to the same motive, I determined to continue that sullen conduct towards her, and fall upon some other method of manifesting my esteem for the daughter: nor was it difficult for me to make her acquainted with my sentiments by the expression of my looks, which I modelled into the characters of humility and love; and which were answered by her with all the sympathy and approbation I could desire. But when I began to consider, that without further opportunities of improving my success, all the progress I had hitherto made would not much avail, and that such opportunities could not be enjoyed without the mother's permission, I concluded it would be requisite to vanquish her coldness and suspicion by my assiduities and respectful behaviour on the road; and she would in all likelihood invite me to visit her at Bath, where I did not fear of being able to cultivate her acquaintance as much as would be necessary to the accomplishment of my purpose. And indeed accident furnished me with an opportunity of obliging her so much, that she could not, with any appearance of good manners, forbear to gratify my inclination.

When we arrived at our dining-place, we found all the eatables in the inn bespoke by a certain nobleman, who had got the start of us; and in all likelihood my mistress and her mother must have dined with Duke Humphrey, had I not exerted myself in their behalf, and bribed the landlord with a glass of wine to curtail his lordship's entertainment of a couple of fowls and some bacon, which I sent with my compliments to the ladies. They accepted my treat with a great many thanks, and desired I would favour them with my company at dinner, where I amused the old gentlewoman so successfully, by maintaining a seemingly disinterested ease in the midst of my civility, that she signified a desire of being better acquainted, and hoped I would be so kind as to see her sometimes at Bath. While I enjoyed myself in this manner, the precise lady had the good fortune to meet with her husband, who was no other than gentleman, or, in other words, valet de chambre, to the very nobleman whose coach stood at the door. Proud of the interest she had in the house, she affected to show her power by introducing the captain to her spouse, as a person who had treated her with great civility; upon which he was invited to a share of their dinner; while the poor lawyer, finding himself utterly abandoned, made application to me, and was, through my intercession, admitted into our company. Having satisfied our appetites, and made ourselves merry at the expense of the person of honour, the civil captain, and complaisant husband, I did myself the pleasure of discharging the bill by stealth, for which I received a great many apologies and acknowledgments from my guests, and we re-embarked at the first warning. The officer was obliged, at last, to appease his hunger with a luncheon of bread and cheese, and a pint bottle of brandy, which he despatched in the coach, cursing the inappetence of his lordship, who had ordered dinner to be put back a whole hour.

Nothing remarkable happened during the remaining part of

our journey, which was finished next day, when I waited on the
ladies to the house of a relation, in which they intended to lodge,
and passing that night at the inn, took lodgings in the morning
for myself.

The forenoon was spent in visiting everything that was worth
seeing in the place, in company with a gentleman to whom Banter
had given me a letter of introduction; and in the afternoon I
waited on the ladies, and found Miss a good deal indisposed with
the fatigue of the journey. As they foresaw they should have
occasion for a male acquaintance to squire them at all public
places, I was received with great cordiality, and had the mother's
commission to conduct them next day to the Long Room, which
we no sooner entered, than the eyes of everybody present were
turned upon us; and when we had suffered the martyrdom of
their looks for some time, a whisper circulated at our expense,
which was accompanied with many contemptuous smiles and
tittering observations, to my utter shame and confusion. I did
not so much conduct as follow my charge to a place where
she seated her mother and herself with astonishing composure,
notwithstanding the unmannerly behaviour of the whole company, which seemed to be assumed merely to put her out of
countenance. The celebrated Mr. Nash, who commonly attends
in this place as master of the ceremonies, perceiving the disposition of the assembly, took upon himself the task of gratifying
their ill-nature still further, by exposing my mistress to the edge
of his wit. With this view he approached us, with many bows
and grimaces, and after having welcomed Miss Snapper to the
place, asked her, in the hearing of all present, if she could inform
him the name of Tobit's dog. I was so much incensed at his
insolence that I should certainly have kicked him where he
stood, without ceremony, had not the young lady prevented
the effects of my indignation, by replying, with the utmost
vivacity, "His name was Nash, and an impudent dog he was."
This repartee, so unexpected and just, raised such an universal
laugh at the aggressor, that all his assurance was insufficient to
support him under their derision; so that, after he had endeavoured to compose himself, by taking snuff, and forcing a
smile, he was obliged to sneak off in a very ludicrous attitude;
while my dulcinea was applauded to the skies for the brilliancy
of her wit, and her acquaintance immediately courted by the
best people of both sexes in the room. This event, with which
I was infinitely pleased at first, did not fail of alarming me, upon
further reflection, when I considered, that the more she was

caressed by persons of distinction, the more her pride would be inflamed, and consequently the obstacles to my success multiplied and enlarged. Nor were my presaging fears untrue. That very night I perceived her a little intoxicated with the incense she had received; and though she still behaved with a particular civility to me, I foresaw that, as soon as her fortune should be known, she would be surrounded with a swarm of admirers, some of whom might possibly, by excelling me in point of wealth, or in the arts of flattery and scandal, supplant me in her esteem, and find means to make the mother of his party. I resolved therefore to lose no time, and being invited to spend the evening with them, found an opportunity, in spite of the old gentlewoman's vigilance, to explain the meaning of my glances in the coach, by paying homage to her wit, and professing myself enamoured of her person. She blushed at my declaration, and in a favourable manner disapproved of the liberty I had taken, putting me in mind of our being strangers to each other, and desiring I would not be the means of interrupting our acquaintance by any such unseasonable strokes of gallantry for the future. My ardour was effectually checked by this reprimand, which was, however, delivered in such a gentle manner that I had no cause to be disobliged; and the arrival of her mother relieved me from a dilemma in which I should not have known how to demean myself a minute longer. Neither could I resume the easiness of carriage with which I came in. My mistress acted on the reserve, and the conversation beginning to flag, the old lady introduced her kinswoman of the house, and proposed a hand at whist.

While we amused ourselves at this diversion, I understood from the gentlewoman that there was to be an assembly next night, at which I begged to have the honour of dancing with Miss. She thanked me for the favour I intended her, assured me she never did dance, but signified a desire of seeing the company; when I offered my service, which was accepted; not a little proud of being exempted from appearing with her in a situation that, notwithstanding my profession to the contrary, was not at all agreeable to my inclination.

Having supped, and continued the game, till such time as the successive yawns of the mother warned me to be gone, I took my leave, and went home, where I made Strap very happy with an account of my progress. Next day I put on my gayest apparel, and went to drink tea at Mrs. Snapper's according to appointment, when I found, to my inexpressible satisfaction, that she was laid up with the toothache, and that Miss was to be entrusted to my care. Accordingly, we set out for the ball-room pretty early in the evening, and took possession of a commodious place, where we had not sat longer than a quarter of an hour, when a gentleman dressed in a green frock came in, leading a young lady, whom I immediately discovered to be the adorable Narcissa! Good Heaven! what were the thrillings of my soul at that instant! my reflection was overwhelmed with a torrent of agitation! my heart throbbed with surprising violence! a sudden mist overspread my eyes! my ears were invaded with a dreadful sound! I paused for want of breath, and, in short, was for some moments entranced! This first tumult subsiding, a crowd of flattering ideas rushed upon my imagination. Everything that was soft, sensible, and engaging in the character of that dear creature, recurred to my remembrance, and every favourable circumstance of my own qualifications appeared in all the aggravation of self-conceit, to heighten my expectation! Neither was this transport of long duration. The dread of her being already disposed of intervened, and overcast my enchanting reverie! My presaging apprehension represented her encircled in the arms of some happy rival, and of consequence for ever lost to me! I was stung with this suggestion, and believing the person who conducted her to be the husband of this amiable young lady, already devoted him to my fury, and stood up to mark him for my vengeance; when I recollected, to my unspeakable joy, her brother, the fox-hunter, in the person of her gallant. Undeceived so much to my satisfaction in this particular, I gazed, in a frenzy of delight, on the irresistible charms of his sister, who no sooner distinguished me in the crowd, than her evident confusion afforded a happy omen to my flame. At sight of me she startled, the roses instantly vanished from her polished cheeks, and returned in a moment with a double glow that overspread her lovely neck, while her enchanting bosom heaved with strong emotion. I hailed these favourable symptoms, and, lying in wait for her looks, did homage with my eyes. She seemed to approve my declaration, by the complacency of her aspect; and I was so transported with her discovery, that more than once I was on the point of making up to her to disclose the throbbings of my heart in person, had not that profound veneration which her presence always inspired, restrained the unseasonable impulse. All my powers being engrossed in this manner, it may easily be imagined how ill I entertained Miss Snapper, on whom I could not now turn my eyes without making comparisons very little to her advantage. It was not even in my power to return distinct answers to the questions she asked from time to time, so that she could not help observing my absence of mind; and having a turn for observation, watched my glances, and tracing them to the divine object, discovered the cause of my disorder. That she might, however, be convinced of the truth of her conjecture, she began to interrogate me with regard to Narcissa, and, notwithstanding all my endeavours to disguise my sentiments, perceived my attachment by my confusion. Upon which she assumed a stateliness of behaviour, and sat silent during the remaining part of the entertainment. At any other time, her suspicion would have alarmed me; but now I was elevated by my passion above every other consideration. The mistress of my soul having retired with her brother, I discovered so much uneasiness at my situation, that Miss Snapper proposed to go home, and while I conducted her to a chair, told me she had too great a regard for me to keep me any longer in torment. I feigned ignorance of her meaning, and having seen her safely at her lodgings, took my leave, and went home in an ecstasy, where I disclosed everything that had happened to my confidant and humble servant Strap, who did not relish the accident so well as I expected, and observed that a bird in hand is worth two in the bush. "But however," said he, "you know best—you know best." Next day, as I went to the Pump-room, in hopes of seeing or hearing some tidings of my fair enslaver, I was met by a gentlewoman, who having looked hard at me, cried, "O Christ! Mr. Random!" Surprised at this exclamation, I examined the countenance of the person who spoke, and immediately recognised my old sweetheart and fellow-sufferer, Miss Williams.

I was mightily pleased to find this unfortunate woman under such a decent appearance, professed my joy at seeing her so well, and desired to know where I should have the pleasure of her conversation. She was as heartily rejoiced at the apparent easiness of my fortune, and gave me to know that she, as yet, had no habitation that she could properly call her own, but would wait on me at any place I should please to appoint. Understanding that she was unengaged for the present, I showed her the way to my own lodgings, where, after a very affectionate salutation, she informed me of her being very happy in the service of a young lady to whom she was recommended by a former mistress deceased, into whose family she had recommended herself by the honest deceit she had concerted while she lived with me in the garret at London. She then expressed a vehement desire to be acquainted with the vicissitudes of my life since we parted, and excused her curiosity on account of the concern she had for my interest. I forthwith gratified her request, and when I described my situation in Sussex, perceived her to attend to my story with particular eagerness. She interrupted me when I had finished that period with, "Good God! is it possible!"—and then begged I would be so good as to continue my relation; which I did as briefly as I could, burning with impatience to know the cause of her surprise, about which I had already formed a very interesting conjecture. When I had brought my adventures down to the present day, she seemed very much affected with the different circumstances of my fortune; and saying with a smile, she believed my distresses were now at a period, proceeded to inform me, that the lady whom she served was no other than the charming Narcissa, who had honoured her with her confidence for some time; in consequence of which trust, she had often repeated the story of John Brown, with great admiration and regard; that she loved to dwell upon the particulars of his character, and did not scruple to own a tender approbation of his flame. I became delirious at this piece of intelligence, strained Miss Williams in my embrace, called her the angel of my happiness, and acted such extravagances, that she might have been convinced of my sincerity, had she not been satisfied of my honour before. As soon as I was in condition to yield attention, she described the present situation of her mistress, who had no sooner reached her lodgings the night before, than she closeted her, and, in a rapture of joy, gave her to know that she had seen me at the ball, where I appeared in the character which she always thought my due, with such advantage of transformation, that unless my image had been engraven on her heart, it would have been impossible to know me for the person who had worn her aunt's livery; that, by the language of my eyes, she was assured of the continuance of my passion for her, and consequently of my being unengaged to any other; and that, though she did not doubt I would speedily fall upon some method of being introduced, she was so impatient to hear of me, that she (Miss Williams) had been sent abroad this very morning, on purpose to learn the name and character I at present bore. My bosom had been hitherto a stranger to such a flood of joy as now rushed upon it. My faculties were overborne by the tide. It was some time before I could open my mouth, and much longer ere I could utter a coherent sentence. At length, I fervently requested her to lead me immediately to the object of my adoration. But she resisted my importunity, and explained the danger of such premature conduct. "How favourable soever," said she, "my lady's inclination towards you may be, you may depend upon it, she will not commit the smallest trespass on decorum, either in disclosing her own, or in receiving a declaration of your passion; and although the great veneration I have for you has prompted me to reveal what she communicated to me in confidence, I know so well the severity of her sentiments with respect to the punctilios of her sex, that, if she could learn the least surmise of it, she would not only dismiss me as a wretch unworthy of her benevolence, but also for ever shun the efforts of your love." I assented to the justness of her remonstrance, and desired she would assist me with her advice and direction. Upon which, it was concerted between us that, for the present, I should be contented with her telling Narcissa that, in the course of her inquiries, she could only learn my name; and that if, in a day or two, I could fall upon no other method of being introduced to her mistress, she would deliver a letter from me, on pretence of consulting her happiness; and say that I met her in the streets, and bribed her to this piece of service. Matters being thus adjusted, I kept my old acquaintance to breakfast, and learned, from her conversation, that my rival, Sir Timothy, had drunk himself into an apoplexy, of which he died five months ago; that the savage was still unmarried; and that his aunt had been seized with a whim which he little expected, and chosen the schoolmaster of the parish for her lord and husband; but matrimony not agreeing with her constitution, she had been hectic and dropsical a good while, and was now at Bath, in order to drink the waters for the recovery of her health; that her niece had accompanied her thither at her request, and attended her with the same affection as before, notwithstanding the mistake she had committed; and that her nephew, who had been exasperated at the loss of her fortune, did not give his attendance out of good-will, but purely to have an eye on his sister, lest she should likewise throw herself away, without his consent or approbation. Having enjoyed ourselves in this manner, and made an assignation to meet next day at a certain place, Miss Williams took her leave; and Strap's looks being very inquisitive about the nature of the communication subsisting between us, I made him acquainted with the whole affair, to his great astonishment and satisfaction.

CHAPTER LVI

I become acquainted with Narcissa's Brother, who invites me to his House, where I am introduced to that adorable Creature—After Dinner, the Squire retires to take his Nap—Freeman, guessing the Situation of my Thoughts, withdraws likewise on pretence of Business—I declare my Passion to Narcissa—Am well received—Charmed with her Conversation—The Squire detains us to Supper—I elude his Design by a Stratagem and get Home sober.

IN the afternoon I drank tea at the house of Mr. Freeman, to whom I had been recommended by Banter; where I had not sat five minutes till the fox-hunter came in, and by his familiar behaviour appeared to be intimate with my friend. I was at first under some concern, lest he should recollect my features; but when I found myself introduced to him as a gentleman from London, without being discovered, I blessed the opportunity that brought me into his company, hoping that, in the course of our acquaintance, he would invite me to his house. Nor were my hopes frustrated; for, as we spent the evening together, he grew extremely fond of my conversation, asked a great many childish questions about France and foreign parts; and seemed so highly entertained with my answers, that, in his cups, he shook me often by the hand, pronounced me an honest fellow, and, in fine, desired our company at dinner next day in his own house. My imagination was so much employed in anticipating the happiness I was to enjoy next day, that I slept very little that night; but rising early in the morning, went to the place appointed, where I met my she-friend, and imparted to her my success with the squire. She was very much pleased at the occasion, which, she said, could not fail of being agreeable to Narcissa, who, in spite of her passion for me, had mentioned some scruples relating to my true situation and character, which the delicacy of her sentiments suggested, and which she believed I would find it necessary to remove, though she did not know how. I was a good deal startled at this insinuation, because I foresaw the difficulty I should find in barely doing myself justice; for, although it never was my intention to impose myself upon any woman, much less on Narcissa, as a man of fortune, I laid claim to the character of a gentleman, by birth, education, and behaviour; and yet, so unlucky had the circumstances of my life fallen out, I should find it a very hard matter to make good my pretensions even to these, especially to the last, which was the most essential. Miss Williams was as sensible as I of this my disadvantage, but comforted me with observing, that when once a woman had bestowed her affections on a man, she cannot help judging of him in all respects with a partiality easily influenced in his favour. She remarked, that although some situations of my life had been low, yet none of them had been infamous; that my indigence had been the crime not of me, but of fortune; and that the miseries I had undergone, by improving the faculties both of mind and body, qualified me the more for any dignified station, and would of consequence recommend me to the good graces of any sensible woman. She therefore advised me to be always open and unreserved to the inquiries of my mistress, without unnecessarily betraying the meanest occurrences of my fate, and trust to the strength of her love and reflection for the rest. The sentiments of this sensible young woman, on this as well as on almost every other subject, perfectly agreed with mine; I thanked her for the care she took of my interests, and promising to behave myself according to her direction, we parted, after she had assured me that I might depend upon her best offices with her mistress, and that she would from time to time communicate to me such intelligence as she should procure relating to my flame. Having dressed myself to the best advantage, I waited for the time of dinner with the most fearful impatience; and as the hour drew nigh, my heart beat with such increased velocity, and my spirits contracted such disorder, that I began to suspect my resolution, and even to wish myself disengaged. At last Mr. Freeman called at my lodgings in his way, and I accompanied him to the house where all my happiness was deposited. We were very kindly received by the squire, who sat smoking his pipe in a parlour, and asked if we chose to drink anything before dinner. Though I never had more occasion for a cordial, I was ashamed to accept his offer, which was also refused by my friend. We sat down, however, and entered into conversation, which lasted half an hour, so that I had time to recollect myself; and, so capricious were my thoughts, even to hope that Narcissa would not appear —when all of a sudden, a servant coming in, gave us notice that dinner was upon the table—and my perturbation returned with such violence, that I could scarce conceal it from the company as I ascended the staircase. When I entered the dining-room, the first object that saluted my ravished eyes was the divine Narcissa, blushing like Aurora, adorned with all the graces that meekness, innocence, and beauty can diffuse! I was seized with a giddiness, my knees tottered, and I scarce had

strength enough to perform the ceremony of salutation, when
her brother, slapping me on the shoulder, cried, "Measter
Randan, that there is my sister." I approached her with eagerness and fear; but in the moment of our embrace, my soul
was agonised with rapture! It was a lucky circumstance for us
both, that my entertainer was not endued with an uncommon
stock of penetration; for our mutual confusion was so manifest,
that Mr. Freeman perceived it, and as we went home together,
congratulated me on my good fortune. But so far was Bruin
from entertaining the least suspicion, that he encouraged me
to begin a conversation with my mistress in a language unknown
to him, by telling her that he had brought a gentleman who
could jabber with her in French and other foreign lingos, as fast
as she pleased; then turning to me, said, "Odds bobs! I wish
you would hold discourse with her in your French or Italiano,
and tell me if she understands it as well as she would be thought
to do—there's her aunt and she will chatter together whole
days in it, and I can't have a mouthful of English for love or
money." I consulted the look of my amiable mistress, and found
her averse to his proposal, which she declined with a sweetness
of denial peculiar to herself, as a piece of disrespect to that part
of the company which did not understand the language in
question. As I had the happiness of sitting opposite to her, I
feasted my eyes much more than my palate, which she tempted
in vain with the most delicious bits carved by her fair hand,
and recommended by her persuasive tongue; but all my other
appetites were swallowed up in the immensity of my love, which
I fed by gazing incessantly on the delightful object. Dinner
was scarce ended, when the squire became very drowsy, and,
after several dreadful yawns, got up, stretched himself, took
two or three turns across the room, begged we would allow him
to take a short nap, and having laid a strong injunction on his
sister to detain us till his return, went to his repose without
further ceremony. He had not been gone many minutes, when
Freeman, guessing the situation of my heart, and thinking he
could not do me a greater favour than to leave me alone with
Narcissa, pretended to recollect himself all of a sudden, and
starting up, begged the lady's pardon for half an hour, for he
had luckily remembered an engagement of some consequence
that he must perform at that instant; so saying, he took his
leave, promising to come back time enough for tea, leaving
my mistress and me in great confusion. Now that I enjoyed
an opportunity of disclosing the pantings of my soul, I had not

the power to use it. I studied many pathetic declarations, but when I attempted to give them utterance, my tongue denied its office; and she sat silent, with a downcast look, full of anxious alarm, her bosom heaving with expectation of some great event. At length I endeavoured to put an end to this solemn pause, and began with, "It is very surprising, madam——" Here the sound dying away, I made a full stop—while Narcissa starting, blushed, and, with a timid accent, answered, "Sir?" Confounded at this note of interrogation, I pronounced, with the most sheepish bashfulness, "Madam!" To which she replied, "I beg pardon—I thought you had spoke to me." Another pause ensued —I made another effort; and though my voice faltered very much at the beginning, made shift to express myself in this manner: "I say, madam, 'tis very surprising that love should act so inconsistent with itself, as to deprive its votaries of the use of their faculties when they have most need of them. Since the happy occasion of being alone with you presented itself, I have made many unsuccessful attempts to declare a passion for the loveliest of her sex—a passion which took possession of my soul, while my cruel fate compelled me to wear a servile disguise so unsuitable to my birth, sentiments, and, let me add, my deserts; yet favourable in one respect, as it furnished me with opportunities of seeing and adoring your perfections. Yes, madam, it was then your dear idea entered my bosom, where it has lived unimpaired in the midst of numberless cares, and animated me against a thousand dangers and calamities." While I spoke thus, she concealed her face with her fan, and when I ceased speaking, recovering herself from the most beautiful confusion, told me, she thought herself very much obliged by my favourable opinion of her, and that she was very sorry to hear I had been unfortunate. Encouraged by this gentle reply, I proceeded, owned myself sufficiently recompensed by her kind compassion for what I had undergone, and declared that the future happiness of my life depended solely upon her. "Sir," said she, "I should be very ungrateful, if, after the signal protection you once afforded me, I should refuse to contribute towards your happiness, in any reasonable condescension." Transported at this acknowledgment, I threw myself at her feet, and begged she would regard my passion with a favourable eye. She was alarmed at my behaviour, entreated me to rise, lest her brother should discover me in that posture, and to spare her, for the present, upon a subject for which she was altogether unprepared. In consequence of this remonstrance,

I rose, assuring her I would rather die than disobey her; but in the meantime begged her to consider how precious the minutes of this opportunity were, and what restraint I put upon my inclinations in sacrificing them to her desire. She smiled with unspeakable sweetness, and said there would be no want of opportunities, provided I could maintain the good opinion her brother had conceived of me; and I, enchanted by her charms, seized her hand, which I well-nigh devoured with kisses. But she checked my boldness with a severity of countenance, and desired I would not so far forget myself to her as to endanger the esteem she had for me; she reminded me of our being almost strangers to each other, and of the necessity there was for her knowing me better before she could take any resolution in my favour; and, in short, mingled so much good sense and complacency in her reproof, that I became as much enamoured of her understanding, as I had been before of her beauty, and asked pardon for my presumption with the utmost reverence of conviction. She forgave my offence with her usual affability; and sealed my pardon with a look so full of bewitching tenderness, that for some minutes my senses were lost in ecstasy! I afterwards endeavoured to regulate my behaviour according to her desire, and turn the conversation upon a more indifferent subject. But her presence was an insurmountable obstacle to my design; while I beheld so much excellence, I found it impossible to call my attention from the contemplation of it! I gazed with unutterable fondness! I grew mad with admiration! "My condition is insupportable!" cried I, "I am distracted with passion! Why are you so exquisitely fair? Why are you so enchantingly good? Why has nature dignified you with charms so much above the standard of women? and, wretch that I am, how dares my unworthiness aspire to the enjoyment of such perfection?"

She was startled at my ravings, reasoned down my transport, and by her irresistible eloquence soothed my soul into a state of tranquil felicity; but, lest I might suffer a relapse, industriously promoted other subjects to entertain my imagination. She chid me for having omitted to inquire about her aunt, who, she assured me, in the midst of all her absence of temper, and detachment from common affairs, often talked of me with uncommon warmth. I professed my veneration for the good lady, excused my omission, by imputing it to the violence of my love, which engrossed my whole soul, and desired to know the situation of her health. Upon which the amiable Narcissa repeated what

I had heard before, of her marriage, with all the tenderness for her reputation that the subject would admit of; told me she lived with her husband hard by, and was so much afflicted with the dropsy, and wasted by a consumption, that she had small hopes of her recovery. Having expressed my sorrow for her distemper, I questioned her about my good friend Mrs. Sagely, who I learned, to my great satisfaction, was still in good health, and who had, by the encomiums she bestowed upon me after I was gone, confirmed the favourable impressions my behaviour at parting had made on Narcissa's heart. The circumstance introduced an inquiry into the conduct of Sir Timothy Thicket, who, she informed me, had found means to incense her brother so much against me, that she found it impossible to undeceive him; but, on the contrary, suffered very much in her own character by his scandalous insinuations; that the whole parish was alarmed, and actually in pursuit of me, so that she had been in the utmost consternation upon my account, well knowing how little my own innocence, and her testimony, would have weighed with the ignorance, prejudice, and brutality of those who must have judged me, had I been apprehended. That Sir Timothy, having been seized with a fit of apoplexy, from which, with great difficulty, he was recovered, began to be apprehensive of death, and to prepare himself accordingly for that great event; as a step to which he sent for her brother, owned, with great contrition, the brutal design he had upon her, and, of consequence, acquitted me of the assault, robbery, and correspondence with her, which he laid to my charge; after which confession, he lived about a month in a languishing condition, and was carried off by a second assault.

Every word that this dear creature spoke, riveted the chains with which she held me enslaved. My mischievous fancy began to work, and the tempest of my passion to wake again, when the return of Freeman destroyed the tempting opportunity, and enabled me to quell the rising tumult. A little while after, the squire staggered into the room, rubbing his eyes, and called for his tea, which he drank out of a small bowl, qualified with brandy, while we took it in the usual way. Narcissa left us in order to visit her aunt; and when Freeman and I proposed to take our leave, the fox-hunter insisted on our spending the evening at his house with such obstinacy of affection, that we were obliged to comply. For my own part, I should have been glad of the invitation, by which, in all likelihood, I should be blessed with more of his sister's company, had I not been afraid of risking her esteem, by entering into a debauch of drinking with him, which, from the knowledge of his character, I foresaw would happen; but there was no remedy. I was forced to rely upon the strength of my constitution, which I hoped would resist intoxication longer than the squire's, and to trust to the good-nature and discretion of my mistress for the rest.

Our entertainer, resolving to begin by times, ordered the table to be furnished with liquor and glasses immediately after tea; but we absolutely refused to set in for drinking so soon, and prevailed upon him to pass away an hour or two at whist, in which we engaged as soon as Narcissa returned. The savage and I happened to be partners at first; and as my thoughts were wholly employed in a more interesting game, I played so ill, that he lost all patience, swore bitterly, and threatened to call for wine if they would not grant him another associate. This desire was gratified, and Narcissa and I were of a side; he won, for the same reason that made him lose before. I was satisfied; my lovely partner did not repine; and the time slipped away very agreeably, until we were told that supper was served in another room.

The squire was enraged to find the evening so unprofitably spent, and wreaked his vengeance on the cards, which he tore, and committed to the flames with many execrations, threatening to make us redeem our loss with a large glass, and quick circulation; and, indeed, we had no sooner supped, and my charmer withdrawn, than he began to put his threats in execution. Three bottles of port (for he drank no other sort of wine) were placed before us, with as many water-glasses, which were immediately filled to the brim, after his example, by each, out of his respective allowance, and emptied in a trice, *to the best in Christendom.* Though I swallowed this and the next as fast as the glass could be replenished, without hesitation or show of reluctance, I perceived that my brain would not be able to bear many bumpers of this sort; and, dreading the perseverance of a champion who began with such vigour, I determined to make up for the deficiency of my strength by a stratagem, which I actually put in practice when the second course of bottles was called for. The wine being strong and heady, I was already a good deal discomposed by the despatch we had made, Freeman's eyes began to reel, and Bruin himself was elevated into a song, which he uttered with great vociferation. When I, therefore, saw the second round brought in, I assumed a gay air, entertained him with a French catch on the subject of drinking, which, though he did not understand it, delighted him highly, and telling him that your choice spirits at Paris never troubled themselves with glasses, asked if he had not a bowl or cup in the house that would contain a whole quart of wine. "Odds niggers!" cried he, "I have a silver caudle cup that holds just the quantity, for all the world—fetch it hither, Numps." The vessel being produced, I bade him decant his bottle into it, which he having done, I nodded in a very deliberate manner, and said, "Pledge you." He stared at me for some time, and crying, "What! all at one pull, Measter Randan!" I answered, "At one pull, sir; you are no milk-sop—we shall do you justice." "Shall you?" said he, shaking me by the hand; "odds then, I'll see it out, an't were a mile to the bottom. Here's to our better acquaintance, Measter Randan"; so saying, he applied it to his lips, and emptied it in a breath. I knew the effect of it would be almost instantaneous; therefore, taking the cup, began to discharge my bottle into it, telling him he was now qualified to drink with the Cham of Tartary. I had no sooner pronounced these words, than he took umbrage at them, and, after several attempts to spit, made shift to stutter out, "A f—t for your Chams of T—Tartary!—I am a f—f—free-born Englishman, worth th—three thousand a year, and v—value no man, damme!" Then, dropping his jaw, and fixing his eyes, he hiccupped aloud, and fell upon the floor as mute as a flounder. Mr. Freeman, heartily glad at his defeat, assisted me in carrying him to bed, where we left him to the care of his servants, and went home to our respective habitations, congratulating each other on our good fortune.

CHAPTER LVII

Miss Williams informs me of Narcissa's approbation of my Flame—I appease the Squire—Write to my Mistress, am blessed with an Answer—Beg leave of her Brother to dance with her at a Ball; obtain his Consent and hers—Enjoy a private Conversation with her—Am perplexed with Reflections—Have the honour of appearing her Partner at a Ball—We are complimented by a certain Nobleman—He discovers some symptoms of a Passion for Narcissa—I am stung with Jealousy—Narcissa, alarmed, retires—I observe Melinda in the Company—The Squire is captivated by her Beauty.

I WAS met next morning, at the usual place, by Miss Williams, who gave me joy of the progress I had made in the affection of her mistress, and blessed me with an account of that dear creature's conversation with her, after she had retired the night before from our company. I could scarce believe her information, when she recounted her expressions in my favour, so much more warm and passionate were they than my most sanguine hopes had presaged; and was particularly pleased to hear that she approved of my behaviour to her brother after she withdrew. Transported at the news of my happiness, I presented my ring to the messenger, as a testimony of my gratitude and satisfaction; but she was above such mercenary considerations, and refused my compliment with some resentment, saying she was not a little mortified to see my opinion of her so low and contemptible. I did myself a piece of justice by explaining my behaviour on this head, and, to convince her of my esteem, promised to be ruled by her directions in the prosecution of the whole affair, which I had so much at heart, that the repose of my life depended upon the consequence.

As I fervently wished for another interview, where I might pour out the effusions of my love without danger of being interrupted, and perhaps reap some endearing return from the queen of my desires, I implored her advice and assistance in promoting this event. But she gave me to understand that Narcissa would make no precipitate compliances of this kind, and that I would do well to cultivate her brother's acquaintance, in the course of which I should not want opportunities of removing that reserve which my mistress thought herself obliged to maintain during the infancy of our correspondence. In the meantime she promised to tell her lady that I had endeavoured, by presents and persuasions, to prevail upon her (Miss Williams) to deliver a letter from me, which she had refused to charge herself with, until she would know Narcissa's sentiments of the matter; and said, by these means she did not doubt of being able to open a literary communication between us, which could not fail of introducing more intimate connections.

I approved of her counsel, and our appointment being renewed for next day, left her with an intent of falling upon some method of being reconciled to the squire, who, I supposed, would be offended with the trick we had put upon him. With this view, I consulted Freeman, who, from his knowledge of the foxhunter's disposition, assured me there was no other method of pacifying him, than that of sacrificing ourselves, for one night, to an equal match with him in drinking. This expedient I found myself necessitated to comply with, for the interest of my passion, and therefore determined to commit the debauch at my own lodgings, that I might run no risk of being discovered by Narcissa in a state of brutal degeneracy. Mr. Freeman, who was to be of the party, went at my desire to the squire, in order to engage him, while I took care to furnish myself for his reception. My invitation was accepted, my guests honoured me with their company in the evening, when Bruin gave me to understand that he had drank many tuns of wine in his life, but was never served such a trick as I had played upon him the night before. I promised to atone for my trespass, and having ordered to every man his bottle, began the contest with a bumper to the health of Narcissa. The toasts circulated with great devotion, the liquor began to operate, our mirth grew noisy, and as Freeman and I had the advantage of drinking small French claret, the savage was effectually tamed before our senses were in the least affected, and carried home in an apoplexy of drunkenness.

I was next morning, as usual, favoured with a visit from my kind and punctual confidante, who telling me she was permitted to receive my letters for her mistress, I took up the pen immediately, and following the first dictates of my passion, wrote as follows:

"DEAR MADAM,—Were it possible for the powers of utterance to reveal the soft emotions of my soul; the fond anxiety, the glowing hopes, the chilling fears, that rule my breast by turns; I should need no other witness than this paper, to evince the purity and ardour of that flame your charms have kindled in my heart. But, alas! expression wrongs my love! I am inspired with conceptions that no language can convey! Your beauty fills me with wonder! your understanding with ravishment, and your goodness with adoration! I am transported with desire, distracted with doubts, and tortured with impatience! Suffer me then, lovely arbitress of my fate, to approach you in person, to breathe in soft murmurs my passion to your ear, to offer the sacrifice of a heart overflowing with the most genuine and disinterested love; to gaze with ecstasy on the divine object of my wishes, to hear the music of her enchanting tongue; and to rejoice in her smile of approbation, which will banish the most intolerable suspense from the bosom of,

"Your enraptured

"R—— R——."

Having finished this effusion, I committed it to the care of my faithful friend, with an injunction to second my entreaty with all her eloquence and influence; and in the meantime went to dress, with an intention of visiting Mrs. Snapper and Miss, whom

I had utterly neglected, and indeed almost forgot, since my dear Narcissa had resumed the empire of my soul. The old gentlewoman received me very kindly, and Miss affected a frankness and gaiety, which, however, I could easily perceive were forced and dissembled; among other things, she pretended to joke me upon my passion for Narcissa, which she averred was no secret, and asked if I intended to dance with her at the next assembly. I was a good deal concerned to find myself become the town-talk on this subject, lest the squire, having notice of my inclinations, should disapprove of them, and, by breaking off all correspondence with me, deprive me of the opportunities I now enjoyed. But I resolved to use the interest I had with him while it lasted; and that very night meeting him occasionally, asked his permission to solicit her company at the ball, which he very readily granted, to my inexpressible satisfaction.

Having been kept awake the greatest part of the night by a thousand delightful reveries that took possession of my fancy, I got up by times, and flying to the place of rendezvous, had in a little time the pleasure of seeing Miss Williams approach with a smile on her countenance, which I interpreted into a good omen. Neither was I mistaken in my presage. She presented me with a letter from the idol of my soul, which, after having kissed it devoutly, I opened with the utmost eagerness, and was blessed with her approbation in these terms:

"SIR,—To say I look upon you with indifference, would be a piece of dissimulation, which I think no decorum requires, and no custom can justify. As my heart never felt an impression that my tongue was ashamed to declare, I will not scruple to own myself pleased with your passion, confident of your integrity, and so well convinced of my own discretion, that I should not hesitate in granting you the interview you desire, were I not overawed by the prying curiosity of a malicious world, the censure of which might be fatally prejudicial to the reputation of

"YOUR NARCISSA."

No anchorite in the ecstasy of devotion ever adored a relique with more fervour than that with which I kissed this inimitable proof of my charmer's candour, generosity, and affection! I read it over an hundred times; was ravished with her confession in the beginning; but the subscription of *Your Narcissa* yielded me such delight as I had never felt before. My happiness was still increased by Miss Williams, who blessed me with a repetition of her lady's tender expressions in my favour, when she received and read my letter. In short, I had all the reason in the world to believe that this gentle creature's bosom was possessed by a passion for me, as warm, though perhaps not so impetuous, as mine for her.

I informed my friend of the squire's consent to my dancing with Narcissa at the ball, and desired her to tell her mistress that I would do myself the honour of visiting her in the afternoon, in consequence of his permission, when I hoped to find her as indulgent as her brother had been complaisant in that particular. Miss Williams expressed a good deal of joy at hearing I was so much in favour with the fox-hunter, and ventured to assure me that my visit would be very agreeable to my mistress, the rather, because Bruin was engaged to dine abroad. This was a circumstance which, I scarce need say, pleased me. I went immediately to the Long Room, where I found him, and affecting to know nothing of the engagement, told him I would do myself the pleasure to wait upon him in the afternoon, and to present his sister with a ticket for the ball. He shook me by the hand, according to custom, and giving me to understand that he was to dine abroad, desired me to go and drink tea with Narcissa notwithstanding, and promised to prepare her for my visit in the meantime.

Everything succeeding thus to my wish, I waited with incredible impatience for the time, which no sooner arrived than I hastened to the scene, which my fancy had preoccupied long before. I was introduced accordingly to the dear enchantress, whom I found accompanied by Miss Williams, who, on pretence of ordering tea, retired at my approach. This favourable accident, which alarmed my whole soul, disordered her also. I found myself actuated by an irresistible impulse; I advanced to her with eagerness and awe, and, profiting by the confusion that prevailed over her, clasped the fair angel in my arms, and imprinted a glowing kiss upon her lips, more soft and fragrant than the dewy rose-bud just bursting from the stem! Her face was in an instant covered with blushes—her eyes sparkled with resentment—I threw myself at her feet and implored her pardon. Her love became advocate in my cause; her look softened into forgiveness; she raised me up, and chid me with so much sweetness of displeasure, that I should have been tempted to repeat the offence, had not the coming in of a servant with the tea-board prevented my presumption. While we were subject to be interrupted or overheard, we conversed about the

pproaching ball, at which she promised to grace me as a
artner; but when the equipage was removed, and we were left
lone, I resumed the more interesting theme, and expressed
myself with such transport and agitation, that my mistress,
earing I would commit some extravagance, rung the bell for
er maid, whom she detained in the room, as a check upon my
ivacity. I was not sorry for this precaution, because I could
nbosom myself without reserve before Miss Williams, who was
he confidante of us both. I therefore gave a loose to the inspira-
ions of my passion, which operated so successfully upon the
ender affections of Narcissa, that she laid aside the constraint
he had hitherto wore, and blessed me with the most melting
eclaration of her mutual flame! It was impossible for me to
orbear taking the advantage of this endearing condescension.
She now gently yielded to my embraces, while I, encircling all
hat I held dear within my arms, tasted in advance the joys of
hat paradise I hoped in a little time wholly to possess! We spent
he afternoon in all the ecstasy of hope that the most fervent
ove, exchanged by mutual vows, could inspire; and Miss
Williams was so much affected with our chaste caresses, which
ecalled the sad remembrance of what she was, that her eyes
vere filled with tears.

The evening being pretty far advanced, I forced myself from
he dear object of my flame, who indulged me in a tender embrace
t parting; and repairing to my lodgings, communicated to my
riend Strap every circumstance of my happiness, which filled
him with so much pleasure, that it ran over at his eyes; and he
prayed heartily that no envious devil might, as formerly, dash
he cup of blessing from my lip. When I reflected on what had
happened, and especially on the unreserved protestations of
Narcissa's love, I could not help being amazed at her omitting
to inquire into the particular circumstances of the life and
fortune of one whom she had favoured with her affection, and
I began to be a little anxious about the situation of her finances,
well knowing that I should do an irreparable injury to the person
my soul held most dear, if I should espouse her without being
able to support her in the rank which was certainly her due.
I had heard indeed, while I served her aunt, that her father had
left her a considerable sum; and that everybody believed she
would inherit the greatest part of her kinswoman's dowry: but
I did not know how far she might be restricted by the old gentleman's will, in the enjoyment of what he had left her; and I was
too well informed of the virtuoso's late conduct, to think my

mistress could have any expectations from that quarter. I confided, however, in the good sense and policy of my charmer, who, I was sure, would not consent to unite her fate with mine before she had fully considered and provided for the consequence

The ball-night being arrived, I dressed myself in a suit I had reserved for some grand occasion; and having drank tea with Narcissa and her brother, conducted my angel to the scene, where she in a moment eclipsed all her female competitors for beauty and attracted the admiration of the whole assembly. My heart dilated with pride on this occasion, and my triumph rejected all bounds, when, after we had danced together, a certain nobleman remarkable for his figure and influence in the *beau monde*, came up, and in the hearing of all present, honoured us with a very particular compliment upon our accomplishments and appearance. But this transport was soon checked, when I perceived his lordship attach himself with great assiduity to my mistress and say some warm things, which, I thought, favoured too much of passion. It was then I began to feel the pangs of jealousy—I dreaded the power and address of my rival—I sickened at his discourse; when she opened her lips to answer, my heart died within me. When she smiled, I felt the pains of the damned. I was enraged at his presumption; I cursed her complaisance; at length he quitted her, and went to the other side of the room. Narcissa, suspecting nothing of the rage that inflamed me, put some questions to me as soon as he was gone, to which I made no reply, but assumed a grim look, which too well denoted the agitation of my breast, and surprised her not a little. She no sooner observed my emotion, than she changed colour, and asked what ailed me? but before I could make answer, her brother, pulling me by the sleeve, bade me take notice of a lady who sat fronting us, whom I immediately, to my vast astonishment, distinguished to be Melinda, accompanied by her mother, and an elderly gentleman, whom I did not know. "Wounds! Mr. Randan," cried the squire, "is she not a delicate piece of stuff? 'Sdeath! I have a good mind—if I thought she was a single person——" Notwithstanding the perplexity I was in, I had reflection enough to foresee that my passion might suffer greatly by the presence of this lady, who in all probability would revenge herself upon me for having formerly disgraced her, by spreading reports to my prejudice. I was therefore alarmed at these symptoms of the squire's admiration; and for some time did not know what reply to make, when he asked my opinion of her beauty. At length I came to a determination, and told him that

her name was Melinda, that she had a fortune of ten thousand
pounds, and was said to be under promise of marriage to a certain
lord, who deferred his nuptials a few months, until he should be
of age. I thought this piece of intelligence, which I had myself
invented, would have hindered him effectually from entertaining
any farther thoughts of her; but I was egregiously mistaken.
The fox-hunter had too much self-sufficiency to despair of
success against any competitor on earth. He therefore made
light of her engagement, saying, with a smile of self-approbation,
"Mayhap she will change her mind—what signifies his being
a lord? I think myself as good a man as e'er a lord in Christendom;—and I'll see if a commoner worth three thousand a year
won't serve her turn." This determination startled me not a
little. I knew he would soon discover the contrary of what I
advanced; and as I believed he would find her ear open to his
addresses, did not doubt of meeting with every obstacle in my
amour that her malice could invent and her influence execute.
This reflection increased my chagrin. My vexation was evident.
Narcissa insisted on going home immediately; and as I led her
to the door, her noble admirer, with a look full of languishment,
directed to her a profound bow, which stung me to the soul.
Before she went into the chair, she asked, with an appearance
of concern, what was the matter with me? and I could
pronounce no more than, "By heaven! I'm distracted."

CHAPTER LVIII

Tortured with Jealousy, I go Home and abuse Strap—Receive a Message
from Narcissa, in consequence of which I hasten to her Apartment, where
her endearing Assurances banish all my Doubts and Apprehensions—In
my Retreat discover somebody in the Dark, whom, suspecting to be a
Spy, I resolve to kill; but, to my great Surprise, am convinced of his being
no other than Strap—Melinda slanders me—I become acquainted with
Lord Quiverwit, who endeavours to sound me with regard to Narcissa—
The Squire is introduced to his Lordship, and grows cold towards me—
I learn from my Confidante that this Nobleman professes honourable Love
to my Mistress, who continues faithful to me, notwithstanding the scan-
dalous Reports she has heard to my Prejudice—I am mortified with an
Assurance that her whole Fortune depends upon the Pleasure of her Brother
—Mr. Freeman condoles me on the decline of my Character, which I
vindicate so much to his Satisfaction, that he undertakes to combat
Fame in my behalf.

HAVING uttered this exclamation, at which she sighed, I went
home in the condition of a frantic bedlamite; and finding the
fire in my apartment almost extinguished, vented my fury upon

poor Strap, whose ear I pinched with such violence, that he roared hideously with pain, and, when I quitted my hold, looked so foolishly aghast, that no unconcerned spectator could have seen him without being seized with an immoderate fit of laughter. It is true, I was soon sensible of the injury I had done, and asked pardon for the outrage I had committed; upon which my faithful valet, shaking his head, said, "I forgive you, and may God forgive you." But he could not help shedding some tears at my unkindness. I felt unspeakable remorse for what I had done, cursed my own ingratitude, and considered his tears as a reproach that my soul, in her present disturbance, could not bear. It set all my passions into a ferment, I swore horrible oaths without meaning or application, I foamed at the mouth, kicked the chairs about the room, and played abundance of mad pranks, that frightened my friend almost out of his senses. At length my transport subsided, I became melancholy, and wept insensibly

During this state of dejection, I was surprised with the appearance of Miss Williams, whom Strap, blubbering all the while, had conducted into the chamber, without giving me previous notice of her approach. She was extremely affected with my condition which she had learned from him, begged me to moderate my passion, suspend my conjectures, and follow her to Narcissa, who desired to see me forthwith. That dear name operated upon me like a charm! I started up, and without opening my lips, was conducted into her apartment through the garden, which we entered by a private door. I found the adorable creature in tears!—I was melted at the sight—we continued silent for some time—my heart was too full to speak—her snowy bosom heaved with fond resentment; at last she sobbing cried, "What have I done to disoblige you?" My heart was pierced with the tender question!—I drew near with the utmost reverence of affection!—I fell upon my knees before her, and kissing her hand, exclaimed, "O! thou art all goodness and perfection! —I am undone by want of merit!—I am unworthy to possess thy charms, which Heaven hath destined for the arms of some more favoured being." She guessed the cause of my disquiet, upbraided me gently for my suspicion, and gave me such flattering assurances of her eternal fidelity, that all my doubts and fears forsook me and peace and satisfaction reigned within my breast.

At midnight I left the fair nymph to her repose, and being let out by Miss Williams, at the garden gate by which I entered, began to explore my way homeward in the dark, when I heard at my back a noise like that of a baboon when he mews and chatters. I turned instantly and perceiving something black, concluded I was discovered by some spy employed to watch for that purpose. Aroused at this conjecture, by which the reputation of the virtuous Narcissa appeared in jeopardy, I drew my sword, and would have sacrificed him to her fame, had not the voice of Strap restrained my arm. It was with great difficulty he could pronounce, "D—d—do! mum—um—um—murder me, if you please." Such an effect had the cold upon his jaws, that his teeth rattled like a pair of castanets. Pleased to be thus undeceived, I laughed at his consternation, and asked what brought him thither? Upon which he gave me to understand, that his concern for me had induced him to follow me to that place, where the same reason had detained him till now; and he frankly owned, that, in spite of the esteem he had for Miss Williams, he began to be very uneasy about me, considering the disposition in which I went abroad, and if I had staid much longer, would have certainly alarmed the neighbourhood in my behalf. The knowledge of this his intention confounded me! I represented to him the mischievous consequences that would have attended such a rash action, and cautioning him severely against any such design for the future, concluded my admonition with an assurance that, in case he should ever act so madly, I would, without hesitation, put him to death. "Have a little patience," cried he, in a lamentable tone, "your displeasure will do the business, without your committing murder." I was touched with this reproach; and, as soon as we got home, made it my business to appease him, by explaining the cause of that transport during which I had used him so unworthily.

Next day, when I went into the Long Room, I observed several whispers circulate all of a sudden, and did not doubt that Melinda had been busy with my character; but I consoled myself with the love of Narcissa, upon which I rested with the most perfect confidence, and going up to the rowly-powly table, won a few pieces from my suspected rival, who, with an easy politeness, entered into conversation with me, and desiring my company at the coffee-house, treated me with tea and chocolate. I remembered Strutwell, and guarded against his insinuating behaviour; nor was my suspicion wrong placed; he artfully turned the discourse upon Narcissa, and endeavoured, by hinting at an intrigue he pretended to be engaged in elsewhere, to learn what connection there was between her and me. But all his finesse was ineffectual; I was convinced of his dissimulation, and gave such general answers to his inquiries, that he was forced to drop the subject, and talk of something else.

While we conversed in this manner, the savage came in with another gentleman, who introduced him to his lordship; and he was received with such peculiar marks of distinction, that I was persuaded the courtier intended to use him in some shape or other; and from thence I drew an unlucky omen. But I had more cause to be dismayed the following day, when I saw the squire in company with Melinda and her mother, who honoured me with several disdainful glances; and when I afterwards threw myself in his way, instead of the cordial shake of the hand, he returned my salute with a cold repetition of "Servant, servant"; which he pronounced with such indifference, or rather contempt, that, if he had not been Narcissa's brother, I should have affronted him in public.

These occurrences disturbed me not a little. I foresaw the brooding storm, and armed myself with resolution for the occasion; but Narcissa being at stake, I was far from being resigned. I could have renounced every other comfort of life with some degree of fortitude; but the prospect of losing her disabled all my philosophy, and tortured my soul into madness.

Miss Williams found me next morning full of anxious tumult, which did not abate when she told me that my Lord Quiverwit, having professed honourable intentions, had been introduced to my lovely mistress by her brother, who had, at the same time, from the information of Melinda, spoke of me as an Irish fortune-hunter, without either birth or estate; who supported myself in the appearance of a gentleman by sharping and other infamous practices; and who was of such an obscure origin, that I did not even know my own extraction. Though I expected all this malice, I could not hear it with temper, especially as truth was so blended with falsehood in the assertion, that it would be almost impossible to separate the one from the other in my vindication. But I said nothing on this head, being impatient to know how Narcissa had been affected with the discovery. That generous creature, far from believing these imputations, was no sooner withdrawn with her confidante, than she inveighed with great warmth against the malevolence of the world, to which only she ascribed the whole of what had been said to my disadvantage; and calling every circumstance of my behaviour to her into review before her, found everything so polite, honourable, and disinterested, that she could not harbour the least doubt of my being the gentleman I assumed. "I have indeed," said she, "purposely forebore to ask the particulars of his life, lest the recapitulation of some misfortunes, which he has undergone, should give him pain: and, as to the article of his fortune, I own myself equally afraid of inquiring into it, and of discovering the situation of my own, lest we should find ourselves both unhappy in the explanation; for alas! my provision is conditional, and depends entirely on my marrying with my brother's consent."

I was thunderstruck with this intelligence; the light forsook my eyes, the colour vanished from my cheeks, and I remained in a state of universal trepidation! My female friend perceiving my disorder, encouraged me with assurances of Narcissa's constancy, and the hope of some accident favourable to our love; and, as a further consolation, gave me to understand that she had acquainted my mistress with the outlines of my life; and that, although she was no stranger to the present low state of my finances, her love and esteem were rather increased than diminished by the knowledge of my circumstances. I was greatly comforted by this assurance, which saved me a world of confusion and anxiety: for I must have imparted my situation one day to Narcissa: and this task I could not have performed without shame and disorder.

As I did not doubt that, by this time, the scandalous aspersions of Melinda were diffused all over the town, I resolved to collect my whole strength of assurance to browbeat the efforts of her malice, and to publish her adventure with the frenchified barber, by way of reprisal. In the meantime, having promised to be at the garden gate about midnight, Miss Williams took her leave, bidding me repose myself entirely on the affection of my dear Narcissa, which was as perfect as inviolable. Before I went abroad, I was visited by Freeman, who came on purpose to inform me of the infamous stories that were raised at my expense. I heard them with great temper, and in my turn disclosed everything that had happened between Melinda and me; and, among other circumstances, entertained him with the story of the barber, letting him know what share his friend Banter had in that affair: he was convinced of the injury my reputation had suffered, and no longer doubting the fountain from whence this deluge of slander had flowed upon me, undertook to undeceive the town in my behalf, and roll the stream back upon its source; but, in the meantime, cautioned me from appearing in public while the prepossession was so strong against me, les I should meet with some affront that might have ba consequences.

CHAPTER LIX

I receive an extraordinary Message at the Door of the Long Room which I however enter, and affront the Squire, who threatens to take th Law of me—Rebuke Melinda for her Malice—She weeps with Vexation— Lord Quiverwit is severe upon me—I retort his Sarcasm—Am receive with the utmost Tenderness by Narcissa, who desires to hear the Stor of my Life—We vow eternal Constancy to one another—I retire—An waked by a Messenger, who brings a Challenge from Quiverwit, whom meet, engage and vanquish.

I THANKED him for his advice, which, however, my pride and resentment would not permit me to follow; for he no soone left me, in order to do justice to my character among his friend and acquaintance, than I sallied out, and went directly to th Long Room. I was met at the door by a servant, who presente to me a billet without a subscription, importing that my presence was disagreeable to the company, and desiring I would take the hint without further disturbance, and bestow myself elsewhere for the future. This peremptory message filled me with indig nation. I followed the fellow who delivered it, and seizing him by the collar, in presence of all the company, threatened to put him instantly to death if he did not discover the scoundrel who had charged him with such an impudent commission, that I might punish him as he deserved. The messenger, affrighted at my menaces and furious looks, fell upon his knees, and told me that the gentleman who ordered him to deliver the letter was no other than Narcissa's brother, who, at that time, stood at the other end of the room, talking to Melinda. I went up to him immediately, and, in the hearing of his inamorata, accosted him in these words, "Look'ee, squire, was it not for one con sideration that protects you from my resentment, I would cane you where you stand, for having had the presumption to send me this scurrilous intimation"; which I tore to pieces and threw in his face: at the same time, darting an angry regard at his mistress, I told her I was sorry she had put it out of my power to compliment her upon her invention, but at the expense of her good nature and veracity. Her admirer, whose courage never rose but in proportion to the wine he had swallowed, instead of resenting my address in what is called an honourable way, threatened to prosecute me for an assault, and took witnesses accordingly; while she, piqued at his pusillanimous behaviour, and enraged at the sarcasm I had uttered against her, endeavoured to make her quarrel a public cause, and wept aloud with spite and vexation. The tears of a lady could not fail of attracting the notice and concern of the spectators, to whom she complained of my rudeness with great bitterness, saying, if she was a man, I durst not use her so. The greatest part of the gentlemen, already prejudiced against me, were offended at the liberty I had taken, as appeared from their looks; though none of them signified their disgust in any other way, except my Lord Quiverwit, who ventured to say, with a sneer, that I was in the right to establish my own character, of which he had now no longer any doubt. Nettled at this severe equivoque, which raised a laugh at my expense, I replied with some warmth, "I am proud of having in that particular got the start of your lordship." He made no answer to my repartee, but with a contemptuous smile, walked off, leaving me in a very disagreeable situation. In vain did I make up to several people of my acquaintance, whose conversation, I hoped, would banish my confusion; everybody shunned me like a person infected, and I should not have been able to bear my disgrace, had not the idea of the ever-faithful and fond Narcissa come to my relief. I quitted the scene of my mortification, and sauntering about the town, happened to wake from my contemplation, when I found myself just opposite to a toy-shop, which I entered, and purchased a ring set with a ruby in the form of a heart, surrounded by diamond sparks, for which I paid ten guineas, intending it for a present to the charmer of my soul.

I was introduced, at the hour appointed, to this divine creature, who, notwithstanding what she had heard to my disadvantage, received me with the utmost confidence and tenderness; and having been informed of the general sketches of my life by Miss Williams, expressed a desire of knowing the particular circumstances, which I related with great candour, omitting, however, some things, that I concluded altogether improper for her ear, and which the reader's reflection will easily suggest. As my story was little else than a recital of misfortunes, the tear of sympathy ceased not to trickle down her enchanting eyes during the whole of the narration, which when I had finished, she recompensed me for my trouble with the most endearing protestations of eternal love. She bewailed her restricted condition, as it was the means of retarding my happiness; told me that Lord Quiverwit, by her brother's permission, had been to drink tea with her that very afternoon, and actually proposed marriage; and seeing me extremely affected with this piece of information, offered to give me a convincing proof of her affection, by espousing me in private, and leaving the rest to fate. I was penetrated with this instance of her regard, but that I might not be outdone in generosity, resisted the bewitching temptation, in consideration of her honour and interest; at the same time, I presented my ring as a pledge of my inviolable attachment, and on my knees implored Heaven to shower its curses on my head, if ever my heart should entertain one thought unworthy of the passion I then avowed. She received my token, gave me in return her picture in miniature, exquisitely drawn, and set in gold; and in the same posture called Heaven to witness, and to judge her flame. Our vows being thus reciprocally breathed, a confidence of hope ensued, and our mutual fondness becoming as intimate as innocence would allow, I grew insensible of the progress of time, and it was morning before I could tear myself from this darling of my soul!—My good angel foresaw what would happen, and permitted me to indulge myself on this occasion, in consideration of the fatal absence I was doomed to suffer.

I went to bed immediately on my return to my lodging, and having slept about two hours, was waked by Strap, who, in great confusion, told me there was a footman below with a letter, which he would deliver to nobody but myself. Alarmed at this piece of news, I desired my friend to show him up to my chamber, and received the following letter, which, he said, required an immediate answer:

"SIR,—When any man injures my honour, let the difference of rank between us be ever so great, I am contented to waive the privilege of my quality, and to seek reparation from him on equal terms. The insolence of your reply to me yesterday in the Long Room I might have overlooked, had not your presumptive emulation in a much more interesting affair, and a discovery which I made this morning, concurred in persuading me to chastise your audacity with my sword. If you, therefore, have spirit enough to support the character you assume, you will not fail to follow the bearer immediately to a convenient place, where you shall be met by

"QUIVERWIT."

Whether I was enervated by the love and favour of Narcissa,

or awed by the superior station of my antagonist, I know not, but I never had less inclination to fight than at this time. However, finding there was a necessity for vindicating the reputation of my mistress, as well as for asserting my own honour, I forthwith rose, and dressing in a hurry, put on my sword, bade Strap attend me, and set out with my conductor, cursing my bad fortune all the way for having been observed in my return from my angel; for so I interpreted his lordship's discovery. When I came within sight of my rival, his lacquey told me he had orders to stop; upon which, I commanded Strap to halt also, while I walked forward, resolving, if possible, to come to an explanation with my challenger before we should come to battle. Nor was an opportunity wanting; for I no sooner approached, than he asked, with a stern countenance, what business I had in Mr. Topehall's garden so early in the morning? "I don't know, my lord," said I, "how to answer a question put to me with such magisterial haughtiness. If your lordship will please to expostulate calmly, you will have no cause to repent of your condescension; otherwise, I am not to be intimidated into any confession." "There is no room for denial," answered he; "I saw you come out with my own eyes." "Did any other person see me?" said I. "I neither know nor care," said he; "I want no other evidence than that of my own senses." Pleased to hear that the suspicion was confined to him alone, I endeavoured to appease his jealousy by owning an intrigue with the waiting-maid; but he had too much discernment to be so easily imposed upon, and told me there was only one way to convince him of the truth of what I alleged, which was no other than renouncing all claim to Narcissa upon oath, and promising, upon honour, never to speak to her for the future. Exasperated at this proposal, I unsheathed my sword, saying, "Heavens! what title have you, or any man on earth, to impose such terms on me!" He did the same, and making towards me with a contracted brow, said I was a villain, and had dishonoured Narcissa. "He's a scandalous villain," I replied, in a transport of fury, "who brands me with that imputation! She is a thousand times more chaste than the mother that bore you; and I will assert her honour with my heart's blood!" So saying, I rushed upon him with more eagerness than address, and endeavouring to get within his point, received a wound in my neck, which redoubled my rage. He excelled me in temper as well as in skill, by which means he parried my thrusts with great calmness, until I had almost exhausted my spirits; and when he perceived me beginning to flag, attacked me fiercely in his turn. Finding himself, however, better opposed than he expected, he resolved to follow his longe and close with me: accordingly, his sword entered my waistcoat, on the side of the breastbone, and running up between my shirt and skin, appeared over my shoulder. I imagined that his weapon had perforated my lungs, and, of consequence, that the wound was mortal; therefore, determined not to die unrevenged, I seized his shell, which was close to my breast, before he could disentangle his point, and keeping it fast with my left hand, shortened my own sword with my right, intending to run him through the heart; but he received the thrust in the left arm, which penetrated up to the shoulder-blade. Disappointed in this expectation, and afraid still that death would frustrate my revenge, I grappled with him, and, being much the stronger, threw him upon the ground, where I wrested his sword out of his hand; and so great was my confusion, instead of turning the point upon him, struck out three of his fore teeth with the hilt. In the meantime, our servants seeing us fall, ran up to separate and assist us; but, before their approach, I was upon my feet, and had discovered that my supposed mortal wound was only a slight scratch. The knowledge of my own safety disarmed me of a good deal of my resentment, and I began to inquire with some concern into the situation of my antagonist, who remained on the ground bleeding plentifully at his mouth and arm; I helped his footman to raise him, and having bound up his wound with my handkerchief, assured him it was not dangerous; I likewise restored his sword, and offered to support him to his house. He thanked me with an air of sullen dignity, and whispering that I should hear from him soon, went away, leaning on his servant's shoulder.

I was surprised at this promise, which I construed into a threat; and resolved, if ever he should call me out again, to use whatever advantage fortune might give me over him in another manner. In the meantime, I had leisure to take notice of Strap, who seemed quite stupefied with horror. I comforted him with an assurance that I had received no damage, and explained the nature of this affair as we walked homeward. By the time I had got into my apartment, I found the wound in my neck stiff and uneasy, and a good deal of clotted blood run down upon my shirt. Upon which, I pulled off my coat and waistcoat, and unbuttoned my collar, that I might dress it with more ease. My friend no sooner perceived my shirt quite dyed with blood, than imagining I had got at least twenty thousand wounds he cried, "O Jesus!" and fell flat on the floor. I stopped the bleeding with a little dry lint, and applying a plaster over it, cleansed myself from the gore, shifted and dressed, while he lay senseless at my feet; so that, when he recovered, and saw me perfectly well, he could scarce believe his own eyes. Now that the danger was past, I was very well pleased with what had happened, hoping that it would soon become known, and, consequently, dignify my character not a little in this place. I was also proud of having shown myself, in some shape, worthy the love of Narcissa, who, I was persuaded, would not think the worse of me for what I had done.

CHAPTER LX

I am visited by Freeman, with whom I appear in Public, and am caressed —Am sent for by Lord Quiverwit, whose Presence I quit in a Passion— Narcissa is carried off by her Brother—I intend to pursue him, and am dissuaded by my Friend—Engage in Play, and lose all my Money—Set out for London—Try my Fortune at the Gaming-table without Success —Receive a Letter from Narcissa—Bilk my Tailor.

WHILE I entertained myself with these reflections, the news of the duel being communicated by some unknown channel, spread all over the town. I was visited by Freeman, who testified his surprise at finding me; for he was told that Lord Quiverwit being dead of his wounds, I had absconded, in order to avoid the cognisance of the law. I asked if people guessed the occasion of the quarrel; and, understanding it was attributed to his lordship's resentment of my reply in the Long Room, confirmed that conjecture, glad to find Narcissa unsuspected. My friend, after I had assured him that my antagonist was in no danger, wished me joy of the event, than which, he said, nothing could happen more opportunely to support the idea he had given of my character to his friends, among whom he had been very assiduous in my behalf.

On the strength of this assurance, I went with him to the coffee-house, where I was saluted by a great many of those very persons who had shunned me the preceding day; and I found everybody making merry with the story of Melinda's French gallant. While I remained in this place, I received a message from Lord Quiverwit, desiring, if I was not engaged, to see me at his house.

Thither I immediately repaired, and was conducted to an

apartment, where I was received by his lordship in bed. When we were left by ourselves, he thanked me, in very polite terms, for having used the advantage fortune had given me over him with such moderation; and asked pardon for any offence his resentment might have prompted him to commit. "I would willingly," said he, "make you my friend; but as it is impossible for me to divest myself of my passion for Narcissa, I am too well convinced of your sentiments to think we shall ever agree on that subject. I took the liberty, therefore, of sending for you, in order to own candidly that I cannot help opposing your success with that young lady; though at the same time, I promise to regulate my opposition by the dictates of justice and honour. This, however, I think proper to advertise you of, that she has no independent fortune; and if you should even succeed in your addresses, you would have the mortification to see her reduced to indigence, unless you have wherewithal to support her; and I am credibly informed of your incapacity that way. Nay, I will confess that, urged by this consideration, I have actually sent notice to her brother of the progress I suspect you have made in her affection, and desired him to take his precautions accordingly." Alarmed and provoked at this information, I told his lordship that I did not see how he could reconcile that piece of conduct with his profession of open dealing, and flung away from him in a passion.

As I walked homeward, in hope of hearing from my mistress as usual, by means of Miss Williams, I was surprised with the waving of a handkerchief from the window of a coach and six that passed by me at full speed; and upon further observation, I saw a servant on horseback riding after it, who I knew by his livery belonged to the squire. Thunderstruck with this discovery, the knowledge of my misfortune rushed all at once on my reflection! I guessed immediately that the signal was made by the dear hand of Narcissa, who, being hurried away in consequence of Lord Quiverwit's message to her brother, had no other method of relating her distress and imploring my assistance. Frantic with this conjecture, I ran to my lodgings, snatched my pistols, and ordered Strap to get post-horses, with such incoherence of speech and disorder, that the poor valet, terrified with the suspicion of another duel, instead of providing what I desired, went forthwith to Freeman, who, being informed of my behaviour, came straight to my apartment, and conjured me so pathetically to make him acquainted with the cause of my uneasiness, that I could not refuse telling him my happiness was fled with Narcissa, and that I must retrieve her, or perish. He represented the madness of such an undertaking, and endeavoured to divert me from it with great strength of friendship and reason. But all his arguments would have been ineffectual, had he not put me in mind of the dependence I ought to have on the love of Narcissa, and the attachment of her maid, who could not fail of finding opportunities to advertise me of their situation; and at the same time demonstrated the injury my charmer's reputation must suffer from my precipitate retreat. I was convinced and composed by these considerations. I appeared in public with an air of tranquillity, was well received by the best company in town, and, my misfortune taking air, condoled accordingly; while I had the satisfaction of seeing Melinda so universally discountenanced, that she was fain to return to London, in order to avoid the scoffs and censure of the ladies of Bath. But though the hope of hearing from the darling of my soul supported my spirits a little while, I began to be very uneasy when, at the end of several weeks, I found that expectation disappointed. In short, melancholy and despondence took possession of my soul; and repining at that Providence which, by acting the stepmother towards me, kept me from the fruition of my wishes, I determined in a fit of despair to risk all I had at the gaming-table, with a view of acquiring a fortune sufficient to render me independent for life, or of plunging myself into such a state of misery as would effectually crush every ambitious hope that now tortured my imagination.

Actuated by this fatal resolution, I engaged in play, and after some turns of fortune, found myself at the end of three days worth a thousand pounds; but it was not my intention to stop here, for which cause I kept Strap ignorant of my success, and continued my career, until I was reduced to five guineas, which I would have hazarded also, had I not been ashamed to fall from a bet of two hundred pounds to such a petty sum.

Having thus executed my scheme, I went home, amazed to find myself so much at ease, and informed my friend Strap of my mischance, with such calmness, that he, imagining I joked, affected to receive the tidings with great equanimity. But both he and I found ourselves mistaken very soon. I had misinterpreted my own stupidity into deliberate resignation; and he had reason to believe me in earnest, when he saw me next morning agitated with the most violent despair, which he endeavoured to alleviate with all the consolation in his power.

In one of my lucid intervals, however, I charged him to take a place in the stage-coach for London, and in the meantime pay my debts in Bath, which amounted to thirty shillings only. Without taking leave of my friends, I embarked, Strap having the good fortune to find a return-horse, and arrived in town without having met with anything remarkable on the road While we crossed Bagshot Heath, I was seized with a sort of inclination to retrieve my fortune, by laying passengers under contribution in some such place. My thoughts were so circumstanced at this time, that I should have digested the crime of robbery, so righteously had I concerted my plan, and ventured my life in the execution, had I not been deterred by reflecting upon the infamy that attends detection.

The apartment I formerly lived in being unengaged, I took possession of it, and next day went in quest of Banter, who received me with open arms, in expectation of having his bond discharged to his liking. But when he understood what had happened, his countenance changed of a sudden; and he told me, with a dryness of displeasure peculiar to himself, that, if he was in my place, he would put it out of fortune's power to play him such another trick, and be avenged of his own indiscretion at once. When I desired him to explain his meaning, he pointed to his neck, raised himself on his tip-toes, and was going away without any further ceremony, when I put him in mind of my indigence, and demanded the five guineas I had formerly lent him. "Five guineas!" cried he. "Zounds! had you acted with common prudence, you might have had twenty thousand in your pocket by this time. I depended upon five hundred from you, as much as if I had had notes for it in the bank; and by all the rules of equity, you are indebted to me for that sum." I was neither pleased nor convinced by this computation, and insisted on my right with such determined obstinacy, that he was fain to alter his tone, and appease my clamour, by assuring me that he was not master of five shillings. Society in distress generally promotes good understanding among people; from being a dun, I descended to be a client, and asked his advice about repairing my losses. He counselled me to have recourse again to the gaming-table, where I succeeded so well before, and put myself in a condition by selling my watch. I followed his directions, and having accommodated him with a few pieces, went to the place, where I lost every shilling.

Then I returned to my lodgings full of desperate resolution and having made Strap acquainted with my fate, ordered him to pawn my sword immediately, that I might be enabled to make another effort. This affectionate creature no sooner understood my purpose, than, seized with insuppressible sorrow at the prospect of my misery, he burst into tears, and asked what I proposed to do, after the small sum he could raise on the sword should be spent? "On my own account," said he, "I am quite unconcerned; for, while God spares me health and these ten fingers, I can earn a comfortable subsistence anywhere; but what must become of you, who have less humility to stoop, and more appetites to gratify?" Here I interrupted him, by saying, with a gloomy aspect, I should never want a resource while I had a loaded pistol in possession. Stupefied with horror at this dreadful insinuation, he stood mute for some time, and then broke out into, "God of his infinite mercy enable you to withstand that temptation of the devil! Consider your immortal soul—there is no repentance in the grave. O Lord! that ever we should come to this.—Are we not enjoined to resign ourselves to the will of Heaven!—where is your patience? *Durum patientia frango*—you are but a young man—there may be many good things in store for you—*Accidit in puncto, quod non speratur in anno*—remember your uncle, Mr. Bowling; perhaps he is now on his voyage homeward, pleasing himself with the hopes of seeing and relieving you; nay, peradventure he is already arrived, for the ship was expected about this time." A ray of hope shot athwart my soul at this suggestion; I thanked my friend for his seasonable recollection, and, after having promised to take no resolution till his return, dismissed him to Wapping for intelligence.

In his absence I was visited by Banter, who being informed of my bad luck at play, told me that fortune would probably be one day weary of persecuting me. "In the meantime," said he, "here is a letter for you, which I received just now enclosed in one from Freeman." I snatched it with eagerness, and knowing the superscription to be of Narcissa's handwriting, kissed it with transport, and having opened it, read:

"It is with great difficulty that I have stolen from the observation of those spies who are set over me, this opportunity of telling you that I was suddenly carried away from Bath by my brother, who was informed of our correspondence by Lord Quiverwit, whom, I since understand, you have wounded in a duel on my account. As I am fully convinced of your honour and love, I hope I shall never hear of such desperate proofs of either for the future. I am so strictly watched, that it will be impossible for you to see me until my brother's suspicions shall

abate, or Heaven contrive some other unforeseen event in ou
behalf. In the meantime you may depend on the constancy and
affection of

"Your own

"NARCISSA."

"P.S. Miss Williams, who is my fellow-prisoner, desires to be
remembered to you. We are both in good health, and only in
pain for you, especially as it will be impracticable for you to
convey any message or letter to the place of our confinement
for which reason, pray desist from the attempt, that, by mis-
carrying, might prolong our captivity.

"N——."

This kind letter afforded me great consolation. I communicated it to Banter, and at the same time showed him her picture
He approved of her beauty and good sense, and could not help
owning that my neglect of Miss Snapper was excusable, when
such a fine creature engrossed my attention.

I began to be reconciled to my fate, and imagined that, if I
could contrive means of subsisting until my uncle should arrive,
in case he was not already at home, he would enable me to do
something effectual in behalf of my love and fortune. I therefore
consulted Banter about a present supply, who no sooner understood that I had credit with a tailor, than he advised me to take
off two or three suits of rich clothes, and convert them into cash,
by selling them at half-price to a salesman in Monmouth Street.
I was startled at this proposal, which I thought savoured a
little of fraud; but he rendered it palatable, by observing, that
in a few months I might be in a condition to do everybody
justice; and in the meantime I was acquitted by the honesty of
my intention. I suffered myself to be persuaded by his salvo,
by which my necessity, rather than my judgment, was convinced; and when I found there were no accounts of the ship
in which my uncle embarked, actually put the scheme in practice,
and raised by it five and twenty guineas, paying him for his
advice with the odd five.

CHAPTER LXI

I am arrested—Carried to the Marshalsea—Find my old Acquaintance Beau Jackson in that Jail—He informs me of his Adventures—Strap arrives, and with difficulty is comforted—Jackson introduces me to a Poet—I admire his Conversation and Capacity—Am deeply affected with my Misfortune—Strap hires himself as a Journeyman Barber.

But this expedient was in a few weeks attended with a consequence I did not foresee; a player having purchased one of the suits which were exposed to sale, appeared in it on the stage one night while my tailor unfortunately happened to be present. He knew it immediately, and inquiring minutely into the affair, discovered my whole contrivance; upon which he came to my lodgings, and telling me that he was very much straitened for want of money, presented his bill, which amounted to fifty pounds. Surprised at this unexpected address, I affected to treat him cavalierly, swore some oaths, asked if he doubted my honour, and, telling him I should take care whom I dealt with for the future, bade him come again in three days. He obeyed me punctually, demanded his money, and finding himself amused with bare promises, arrested me that very day in the street. I was not much shocked at this adventure, which, indeed, put an end to a state of horrible expectation; but I refused to go to a spunging house, where I heard there was nothing but the most flagrant imposition; and a coach being called, was carried to the Marshalsea, attended by a bailiff and his follower, who were very much disappointed and chagrined at my resolution.

The turnkey, guessing from my appearance that I had money in my pocket, received me with the repetition of the Latin word *depone*, and gave me to understand that I must pay beforehand for the apartment I should choose to dwell in. I desired to see his conveniences, and hired a small paltry bedchamber for a crown a week, which, in any other place, would have let for half the money. Having taken possession of this dismal habitation, I sent for Strap, and my thoughts were busied in collecting matter of consolation to that faithful squire, when somebody knocked at my door, which I no sooner opened, than a young fellow entered, in very shabby clothes and marvellous foul linen. After a low bow, he called me by my name, and asked if I had forgot him. His voice assisted me in recollecting his person, whom I soon recognised to be my old acquaintance

Jackson, of whom mention is made in the first part of my memoirs. I saluted him cordially, expressed my satisfaction of finding him alive, and condoled him on his present situation which, however, did not seem to affect him much, for he laughed very heartily at the occasion of our meeting so unexpectedly in this place. Our mutual compliments being passed, I inquired about his amour with the lady of fortune, which seemed to be so near a happy conclusion when I had the pleasure of seeing him last; and, after an immoderate fit of laughter, he gave me to understand that he had been egregiously bit in that affair. "You must know," said he, "that a few days after our adventure with the bawd and her b—ches, I found means to be married to that same fine lady you speak of, and passed the night with her at her lodgings, so much to her satisfaction, that early in the morning, after a good deal of snivelling and sobbing, she owned, that, far from being an heiress of great fortune, she was no other than a common woman of the town, who had decoyed me into matrimony, in order to enjoy the privilege of a *femme couverte*; and that, unless I made my escape immediately, I should be arrested for a debt of her contracting, by bailiffs employed and instructed for that purpose. Startled at this intimation, I rose in a twinkling, and taking leave of my spouse with several hearty damns, got safe into the verge of the court, where I kept snug until I was appointed surgeon's mate of a man-of-war at Portsmouth; for which place I set out on Sunday, went on board of my ship, in which I sailed to the Straits, where I had the good fortune to be made surgeon of a sloop that came home a few months after, and was put out of commission; whereupon I came to London, imagining myself forgotten, and freed from my wife and her creditors; but had not been in town a week before I was arrested for a debt of hers, amounting to twenty pounds, and brought to this place, where I have been fixed by another action since that time. However, you know my disposition; I defy care and anxiety; and being on the half-pay list, make shift to live here tolerably easy." I congratulated him on his philosophy, and remembering that I was in his debt, repaid the money he formerly lent me, which, I believe, was far from being unseasonable. I then inquired about the economy of the place, which he explained to my satisfaction; and after we had agreed to mess together, he was just going to give orders for dinner, when Strap arrived.

I never in my life saw sorrow so extravagantly expressed in any countenance as in that of my honest friend, which was, ndeed, particularly adapted by nature for such impressions. When we were left by ourselves, I communicated to him my disaster, and endeavoured to console him with the same arguments he had formerly used to me, withal representing the fair chance I had of being relieved in a short time by Mr. Bowling. But his grief was unutterable; he seemed to give attention without listening, and wrung his hands in silence; so that I was in a fair way of being infected by his behaviour, when Jackson returned, and perceiving the deference I paid to Strap, although in a footman's habit, distributed his crumbs of comfort with such mirth, jollity, and unconcern, that the features of the distressed squire relaxed by degrees; he recovered the use of speech, and began to be a little more reconciled to this lamentable event. We dined together on boiled beef and greens, brought from a cook's shop in the neighbourhood; and although this meal was served up in a manner little corresponding with the sphere of life in which I had lately lived, I made a virtue of necessity, ate with good appetite, and treated my friends with a bottle of wine, which had the desired effect of increasing the good humour of my fellow-prisoner, and exhilarating the spirits of Strap, who now talked cavalierly of my misfortune.

After dinner, Jackson left us to our private affairs; when I desired my friend to pack up all our things and carry them to some cheap lodging he should choose for himself in the neighbourhood of the Marshalsea, after he had discharged my lodging, for which purpose I gave him money. I likewise recommended to him the keeping of my misfortune secret, and saying to my landlord, or any other who should inquire for me, that I was gone into the country for a few weeks; at the same time I laid strong injunctions upon him to call every second day upon Banter, in case he should receive any letter for me from Narcissa, by the channel of Freeman; and by all means to leave a direction for himself at my uncle's lodgings in Wapping, by which I might be found when my kinsman should arrive.

When he departed to execute these orders, which, by the bye, were punctually performed that very night, I found myself so little seasoned to my situation, that I dreaded reflection, and sought shelter from it in the company of the beau, who, promising to regale me with a lecture upon taste, conducted me to the common side, where I saw a number of naked miserable wretches assembled together. We had not been here many minutes, when a figure appeared, wrapt in a dirty rug, tied about his loins with two pieces of list, of different colours, knotted together; having a black bushy beard, and his head covered with a huge mass of brown periwig, which seemed to have been ravished from the head of some scarecrow. This apparition, stalking in with great solemnity, made a profound bow to the audience, who signified their approbation by a general response of "How d'ye do, doctor?" He then turned towards us, and honoured Jackson with a particular salutation. Upon which my friend, in a formal manner, introduced him to me by the name of Mr. Melopoyn. This ceremony being over, he advanced into the middle of the congregation, which crowded around him, and hemming three times, to my utter astonishment, pronounced, with great significance of voice and gesture, a very elegant and ingenious discourse upon the difference between genius and taste, illustrating his assertions with apt quotations from the best authors, ancient as well as modern. When he had finished his harangue, which lasted a full hour, he bowed again to the spectators, not one of whom, I was informed, understood so much as a sentence of what he had uttered. They manifested, however, their admiration and esteem by a voluntary contribution, which, Jackson told me, one week with another, amounted to eighteenpence. This moderate stipend, together with some small presents that he received for making up differences and deciding causes amongst the prisoners, just enabled him to breathe and walk about, in the grotesque figure I have described. I understood, also, that he was an excellent poet, and had composed a tragedy, which was allowed by everybody who had seen it to be a performance of great merit; that his learning was infinite, his morals unexceptionable, and his modesty invincible. Such a character could not fail of attracting my regard; I longed impatiently to be acquainted with him, and desired Jackson would engage him to spend the evening in my apartment. My request was granted, he favoured us with his company, and in the course of our conversation, perceiving that I had a strong passion for the *Belles Lettres*, acquitted himself so well on that subject, that I expressed a fervent desire of seeing his productions. In this point, too, he gratified my inclination; he promised to bring his tragedy to my room next day, and in the meantime entertained me with some detached pieces, which gave me a very advantageous idea of his poetical talent. Among other things, I was particularly pleased with some elegies in imitation of Tibullus; one of which I beg leave to submit to the reader, as a specimen of his complexion and capacity.

Where now are all my flattering dreams of joy?
Monimia, give my soul her wonted rest:—
    Since first the beauty fix'd my roving eye,
Heart-gnawing cares corrode my pensive breast!

Let happy lovers fly where pleasures call,
With festive songs beguile the fleeting hour;
    Lead beauty through the mazes of the ball,
Or press her wanton in love's roseate bower.

For me, no more I'll range th' empurpled mead,
Where shepherds pipe, and virgins dance around;
    Nor wander through the woodbine's fragrant shade
To hear the music of the grove resound.

I'll seek some lonely church, or dreary hall,
Where fancy paints the glimm'ring taper blue,
    Where damps hang mould'ring on the ivy'd wall,
And sheeted ghosts drink up the midnight dew.

There, leagu'd with hopeless anguish and despair,
Awhile in silence o'er my fate repine:
    Then, with a long farewell to love and care,
To kindred dust my weary limbs consign.

Wilt thou, Monimia, shed a gracious tear
On the cold grave where all my sorrows rest;
    Strew vernal flowers, applaud my love sincere,
And bid the turf lie easy on my breast?

I was wonderfully affected with this pathetic complaint, which seemed so well calculated for my own disappointment in love, that I could not help attaching the idea of Narcissa to the name of Monimia, and of forming such melancholy presages of my passion, that I could not recover my tranquillity, and was fain to have recourse to the bottle, which prepared me for a profound sleep, that I could not otherwise have enjoyed. Whether these impressions invited and introduced a train of other melancholy reflections, or my fortitude was all exhausted in the effort I made against despondence during the first day of my imprisonment, I cannot determine; but I awoke in the horrors, and found my imagination haunted with such dismal apparitions, that I was ready to despair; and I believe the reader will own I had no great cause to congratulate myself, when I considered my situation. I was interrupted in the midst of these gloomy apprehensions by the arrival of Strap, who contributed not a little to the re-establishment of my peace by letting me know that he had hired himself as a journeyman barber; by which means he would be able not only to save me a considerable expense, but even make shift to lay up something for my subsistence after my money should be spent, in case I should not be relieved before.

CHAPTER LXII

I read Melopoyn's Tragedy, and conceive a vast opinion of his Genius—
He recounts his Adventures.

WHILE we ate our breakfast together, I made him acquainted
with the character and condition of the poet, who came in with
his play at that instant, and imagining we were engaged about
business, could not be prevailed upon to sit; but, leaving his
performance, went away. My friend's tender heart was melted
at the sight of a gentleman and Christian (for he had a great
veneration for both these epithets) in such misery; and assented,
with great cheerfulness, to a proposal I made of clothing him
with our superfluities; a task with which he charged himself,
and departed immediately to perform it.

He was no sooner gone, than I locked my door, and sat down
to the tragedy, which I read to the end with vast pleasure, not
a little amazed at the conduct of the managers who had rejected
it. The fable, in my opinion, was well chosen and naturally
conducted; the incidents interesting, the characters beautifully
contrasted, strongly marked, and well supported; the diction
poetical, spirited, and correct; the unities of the drama maintained with the most scrupulous exactness; the opening gradual
and engaging, the *peripeteia* surprising, and the catastrophe
affecting. In short, I judged it by the laws of Aristotle and
Horace, and could find nothing in it exceptionable, but a little
too much embellishment in some few places, which objection
he removed to my satisfaction by a quotation from Aristotle's
Poetics, importing that the least interesting parts of a poem
ought to be raised and dignified by the charms and energy
of diction.

I revered his genius, and was seized with an eager curiosity
to know the particular events of a fortune so unworthy of his
merit. At that instant Strap returned with a bundle of clothes,
which I sent with my compliments to Mr. Melopoyn, as a small
token of my regard, and desired the favour of his company to
dinner. He accepted my present and invitation, and in less
than half an hour made his appearance in a decent dress, which
altered his figure very much to his advantage. I perceived, by
his countenance, that his heart was big with gratitude, and
endeavoured to prevent his acknowledgments, by asking pardon
for the liberty I had taken; he made no reply, but, with an aspect

full of admiration and esteem, bowed to the ground, while the tears gushed from his eyes. Affected with these symptoms of an ingenuous mind, I shifted the conversation, and complimented him on his performance, which, I assured him, afforded me infinite pleasure. My approbation made him happy; dinner being served, and Jackson arrived, I begged their permission for Strap to sit at table with us, after having informed them that he was a person to whom I was extremely obliged; they were kind enough to grant that favour, and we ate together with great harmony and satisfaction.

Our meal being ended, I expressed my wonder at the little regard Mr. Melopoyn had met with from the world; and signified a desire of hearing how he had been treated by the managers of the playhouses, to whom I understood from Jackson he had offered his tragedy without success. "There is so little entertaining in the incidents of my life," said he, "that I am sure the recital will not recompense your attention; but, since you discover an inclination to know them, I understand my duty too well to disappoint your desire.

"My father, who was a curate in the country, being, by the narrowness of his circumstances, hindered from maintaining me at the university, took the charge of my education upon himself, and laboured with such industry and concern in the undertaking, that I had little cause to regret the want of public masters. Being at great pains to consult my natural bias, he discovered in me, betimes, an inclination for poetry; upon which he recommended me to an intimate acquaintance with the classics, in the cultivation of which he assisted me with paternal zeal and uncommon erudition. When he thought me sufficiently acquainted with the ancients, he directed my studies to the best modern authors, French and Italian, as well as English, and laid a particular injunction upon me to make myself master of my mother tongue.

"About the age of eighteen, I grew ambitious of undertaking a work of some consequence; and, with my father's approbation, actually planned the tragedy you have read; but, before I had finished four acts, that indulgent parent died, and left my mother and me in very indigent circumstances. A near relation, compassionating our distress, took us into his family, where I brought my fable to a conclusion; and soon after that period my mother quitted this life. When my sorrow for this melancholy event had subsided, I told my kinsman, who was a farmer, that having paid my last duty to my parent, I had now no attachment to detain me in the country, and therefore wa resolved to set out for London, and offer my play to the stage where I did not doubt of acquiring a large share of fame as wel as fortune; in which case I should not be unmindful of m friends and benefactors. My cousin was ravished with th prospect of my felicity, and willingly contributed towards th expense of fitting me out for my expedition.

"Accordingly I took a place in the waggon, and arrived i town, where I hired an apartment in a garret, willing to live a frugal as possible, until I should know what I had to expec from the manager to whom I intended to offer my play; for though I looked upon myself as perfectly secure of a goo reception, imagining that a patentee would be as eager t receive, as I to present my production, I did not know whethe or not he might be pre-engaged in favour of another author, a circumstance that would certainly retard my success. On thi consideration, too, I determined to be speedy in my application and even to wait upon one of the managers the very next day For this purpose, I inquired of my landlord if he knew where either or both of them lived; and he, being curious to know my business, and at the same time appearing to be a very honest, friendly man (a tallow-chandler), I made him acquainted with my design; upon which he told me that I went the wrong way to work; that I would not find such easy access to a manager as I imagined; and that, if I delivered my performance without proper recommendation, it would be as one to a thousand if ever it should be minded. 'Take my advice,' said he, 'and your business is done. One of the patentees is a good Catholic, as I am, and uses the same father who confesses me. I will make you acquainted with this good priest, who is an excellent scholar, and if he should approve of your play, his recommendation will go a long way in determining Mr. Supple to bring it on the stage.' I applauded his expedient, and was introduced to the friar, who, having perused the tragedy, was pleased to signify his approbation, and commended me, in particular, for having avoided all reflections upon religion. He promised to use all his influence with his son Supple in my behalf, and to inform himself that very day at what time it would be proper for me to wait upon him with the piece. He was punctual in performing his engagement, and next morning gave me to understand that he had mentioned my affair to the manager, and that I had no more to do than to go to his house any time in the forenoon, and make use of his name, upon which I should find immediate admittance. I took this advice, put my performance in my bosom, and, having received directions, went immediately to the house of Mr. Supple, and knocked at the door, which had a wicket in the middle, faced with a network of iron. Through this a servant having viewed me for some time, demanded to know my business. I told him my business was with Mr. Supple, and that I came from Mr. O'Varnish. He examined my appearance once more, then went away, returned in a few minutes, and said his master was busy, and could not be seen. Although I was a little mortified at my disappointment, I was persuaded that my reception was owing to Mr. Supple's ignorance of my errand; and, that I might meet with no more obstructions of the same kind, I desired Mr. O'Varnish to be my introductor the next time. He complied with my request, and obtained immediate admittance to the manager, who received me with the utmost civility, and promised to read my play with the first convenience. By his own appointment, I called again in a fortnight, but he was gone out; I returned in a week after, and the poor gentleman was extremely ill; I renewed my visit in a fortnight after that, and he assured me he had been so much fatigued with business, that he had not been able as yet to read it to an end; but he would take the first opportunity; and, in the meantime, observed that what he had just seen of it was very entertaining. I comforted myself with this declaration a few weeks longer, at the end of which I appeared again before his wicket, was let in, and found him laid up with the gout. I no sooner entered his chamber, than, looking at me with a languishing eye, he said, 'Mr. Melopoyn, I'm heartily sorry for an accident that has happened during my illness. You must know that my eldest boy, finding your manuscript upon the table in the dining-room, where I used to read it, carried it into the kitchen, and leaving it there, a negligent wench of a cook-maid, mistaking it for waste paper, has expended it all but a few leaves in singeing fowls upon the spit. But I hope the misfortune is not irreparable, since, no doubt, you have several copies.'

"I protest to you, my good friend, Mr. Random, I was extremely shocked at this information; but the good-natured gentleman seemed to be so much affected with my misfortune, that I suppressed my concern, and told him that, although I had not another copy, I should be able to retrieve the loss by writing another from my memory, which was very tenacious. You cannot imagine how well pleased Mr. Supple was at this assurance; he begged I would set about it immediately, and carefully revolve and recollect every circumstance, before I pretended to commit it to paper, that it might be the same individual play that he had perused. Encouraged by this injunction, which plainly demonstrated how much he interested himself in the affair, I tasked my remembrance and industry, and in three weeks produced the exact image of the former, which was conveyed to him by my good friend, Father O'Varnish, who told me next day that Mr. Supple would revise it superficially, in order to judge of its sameness with the other, and then give his final answer. For this examination I allotted a week; and in full confidence of seeing it acted in a little while, demanded an audience of the manager when that term was expired. But alas! the season had slipped away insensibly; he convinced me that, if my play had been put into rehearsal at that time, it could not have been ready for performing until the end of March, when the benefit nights came on; consequently it would have interfered with the interest of the players, whom it was not my business to disoblige.

"I was fain to acquiesce in these reasons, which to be sure were extremely just, and to reserve my performance for the next season, when he hoped I would not be so unlucky. Although it was a grievous disappointment to me, who by this time began to want both money and necessaries: having, on the strength of my expectation from the theatre, launched out into some extravagances, by which the sum I brought to town was already almost consumed. Indeed, I ought to be ashamed at this circumstance of my conduct; for my finances were sufficient, with good economy, to have maintained me comfortably a whole year. You will perhaps be amazed when I tell you that in six months I expended not a farthing less than ten guineas: but when one considers the temptations to which a young man is exposed in this great city, especially if he is addicted to pleasure, as I am, the wonder will vanish, or at least abate. Nor was the cause of my concern limited to my own situation entirely: I had writ an account of my good reception to my kinsman, the farmer, and desired him to depend upon me for the money he had kindly accommodated me with about the end of February; which promise I now found myself unable to perform. However, there was no remedy but patience. I applied to my landlord, who was a very good-natured man, candidly owned my distress, and begged his advice in laying down some plan for my subsistence. He readily promised to consult his confessor on the subject, and told me I was welcome, in the meantime, to lodge and board with him, until fortune should put it in my power to make restitution.

"Mr. O'Varnish, being informed of my necessity, offered to introduce me to the author of a weekly paper, who, he did not doubt, would employ me in that way, provided he should find me duly qualified; but, upon inquiry, I understood that this journal was calculated to foment divisions in the commonwealth, and therefore I desired to be excused from engaging in it. He then proposed that I should write something in the poetical way, which I might dispose of to a bookseller for a pretty sum of ready money, and perhaps establish my own character into the bargain; this event would infallibly procure friends, and my tragedy would appear next season to the best advantage, by being supported both by interest and reputation. I was charmed with this prospect, and having heard what friends Mr. Pope acquired by his pastorals, set about a work of that kind, and in less than six weeks composed as many eclogues, which I forthwith offered to an eminent bookseller, who desired me to leave them for his perusal, and he would give me an answer in two days. At the end of that time I went to him, when he returned the poems, telling me they would not answer his purpose, and sweetened his refusal by saying there were some good clever lines in them. Not a little dejected at this rebuff, which I learned from Mr. O'Varnish was owing to the opinion of another author, whom this bookseller always consulted on these occasions, I applied to another person of the same profession who told me the town was cloyed with pastorals, and advised me, if I intended to profit by my talents, to write something satirical or luscious, such as *The Button Hole, Shockey and Towzer, The Leaky Vessel*, etc.—and yet this was a man in years, who wore a reverend periwig, looked like a senator, and went regularly to church. Be that as it will, I scorned to prostitute my pen in the manner he proposed, and carried my papers to a third, who assured me that poetry was entirely out of his way; and asked if I had got never a piece of secret history, thrown into a series of letters, or a volume of adventures, such as those of Robinson Crusoe and Colonel Jack, or a collection of conundrums, wherewith to entertain the plantations? Being quite unfurnished for this dealer, I had recourse to another with as little success; and I verily believe was rejected by the whole trade.

"I was afterwards persuaded to offer myself as a translator, and accordingly repaired to a person who was said to entertain numbers of that class in his pay; he assured me he had already a great deal of that work on his hands, which he did not know what to do with; observed that translation was a mere drug, that branch of literature being overstocked with an inundation of authors from North Britain; and asked what I would expect per sheet for rendering the Latin classics into English. That I might not make myself too cheap, I determined to set a high price upon my qualifications, and demanded half a guinea for every translated sheet. 'Half a guinea!' cried he, staring at me, then paused a little, and said, 'he had no occasion for my service at present.' I found my error, and, resolving to make amends, fell one-half in my demand; upon which he stared at me again, and told me his hands were full. I attempted others, without finding employment, and was actually reduced to a very uncomfortable prospect, when I bethought myself of offering my talents to the printers of halfpenny ballads, and other such occasional essays as are hawked about the streets. With this view, I applied to one of the most noted and vociferous of this tribe, who directed me to a person whom I found entertaining a whole crowd of them with gin, bread, and cheese; he carried me into a little back parlour, very neatly furnished, where I signified my desire of being enrolled among his writers; and was asked what kind of composition I professed? Understanding that my inclination leaned towards poetry, he expressed his satisfaction, telling me one of his poets had lost his senses, and was confined in Bedlam, and the other was become dozed with drinking drams; so that he had not done anything tolerable these many weeks. When I proposed that we should enter into terms of agreement, he gave me to understand that his bargains were always conditional, and his authors paid in proportion to the sale of their works.

"Having therefore settled these conditions, which, I do assure you, were not very advantageous to me, he assigned me a subject for a ballad, which was to be finished in two hours; and I returned to my garret in order to perform his injunction. As the theme happened to suit my fancy, I completed a pretty sort of an ode within the time prescribed, and brought it to him big with hope of profit and applause. He read it in a twinkling, and, to my utter astonishment, told me it would not do, though indeed he owned I wrote a good hand, and spelled very well, but my language was too high-flown, and of consequence not at all adapted to the capacity and taste of his customers. I promised to rectify that mistake, and in half an hour humbled

my style to the comprehension of vulgar readers; he approved
of the alteration, and gave me some hopes of succeeding in time,
though he observed that my performance was very deficient
in the quaintness of expression that pleases the multitude;
however, to encourage me, he ventured the expense of printing
and paper, and, if I remember aright, my share of the sale
amounted to fourpence halfpenny.

"From that day I studied the Grub Street manner with great
diligence, and at length became such a proficient, that my
works were in great request among the most polite of the
chairmen, draymen, hackney coachmen, footmen, and servant-
maids. Nay, I have enjoyed the pleasure of seeing my productions
adorned with cuts, pasted upon the wall as ornaments in beer
cellars and cobblers' stalls, and have actually heard them sung
in clubs of substantial tradesmen. But empty praise, you know,
my dear friend, will not supply the cravings of nature. I found
myself in danger of starving in the midst of all my fame; for of
ten songs I composed, it was well if two had the good fortune
to please. For this reason I turned my thoughts to prose, and,
during a tract of gloomy weather, published an apparition
on the substance of which I subsisted very comfortably a whole
month; I have made many a good meal upon a monster; a rape
has often afforded me great satisfaction; but a murder, well
timed, was my never-failing resource. What then? I was a most
miserable slave to my employers, who expected to be furnished
at a minute's warning with prose and verse, just as they thought
the circumstances of the times required, whether the inclination
was absent or present. Upon my sincerity, Mr. Random, I have
been so much pestered and besieged by those children of clamour,
that life became a burden to me.

CHAPTER LXIII

The Continuation and Conclusion of Mr. Melopoyn's Story.

"I MADE shift, notwithstanding, to maintain myself till the
beginning of next winter, when I renewed my addresses to my
friend Mr. Supple, and was most graciously received. 'I have
been thinking of your affair, Mr. Melopoyn,' said he, 'and am
determined to show how far I have your interest at heart, by
introducing you to a young nobleman, of my acquaintance,
who is remarkable for his fine taste in dramatic writings, and is,

besides, a man of such influence, that, if once he should approve of your play, his patronage will support it against all the efforts of envy and ignorance: for I do assure you that merit alone will not bring success. I have already spoke of your performance to Lord Rattle, and if you will call at my house in a day or two, you shall have a letter of introduction to his lordship.' I was sensibly touched with this mark of Mr. Supple's friendship, and looking upon my affair as already done, went home and imparted my good fortune to my landlord, who, to render my appearance more acceptable to my patron, procured a suit of new clothes for me on his own credit.

"Not to trouble you with idle particulars, I carried my tragedy to his lordship's lodgings, and sent it up, along with Mr. Supple's letter, by one of his servants, who desired me, by his lord's order, to return in a week. I did so, and was admitted to his lordship, who received me very courteously, told me he had perused my play, which he thought, on the whole, was the best *coup d'essai* he had ever seen; but that he had marked some places in the margin which he imagined might be altered for the better. I was transported with this reception, and promised, with many acknowledgments of his lordship's generosity, to be governed solely by his advice and direction. 'Well then,' said he, 'write another fair copy with the alterations I have proposed, and bring it to me as soon as possible; for I am resolved to have it brought on the stage this winter.' You may be sure I set about this task with alacrity; and though I found his lordship's remarks much more numerous, and of less importance, than I expected, I thought it was not my interest to dispute upon trifles with my patron; therefore new modelled it, according to his desire, in less than a month.

"When I waited upon him with the manuscript, I found one of the actors at breakfast with his lordship, who immediately introduced him to my acquaintance, and desired him to read a scene of my play. This task he performed very much to my satisfaction, with regard to emphasis and pronunciation; but he signified his disgust at several words in every page, which I presuming to defend, Lord Rattle told me, with a peremptory look, I must not pretend to dispute with him, who had been a player these twenty years, and understood the economy of the stage better than any man living. I was forced to submit, and his lordship proposed the same actor should read the whole play in the evening before some gentlemen of his acquaintance, whom he would convene at his lodgings for that purpose.

"I was present at the reading; and I protest to you, my dear friend, I never underwent such a severe trial in the whole course of my life as at that juncture; for although the player might be a very honest man, and a good performer, he was excessively illiterate and assuming, and made a thousand frivolous objections, which I was not permitted to answer. However, the piece was very much applauded on the whole; the gentlemen present, who, I understood, were men of fortune, promised to countenance and support it as much as they could; and Lord Rattle assuring me that he would act the part of a careful nurse to it, desired me to carry it home, and alter it immediately according to their remarks. I was fain to acquiesce in his determination, and fulfilled his injunctions with all the expedition in my power: but before I could present the new copy, my good friend Mr. Supple had disposed of his property and patent to one Mr. Brayer; so that fresh interest was to be made with the new manager. This task Lord Rattle undertook, having some acquaintance with him, and recommended my performance so strongly that it was received.

"I looked upon myself now as upon the eve of reaping the fruits of all my labour. I waited a few days in expectation of its being put into rehearsal, and wondering at the delay, applied to my worthy patron, who excused Mr. Brayer, on account of the multiplicity of business in which he was involved, and bade me beware of teasing the patentee. I treasured up this caution, and exerted my patience three weeks longer; at the end of which his lordship gave me to understand that Mr. Brayer had read my play, and owned it had indubitable merit; but as he had long been pre-engaged to another author, he could not possibly represent it that season; though, if I would reserve it for the next, and, in the interim, make such alterations as he had proposed by observations on the margin, I might depend upon his compliance.

"Thunderstruck at this disappointment, I could not, for some minutes, utter one syllable. At length, however, I complained bitterly of the manager's insincerity in amusing me so long, when he knew from the beginning that he could not gratify my desire. But his lordship reprimanded me for my freedom, said Mr. Brayer was a man of honour, and imputed his behaviour with respect to me to nothing else but forgetfulness. And indeed I have had some reason, since that time, to be convinced of his bad memory; for, in spite of appearances, I will not allow myself to interpret his conduct any other way. Lord Rattle, observing me very much affected with my disappointment, offered his interest to bring on my play at the other house, which I eagerly accepting, he forthwith wrote a letter of recommendation to Mr. Bellower, actor, and prime minister to Mr. Vandal, proprietor of that theatre; and desired me to deliver it with my tragedy without loss of time. Accordingly, I hastened to his house, where, after having waited a whole hour in a lobby, I was admitted to his presence, and my performance received with great state. He told me he was extremely busy at present, but he would peruse it as soon as possible, and bade me call again in a week. I took my leave not a little astonished at the pert and supercilious behaviour of this stage-player, who had not treated me with good manners; and began to think the dignity of a poet greatly impaired since the days of Euripides and Sophocles; but all this was nothing in comparison to what I have since observed.

"Well, Mr. Random, I went back at the appointed time, and was told that Mr. Bellower was engaged, and could not see me. I repeated my visit a few days after, and, having waited a considerable time, was favoured with an audience, during which he said he had not as yet read my play. Nettled at this usage, I could contain myself no longer, but telling him I imagined he would have paid more deference to Lord Rattle's recommendation, demanded my manuscript with some expressions of resentment. 'Ay,' said he, in a theatrical tone, 'with all my heart.' Then pulling out a drawer of the bureau at which he sat, he took out a bundle, and threw it upon a table that was near him, pronouncing the word 'There' with great disdain. I took it up, and perceiving, with some surprise, that it was a comedy, told him it did not belong to me; upon which he offered me another, which I also disclaimed. A third was produced, and rejected for the same reason. At length he pulled out a whole handful, and spread them before me, saying, 'There are seven— take which you please—or take them all.' I singled out my own, and went away, struck dumb with admiration at what I had seen—not so much on account of his insolence, as of the number of new plays, which from this circumstance I concluded were yearly offered to the stage. You may be sure I did not fail to carry my complaint to my patron, who did not receive it with all the indignation I expected; but taxed me with precipitation, and told me I must lay my account with bearing the humours of the players, if I intended to write for the stage. 'There is now no other remedy,' said he, 'but to keep it till the next season for Mr. Brayer, and alter it at your leisure, in the summer, according to his directions.' I was now reduced to a terrible alternative, either to quit all hopes of my tragedy, from which I had all along promised myself a large share of fortune and reputation, or to encounter eight long months of adversity in preparing for and expecting its appearance. This last penance, painful as it was, seemed most eligible to my reflection at that time, and therefore I resolved to undergo it.

"Why should I tire you with particulars of no consequence? I wrestled with extreme poverty until the time of my probation was expired; and went to my Lord Rattle, in order to remind him of my affair, when I understood, to my great concern, that his lordship was just on the point of going abroad, and, which was still more unfortunate for me, Mr. Brayer had gone into the country, so that my generous patron had it not in his power to introduce me personally, as he intended. However, he wrote a very strong letter to the manager in my favour, and put him in mind of the promise he had made in behalf of my play.

"As soon as I was certified of Brayer's return, I went to his house with this letter, but was told he was gone out. I called again next day early in the morning, received the same answer, and was desired to leave my name and business; I did so, and returned the day after, when the servant still affirmed that his master was gone abroad, though I perceived him, as I retired, observing me through a window. Incensed at this discovery, I went to a coffee-house hard by, and enclosing his lordship's letter in one from myself, demanded a categorical answer. I sent it to his house by a porter, who returned in a few minutes, and told me Mr. Brayer would be glad to see me at that instant. I obeyed the summons, and was received with such profusion of compliments and apologies, that my resentment immediately subsided, and I was even in pain for the concern which this honest man showed at the mistake of his servant, who, it seems, had been ordered to deny him to everybody but me. He expressed the utmost veneration for his good and noble friend Lord Rattle, whom he should be always proud to serve; promised to peruse the play with all despatch, and give me a meeting upon it; and, as a testimony of his esteem, made me a present of a general order for the season, by which I should be admitted to any part of the theatre. This was a very agreeable compliment to me, whose greatest pleasure consisted in seeing dramatic performances; and you need not doubt that I often availed myself of my privilege. As I had an opportunity of being behind the scenes when I pleased, I frequently conversed with Mr. Brayer about my play, and asked when he intended to put it into rehearsal; but he had always so much business upon his hands, that it remained with him unopened a considerable while; and I became very uneasy about the season, that wasted apace, when I saw in the papers another new play advertised, which had been written, offered, accepted, and rehearsed in the compass of three months. You may easily guess how much I was confounded at this event. I own to you that, in the first transports of my anger, I suspected Mr. Brayer of having acted towards me in the most pitiful perfidious manner; and was actually glad at his disappointment in the success of his favourite piece, which, by the strength of art, lingered till the third night, and then died in a deplorable manner. But, now that passion has no share in my reflection, I am willing to ascribe his behaviour to his want of memory or want of judgment, which, you know, are natural defects, that are more worthy of compassion than reproach.

"About this time I happened to be in company with a gentle-woman, who, having heard of my tragedy, told me she was acquainted with the wife of a gentleman, who was very well known to a lady, who had great interest with a person who was intimate with Earl Sheerwit, and that, if I pleased, she would use her influence in my behalf. As this nobleman had the character of a Mæcenas in the nation, and could stamp a value upon any work by his sole countenance and approbation, I accepted her offer with eagerness, in full confidence of seeing my reputation established, and my wishes fulfilled in a very short time, provided that I should have the good fortune to please his lordship's taste. I withdrew the manuscript from the hands of Mr. Brayer, and committed it to the care of this gentlewoman, who laboured so effectually in my interest, that in less than a month it was conveyed to the earl, and, in a few weeks after, I had the satisfaction to hear that he had read and approved it very much. Transported with this piece of intelligence, I flattered myself with the hopes of his interesting himself in its favour; but hearing no more of this matter in three whole months, I began—God forgive me!—to suspect the veracity of the person who brought me the good tidings; for I thought it impossible that a man of his rank and character, who knew the difficulty of writing a good tragedy, and understood the dignity of the work, should read and applaud an essay of this kind without feeling an inclination to befriend the author, whom his counte-

nance alone could raise above dependence. But it was not long
before I found my friend very much wronged by my opinion.

"You must know that the civilities I had received from Lord
Rattle, and the desire he manifested to promote the success of
my play, encouraged me to write an account of my bad fortune
to his lordship, who condescended so far as to desire, by letter,
a young squire of a great estate, with whom he was intimate,
to espouse my cause, and, in particular, make me acquainted
with one Mr. Marmozet, a celebrated player, who had lately
appeared on the stage with astonishing éclat, and bore such
sway in the house where he acted, that the managers durst not
refuse anything he recommended. The young gentleman whom
Lord Rattle had employed for this purpose, being diffident of
his own interest with Mr. Marmozet, had recourse to a nobleman
of his acquaintance, who, at his solicitation, was so good as to
introduce me to him; and the conversation turning upon my
performance, I was not a little surprised, as well as pleased, to
hear that Earl Sheerwit had spoken very much in its praise,
and even sent Mr. Marmozet the copy, with a message expressing
a desire that he would act in it next season. Nor was the favourite
actor backward in commending the piece, which he mentioned
with some expressions of regard, that I do not choose to repeat;
assuring me that he would appear in it, provided he should be
engaged to play at all during the ensuing season. In the meantime, he desired I would give him leave to peruse it in the
country, whither he intended to remove next day, that he might
have leisure to consider and point out such alterations as might,
perhaps, be necessary for its representation; and took my
direction, that he might communicate by letter the observations
he should make. Trusting to these assurances, and the interest
which had been made in my behalf, I hugged myself in the
expectation of seeing it not only acted, but acted to the greatest
advantage; and this I thought could not fail of recompensing
me in an ample manner for the anxiety and affliction I had
undergone. But six weeks being elapsed, I did not know how to
reconcile Mr. Marmozet's silence with his promise of writing to
me in ten days after he set out for the country; however, I was
at last favoured with a letter, importing that he had made some
remarks on my tragedy, which he would freely impart at meeting,
and advising me to put it, without loss of time, into the hands
of that manager who had the best company, as he himself was
quite uncertain whether or not he should be engaged that winter.
I was a good deal alarmed at this last part of his letter, and

advised about it with a friend, who told me it was a plain indication of Mr. Marmozet's desire to get rid of his promise; that his pretended uncertainty about acting next winter was no other than a scandalous evasion; for, to his certain knowledge, he was already engaged, or at least in terms with Mr. Vandal; and that his design was to disappoint me, in favour of a new comedy, which he had purchased of the author, and intended to bring upon the stage for his own advantage. In short, my dear sir, this person, who, I must own, is of a sanguine complexion, handled the moral character of Mr. Marmozet with such severity, that I began to suspect him of some particular prejudice, and put myself upon my guard against his insinuations. I ought to crave pardon for this tedious narration of trivial circumstances, which, however interesting they may be to me, must certainly be very dry and insipid to the ear of one unconcerned in the affair. But I understand the meaning of your looks, and will proceed. Well, sir, Mr. Marmozet, upon his return to town, treated me with uncommon complaisance, and invited me to his lodgings, where he proposed to communicate his remarks, which I confess were more unfavourable than I expected; but I answered his objections, and, as I thought, brought him over to my opinion; for, on the whole, he signified the highest approbation of the performance. In the course of our dispute, I was not a little surprised to find this poor gentleman's memory so treacherous, as to let him forget what he had said to me, before he went out of town, in regard to Earl Sheerwit's opinion of my play, which he now professed himself ignorant of; and I was extremely mortified at hearing from his own mouth, that his interest with Mr. Vandal was so very low, as to be insufficient of itself to bring a new piece upon the stage. I then begged his advice; and he counselled me to apply to Earl Sheerwit for a message in my favour to the manager, who would not presume to refuse anything recommended by so great a man; and he was so kind as to promise to second this message with all his power. I had immediate recourse to the worthy gentlewoman, my friend already mentioned, which opened the channels of her conveyance with such expedition, that in a few days I had the promise of the message, provided I could assure myself of Mr. Vandal's being unengaged to any other author; for his lordship did not choose to condescend so far, until he should understand that there was a probability (at least) of succeeding; at the same time that blessed me with this piece of news, I was startled at another, by the same channel of communication; which was, that Mr. Marmozet, before he advised me to this application, had informed the earl that he had read my play, and found it altogether unfit for the stage. Though I could not doubt the certainty of this intelligence, I believed there was some misapprehension in the case; and without taking any notice of it, told Mr. Marmozet the answer I had been favoured with; and he promised to ask Mr. Vandal the question proposed. I waited upon him in a day or two, when he gave me to understand that Mr. Vandal having professed himself free of all engagements, he had put my play into his hands, and represented it as a piece strongly recommended by Earl Sheerwit, who, he assured him, would honour him with a message in its favour; and he desired me to call for an answer at Mr. Vandal's house in three days. I followed his directions, and found the manager, who, being made acquainted with my business, owned that Mr. Marmozet had given him a manuscript play, but denied that he had mentioned Earl Sheerwit's name. When I informed him of the circumstances of the affair, he said he had no engagement with any author; that he would read my tragedy forthwith, and did not believe he should venture to reject it in contradiction to his lordship's opinion, for which he had the utmost veneration, but put it into rehearsal without loss of time. I was so much intoxicated with this encouragement, that I overlooked the mysterious conduct of Mr. Marmozet, and attended the manager at the time appointed, when, to my infinite confusion, he pronounced my play improper for the stage, and rejected it accordingly. As soon as I could recollect myself from the disorder into which this unexpected refusal had thrown me, I expressed a desire of hearing his objections, which were so groundless, indistinct, and unintelligible, that I persuaded myself he had not at all perused the piece, but had been prompted by somebody, whose lessons he had not rightly retained. However, I have been since informed that the poor man's head, which was not naturally very clear, had been disordered with superstition, and that he laboured under the tyranny of a wife and the terrors of hell-fire at the same time. Precipitated, in this manner, from the highest pinnacle of hope to the abyss of despondence, I was ready to sink under the burden of my affliction, and, in the bitterness of my anguish, could not help entertaining some doubts of Mr. Marmozet's integrity, when I recollected and compared the circumstances of his conduct towards me. I was encouraged in this suspicion by being told that my Lord Sheerwit had spoke of his character with great contempt, and, in particular, resented his insolence in opposing his own taste to that of his lordship concerning my tragedy. While I hesitated between different opinions of the matter, that friend, who, as I told you before, was a little hot-headed, favoured me with a visit, and having heard a circumstantial account of the whole affair, could not contain his indignation, but affirmed, without ceremony, that Marmozet was the sole occasion of my disappointment; that he had acted from first to last with the most perfidious dissimulation, cajoling me with insinuating civilities, while he underhand employed all his art and influence to prejudice the ignorant manager against my performance; that nothing could equal his hypocrisy but his avarice, which engrossed the faculties of his soul so much, that he scrupled not to be guilty of the meanest practices to gratify that sordid appetite; that in consequence of this disposition, he had prostituted his honour in betraying my inexperience, and in undermining the interest of another author of established reputation, who had also offered a tragedy to the stage, which he thought would interfere with the success of the comedy he had bought, and determined to bring on at all events.

"I was shocked at the description of such a monster, which I could not believe existed in the world, bad as it is, and argued against the asseverations of my friend, by demonstrating the bad policy of such behaviour, which could not fail of entailing infamy upon the author; and the small temptation that a man of Mr. Marmozet's figure and success could have to consult his interest in such a grovelling manner, which must create contempt and abhorrence of him in his patrons, and effectually deprive him of the countenance and protection he now enjoys in such an eminent degree. He pretended to laugh at my simplicity, and asked if I knew for which of his virtues he was so much caressed by the people of fashion. 'It is not,' said he, 'for the qualities of his heart, that this little parasite is invited to the tables of dukes and lords, who hire extraordinary cooks for his entertainment. His avarice they see not, his ingratitude they feel not, his hypocrisy accommodates itself to their humours, and is of consequence pleasing; but he is chiefly courted for his buffoonery, and will be admitted into the choicest parties of quality for his talent of mimicking Punch and his wife Joan, when a poet of the most exquisite genius is not able to attract the least regard.' God forbid, Mr. Random, that I should credit assertions that degrade the dignity of our superiors so much, and represent that poor man as the most abject of all beings!

No! I looked upon them as the hyperboles of passion; and though that comedy of which he spoke did actually appear, I dare not doubt the innocence of Mr. Marmozet, who, I am told, is as much as ever in favour with the earl: a circumstance that surely could not be, unless he had vindicated his character to the satisfaction of his lordship. Pray forgive this long digression, and give the hearing a little longer; for, thank Heaven! I am now near the goal.

"Baffled in all my attempts, I despaired of seeing my play acted; and bethought myself of choosing some employment that might afford a sure, though mean subsistence; but my landlord, to whom I was by this time considerably indebted, and who had laid his account with having his money paid all in a heap, from the profits of my third night, could not brook his disappointment, therefore made another effort in my behalf, and, by dint of interest, procured a message from a lady of fashion to Mr. Brayer, who had always professed a great veneration for her, desiring that he would set up my play forthwith, and assuring him that she and all her friends would support it in the performance. To strengthen my interest, she engaged his best actors in my cause; and, in short, exerted herself so much, that it was again received, and my hopes began to revive. But Mr. Brayer, honest man, was so much engrossed by business of vast consequence, though to appearance he had nothing at all to do, that he could not find time to read it until the season was pretty far advanced; and read it he must, for, notwithstanding his having perused it before, his memory did not retain one circumstance of the matter.

"At length he favoured it with his attention, and, having proposed certain alterations, sent his duty to the lady who patronised it, and promised, on his honour, to bring it on next winter, provided these alterations should be made, and the copy delivered to him before the end of April. With an aching heart, I submitted to these conditions, and performed them accordingly. But fortune owed me another unforeseen mortification; Mr. Marmozet, during the summer, became joint patentee with Mr. Brayer; so that, when I claimed performance of articles, I was told he could do nothing without the consent of his partner, who was pre-engaged to another author.

"My condition was rendered desperate by the death of my good friend and landlord, whose executors obtained a judgment against my effects, which they seized, turned me out into the streets naked, friendless. and forlorn; there I was arrested at the suit of my tailor, and thrown into this prison, where I have made shift to live these five weeks on the bounty of my fellow-prisoners, who, I hope, are not the worse for the instruction and good offices by which I manifest my gratitude; but, in spite of all their charitable endeavours, my life was scarce tolerable, until your uncommon benevolence enabled me to enjoy it with comfort."

CHAPTER LXIV

I am seized with a deep Melancholy, and become a Sloven—Am relieved by my Uncle—He prevails upon me to engage with his Owners as Surgeon of the Ship which he commands—He makes me a considerable Present—Entertains Strap as his Steward—I take leave of my Friends and go on Board—The Ship arrives in the Downs.

I SHALL not make any reflections on this story, in the course of which the reader must perceive how egregiously the simplicity and milky disposition of this worthy man had been duped and abused by a set of scoundrels, who were so habituated to false-hood and equivocation, that I verily believe they would have found the utmost difficulty in uttering one syllable of truth, though their lives had depended upon their sincerity. Notwith-standing all that I had suffered from the knavery and selfishness of mankind, I was amazed and incensed at the base indifference which suffered such uncommon merit as he possessed to languish in obscurity, and struggle with all the miseries of a loathsome jail; and should have blessed the occasion that secluded me from such a perfidious world, had not the remembrance of the amiable Narcissa preserved my attachment to that society of which she constituted a part. The picture of that lovely creature was the constant companion of my solitude. How often did I contem-plate the resemblance of those enchanting features that first captivated my heart! How often did I weep over those endearing scenes which her image recalled; and how often did I curse my perfidious fate for having robbed me of the fair original! In vain did my imagination flatter me with schemes of future happiness; surely reason always interposed, and, in a moment, overthrew that unsubstantial fabric, by chastising the extravagance of my hope, and representing my unhappy situation in the right point of view. In vain did I fly for refuge to the amusements of the place, and engage in the parties of Jackson, at cards, billiards, ninepins, and fives; a train of melancholy thoughts took possession of my soul, which even the conversation of Melopoyn could not divert. I ordered Strap to inquire every day at Banter's lodgings, in expectation of hearing again from my charmer; and my disappointment considerably augmented my chagrin. My affectionate valet was infected with my sorrow, and often sat with me whole hours without speaking, uttering sigh for sigh, and shedding tear for tear. This fellowship increased our distemper; he became incapable of business, and was discarded by his master; while I, seeing my money melt away, without any certainty of deliverance, and, in short, all my hopes frustrated, grew negligent of life, lost all appetite, and degenerated into such a sloven, that during the space of two months I was neither washed, shifted, nor shaved; so that my face, rendered meagre with abstinence, was obscured with dirt, and overshadowed with hair, and my whole appearance squalid and even frightful; when, one day, Strap brought me notice that there was a man below who wanted to speak with me. Roused at this intelligence, and in full hopes of receiving a letter from the dear object of my love, I ran downstairs with the utmost precipitation, and found, to my infinite surprise, my generous uncle Mr. Bowling. Transported at the sight, I sprung forward to embrace him. Upon which he started aside with great agility, drew his hanger, and put himself upon his guard, saying, "Avast, brother, avast! sheer off!—Yoho! you turnkey, why don't you keep a better look-out? here's one of your crazy prisoners broke from his lashings, I do suppose." I could not help laughing heartily at his mistake; but this I soon rectified by my voice, which he instantly recollected, and shook me by the hand with great affection, testifying his concern at seeing me in such a miserable condition.

I conducted him to my apartment, where, in presence of Strap, whom I introduced to him as one of my best friends, he gave me to understand that he was just arrived from the Coast of Guinea, after having made a pretty successful voyage, in which he acted as mate, until the ship was attacked by a French privateer; that the captain being killed during the engagement, he had taken the command, and was so fortunate as to sink the enemy; after which exploit he fell in with a merchant ship from Martinico, laden with sugar, indigo, and some silver; and, by virtue of his letter of marque, attacked, took, and brought her safe in Kinsale, in Ireland, where she was condemned as a lawful prize; by which means he had not only got a pretty sum of money, but also acquired the favour of his owners, who had already conferred upon him the command of a large ship, mounted with twenty nine-pounders, ready to sail upon a very advantageous voyage, which he was not at liberty to discover. And he assured me, that it was with the greatest difficulty that he had found me, in consequence of a direction left for him at his lodgings at Wapping.

I was rejoiced beyond measure at this account of his good fortune; and, at his desire, recounted all the adventures that had happened to me since we parted. When he understood the particulars of Strap's attachment to me, he squeezed his hand very cordially, and promised to make a man of him; then giving me ten guineas for my present occasion, took a direction for the tailor who arrested me and went away in order to discharge the debt, telling me at parting that he would soon fetch up all my leeway with a wet sail.

I was utterly confounded at this sudden transition, which affected me more than any reverse I had formerly felt; and a crowd of incoherent ideas rushed so impetuously upon my imagination, that my reason could neither separate nor connect them, when Strap, whose joy had manifested itself in a thousand fooleries, came into my room with his shaving utensils, and, without any previous intimation, began to lather my beard, whistling with great emotion all the while. I started from my reverie, and being too well acquainted with Strap to trust myself in his hands while he was under such agitation, desired to be excused, sent for another barber, and suffered myself to be trimmed. Having performed the ceremony of ablution, I shifted, and dressing in my gayest apparel, waited for the return of my uncle, who was agreeably surprised at my sudden transformation.

This beneficent kinsman had satisfied my creditor, and obtained an order for my discharge, so that I was no longer a prisoner; but as I had some reluctance to part with my friends and fellows in distress, I prevailed upon Mr. Bowling to favour us with his company, and invited Mr. Melopoyn and Jackson to spend the evening at my apartment, where I regaled them with a supper, good wine, and the news of my release, on which they heartily congratulated me, notwithstanding the loss of my company, which, they were pleased to say, they should severely feel. As for Jackson, his misfortune made so little impression on himself, and he was altogether so loose, indifferent, and indiscreet, that I could scarce pity his situation. But I had conceived a veneration and friendship for the poet, who was in all respects an object much more worthy of compassion and regard. When our guests withdrew, and my uncle had retired, with an intention to visit me next morning, I made up a bundle of some linen and other necessaries, and bidding Strap carry them to Mr. Melopoyn's lodgings, went thither myself and pressed it upon his acceptance, with five guineas, which, with much difficulty, he received, assuring me, at the same time, that he should never have it in his power to make satisfaction. I then asked if I could serve him any other way? To which he answered, "You already have done too much"; and unable to contain the emotions of his soul any longer, burst into tears and wept aloud. Moved at this spectacle, I left him to his repose; and when my uncle returned in the morning, represented his character in such favourable light, that the honest seaman was affected with his distress, and determined to follow my example, in presenting him with five pieces more. Upon which, that I might save him some confusion, I advised Mr. Bowling to enclose it in a letter to be delivered by Strap after we should be gone.

This was accordingly done. I took a formal leave of all my acquaintance in the jail; and just as I was about to step into an hackney-coach at the gate, Jackson calling me, I returned, and he asked me in a whisper if I could lend him a shilling? His demand being so moderate, and in all likelihood the last he would make upon me, I slipped a guinea into his hand, which he no sooner perceived, than he cried, "O Jesus! a guinea!" then laying hold of a button of my coat, broke out into an immoderate fit of laughter; and when his convulsion was ended, told me I was an honest fellow, and let me go. The coachman was ordered to drive to Mr. Bowling's lodgings, where, when we arrived, he entered into a serious discourse with me on the subject of my situation, and proposed that I should sail with him in quality of his surgeon; in which case he would put me in a method of getting a fortune in a few years by my own industry; and assured me that I might expect to inherit all that he should die possessed of, provided I should survive him. Though I was penetrated with a sense of his generosity, I was startled at a proposal that offered violence to my love, and signified my sentiments on that head, which he did not seem to relish, but observed that love was the fruit of idleness; that, when once I should be employed in business, and my mind engaged in making money, I should be no more troubled with these silly notions, which none but your fair-weather Jacks, who have nothing but their pleasure to mind, ought to entertain. I was piqued at this insinuation, which I looked upon as a reproach, and without giving myself time to deliberate, accepted his offer. He was overjoyed at my compliance, carried me immediately to his chief owner, with whom a bargain was struck; so that then I could not retract with honour, had I been ever so much averse to the agreement. That I might not have time to cool, he bade me draw out a list of medicines for a complement of five hundred men, adapted to the distempers of hot climates, and sufficient for a voyage of eighteen months, and carry it to a certain wholesale apothecary, who would also provide me in two well-qualified mates. While I was thus employed, Strap came in, and looked very blank when he understood my resolution. However, after a pause of some minutes, he insisted upon going along with me; and at my desire was made ship's steward by Captain Bowling, who promised to be at the expense of fitting him out, and to lend him two hundred pounds to purchase an adventure.

When I had delivered my list of medicines, chosen a couple of my own countrymen for mates, and bespoke a set of chirurgical instruments, my uncle told me that, by his last voyage, he had cleared almost three thousand pounds, one-third of which he would immediately make over and put into my hands; that he would procure for me credit to the value of as much more, in such goods as would turn to best account in the country to which we were bound; and that, although he looked upon my interest as his own, he would keep the remaining part of his fortune in his own disposal, with a view of preserving his independence, and a power of punishing me, in case I should not make a good use of what he had already bestowed.

Without troubling the reader with an account of the effect which this surprising generosity had upon my mind, I shall only say that his promises were instantly performed, and an invoice of merchandise proper for the voyage presented to me, that I might purchase the goods and ship them with all expedition. In the midst of this hurry, the remembrance of my charming Narcissa often interposed, and made me the most miserable of all mortals. I was distracted with the thought of being torn from her, perhaps for ever; and though the hope of seeing her again might have supported me under the torments of separation, I could not reflect upon the anguish she must feel at parting with me, and the incessant sorrows to which her tender bosom would be exposed during my absence, without being pierced with the deepest affliction. As my imagination was daily and nightly upon the rack to invent some method of mitigating this

cruel stroke, or at least of acquitting my love and honour in
the opinion of this gentle creature, I at length stumbled upon
an expedient, with which the reader will be made acquainted
in due time; and, in consequence of my determination, became
less uneasy and disturbed.

My business being finished and the ship ready to sail, I resolved
to make my last appearance among my acquaintance at the
other end of the town, where I had not been since my imprisonment; and as I had, by the advice of my uncle, taken off some
very rich clothes for sale, I put on the gayest suit in my possession, and went in a chair to the coffee-house I used to frequent,
where I found my friend Banter so confounded at the magnificence of my dress, that, when I made up to him, he gazed at
me with a look of astonishment, without being able, for some
minutes, to open his lips; then pulling me aside by the sleeve,
and fixing his eyes on mine, accosted me in this manner:
"Random, where the devil have you been? eh!—What is the
meaning of all this finery?—Oho! I understand you.—You are
just arrived from the country! what! the roads are good, eh!—
Well, Random, you are a bold fellow, and a lucky fellow!—
but take care, the pitcher goes often to the well, but is broke
at last." So saying, he pointed to his collar; by which gesture,
and the broken hints he had ejaculated, I found he suspected
me of having robbed on the highway; and I laughed very
heartily at his supposition. Without explaining myself any
further, I told him he was mistaken in his conjecture; that I
had been for some time past with the relation of whom he had
frequently heard me speak; and that, as I should set out next
day upon my travels, I had come to take my leave of my friends,
and to receive of him the money he had borrowed from me,
which, now that I was going abroad, I should certainly have
occasion for. He was a little disconcerted at this demand; but,
recollecting himself in a moment, swore in an affected passion
that I had used him extremely ill, and he would never forgive
me, for having, by this short warning, put it out of his power
to free himself of an obligation he could no longer bear. I could
not help smiling at this pretended delicacy, which I commended
highly, telling him he needed not to be uneasy on that score,
for I would give him a direction to a merchant in the city, with
whom I would leave a discharge for the sum, to be delivered
upon payment. He professed much joy at this expedient, and
with great eagerness asked the person's name and place of
abode, which he forthwith wrote in his pocket-book, assuring

me that he should not be long in my debt. This affair, which I
knew he would never after think of, being settled to his satisfaction, I sent cards to all my friends, desiring the favour of
their company at a tavern in the evening, when they honoured
my invitation, and I had the pleasure of treating them in a very
elegant manner, at which they expressed equal admiration as
applause. Having enjoyed ourselves till midnight, I took my
leave of them, and was well-nigh stifled with caresses. Next
day I set out with Strap in a post-chaise for Gravesend, where
we went on board, and, the wind serving, weighed anchor in
less than twelve hours. Without meeting with any accident,
we reached the Downs, where we were obliged to come to an
anchor, and wait for an easterly wind to carry us out of the
Channel.

CHAPTER LXV

I set out for Sussex—Consult Mrs. Sagely—Achieve an Interview with
Narcissa—Return to the Ship—We get clear of the Channel—I learn our
Destination—We are chased by a large Ship—The Company are dismayed,
and encouraged by the Captain's speech—Our Pursuer happens to be an
English Man-of-war—We arrive at the Coast of Guinea, purchase 400
Negroes, sail for Paraguay, get safe into the River of Plate, and sell our
Cargo to great Advantage.

IT was now I put in execution the scheme I had projected at
London; and asking leave of the captain for Strap and me to
stay on shore till the wind should become favourable, my request
was granted, because he had orders to remain in the Downs
until he should receive some despatches from London, which
he did not expect in less than a week. Having imparted my
resolution to my trusty valet, who (though he endeavoured to
dissuade me from such a rash undertaking) would not quit me
in the enterprise, I hired horses, and set out immediately for
that part of Sussex where my charmer was confined, which was
not above thirty miles distant from Deal, where we mounted.
As I was perfectly well acquainted with the extent of the squire's
estate and influence, I halted within five miles of his house,
where we remained till the twilight, at which time we set forward, and, by the favour of a dark night, reached a copse about
half a mile from the village where Mrs. Sagely lived. Here we
left our horses tied to a tree, and went directly to the house of
my old benefactress, Strap trembling all the way, and venting

ejaculatory petitions to Heaven for our safety. Her habitation being quite solitary, we arrived at the door without being observed, when I ordered my companion to enter by himself, and, in case there should be company with her, deliver a letter which I had writ for that purpose, and say that a friend of hers in London, understanding that he intended to travel this road, had committed it to his care. He rapped at the door, to which the good old matron coming, told him, that being a lone woman, he must excuse her if she did not open it until he had declared his name and business. He answered that his name was unknown to her, and that his business was to deliver a letter, which, to free her from all manner of apprehension, he would convey to her through the space between the door and threshold. This he instantly performed; and she no sooner read the contents, which specified my being present, than she cried, "If the person who wrote this letter be at hand, let him speak, that I may be assured by his voice whether or not I may safely admit him." I forthwith applied my mouth to the keyhole and pronounced, "Dear mother, you need not be afraid; it is I, so much indebted to your goodness, who now crave admittance." She knew my voice, and opening the door immediately, received me with a truly maternal affection, manifesting, by the tears she let fall, her concern lest I should be discovered, for she had been informed of everything that had happened between Narcissa and me, from the dear captive's own mouth.

When I explained the motive of my journey, which was no other than a desire of seeing the object of my love before I should quit the kingdom, that I might in person convince her of the necessity I was under to leave her, reconcile her to that event, by describing the advantages that in all probability would attend it, repeat my vows of eternal constancy, and enjoy the melancholy pleasure of a tender embrace at parting; I say, when I had thus signified my intention, Mrs. Sagely told me that Narcissa, upon her return from Bath, had been so strictly watched, that nobody but one or two of the servants, devoted to her brother, was admitted to her presence; that afterwards she had been a little enlarged, and was permitted to see company, during which indulgence she had been several times at her cottage; but of late she had been betrayed by one of the servants, who discovered to the squire that he had once carried a letter from her to the post-house, directed to me; upon which information she was now more confined than ever, and that I could have no chance of seeing her, unless I would run the risk of getting into the garden, where she and her maid were every day allowed to take the air, and lie hid until I should have an opportunity of speaking to them—an adventure attended with such danger that no man in his right wits would attempt it. This enterprise hazardous as it was, I resolved to perform, in spite of all the arguments of Mrs. Sagely, who reasoned, chid, and entreated by turns, and the tears and prayers of Strap, who conjured me on his knees, to have more regard to myself, as well as to him, than to attempt my own destruction in such a precipitate manner. I was deaf to everything but the suggestions of my love; and ordering him to return immediately with the horses to the inn from whence we set out, and wait for my coming in that place, he at first peremptorily refused to leave me, until persuaded him that, if our horses should remain where they were till daylight, they would certainly be discovered, and the whole county alarmed. On this consideration, he took his leave in a sorrowful plight, kissed my hand, and weeping, cried, "God knows if ever I shall see you again."—My kind landlady, finding me obstinate, gave me her best advice how to behave in the execution of my project; and, after having persuaded me to take a little refreshment, accommodated me with a bed, and left me to my repose. Early in the morning I arose, and armed with a couple of loaded pistols and a hanger, went to the back of the squire's garden, climbed over the wall, and, according to Mrs. Sagely's direction, concealed myself in a thicket, hard by an alcove that terminated a walk at a good distance from the house which (I was told) my mistress chiefly frequented. Here I absconded from five o'clock in the morning to six in the evening without seeing a human creature: at last I perceived two women approaching, whom, by my throbbing heart, I soon recognised to be the adorable Narcissa and Miss Williams. I felt the strongest agitation of soul at the sight; and guessing that they would repose themselves in the alcove, stepped into it unperceived, and laid upon the stone table a picture of myself in miniature, for which I had sat in London, purposing to leave it with Narcissa before I should go abroad. I exposed it in this manner as an introduction to my own appearance, which, without some previous intimation, I was afraid might have an unlucky effect upon the delicate nerves of my fair enslaver; and then withdrew into the thicket, where I could hear their discourse, and suit myself to the circumstances of the occasion. As they advanced I observed an air of melancholy in the countenance of Narcissa blended with such unspeakable sweetness, that I could scarce refrain from flying into her arms, and kissing away the pearly drop that stood collected in each bewitching eye. According to my expectation, she entered the alcove, and perceiving something on the table, took it up. No sooner did she cast her eye upon the features, than, startled at the resemblance, she cried, "Good God!" and the roses instantly vanished from her cheeks, Her confidante, alarmed at this exclamation, looked at the picture, and, struck with the likeness, exclaimed, "O Jesus! the very features of Mr. Random!" Narcissa having recollected herself a little, said, "Whatever angel brought it hither as a comfort to me in my affliction, I am thankful for the benefit, and will preserve it as the dearest object of my care." So saying, she kissed it with surprising ardour, shed a flood of tears, and then deposited the lifeless image in her lovely bosom. Transported at these symptoms of her unaltered affection, I was about to throw myself at her feet, when Miss Williams, whose reflection was less engaged than that of her mistress, observed that the picture could not transport itself hither, and that she could not help thinking I was not far off. The gentle Narcissa, startling at this conjecture, answered, "Heaven forbid! for although nothing in the universe could yield me satisfaction equal to that of his presence for one poor moment, in a proper place, I would rather forfeit his company—almost for ever, than see him here, where his life would be exposed to so much danger." I could no longer restrain the impulse of my passion, but, breaking from my concealment, stood before her, when she uttered a fearful shriek, and fainted in the arms of her companion. I flew towards the treasure of my soul, clasped her in my embrace, and, with the warmth of my kisses, brought her again to life. O! that I were endowed with the expression of a Raphael, the graces of a Guido, the magic touches of a Titian, that I might represent the fond concern, the chastened rapture, and ingenuous blush that mingled in her beauteous face when she opened her eyes upon me, and pronounced, "O heavens! is it you?"

I am afraid I have already encroached upon the reader's patience with the particulars of this amour, on which, I own, I cannot help being impertinently circumstantial. I shall therefore omit the less material passages of this interview, during which I convinced her reason, though I could not appease the sad presages of her love, with regard to the long voyage and dangers I must undergo. When we had spent an hour (which was all she could spare from the barbarity of her brother's vigilance) in lamenting over our hard fate, and in repeating our reciprocal vows, Miss Williams reminded us of the necessity there was for our immediate parting; and sure, lovers never parted with such sorrow and reluctance as we. But because my words are incapable of doing justice to this affecting circumstance, I am obliged to draw a veil over it, and observe that I returned in the dark to the house of Mrs. Sagely, who was overjoyed to hear of my success, and opposed the tumults of my grief with such strength of reason, that my mind regained in some measure its tranquillity; and that very night, after having forced upon the good gentlewoman a purse of twenty guineas, as a token of my gratitude and esteem, I took my leave of her, and set out on foot for the inn, where my arrival freed honest Strap from the horrors of unutterable dread.

We took horse immediately, and alighted early next morning at Deal, where I found my uncle in great concern on account of my absence, because he had received his despatches, and must have weighed with the first fair wind, whether I had been on board or not. Next day, a brisk easterly gale springing up, we set sail, and in eight and forty hours got clear of the Channel.

When we were about two hundred leagues to westward of the Land's End, the captain taking me apart into the cabin, told me that, now he was permitted by his instructions, he would disclose the intent and destination of our voyage: "The ship," said he, "which has been fitted out at a great expense, is bound for the coast of Guinea, where we shall exchange part of our cargo for slaves and gold dust; from thence we will transport our negroes to Buenos Ayres in New Spain, where, by virtue of passports obtained from our own court and that of Madrid, we will dispose of them and the goods that remain on board for silver, by means of our supercargo, who is perfectly well acquainted with the coast, the lingo, and inhabitants." Being thus let into the secret of our expedition, I borrowed of the supercargo a Spanish grammar, dictionary, and some other books of the same language, which I studied with such application, that, before we arrived in New Spain, I could maintain a conversation with him in that tongue. Being arrived in the warm latitudes, I ordered, with the captain's consent, the whole ship's company to be blooded and purged, myself undergoing the same evacuation, in order to prevent those dangerous fevers to which northern constitutions are subject in hot climates; and I have reason to believe that this precaution was not unserviceable, for we lost but one sailor during our whole passage to the coast.

One day, when we had been about five weeks at sea, we

descried to windward a large ship bearing down upon us with all the sail she could carry. Upon which my uncle ordered the studding sails to be hoisted, and the ship to be cleared for engaging; but finding that, to use the seaman's phrase, we were very much wronged by the ship which had us in chase, and which by this time had hoisted French colours, he commanded the studding sails to be taken in, the course to be clewed up, the maintop sail to be backed, the tompions to be taken out of the guns, and every man to repair to his quarters. While everybody was busied in the performance of these orders, Strap came upon the quarter-deck, trembling, and looking aghast, and, with a voice half suppressed by fear, asked if I thought we were a match for the vessel in pursuit of us? Observing his consternation, I said, "What! are you afraid, Strap?" "Afraid!" he replied, "n—n—o; what should I be afraid of? I thank God, I have a clear conscience; but I believe it will be a bloody battle, and I wish you may not have occasion for another hand to assist you in the cockpit." I immediately perceived his drift, and making the captain acquainted with his situation, desired he might be stationed below with me and my mates. My uncle, incensed at his pusillanimity, bade me send him down instantly, that his fear might not infect the ship's company; whereupon I told the poor steward that I had begged him for my assistant, and desired him to go down and help my mates to get ready the instruments and dressings. Notwithstanding the satisfaction he must have felt at these tidings, he affected a shyness of quitting the upper deck; and said he hoped I did not imagine he was afraid to do his duty above board; for he believed himself as well prepared for death as any man in the ship, no disparagement to me or the captain. I was disgusted at this affectation, and, in order to punish his hypocrisy, assured him he might take his choice either of going down to the cockpit with me, or of staying upon deck during the engagement. Alarmed at this indifference, he replied, "Well, to oblige you, I'll go down; but, remember, it is more for your sake than my own." So saying, he disappeared in a twinkling, without waiting for an answer. By this time we could observe two tier of guns in the ship which pursued us, and which was now but two short miles astern. This discovery had an evident effect upon the sailors, who did not scruple to say that we should be torn to pieces, and blown out of the water, and that, in case any of them should lose their precious limbs, they must go a-begging for life, for there was no provision made by the merchants for those poor souls who were maimed in their service. The captain, understanding this backwardness, ordered the crew abaft, and spoke to them thus: "My lads, I am told you hang an a—se. I have gone to sea thirty years man and boy, and never saw English sailors afraid before. Mayhap you think I want to expose you for the lucre of gain. Whosoever thinks so, thinks a damned lie, for my whole cargo is insured; so that, in case I should be taken, my loss would not be great. The enemy is stronger than we, to be sure. What then? have we not a chance for carrying away one of her masts, and so get clear of her? If we find her too hard for us, 'tis but striking at last. If any man is hurt in the engagement, I promise on the word of an honest seaman to make him a recompense according to his loss. So now, you that are lazy, lubberly, cowardly dogs, get away, and skulk in the hold and bread-room; and you that are jolly boys, stand by me, and let us give one broadside for the honour of Old England." This eloquent harangue was so well adapted to the disposition of his hearers, that one and all of them, pulling off their hats, waved them over their heads, and saluted him with three cheers; upon which he sent his boy for two large case bottles of brandy, and having treated every man with a dram, they repaired to their quarters, and waited impatiently for the word of command. I must do my uncle the justice to say that, in the whole of his disposition, he behaved with the utmost intrepidity, conduct, and deliberation. The enemy being very near, he ordered me to my station, and was just going to give the word for hoisting the colours and firing, when the supposed Frenchman hauled down his white pennant, jack, and ensign, hoisted English ones, and fired a gun ahead of us. This was a joyful event to Captain Bowling, who immediately showed his colours and fired a gun to leeward. Upon which the other ship ran alongside of us, hailed him, and giving him to know that she was an English man-of-war of forty guns, ordered him to hoist out his boat and come on board. This command he obeyed with the more alacrity, because, upon inquiry, he found that she was commanded by an old messmate of his, who was overjoyed to see him, detained him to dinner, and sent his barge for the super-cargo and me, who were very much caressed on his account. As this commander was destined to cruise upon the French, in the latitude of Martinico, his stem and quarters were adorned with white fleurs-de-lis, and the whole shell of the ship so much disguised for a decoy to the enemy, that it was no wonder my uncle did not know her, although he had sailed on board of her many years. We kept company with her four days, during which time the captains were never asunder, and then parted, our course lying different from hers.

In less than a fortnight after our separation, we made the land of Guinea, near the mouth of the River Gambia, and trading along the coast as far to the southward of the line as Angola and Bengula, in less than six months disposed of the greatest part of our cargo, and purchased four hundred negroes, my adventure having been laid out in gold dust.

Our complement being made up, we took our departure from Cape Negro, and arrived in the Rio de la Plata in six weeks, having met with nothing remarkable in our voyage, except an epidemic fever, not unlike the jail distemper, which broke out among our slaves and carried off a good many of the ship's company; among whom I lost one of my mates, and poor Strap had well-nigh given up the ghost. Having produced our passport to the Spanish governor, we were received with great courtesy, sold our slaves in a very few days, and could have put off five times the number at our own price; though we were obliged to smuggle the rest of our merchandise, consisting of European bale goods, which, however, we made shift to dispose of at a great advantage.

CHAPTER LXVI

I am invited to the Villa of a Spanish Don, where we meet with an English Gentleman and make a very interesting Discovery—We leave Buenos Ayres and arrive at Jamaica.

OUR ship being freed from the disagreeable lading of negroes, to whom, indeed, I had been a miserable slave since our leaving the coast of Guinea, I began to enjoy myself, and breathe with pleasure the pure air of Paraguay, this part of which is reckoned the Montpellier of South America, and has obtained, on account of its climate, the name of Buenos Ayres. It was in this delicious place that I gave myself entirely up to the thoughts of my dear Narcissa, whose image still kept possession of my breast, and whose charms, enhanced by absence, appeared to my imagination, if possible, more engaging than ever! I calculated the profits of my voyage, which even exceeded my expectation; resolved to purchase a handsome sinecure upon my arrival in England, and, if I should find the squire as averse to me as ever, marry his sister by stealth; and in case our family should increase, rely upon the generosity of my uncle, who was by this time worth a considerable sum.

While I amused myself with these agreeable projects, and the transporting hopes of enjoying Narcissa, we were very much caressed by the Spanish gentlemen, who frequently formed parties of pleasure for our entertainment, in which we made excursions a good way into the country. Among those who signalised themselves by their civility to us, there was one Don Antonio de Ribera, a very polite young gentleman, with whom I had contracted an intimate friendship, who invited us one day to his country house, and, as a further inducement to our compliance, promised to procure for us the company of an English signior, who had been settled in those parts many years, and acquired the love and esteem of the whole province by his affability, good sense, and honourable behaviour.

We accepted his invitation, and set out for his villa, where we had not been longer than an hour, when the person arrived in whose favour I had been so much prepossessed. He was a tall man, remarkably well-shaped, of a fine mien and appearance, commanding respect, and seemed to be turned forty; the features of his face were saddened with a reserve and gravity, which in other countries would have been thought the effect of melancholy; but here appeared to have been contracted by his commerce with the Spaniards, who are remarkable for that severity of countenance. Understanding from Don Antonio that we were his countrymen, he saluted us all round very complaisantly, and fixing his eyes very attentively on me, uttered a deep sigh. I had been struck with a profound veneration for him at his first coming into the room; and no sooner observed this expression of his sorrow, directed, as it were, in a particular manner to me, than my heart took part in his grief. I sympathised involuntarily, and sighed in my turn. Having asked leave of our entertainer, he accosted us in English, professed his satisfaction at seeing so many of his countrymen in such a remote place, and asked the captain, who went by the name of Signior Thoma, from what part of Britain he had sailed, and whither he was bound. My uncle told him that we had sailed from the River Thames, and were bound for the same place by the way of Jamaica, where we intended to take in a lading of sugar.

Having satisfied himself in these and other particulars about the state of the war, he gave us to understand that he had a longing desire to revisit his native country, in consequence of which he had already transmitted to Europe the greatest part of his fortune in neutral bottoms, and would willingly embark the rest of it with himself in our ship, provided the captain had no objection to such a passenger. My uncle very prudently replied, that for his part he should be glad of his company, if he could procure the consent of the governor, without which he durst not admit him on board, whatever inclination he had to oblige him. The gentleman approved of his discretion, and, telling him that there would be no difficulty in obtaining the connivance of the governor, who was his good friend, shifted the conversation to another subject.

I was overjoyed to hear his intention, and already interested myself so much in his favour, that, had he been disappointed, I should have been very unhappy. In the course of our entertainment, he eyed me with uncommon attachment; I felt a surprising attraction towards him; when he spoke, I listened with attention and reverence; the dignity of his deportment filled me with affection and awe: and, in short, the emotions of my soul, in presence of this stranger, were strong and unaccountable!

Having spent the best part of the day with us, he took his leave, telling Captain Thoma that he should hear from him in a short time. He was no sooner gone, than I asked a thousand questions about him of Don Antonio, who could give me no other satisfaction, than that his name was Don Rodrigo, that he had lived fifteen or sixteen years in these parts, was reputed rich, and supposed to have been unfortunate in his younger years, because he was observed to nourish a pensive melancholy, even from the time of his first settlement among them; but that nobody had ventured to inquire into the cause of his sorrow, in consideration of his peace, which might suffer in the recapitulation of his misfortunes.

I was seized with an irresistible desire of knowing the particulars of his fate, and enjoyed not one hour of repose during the whole night, by reason of the eager conceptions that inspired me with regard to his story, which I resolved, if possible, to learn. Next morning, while we were at breakfast, three mules richly caparisoned arrived with a message from Don Rodrigo, desiring our company, and that of Don Antonio, at his house, which was situated about ten miles farther up in the country. I was pleased with this invitation, in consequence of which we mounted the mules which he had provided for us, and alighted at his house before noon. Here we were splendidly entertained by the generous stranger, who still seemed to show a particular regard for me, and, after dinner, made me a present of a ring set with a beautiful amethyst, the production of that country, saying, at the same time, that he was once blessed with a son, who, had he lived, would have been nearly of my age. This observation, delivered with a profound sigh, made my heart throb with violence; a crowd of confused ideas rushed upon my imagination, which while I endeavoured to unravel, my uncle perceived my absence of thought, and tapping me on the shoulder, said, "Oons! are you asleep, Rory!" Before I had time to reply, Don Rodrigo, with uncommon eagerness of voice and look, pronounced, "Pray, captain, what is the young gentleman's name?"—"His name," said my uncle, "is Roderick Random." "Gracious Powers!" cried the stranger, starting up, —"and his mother's?"—"His mother," answered the captain, amazed, "was called Charlotte Bowling." "O bounteous Heaven!" exclaimed Don Rodrigo, springing across the table, and clasping me in his arms, "my son! my son! have I found thee again?—do I hold thee in my embrace, after having lost and despaired of seeing thee so long?" So saying, he fell upon my neck and wept aloud with joy; while the power of nature operating strongly in my breast, I was lost in rapture, and while he pressed me to his heart, let fall a shower of tears into his bosom. His utterance was choked up a good while by the agitation of his soul. At length he broke out into, "Mysterious Providence!—O my dear Charlotte! there yet remains a pledge of our love; and such a pledge!—so found!—O Infinite Goodness! let me adore thy all-wise decrees!" Having thus expressed himself, he kneeled upon the floor, lifted up his eyes and hands to heaven, and remained some minutes in a silent ecstasy of devotion. I put myself in the same posture, adored the All-good Disposer in a prayer of mental thanksgiving; and when his ejaculation was ended, did homage to my father, and craved his parental blessing. He hugged me again with unutterable fondness, and having implored the protection of Heaven upon my head, raised me from the ground, and presented me as his son to the company, who wept in concert over this affecting scene. Among the rest, my uncle did not fail to discover the goodness and joy of his heart. *Albeit unused to the melting mood,* he blubbered with great tenderness, and wringing my father's hand, cried, "Brother Random, I'm rejoiced to see you—God be praised for this happy meeting." Don Rodrigo, understanding that he was his brother-in-law, embraced him affectionately, saying, "Are you my Charlotte's brother?—Alas! unhappy Charlotte! but why should I repine? we shall meet again never more to part!—Brother, you are truly welcome. Dear son, I am transported with unspeakable joy!—This day is a jubilee—my friends and servants shall share my satisfaction."

While he despatched messengers to the gentlemen in the neighbourhood to announce this event, and gave orders for a grand entertainment, I was so much affected with the tumults of passion which assailed me on this great, sudden, and unexpected occasion, that I fell sick, fevered, and in less than three hours became quite delirious; so that the preparations were countermanded, and the joy of the family converted into grief and despair. Physicians were instantly called, I was plentifully blooded in the foot, my lower extremities were bathed in a decoction of salutiferous herbs; in ten hours after I was taken ill I enjoyed a critical sweat, and next day felt no remains of the distemper, but an agreeable lassitude, which did not hinder me from getting up. During the progress of this fever, which from the term of its duration is called *ephemera*, my father never once quitted my bedside, but administered the prescriptions of the physicians with the most pious care; while Captain Bowling manifested his concern by the like attendance. I no sooner found myself delivered from the disease, than I bethought myself of my honest friend, Strap; and resolving to make him happy forthwith in the knowledge of my good fortune, told my father in general that I had been infinitely obliged to this faithful adherent, and begged he would indulge me so far as to send for him, without letting him know my happiness, until he could receive an account of it from my own mouth.

My request was instantly complied with, and a messenger with a spare mule detached to the ship, carrying orders from the captain to the mate to send the steward by the bearer. My health being, in the meantime, re-established, and my mind composed, I began to relish this important turn of my fortune, in reflecting upon the advantages with which it must be attended; and as the idea of my lovely Narcissa always joined itself to every scene of happiness I could imagine, I entertained myself now with the prospect of possessing her in that distinguished sphere to which she was entitled by her birth and qualifications. Having often mentioned her name while I was deprived of my senses, my father guessed that there was an intimate connection between us, and discovering the picture which hung in my bosom by a ribbon, did not doubt that it was the resemblance of my amiable mistress. In this belief he was confirmed by my uncle, who told him that it was the picture of a young woman to whom I was under promise of marriage. Alarmed at this piece of information, Don Rodrigo took the first opportunity of questioning me about the particulars of this affair, which when I had candidly recounted, he approved of my passion, and promised to contribute all in his power towards its success. Though I never doubted his generosity, I was transported on this occasion, and throwing myself at his feet, told him he had now completed my happiness; for, without the possession of Narcissa, I should be miserable among all the pleasures of life. He raised me with a smile of paternal fondness; said that he knew what it was to be in love; and observed that if he had been as tenderly beloved by his father as I was by mine, he should not now perhaps have cause—here he was interrupted by a sigh, the tear rushed into his eye, he suppressed the dictates of his grief, and the time being opportune, desired me to relate the passages of my life, which my uncle had told him were manifold and surprising. I recounted the most material circumstances of my fortune, to which he listened with wonder and attention, manifesting from time to time those different emotions which my different situations may be supposed to have raised in a parent's breast, and, when my detail was ended, blessed God for the adversity I had undergone, which, he said, enlarged the understanding, improved the heart, steeled the constitution, and qualified a young man for all the duties and enjoyments of life, much better than any education which affluence could bestow.

When I had thus satisfied his curiosity, I discovered an inclination to hear the particulars of his story, which he gratified, by beginning with his marriage, and proceeded to the day of his disappearing, as I have related in the first part of my memoirs. "Careless of life," continued he, "and unable to live in a place where every object recalled the memory of my dear Charlotte, whom I had lost through the barbarity of an unnatural parent, I took my leave of you, my child, then an infant, with a heart full of unutterable woe, but little suspecting that my father's unkindness would have descended to my innocent orphan; and setting out alone at midnight for the nearest seaport, early next morning got on board a ship, bound as I had heard for France, and bargaining with the master for my passage, bade a long adieu to my native country, and put to sea with the first fair

wind. The place of our destination was Granville; but we had
the misfortune to run upon a ridge of rocks near the Island of
Alderney, called the Caskets, where the sea running high, the
ship went to pieces, the boat sunk alongside, and every soul on
board perished, except myself, who, by the assistance of a
grating, got ashore on the coast of Normandy. I went directly
to Caen, where I was so lucky as to meet with a count whom I
had formerly known in my travels. With this gentleman I set
out for Paris, where I was recommended by him and other
friends as a tutor to a young nobleman, whom I accompanied
to the court of Spain. There we remained a whole year, at the
end of which my pupil being recalled by his father, I quitted my
office, and staid behind, by the advice of a certain Spanish
grandee, who took me into his protection, and introduced me to
another nobleman, who was afterwards created viceroy of Peru.
He insisted on my attending him to his government in the
Indies, where, however, by reason of my religion, it was not
in his power to make my fortune any other way than by encouraging me to trade, which I had not long prosecuted, when
my patron died, and I found myself in the midst of strangers,
without one friend to support or protect me. Urged by this
consideration, I sold my effects, and removed to this country,
the governor of which, having been appointed by the viceroy,
was my intimate acquaintance. Here has Heaven prospered my
endeavours during a residence of sixteen years, in which my
tranquillity was never invaded, but by the remembrance of your
mother, whose death I have in secret mourned without ceasing,
and the reflection of you, whose fate I could never learn, notwithstanding all my inquiries, by means of my friends in France, who,
after the most strict examination, could give me no other account, than that you went abroad six years ago, and was never
after heard of. I could not rest satisfied with this imperfect
information, and though my hope of finding you was but
languid, resolved to go in quest of you in person; for which
purpose I have remitted to Holland the value of twenty
thousand pounds, and am in possession of fifteen thousand
more, with which I intended to embark myself on board of
Captain Bowling, before I discovered this amazing stroke
of Providence, which you may be sure has not altered my
intention."

My father having entertained us with this agreeable sketch
of his life, withdrew, in order to relieve Don Antonio, who, in his
absence, had done the honours of his house; and I was just

dressed for my appearance among the guests, when Strap arrived from the ship.

He no sooner entered the grand apartment in which I was, and saw the magnificence of my apparel, than his speech was lost in amazement, and he gaped in silence at the objects that surrounded him. I took him by the hand, observed that I had sent for him to be a witness and sharer of my happiness, and told him I had found a father. At these words he started, and after having continued some minutes with his mouth and eyes wide open, cried, "Aha!—odd, I know what! go thy ways, poor Narcissa, and go thy ways, somebody else—well—Lord, what a thing is love!—God help us! are all our mad pranks and protestations come to this? and have you fixed your habitation in this distant land? God prosper you!—I find we must part at last—for I would not leave my poor carcass so far from my native home for all the wealth in the universe!" With these ejaculations, he began to sob and make wry faces; upon which I assured him of his mistake, both in regard to Narcissa and my staying at Paraguay, and informed him, as briefly as I could, of the great event which had happened. Never was rapture more ludicrously expressed than in the behaviour of this worthy creature, who cried, laughed, whistled, sung, and danced all in a breath. His transport was scarce over, when my father entered, who no sooner understood that this was Strap, than he took him by the hand, saying, "Is this the honest man who befriended you so much in your distress? you are welcome to my house, and I will soon put it in the power of my son to reward you for your good offices in his behalf; in the meantime, go with us, and partake of the repast that is provided." Strap, wild as he was with joy, would by no means accept of the proffered honour, crying, "God forbid!—I know my distance—your worship shall excuse me." And Don Rodrigo finding his modesty invincible, recommended him to his major-domo, to be treated with the utmost respect; while he carried me into a large saloon, where I was presented to a numerous company, who loaded me with compliments and caresses, and congratulated my father in terms not proper for me to repeat.

Without specifying the particulars of our entertainment, let it suffice to say it was at the same time elegant and sumptuous, and the rejoicings lasted two days. After which, Don Rodrigo settled his affairs, converted his effects into silver and gold, visited and took leave of all his friends, who were grieved at his departure, and honoured me with considerable presents; and coming on board of my uncle's ship, with the first favourable wind we sailed from the Rio de la Plata, and in two months came safe to an anchor in the harbour of Kingston, in the Island of Jamaica.

CHAPTER LXVII

I visit my old Friend Thomson—We set sail for Europe—Meet with an odd Adventure—Arrive in England—I ride across the Country from Portsmouth to Sussex—Converse with Mrs. Sagely, who informs me of Narcissa's being in London—In consequence of this Intelligence, I proceed to Canterbury—Meet with my old Friend Morgan—Arrive at London—Visit Narcissa—Introduce my Father to her—He is charmed with her good Sense and Beauty—We come to a Determination of demanding her Brother's Consent to our Marriage.

I INQUIRED, as soon as I got ashore, about my generous companion, Mr. Thomson; and hearing that he lived in a flourishing condition upon the estate left him by his wife's father, who had been dead some years, I took horse immediately, with the consent of Don Rodrigo, who had heard me mention him with great regard, and in a few hours reached the place of his habitation.

I should much wrong the delicacy of Mr. Thomson's sentiments, to say barely he was glad to see me. He felt all that the most sensible and disinterested friendship could feel on this occasion; introduced me to his wife, a very amiable young lady, who had already blessed him with two fine children; and being as yet ignorant of my circumstances, frankly offered me the assistance of his purse and interest. I thanked him for his generous intention, and made him acquainted with my situation, on which he congratulated me with great joy, and after I had staid with him a whole day and night, accompanied me back to Kingston, to wait upon my father, whom he invited to his house. Don Rodrigo complied with his request, and having been handsomely entertained during the space of a week, returned extremely well satisfied with the behaviour of my friend and his lady, to whom, at parting, he presented a very valuable diamond ring, as a token of his esteem. During the course of my conversation with Mr. Thomson, he gave me to understand that his and my old commander, Captain Oakum, was dead some months; and that, immediately after his death, a discovery had been made of some valuable effects that he had feloniously secreted out of a prize, by the assistance of Doctor Mackshane, who was now actually in prison on that account, and being destitute of friends, subsisted solely on the charity of my friend, whose bounty he had implored in the most abject manner, after having been the barbarous occasion of driving him to that terrible extremity on board of the *Thunder*, which we have formerly related. Whatsoever this wretch might have been guilty of, I applauded Mr. Thomson's generosity towards him in his distress, which wrought so much upon me also, that I sent him ten pistoles, in such a private manner that he could never know his benefactor.

While my father and I were caressed among the gentlemen on shore, Captain Bowling had written to his owners by the packet, which sailed a few days after our arrival, signifying his prosperous voyage hitherto, and desiring them to insure his ship and cargo homeward-bound; after which precaution, he applied himself so heartily to the task of loading his ship, that, with the assistance of Mr. Thomson, she was full in less than six weeks. This kind gentleman likewise procured for Don Rodrigo bills upon London for the greatest part of his gold and silver, by which means it was secured against the risk of the seas and the enemy; and, before we sailed, supplied us with such large quantities of all kinds of stock, that not only we, but the ship's company, fared sumptuously during the voyage.

Everything being ready, we took our leave of our kind entertainers, and, going on board at Port Royal, set sail for England on the first day of June. We beat up to windward with fine easy weather; and one night, believing ourselves near Cape Tiberoon, lay to, with an intention to wood and water next morning in the bay. While we remained in this situation, a sailor, having drank more new rum than he could carry, staggered overboard, and notwithstanding all the means that could be used to preserve him, went to the bottom and disappeared. About two hours after this melancholy accident happened, as I enjoyed the cool air on the quarter-deck, I heard a voice rising, as it were, out of the sea, and calling, "Ho, the ship, ahoy!" Upon which one of the men upon the forecastle cried, "I'll be damned, if that ain't Jack Marlinspike, who went overboard!" Not a little surprised at this event, I jumped into the boat that lay alongside, with the second mate and four men, and, rowing towards the place from whence the voice (which repeated the hail) seemed to proceed, we perceived something floating upon the water; when we had rowed a little farther, we discerned it to be a man riding upon a hencoop, who, seeing us approach,

pronounced with a hoarse voice, "Damn your bloods! why did
you not answer when I hailed?" Our mate, who was a veritable
seaman, hearing this salute, said "By Gad, my lads, this is none
of our men. This is the devil—pull away for the ship." The
fellows obeyed his command without question, and were already
some fathoms on our return, when I insisted on their taking up
the poor creature, and prevailed upon them to go back to the
wreck; which when we came near the second time, and signified
our intention, we received an answer of, "Avast, avast,—what
ship, brother?" Being satisfied in this particular, he cried,
"Damn the ship, I was in hopes it had been my own—where are
you bound?" We satisfied his curiosity in this particular too;
upon which he suffered himself to be taken on board, and, after
having been comforted with a dram, told us, he belonged to the
Vesuvio man-of-war, upon a cruise off the Island of Hispaniola;
he had fallen overboard about four and twenty hours ago, and
the ship being under sail, they did not choose to bring to, but
tossed a hencoop overboard for his convenience, upon which
he was in good hopes of reaching the Cape next morning; howsomever, he was as well content to be aboard of us, because
he did not doubt that we should meet his ship; and, if he had
gone ashore in the bay, he might have been taken prisoner by
the French. My uncle and father were very much diverted with
the account of this fellow's unconcerned behaviour; and, in two
days, meeting with the *Vesuvio*, as he expected, sent him on
board of her, according to his desire.

Having beat up successfully the Windward Passage, we
stretched to the northward, and falling in with a westerly wind,
in eight weeks arrived in soundings, and in two days after made
the Lizard. It is impossible to express the joy I felt at the sight
of English ground! Don Rodrigo was not unmoved, and Strap
shed tears of gladness. The sailors profited by our satisfaction;
the shoe that was nailed to the mast being quite filled with our
liberality. My uncle resolved to run up into the Downs at once;
but the wind shifting when we were abreast of the Isle of Wight,
he was obliged to turn into St. Helen's and come to Spithead,
to the great mortification of the crew, thirty of whom were
immediately pressed on board of a man-of-war.

My father and I went ashore immediately at Portsmouth,
leaving Strap with the captain to go round with the ship and
take care of our effects; and I discovered so much impatience to
see my charming Narcissa, that my father permitted me to ride
across the country to her brother's house; while he should hire

a post-chaise for London, where he would wait for me at a place to which I directed him.

Fired with all the eagerness of passion, I took post that very night, and in the morning reached an inn about three miles from the squire's habitation; here I remained till next morning, allaying the torture of my impatience with the rapturous hope of seeing that divine creature, after an absence of eighteen months, which, far from impairing, had raised my love to the most exalted pitch! Neither were my reflections free from apprehensions, that sometimes intervened in spite of all my hope, and represented her as having yielded to the importunity of her brother, and blessed the arms of an happy rival. My thoughts were even maddened with the fear of her death; and when I arrived in the dark at the house of Mrs. Sagely, I had not for some time courage to desire admittance, lest my soul should be shocked with dismal tidings. At length, however, I knocked, and no sooner certified the good gentlewoman of my voice, than she opened the door and received me with a most affectionate embrace, that brought tears into her aged eyes. "For Heaven's sake! dear mother," cried I, "tell me, how is Narcissa? is she the same that I left her?" She blessed my ears with saying, "She is as beautiful, in as good health, and as much yours as ever." Transported at this assurance, I begged to know if I could not see her that very night; when this sage matron gave me to understand that my mistress was in London, and that things were strangely altered in the squire's house since my departure; that he had been married a whole year to Melinda, who at first found means to wean his attention so much from Narcissa, that he became quite careless of that lovely sister, comforting himself with the clause in his father's will by which she should forfeit her fortune by marrying without his consent; that my mistress, being but indifferently treated by her sister-in-law, had made use of her freedom some months ago, and gone to town, where she was lodged with Miss Williams, in expectation of my arrival; and had been pestered with the addresses of Lord Quiverwit, who, finding her heart engaged, had fallen upon a great many shifts to persuade her that I was dead; but finding all his artifices unsuccessful, and despairing of gaining her affection, he had consoled himself for her indifference, by marrying another lady some weeks ago, who had already left him on account of some family uneasiness. Besides this interesting information, she told me that there was not a great deal of harmony between Melinda and the squire, who

was so much disgusted at the number of gallants who continued
to hover about her even after marriage, that he had hurried her
down into the country, much against her own inclination, where
their mutual animosities had risen to such a height, that they
preserved no decency before company or servants, but abused
one another in the grossest terms.

This good old gentlewoman, to give me a convincing proof of
my dear Narcissa's unalterable love, gratified me with a sight
of the last letter she had favoured her with, in which I was mentioned with so much honour, tenderness, and concern, that my
soul was fired with impatience, and I determined to ride all
night, that I might have it the sooner in my power to make her
happy. Mrs. Sagely perceiving my eagerness, and her maternal
affection being equally divided between Narcissa and me, begged
leave to remind me of the sentiments with which I went abroad,
that would not permit me for any selfish gratification to prejudice
the fortune of that amiable young lady, who must entirely
depend upon me after having bestowed herself in marriage. I
thanked her for her kind concern, and as briefly as possible
described my flourishing situation, which afforded this humane
person infinite wonder and satisfaction. I told her, that now I
had an opportunity to manifest my gratitude for the obligations
I owed, I would endeavour to make her old age comfortable and
easy; as a step to which, I proposed she should come and live
with Narcissa and me. This venerable gentlewoman was so much
affected with my words, that the tears ran down her ancient
cheeks; she thanked Heaven that I had not belied the presages
she had made, on her first acquaintance with me; acknowledging
my generosity, as she called it, in the most elegant and pathetic
expressions; but declined my proposal, on account of her attachment to the dear melancholy cottage where she had so peacefully
consumed her solitary widowhood. Finding her immovable on
this subject, I insisted on her accepting a present of thirty
guineas, and took my leave, resolving to accommodate her with
the same sum annually, for the more comfortable support of the
infirmities of old age.

Having rode all night, I found myself at Canterbury in the
morning, where I alighted to procure fresh horses; and, as I
walked into the inn, perceived an apothecary's shop on the
other side of the street, with the name of Morgan over the door.
Alarmed at this discovery, I could not help thinking that my old
messmate had settled in this place; and, upon inquiry, found
my conjecture true, and that he was married lately to a widow

in that city, by whom he had got three thousand pounds. Rejoiced at this intelligence, I went to his shop as soon as it was open, and found my friend behind the counter, busy in preparing a glyster. I saluted him at entrance with, "Your servant, Mr. Morgan." Upon which he looked at me, and replying, "Your most humble servant, goot sir!" rubbed his ingredients in the mortar, without any emotion. "What!" said I, "Morgan, have you forgot your old messmate?" At these words he looked up again, and starting, cried, "As Got is my—sure it cannot—yes, by my salfation, I pelieve it is my dear friend Mr. Random." He was no sooner convinced of my identity, than he threw down the pestle, overset the mortar, and jumping over the board, swept up the contents with his clothes, flew about my neck, hugged me affectionately, and daubed me all over with turpentine and the yolks of eggs, which he had been mixing when I came in. Our mutual congratulations being over, he told me that he found himself a widower upon his return from the West Indies; that he had got interest to be appointed surgeon of a man-of-war, in which capacity he had served some years, until he married an apothecary's widow, with whom he now enjoyed a pretty good sum of money, peace and quiet, and an indifferent good trade. He was very desirous of hearing my adventures, which I assured him I had not time to relate, but told him in general, my circumstances were very good, and that I hoped to see him when I should not be in such a hurry as at present. He insisted, however, on my staying breakfast, and introduced me to his wife, who seemed to be a decent sensible woman, pretty well stricken in years. In the course of our conversation he showed the sleeve buttons I had exchanged with him at our parting in the West Indies, and was not a little proud to see that I had preserved his with the same care. When I informed him of Mackshane's condition, he seemed at first to exult over his distress; but, after a little recollection, said, "Well, he has paid for his malice, I forgife him, and may Got forgife him likewise." He expressed great concern for the soul of Captain Oakum, which he believed was now gnashing its teeth; but it was some time before I could convince him of Thomson's being alive, at whose good fortune, nevertheless, he was extremely glad.

Having renewed our protestations of friendship, I bade the honest Welshman and his spouse farewell, and taking post-horses, arrived at London that same night, where I found my father in good health, to whom I imparted what I had learned of Narcissa. This indulgent parent approved of my intention of marrying her, even without a fortune, provided her brother's consent could not be obtained; promised to make over to me in a few days a sufficiency to maintain her in a fashionable manner, and expressed a desire of seeing this amiable creature, who had captivated me so much. As I had not slept the night before, and was besides fatigued with my journey, I found myself under a necessity of taking some repose, and went to bed accordingly; next morning about ten o'clock, took a chair, and according to Mrs. Sagely's directions, went to my charmer's lodgings and inquired for Miss Williams. I had not waited in the parlour longer than a minute, when this young woman entered, and no sooner perceived me, than she shrieked and ran backward; but I got between her and the door, and clasping her in my arms, brought her to herself with an embrace. "Good Heaven," cried she, "Mr. Random, is it you indeed? my mistress will run distracted with joy." I told her it was from an apprehension that my sudden appearance might have some bad effect on my dear Narcissa, that I had desired to see her first, in order to concert some method of acquainting her mistress gradually with my arrival. She approved of my conduct, and, after having yielded to the suggestions of her own friendship, in asking if my voyage had been successful, charged herself with that office, and left me glowing with desire of seeing and embracing the object of my love. In a very little time I heard somebody come downstairs in haste, and the voice of my angel pronounce, with an eager tone, "O Heaven! is it possible! where is he?" How were my faculties aroused at this well-known sound! and how was my soul transported, when she broke in upon my view, in all the bloom of ripened beauty! *Grace was in all her steps, heaven in her eye, in every gesture dignity and love!*—You whose souls are susceptible of the most delicate impressions, whose tender bosoms have felt the affecting vicissitudes of love, who have suffered an absence of eighteen long months from the dear object of your hope, and found at your return the melting fair, as kind and as constant as your heart could wish, do me justice on this occasion, and conceive what unutterable rapture possessed us both, while we flew into each other's arms! This was no time for speech,—locked in a mutual embrace, we continued some minutes in a silent trance of joy!—When I thus encircled all that my soul held dear, while I hung over her beauties,— beheld her eyes sparkle, and every feature flush with virtuous fondness; when I saw her enchanting bosom heave with undissembled rapture, and knew myself the happy cause—Heavens!

what was my situation! I am tempted to commit my paper to the flames, and to renounce my pen for ever, because its most ardent and lucky expression so poorly describes the emotions of my soul. "O adorable Narcissa," cried I; "O miracle of beauty, love, and truth! I at last fold thee in my arms! I at last can call thee mine! No jealous brother shall thwart our happiness again; fortune hath at length recompensed me for all my sufferings, and enabled me to do justice to my love." The dear creature smiled ineffably charming, and with a look of bewitching tenderness, said, "And shall we never part again?" "Never," I replied, "thou wondrous pattern of all earthly perfection! never, until death shall divide us! By this ambrosial kiss, a thousand times more fragrant than the breeze that sweeps the orange grove, I never more will leave thee!"

As my first transport abated, my passion grew turbulent and unruly. I was giddy with standing on the brink of bliss, and all my virtue and philosophy were scarce sufficient to restrain the inordinate sallies of desire. Narcissa perceived the conflict within me, and, with her usual dignity of prudence, called off my imagination from the object in view, and with eager expressions of interested curiosity, desired to know the particulars of my voyage. In this I gratified her inclination, bringing my story down to the present hour. She was infinitely surprised at the circumstance of my finding my father, which brought tears into her lovely eyes. She was transported at hearing that he approved my flame, discovered a longing desire of being introduced to him, congratulated herself and me upon my good fortune, and observed that this great and unexpected stroke of fate seemed to have been brought about by the immediate direction of Providence. Having entertained ourselves some hours with the genuine effusions of our souls, I obtained her consent to complete my happiness as soon as my father should judge it proper, and applying with my own hands a valuable necklace, composed of diamonds and amethysts set alternately, which an old Spanish lady at Paraguay had presented me with, I took my leave, promising to return in the afternoon with Don Rodrigo. When I went home, this generous parent inquired very affectionately about the health of my dear Narcissa, to whom that I might be the more agreeable, he put into my hand a deed, by which I found myself in possession of fifteen thousand pounds, exclusive of the profits of my own merchandise, which amounted to three thousand more. After dinner I accompanied him to the lodging of my mistress, who, being dressed for the occasion, made a most dazzling appearance. I could perceive him struck with her figure, which I really think was the most beautiful that ever was created under the sun. He embraced her tenderly, and told her he was proud of having a son who had a spirit to attempt and qualifications to engage the affections of such a fine lady. She blushed at this compliment, and with eyes full of the softest languishment turned upon me, said she should have been unworthy of Mr. Random's attention, had she been blind to his extraordinary merit. I made no other answer than a low bow. My father, sighing, pronounced, "Such once was my Charlotte!" while the tear rushed into his eye, and the tender heart of Narcissa manifested itself in two precious drops of sympathy, which, but for his presence, I would have kissed away. Without repeating the particulars of our conversation, I shall only observe that Don Rodrigo was as much charmed with her good sense as with her appearance; and she was no less pleased with his understanding and polite address. It was determined that he should write to the squire, signifying his approbation of my passion for his sister, and offering a settlement which he should have no reason to reject; and that, if he should refuse the proposal, we would crown our mutual wishes without any farther regard to his will.

CHAPTER LXVIII

My father makes a Present to Narcissa—The Letter is despatched to her Brother—I appear among my Acquaintance—Banter's Behaviour—The Squire refuses his Consent—My Uncle comes to Town Approves of my Choice—I am Married—We meet the Squire and his Lady at the Play— Our Acquaintance is courted.

AFTER having spent the evening to the satisfaction of all present, my father addressed himself thus to Narcissa, "Madam, give me leave to consider you hereafter as my daughter, in which capacity I insist upon your accepting this first instance of my paternal duty and affection." With these words he put into her hand a banknote of £500, which she no sooner examined, than, with a low curtsey, she replied, "Dear sir, though I have not the least occasion for this supply, I have too great a veneration for you to refuse this proof of your generosity and esteem, which I the more freely receive, because I already look upon Mr. Random's interest as inseparably connected with mine." He was extremely well pleased with her frank and ingenuous reply; upon which we saluted, and wished her good night. The letter, at my request, was despatched to Sussex by an express, and in the meantime, Don Rodrigo, to grace my nuptials, hired a ready-furnished house, and set up a very handsome equipage.

Though I passed the greatest part of the day with the darling of my soul, I found leisure sometimes to be among my former acquaintance, who were astonished at the magnificence of my appearance. Banter, in particular, was confounded at the strange vicissitudes of my fortune, the causes of which he endeavoured in vain to discover, until I thought fit to disclose the whole secret of my last voyage, partly in consideration of our former intimacy, and partly to prevent unfavourable conjectures which he and others, in all probability, would have made in regard to my circumstances. He professed great satisfaction at this piece of news, and I had no cause to believe him insincere, when I considered that he would now look upon himself as acquitted of the debt he owed me, and at the same time flatter himself with hopes of borrowing more. I carried him home to dinner with me, and my father liked his conversation so much, that, upon hearing his difficulties, he desired me to accommodate him for the present, and inquire if he would accept of a commission in the army, towards the purchase of which he would willingly lend him money. Accordingly, I gave my friend an opportunity of being alone with me, when, as I expected, he told me that he was just on the point of being reconciled to an old rich uncle, whose heir he was, but wanted a few pieces for immediate expense, which he desired I would lend him, and take his bond for the whole. His demand was limited to ten guineas; and when I put twenty into his hand, he stared at me for some moments; then putting it into his purse, said, "Ay, 'tis all one,—you shall have the whole in a very short time." When I had taken his note, to save the expense of a bond, I expressed some surprise that a fellow of his spirit should loiter away his time in idleness, and asked why he did not choose to make his fortune in the army? "What!" said he, "throw away my money upon a subaltern's commission, to be under the command of a parcel of scoundrels, who have raised themselves above me by the most infamous practices! No, I love independency too well to sacrifice my life, health, and pleasure for such a pitiful consideration." Finding him averse to this way of life, I changed the subject and returned to Don Rodrigo, who had just received the following epistle from the squire:

"SIR,—Concerning a letter which I received, subscribed R. Random, this is the answer. As for you, I know nothing of you. Your son, or pretended son, I have seen;—if he marries my sister, at his peril be it; I do declare, that he shall not have one farthing of her fortune, which becomes my property, if she takes a husband without my consent. Your settlement, I do believe, is all a sham, and yourself no better than you should be; but if you had all the wealth of the Indies, your son shall never match in our family, with the consent of

"ORSON TOPEHALL."

My father was not much surprised at this polite letter, after having heard the character of the author; and as for me, I was even pleased at his refusal, because I now had an opportunity of showing my disinterested love. By his permission I waited on my charmer; and, having imparted the contents of her brother's letter at which she wept bitterly, in spite of all my consolation and caresses, the time of our marriage was fixed at the distance of two days. During this interval, in which my soul was wound up to the last stretch of rapturous expectation, Narcissa endeavoured to reconcile some of her relations in town to her marriage with me; but, finding them all deaf to her remonstrances, either out of envy or prejudice, she told me with the most enchanting sweetness, while the tears bedewed her lovely cheeks, "Sure the world will no longer question your generosity, when you take a poor forlorn beggar to your arms." Affected with her sorrow, I pressed the fair mourner to my breast, and swore that she was more dear and welcome on that account, because she had sacrificed her friends and fortune to her love for me. My uncle, for whose character she had a great veneration, being by this time come to town, I introduced him to my bride; and although he was not very much subject to refined sensations, he was struck dumb with admiration at her beauty. After having kissed and gazed at her for some time, he turned to me, saying, "Odds bobs, Rory! here's a notable prize, indeed, finely built and gloriously rigged, i'faith! if she ain't well manned when you have the command of her, sirrah, you deserve to go to sea in a cockleshell. No offence, I hope, niece; you must not mind what I say, being, as the saying is, a plain seafaring man; thof, may-hap, I have as much regard for you as another." She received him with great civility, told him she had longed a great while to see a person to whom she was so much indebted for his generosity to Mr. Random; that she looked upon him as her uncle, by which name she begged leave to call him for the future; and that she was very sure he could say nothing that would give her the least offence. The honest captain was transported at her courteous behaviour, and insisted upon giving her away at the ceremony, swearing that he loved her as well as if she was his own child, and that he would give two thousand guineas to the first fruit of our love, as soon as it could squeak. Everything being prepared for the solemnisation of our nuptials, which were to be performed privately at my father's house, the auspicious hour arrived, when Don Rodrigo and my uncle went in the coach to fetch the bride and Miss Williams; leaving me with a parson, Banter, and Strap, neither of whom had as yet seen my charming mistress. My faithful valet, who was on the rack of impatience to behold a lady of whom he had heard so much, no sooner understood that the coach was returned, than he placed himself at a window to have a peep at her as she alighted; and when he saw her, clapped his hands together, turned up the white of his eyes, and, with his mouth wide open, remained in a sort of ecstasy, which broke out into, "*O Dea certe! qualis in Eurotæ ripis, aut per juga Cynthi, exercet Diana choros!*" The doctor and Banter were surprised to hear my man speak Latin; but when my father led Narcissa into the room, the object of their admiration was soon changed, as appeared in the countenances of both. Indeed, they must have been the most insensible of all beings, could they have beheld, without emotion, the divine creature that approached! She was dressed in a sack of white satin, embroidered on the breast with gold; the crown of her head was covered with a small French cap, from whence descended her beautiful hair in ringlets that waved upon her snowy neck, which dignified the necklace I had given her; her looks glowed with modesty and love; and her bosom, through the veil of gauze that shaded it, afforded a prospect of Elysium! I received this inestimable gift of Providence as became me; and in a little time the clergyman did his office, my uncle, at his own earnest request, acting the part of a father to my dear Narcissa, who trembled very much, and had scarce spirits sufficient to support her under this great change of situation. Soon as she was mine by the laws of heaven and earth, I printed a burning kiss upon her lips, my father embraced her tenderly, my uncle hugged her with great affection, and I presented her to my friend Banter, who saluted her in a very polite manner; Miss Williams hung round her neck, and wept plentifully; while Strap fell upon his knees, and begged to kiss his lady's hand, which she presented with great affability. I shall not pretend to describe my own feelings at this juncture; let it suffice to say that, after having supped and entertained ourselves till ten o'clock, I cautioned my Narcissa against exposing her health by sitting up too late, and she was prevailed upon to withdraw with her maid to an apartment destined for us. When she left the room, her face was overspread with a blush that set all my blood in a state of fermentation, and made every pulse beat with tenfold vigour! She was so cruel as to let me remain in this condition a full half-hour; when no longer able to restrain my impatience, I broke from the company, burst into her chamber, pushed out her confidante, locked the door, and found her—O heaven and earth!—a feast a thousand times more delicious than my most sanguine hope presaged!—But let me not profane the chaste mysteries of Hymen. I was the happiest of men!

In the morning I was waked by three or four drums, which Banter had placed under the window; upon which I withdrew the curtain, and enjoyed the unspeakable satisfaction of contemplating those angelic charms which were now in my possession! *Beauty which, whether sleeping or awake, shot forth peculiar graces!* The light darting upon my Narcissa's eyes, she awoke also, and recollecting her situation, hid her blushes in my bosom. I was distracted with joy! I could not believe the evidence of my senses, and looked upon all that had happened as the fictions of a dream! In the meantime my uncle knocked at the door, and bade me turn out, for I had had a long spell. I rose accordingly, and sent Miss Williams to her mistress, myself receiving the congratulations of Captain Bowling, who rallied me in his sea phrase with great success. In less than an hour Don Rodrigo led my wife in to breakfast, where she received the compliments of the company on her looks, which, they said, if possible, were improved by matrimony. As her delicate ears were offended with none of those indecent ambiguities which are too often spoke on such occasions, she behaved with dignity, unaffected modesty, and ease; and, as a testimony of my affection and esteem, I presented her, in presence of them all, with a deed, by which I settled the whole fortune I was possessed of on her and her heirs for ever. She accepted it with a glance of most tender acknowledgment, observed that she could not be surprised at anything of this kind I should do, and desired my father to take the trouble of keeping it, saying, "Next to my own Mr. Random, you are the person in whom I ought to have the greatest confidence." Charmed with her prudent and ingenuous manner of proceeding, he took the paper, and assured her that it should not lose its value while in his custody.

As we had not many visits to give and receive, the little time we staid in town was spent in going to public diversions, where I have the vanity to think Narcissa was seldom eclipsed. One night in particular, we had sent our footman to keep one of the stage boxes, which we no sooner entered, than we perceived in the opposite box the squire and his lady, who seemed not a little surprised at seeing us. I was pleased at this opportunity of confronting them; the more because Melinda was robbed of all her admirers by my wife, who happened that night to out-shine her sister both in beauty and dress. She was piqued at Narcissa's victory, tossed her head a thousand different ways, flirted her fan, looked at us with disdain, then whispered to her husband, and broke out into an affected giggle; but all arts proved ineffectual, either to discompose Mrs. Random, or to conceal her own mortification, which at length forced her away long before the play was done. The news of our marriage being spread with many circumstances to our disadvantage, by the industry of this malignant creature, a certain set of persons, fond of scandal, began to inquire into the particulars of my fortune, which they no sooner understood to be independent, than the tables were turned, and our acquaintance courted as much as it had been despised before. But Narcissa had too much dignity of pride to encourage this change of conduct, especially in her relations, whom she could never be prevailed upon to see after the malicious reports they had raised to her prejudice.

CHAPTER LXIX

My Father intends to revisit the Place of his Nativity—We promise to accompany him—My Uncle renews his Will in my favour, determining to go to Sea again—We set out for Scotland—Arrive at Edinburgh—Purchase our Paternal Estate—Proceed to it—Halt at the Town where I was educated—Take up my Bond to Crab—The Behaviour of Potion and his Wife, and one of my female Cousins—Our Reception at the Estate—Strap marries Miss Williams, and is settled by my Father to his own Satisfaction—I am more and more happy.

My father intending to revisit his native country, and pay the tribute of a few tears at my mother's grave, Narcissa and I resolved to accompany him in the execution of his pious office, and accordingly prepared for the journey; in which, however, my uncle would not engage, being resolved to try his fortune once more at sea. In the meantime he renewed his will in favour of my wife and me, and deposited it in the hands of his brother-in-law. While I, that I might not be wanting to my own interest, summoned the squire to produce his father's will at Doctors' Commons, and employed a proctor to manage the affair in my absence.

Everything being thus settled, we took leave of all our friends in London, and set out for Scotland, Don Rodrigo, Narcissa, Miss Williams, and I in the coach, and Strap with two men in livery on horseback. As we made easy stages, my charmer held it out very well till we arrived at Edinburgh, where we proposed to rest ourselves some weeks.

Here Don Rodrigo having intelligence that the fox-hunter had spent his estate, which was to be exposed to sale by public auction, he determined to make a purchase of the spot where he was born, and actually bought all the land that belonged to his father.

In a few days after this bargain was made, we left Edinburgh, in order to go and take possession; and, by the way, halted one night in that town where I was educated. Upon inquiry, I found that Mr. Crab was dead; whereupon I sent for his executor, paid the sum I owed, with interest, and took up my bond. Mr. Potion and his wife, hearing of our arrival, had the assurance to come to the inn where we lodged, and send up their names, with a desire of being permitted to pay their respects to my father and me; but their sordid behaviour towards me when I was an orphan, had made too deep an impression on my mind to be effaced by this mean mercenary piece of condescension. I therefore rejected their message with disdain, and bade Strap tell them that my father and I desired to have no communication with such low-minded wretches as they were.

They had not been gone half an hour, when a woman, without any ceremony, opened the door of the room where we sat, and, making towards my father, accosted him with, "Uncle, your servant—I am glad to see you." This was no other than one of my female cousins, mentioned in the first part of my memoirs, to whom Don Rodrigo replied, "Pray, who are you, madam?" "O!" cried she, "my cousin Rory there knows me very well.— Don't you remember me, Rory?" "Yes, madam," said I; "for my own part, I shall never forget you. Sir, this is one of the young ladies who, as I formerly told you, treated me so humanely in my childhood!" When I pronounced these words, my father's resentment glowed in his visage, and he ordered her to be gone, with such a commanding aspect, that she retired in a fright, muttering curses as she went downstairs. We afterwards learned that she was married to an ensign, who had already spent all her fortune; and that her sister had bore a child to her mother's footman, who is now her husband, and keeps a petty alehouse in the country.

The fame of our flourishing condition having arrived at this place before us, we got notice that the magistrates intended next day to compliment us with the freedom of the town; upon which my father, considering their complaisance in the right point of view, ordered the horses to the coach early in the morning.

We proceeded to our estate, which lay about twenty miles from this place; and when we came within half a league of the house, were met by a prodigious number of poor tenants, men, women, and children, who testified their joy by loud acclamations, and accompanied our coach to the gate. As there is no part of the world in which the peasants are more attached to their lords than in Scotland, we were almost devoured by their affection. My father had always been their favourite, and now that he appeared their master, after having been thought dead so long, their joy broke out into a thousand extravagances. When we entered the courtyard, we were surrounded by a vast number, who crowded together so closely to see us, that several were in danger of being squeezed to death; those who were near Don Rodrigo fell upon their knees, and kissed his hand, or the hem of his garment, praying aloud for long life and prosperity to him; others approached Narcissa and me in the same manner; while the rest clapped their hands at a distance, and invoked Heaven to shower its choicest blessings on our heads! In short, the whole scene, though rude, was so affecting, that the gentle partner of my heart wept over it, and my father himself could not refrain from dropping a tear.

Having welcomed his daughter and me to his house, he ordered some bullocks to be killed, and some hogsheads of ale to be brought from the neighbouring village, to regale these honest people, who had not enjoyed such a holiday for many years before.

Next day we were visited by the gentlemen in the neighbourhood, most of them our relations, one of whom brought along with him my cousin the fox-hunter, who had stayed at his house since he was obliged to leave his own. My father was generous enough to receive him kindly, and even promised to purchase for him a commission in the army, for which he expressed great thankfulness and joy.

My charming Narcissa was universally admired and loved for her beauty, affability, and good sense; and so well pleased with the situation of the place, and the company round, that she has not as yet discovered the least desire of changing her habitation.

We had not been many days settled, when I prevailed upon my father to pay a visit to the village where I had been at school. Here we were received by the principal inhabitants, who entertained us in the church, where Mr. Syntax the schoolmaster, my tyrant being dead, pronounced a Latin oration in honour of our family. And none exerted themselves more than Strap's father and relations, who looked upon the honest valet as the first gentleman of their race, and honoured his benefactors accordingly. Having received the homage of this place, we retired, leaving forty pounds for the benefit of the poor of the parish, and that very night, Strap being a little elevated with the regard that had been shown to him, and to me on his account, ventured to tell me that he had a sneaking kindness for Miss Williams, and that, if his lady and I would use our interest in his behalf, he did not doubt that she would listen to his addresses. Surprised at this proposal, I asked if he knew the story of that unfortunate young gentlewoman. Upon which he replied, "Yes, yes, I know what you mean—she has been unhappy, I grant you—but what of that? I am convinced of her reformation; or else you and my good lady would not treat her with such respect.—As for the censure of the world, I value it not a fig's end—besides, the world knows nothing of the matter." I commended his philosophy, and interested Narcissa in his cause; who interceded so effectually, that, in a little time, Miss Williams yielded her consent, and they were married with the approbation of Don Rodrigo, who gave him five hundred pounds to stock a farm, and made him overseer of his estate. My generous bedfellow gave her maid the same sum; so that they live in great peace and plenty within half a mile of us, and daily put up prayers for our preservation.

If there be such a thing as true happiness on earth, I enjoy it. The impetuous transports of my passion are now settled and mellowed into endearing fondness and tranquillity of love, rooted by that intimate connection and interchange of hearts, which nought but virtuous wedlock can produce.—Fortune seems determined to make ample amends for her former cruelty; for my proctor writes that, notwithstanding the clause in my father-in-law's will, on which the squire founds his claim, I shall certainly recover my wife's fortune, in consequence of a codicil annexed, which explains that clause, and limits her restriction to the age of nineteen, after which she was at her own disposal. I would have set out for London immediately after receiving this piece of intelligence, but my dear angel has been qualmish of late, and begins to grow remarkably round in the waist; so that I cannot leave her in such an interesting situation, which I hope will produce something to crown my felicity.

FINIS

Date

Study

JUN 29 1955
MAR 23 76